KELLY HASHWAY

To Ayla with love.

CURSE OF THE GRANVILLE FORTUNE

KELLY HASHWAY

CHAPTER ONE

I was about to climb the biggest bike ramp at the park when the vision hit me. Some people might think having visions was cool. For me, it was a curse.

I clutched the handlebars, trying to steady the bike, but my hands and arms tingled with a warmth that made me sweat like a freak. Not now! I couldn't have a vision here. Holly would think I was having a fit or something and run home to tell Mom.

"J.B., what's wrong?" Holly asked as my bike swerved.

I'd never told anyone about the visions. I didn't want to be labeled a head case and forced to see some shrink, but I felt Holly's eyes on me as my body shook. What choice did I have? I purposely missed the ramp and crashed into a bush, hoping the accident would cover up the strange things that were about to happen to me.

My eyes shut at the exact moment of the collision,

and the vision flooded my brain.

You three who bring disgrace to your families shall suffer great misfortune. Your lives shall be cursed until you return what was taken this night.

The old woman's voice thundered in my ears, but I couldn't see anything except the brilliant white light surrounding my body. A warm electric current pulsed through my veins. I felt like I was floating, but something weighed me down by my shoulders. Something familiar. I wasn't alone. There were two others with me. I couldn't see their faces through the white light, but I knew they were there.

As usual, the vision had come at the worst possible time—when someone was around to see it. When someone was around to find out my secret. I was cursed. Cursed for something I didn't even do. I'd had the vision since I was four, maybe before that, but I couldn't remember. It was always the same. Some woman cursing me for stealing, but I never stole anything.

"J.B.!" Holly screamed. "Get up! We have to get out of here!"

I opened my eyes, trying to focus on Holly's face. My head throbbed—a combination of the mind-numbing vision and the crash. Holly pointed toward the forest at the edge of the park and yanked me to my feet.

"Easy. I just nosedived into a bush. Could you give me a sec?" I wiped my brow with the sleeve of my sweatshirt and took a deep breath.

Holly opened her mouth to speak, but it wasn't *her* voice I heard.

"Knife!" the scratchy voice cried out.

Holly hid behind me, burying her head in my back. I looked toward the forest and saw a grisly looking man wandering out of the trees. His clothes were torn, and he was covered in mud and leaves. I could barely see his skin through all the muck.

"Grim!" the man cried. He sounded like he was in desperate need of water.

The guy had to be crazy. I didn't feel bad for thinking that because most people would think I was crazy, too, if they knew about my recurring vision.

Holly tugged on my arm. "Let's get out of here!"

The guy wandered around, stumbling over his own feet. What had happened to him inside the forest? I hung out at the park all the time, but I'd never gone into the woods.

Holly hopped on her bike and started to pedal, but her shoelace tangled in the chain. She fell sideways into the same bush I'd just gotten out of. Typical Holly. She couldn't do anything without getting hurt.

The crash got the crazy guy's attention. He cocked his head in our direction and locked eyes with me.

I rushed over to Holly and yanked her shoelace free. I was helping her up when I spotted a beat up gray Ford Focus at the edge of the park gate. The front end was dented and the headlight was cracked. It was Dad's car. He didn't have the money to get it fixed after someone hit him in a parking lot. What was he doing here? Why wasn't he at work?

"Grim!" the man cried, reaching his hand toward Holly and me.

"Go!" I shouted at Holly. She pedaled out of the park. I grabbed my bike, hoping it didn't get too banged up in the crash, and sped out of there as fast as I could.

Holly turned right, heading for home, but I stopped at the gate and hid my bike behind a tree. I could see Dad talking on his cell phone in the front seat of his car. I crept over to the passenger side and tapped on the window. Dad jumped, dropping his phone in his lap. His eyes widened when he saw me. I tapped the window again, but Dad scrambled for his phone and held up his finger to me. He didn't open the window until he finished his call.

"Who were you talking to?" I asked.

"J.B., I can't talk right now." Dad was looking past me to the park. "You should go home. Right now." Why was he trying to get rid of me?

I turned back toward the park. The man wasn't

there, but Dad kept searching for something.

"Dad, why are you here? I thought you started some big new case today," I said. Dad had started his own law firm about two years ago. Beaumonte and Associates. Now, he was gone all the time, even though he barely made enough money to pay the bills.

"I don't have time to talk about this right now. Just go home," Dad said, still not looking at me.

What else was new? Dad never had time for me anymore. We used to spend every Saturday watching James Bond movies. I'd wanted to be James Bond since I was four. That was why everyone calls me J.B. instead of Jack Beaumonte. Dad was the one who gave me the nickname. Now, I wasn't sure I wanted it anymore.

I was angry and tired of being ignored. I thought about blocking Dad's view of the park. Maybe then he'd have to look at me. But I saw a black leather-bound book sticking out of Dad's briefcase. His case journal. If he didn't have his notes for the case, he'd have to come home. He wouldn't even notice if I took the book. He was too wrapped up looking for the crazy guy in the park. I reached my hand in the window, but Dad's voice made me yank it back out.

"J.B., please go home before—"

Sirens blared and two police cars screeched to a stop in front of the park. News vans followed behind them. Dad got out of the car in a hurry.

"Tell your mother I'll be working late," he said, running toward the police officers.

Were they the ones Dad had called? He seemed to know they were on their way, and he sure wanted me to get out of there. Looking at Dad, I knew he'd changed. He was like a stranger to me now.

I reached through the car window, grabbed the case journal, and stuffed it under my sweatshirt. If I was going to be cursed for stealing, I might as well steal something. I ran back to my bike and took off for the other side of the park. I stopped behind a row of pine trees. I could see through them, but they kept me pretty well hidden from Dad and the police.

"What's that?" Holly asked, pulling up next to me and pointing to the lump in my sweatshirt.

"I thought you went home," I said, pulling out the journal.

"I got one block and realized you weren't behind me, so I headed back." Holly squinted at me. "What are you doing with Dad's case journal?"

I didn't know how to explain why I took it. I was mad at Dad for wanting me gone, and I was confused about why he was even here.

"Dad's here. I went over to see what he was doing, and I caught him on his cell. I think he called the police."

Holly shrugged. "So? There's a crazy person loose

in the park. He should've called the police. Besides, he was probably trying to protect us."

I shook my head. "He didn't know we were here, and he looked guilty when I caught him on the phone. He kept staring past me like he was trying to see the crazy guy."

Holly wrinkled her forehead. "So, he *did* know the guy was there."

"Probably, yeah. But he couldn't see him from the car. He was searching for him." I threw my head back, frustrated that Holly kept questioning me. "Listen, you can go home if you want, but I'm going to see what Dad's up to. He acted really weird, and I want to know why."

Holly crossed her arms and leaned back on her bike seat, almost falling in the process. I ignored her and turned back to the park. The police were helping the man into the back of a squad car. Dad said something to one of the cops and got in his car. I wondered where he was going. I doubted it was to work.

The news vans packed up and left. They'd gotten to the park so fast. Had Dad called them, too?

"Now what?" Holly asked.

I squeezed the journal in my hands. "We check out Dad's journal." I flipped through the pages. Most of them were blank. I knew Dad's law firm wasn't doing well, but this was weird. I opened to the first page.

"Read it," Holly said.

I cleared my throat. "'Braeden Forest looks like any other forest from the outside, but once inside, a person's worst nightmares become a reality. There are hundreds of seemingly identical paths, and each one leads to dangerous and frightening beasts. The forest is also home to the infamous Grimault thieves.'" I stopped reading. From the moment I'd opened the journal, something had been bothering me, but I couldn't put my finger on it until now. "This is *Mom's* handwriting."

"What? Let me see!" Holly leaned over and studied the writing. "You're right! Why would she write in Dad's case journal?"

"Mom and Dad are hiding something. Here, listen. It says, 'The Grimault thieves are descendants of Aristede Grimault who sailed here from France in 1809 shortly after being cursed for stealing the Granville fortune along with Sebastien Granville and Jean Beaumonte.'" I almost dropped the journal as I met Holly's stare.

"Jean Beaumonte? We have to be related to him, right?" Holly said.

"I guess so." I felt strange all of a sudden, like I'd heard this before.

Holly tapped the page. "What else does it say?"

I forced my eyes to focus on the journal. "'Aristede

was never heard from again. There was no contact between him and either of his accomplices. And the curse remains intact until the wrongdoers restore the Granville fortune to its rightful owners.'" The curse. The three people. I *had* heard this before. It was my vision! The old woman had cursed Jean and his two friends. Now, I was cursed because of it. My whole family was cursed.

It made sense now. All of it. Strange things happened around my family, things we couldn't explain. Like Holly's accidents, her trips to the hospital with broken bones and rare illnesses. Dad couldn't pay the bills no matter how much he worked because all his cases fell apart before he got paid. Mom had this weird way of making things break in her bare hands—including one potential employer's hand when she shook it. And I had these stupid visions that took over my whole body and turned me into a total freak!

"We're cursed!" Holly yelled. "All because some relative of ours stole something hundreds of years ago?"

I didn't know what to say. I wasn't about to come clean about my visions.

"Don't just sit there. Keep reading!" Holly demanded.

I nodded. "'The Grimault thieves discovered the forest was a safe place to live because no one would enter the woods on account of its mystical power to make a person's fears come to life. However, there have been a few recorded incidents of men who have entered the forest and have never been heard from again. The Grimault thieves are rumored to have settled there in search of the lost Granville fortune.' That's all it says."

I couldn't believe it. I'd played at Bradley Park all my life, and my parents never mentioned the forest was dangerous. Of course, they never mentioned our family was cursed either. It'd been torture trying to keep the visions a secret from my parents so they wouldn't think I was crazy. Now, it turned out I only thought I was crazy because my parents didn't tell me about the family curse.

"There's a fortune buried in those woods?" Holly asked.

"That's what Mom wrote in the journal."

"I'm going to ask her about this," Holly said.

"Wait." I knew it wouldn't be that easy. My parents had kept this from me for nine years. "Mom and Dad hid this from us all our lives. What makes you think they'll tell us about it now?"

"Because we found out about it. They have to tell us the truth."

"Or they could just ground us for stealing Dad's journal," I said, tucking the book back under my sweatshirt and turning my bike toward the road.

"*You* stole the journal. I'm not getting in trouble for that," Holly said, turning her bike around, too.

"Whatever. I want answers, and I'll find them myself. I say we explore the forest."

"You're crazy. We find out we're cursed and you want to go into a scary forest that's full of thieves?"

Holly's face was so pale she looked sick, and that gave me an idea. "We're going into Braeden Forest when Mom goes food shopping this afternoon."

"But—" Holly protested as I took off for home.

CHAPTER TWO

I left my bike on the lawn and crept to the front door. I turned to Holly and put a finger to my lips, silently praying that she'd actually be quiet and not knock over the coat rack. Mom couldn't know we were home yet.

"Wait," Holly whispered. "Food shopping with Mom is one of our weekly chores. How are we going to get out of it?"

"Just be quiet and leave the rest to me." I opened the door slowly, hoping it wouldn't creak, and peeked my head in. I could see the kitchen and the living room. Both were empty. I guessed Mom was in the upstairs den posting more of Grandma's antiques on eBay. I shut the door behind us with only the tiniest click. So far so good.

I ducked into the bathroom, pulling Holly behind me. I grabbed the baby powder from the medicine cabinet and handed it to her. "Dab some of this on your face so you look pale," I said.

"Why? What are we doing?"

"Not we. *You*. I'll tell Mom you fell off your bike and got the wind knocked out of you. She won't have any trouble believing that, especially since you still have leaves in your hair." I pointed to the clump of leaves stuck in her ponytail.

"Why didn't you tell me?" Holly tried to grab them, but I stopped her.

"Leave them. We want Mom to see you like this."

"Ugh! Fine," Holly said with a huff.

"And practice moaning for your pretend stomachache. Getting the wind knocked out of you isn't enough. We have to make sure Mom won't think you'll feel better in an hour and just postpone the shopping."

"What if I say my ribs hurt? I could pretend I cracked one," Holly said with a smile. As usual, she wasn't thinking ahead.

"If Mom thinks you broke a rib, she'll take you to the emergency room to have it X-rayed. Stick to the stomachache. Got it?" I gave her a serious look to make sure she didn't try to come up with any other injuries that would ruin my plan.

"Fine. Pale face and stomachache," Holly said. Then she muttered, "How boring."

I ran into the kitchen to heat up a bowl of canned soup. Without letting it cool, I ate two spoonfuls. It burned my tongue, but I forced myself to swallow. Then I put the bowl on the coffee table in the living room.

Holly walked into the room as I finished rearranging the pillows on the couch to make it look like she'd been lying there. I looked Holly up and down. Her face was definitely pale, but something was wrong. "Did you take some leaves out of your hair?"

"Just a couple."

"Holly!" I said in a loud whisper.

"Fine." She ran to the bathroom and came back a second later with the rest of the leaves in her hair. "How's that?"

"Better. Now I'm going to help you up to bed." I took her by the arm and led her to the stairs. We only made it up three steps before running into Mom.

"Good, you're home. I'm about to make lun—" With one look at Holly, Mom stopped. "Sweetie, are you all right? You look pale."

"That's what I thought," I said before Holly could get a word in. "She tried to go up the big ramp at the park, and she fell in a bush. I think she got the wind knocked out of her. I brought her home and made her some soup, but she could only get a few bites down. I'm taking her up to bed so she can rest."

"Thank you, J.B.," Mom said. "Holly's lucky to have such a good brother." I stuck my tongue out at Holly as

Mom took her arm.

Once Holly was back in bed, I mouthed the word "moan."

"Ohh!" Holly held her hands to her stomach. "My stomach." I had to admit she was pretty good at pretending to be sick.

"Sweetie, why on earth did you try to go on the big bike ramp? You know you're not—" Mom paused, not wanting to offend Holly. "You need to be more careful."

"J.B. dared me." Holly slowly raised her hand and pointed at me. My jaw dropped. Now she'd gone too far.

"Jack Beaumonte!" It was never good when Mom used my full name. "You're supposed to look out for your sister, not get her hurt."

"Sorry." I lowered my head, pretending to be ashamed. "Let me make up for it. I'll stay home with Holly while you go shopping. I'll get her whatever she needs."

"The grocery shopping. I completely forgot. I don't want to leave Holly in this condition. The shopping will have to wait." She patted Holly's hand.

"No!" I said, a little too enthusiastically. "I mean, it can't wait. Holly and I finished all the food in the fridge last night." We never had much food in the fridge to begin with, so it wasn't hard to do. "Besides, it's not like you can wait for Dad to get home. We'd all starve to death by then." No arguing with that.

"You're right. We don't even have anything for dinner." Mom wrinkled her forehead.

"Mom," Holly said in a weak voice. "I'm probably going to sleep all afternoon, but if I need anything, J.B. will get it for me."

"Right," I agreed, hoping I didn't sound too eager to get rid of her.

"Well, if you think you'll be all right, I'll run into town and grab the necessities as quickly as I can. I'll leave my cell on. If you need me, call and I'll come right home. Can I get you anything before I leave?"

Holly shook her head.

Mom kissed her cheek. "What is it, dear?" she asked.

I stared at Holly, afraid she'd somehow ruined the plan. The worried look on her face didn't make me relax any.

"Just my stomach," Holly said. "I'm sure I'll feel better after a nap."

"I'll be home as soon as I can," Mom said. Then she whispered to me, "Take good care of her, and call me if she gets any worse."

As soon as I saw Mom's face, I knew why Holly had looked so worried. Mom had kissed Holly's baby-powdered cheek, covering her lips in white powder.

"Sure," I managed to say.

We stayed in Holly's room, listening for Mom's car pulling out of the driveway. My heart raced. Mom usually checked her makeup in the rearview mirror before she went anywhere. I crept to the window and peeked around the curtains. The blue sedan was backing out. I breathed a sigh of relief.

"Did you see her lips?" Holly said.

"Come on. We don't have much time." I stashed Dad's journal under my bed and ran down to the kitchen. As I stuffed granola bars in my pockets, I spotted a rope hanging from a hook on the garage door. I wasn't sure what it was doing there, but I figured we shouldn't go into the forest empty-handed, so I took the rope and wound it up.

"What's that for?" Holly asked.

"I'm not sure. Maybe we can use it to climb trees if we see any wolves or bears."

"Bears?" Holly's voice quivered. "Do you really think we should go into the forest? I mean, I'm pretty sure bears can climb trees. How would we get away from them?"

"Don't you want to break this curse? Or do you like getting hurt all the time and never having any money?" I wanted to make her angry. If Holly were angry, she'd forget about being scared.

"Let's go," Holly said, tearing the leaves from her hair.

I finished winding the rope into a big loop and draped it across my neck and shoulder like a sash. As I turned toward the door, the painting above the fireplace caught my eye. I'd never paid attention to it before. A bunch of trees with two paths leading into them—big deal. But after reading Dad's journal and seeing the crazy guy wandering out of the forest, I wanted to look at the painting. I walked over and took it off the wall.

"What are you doing? We have to hurry," Holly said, tapping her watch.

"I think this is—" I turned the painting over. There was writing on the back in faded, curvy script. "Braeden Forest."

"So?"

I couldn't believe she didn't see why this was important. "First, some crazy guy comes out of the forest. Then, we find out our family is cursed. And the painting that's been in our house forever is of the forest where the stolen Granville fortune is buried! It's all connected."

"You think the crazy guy has something to do with the curse?" Holly asked.

"It seems like it." I had a crazy idea that maybe the painting was more than art. I took it into Dad's office and grabbed the scissors off the desk.

Holly ran after me. "Stop! Mom's going to kill you!"

she said, as I stabbed the corner of the painting.

I ignored her and cut the canvas along the frame.

"Why did you do that?"

"This has to be a clue." I rolled up the painting. "Come on. We'll bike back to the park." I pushed her out the door before she could yell at me anymore.

The gated entrance to the park was locked with yellow police tape draped across it, so we stashed our bikes in the bushes and climbed over the gate. As soon as we were in the park, we headed straight past the swings to the forest.

I checked the painting. "That's weird. There are two paths entering the forest in the painting, but there's only one path in front of us." I closed my eyes and pictured the crazy guy coming out of the woods. He came out of the trees, not the path. "There has to be another path behind these bushes." I put the painting on the merry-go-round and started shoving branches out of the way. Sure enough, there was another path. "There's a trail! Let's go!"

"What about the painting? Are you going to leave it on the merry-go-round?"

"It only shows the entrance. Why would we need to bring it?"

Holly shrugged and followed me down the overgrown path.

At first, Braeden Forest looked like any other

forest. But after walking for about ten minutes, it got dark and following the path got a lot more difficult.

"The sunlight can't get through all these trees. It looks like nighttime in here," I said.

"Yeah, and the trees are spooky. Their branches look like bony, wrinkled arms."

I followed Holly's stare to a large oak tree. The bark was cracked and peeling. Some of the branches spidered out at the ends, making them look like wrinkly hands and fingers.

"The trees over there look like they have faces." I pointed up ahead. The bark was peeling off in weird patterns that looked like ghoulish faces. One reminded me of my great uncle Lester, and that didn't make me feel better because he gave me the creeps.

A branch brushed against my shoulder. I jumped. There wasn't any wind to make the branches sway. Holly raised a shaky hand and pointed behind me. I turned to see the tree reaching out to grab me as if it were a person. "The trees are alive!"

CHAPTER THREE

Bark splintered as the branches bent like fingers and swatted at us. The faces in the trees snarled at me, making me stumble backwards.

"Run!" I pushed Holly down the path. The bony wooden fingers of an oak tree grazed my arm.

"The path splits up ahead!" Holly yelled. "Which way should we go?"

"We can't get lost, or we'll never make it back home before Mom."

"Give me the granola bars you brought."

How could she think about food at a time like this? We were being attacked by a bunch of hundred-year-old trees! "We can't stop to eat!"

"We can break the granola bars into little pieces and drop them on the ground to mark the paths we take."

"Good thinking!" I took the granola bars from my pocket and tossed them to Holly. "You mark the trail.

I'll lead the way." I glanced over my shoulder. No trees were chasing us. They were still firmly rooted in the ground, and we were out of reach of their limbs. "We can slow down now."

Holly stopped and bent at the waist while she caught her breath. "What *was* that back there?"

I shivered, remembering the feel of the tree's bony fingers sliding across my back. "The journal said the forest makes your worst nightmares become a reality. We were talking about the scary faces in the bark and how the branches looked like arms. Our fears came to life." I was beginning to understand how that guy had gone crazy in here.

"Do you really think everything Mom wrote in the journal is true? The curse? The buried fortune?" Holly asked, grabbing my arm.

I knew it was. "Just keep your scary thoughts to yourself, and we'll be fine," I said.

We pushed through leaves and fallen branches. I was about to step over another fallen tree when I heard twigs breaking. I stopped and stuck my arm out in front of Holly. The noise had come from somewhere to our left, but a bush blocked my view.

"Stay still. There's something up ahead. It's probably a squirrel, but keep quiet until we know for sure." I tried to sound calm so Holly wouldn't panic, but a loud cracking sound made my efforts useless.

"What was that?" Holly stepped behind me and buried her head between my shoulder blades.

I was afraid to think of what it might be. I didn't know if the forest only made the things said out loud come to life or if it could read thoughts, too. I moved the branches of the bush to get a better look. A deer ran through some fallen trees. I let go of the breath I'd been holding.

"Is it bears?" Holly asked.

My whole body tensed. Holly had volunteered another scary suggestion to the forest. I looked around, but I couldn't see a bear anywhere. Leaves rustled and another cracking sound came from high in a tree. Three large branches fell to the ground in front of us. Only these weren't normal tree limbs. They were shaped like bears. Big green, leafy bears! Once again, our imaginations had turned the forest into living creatures ready to devour us.

I kept an eye on the bears to make sure they didn't move. The one closest to me was the largest. The leaves making up the bear's mouth were spaced out, exposing its big green teeth. I wasn't willing to bet those teeth would crumble apart like regular leaves. I was way past thinking anything in this forest was ordinary.

Holly squeezed my arm tighter. "What do we do?"

"I don't think they see us. Let's back up and go

down another path. Move as quietly as you can."

"Okay." Holly's voice shook. She took a step away from me and stopped. She could see the bears now, and she shivered with fear.

I nudged her with my elbow. She backed up slowly, her eyes never leaving the bears. I saw the fallen tree branch on the ground just as Holly stepped on it. I reached out to her, but I was too slow. Holly's feet came out from under her, and she fell backward into a pile of leaves.

"Ow!" she yelled.

The bears let out deep rumbling growls. I yanked Holly to her feet. "Run!"

The bears charged after us. I pushed Holly to run faster, but I knew we couldn't outrun bears. I followed the trail of granola and got an idea.

"Throw the granola bars on the ground," I yelled. "Maybe the bears will stop to eat them." If tree-bears actually ate. They sure seemed to want to eat Holly and me.

Holly turned and threw the granola bars at the bears, hitting one of them on the nose. A few leaves fell to the ground. The bears were stunned at first, but then their noses twitched in the air. All three rushed to the spot where the bars landed.

"It worked!" Holly said.

"Keep running!" We had to get off this path, or the

bears would follow our granola trail right to us.

We reached the fork and ran a little way down the other path before stopping to catch our breath. I threw my head back and rested my hands on my hips. Holly leaned against a tree.

She looked at her feet, avoiding my eyes. "I'm sorry. It's my fault those trees turned into—" She paused, and I was grateful that she'd caught herself before she created more bears for us to deal with. "I couldn't keep my fears to myself. Me and my big mouth."

I wasn't sure how much was Holly's fault and how much could be blamed on our family's curse. "We know how the forest works now. We won't say anything that could be the least bit scary. That won't be hard." I wasn't sure that was true, but I needed to convince Holly it was. "Let's keep going."

"But we don't have any way to mark a trail anymore. How will we find our way back home?" Holly asked.

"We'll take the paths on the left. Then when we turn around, all the paths we took will be on the right since we'll be facing the opposite direction. That should be easy enough to remember."

Holly nodded.

We walked for a few minutes until we came to a stream. It seemed strange that a stream running through a forest would be so wide. What surprised me even more was that the stream had a strong current that crashed against the big, jagged rocks sticking out of it.

"We can't swim across it with a current that strong," Holly said.

Going in the stream was out of the question. I scanned the surrounding trees overhanging the water.

"How do you feel about swinging across the stream on this rope?" I asked, removing the rope from across my chest. I threw one end up into an oak tree along the stream. I looped the rope around a branch and held both ends in my hands.

"Like a rope swing?"

"Exactly. I'll swing over, and then you'll grab onto the rope as it swings back."

"Sounds dangerous," Holly said. "If we miss, the current will pull us to who knows where."

I wasn't giving up. "We have to keep going," I said. "We have to end the curse."

Holly took a deep breath and exhaled louder than necessary. She shook her head, almost like she couldn't believe what she was saying. "Okay, let's do this—before I change my mind."

I smiled. Holly was being really brave considering what we'd already faced inside the forest. I took a few steps backward, and with a running start, I swung over the stream. My eyes focused on the water, expecting to see a large octopus reaching up to grab me. Thankfully, the forest couldn't read minds. I landed hard on the other side, but I made it. Now, it was Holly's turn. She jumped up and grabbed the rope as it swung back to her. Following my example, Holly swung over the stream.

It would've worked well if we were the same height, but Holly was shorter than me and couldn't reach the other side. She started to swing back. Without thinking, I reached for her legs and pulled her to me. We landed on the ground in a heap. I broke Holly's fall, but she cut her leg on a rock and had rope burns on her hands.

"Are you okay?" I asked.

"I've done worse," Holly said. "Thanks for catching me."

"Don't thank me yet. I couldn't grab the rope, and now we have no way of getting back across the stream."

"How are we going to get home?" Her voice was full of panic.

"I don't know." This was turning out to be some curse.

CHAPTER FOUR

I sat by the stream, trying to find the courage to keep going. I had to find out more about the curse. Then, there was the crazy guy at the park. As awful as those enchanted trees and bears were, I didn't think they were what had caused that man to go insane. That worried me. Holly and I were lucky to be alive, and I wasn't sure if I could handle what else might be lurking in the forest. Still, I knew I had to get up and figure out what to do next. Holly was counting on me.

"Come on," I said, getting to my feet. "There has to be another way out of the forest."

Holly's eyes were glassy, and the corners of her mouth twitched like she was about to cry. But she got up and followed me down the path.

"Mom should be getting home soon," Holly said, glancing at her watch. "We'll never make it back in ti—ahh!" Holly tripped over a large rock and stumbled to the ground.

"Are you okay?" I asked.

"I don't know. I landed funny on my ankle." She tried to flex her foot, but it barely moved before she stopped. "Ouch, it really hurts," she said, rubbing her ankle.

"Here, I'll help you up." I pulled her to her feet, but she fell forward on me in pain.

"I can't stand on it." Holly's eyes filled with tears.

"Put your arm over my shoulder and lean on me like a crutch. That way you don't have to put any pressure on your ankle when you walk."

"I'm sorry," Holly said, leaning on me. "Why is it always me getting hurt?"

I laughed. "Look at the bright side. Thanks to the curse, the clumsiness isn't entirely your fault."

"Thanks a lot, big brother," Holly said with a sarcastic smirk. I smiled. I liked it when Holly called me big brother, even though I'm only a year older than she is. Exactly a year. She was born on my first birthday.

After walking about ten feet, Holly cringed in pain. Tears streamed down her face. Her injury wasn't that bad, and I figured her crying had more to do with being scared than with her ankle.

"Are you all right?" I asked.

"I need to rest for a minute."

"There's a cave up there. Can you make it?"

"I guess," she whimpered.

I helped Holly to the cave, and she sighed as she sat down on the dirt. "Much better," she said. She folded her sock down and checked her ankle for bruises. There weren't any.

Her injury didn't look bad at all, so I decided I should check out the trail while she rested. "I'm going to scout out the path ahead. Will you be all right on your own for a few minutes?"

"Yeah. I just wish we still had our granola bars. I'm starving."

I was hungry, too, but I was trying not to think about it. "I'll be right back."

The path looked clear, but a vulture circled above me. After a few turns, it stopped circling and flew off to join a group of its friends nearby. I turned around and ran back to the cave. I kept glancing at the sky to make sure the flock hadn't followed me. After several feet, I saw no sign of the vultures. Instead, I heard a low, rumbling growl.

I stopped dead in my tracks. A large gray wolf stood between me and the cave. I'd never seen a wolf up close, but I knew this one wasn't like any other wolf on the planet. It looked like a giant boulder, which could only mean one thing—Holly had struck again! The hair on the wolf's back stuck straight up as it slowly stalked its way toward Holly, who was backed up against the wall of the cave.

Holly stared at the wolf, and it growled even louder.

"Don't make eye contact. It will think you're challenging it," I whispered.

The wolf swung his head around to look at me. I jumped at the sight of its huge stone fangs. I was a little relieved when it turned back toward Holly.

The wolf twitched its nose and hungrily snapped its teeth together. I inched closer to the cave, trying to get to Holly.

"What do we do?" she whispered.

I surveyed the woods, searching for anything that could be used as a weapon, but there was nothing in sight—at least nothing strong enough to break stone. I turned back toward the cave and saw a pair of mossy green eyes behind Holly. Another stone wolf slowly inched toward her, snarling and baring its sharp teeth.

"Don't move," I whispered as calmly as possible, but Holly whipped her head around to see what I was staring at.

She screamed. She was completely defenseless, and there was nothing I could do to help.

"What do I do?" She didn't have to wait for an answer. The wolf inside the cave lunged. Holly raised her arms to shield her head and threw herself on the ground. I thought she was a goner. It took me a few seconds to realize that the wolf hadn't lunged at Holly. It was attacking the other wolf at the entrance to the cave. Chunks of rock flew through the air as the two stone wolves collided.

"They're fighting!" I yelled. "We have to get out of here!"

Holly sprang to her feet and ran out of the cave, despite her sore ankle. I grabbed her arm and pulled her along. We sprinted to the next fork in the path, and, once again, I chose the path on the left. We were far enough away from the two wolves, so we stopped to catch our breath.

"Where did those things come from?" I was accusing more than asking.

Holly covered her face with her hands. "I'm sorry. I fell asleep, and I had a nightmare. It was about wolves, and, well, you know I talk in my sleep."

"I can't believe you fell asleep in this place with all the scary things around!" Holly was on the verge of tears.

I took a deep breath. "Sorry. We're both under a lot of stress thanks to this forest and the curse and whatever else Mom and Dad are hiding from us. It's not your fault."

Holly squeezed her eyes shut, and I put my hand on her shoulder to let her know I wasn't mad. Scared was more like it.

CHAPTER FIVE

I ripped off part of my undershirt and wrapped Holly's ankle for support. The shirt wasn't going to help much, but Holly believed me when I said it would. Before long, I was leading her down the path again. The sun was high in the sky, and so were the vultures. Holly still wasn't moving quickly, but at least she didn't need to lean on me anymore. No matter how sore her ankle was, I wasn't about to stop and let her rest in any more caves.

"We should stay under these overhanging trees," I said, watching the vultures.

"Why do you keep looking up?" Holly asked as she leaned one hand on a tree and stepped over a fallen branch.

"Well, first of all, I noticed it's getting late. Mom's definitely home by now."

"She's going to think we were kidnapped or something," Holly said.

"I don't think so. There's a big blank spot above the fireplace where the painting used to be. Mom's bound to notice it. She'll figure out what we did. Especially if she goes to the park and finds the painting on the merry-go-round."

"Should we turn around and head home?" Holly asked.

"We can't. We'd have to walk back past that cave, and we definitely wouldn't be lucky enough to get by those stone wolves again." I couldn't believe I'd said that out loud. Holly and I froze, afraid the forest would create more stone wolves or that the ones Holly had made earlier would magically appear. Nothing happened. "I guess the forest knows the difference between talking about the past and voicing our fears." I relaxed a little, but Holly still looked nervous.

"What if Mom comes looking for us? All those things our fears created might get her."

I had to bite my tongue when Holly said *our* fears— as if *I* had anything to do with the bears or wolves. I'd learned my lesson after the living tree people. "I don't think Mom would come after us by herself. She knows there are hundreds of different paths in these woods. She wrote about them in the journal. She wouldn't have any way of knowing which paths we took. We should keep walking and try to find another way out."

Holly nodded, but I could tell by the way she

chewed on her lower lip something still bothered her. "Hey, J.B.? When I asked you why you kept looking at the sky, you said 'first of all' and explained about the time, but what's second of all?"

"I don't want to scare you, but do you remember when I left you in the cave and scouted out the path?"

She shivered. "Don't remind me!"

"Well, I found something."

"The Grimault thieves?"

"No. Vultures. They've been circling overhead."

"I thought vultures only ate dead animals."

The vultures spiraled through the air. One flew low enough that I could see its sharp talons. "I don't think we're in any danger." I hoped I was right.

I was exhausted, and my stomach growled so loudly that I looked around expecting to see a growling bear—real or the leafy variety.

"Why can't we come across a fruit tree?" Holly asked, rubbing her stomach. "Any chance that thinking aloud works for good things, too?"

I considered it for a second, but no magical fruit trees appeared. I assumed the forest only tuned into fears. "I'm hungry too, but I'm more worried about finding water. I thought we'd find another stream somewhere, or if that stream we crossed earlier today was big enough, maybe we'd come across it again."

"But we haven't changed directions, and I think

we're walking away from the stream." Holly's eyes watered. She was giving up hope of finding water and, more importantly, of ever getting home.

"I'm sure we'll find water soon," I said, but I wasn't convinced. I was trying to be brave for Holly, but I'd never been so scared in my life. We'd never be able to retrace our steps and go home. Even if we were lucky enough to get past the wolves a second time, Holly wouldn't be able to cross that stream with her sore ankle. Especially without the rope.

"How long have the vultures been circling above us?" Holly asked.

"I don't know. Why?"

"Do you think we could follow them to find water? If they live in this forest, they must know where to find water."

"That's true. But, if we follow the vultures, we'll have to stop taking the paths on the left. How will we get home if we can't find another way out of here? We won't be able to retrace our steps."

"I don't think we have a choice. If we don't find water, we won't need to worry about how to get home. We won't be *alive* to worry about how to get home."

"Then we need to take this path on the right because the vultures just changed directions," I said.

The vultures started turning in all directions like

they were playing a game. We couldn't stay on the paths anymore, and I had to let Holly lean on me again as we pushed through the bushes and climbed over boulders.

I was about to give up on the plan when I heard the sound of crashing waves. The sun was getting lower in the sky, but I could see a beach beyond the trees up ahead.

"We're out!" I yelled, running for the sand. The forest went all the way to the shore. I threw my body down on the cool, soft sand and let out a cheer. "We can walk to town from here and call Mom."

Holly walked over to me, but she wasn't nearly as relieved as I was to be out of the woods. "J.B., look!" She pointed a shaky finger down the beach.

To our left, a string of caves lined the coast. I knew she was thinking about the wolves. I was about to tell her we were perfectly safe when I heard something moving in the cave closest to us. I jumped up.

"Wolf!" Holly screamed, and she darted back into the woods.

"Wait!" I yelled, but I didn't even look in her direction. My eyes were glued to the cave, or, more specifically, the girl coming out of the cave. She was about my age. Her hair was dark brown, and the ends had the slightest little curl. She was easily the most beautiful girl I'd ever seen, but it was her eyes

I couldn't look away from. They were the deepest shade of blue-green. I was so shocked by their color I stumbled backward.

She jumped when she saw me. "Are you okay?" she asked.

Blood rushed to my cheeks, and I couldn't form words. She repeated her question, staring at me like I was a complete mental case. I shook my head, forcing myself to snap out of the weird trance I was in. "I'm fine."

"Is your friend okay?" the girl said, looking toward the woods. I spotted Holly peering out from behind a large pine tree at the edge of the forest.

"Oh, yeah. She's my younger sister. We were born exactly a year apart." Why was I babbling?

"You have the same birthday? What are the odds of that?" she said, brushing back a strand of hair that had fallen across her face. "I think I'd like sharing my birthday with someone. I kind of always wished I had a twin."

"Yeah, I bet it's fun to be a twin. You should try it. I mean—" What was *wrong* with me?

I turned away, wanting to shrink from embarrassment, and I felt Holly's hand on my shoulder. "You should try it?" she whispered with a laugh. Of course she'd heard that!

Holly sized up the girl and winked at me. She knew

I had a crush. I glared at her, silently begging her to shut up. Although, I didn't think she could do anything to make me feel more embarrassed.

"I should go," the girl said, fidgeting uncomfortably.

"Wait," Holly said. "I'm Holly. You've met my brother, J.B."

"Sort of." She glanced at me, taking another step back. "I have to go." She motioned to the cave behind her and ducked inside.

Holly shrugged. "Was it something I said?"

"More likely something *I* said. I was a babbling idiot! Nothing I said made sense." I kicked a clump of wet sand.

"You're right. It didn't." Holly laughed.

I was about to retaliate when the girl came walking out of the cave again. Holly stopped laughing and grabbed my arm. "She's got a knife! She must be one of the Grimault thieves! Run!"

I didn't have time to react. Holly took off again, but this time she didn't duck behind a tree. She kept going.

"I didn't mean to scare her." The girl held a broken seashell in her hand, not a knife. "I'm Noelle."

"What are you doing here?" I asked.

Noelle just stared at me.

"Look, I'm sorry about before. My sister and I ran into some scary animals in the forest, and I guess I'm still a little shaky."

Noelle's face lit up. "Did you see anyone else in the woods? A man?"

"No. Why?"

"I'm looking for my dad. He's missing. I saw him in the forest, and well—he was in trouble." She looked away.

"You saw him in there?"

"Sort of. He was in the caves first." Noelle's hands shook, and she dropped the seashell in the sand. I picked it up and handed it to her. Our fingers touched, and a surge of electricity shot up my arm. We both jumped backward.

"Sorry, static electricity, I guess."

Noelle squinted at me. "Can you keep a secret?"

"Absolutely."

"I had this dream about my dad. He was wandering around in these woods, and he was mumbling. When I woke up this morning, my whole body was shaking and he was gone."

I wasn't sure what to say. I didn't want to make her worry even more, but I couldn't keep the truth about this forest a secret. Not if she was planning to go looking for her dad. "Listen, Noelle, these woods aren't like anything you've ever seen. Any and every scary thing you can imagine—it all comes to life in there."

I expected her to laugh or yell at me for trying to scare her, but Noelle didn't look surprised.

"I know. I saw it in my dream. I can't tell you how, but I knew the dream was real. I knew it was really happening." She looked down the shoreline, avoiding my eyes. "You probably think I'm crazy."

"No, not at all. After what I've seen in the forest, I think *I* might be the crazy one."

Noelle turned back to me and smiled. "Will you help me look for my father?"

I nodded. "But first, we have to find my sister. Before something else does."

CHAPTER SIX

The forest was the last place I wanted to be, especially after finding a way out of it. But, I couldn't say no to Noelle, and I couldn't leave Holly alone to voice her scary thoughts either.

"Holly? Where are you?" I hoped she wasn't lying in a ditch somewhere. "Holl—"

"Ca-caw!" Only Holly would think to make fake birdcalls.

Noelle and I stopped. We looked all around, but Holly was nowhere to be seen. I was getting impatient. This wasn't the place to be fooling around. "Where are you? I know that's you."

She answered with another birdcall.

"Are you sure that's your sister?" Noelle asked. "It sounds like a vulture."

I wanted to kick myself for forgetting to tell Noelle how the forest worked. Now she'd suggested a creature for us to deal with. I immediately whipped my head toward the trees. The branch directly above us started transforming into a giant vulture. As if the real ones weren't scary enough.

"Quick, get in that bush!" I yelled.

"What? I'm not getting in a sticker bush." The oversized bird swooped down at Noelle, and she dove for the bush.

I reached out and grabbed the tail of the bird as it pecked at Noelle. I started ripping the leaves out like feathers and the bird turned on me. Noelle leaped out of the bush and grabbed hold of the bird's wing. I got a hand on the other wing, and we pulled in opposite directions. The tree branch broke apart, and the leaves fell to the ground.

"Take that, forest!" I said, breathing heavily. I was really tired of this place.

"What *was* that?" Noelle's face was ghostly white.

"I forgot to tell you that the forest can hear you. If you imagine something scary and say it out loud, the forest makes it real. It only hears the nightmarish stuff, too. So, wishing for things like food or water doesn't get you anything." I kicked the pile of leaves, making sure the bird wasn't about to come back to life.

"I made the forest create that thing?"

"Don't sweat it. Holly and I created lots of scary creatures." I didn't go into details about the bears, wolves, and tree people. I didn't want to test the boundaries between remembering scary things and creating new ones.

Noelle looked like she was about to pass out when Holly stepped out from behind a bush. She had branches and leaves tucked into her clothing. I couldn't help laughing. "Nice job at the camouflage, but bushes don't wear sneakers."

"You couldn't find me, so obviously I did a pretty good job," Holly sneered. She squinted at Noelle. "Way to create an attack bird."

"Whoa!" I said, feeling strangely protective of Noelle. "Do you really want to compare who's made what come to life in this forest? Because I think your handiwork back at the cave would win."

Holly glared at me. "Whatever. Let's just get back to shore and away from this forest."

I grabbed her arm. "We can't leave yet. I promised Noelle we'd help her look for her dad. He's lost in here." I leaned closer and whispered, "Besides, I'm not ready to give up on breaking the curse." I hoped Noelle hadn't heard that part. I hadn't made the best first impression and didn't want her to know I was a cursed freak.

"Are you crazy?" Holly swung her arm out from my grip. "If you want to stay in this horrible place, be my guest. I'm going home." She turned, and her tree branch camouflage caught on a sticker bush. She started ripping the leaves from her clothing. "A little help, please!"

"And you want to go back to the shore on your own? You couldn't even make it two steps without needing my help."

Noelle bent down and picked something up off the ground. It was so dirty I couldn't tell what it was. "No, no, no!" She shook her head.

"What is it?" I asked.

"My dad's watch—or what's left of it." I took the watch from her, and we shocked each other again as our fingers touched.

"Sorry," I mumbled, but Noelle was too upset to care about a little static electricity. The watchband was chewed up, and the face was cracked. It looked like an animal had been using it as a chew toy. "It probably fell off and some squirrels thought it was food."

Noelle's lower lip quivered. "Probably. But this means my dream definitely was real. He was here and something bad happened to him."

Holly sighed and said, "If we're really going back through this forest, let's get it over with."

"Thanks," Noelle said in a soft voice.

"But this time, I get to lead." Before I could protest, Holly hopped onto a trail and took off like she knew where she was going. She even started skipping and humming "Lions and Tigers and Bears" as if she were Dorothy in *The Wizard of Oz*. But soon she got carried away and started singing her own version out loud, "Wolves and vultures and bears, oh my!"

I quickly covered her mouth. We all froze, waiting to see Holly's latest forest creations. The bush next to us started to move and wood splintered somewhere above us. "Run!" I yelled. We sprinted to the next fork in the trail.

"Go that way," Noelle said, pointing to the path on the left. "I'll try to lure the creatures this way."

Was she crazy? She was no match for the forest creatures. "We can't split up. Our only chance is to stay together." I grabbed her sleeve and tugged her to the left with Holly and me. But Noelle wiggled out of her jacket and tossed it on the trail to the right.

"Go!" she yelled, pushing me down the other path. "Maybe my jacket will confuse them. They'll think we took the other path."

We ran until we couldn't run anymore. My legs were like jelly, stumbling over the tiniest pebbles. Noelle's plan must have worked because there weren't any forest creatures behind us. "Let's slow down," I said, out of breath. "It's getting dark. We should find shelter for the night."

"What about my dad?" Noelle asked. "I have to find him."

"It'll be too dark to search soon, and we need to find shelter from—" I stopped. My mind swarmed with thoughts of all the terrible things in the forest we might need shelter from during the night.

"Go ahead. Say it!" Holly yelled. "All the terrifying things I've created? The scary things I'll probably talk about while I'm having nightmares? I can't take this anymore. Why did we even come here?" She sank to her knees and cried.

I knelt down beside her and put my arm around her shoulders. "I'm sorry I dragged you into this, but I couldn't ignore the journal. Not if there's a way to end the curse."

She nodded. "What are we going to do?" Her red, swollen eyes pleaded with me to find a way out of all this. I'm her big brother, and I'd gotten her lost inside a scary enchanted forest.

I sighed. "We're going to find shelter. In the morning, we're going to break the curse and find a way out of this forest."

Holly used her sleeve to wipe the tears from her eyes. Then, she gave me a thin smile to let me know she was ready to move on.

I turned around to tell Noelle we were ready to go, but she was gone. "Noelle?" My eyes frantically searched the woods.

"You don't think something got her, do you?" Holly

asked, jumping to her feet.

I felt sick. I knew what Noelle had done. "She went to find her dad." She was alone in the woods with danger lurking around every corner, and it was my fault.

"What do we do now? Even if we find her, we can't force her to stay with us."

Holly was right, and it wasn't safe to walk in the dark, so we started searching for shelter—without Noelle. With each step, the path got more difficult to see. The trees and bushes overhanging the path blocked what little daylight was left. I had to walk with my arms up to protect my face from getting scratched by branches.

"That's strange." I squinted at something big and dark up ahead.

"What is it?" Holly asked. "And please don't tell me that large blob is the backside of a b—"

I covered her mouth before she could finish her sentence and put us in danger again. "Please think about what you're saying *before* you say it." She nodded, and I lowered my hand.

"Sorry," she said, biting her lip.

We walked closer to the object, and I smiled. "It's our home for the night." I grabbed Holly's hand and pulled her toward a large tree that had been split in half, probably by lightning. The top of the tree had fallen over onto an enormous boulder, and moss had grown on the tree and rock, forming a sort of roof. "There's just enough room under here for us to sleep."

"We're going to sleep under a fallen tree?" Holly asked.

"It's the best shelter we're going to find, unless you want to try to make our way back to the cave with the—"

"This looks great!" Holly interrupted.

"Good. Let's get some rest."

I needed to sleep after the day I'd had. Between all the walking and escaping dangerous animals, I was wiped. But, knowing that the fallen tree didn't provide much protection from those animals made it almost impossible to even close my eyes. I wondered how Noelle was doing.

CHAPTER SEVEN

Every time I closed my eyes, I heard rustling in the woods and my eyes popped open. So, when the sun finally came up in the morning, I was more than ready to start searching for the Granville fortune. I had to break the curse, even if it meant not seeing Noelle again.

I nudged Holly's shoulder. "Wake up."

"Don't eat me!" she screamed. Her arms flailed in front of her face.

There wasn't much room, but I backed up as much as I could to avoid getting hit. "Holl, it's me."

She sprang up and hit her head on the tree limb above her. "Ouch!" she yelled, placing a hand on the top of her head.

She'd done it again! "Let's not start the day with another injury. If you keep this up, I won't have a shirt left to wrap your wounds in."

"Very funny." She narrowed her eyes at me. "I

think I can take your shirt off my ankle. It feels a little better."

"Good, because we have no idea what the forest has in store for us today."

I hated not knowing what to expect. It would've been nice to think that as long as we didn't voice our fears, we'd get through the woods with no problems, but I was willing to bet the heart of the forest was going to be the scariest of all. And I guessed we were heading toward it.

"I've never been this hungry or thirsty in my life," Holly said, letting out a groan. "My stomach is past the point of growling. It just hurts!"

"I know what you mean. We could try to follow the vultures again—if we come across them." I scanned the sky, but it was clear. "We don't know which way they went after we left them last night."

"Ugh! Can't something go right for once?"

"At least it looks like the weather will be nice today," I said, trying to be optimistic, but there really wasn't any bright side to the situation. We were cursed, hungry, lost, and doomed to be grounded for life if we ever made it home. We walked for hours until we heard mumbled voices.

"Did you hear that?" Holly asked, tugging on my sleeve.

"Shh!" I warned her. The last thing we needed

was her imagination getting us into trouble again. I pushed aside a large branch. Not more than twenty-five feet ahead was a small clearing and two kids. The taller one couldn't have been more than seventeen or eighteen, and the shorter one was about my age. "Get down," I whispered, pulling Holly behind a large bush. "There are two guys in that clearing." The boys must be brothers. The resemblance was strong—tall, dark, shaggy hair, and muscular.

"Maybe they could help us."

"I don't know. They look mean." Both boys scowled as they talked.

"You don't think they're the thieves, do you? The ones from the journal?" Holly said, reading my mind.

"Don't worry. If they are the Grimault thieves, they're just searching for the Granville fortune. Besides, it's not like we have any valuables for them to steal." Holly opened her mouth to protest, but I cut her off. "Be quiet. I want to hear what they're saying." I leaned forward, but the boys were too far away. "I can't hear them."

"Do they have any food with them?" Holly asked.

Just like Holly—controlled by her stomach. "No, but the older one is holding—" My eyes widened.

Holly poked me between my shoulder blades. "What?"

"I think it's the painting we left at the park." What

if they figured out they weren't alone in the woods? That someone else was trying to find the fortune?

"Mom would've taken the painting home with her."

"What if they found it before Mom did?"

"What if Mom was in the park when they found the painting? They could've done something to her," Holly said.

"We have to follow them and see if that's true." I wanted to stay calm, but there were a million thoughts in my head and not one was good.

"What are they doing now?" Holly asked, tilting her head to see around me.

I peered over the bush. "They're leaving. Come on, but be quiet."

We followed the two guys to a campsite. Four green tents were pitched around a large campfire. The guys entered one of the tents.

"What is this place?" Holly asked once we were safely hidden behind a large boulder.

"I guess this is where the Grimaults are camping out while they search for the fortune. We should look around while they're in that tent."

"What if someone comes out while we're snooping?"

"We'll have to stay behind the trees and only go into the camp when it's absolutely necessary."

Holly's face lit up. "Look! There's bread and water by the fire. Do you think we could get to it without being seen?"

I surveyed the area, searching for the best path to the fire. "I think we should circle around to the other side by that tent. Then I'll run out and grab the canteen and bread."

"There aren't as many trees to hide behind over there," Holly said.

"You're right. You better stay here. Hide behind this tree and keep out of sight. I'll get the food."

"Be careful."

I crept from tree to tree, checking each of the tents to make sure no one was coming into the clearing. I made my way to the tent closest to the fire and gave Holly a little wave to let her know where I was. Then, I ran into the center of the camp, but I saw a look of panic on Holly's face just as I got to the bread. I had no idea what was wrong, so I grabbed the food. As I turned around, I saw the boots of one of the thieves stepping out of a tent. It was the younger one. Luckily, he was looking at what I assumed was the painting of Braeden Forest that he held in his hands. I didn't hesitate. I ran as fast as I could back into the trees.

I ducked behind the nearest tree, leaning my back against the trunk and holding my breath in fear. My heart pounded so loudly I was sure the thief would hear it and find me.

"Hey, where's my bread and water?"

My body trembled as I clutched the canteen and loaf of bread to my chest.

"What are you yelling about, Edward?"

I peeked around the tree and saw the older boy coming out of his tent, rubbing his eyes. "I was trying to sleep."

"Garret, did you eat my food?"

"What food? I told you I'm trying to sleep. You know I'm on patrol tonight, so keep quiet and let me rest," Garret grumbled as he disappeared inside the tent.

I froze, afraid even the smallest step would give me away. My eyes darted in all directions, looking for Holly. I didn't see her anywhere. I took that as a good sign. If I couldn't see her, hopefully neither could Edward.

"Someone stole my food!" Edward kicked at the logs in the fire. His boot hit the flames and caught on fire. He yelled and jumped up and down, trying to stamp out the flames that were probably burning a hole through to his foot.

I ran to the next tree and caught a glimpse of Holly, still backed up against the oak tree. I tried to motion to her, but she was looking the other way. Edward was still trying to put out his flaming boot, so I ran to Holly and grabbed her arm. Before she saw it was me, she let out a bloodcurdling scream.

CHAPTER EIGHT

I covered Holly's mouth with my hand, but it was too late. Edward stopped stamping his boot against the ground and looked in every direction. I pushed Holly into the cover of the trees, and as I turned back to see what Edward was doing, my eyes locked with his. Neither of us moved.

Holly tugged on my arm. "Let's get out of here!"

I stayed frozen in place. Thoughts of fortune, curses, and Noelle all jumbled together in my mind. Chills ran down my spine. I knew I should run, but I was strangely drawn to the camp. Something about Edward seemed almost familiar. Like I'd met him before. I didn't have time to explain this to Holly because the other thief, Garret, came running into the center of the camp, holding a large knife.

"Who screamed?" asked Garret.

"They—" Edward stopped and stared at the fire still burning through his boot. He stomped so hard on the ground that enough dirt kicked up and put out the flame. "They went into the trees. Two of them." Edward pointed in our direction. "They stole my food!"

I pushed Holly through the trees. "Run!"

Holly swatted at the tree branches. "Why are we running through all this? It's slowing us down!"

"Those guys live in this forest. They know the paths better than we do. This is our only chance of getting away. But we have to stop talking, or they'll follow the sound of our voices."

I ran so fast I could hardly speak, but I managed to whisper, "This way," between all my huffing and puffing. Holly and I ducked under the branch of a large elm tree. I looked back to see how close Edward and Garret were, but I didn't see them. "Where did they go?"

"I don't know. I've been trying to keep up with—" Holly didn't finish her sentence. She screamed instead.

I whipped my head around and saw Edward and Garret blocking our path. Holly and I ran right into their arms. I felt like a fool for not realizing the thieves probably knew all the shortcuts through the forest.

"Gotcha!" Garret yelled.

I didn't even try to scream for help. It would've been useless. The only other people around were more Grimault thieves.

"What were you doing at our camp? And how

did you get by the traps we set on the paths?" Garret asked.

"We're lost. Please don't hurt us," Holly said in a shaky voice. Garret held her by her ponytail, and she was craning her neck to look at him.

"You expect us to believe you're lost?" Garret said. "No one in their right mind comes into Braeden Forest. This place will eat you alive if you don't know how to get around its enchantments."

"What did you do with our mother?" I demanded, trying to sound tough. It wasn't easy, considering these guys were terrifying. Edward looked normal enough, but I got this weird feeling around him—like my skin was crawling or something.

"Your mother's here, too?" Edward said, squeezing my arms. His hands felt unusually warm through my shirt.

"So, you found the painting before our mom did," I said, more as a statement than a question.

"What painting?" Edward and Garret asked as they exchanged a puzzled look.

"I saw you looking at it back at your camp."

"A painting—yeah, that's what we were looking at!" Garret laughed, and I could tell he was being sarcastic. I *really* didn't like him.

"You don't have our mother held prisoner?" Holly asked.

"She brings up a good point. Kidnapping could make us a fortune. It'd come in handy if we don't find—" Garret stopped himself. He obviously didn't want to mention the Granville fortune in front of Holly and me, and I wasn't going to tell him we already knew about it. Something told me it'd be the end of us. "Where did you say you lived?" he asked.

"Let us go! We aren't going to tell you anything!" I struggled to break free from Edward's grasp, but it was no use.

"Let's take them back to the camp and figure out what we're going to do with them," Edward said.

I wasn't about to go without a fight. I looked at the burn mark on Edward's right boot, and I got an idea. I raised my foot and with all my might, I stomped on Edward's wounded foot.

"Ow!" Edward let go of me and grabbed his foot. I reached for Holly's hand and tried to pull her from Garret's grasp, but he was too strong. The only thing I succeeded in doing was getting Holly's hair pulled.

Holly yelled. Then she looked me in the eyes. "Run, J.B.!"

I stood there staring at Holly. I didn't want to get away if it meant leaving her behind.

"Go!" she insisted, giving me a look I knew well. She'd come up with a plan of her own. I turned and ran.

I had to trust that Holly'd figured out how to get free from Garret. Still, I didn't want to run too far, so I hid behind a bush just close enough for me to keep an eye on her. Garret stood with his mouth gaping open, caught off guard by the fact that I'd left my sister stranded there. Holly didn't waste any time. She angled her head, which couldn't have been easy since Garret still had a grip on her hair, and she bit down on his free arm. Garret yelled and let go. While he rubbed his arm, Holly took off.

I smiled so wide my molars were probably showing. That was Holly. A biter since birth.

CHAPTER NINE

When she got close enough, I pulled Holly behind the bush. This time, she didn't scream. She threw her arms around me and squeezed me harder than I'd ever been hugged. Normally, I'm not the hugging type, but I was relieved Holly's plan had worked and she was free from Garret.

As soon as she let go of me, I put a finger to my lips. I heard Garret and Edward's voices before I saw them, and I motioned for Holly to stay still.

"Which way did they go?" Garret said.

From where I crouched, I could only see their boots, but that was enough to make sure Holly and I stayed out of sight until the coast was clear.

"They couldn't have gone far," Edward said.

"Exactly, so why haven't we spotted them?" Garret practically screamed. I expected thieves to be a little stealthier than these two. Who didn't know that screaming was not a good idea when you're trying to sneak up on someone?

"They must be hiding," Edward said.

A lump formed in my throat. Edward was no dummy. He was probably searching the bushes.

"We can't look behind every tree for them, but we also can't let them escape and tell people we're here."

"Relax, Garret. They won't make it out of this forest alive with all the wild animals in here. Not to mention the creatures this place creates," Edward said.

"Yeah," Garret growled. "They don't even have any weapons."

"Let's head back to camp. I need to take a look at this burn on my foot."

"I should probably wash my arm. Who knows what diseases that little twerp has? I can't believe she bit me!"

Holly squeezed her hands into fists, but I covered her mouth with one hand and held her arm with the other. When I couldn't see Garret and Edward anymore, I stood up and sighed with relief. "I didn't want to leave you, but when I saw the look on your face, I knew you'd thought of your own way to escape."

"I can't get the taste of that dirty, disgusting thief's arm out of my mouth," Holly said.

"Here, you can rinse your mouth with some of this

water." I grabbed the canteen I'd hidden behind the bush.

Holly's eyes widened at the sight of food. "I can't believe you held on to the bread and water through all that. I would've dropped them."

"My stomach wouldn't let me. I'm starving!"

"Me too! Break off a piece of bread for me."

"It's kind of squished because I was gripping it so tightly, and it feels like it's getting stale."

"I don't care," Holly said, shoving the food in her mouth.

While we sat in our hiding place eating the stolen bread and drinking water, I tried to decide what to do next. I wasn't sure how Noelle was managing on her own. I hoped she didn't run into Garret and Edward. Before I knew it, we'd devoured the food, and I still didn't have a plan. To make matters worse, I felt another vision coming on. I turned away from Holly. Luckily, she was too busy eating crumbs off her shirt to notice me sweating. I splashed some water on my face, hoping to shock myself out of it. The vision came anyway, but it was calmer. I didn't shake as much, and my head felt clearer afterwards. I started to make sense of the weird things that had happened.

"The crazy guy in the park kept saying 'knife' and 'grim,'" I said, testing my idea on Holly.

"Garret had a knife."

I nodded. "And 'grim' was supposed to be Grimault." I was sure the Grimault thieves had driven that poor man insane. Garret and Edward were young, but the rest of their family was in the woods, too. I hoped we wouldn't meet them.

"Do you still want to search for the Granville fortune?" Holly asked.

As much as I didn't want to be anywhere near the Grimault thieves, I knew the fortune was the answer to ending the curse. "Yeah," I answered. "But we have to find Noelle, too."

"Why?"

"She's all alone. She could be in trouble, and we're the only ones who know she's here."

Holly grunted and threw a rock at the tree behind me. I ducked as it ricocheted off the peeling bark and just missed hitting me in the head. "*She* walked away from *us*, remember?"

"She was upset. She thought we weren't going to help her find her dad. How would you feel if it was Dad or Mom who went missing in this place? You'd be out of your mind, too." Holly bit her lip and refused to look me in the eye. That usually meant she was thinking about what I'd said but didn't want to give in. "What if Garret and Edward or any of the other Grimault thieves find her? The others could be much bigger and stronger. She wouldn't stand a chance."

Holly finally looked at me. "I guess we have to try to help her."

"Thanks, Holl." I couldn't fight back my smile.

"So, now what?" she asked.

"We try not to run into any more Grimault thieves."

"How do we do that?"

"They walked that way," I said, pointing to the right. "So we'll go the other way. I saw a path back where Edward and Garret caught us."

It didn't take long to find our way back to the path, but it did take longer than it should have since I kept pulling Holly behind trees at the smallest sound. Since the forest was full of squirrels and other little creatures, that happened often.

"I thought we finished all the water," Holly said, pointing to the empty canteen in my hand.

"We did, but I figured we should hold on to it in case we find that stream. We could refill it." I looped the strap of the canteen around my neck so I had both hands free.

"Good thinking, but I'm hoping we get out of here soon enough that we won't have to worry about finding more water."

"That's a nice thought, but we probably won't be that lucky. We're cursed, remember?"

"Yeah, but this path seems different than the others. We've been on it for a while, and it hasn't split into two like the rest of them."

"That *is* strange. Now that I think about it, the path has been curving to the right. But that means—" I stopped, afraid to finish my thought.

"We're heading right back to the thieves' camp!" Holly said.

"We have to get off this path!" I grabbed Holly's arm and pulled her into the trees to the left of the path.

As we ducked behind a large tree, I heard voices. *Garret and Edward.* That explained why they were able to cut us off earlier. The path looped around their camp.

Through the trees, I could see the campfire. Garret and Edward were standing by it. Garret had his arm wrapped in a white shirt. A smile crept across Holly's face when she saw it. I didn't move a muscle as I watched another thief join Edward and Garret. Even though I could only see his back, the moment he spoke, I knew nothing I'd faced in Braeden Forest was as frightening as the realization of who the figure was that stood before me.

"It's Dad!"

CHAPTER TEN

Dad talked to Edward and Garret like he'd known them for years. He'd kept things from me before, but this went way beyond any little white lie. There was a huge difference between being a lawyer and being a thief.

"What's Dad doing with the Grimault thieves?" Holly asked.

"Shh!" I leaned in as close as I could without being seen. Dad handed Garret and Edward some silver coins.

Garret flipped one in the air and smiled. "Hopefully, we'll have the rest soon. We've been living off practically nothing, but that will change once we find the Granville fortune."

Dad removed a piece of paper from his pocket and showed it to Garret, who looked very happy. "It was given to me by my father, a very dear friend of your grandfather."

Dad and Grandpa both knew the Grimaults? Was Dad working with them to scare that poor guy and get the park closed so they could search for the fortune?

"Edward, go get Dad," Garret said. "He'll want to see this right away." Garret led Dad to the big rocks surrounding the campfire, and they sat down.

I turned to Holly. She was frozen in disbelief, and I knew exactly how she felt. I couldn't believe the man I'd known all my life was a thief. He'd been sneaking around behind our backs and lying to our faces. Did Mom know about this?

Why would Dad want to steal the Granville fortune if it had to be returned in order to end the curse? I had to find out what was going on. I turned back to the camp and saw Edward returning with another thief in his early twenties. Definitely not their father.

"What do you think those coins are?" Holly asked. Garret was still flipping his in the air. "And where did Dad get them? We're practically broke."

"They're part of the Granville fortune," came a soft voice behind us. "Silver coins with the family crest imprinted on them." Noelle looked like she hadn't slept in days.

"Look who it is," Holly said, sounding as unfriendly as possible.

"Lay off!" I said. I was so happy to see Noelle and not just because I'd been worried about her being alone in the forest. I felt different when she was around. I felt like Noelle and I were supposed to be together somehow.

"Looks like a party," Noelle said, pointing to the group of thieves. The three boys were sitting on the ground listening to my dad like they were one big happy family. It made my stomach turn. Dad couldn't even make time to share a meal with *me*.

"Where have you been?" I asked Noelle.

"I found this camp after I left you guys. I've been staying close to it. I thought maybe my dad would show up here looking for help. He hasn't." She lowered her eyes.

"Noelle, I feel awful about what happened. I didn't mean we weren't going to help you."

Noelle raised her eyes to mine. "My dream was so awful. I had to find my dad. I didn't mean to make you feel bad when I left."

Holly tapped her foot. "What is *with* you two? We're in a freaky forest that preys on our fears and is full of thieves—and one of them is our dad. Who cares who hurt whose feelings?"

She was right. We didn't have time for apologies. I had to figure out what Dad was doing with the Grimaults.

"Wait a minute. *Your* dad's here, too?" Noelle looked accusingly at me.

I shook my head. "We had no idea he was here. He's supposed to be on some big court case. He's a lawyer. Or at least that's what he told us."

Noelle touched my shoulder. Again, we shocked each other. "Sorry," she said, staring at her hand. "And you don't owe me any explanations. We don't even know each other."

"That's right. We don't," Holly chimed in. "It's really hard to hear what they're saying with you two chatting away." She flipped her head around to watch the camp again.

"Maybe I can help," Noelle said. "I've been watching them, and I've figured out a few things." She peeked through the branches. "Trent is the really muscular one. He's twenty-two. I know because he's constantly reminding Garret and Edward that he's older than them. Trent's their cousin. He likes to pretend he's in charge, but no one listens to him."

"How old are *you*?" Holly asked.

"Almost ten." Noelle looked like she was about to say more, but she changed her mind.

"So, they're one big happy family of thieves, huh?" I asked.

"Not quite. Edward and Garret get along pretty well, as long as Edward listens to Garret. Garret thinks he's like second-in-command or something. Trent hates it when Garret tells him what to do, so they fight a lot."

"What about their father?"

"Morgan Grimault. He makes the kids work day and night while he does who knows what inside that tent." Noelle shivered.

"What's wrong?" I asked.

"Morgan's scary. I've heard the others talking about some of the awful things he's done to people who've come near the forest." Noelle choked on the words, and I knew exactly what she was thinking. Morgan was responsible for her father's disappearance. I stared at my dad. He didn't look like he was in any danger. I wasn't sure if I felt relieved that he didn't have to worry about the Grimaults hurting him or if I was terrified that he seemed to belong with them.

"Dad's the scary one," Holly said. "He's been lying to us about all those business trips. I bet this is where he's been going. He's a thief!"

I'd always resented the fact that Dad was never home, but I couldn't believe he was a thief. On the rare occasions when he did stay home, he was the greatest father ever. That was why I hated his job so much. It took him away from me. "They're going to hear you," I warned Holly. She wasn't being loud at all. I just didn't want to listen to her talk about Dad like that.

"I'm not going to stand around and wait to be caught again," Holly said, tugging on my arm. She turned to Noelle. "If you're coming with us, then let's go."

I broke loose from Holly's grip. "Hang on. Someone else came out of that tent."

Noelle gulped. "It's Morgan."

He looked about fifty and wore a long trench coat. He had a red scarf around his neck and a large knife—twice the size of Garret's—hanging from his belt. The knife wasn't the most disturbing thing about him. He had enormous bushy black eyebrows that looked like giant caterpillars, a grisly black beard, and a mustache that curled at the ends.

Noelle, Holly, and I ducked behind the bushes.

"What do we have here?" Morgan asked, walking over to the fire.

"Sorry to wake you," Garret said, "but I figured you'd want to hear what Bruce has to say as soon as possible."

Morgan nodded and addressed my father. "I'm Morgan Grimault. My boys and I arrived about a month ago to search for the fortune my great-great-great-great-great-grandfather Aristede hid in this forest. Edward tells me you're the son of my father's friend Eli, and you've brought me a piece of the map showing the location of the fortune."

Dad stood up and removed a paper from his pocket. "That's right. I know the search is a family affair, but my father came across this and asked me to bring it to you." He handed the map to Morgan.

"Let's see." Morgan examined the map by the light of the fire.

"All of the maps are drawn to look slightly different than the real forest. Once we find all of the differences, we'll know where to look for the fortune." Morgan stroked his beard as he studied the paper.

"So, each map is part of a larger treasure map?" my dad asked.

"Exactly," Morgan said, and his face twisted in anger. "This map wasn't drawn by Aristede. He drew the first one, and I can't locate the fortune without it. We must still be missing one map!" He threw the map to the ground and stormed back to his tent. Garret followed him. Trent shrugged and went into his own tent.

"I was certain I had the only remaining map," Dad said. Worry lines creased his forehead.

"Dad's been searching all his life for the maps his ancestors left behind," Edward said. "They were hidden in places where only our family would find them."

"Are they all drawings of the same part of the forest?" Dad asked.

"No. Each map shows a different section of the forest. They contain things that *aren't* in the forest. The additional items are the clues to where the fortune is buried. The older maps are more difficult to read because the forest has changed over time, and some things that used to be in the forest might not be here now."

"How do you know some maps are older than others? Weren't they all drawn at the same time?"

Edward shook his head. "Aristede drew the first map, and with each generation of Grimaults, someone else has drawn a map. The fortune was meant to remain hidden until now."

I turned to Holly. "That doesn't make sense. Why would Aristede leave the fortune for someone else?"

"Maybe he wanted his family to be cursed like he was," she said.

Noelle's eyes widened. "How do you know they're cursed?"

"Because we are, too. Thanks to our ancestor who stole the Granville fortune." Holly practically spit the words out.

Noelle squinted at Holly, and this time I wasn't sure what Holly had done to provoke it.

"Let's just keep an eye on Dad," I said, motioning toward the camp.

Edward was still explaining the maps. "My grandfather was the last person to draw a map. When he died, he left the map to my dad as the first clue to the location of the fortune."

"How did each generation know what to draw?" my dad asked.

"They were each told a part of the story about the

hidden fortune so that they could draw the necessary map. Aristede told Ulysses every part of the story except for what Aristede drew himself. Then, Ulysses told Gerard the remaining part of the story with the exception of what Ulysses and Aristede drew. And so on. No one, except for Aristede, ever knew the exact location of the fortune."

"So if Aristede was Morgan's great-great-great-great-great-grandfather, that means there must be a total of..." Dad paused as he counted out five great-grandfathers, a grandfather, and a father on his fingers. "Seven maps."

"We thought the map you brought was the final piece since it was the seventh, but one of the maps must be a fake because Aristede's is still missing."

"There must be some way to figure out which map is fake."

"Dad carries a list of his ancestors so we can keep track of the maps we still need. I know where he keeps it. Wait here." Edward headed toward Morgan's tent and disappeared inside.

"Something isn't right," I whispered. "For someone trying to help the Grimaults locate the fortune, Dad doesn't know much about it. And our name isn't Grimault, so how did Dad or Grandpa get one of the maps?"

Edward returned with a slip of paper in his hands. "We've been recovering the maps from the most recently drawn to the oldest. Take a look."

Dad and Edward had their backs to me, so I figured it was safe to move a little closer. I ducked behind a tree and motioned for Holly and Noelle to follow.

"How do you match the map to the person who drew it?" Dad asked.

"They're initialed in the bottom right-hand corner."

Dad picked up the map Morgan had thrown. "This one has the initials GG. That means it was drawn by..." he looked at the list of names, "Gerard Grimault."

"But we already found his map. See, it's checked off," Edward said.

"So, one of the maps with the initials GG is a fake."

"You better hope it isn't the map you brought," Edward warned. He led my father into one of the tents.

"Let's go," Holly whispered.

"Dad may be in trouble. Didn't you hear Edward? The map Dad brought must be a fake. I knew he wasn't really a thief."

"What are you talking about? You saw the look on Dad's face when Morgan said the map wasn't the last piece they were looking for. Dad was as surprised as the rest of them."

"There must be some explanation we aren't seeing. I'm not leaving here until I find out what's really going on!"

"What do you plan on doing? You can't storm into

those tents and tell Dad to take us home. Those guys would kill you!"

"I'm not going to talk to Dad or any of those other thieves—"

"*Other* thieves? I thought you said you didn't believe Dad *was* a thief?"

"I don't. That's not what I meant!" I balled my hands into fists. "If Morgan thinks Dad's map is a fake, he might hurt him. I'm not going to let that happen."

Holly threw her arms in the air. "You can't fight a group of armed thieves."

"I'm not leaving Dad alone with these guys. If you don't want to stay and help me, then leave. Find your own way home!" Tears burned my eyes. Noelle stepped away, giving Holly and me some privacy.

"Do you really want to risk our lives for him? He's never there for us."

She was right. Dad had missed so many important events in our lives. But what about the good times? I had to hold on to those, no matter how angry I was with him.

"We've been focused on Dad, but this isn't just about him," I said. "It's about the curse. We need to end it, with or without Dad's help."

Holly nodded. "You're right."

With or without Dad's help. Why did I have a feeling it'd be without?

CHAPTER ELEVEN

Holly, Noelle, and I were no match for a gang of thieves. Still, I couldn't sit there and do nothing, so I took a deep breath and tried to gather all the courage I could. Then, I led us through the trees surrounding the camp and started searching for Dad.

"He's not in there," I whispered after peeking into a tent.

"We saw Dad go in there with Edward. We only turned our backs to the camp for a minute. Where could he have gone?"

I didn't get a chance to answer Holly's question because a heavy hand slammed down hard on my right shoulder. I turned to meet Trent's evil stare.

"What do we have here? Garret and Edward said they found two kids wandering around earlier, but it looks like we have another now." Trent grinned eerily at Noelle.

"Let go of him," Holly said. She was trying to sound

brave, but her voice was shaky.

Trent grabbed Holly by her ponytail. "I heard what you did to Garret, so don't get any ideas about trying to bite me. I'm much stronger than he is."

Holly winced as Trent yanked her hair.

I squirmed, trying to get free, but Trent was even stronger than the others. His muscles were so huge they looked like they were going to burst right through his shirt. What was Morgan feeding these guys? They definitely didn't get this strong off bread and water.

"Trent? Is that you?" Garret asked. He yawned as he walked out of his tent.

"Yeah. I found those two little snoops you were talking about earlier, and they've got another one with them now," Trent said.

Garret grabbed Noelle's arm and turned to Holly and me. "Not very bright, are you, stumbling into our camp twice in the same day? You don't really think you're clever enough to escape again, do you?"

"We were clever enough to steal your bread and water," Holly said.

Garret's face reddened. He stormed over to me and ripped the canteen from around my neck. It felt like my head was going to come off with it.

"I'll show you what we do to thieves around here!" he said, throwing the canteen on the ground.

"Aren't you all thieves?" asked Holly.

I didn't know where Holly's newfound confidence was coming from, but I was worried she was going to get us killed.

"What did you do with my father?" Noelle asked. "He came here yesterday."

Garret and Trent exchanged glances and started laughing. "Sweetie, nobody comes here and lives to tell about it," Trent said.

"No!" Noelle slumped forward like she was in pain. Garret had to hold her up. I wanted to reach out to her, but Trent's grip was too tight.

"What are you going to do to us?" Holly demanded.

"I'll let my father decide that in the morning," Garret said. "In the meantime, you'll spend the night in Trent's tent." He turned to Trent. "I'm on patrol tonight, so you'll have to keep an eye on them."

"Fine," Trent said through gritted teeth. I could tell Trent resented having to take orders from his younger cousin, especially since he'd been assigned to babysit for the night.

Once we were inside the tent, Garret made Trent repeat his orders back to him three times before he was satisfied enough to leave. The only things in the tent were a duffle bag and a bed, which was actually a bale of hay. Trent moved his bed to block the entrance to the tent.

"Sit over there against the far end," Trent said. He

removed his boots and sat on the bed. "I'm staying right here, so don't get any ideas about trying to escape. You'll never get past me."

I walked across the tent and sat against the canvas. Noelle rested her head on her knees and continued to cry. Surprisingly, Holly put her arm around Noelle's shoulders. Even *she* sympathized with Noelle's loss. I glared at Trent. "We're kids. Can't you let us go?"

"That isn't my decision, not that I would anyway. I suggest you get some rest. Who knows what Uncle Morgan will do with you in the morning." Trent started laughing.

"What's so funny?" I asked, not sure I really wanted to know.

Trent lay back on his bed. "I was thinking about what Uncle Morgan did to Sticky Fingers Sam. He said he had some information that might help us find the fortune, but Garret caught him stealing from us. When Uncle Morgan found out, he covered Sam in honey and left him tied to a tree near the seaside entrance to the forest." Trent was laughing so hard I could barely understand him.

"What happened to him?" I asked, my words getting caught in my throat as I imagined what else Morgan might have done to Sam.

"Don't really know. Uncle Morgan nicknamed him Sweetcheeks because the squirrels and vultures were eating the sweet honey off Sam's cheeks when we left him."

I didn't see how anyone could find that funny. They'd left that poor guy to die. These thieves were getting more horrifying by the minute.

Noelle wiped her face with her sleeve. "You killed him!" She jumped to her feet and lunged at Trent.

Holly grabbed Noelle's arm, but Noelle easily broke free. I put her in a bear hug from behind. She fought me, swinging her arms at my hands. We shocked each other again, and luckily it snapped Noelle out of her attack. She slumped into my arms. Holly got to her feet and helped me sit Noelle down.

Trent sat straight up on his bed. "I'd keep her under control if I were you. We wouldn't want the little sweetie to get hurt."

Noelle scowled at Trent. I was afraid she was going to pounce again, but instead she asked in a weak voice, "Why did you do it? Why couldn't you just send him away?"

"We couldn't take a chance of letting him get out of these woods alive. This camp is a secret. No one who comes across it ever gets out alive."

I gulped, and Noelle's sobbing got louder. We'd been safer in the woods on our own, even with the forest preying on our fears, than we were with the Grimaults. I sat huddled against the wall for a long time, thinking about how hopeless the situation was when I heard the faint sound of snoring.

"Trent's asleep," I whispered.

"So?" Holly said. "He's blocking the entrance."

She was right, but we couldn't stay here and wait for whatever it was Morgan was going to do to us. I stared at Trent's bed, thinking the enchanted forest could actually help us for the first time.

"Holl, I've got a crazy idea."

"I'm listening, but I'm warning you I've had my fill of crazy in the past few days."

"I think we might be able to use the forest to help us get away from Trent." Holly and Noelle looked at me like I'd completely lost it. "His bed is a bale of hay. Maybe we could make it change into something that'd hold him back long enough for us to run away."

"But it'd be blocking the doorway, too," Holly said. "We'd have to fight our way around it."

"It's worth a try. Trent will use his knife to hack up the hay, and even if we don't get away, we'll be right back where we are now. No matter how mad Trent gets, he won't do anything to us until Morgan wakes up."

"I guess, but does that mean we're going to leave Dad here?" Holly asked.

"No," I said without hesitation. "We're going to search for him. Garret's supposed to patrol all night for intruders. Maybe Dad's on patrol, too."

"That would explain why he wasn't in any of the tents," Holly said.

"We'll keep looking for your father, too," I said to Noelle. "These guys are thieves, and I'll bet they're also liars. Who knows if they've really met your dad?"

Noelle looked at me through swollen eyes. "Thanks."

I took a deep breath. My plan had the potential to backfire badly, but it was the only thing I could come up with. I chose my words carefully and pointed to Trent's bed. "Trent's bed looks like a—" I looked at Holly and silently communicated an apology, "big yellow bear wrapping him in a hug."

Immediately, the hay bent and twisted into the form of a large bear. It wrapped its arms around Trent. The bear growled in response to Trent's snoring, and Trent startled out of his sleep. Holly, Noelle, and I jumped up and ran for the tiny space between the tent door and the bear-hugging duo. I grabbed Trent's bandana and shoved it in his mouth to keep him from screaming. We burst out of the tent and sprinted into the woods.

"I hate to say it, but we're going to have to get back onto one of the paths if we want to find our way through these woods in the dark," I said.

"If you want to find your dad, our best chance is

to get back on the trail that circles the camp," Noelle said.

Holly slowed to a stop. "No way!"

Noelle and I stopped, too. I couldn't hear the thieves or the growling bear, so I figured it was safe to take a second to think. "She's right, Holly. Look, we're getting the hang of this forest, and we've gotten away from the thieves more than once. We can do this. Dad would do it for us. It's probably why he's in Braeden Forest in the first place."

"Are you sure about that?" Holly asked, crossing her arms. "Can you really forget about how he's never around anymore? And what about the secrets he's been keeping? Why would seeing him here make you forgive him all of a sudden?"

"That's not what I'm doing. I'm still mad at him. It's just—" I couldn't explain how I felt because I didn't understand it myself. "Let's not argue. We need to move before the sun comes up and someone sees us."

"I think the path is somewhere over there," Noelle said, pointing to our right.

We managed to find our way back to the path. After about ten minutes, I began to move more confidently through the forest.

"Hold up, J.B.," Holly said. "I don't think we've been on this section of the path before."

Something tightened around my ankle, and I was

swept upside-down. I looked at Holly and realized I was dangling from a tree, caught up in some sort of rope netting.

"Are you all right?" Noelle asked.

"I'm fine. The thieves must have placed traps along the trail so no one would find their camp." I struggled to sit up in the netting. The rope was rough, and it dug into my arms and legs.

"Garret mentioned something about traps when he caught us earlier," Holly said. "How are we going to get you down from there?"

"We need something to cut the rope. Look for a sharp rock."

Holly searched the ground, feeling along the grass and dirt. "It's still kind of dark. I can't really see well, but I don't think there are any sharp—" Holly screamed and grabbed Noelle's arm.

I watched helplessly as they both were scooped up into another net. I closed my eyes and tried to pretend I was anywhere other than dangling from the trees with no way to get free.

CHAPTER TWELVE

It was bad enough that *I'd* gotten caught in a net, but I didn't think things could get any worse now that Holly and Noelle were dangling beside me. If I'd had even a little luck, Holly would've found a sharp rock before she reached headfirst into the trap. Or, at least she wouldn't have pulled Noelle into the trap with her so one of us would've been free.

"Ow! That's my foot!" Holly whined.

"At least you're not upside-down!" Noelle said, squirming in the net.

"Would you two knock it off?" I was sick of their arguing.

"Quit moving around!" Holly yelled.

"I wouldn't be stuck up here if you hadn't grabbed me! So lay off!" Noelle said.

The only time they'd gotten along was when Garret told Noelle about her dad. Holly must have forgotten all about that because she was back to her usual self.

"Fighting isn't helping. We need to find a way out of here."

They stopped squirming. Holly blew a few strands of hair out of her face. "How do you suggest we get down from here, big brother?"

"I don't think getting down is going to be a problem," Noelle said.

"Did you think of a way to get out of these nets?" I asked.

"Yeah." Noelle's voice shook. "I'm pretty sure *he'll* cut us down." She pointed down the path.

I shifted my weight and saw a shadowy figure walking our way. "Please be Dad," I muttered. Deep down, I knew the person walking toward us wasn't my dad. The panic in Noelle's voice meant she knew it, too.

"Garret," I mumbled as he walked up to the traps.

"You? How did you get away from Trent?" Garret asked. His face twisted in a combination of confusion and anger.

"I guess we *were* clever enough to escape again!" Holly said, using Garret's words against him.

"Wait until I cut you down from there!"

"You can't hurt us. You can't do anything without your father's orders," I said, hoping it was true.

"Not a problem. I'm dying to see what he has planned for you." Garret yanked the knife from his belt loop and swung it at the rope tied around the tree trunk.

I landed hard on my back. "Ouch!" I thrashed around for a minute, trying to get out of the net, but I couldn't find an opening anywhere. I looked up at Garret, and the smirk on his face said it all. He hadn't cut us free. He'd only cut the nets down from the tree. "How are we supposed to go back to the camp if we're stuck in these ropes?" I asked.

"Simple." Garret grabbed hold of the two nets and dragged them behind him.

"Ow!" Holly winced. "Great, where was that sharp rock when I needed it earlier?"

"What was that about not being able to hurt you?" Garret asked. He laughed like a crazy person as he dragged us back to camp. He struggled to pull our weight, but apparently causing us pain was worth the struggle.

Luckily, we hadn't gotten far before we were captured because Garret didn't have to drag us for long. I was grateful I was wearing long sleeves and jeans. Otherwise, I would've been cut to shreds by all the gravel and fallen tree branches Garret pulled us through—no doubt on purpose.

Edward walked into the camp from the other direction the same time we did. He stared directly at us. I was about to tell him to stop staring when Trent came running out of his tent. His clothes were torn to shreds, and his hair stuck out in all directions. He yanked the bandana out of his mouth and rushed over to us. "I'm going to kill you little brats!"

Garret stepped in front of him, letting the ropes fall to the ground. "You were supposed to guard them!"

I had to smile, even if only for a second. At least I'd succeeded in getting Trent in trouble.

"My bed attacked me while I was—" Trent stammered.

"While you were what?" Garret didn't wait for an answer. He shoved Trent in the chest. "You fell asleep!"

"Maybe I would've been able to stay awake if you and Edward hadn't kept me up all day yelling and finding stupid ways to prove who's tougher!" Trent yelled, regaining his confidence.

"What's going on out here?" I turned my head to see Morgan standing in the entrance of his tent. One look told me he wasn't a morning person. He squinted against the sunlight and scowled at me.

"I caught these kids snooping around last night and—" Garret began.

"*You* caught them? Don't you mean *I* caught them?" Trent said.

"Yeah, that's right. You caught them and then let them escape! I found them in one of the traps!" Garret yelled.

"Enough!" Morgan's voice echoed through the trees. "Who are these children? Cut them free."

Edward rushed over to help Noelle to her feet. I stared at Morgan, wondering what he was going to do to us.

"Don't even think about moving," Morgan said. "If you want to live, you'll do as I say. I'm a very busy man, and I won't have three kids getting in my way."

"Uncle Morgan, I'd be happy to take care of them for you," Trent said. I suspected he was trying to suck up so he wouldn't be punished for letting us escape.

"That won't be necessary. We won't be staying here much longer. We're only missing one piece of the treasure map. We still don't know the exact location, but I think we might be able to begin our search. It seems that one of the maps drawn by Gerard is a fake. I've come to the conclusion that our new friend Bruce may not be a friend after all. The map he brought is different than the others."

"No!" Holly had tears in her eyes.

"Shh!" I warned her. "Don't say a word."

Luckily, Morgan was so caught up talking about the fortune he didn't hear Holly. "The only remaining piece of the puzzle is the map drawn by Aristede. I had a feeling it would be more difficult to find since it's the oldest," he said.

"Let's look at all the maps together. Maybe we

won't need Aristede's if we can figure out the clues in the rest," Garret suggested.

Morgan took six maps from his pocket and laid them on the ground in front of the fire. I watched as the thieves studied them. The only one who wasn't looking at the maps was Trent. He was keeping a close eye on Holly, Noelle, and me. There was no way to escape. I wasn't really upset that I couldn't get away. I wanted to know more about the fortune. It was the key to ending the curse.

Finally, Morgan spoke. "In each map, one part of the forest is drawn incorrectly. The clue is in which path to take. A large tree blocks this path in Bernard's map, but there is no such tree in the actual forest. Therefore, that's the clue. We must take that path."

"That's just what your father told you," Trent said. "We don't know if it's true."

Morgan turned and glared at Trent. "What was that about my father?"

Trent gulped. "Uh—I just meant that we don't really know where the clues are hidden in the maps. We need to see that part of the forest before we can be sure."

"I hate to agree with Trent," Garret said, "but we can't be sure where the clues are until we see them for ourselves. Like you said, no one, aside from Aristede himself, knows the true location of the fortune."

Garret was defending Trent! Things were getting weird, and I wanted to get out of here. Having the maps would make it easier to find the fortune, but these guys were crazy.

"I see your point," Morgan said. "Though I'd be more careful how you say things about our family in the future, Trent." Morgan placed his hand on his knife. The message was clear. Another comment like that and Trent would find himself at the sharp end of a knife.

"Yes, sir," Trent said, looking as surprised as I was that he'd escaped punishment.

"Now, we do know that each map contains something that isn't present in the forest and that's the clue," Morgan said, returning his attention to the maps.

"Hey, that's like our painting," Holly said. "There were two paths, but when we entered the forest, one of those paths was overgrown with trees."

"What did you say?" Morgan asked as if she'd said the most interesting thing in the world.

Holly grabbed my arm and stepped closer to me.

Noelle's head snapped up, and she squinted at me.

"They thought we had a painting of theirs when we caught them earlier," Garret said.

"But you didn't. It was one of your treasure maps," I said. Noelle stared at me so intently my cheeks got warm.

"We were trying to locate the part of the forest drawn in Bernard's map," Garret told his father. "In case we weren't able to recover the final piece of the treasure map."

"Why did you think we had your painting?" Edward asked me.

I didn't know if I should tell them the real reason, which was that the painting and the maps looked very similar. The last thing I wanted was to help the guys who were holding us captive and who may have hurt Dad. Then, I thought of something. If the thieves wanted the painting, they'd have to help us find our way back to the entrance of the forest where we'd left it.

"We're waiting!" Morgan stomped his foot in the dirt.

I took a deep breath. "We thought you had our painting because the maps you're trying to gather look like it. Only ours is a painting."

"What part of the forest is illustrated on this painting?" Morgan spoke so fast I had trouble understanding him.

"It's the entrance by the park," Holly said.

Noelle smiled, and I couldn't make sense of her sudden interest in the fortune.

"The entrance," Morgan repeated, looking over all six maps. "Of course! That's the missing piece. We need to know where to *begin* the search!"

"We've been assuming the search began by the seaside entrance," Garret said. "That must be why we couldn't locate any of the areas drawn on the maps. We have to start at the park."

"Yes! It makes sense now!" Morgan yelled.

"But, Dad, why would one of the pieces be a painting?" Edward asked. "Why is it different from the others?"

"Because Aristede was a painter!" Morgan said, grinning so wide he looked insane.

CHAPTER THIRTEEN

After reading Dad's journal, I'd had a feeling the painting was a clue, but I never thought it'd be something like this. What I really didn't understand was how something so important to the Grimaults had ended up in *my* living room.

"How did these kids get our ancestor's painting?" Garret asked, reading my mind.

"I'm not sure," Morgan said, "but they're obviously special." He smiled at Holly and me. "Consider yourselves my guests of honor. You'll be coming with us on our search."

"You want to take them with us to find the fortune?" Trent asked.

"No, I want them to take us to the painting." Morgan's cheerful expression was instantly replaced by a sinister and intimidating look. "Now, where is it?"

"We left it at the park, but we don't know how to get back there," I said. "We've been lost for days."

"Then we better get started. Boys, get your knives, fill the canteens with water, and grab some bread." Morgan gathered the maps and placed them in his pocket.

Holly tugged on my sleeve and whispered, "Why are we helping them?"

"Because they're going to take us back to the park. Then we might be able to get help, like the police or someone who'd take care of these guys, so we can find the Granville fortune."

"You don't really think these guys are going to let us go when we find the painting, do you? What if the painting isn't even there? Mom may have found it by now."

"What other choice do we have? Besides, the walk back through the forest will give us time to think of a better idea."

I raised my head and saw Edward coming toward us.

"My dad says you're traveling with me," he said, looking at Noelle. He turned to Holly and me. "Don't get any ideas about making a run for it. You'll never make it through this forest without our protection." It sounded more like a warning than a threat.

"We know," I said. "We won't try to escape."

"Good, let's go."

My eyes darted in every direction as I followed Edward. Around each turn, I expected to see the wolves or bears Holly had created earlier, but the forest was quiet. I started thinking the journey home was going to be easy—until I saw the stream. The current was even rougher than I remembered.

"I forgot about the stream," Holly said. "We'll never get across it without our rope."

"I don't think we can swim across this, Dad," Garret said. "The current is too strong, and the water is full of jagged rocks."

Morgan stood at the water's edge. "You say you crossed this stream on your way into the forest?" he asked me.

"Answer him!" Garret said, shoving me hard on the back.

I stumbled forward, but Noelle caught me by the arm before I fell. She shocked me and immediately let go. "We draped a rope over a tree branch to swing across the water," I said.

"Where's the rope?" Morgan asked.

"We left it hanging on the tree, but this isn't where we crossed the stream," I answered.

Morgan furrowed his brow. After what seemed like a lifetime of silence, he finally spoke. "The only way to cross is by using the rocks to our advantage."

"What's that supposed to mean?" I asked.

"The rocks are close enough together that we should be able to jump from one to another to get across the water."

"What if we fall in? That current will pull us out to who knows where!" Holly's voice trembled.

Morgan waved his arm and said, "Come on! We're wasting time."

"Wait!" I protested. "The three of us aren't as tall as you guys. Our legs aren't long enough to jump across those rocks."

"Move!" Garret said, pushing me toward the stream.

"It'll be fine. Edward says they've done stuff like this before," Noelle said in a low voice as she marched past me. How could she be so trusting?

The thieves began crossing the river in pairs. Edward and Noelle crossed the stream first with Edward leading the way. Once Edward safely jumped onto the first rock, he turned and extended his arm to Noelle who joined him. They continued like this to the other side of the stream.

Holly and I were each paired with a thief to cross the stream. I went first with Garret. I didn't like the idea of being separated from Holly, but after watching some of these guys struggle to get across the stream, I realized being paired with a long-legged thief was our only chance to safely cross the rough water. I slipped once, but Garret grabbed my arm and pulled me onto the rock. Trent insisted he could cross the water alone, and no one had any objection to him trying. He stumbled a little, but he made it safely to the other side.

The last pair to cross was Holly and Morgan. I had a feeling Morgan wasn't crossing last in order to make sure everyone made it safely. He probably didn't want to risk his own life trying to see if his plan would work. Some father he was.

Holly stood at the water's edge. "I'm not going. If I slip, he'll probably just save himself."

"You can't stay behind," I shouted.

Holly huffed but gave in, refusing to grab Morgan's hand as she jumped from rock to rock. She leaped and fell belly down onto each rock. She was getting pretty banged up, but I couldn't blame her for not wanting to put her life in Morgan's hands.

Holly and Morgan reached the final rock, and I noticed the land was farther away than Holly could jump on her own. "You're going to have to let him help you!" I yelled.

"I'm not going to make it! This rock is too narrow and pointy. I can't get any kind of running start. The stupid thing looks like a shark's fin."

"No!" I yelled. I watched in horror as the rock beneath Holly's feet transformed into a gray shark.

Holly splashed into the water. The shark turned in her direction with its jaws wide open.

The current was strong, and it pulled Holly downstream. I got down on the ground and reached for her, but she was too far away.

"Move!" Morgan said, pushing me aside. He drew his knife from his belt and hit the shark between the eyes. The knife didn't harm the rock shark, but the creature kept attacking *it* instead of going for Holly.

"Help!" Holly yelled.

I stared in terror at the jagged rock in her path. Before I could do anything, Edward rushed past Morgan. He reached out and grabbed Holly by the back of her shirt. I ran over and helped Edward pull Holly out of the water. She trembled as we set her down on the ground.

I put my arm around her shoulders. "Are you okay?" I could barely get the words out. I'd almost lost my sister.

"I think so," Holly said through chattering teeth.

"Let's continue," Morgan said. "It's getting dark, and we need to find a safe place to rest for the night." He walked over to Holly and me, extended a hand to each of us, and pulled us to our feet. He removed his jacket and handed it to Holly. "Put this on. You must be freezing in those wet clothes."

"Th-thanks," Holly said, taking the coat. She gave me a puzzled look, and I shrugged.

I didn't know what to make of Morgan's kind gesture. In a way, it made me more nervous than when he was being cruel.

CHAPTER FOURTEEN

The air was getting cold, and I wished I had a jacket, too, even if it did belong to a thief. Morgan wanted Garret and Edward by his side, so he told Trent he was on babysitting duty. So much for the moment of kindness. Trent fell back behind Holly, Noelle, and me while the rest of the group walked ahead of us. Noelle hadn't even looked at me since the incident at the stream. Her eyes were glued to Edward. I thought she would've checked on Holly after a rock shark had almost eaten her.

The sun was setting, and I couldn't see very far in front of me. I wasn't sure how we were going to find shelter.

"I hope they don't make us sleep in a cave," Holly said, visibly shivering under Morgan's jacket.

"It would be better than sleeping in the open."

"Not if there's a hungry W-O-L-F in the cave."

"Well, as long as you keep your mouth shut, the

forest won't create one." Why couldn't she get the hang of this place? It was scary, but it wasn't that complicated. You didn't talk about the frightening things you imagined while you were here. Of course, I was convinced the forest put those scary thoughts into our heads, hoping we'd say them aloud.

I saw something shiny out of the corner of my eye. Trent was swinging his knife back and forth in the air, like he was fighting someone who wasn't really there. He grunted and stabbed the knife straight out in front of him. I rolled my eyes. He was like a child in a big, scary, muscular body. At least he wasn't paying attention to Holly and me.

"Why do you think Morgan saved me back there?" Holly asked. "He only needs one of us. He could have let me drown. Or get eaten." She lowered her head. At least she realized she was the one who had put herself in danger of both being shark food and drowning.

"Morgan's sudden mood swings can only mean one thing," I said. "He wants that painting so much he was willing to save you to get it. He knew I wouldn't help him if he let you get eaten by that shark."

"But why did he give me his coat? That was weird. You don't think he has a daughter, do you? Maybe I remind him of her?"

"This is a family thing—searching for the fortune. She'd be here."

"You're probably right. Father of the year over there, taking his kids with him to this dangerous forest to search for some fortune that may or may not be here."

"At least they're together. Dad's never taken me to work with him," I said. The Grimaults may be dysfunctional, but they acted like a family. I glanced at Edward and Garret. They looked at their father like he was the greatest man on earth. For a second, I envied them. My eyes fell on Noelle who was walking very close to Edward. She seemed to almost fit in with them—well, with Edward at least.

Holly patted my shoulder. "If it makes you feel any better, Dad's somehow involved in this. So, we're not that different from Morgan's kids."

"Except Dad didn't tell us about it."

"No, he didn't," Holly agreed. "But the worst part of all this is I'm ashamed of Dad."

I didn't know what to say. Part of me agreed, but I didn't have time to think about it because everyone suddenly stopped walking. I looked around to see if Morgan had found a place to sleep, but all I saw was wide-open space. The thieves took off their boots and claimed trees to lean against.

"What are we doing?" Holly asked.

"Camping for the night," Garret said. He walked over to Holly and me, holding two red bandanas in his hands. He looked at Trent, who was still swinging his knife in the air. As soon as Trent noticed Garret staring at him, he put his knife back into its holder on his belt.

"There was a bee," Trent said.

Garret rolled his eyes. "Sure there was."

"We can't camp here. There's nothing to shelter us from wild animals," I told Garret.

"We're going to take turns standing guard." Garret rolled one of the bandanas long-ways. "Turn around."

"Huh?" I couldn't see the point in blindfolding us.

"You don't think we're going to let you escape the minute we fall asleep, do you? We're tying your hands behind your back. That way you won't even think about trying to get away."

"But you said someone would be on guard. We wouldn't be able to escape." I didn't want to have my hands tied. My mind flashed with images of all the scary things in the forest that could attack me while I was helpless to defend myself.

"The purpose of the lookout isn't to keep an eye on you. His job is to protect the rest of us from wild animals. Now turn around," Garret said.

As much as I didn't want to, I turned around and placed my wrists together. Once Holly and I were tied up, Garret pointed to the ground next to a tree about six feet away. I walked over and leaned my back against the bark. I inched down to the ground to avoid falling hard on my butt. I was happy to see Holly do the same. At least that was one injury prevented. At the next tree over, Edward was tying Noelle's hands. He whispered something to her before walking back to his father. Noelle turned in my direction and shrugged. She squatted down and leaned against her tree.

The thieves fell asleep almost instantly. Noelle and Edward were sharing a tree, but she was leaning as far away from him as possible. Maybe she didn't trust him after all. She was so difficult to read. Trent was on guard, walking around us in a big loop. He had his knife out in front of him, but he wasn't swinging it around this time. He looked serious. I closed my eyes and pretended to sleep. I heard Trent's footsteps on the gravel. After a few minutes, I opened my eyes just enough to peek at Trent. He wasn't circling the camp anymore. Maybe he'd heard something and gone to check it out. I nudged Holly.

"We have to get away from these guys."

"We can't walk around with our hands tied," Holly said.

"We need to steal a knife to cut off these bandanas."

"Definitely."

I looked around. Out of Edward, Garret, or Morgan, my options weren't good. I decided Edward was my best bet. The other two flat out scared me. Edward was lying on his back with his arms behind his head.

The knife on his belt was exposed.

Holly nodded and mouthed, "Go ahead." I was about to ask why I had to be the one to steal the knife, but I didn't because I knew Holly was too clumsy to do it. She'd probably fall face first into Edward's armpit.

I took one last look around for Trent, and I scooted on my knees over to Edward. It wasn't going to be easy to get the knife with my hands tied behind me. I couldn't see what I was doing. Holly tilted her head to the left, so I scooted over, feeling for the knife. As I wrapped my fingers around the handle, Edward stirred. I froze. I was leaning awkwardly over Noelle, and I was afraid I was going to fall on her. Her body shook for a moment, and she opened her eyes. I was shocked she didn't scream. Instead, she sat up and effortlessly slipped the bandana from her wrists. Then, she removed the knife from Edward's belt loop and cut me free. We tiptoed over to Holly, and Noelle cut her free, too.

"How'd you get yours off so easily?" Holly asked Noelle.

"I told Edward I wanted to help them find the fortune, and that it wasn't necessary to tie me up because I wouldn't run away. I guess he believed me," Noelle said.

"I saw you shake. Are you okay?" I asked.

"I do that when I dream sometimes." Noelle

looked away like she was embarrassed, so I took the knife from her and returned it to Edward's belt. Having a knife for protection was probably a good thing, but I'd never be able to use it.

I decided we should keep following the path we were on before we'd camped. We tiptoed around the side of a large tree and heard a rumbling sound.

Holly gave me a look, as if to ask, "What is that?"

"Wait here," I whispered. I peeked around the tree. In the moonlight, I could see Trent slumped on the ground, sound asleep and snoring. I waved the girls on, and we passed with no problem.

"Wait until Morgan finds out he let us escape again," Holly said once we were too far away to wake Trent.

"Forget Morgan. Garret will kill Trent long before Morgan gets to him," Noelle told us.

"Why aren't you staying to help them find the fortune? You told Edward you would," Holly said. Her voice was full of attitude. "It's not like you even cared that I almost died in that stream. You haven't said two words to us in hours."

"Sorry, but I've been trying to figure these guys out. Like Edward," Noelle said. "He's—odd. One minute he's all wrapped up in his dad and the search, and the next he's being nice to me." She kicked a pebble on the ground. Did she feel bad about breaking her promise to Edward by escaping with Holly and me?

We walked for a few minutes in silence. I hoped we were heading toward the park, and the familiar sight up ahead let me know we were. Unfortunately, it was a familiar sight I didn't want to see. About twenty yards in front of me were the three green, leafy bears Holly had accidentally created on our way into the forest days ago. I froze, hoping the bears wouldn't be able to see us in the darkness, but I heard them snort. They'd picked up our scent.

"What do we do? We don't have granola bars this time," Holly said, grabbing my arm.

"We've got to climb this tree and fast!" I motioned to the oak tree beside us.

The bears turned and charged. I pushed Noelle after Holly.

"Hurry!" I shouted, climbing up the tree behind Noelle.

"Bears can climb trees!" Holly yelled. She was having trouble climbing. Morgan's jacket was weighing her down.

One of the bears was already climbing the tree. Holly was right. It was a good climber. The bear stopped just below me and swung its huge paw at my leg.

"Go higher!" I yelled.

"I can't! The branches are too thin," Holly said.

The bear growled and swatted at my leg again. My jeans ripped, and razor sharp claws sliced my skin. "Ow!" Warm blood trickled down my right calf.

Holly squirmed out of Morgan's coat, almost falling in the process.

"What are you doing?" I yelled.

"Lean as close to the tree as you can. I have an idea," Holly said, holding the jacket away from her body.

Noelle and I hugged the tree. What was Holly doing? The bear wasn't going to chase a coat.

Holly dropped the coat, and it fell on the bear's head. The bear flailed its paws and tumbled to the ground, jacket and all.

"That was awesome!" I said. I watched the bear wiggling on the ground, whining from the fall.

My celebration was cut short because the other two bears had reached the tree. They fought for a minute, but the larger of the two won and started to climb.

I was about to become dinner, but then I heard a loud noise. I looked down and saw someone hiding behind a big boulder. He was banging a canteen against the rock. The noise startled the two uninjured bears, but they didn't back away. They advanced on the rock to investigate the sound. I heard wood snapping and saw the flicker of a flame. Whoever it was lit a tree branch on fire and waved it at the bears. The flames licked at the leafy bears, and the one's nose caught fire. It whined and ran off with the other bears following.

Trent walked out from behind the boulder. I hadn't thought the sight of a Grimault thief would make me even a little bit happy, but we would've been bear food if it weren't for Trent.

Trent yelled as he stormed up to the tree. "You kids have made me look bad for the last time!" He threw the flaming tree branch to the ground and stomped out the fire.

Holly gave me a worried look and squeezed the tree.

"You can't hurt us," I said. "If you do, Morgan will know you let us escape again. What do you think he'll do to you if he finds out?"

"Yeah, maybe he'll tie *you* up and leave you to the wolves," Holly taunted. I suspected her confidence would disappear the minute she stepped back on the ground where Trent could reach her.

Trent stared at us. Morgan would never forgive him for losing us a second time. Trent needed to get us back to the camp before everyone woke up.

"This is what's going to happen," he said. "You're going to climb down from that tree and come with me back to our camp. Then, I'm tying you up again, so no one will know you escaped." He took his knife from his belt and pointed it in our direction. "If you even so much as think about telling Uncle Morgan what happened here, I'll kill you before you can get the words out." He looked at Noelle. "Got that, sweetie?"

"Don't call me sweetie," Noelle growled back at him.

We didn't have any choice, so we climbed down from the tree. Trent picked up Morgan's jacket and threw it at Holly. "Put this back on."

"It's ripped," she said as she placed the jacket on her body. A large gash ran down the side from the bear's claws. "Morgan is definitely going to notice a rip this big. What are we going to tell him?"

Trent thought for a moment. "Tell him you rolled on a sharp rock while you were sleeping. Now come on! We have to get back before anyone notices you're gone," he said, shoving us in the direction of the camp.

The others were still asleep, so Trent used new bandanas to tie our hands. He was really rough and tied the bandanas so tight my wrists burned.

"Tight enough for you, sweetie?" Trent said as he tied Noelle's wrists. She looked like she was about to scream, but she turned and walked back to the tree where Edward was sleeping. Her eyes flickered in my direction before she shut them.

Trent shoved Holly and me to the ground. He sat against a tree facing us and polished his knife with a bandana. I knew he was trying to intimidate us with the weapon, but he was also keeping himself busy so he wouldn't fall asleep again. He wasn't going to let us get away a third time.

CHAPTER FIFTEEN

Those bears weren't far from where we were camped. Even if the one burned into a pile of ashes, it still left two out there. That thought wouldn't allow me to keep my eyes closed for long. When I finally did shut my eyes, I had one of my visions, and I didn't even try to sleep after that. I was actually happy when Morgan woke up at the first crack of dawn.

He ran around, kicking his sleeping sons. "Get up! We need to get an early start. Today is the day we find my fortune!"

Garret and Edward moaned, but they got up and put on their boots. Noelle sat up clumsily, her hands firmly tied behind her. Edward drew his knife and cut her loose. They whispered back and forth, but I couldn't hear a word of it. The only one who wasn't getting ready for another day's search was Trent. He was asleep against the oak tree facing Holly and me. Morgan was too excited to notice Trent, but Garret saw him and stormed over. He smacked Trent on the side of the head with his canteen. The cap was loose and water splashed all over Trent's face.

"Ouch! What was that for?" Trent asked, wiping his face with his sleeve.

"You fell asleep again! I'm not sure why Dad keeps you around. You're worthless!"

I elbowed Holly and smiled. Seeing Trent get in trouble almost made up for my hands being numb thanks to how tightly he'd tied them.

Trent jumped to his feet and yelled in Garret's face, "How do you expect me to search for the fortune all day *and* stay up to patrol all night?"

"You weren't supposed to patrol all night. You were supposed to wake Edward for the second shift!"

"How do you know I didn't? Maybe Edward fell asleep!"

"Don't lie to me!" Garret said, shoving Trent in the chest and knocking him into the oak tree.

I stepped in front of Holly to shield her if a fight broke out.

"What's going on?" Edward asked, walking over to Garret. Noelle tagged closely behind him. "Dad wants to get started."

Garret nodded. "This isn't over," he said to Trent and stormed off to his father's side.

Edward glared at Trent. "What's in your hair?"

I squinted at the chunky, white goo on the side of his head.

"Oh, it's owl poop," Trent said, using his bandana to wipe the rest of the remains from his hair.

Edward gave Trent a disgusted look, and he walked off to catch up with Garret and Morgan.

"So that's what woke you last night. You were sound asleep when we passed by," I said, trying not to laugh.

Trent's eyes burned into mine. He reached into his pocket, and I backed up, afraid of what he might do. Luckily, Garret returned.

"We're almost ready," Garret told Trent. "Remove their bandanas before we go. It'll be too difficult for them to keep up if their hands are tied." Out of nowhere, Garret turned to Holly and grabbed hold of Morgan's jacket. "What happened to my father's coat?"

"Oh, I—" Holly looked to Trent for help.

"You had something to do with this?" Garret accused Trent.

"They tried to escape again last night. I had to get a little rough with the girl," Trent said.

Holly's jaw dropped. I nudged her with my foot, warning her to keep quiet.

"Fine. Keep a closer eye on them so they don't try anything while we're searching for the fortune. Dad won't be happy if anything goes wrong, and you don't want to have to answer to him," Garret said, and he walked away.

Trent cut the bandanas from our wrists. I waited until he put his knife away before confronting him about what he'd told Garret.

"If you get us in trouble with Morgan, we'll tell him what really happened last night," I said.

"The only chance you had to get me in trouble with Uncle Morgan was if he caught us returning to camp last night. Now it's your word against mine, and there's no way he'd believe you over me. So, I'd watch the tone you take with me, or you might have an unfortunate accident on our journey today." I knew he wouldn't hesitate to hurt Holly and me if he thought he could make it look like an accident.

Holly gulped, and I was almost happy to see Edward walking back over to us.

"Dad said you're supposed to go on up ahead. I'm going to watch them," Edward told Trent.

Trent didn't hide his disappointment, but he did what Edward told him. Everyone was ready to start the search again, so we headed toward the park to find the last piece of the treasure map.

"I never should've trusted Trent to keep his word. I should've told Garret I ripped the coat in my sleep," Holly whispered.

I looked at Edward to see if it was safe for Holly and me to talk. He was talking to Noelle again. His face was serious, and he was keeping his eyes straight ahead of him. He probably didn't want his family to notice he was being nice to Noelle. At least Noelle was keeping him preoccupied so Holly and I could talk. "You can't trust a thief," I finally answered.

"You can say that again." Holly's eyes dropped to the ground. No question about it, she was thinking about Dad.

"We don't know for sure if—" I didn't want to mention Dad's name in case anyone was trying to eavesdrop. "I mean, we don't know what You-know-who is doing in the forest, so don't jump to conclusions."

"He acted just like one of them!" Holly said, forgetting to keep her voice down.

Garret glared at us from up ahead. "Shut up before I shut you up!"

Holly and I bowed our heads and kept our eyes down. After a few minutes, Garret walked over to talk to Edward. Garret looked in my direction once before he and Edward got caught up in a conversation. Noelle stepped away from them.

"What about Noelle?" Holly whispered. "I don't get her at all."

"Me either. She's getting pretty comfortable with

Edward, but she tried to escape with us last night. It doesn't add up."

"Talking about me?" Noelle whispered, coming up alongside me.

Holly turned away, refusing to acknowledge Noelle's presence.

"What's the deal with Edward?" I asked her. "You've been talking to him a lot."

Noelle raised her eyes to mine. "He's different from the rest of his family. He's nice, and he keeps Trent off my case." She glared in Trent's direction. "If he calls me sweetie one more time, I swear I'll punch him."

I nodded. "Edward does seem different than the rest of them. Nicer."

"It's hard to explain, but I know he wouldn't hurt me or let the others hurt me either." Noelle gave me a half smile and walked back over behind Edward and Garret.

"I don't like her," Holly said, stepping closer to me.

Edward and Garret stopped talking, so I motioned for Holly to be quiet. We walked in silence for hours. Garret watched Holly and me so closely that we weren't able to talk anymore. Our pace slowed. We were all getting tired of the search. Our feet practically dragged from boredom and exhaustion.

Morgan noticed everyone's attitudes and shouted, "This is a celebration! My fortune will soon be at hand! Let's have a song!" He was the only one who was still excited about finding the fortune, but the others joined in and sang anyway.

After four verses, I realized I was humming along. Holly gave me a dirty look.

I shrugged. "It's kind of catchy."

"Where do you think Dad is?" Holly asked.

"Shh! Don't talk about him in front of the others. Until we find out what's really going on, we can't let them know he's our father."

"Don't worry. They can't hear us over their singing."

"I thought I told you two to shut up!" Garret said.

"No, they can't hear us," I mumbled sarcastically. I turned to Garret and said, "We were singing along."

"You *should* be celebrating. It's a wonder Dad's letting you come along. It's not as though you remember how to get back to the park."

I stiffened. I'd been hoping no one would notice that. "Actually, I remember passing through here. Don't you, Holly?"

"Oh, yeah." Holly nodded, following my lead. "We're definitely heading in the right direction."

I was trying to play along so Garret wouldn't convince Morgan to get rid of Holly and me, and the sound of the growling wolf sticking his head out of the cave up ahead let me know that we really were retracing our steps.

"What do you want us to do, Dad?" Garret asked. He stopped the group and stood face to face with the giant rock wolf. He held up his knife in defense. Edward was behind him, standing protectively in front of Noelle.

"Get rid of it! That's why we brought weapons!" Morgan said. He was at the back of the group now. Some fearless leader.

"No!" I yelled. "That thing will mangle your puny little knives. We need something bigger and stronger." I looked at the pile of rocks on the ground near the cave, and I had a feeling it was the remains of the other rock wolf. That must have been some fight Holly and I missed when we ran away. "We need another rock wolf."

Holly wrinkled her forehead. "You can't be serious! After what almost happened last time?"

"Dad, what do you want me to do?" Garret asked more urgently.

"Create another wolf," Morgan said, looking me in the eyes.

"You're taking advice from *him*?" Trent asked.

Morgan glared at Trent. "I've been hearing a lot of negative comments about you lately. You're falling asleep on the job, questioning my orders, and speaking ill of our family's fortune," Morgan counted off on his fingers like he'd forgotten about the wolf that was ready to eat us all. "I'll give you one chance to defend yourself, or we'll be feeding *you* to the wolf."

I didn't think wolves—even stone ones—understood English, but this one sure seemed to. It crouched low to the ground, ready to pounce.

"The wolf's going to attack!" I yelled. I didn't wait for a response. I stared at the pile of rocks and shouted, "Those rocks look like a giant wolf ready to attack one of its kind." I hoped I'd chosen my words carefully enough. The pile of rocks shifted and rumbled as they transformed into a *giant*—poor choice of words on my part—wolf in a low crouch. It let out a deep growl and lunged at the other wolf. Their jaws locked on each other, and pieces of rock flew everywhere. "Run!" I yelled.

No one hesitated. We ran past the cave and didn't look back.

CHAPTER SIXTEEN

I was more than a little surprised to see a bunch of tough thieves running away from a fight. I was even more surprised that Morgan had listened to *me*, especially since my plan involved creating another rock wolf.

"Uncle Morgan must be losing his mind!" Trent mumbled under his breath.

"Dad?" Garret said in a low voice. "Trent should be punished for his lack of loyalty to you, and I'd be happy to carry out any punishment you see fit. But, I can't help wondering why we're taking these kids with us. We don't need them."

I gulped. Garret was right. They didn't need us. I leaned closer, hoping to find out Morgan's reason for keeping us around. Luckily, they were too busy to notice me.

"Until we know how they got Aristede's painting, they're staying in my sight," Morgan said. "I can't believe they'd stumble upon something as important as the last remaining piece of my treasure map."

Morgan looked in my direction, so I stepped closer to Holly.

"Why does he keep looking at us? It's creepy," Holly whispered out of the corner of her mouth. She hadn't overheard the conversation between Morgan and Garret, and I figured that was a good thing. Keeping her on a need-to-know basis was probably my best bet. I couldn't have her freaking out and getting us in any more trouble. "Oh no, he's coming over here," she said.

Morgan walked alongside me for a while without saying a word. I hated not knowing what he was up to. Holly stared at the ground, trying to avoid eye contact with Morgan.

"Hungry?" Morgan asked, holding out two pieces of bread.

"Thank you," I said, taking Holly's piece, too, so she didn't have to move any closer to Morgan.

"So, where did you say you got the painting?" he asked.

"I didn't say." I was trying to keep the edge out of my voice, but it wasn't easy to be nice to this guy when I was imagining all the things he could do to Holly and me once he got what he was after.

"Oh? I could've sworn you said something about it. Well, where *did* you get it?" His tone still sounded friendly, but his smile was completely forced.

"At an antique store in town," I lied. I took another bite of bread and tried to act casual. Holly immediately looked at me. I sighed and bowed my head. I knew she hadn't meant to, but she'd just given me away.

"An antique store?" Morgan's face turned twelve different shades of red, and he balled his hands into fists. "You don't really expect me to believe that, do you? Each map was carefully hidden where only a Grimault could find it. There's no way the most important map would be in an antique store where anyone could buy it. Now, tell me the truth!"

Noelle widened her eyes at me, and I got the feeling she wanted me to make up another lie. A *better* lie.

"Well, we—"

"J.B., look!" Holly said. She dropped her bread on the ground and pointed up ahead. I expected to see a wild animal, but instead I saw my dad walking toward us. "D—" Holly began, but I shoved the rest of my bread into her mouth to stop her.

"Bruce!" Morgan growled. He put one hand up, motioning for everyone else to stay where they were, and he marched up to my dad. "How dare you show your face after you tried to pass off that phony drawing as a piece of my treasure map."

My hands shook. I was sure the Grimaults were going to attack my dad.

"Let me explain," Dad said, putting his hands up in surrender. "Edward and I determined the map I brought may have been fake, so I headed home, planning to search my father's belongings for another map. Only, I never made it home because I took a wrong turn and ended up heading in the opposite direction. I found *this* at the other end of the forest." He handed the painting to Morgan.

He really *was* helping Morgan. Something wasn't right. If he found the painting in the park, he *was* heading home. He hadn't taken a wrong turn. I studied his face, but his expression was blank—unreadable.

Trent, Garret, and Edward pointed their knives at my dad, waiting for their orders. Noelle stepped toward Holly and me. Morgan studied the painting, and I thought his eyes might pop out of his head. He smiled and said, "It's signed AG! At last! The final piece! Bruce, you took a big chance returning here after your map turned out to be a fake."

Dad reached out and shook Morgan's hand. "As I told you earlier, I'm here to help you find the fortune. It belongs with its rightful owner." Morgan's eye twitched slightly, but he nodded in response.

Dad kept talking to Morgan as if Holly and I weren't there. How could he pretend not to recognize us? I stared at him, trying to find some sign he'd come to save us.

"New recruits?" he asked, pointing at Holly and me. "Your family's bigger than I thought."

"Oh, don't worry about them. They had the painting and were going to help us find it, but we don't need them anymore thanks to you." Morgan slapped my father on the back.

"What do you mean you don't need us anymore?" Holly asked with a shaky voice.

Noelle crept back over to Edward and whispered something in his ear. He shrugged in response.

"I have the painting. Why should I keep you kids around?" Morgan said, still mesmerized by the painting.

"Dad!" Edward said in a panic.

"Oh, fine. The other girl can stay. She hasn't been a problem like these two." He glared at Holly and me.

Was that what Noelle had whispered to Edward? Was she trying to protect herself? I had to get Holly and me out of here. Unlike Noelle, we didn't have anyone protecting us.

A rush of adrenaline sent my brain into overdrive. "You can't get rid of us because you still don't know how we got the painting, and we're not going to tell you until you agree to let us go," I said.

"You're making demands of me?" Morgan laughed, but his face turned red. "Tell me how you got Aristede's painting, or I'll kill you both right now!" He drew his knife and shook it at me.

"Wait!" Dad said, taking a step toward me. "Perhaps you might let me try getting it out of them."

Morgan furrowed his brow. "What makes you think you'll have better luck?"

"I have children of my own. Ones who aren't as disciplined as your boys. I know how to talk to them."

"You might have kids, but that doesn't mean you know them or that you know how to be a father," Holly said. Her eyes filled with tears. I was too angry to cry. Dad had basically said Edward and Garret were better kids than Holly and me.

Morgan moved toward Holly, but Dad put out his hand to stop him. "Please, let me try. You have more important things to focus on. You're about to locate the fortune."

Morgan nodded. "Fine, but while you're at it, lead us in the direction you came from. I need to find the back entrance to the forest. The one by the park."

"Follow me," Dad said. He turned to Holly and me. "You two can help lead the way."

I thought I saw Dad wink at me, but I wasn't sure if it was wishful thinking. I looked at Holly to see if she'd noticed it, but she was staring at the ground. We walked in silence until we came to a clearing. A clearing I knew well.

"The park!" I yelled.

Holly smiled. "Maybe someone will see us! Mom probably has the police searching here." She waved her arms in the air, but Garret yanked them down to her sides.

"Another move like that and you'll be wolf food," he growled in her ear.

I pulled Holly away from Garret. "Don't touch her!" He wasn't the least bit afraid of me. He stepped closer and curled his upper lip.

"Let me through," Morgan said, pushing his way to the front of the group. "Let's see here. What's present in the painting but not in the forest? Oh, yes! There should be another path around here."

"You have the painting, and we're out of the forest. Now, let us go," I said.

"So you can run home and tell your mommy all about us? No, you're not going anywhere. I know a nice cave a little way back where we can leave you two. You'll let me know which rock wolf won the fight, won't you?" Morgan laughed, and Garret smiled in amusement.

I thought about telling Holly to run for it, but we were outnumbered. She'd never get away.

"Do you know where the other path is?" Dad asked me.

"What?" Morgan said, his mood changing in a split second.

"I thought they might know where the other path is. It's their painting, right?"

"It's *my* painting!" Morgan corrected him.

"Of course it belongs to you. What I meant was they *had* the painting, so they might be more familiar with it since it was in their possession."

Morgan glared at Holly and me. "*Do* you know where the second path is?"

I wasn't sure if we should tell them anything since Morgan wasn't going to let us go anyway.

"Well?" Morgan yelled.

Holly jumped and nodded at me. She wanted me to cooperate, and I didn't see any other option.

"Yes. We took that path," I said.

"I suppose we should keep them around," Dad said. "They could be useful."

"Fine," Morgan grumbled. "But keep them out of my way."

Dad nodded. "I'll take charge of them for you."

"Show us the path from the painting," Morgan ordered.

"It's to the right of this one. Those tree branches are covering it up." I pointed to the spot where the path was overgrown.

Trent, Garret, and Edward uncovered the path, and Morgan made me lead the way. Dad had saved us from being thrown to the wolves, but he still pretended not to know us. I hoped he was keeping the secret for the same reason I was—so no one got hurt by the Grimaults.

I barely paid attention to where I was going. My mind was too clouded to think straight, but I was forced back to reality when I heard Noelle's piercing scream. I whipped my head around to see one of the creepy trees Holly and I had brought to life had Noelle locked tightly in its gnarly bark arms.

CHAPTER SEVENTEEN

A branch twisted around her head, muffling her screams. Edward and I rushed to her. He drew his knife and started slashing at the base of the branches where they connected to the trunk. Noelle's eyes widened as Edward's knife came dangerously close to her arm. The knife wasn't big enough to make any real slices in the branches, so I pushed Edward aside.

"That's not working!" I tugged on the branch around Noelle's waist. Edward glared at me, but he threw the knife to the ground and helped me. Another limb swatted at Edward's head. We needed help, but the others were fighting off attacks by the rest of the trees. Edward and I were going to have to find a way to free Noelle.

"I have an idea," I said, looking into Noelle's terrified eyes. Her mouth was still covered, so I didn't wait for a response. I put my hand on her shoulder. "Edward, give me a boost! I'm going to jump on the branch around Noelle's waist to get the tree to give a little. When it loosens its grip, you pull Noelle free."

Edward bent down and interlocked his fingers so I could step in them like a stirrup. I placed my left hand on his shoulder for balance. Without warning, my entire body got warm, warmer, hot. My arms and legs tingled so much I could barely think straight. I figured I was having another vision, but Noelle's eyes darted back and forth between Edward and me. She felt it, too. Edward studied his arms like he'd never seen them before. He was as shocked and confused as I was. Our eyes met, and he shook his head, yelling, "Jump!"

I snapped out of it and jumped on the branch, stomping as hard as I could. The limb shook under me and splintered. With a final stomp, the branch and I both fell to the ground. Edward didn't hesitate. He grabbed Noelle and pulled her to him. They landed in a heap on the ground.

"Come on!" I yelled, getting to my feet. I took Noelle's hand and pulled her up. Edward grabbed his knife off the trail and ran to help Garret, who was being attacked by a large oak. Trent reached into his back pocket and pulled out his lighter.

"No! You'll burn down the whole forest!" I jumped on his back and pried the lighter from his hand. The only reason I was successful was that I'd taken him by surprise. Once the shock wore off, he effortlessly flung me to the ground.

"Give that back. It was my grandfather's lighter." Trent ripped it from my fingers.

Morgan let out a primal yell, startling everyone. Even the trees shivered. "Run for it!" He didn't wait to see if we were following orders. He took off, leaving us to fight our way through the branches that narrowly missed grabbing hold of him. Garret took his boot off and used it to hit the trees as we ran. He looked funny, hobbling along with one shoeless foot, but it worked. Most of the skinnier branches broke on impact. We made it past the living trees and were forced to stop when we came to the mouth of a large, pitch-black cave blocking the path. This wasn't the way Holly and I had gone after we'd fought off the trees the first time.

"Now what?" Holly asked, out of breath.

Morgan flipped through the maps. "None of the maps show this cave! We must've made a wrong turn. We have to go back!"

"No way!" I blurted out. All eyes turned to me. I had to think of something and fast. I scanned the outside of the cave. It was huge, almost like the cave cut through the mountain bordering the outer edge of the forest. The path led straight into the cave, which meant we had to go inside. "I think the cave might actually be a tunnel," I said.

"A tunnel?" Noelle asked.

"The path leads into it. I doubt it's a dead end. All the other trails have been connected or led somewhere. This one must, too." I shrugged at Morgan. "Unless you want to give up the search, we have to go in there."

"No one's giving up!" He stepped toward me, stopping inches from my face. "If you're wrong about this, I'll make sure you don't get past those trees on our way back."

I forgot how to breathe. I was guessing. I had no idea how to read the maps or how to navigate the forest.

Trent whipped out his lighter and led the way into the cave. We could barely see, and we had to make a human chain to avoid stepping on each other. I was holding on to Holly and Noelle's trembling arms. We walked through the darkness, guided only by the faint flicker of Trent's lighter.

"Looks like we're going down," Trent called from the front of the line. "There are some steps, and they're steep."

Holly and Noelle squeezed my arms. My foot slipped a little on the first step. The stones were really uneven. Holly was lucky she had Dad and me on either side of her. She never would've made it down these steps on her own without falling. At the bottom, the tunnel opened up into a pretty big enclosed space. We were underground.

The walls were rusty brown and looked like dust clouds hardened into solid forms. Trent stopped to point at a small red arrow drawn on the wall. "It's written in blood," he said.

"Aristede must have marked the way through the tunnel. Keep moving," Morgan said, pushing Trent along.

Our feet stirred up the dirt on the ground, making it even harder to see. A fluttering sound overhead drew everyone's attention to the ceiling. Brown fruit bats hung upside-down in huge clusters. Holly's nails dug into my arm as a bat darted through the dark alcove. Once we got past the bats, the trail narrowed and wound through a darker labyrinth of eerie rock formations. The tunnel started to look like a giant mouth with enormous jagged teeth.

I heard Holly gulp. "Keep the bad thoughts to yourself," I whispered. The last thing we needed was her saying something that'd make us all cave food.

I struggled to breathe. The air inside the cramped tunnel was hot and humid. The ceiling sloped downward, and we had to hunch at the waist. After several more steps, Noelle and Holly let go of my arms. We were facing a solid rock wall.

"What?" I murmured. The sides of the cave had

opened up so we had a little room to turn around. I twisted to the right and saw Morgan advancing on me, his knife drawn.

"I told you you'd pay if this wasn't the right way to go!" he said.

"Trent, shine that lighter on the wall over here!" Dad yelled. "There's another trail marker."

Trent awkwardly made his way through the group and lifted his lighter to the wall. A faint red arrow pointed straight up to a circular hole in the ceiling of the cave. The space was just big enough for a person to squeeze through. There were no steps like there had been at the entrance. We were going to have to climb out.

"Garret, you go first," Morgan said. "Trent, you'll go last since you have the lighter. We'd be in the dark without you."

Garret reached up, placed his hand in a recessed spot on the wall, and began to climb. We took turns scaling the walls until we were finally out of the tunnel. The air on the surface felt unusually cold after being underground. I swallowed painfully. My mouth was as dry as cotton, and I could taste the gritty dirt from the cave floor that covered most of my body. We all looked like we'd climbed out of our own graves.

Morgan's eyes narrowed on me. "I guess it's your lucky day."

I didn't think any of us had an ounce of luck thanks to our ancestors and the curse. Noelle gave me a half smile. I felt bad that she'd gotten wrapped up in all this when she wasn't even cursed.

We moved quickly through the trails. Every time Morgan recognized a part of the forest from one of his maps, he pushed his way to the front of the group and studied the map to determine the next path to choose. After a while, the group came to a sudden halt.

"Get into the cover of the trees!" Garret whispered as he sidestepped behind a tall oak.

I imagined all sorts of wild beasts ferocious enough to scare a crew of armed thieves. Someone grabbed my arm, and I was shocked to see it was Dad. He pulled me behind a bush. I looked directly into his eyes, hoping to see even a glimpse of the father I'd always known, but he stared far off into the woods. I turned to see what he was looking at. The hairiest looking beast I'd ever seen stood next to a large boulder. It had wiggling furry arms all over its body.

Holly gasped and buried her head in my shoulder. "What is it?"

"I'm hoping it goes away before we have a chance to find out," I said, but I barely got the words out of my mouth before the creature started coming right at us.

CHAPTER EIGHTEEN

The creature wasn't like anything I'd ever seen before—even in this place. Grimaults had their knives drawn, ready to fight, but I could tell they were scared. Beads of sweat streamed down Garret's face. I hoped the thieves wouldn't take off running for their lives, leaving Holly, Noelle, and me unarmed and helpless against the beast. Noelle stared wide-eyed in horror. Her entire body shook. As the creature got closer, I heard a strange chittering sound and a loud squawk. Large wings rose up from the creature's head. Some sort of slime dripped off the beast's body, leaving a gooey trail on the ground.

"Ew!" Holly covered her eyes.

A man's face appeared beneath the wings. It wasn't a giant hairy beast at all. It was a man, about forty years old, with a vulture perched on the back of his neck and squirrels covering him from head to toe.

"Well, if it isn't Sticky Fingers Sam, or should I call

you Sweetcheeks?" Garret said, stepping out from behind the oak tree.

Noelle sobbed uncontrollably. She'd gotten really upset when Trent told us what Morgan had done to Sam. Seeing him in person now must have been too much to handle.

Morgan stormed up to Sam with his knife raised. "We left you for dead, and believe me you're going to wish you were!"

As soon as Morgan came near Sam, the vulture swooped down from Sam's neck and landed on Morgan's head. It pecked furiously at his hat.

"Get it off!" Morgan yelled.

Garret ran to his father and swung his knife at the vulture. Morgan's eyes widened, and he ducked each time Garret swung the knife.

Sam threw his head back and laughed. He whistled loudly, and the vulture returned to his shoulder. "It looks like my friend doesn't like the tone you've taken with me, Morgan."

"Don't talk to my father like that," Edward said. I was startled by the forcefulness in his voice. He'd been unusually quiet for a while now. "You're not one of us anymore. You're a thief and a traitor!"

"Ah, yes, I'm a thief, but who here isn't?" Sam asked. His eyes lingered on Noelle for a moment, and then he glanced at Holly and me. "Recruiting them a little young, aren't you, Morgan? Looks like you could use me back on the team."

"You can't seriously think—" Garret began.

"Silence!" Morgan shouted. He stepped between Garret and Sam. "How did you escape? When we left you tied to that tree these animals were feasting on you!"

"That's where you're wrong. These animals were feasting on the honey you covered me in. Some of the honey dripped onto the ropes you used to tie me. When the squirrels nibbled the honey, they chewed right through the rope, and my watch incidentally."

"Even if you were free from the ropes, you still had hungry animals to get away from," Garret said, keeping his distance.

"I didn't need to get away from them. They liked me. I was giving them food. All I had to do to keep them from turning on me was continue feeding them. So, I kept taking sap from the trees and rubbing it on my clothes. The next thing I knew, I had loyal protectors."

"Why didn't you leave the forest?" Garret asked.

"Because I provided you with information about the Granville fortune, and I want my reward. I'm not leaving here without it."

"You're not getting any of that fortune! It's ours!" Trent yelled.

"Still got quite the temper, huh, Trent?" Sam said.

"The fact of the matter is I know these woods better than all of you. While you've been staying at your campsite, I've been living out here. I know my way around in the dark. You need me."

Morgan scratched his chin. "You think you know where the fortune is?"

Sam shook his head, and I swore the vulture shook its head, too. "No, but I'll easily recognize the clues on your maps. Plus, the animals in this forest love me. I'll keep them out of your way."

Morgan stared at Sam, contemplating what to do. No one moved, and I thought I saw Dad and Sam exchange a look.

I leaned close to Holly and whispered, "Why would anyone want to rejoin a group of thieves? Especially after they tried to kill him?" She shrugged.

Before I could say more, Morgan spoke. "Fine. You'll help us. Now, let's go. I want my fortune." He motioned for Sam to lead the way.

Garret walked slowly to Morgan at the back of the group. "Dad, are you sure about this?"

"I have no intention of sharing my fortune with that traitor, but I do like the idea of having Sam's help to locate it. I'm going to let Sam think he's part of the team again until the fortune is found. Then, I'll dispose of him," Morgan said.

"Morgan's desperate to find that fortune," I

whispered to Holly once we were heading to the next location on the maps.

"Sam must know Morgan's not the type to forgive and forget. Why is he doing this?" Holly asked.

"I don't know, but I almost feel sorry for Sweetcheeks." Noelle sniffled. "Don't worry. He's probably not as scary as he looks," I said, trying to reassure her, but she kept her eyes locked on Sam.

"This is ridiculous! Sam doesn't deserve any of the fortune!" Trent complained.

"Trent's mad because Sam made him look bad," Edward whispered to me.

I jumped. Why would he tell me this? We didn't exactly like each other, and my name wasn't Grimault. "How?" I asked.

"Trent's the one who introduced Sam to my dad. They met at the pool hall downtown. Trent must've been running his mouth about the fortune, and Sam said he thought he could help. Sam did have some useful information for us, so Dad let him tag along. But after just a few hours, Garret caught Sam stealing from us. Dad blamed Trent for bringing Sam here. It's been downhill for Trent ever since."

"That explains a lot," I said. "Why are you telling me this?"

Edward shrugged. "I don't know. It can't hurt to tell you. It's not like Dad's going to let—"

"You figure we're dead meat, so why not tell us what's really going on?" I asked.

Edward shook his head. "Look, I was trying to be, you know, nice. I think Dad should let the three of you go. There's no reason to keep you hostage. We'll be out of here as soon as we find the fortune."

Holly scrunched up her forehead. "You really don't want your dad to hurt us?"

"No," Edward said.

"Then why'd you try to catch us earlier?" I asked, remembering how mean he'd seemed when I'd first met him.

"You stole my food, and I burned my foot because of you. You would've been mad, too."

I couldn't argue. I would've reacted the same way in his place.

"He doesn't want to be here," Noelle said, joining our conversation. "That's why I've been talking to him. He doesn't want us to get hurt. He's only following his dad's orders." She smiled at Edward.

Out of the corner of my eye, I saw Trent reach toward his belt. He took a piece of bread from his pocket. Just as it touched his mouth, two squirrels leaped off Sam and stole the bread from Trent's hand. "Hey! Get your syrupy paws off me!" As if they were offended, the squirrels clawed at Trent's hand a few times and jumped back onto Sam. "Ow!" Trent wiped his hand on his pants. "You better keep those creatures to yourself or I'll—" He didn't get to finish his threat because the vulture on Sam's shoulders turned and squawked at him.

Sam laughed as Trent backed away from the vulture. I smiled again. I was starting to like Sam.

Sam really was helpful when it came to finding the clues on the maps. The search went much quicker. Before long, we came to a large tree in between two paths.

Morgan cleared his throat. "This is the final map, so the location of the fortune is hidden somewhere on it." He studied the map for several minutes. "This doesn't make sense. All of the other maps indicated which paths to choose by adding something that didn't exist in the forest to the correct path. I can't find what was added on this map."

Sam took a turn studying the map, but even he couldn't decipher it. "There isn't anything added to either of the paths on the map. Are you sure this map isn't a fake?"

"This map was drawn by my father. I know for certain it's authentic. Keep looking!" Morgan yelled. His patience with the search had obviously run out.

"Maybe all the honey is blurring his vision," Trent said. The look on Morgan's face said it wasn't the time for jokes.

Edward and Garret didn't have any luck reading

the map either, so they let my dad take a turn. No one could find any difference between the paths in the forest and the ones drawn on the map.

"I want my fortune!" Morgan yelled. His face turned purple with rage.

"J.B. is good at figuring out things like that," Holly said.

"What?" Why had Holly said that? Now I was going to have to figure out where the fortune was buried, and Morgan was going to kill me if I failed.

"I bet he could help you, if you promise to let us go," Holly said.

It wasn't her best idea, but I couldn't think of any other way to save us. I stared Morgan in the eyes. "Yeah, I'll help, as long as you let Holly, Noelle, and me go once you've found the fortune. You'll be able to leave the forest, so you won't have to worry about us telling anyone you're here," I said.

"You don't get it, do you? *I'm* in charge here! *I* make the demands, not you!" Morgan growled. "Now, we'll see how good you are at solving puzzles, but the only reward you'll get is being able to live long enough for me to get my hands on the fortune!"

"Why should we help you if you're going to kill us anyway?" I asked.

"Because if you don't, I'll kill you sooner." Morgan paused and pointed his knife at Holly. "I think I'll start with her."

"No! I'll help you. Just leave her alone!" I said, putting my arm up in front of Holly. I looked at Dad standing there, not doing a thing.

"Here!" Morgan shoved the final map into my hand.

Everyone stared at me, and it made me even more nervous. I compared the drawing to the forest. There *was* a difference. "I see something." I had to be right about this. Otherwise, we were done for.

"Where?" Noelle asked, looking over my shoulder.

"Here." I pointed to the base of the tree in the drawing. "The map shows *three* big roots from the tree going into the ground. But the tree in front of us only has *two* roots. The fortune must be buried where the third root is in the drawing."

Edward smiled at me. "This is the final map, so the clue is where the fortune is buried, not which path to take."

"J.B., you're a genius!" Noelle said.

"Give me that map. I want to see what you're talking about." Morgan yanked the map from my hands and examined it. A smile spread across his face. "Dig!" he ordered. "Right there, in the middle of those two roots."

"We don't have any shovels," Garret said. How hadn't I noticed it before? The thieves must not have had any faith in finding the fortune. Otherwise, they would've brought shovels.

"Use your knives to dig up the dirt. I don't care how you do it. Just get me my fortune!"

I wanted to get the fortune and end the curse, but there was no way the Grimaults would let me do that. I grabbed Holly's arm and took a step back. This was our best opportunity to escape. The thieves were on their hands and knees digging up the dirt beneath the tree. Holly read my mind and nodded. I tapped Noelle on the arm and motioned for her to come with us. She shook her head. I didn't want to leave her, but I couldn't waste time either. I had to get Holly out of this place. Besides, I was sure Edward would do his best to protect Noelle.

Holly and I tiptoed backward, trying not to make a sound. Once we were about twenty feet away, I took off at a sprint. I didn't think anyone was paying attention to us, but I was wrong. As we came to a bend in the path, someone grabbed us from behind. Without looking, I knew it was Dad.

"What are you doing?" Holly cried. "Why won't you help us, D—"

Dad covered Holly's mouth with his hand, and she sobbed in our father's arms. "It's all right, Morgan. I've got them. Keep digging."

I couldn't believe my ears. I'd been defending Dad to Holly since we'd first seen him with the thieves. Now, I wondered if Holly had been right all along.

CHAPTER NINETEEN

I was feeling totally helpless for about the hundredth time since I'd come into the forest. There was nothing to do but watch as the Grimault thieves unearthed the Granville fortune. It was a slow process. Since they didn't have any shovels, they had to soften the dirt with their knives and scoop it aside with their hands. By the time they reached the fortune, they were sweaty and covered with dirt. Except Morgan. He'd made his family do all the work while *he* stood back and watched.

"It's heavy," Garret said as he and the others placed the chest in front of Morgan.

Noelle stepped closer, staring in amazement.

Morgan pushed everyone aside and used his bandana to wipe the dirt off the top of the chest. He knelt down next to it and placed a hand on each side of the lid. "Before we open it, let's have a moment of silence." Morgan bowed his head, and the others dropped to their knees behind him and bowed their heads as well.

Dad was participating, too. I shook my head and said, "I guess you were right, Holl. He isn't who I thought he was."

Holly nodded and a tear rolled down her cheek.

Morgan raised his head and slowly lifted the lid of the chest. The hinges were rusted with age, and they squeaked as the lid opened. From where I stood, I had a clear view of the fortune, and I couldn't help but smile. There were large silver coins and priceless antiques. All along, I hadn't been convinced we'd ever find the fortune, and now here it was an arm's length away. I wanted to reach out and touch the coins, but I was afraid Morgan would cut off my hand.

Morgan threw himself on top of the chest. "At last, it's mine!"

"That's what you think!" Noelle said. She grabbed the knife out of Edward's hand and stormed up to Morgan. "This fortune doesn't belong to you. It was stolen from the Granville family, and I'm going to see it's returned."

Morgan's face turned crimson, and the big vein in his forehead stuck out so far it looked like a giant worm. He stood up and glared at Noelle. "How would you know where this fortune came from?" He turned accusingly to Edward. "What have you told her?"

Edward took a step back and Noelle jumped to his defense. "He didn't tell me anything. I know all about the Granville fortune and the people who stole it."

And then I remembered. Noelle had told Holly and me the coins Dad had given to Garret were pieces of the Granville fortune, imprinted with the family crest. How had she known that? I hadn't asked her because I was so surprised to see her again. I'd completely forgotten about it.

Everyone stared at Noelle. She shook the knife at Morgan. He could've easily ripped the knife from her fingers, but he smiled instead.

"You're a smart one. Although, I'm not convinced Edward didn't tell you more than he should have." Morgan gave Edward a disapproving look, and Edward lowered his head. Morgan turned back to Noelle and snatched the knife away from her. "Still, I'd love to hear what you know about the fortune and where you heard it."

Noelle stumbled backward into Sam. The vulture squawked and raised its wings, but Sam tossed it a piece of bread to keep it from attacking Noelle. She turned to face Sam and started to cry.

"I want answers!" Morgan yelled, stabbing the knife into the tree behind him. "First, these two find our camp." He pointed a shaky hand at Holly and me. "Then, they tell me they have the final piece of my family's treasure map. Bruce shows up with silver coins and information for me. Don't even get me started on Sam. Now you—" he turned back to Noelle, "you somehow know all about the Granville fortune. How is it that so many people know about *my* fortune? This was supposed to be a secret. A secret only I'd benefit from."

"What do you mean only you?" Trent asked. "You said we'd each get a share of the fortune. We've done more than you have to find it. All you did was sleep in your tent while the rest of us searched and went out for food and supplies. You didn't even help dig up the chest!"

I expected Garret to come to his father's defense, but he looked at his dad and waited for an answer. He must've been questioning him, too. I could almost sympathize with him.

Morgan met his sons' stares. "Is this how you *all* feel?" Garret and Edward looked away, losing their nerve to go against their father.

My dad stepped up and put his face right in Morgan's. "It's not how we *all* feel. A few of us believe this fortune should be returned to the Granville family. Isn't that right, Noelle?" Noelle looked like she was in shock, and I couldn't blame her. I was, too.

Morgan inhaled deeply, making his nostrils flare. "I was right. You aren't a friend at all."

Dad straightened up, and somehow he seemed taller than usual. "No, I'm not, and I'm going to see that this chest is returned to its rightful owner. No matter what it takes."

Morgan didn't respond. He seemed to be calculating his next move. Just when I thought things couldn't get any more bizarre, Sam walked over and shook Dad's hand. "Good to see you again, Bruce."

"You've got that right. I thought you were dead," Dad said. "Got yourself some pets I see."

"They're the best protection I could ask for," Sam replied, tossing another piece of bread to the vulture.

"What's going on?" Edward asked. That's what I wanted to know.

"You should really do background checks on your recruits, Morgan," Sam said. "All I had to do was let Trent beat me in a few games of pool, and he told me everything I needed to know about you and the fortune. You took me aboard just as easily, without any questions."

"Why you little!" Trent reached for Sam, but Noelle stuck her foot out and tripped him.

"Keep your hands off him!" Noelle said.

Trent scowled at her. "Edward you better control your little sweetie over here before I—"

Without warning, Noelle landed a right hook on Trent's jaw. "Don't call me sweetie!"

Trent got to his feet, rubbing his jaw. He took a step toward Noelle, but Edward blocked him.

"Noelle, what's gotten into you?" Edward asked.

"I'm tired of pretending. I'm tired of keeping secrets. I wanted to tell you and J.B. who I really am, but I couldn't. I was worried about my dad. When he showed up, I was afraid you'd hurt him if I told you." She turned to face Sam. "I thought you were dead. Trent told me what they did to you, and I had a dream you were lost in these woods. I came looking for you. When I saw you, I thought you were something I created from my own fears. This forest does that somehow. I didn't think you were real."

Sam was Noelle's father! Of course! He'd said the squirrels chewed through his watch—the watch Noelle had found. It also explained Noelle's reaction when we'd first seen Sam. But why had Sam helped Morgan? And how had my dad gotten involved? My head felt like it might explode.

Everyone stared wide-eyed as Sam removed his jacket, covered in squirrels, and gently placed it on the ground. He walked over to Noelle and hugged her. "I'm sorry, sweetheart. I never meant to put you through all this." Noelle sobbed in her dad's arms.

"What's going on?" Morgan yelled. "Who are all you people?"

Sam draped one arm across Noelle's shoulders.

"We're Granvilles, and that's *our* fortune you've found."

Noelle turned to me. "My ancestor, Sebastien, stole this from his family a long time ago, dooming his descendants to be cursed until it was returned."

I knew the story. I'd read about it in Dad's journal, and I'd had visions about the curse. Now, here we all were. Together. The three cursed families that started this. The three cursed families that had to end this.

"And who are *you*?" Morgan growled at my father.

"Bruce Beaumonte."

"Beaumonte? I should have known." Morgan let out a primal yell.

Noelle smiled at me. "I figured out who you were when we were spying on the camp. Holly mentioned your ancestor and you guys being cursed."

I remembered the look on Noelle's face when Holly had told her. Now I understood why she'd gotten so upset.

My dad put a hand on Noelle's shoulder. "I recognized you immediately. Your father carries your picture with him, and he looks at it every chance he gets."

"You two were working together to find the fortune," Morgan said through gritted teeth.

Dad nodded. "We knew you'd keep it for yourself instead of returning it and breaking the curse. We've been working as private investigators for years, with *you* being our top case. Of course, you didn't make things easy for us, seeing as you captured our kids."

Dad looked at Holly and me, and I could barely fight back the tears. It had been lie after lie. He wasn't a lawyer. He was a private investigator. He'd been leaving me to spy on the Grimaults. I figured it was better than being a thief, but Dad was as much a stranger to me right now as he was to Morgan.

Morgan lunged at Dad. I grabbed the loaf of bread sticking out of Dad's pocket, hoping it was stale. Stepping forward, I swung it at Morgan's knife. The bread shattered, leaving crumbs in my hands. I blew the crumbs in his face, aiming right for his eyes. I'd hoped to temporarily blind him, but the crumbs scattered and stuck to the sweat on his cheeks and brow instead. Sam's squirrels chittered and leaped onto Morgan, nibbling at the breadcrumbs.

"Get them off me!" Morgan screamed. He fell to the ground, dropping his knife, and swatted at the squirrels.

"I wouldn't move around so much," Sam said. "They have sharp teeth!"

"Garret! Edward!" Morgan yelled. Garret and Edward didn't move. The corners of Trent's mouth twitched as he fought back a smile. He must've been enjoying this after all Morgan had put him through.

Realizing he was on his own, Morgan buried his face in the dirt, scaring most of the squirrels away. He grabbed for his knife on the ground in front of him. Dad went for it, too, but Morgan was closer. I picked up what was left of the bread and flung it on Morgan's back. This time the vulture swooped down for it, pinning Morgan to the ground.

Dad pulled me away from Morgan. "Thanks, J.B., but I've got it from here," he said. I wanted to hug him, but I couldn't move.

Dad and Sam grabbed Morgan's arms and yanked him to his feet. Garret drew his knife and advanced on Holly. She screamed as he wrapped one arm tightly around her shoulders and placed the knife against her cheek.

"Let my father go or she dies!" Garret yelled.

Dad and Sam stared in horror. "Easy now," Dad said in a soft voice. "No one has to get hurt."

"That's right," Garret agreed. "As long as you stay out of our way. We're taking the fortune, and we're leaving. If you can't agree to that, it'll cost you her life." He squeezed Holly, and she started to cry.

Sam, Noelle, my dad, and I all looked back and forth at each other. As much as we wanted to return the Granville fortune and break the curse, we couldn't trade Holly's life to do it.

Trent walked toward my dad and motioned for him

to let go of Morgan. Dad looked at Holly and released his grip. Sam did the same. Garret pushed Holly to the ground and rushed to his father's side. Noelle and I helped Holly up, and our fathers stood protectively in front of us. We faced each other in two groups. The Grimaults versus the Granvilles and Beaumontes. With one exception. Edward stood in the middle.

Morgan glared at his son with even more disapproval than I'd seen him give Trent. "Choose your side, but make sure you're certain. If you turn your back on me now, you'll no longer be a son to me. You'll be my enemy." He spoke slowly, making sure Edward understood each word.

"Edward, come on!" Garret begged.

Noelle mouthed something to Edward. I figured she was asking him to stay with us. Part of me wanted him to. After all, he did seem different than the rest of his family. He was more human than they were.

Edward looked at me, and then he turned to Noelle and whispered, "I'm sorry." He rushed to the chest and grabbed an end. Garret smiled and took the other. Together, they picked it up and walked off. Dad and Sam started to protest, but Morgan put his hand up to stop them.

He motioned for Trent to follow Garret and Edward, leaving him alone with us. Morgan smirked. "Those branches look like a huge claw reaching down to squeeze you all in its fist!" he yelled, focusing his eyes on the limbs dangling over our heads. Without waiting to see his creation, Morgan took off after his family and the Granville fortune.

We tried to run, but the transformation happened too quickly. In one swift motion, we were scooped off the trail by the large leafy claw. The finger-like branches tightened around us. Sam and his vulture were near my right shoulder. The vulture released its feet from Sam's neck and clawed at the leaves, ripping them to shreds. It had the right idea. The branches were too thick to break, but the leaves were easy to damage. I started biting the leaves in front of my face, spitting them out and going back for more. I must've looked like a savage animal, but it seemed to be working. I could feel the tree's grip on me weakening. "Rip the leaves!" I yelled. "It should make the claw release its grip."

Dad's left arm was free, and he yanked handfuls of leaves at a time. Holly jumped at the opportunity to bite something. Sam and Noelle were pinned together with very little wiggle room, but they did their best. Leaves flew through the air. We had to be close to making the branches bare, but the tree wasn't letting go.

I looked at Sam and Noelle. They were the only ones facing the bottoms of the branches. "Try to break the ends of the branches. They're the thinnest points. Maybe it will weaken the tree enough to free us!"

Noelle managed to get one hand around a branch. She looked like she was arm wrestling with it. Finally, I heard a snap. Noelle and Sam fell to the ground. Sam whistled to the vulture. In seconds, I felt the bird's beak biting the branch behind my head. The tree snapped again, and I fell. The vulture continued to break the branches until we were all free.

The bare branches hung lifelessly toward the ground. It was over. Of course, since the Grimaults stole the Granville fortune, we were still cursed, so the future didn't look good for any of us.

Dad put his hand on my shoulder. "You okay, J.B.?"

I nodded.

"Let's go home," he said, giving me a half smile.

No one said a word as we made our way back to Bradley Park and out of the forest for good.

CHAPTER TWENTY

I didn't fully remember leaving Braeden Forest or even saying goodbye to Noelle and Sam, but I woke up in the morning safe in my own bed. My thoughts were so cloudy I wondered if it all had been a bad dream. Something my overactive imagination had cooked up. I threw on clean clothes and went to check on Holly. She was sound asleep when I walked into her room, but the worn-out look on her face told me Braeden Forest hadn't been merely a nightmare. It'd been a real-life horror Holly and I had lived through for several long days.

"How are you feeling, pal?" Dad asked from the doorway.

I turned to face him, unsure if I even recognized him after all I'd been through. He looked completely exhausted. Exactly how I felt. "I don't know. Are you asking as my dad? Or as Bruce, the thief? Or how about as a private investigator?"

Holly moaned and opened her eyes. "What's going on?"

"It's okay, sweetheart. You're home now," Dad said. He walked over and brushed the hair from Holly's face.

"No, it's not okay!" I exploded. Everything that had happened left me questioning who my dad really was. I felt betrayed and couldn't hold back my feelings any longer. "Why didn't you tell us about the family curse? Why did you go after the Grimaults by yourself? Why did you pretend you didn't know us?"

"Whoa! One question at a time," he said, putting his hands up in surrender.

Holly sat up in bed, and I sat next to her so we were both facing Dad, who slumped down at the foot of the bed.

He took a deep breath before he began. "First of all, I'm not a lawyer. I work as a private investigator."

"Why the secrecy?" I asked. "You could've at least been honest about your job."

"Sam and I only take on special cases, and Sam uses a fake name to conceal his identity as a member of the Granville family. Our primary goal has always been to recover the stolen Granville fortune and break the curse that's plagued our families for years. We had to be secretive so the Grimaults didn't discover who we were or what we were doing. If Morgan heard about two private investigators in the area, he would've gotten suspicious. So, we told everyone we were lawyers. It's all been kept very secretive to stay off Grimault's radar. It's not a great life, but we have the curse to thank for that."

"And what exactly is the curse?" Holly asked. "What does it do to us?"

"You saw what the forest could do. Well, the curse was helping fuel that power. Our biggest fears come to life. Holly's fear of hospitals. My fear of not being able to provide for and protect you. Your mother's fear of things falling to pieces." Dad looked at me, probably wondering how the curse affected me. I turned away. I couldn't admit to my fear—that I was losing my mind.

I thought about how this had all started. "You were at the park when that guy came wandering out of the forest. That wasn't a coincidence. You knew he'd be there."

Dad lowered his head. I could tell he was sorry for betraying us. "You have to understand I was trying to protect our family. Sam and I had to make sure the forest was cut off from the public. We didn't want any innocent people to get hurt wandering into the woods and coming across one of the Grimaults. Sam has a connection at the police station, so he was able to get released even after he'd convinced everyone he'd lost his mind. The second they let him go, he went into the forest to find Morgan."

Sam was the crazy man at the park. I hadn't even recognized him underneath all the dirt.

"But why did Sam go looking for the Grimaults on his own?" I asked.

"He insisted on it. He thought it'd be best to get on the inside and help Morgan locate the fortune. I was supposed to come in and help Sam recover the fortune and break the curse. I felt awful when he didn't return. If anything had happened to him, it would've been my fault."

"Something did happen to him. They tortured him! They tied his hands and left him to be eaten!" Dad put his head in his hands. I knew this had been tough on him, too, but I needed to understand what had happened in the forest, no matter how difficult it was for him to talk about.

"Noelle went into the forest to search for him. She could've been killed! All because you and Sam lied to us!" I couldn't control my anger. I knew Dad and Sam had thought they were protecting their families, but they'd ended up putting us in *more* danger.

"I didn't have a choice. Only your mother knew the truth. The Grimaults have been coming here for generations to search for the fortune. They're greedy people. They knew the fortune would be difficult to find without all the maps, but that didn't stop them from trying."

"Where did you get a map?" Holly asked.

"I drew it. Sam and I had been in the forest numerous times, and we chose a place to use as the setting for a fake map. It was a long shot, but I had to bring Morgan something that would make him accept me as the son of his father's friend.

"It wasn't until much later that I discovered I really did possess a piece of the treasure map. I knew Aristede made the painting of the forest," Dad said, looking me in the eyes. "The one from our living room. But I had no idea it was part of the treasure map until Edward showed me the other maps back at the campsite. After talking to Edward, I went back to Bradley Park, intending to head home and retrieve the painting, but I found the painting on the merry-go-round where you'd left it. That's when I got your mother's panicked voice mails on my cell. She said you two had taken the painting and were missing. I knew you'd gone into the forest, so I had to find you *and* the fortune. When I came across the Grimaults holding you captive, I had to pretend I didn't know you so Morgan wouldn't harm you."

"So, you did wink at me?" I asked.

"Yes. I wasn't sure if you saw that, but I wanted to give you a sign I was there to help. Luckily, you played right along."

"We weren't playing along. We thought you were

really a thief. We were terrified!" Holly said, squeezing the sheets in her fists.

"I'm sorry, honey. I wanted to tell you, but I couldn't chance Morgan hurting you."

"Why did you stop us when we tried to escape?" Holly asked.

"You saw what that place is capable of creating. It was too dangerous to let you wander through the forest alone."

My mind was racing trying to make sense of it all. I nearly kicked myself for forgetting to ask about Noelle. "How's Noelle? And Sam?"

Dad laughed. "Is this your first crush or did I miss one along the way?"

Man, I thought one girl was pretty and everyone had to get on my case about it.

"Noelle is fine, J.B.," Dad said. "I spoke with Sam this morning. You can call her later if you'd like."

I wasn't even sure she'd want to talk to me after all that had happened, but I was glad she was safe. One question still bothered me. "Why did we have that old painting in our living room?"

Dad folded his hands in his lap. "Jean Beaumonte helped steal the Granville fortune, as you now know." He gave me a stern look and added, "By the way, I want my journal back." I swallowed hard, expecting a lecture on stealing, but Dad continued with his explanation. "Everyone in our family has tried to find the Granville fortune and return it so we could break the curse. We discovered Aristede's painting, and it's been passed down with each generation of Beaumontes as a reminder that we had to stop the Grimaults from stealing the Granville fortune again."

"So this is a family business, just like the search for the fortune was in the Grimault family?" I asked.

"Yes. I was hoping the curse would be broken before you were old enough to join the search. But now that the Grimaults got away with the fortune—"

"Anyone hungry?" Mom walked into the room carrying a tray of milk and blueberry pancakes. She placed the tray on Holly's nightstand.

"Mom!" Holly cried. She jumped up and hugged her. I tried to hold back and act tough, but I couldn't fight the urge to hug my mom.

"I'm so happy you two are all right. I was so worried about you," Mom said. Tears streamed down her cheeks.

"We're sorry we lied to you," Holly said.

"I think your father and I are partially to blame. We shouldn't have kept this from you," Mom said.

We all sat on the bed, and Holly and I dug into the pancakes.

"How are you part of this, Mom?" I asked with my mouth full.

"I worked with your father up until you were born, J.B. Then, I upgraded to a better job." She squeezed my hand and Holly's. I wasn't sure I'd consider being a mom an upgrade, but she sure seemed to love it.

"What about the journal? You wrote it," I added.

"I still help out, doing research, keeping notes, things like that."

I still wondered about one thing. "Why did you let us hang out at the park if the forest was dangerous?"

Dad sighed. "All your friends hung out there. It would've been too difficult to stop you without telling you about the curse. Plus, the Grimaults used the seaside entrance to the forest, and they never would've exposed themselves to a park full of people. The park itself was safe.

"Understand that we can't tell you everything about my job, especially since finding Morgan now will be more difficult than ever. He knows Sam and I will be looking for him so we can return the Granville fortune to its rightful owners." Dad shook his head, obviously not wanting to think about that right now. "But I'll try to be more honest with you."

I appreciated him explaining all of this to me, and I wanted to promise to be honest with him, too. But I couldn't. Especially since I was about to go back into Braeden Forest.

CHAPTER TWENTY-ONE

Ever since I'd gotten up, I'd had this nagging urge to return to those woods. It didn't make any sense, but I couldn't ignore it. The big problem was getting away from Holly and my parents long enough to find out what was calling me back to the place where I'd almost died several times.

"Thanks for the pancakes, Mom. They're great, but I think I need to take a walk and clear my head. That's okay, isn't it?" I asked, getting up and heading to the door.

Mom looked hesitant to let me go, but Dad said, "Sure, champ. Just don't go too far. You've been through a lot and must be exhausted." He looked guilty. Normally, I would've been glad he understood what he'd put me through, but the fact that I was lying to him made *me* feel guilty, too.

"Wait a minute!" Mom said, picking up two wrapped presents on Holly's desk. Birthday presents...I forgot it was my birthday.

"Happy birthday to you," Mom sang, as she handed Holly and me the gifts.

Holly dug right in. Not even traumatic experiences could ruin a birthday for her. My parents were staring at me, so I unwrapped my present, too.

"A cell phone! Finally!" Holly shrieked.

Dad smiled. "We weren't sure if you were ready for this responsibility, but, given recent events, I think we made the right decision."

"No way would you get cell phone reception in that forest," Holly said. She didn't know when to keep her mouth shut, but hearing her talk about the forest reminded me I had somewhere to be.

"Thanks, Mom and Dad. This is great. I think I'll go for that walk now." I put the box down on Holly's desk.

Dad picked up the phone and handed it to me. "It's already programmed, so take it with you in case you get tired and want us to pick you up."

I smiled. "Sure, Dad."

"I'll go with you," Holly said, kicking off the covers.

"Actually, I kind of want to be alone." I felt bad blowing off Holly, but what I had to do, whatever it was, I had to do alone. "I won't be long," I said. I started running the minute my foot hit the stairs. I bolted through the front door, letting it slam behind me. I was worried Dad or Holly would look out the window to see where I was heading, so I took a detour to the park.

The police tape hung across the entrance gate, so I climbed over it like last time. I headed straight for the forest. My body was on autopilot, which was good because I didn't have a clue what I was doing. Was I really going into those woods again? Armed with nothing more than a cell phone that probably wouldn't get reception?

A squeaking sound broke my trance. The merry-go-round moved. Noelle gracefully jumped off it, landing a few feet in front of me.

"Right on time," she said.

On time for what? I was about to ask when Edward came walking over to us from the woods.

"*You*? I thought you and your family would be halfway to France by now," I said. I still wasn't sure how I felt about Edward.

"Why are we all here? I mean, I knew we'd all meet here. I saw you both coming," Noelle said. "I must've fallen asleep on the merry-go-round, and I had a dream we'd all be here." She blushed. "Does that sound silly?"

I shook my head. "No. I felt like I *had* to come here. Like something was pulling me in this direction. You had another one of your dreams? Do you have them a lot?"

"Not a lot."

"You're not the only one who has them," I said. "But they're not dreams. They're visions. I've had them since I was little."

Edward stepped closer, but he was staring into the distance. "I've had them, too."

"Why are we here?" Noelle asked, looking at me as if I somehow had all the answers.

"I think I know," Edward said, finally making eye contact with us. "I had a vision about Aristede, Jean, and Sebastien getting cursed by an old woman wearing that necklace." He pointed to a blue-green stone dangling from Noelle's neck. She reached up and brushed her fingers against it. She hadn't been wearing it in the forest.

"I found this in the attic. It belonged to one of my ancestors. It's supposed to be really old."

"It is," Edward said.

It was my vision! Edward had seen my vision—the curse, the old woman, feeling like I was floating yet connected to something at the same time. I should've been totally freaked out, but I felt at ease for the first time. I felt...complete. We weren't drawn to the forest. We were drawn to each other, like we had been since we'd met. Somehow, Noelle and Edward were answering questions I'd had for years. It gave me a strange idea. "This may sound crazy, but I think you can show us your vision."

"What?" Noelle and Edward asked.

"I think that if we all touch—you know, like make a connection for the vision to travel through."

"Man, I am *not* holding your hand," Edward said.

I pictured my vision. "We can put our hands on each other's shoulders. We'll make a sort of triangle with our bodies. What do you think?"

"I'll try it," Noelle said with a shrug.

Edward nodded. "I guess."

We moved closer, awkwardly reaching our hands out and resting them on each other's shoulders. My fingertips began to tingle, and the hair on my arms stood up. Edward and Noelle must have felt the same way because they stared at their hands. I'd thought the forest had somehow been creating the static electricity between Noelle and me, but it was something else altogether.

"What do we do now?" Noelle asked. "I've only ever had visions when I was asleep."

I'd never seen our faces in my vision, but somehow I knew what we had to do. "We close our eyes, and Edward pictures his vision in his mind. If he sees it, we should see it, too."

"How do you know that?" Noelle asked.

"I saw us doing it," I answered. "It's the vision I've been having since I was four."

I expected Noelle and Edward to be confused by this, but there was something weird about the three of us together. It was doing something to us. We were sharing the same emotions. We, as a group, held the answers to our questions. "Ready?" I asked, eager to try this.

Edward and Noelle nodded and closed their eyes. I closed mine, too. An intense warmth passed through my body. The same warmth I'd felt every time Edward and I touched back in the forest. An image immediately popped into my head. I'd thought calling up the vision would take some practice, but it came as easily as breathing.

It was dark, but I could see three boys about seventeen or so. They crept through the night, dressed in black. One of them had wavy hair that was kind of long and shaggy. He led the way to a stone tower. It looked like they were outside a giant castle. They reached a large wooden door, and the shaggy-haired one pulled a key from his pocket. He slipped it into the lock and opened the door.

The tallest boy pushed his way into the room. He opened the sack in his hands and began stuffing silver coins, jewelry, and other expensive objects inside.

"That's enough, Aristede. We don't have time to take everything. The party will be ending soon, and the guests will be heading this way," the skinny one said.

"Jean's right. I've already bagged the most expensive things. This should be more than enough to get us overseas," the shaggy-haired one replied.

Aristede nodded, but he continued to grab things on his way to the door. They were stopped by a hunched-over figure in the doorway.

An elderly woman with long flowing gray hair pointed a bony finger at the boys. "You three who bring disgrace to your families shall suffer great misfortune. Your lives shall be cursed until you return what was taken this night." The blue-green stone dangling from her neck sparkled in the darkness. A brilliant white light shot from the woman's eyes. She let out a painful cry and collapsed on the ground.

The shaggy boy rushed to her and whispered, "I'm sorry, Grandmother."

"Sebastien, let's go before anyone else comes," Jean urged, pushing him through the doorway.

The warmth left my body as the vision faded away. I opened my eyes and met Edward's stare. He had seen this before, but he looked shocked, sharing Noelle's and my response.

Noelle shook her head. "That was..." She couldn't finish her statement, but she didn't need to. Edward and I nodded.

"So that's how it all started," Edward said. "The curse."

Noelle had tears in her eyes. "It makes sense now. Sebastien's grandmother."

Before I could ask what she meant, I understood. In Edward's vision, Sebastien hadn't looked surprised by his grandmother's power.

A strange tingling, like static electricity, shot up my arms, and I was warm all over. From the looks on Edward and Noelle's faces, they felt it, too. Instinctively, we closed our eyes as another vision flashed before us.

The old woman was sitting in her room, talking to another woman about half her age. The old woman's eyes were almost white. She was blind.

"The sight is gone." She bowed her head and sighed. "I don't know what went wrong. The boys have stolen our great fortune. They've separated, and now none of them has any of my power. It will remain in their bloodlines until three who are ready to use it come along. Three who will restore what we have lost," the old woman said.

"Mother, surely you can talk to them. Make them see," the younger woman replied.

"It's useless. Sebastien has left. He has shamed this family and taken our most precious gift with him. We are at a loss."

The vision faded away.

"That was intense," Noelle said, breathing heavily.

"I don't know if I can handle much more of this."

Edward looked down at his arms. "You're going to have to," he said.

Our eyes shut, almost like an involuntary response to the vision flooding our thoughts. This one was different. A hospital maternity ward. Three babies born on the same day, at the same time. Jack Beaumonte, Noelle Granville, and Edward Grimault.

The tingling stopped, and the vision ended as abruptly as it had started. We stared at each other in silence. *We* were the three, the ones who'd inherited the old woman's gift of sight.

"We have the same birthday?" Edward looked frazzled. He dropped his arms to his sides and glanced away.

My new cell phone vibrated in my pocket. Probably Holly wondering where I was. She wouldn't have understood this. I ignored the call.

"Happy tenth birthday. Some present, huh?" Noelle giggled nervously.

"Holly isn't going to like this," I said. I could imagine how she'd react to finding out she had to share her birthday with Noelle and Edward. Holly didn't even like having to share the day with *me*, and it'd been my birthday first.

"You can't tell her. We can't tell anyone. At least not yet." Noelle looked scared, and I couldn't blame her. We weren't like other people.

I nodded. "You're right. Our dads don't seem to know about this part of the curse. I'm not sure we should tell them, not until we figure out what this means." Dad had tried to keep the curse a secret to protect me. I had to keep *this* a secret to protect him. We had more in common than I'd thought.

"My dad took off in the middle of the night," Edward said. "He didn't even tell Garret or me where he was heading." I could hear the disappointment in his voice, and I knew how he felt.

"You can't tell Garret or Trent, either," Noelle said.

Edward nodded. "We don't tell anyone."

"Good. We all agree." It seemed odd saying it aloud. We weren't exactly three people *I* would've put together, but we seemed to see eye-to-eye somehow.

Noelle met my stare. "We *share* the woman's gift."

I nodded. "That's why we each see something different. Edward sees things that have already happened, you see things as they're happening, and I see things that haven't happened yet."

"The past, present, and future," Noelle said.

There had been a purpose to the curse. It wasn't meant to simply punish the boys for stealing the Granville fortune. The gift of sight that went with it was meant to change them, to make them see the error in the path they'd chosen, and to correct it. Only they didn't do that. They'd split up. The only way the gift of sight truly worked was if the three—now us—stayed together. I wondered if Noelle and Edward understood that. We couldn't split up the way Sebastien, Aristede, and Jean did or the curse would never end. We had to fulfill what the old woman wanted our ancestors to do. "In the vision, the old woman said we have to use the gift to return what was lost on the night of the curse."

"My family's fortune," Noelle said.

"Right, but it was split up. Isn't that what Sebastien's grandmother meant when she said the boys separated?" I asked.

"Probably," Edward said. "Aristede's fortune wasn't exactly as big as my dad thought it'd be. There must be more out there somewhere." He looked toward the forest.

"I don't think it's in there," I said. "Sebastien and Jean would've hidden their portions of the fortune in other places since they separated."

"We have to find those places if we want the curse to end," Noelle said, but she didn't sound as eager as she'd been before. We didn't have any maps or other clues to help us find what Sebastien and Jean had stolen, and not even Edward had a clue where *his* father had run off with the fortune. We were still missing all three parts.

"So we work together?" Edward asked, looking back and forth between Noelle and me.

"It looks that way," Noelle answered, giving us both a half smile.

From this moment forward, we were all changed. Like it or not, we were the ones who had been chosen to break the curse.

I looked at Edward and Noelle, my second family of sorts, destined to be linked forever by this shared sight. "It's up to us," I said. "We are the three."

ACKNOWLEDGEMENTS

There are so many people I want to thank because this was actually the very first book I ever wrote. The book went through several major changes, including a genre change and age level change. It's been a crazy but fun journey with J.B. and the gang. First I have to thank my mother, Patricia Bradley, and my sister, Heather DeRobertis, for encouraging me to pursue my dream of writing a novel and reading countless versions of this story. A huge thanks to my critique group, Shauna, Katrina, Katie, Terrie, Cindy, Taurean, Leslie, and Londy for all your amazing feedback. Lauren Hammond, thank you for believing in this book.

To Georgia McBride and the team at Georgia McBride Media Group, thank you for seeing the potential in this series from the start. To my editor, Ashlynn Yuhas, thank you for helping me polish this story and making it that much better. To Nicole LaVigne and Kerry Genova I appreciate your careful attention in making each word count. To my cover designer, what can I say but wow! You brought J.B. and Holly to life, and I couldn't be happier with your portrayal of them.

To my daughter, Ayla, I promise not to tell you to go to sleep when you're reading this book in bed at night. As always, this book is for you, my greatest joy and inspiration. Ryan, you are the most supportive husband in the world and I love you for it. To my father, Martin Bradley, I can't thank you enough for the way you promote my books to everyone you meet.

Kelly's Coven, you are all superstars! I couldn't do this without you and your support. Thank you a million times over for being the best street team ever. To the book bloggers, readers, and my fellow writers, thank you for sharing my career with me. I love you all!

KELLY HASHWAY

Kelly Hashway grew up reading R.L. Stein's Fear Street novels and writing stories of her own, so it was no surprise to her family when she majored in English and later obtained a masters degree in English Secondary Education from East Stroudsburg University. After teaching middle school language arts for seven years, Hashway went back to school and focused specifically on writing. She is now the author of three young adult series, one middle grade series, and several picture books. She also writes contemporary romance under the pen name Ashelyn Drake. When she isn't writing,

Hashway works as a freelance editor for small presses as well as for her own list of clients. In her spare time, she enjoys running, traveling, and volunteering with the PTO. Hashway currently resides in Pennsylvania with her husband, daughter, and two pets.

OTHER MONTH9BOOKS AND TANTRUM BOOKS TITLES YOU MIGHT LIKE:

TRACY TAM: SANTA COMMAND

KING OF THE MUTANTS

THE THREE THORNS: BROTHERHOOD OF THE SHIELD
BOOK 1

DAWN OF THE JED

LUCAS MACKENZIE AND THE LONDON MIDNIGHT
GHOST SHOW

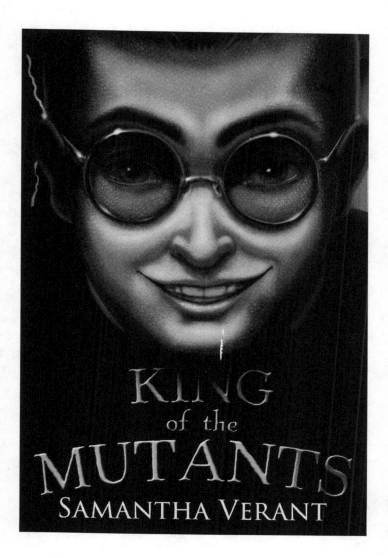

KING
of the
MUTANTS
SAMANTHA VERANT

TRACY TAM
SANTA COMMAND

KRYSTALYN DROWN

THE
BROTHERHOOD
AND THE
SHIELD
THE THREE THORNS

MICHAEL GIBNEY

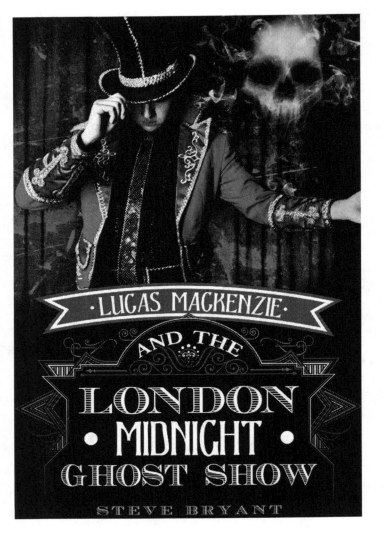

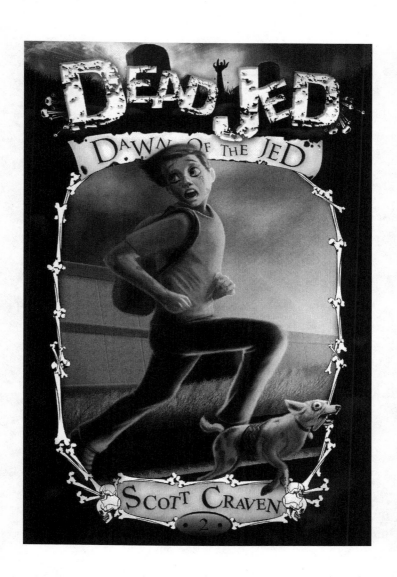

The Philosophy of Rawls

A Collection of Essays

Series Editors

Henry S. Richardson
Georgetown University

Paul J. Weithman
University of Notre Dame

A GARLAND SERIES
READINGS IN PHILOSOPHY
ROBERT NOZICK, *ADVISOR*
HARVARD UNIVERSITY

Contents of the Series

The Two Principles
and Their Justification

Edited with an introduction by

Henry S. Richardson
Georgetown University

GARLAND PUBLISHING, INC.
A MEMBER OF THE TAYLOR & FRANCIS GROUP
New York & London
1999

Library of Congress Cataloging-in-Publication Data

The two principles and their justification / edited with an introduction
  by Henry S. Richardson.
         p.   cm. — (The philosophy of Rawls ; 2)
      "A Garland series, readings in philosophy."
      Includes bibliographical references.
      ISBN 0-8153-2926-1 (alk. paper)
         1. Justice. 2. Fairness. 3. Liberty. 4. Rawls, John 1921—
  Contributions in political science.
  I. Richardson, Henry S. II. Series.

  JC578.T84 1999
  323.44—dc21   99-048604

Printed on acid-free, 250-year-life paper
Manufactured in the United States of America

Contents

Series Introduction

John Rawls is the pre-eminent political philosopher of our time. His 1971 masterpiece, *A Theory of Justice*, permanently changed the landscape of moral and political theory, revitalizing the normative study of social issues and taking stands about justice, ethics, rationality, and philosophical method that continue to draw followers and critics today. His *Political Liberalism* (rev. ed., 1996) squarely faced the fundamental challenges posed by cultural, religious, and philosophical pluralism. It should be no surprise, then, that turn-of-the-century searches of the periodical indices in philosophy, economics, law, the humanities, and related fields turn up almost three thousand articles devoted to a critical discussion of Rawls's theory. In these Volumes we reprint a wide-ranging selection of the most influential and insightful articles on Rawls.

While it was impossible, even in a collection of this size, to reprint all of the important material, the selection here should provide the student and scholar with a route into all of the significant controversies that have surrounded Rawls's theories since he first began enunciating them in the nineteen-fifties — issues that the Introductions to each Volume of this series delineate. Eight criteria guided our selection. First, these volumes form part of a series devoted to *secondary* literature. We reprint no articles by Rawls: most of these have just appeared together for the first time in his *Collected Papers*.[1] Second, we reprint only self-contained articles published in English, rather than selections from books or articles in other languages. Third, the articles reprinted here are all *about* Rawls's view, as opposed to being original reflections inspired by Rawls's work. Fourth, we aimed for a broad coverage of controversies and of the main features of Rawls's theory that they surround. Since the Volumes are organized in terms of these controversies, we include very few overall assessments or book reviews. Some central elements of Rawls's theory, while relatively novel and well-articulated, have not been controversial enough to draw critical fire in the secondary literature. The Volume Introductions mention many of these features. Fifth, we aimed to include the most influential articles that have appeared. In identifying these, we used a systematic search of the citation indices to supplement our own judgment. Naturally, we also took special notice of pieces cited by Rawls himself. Sixth, we sought to reprint articles by a large number of authors representing the widest possible range of points of view. In some cases, this meant refraining from reprinting a certain article because its author was already well represented in the selections. Seventh, we have sought to exhibit through our selections the broadly interdisciplinary influence of Rawls's writings. We have included articles by political theorists, economists, lawyers, religious thinkers, and social scientists as well as by philosophers. Eighth, we have favored including articles that are now relatively hard to find. For this reason, with the exception of H.L.A. Hart's exceptionally influential essay, we refrained from including any of the fine articles that were reprinted in Norman Daniels's 1975 collection, *Reading Rawls*,[2] which the reader interested in the early reception of Rawls's views should consult.

Utilizing all of these selection criteria did not leave us without painful choices. The secondary literature on Rawls is so deep that another set of five volumes could cover all the main issues with a completely non-overlapping set of fine articles. Some articles unfortunately had to be cut because of their sheer length: dropping one of them allowed us to include two or three others. Others, more arbitrarily, fell victim to the high permissions costs set by their initial publishers. We particularly regret that it proved impossible to find a short enough, self-contained essay by Robert Nozick that would have represented his trenchant libertarian critique of Rawls. While we do include (in Vol. 3) some of the secondary literature that responds to and picks up on Nozick's influential arguments, one should consult Nozick's *Anarchy, State, and Utopia* (1974) to appreciate their richness, subtlety, and power.[3]

The five volumes are arranged in roughly chronological order. The first volume includes articles on Rawls's early statements of his view and on its central contractarian ideas. Volume 2 covers the two principles of justice as fairness and Rawls's most general ideas about their justification. Volume 3 focuses on the concrete implications of Rawls's view and on the debates between Rawls and his utilitarian, perfectionist, libertarian, conservative, radical, and feminist critics. Volume 4 treats of Rawls's moral psychology and his attempt to accommodate the value of community. Volume 5, on Rawls's most recent work, is entitled "Reasonable Pluralism."

The serious student of Rawls's initial impact is greatly assisted by *John Rawls and His Critics: An Annotated Bibliography*, put together by J.H. Wellbank, Denis Snook, and David T. Mason, which catalogues and provides abstracts for most of the secondary literature in English prior to 1982.[4] While this work was of great help with that earlier period, completing the onerous task of collecting and sorting through the voluminous secondary literature, which has since continued to balloon, would not have been possible without the able and thorough research assistance of Rachael Yocum. We are grateful to the Dean of Georgetown College and to the Graduate School of Georgetown University for their generosity in supporting this research assistance.

Henry S. Richardson
Paul J. Weithman

Notes

[1] John Rawls, *Collected Papers*, ed. Samuel Freeman (Cambridge, Mass.: Harvard University Press, 1999).

[2] Norman Daniels, ed., *Reading Rawls* (N.Y.: Basic Books, 1975).

[3] Robert Nozick, *Anarchy, State, and Utopia* (N.Y.: Basic Books, 1974).

[4] J.H. Wellbank, Denis Snook, and David T. Mason, *John Rawls and His Critics: An Annotated Bibliography* (New York: Garland, 1982).

Volume Introduction

The articles in the present volume reflect the critical discussion of the two principles of justice as fairness — Rawls's theory — and his most general ideas about their justification, namely Kantian constructivism and reflective equilibrium. For articles on the development and main outlines of the social contract apparatus to which Rawls appeals in articulating one strand of argument for his principles, see Vol. 1. Here, instead, we initially turn to controversies generated by those principles themselves. Since some of the criticisms raised in this literature led Rawls to revise his formulation of the principles, it would be well to start with the final formulation of them in his 1971 book, *A Theory of Justice* [*TJ*]:[1]

First Principle

Each person is to have an equal right to the most extensive total system of equal basic liberties compatible with a similar system of liberty for all.

Second Principle

Social and economic inequalities are to be arranged so that they are both:
(a) to the greatest benefit of the least advantaged, consistent with the just savings principle,
and
(b) attached to offices and positions open to all under conditions of fair equality of opportunity.

Famously, Rawls ranks the first principle "lexically" ahead of the second, so that no consideration of distributive justice may interfere with promoting equal basic liberties. He also ranks the second principle, with its two parts, lexically ahead of considerations of efficiency or welfare. Part (a) of the second principle, which Rawls calls the "difference principle," has been far more controversial than part (b).

As noted in the Introduction to Volume 1, one of the most distinctive aspects of Rawls's approach has been his understanding of principles as open-textured and as consequently standing in need of interpretation and specification. This "final statement" of his two principles represents a filling out of provisional versions in *TJ* which, in turn, are more definite than the "general conception" of justice as fairness that he there introduced as an expository device but has since dropped. His later writings do, however, make use of more general versions of the ideals of justice as fairness, including the idea of society as a system of fair cooperation, which he describes in *Political Liberalism* (*PL*) as the "fundamental organizing idea of justice as fairness."[2] In *TJ*, an important strand of his argument involves considering four alternative interpretations of the second principle (set out on 65), involving weaker and stronger readings of equal opportunity and weaker and stronger readings of the ideal of reciprocal advantage. The last — the difference principle — has been the most controversial aspect of Rawls's principles. (The question of intergenerational justice, of which Rawls's discussion of "just savings" was a pioneering treatment, is a relatively technical and difficult subject that is touched upon by Leininger's article in this Volume and Kavka's and Barry's articles in Vol. 3.[3])

The first principle, however, has also received its share of critical attention. As Rawls acknowledges in *PL* (289), H.L.A. Hart's critical essay (reprinted here) led him to see a need to recast his argument for the first principle and its priority.[4] Rather than simply taking it as a fact that individuals are deeply attached to their conceptions of the good and fiercely protective of their freedom to pursue them, Rawls came, after thinking through Hart's criticisms, to feel the need to appeal to a richer ideal of persons as having the moral powers to frame and to pursue conceptions of justice and of their good, an ideal which is no longer imputed to the parties to his hypothetical social contract (the parties in the "original position" [OP]: see Vol. 1) but rather is seen as being embodied in the moral constraints on their choice (see *PL*, 370). Hart's criticisms also led to a minor reformulation of the first principle, replacing the idea of a "most extensive" scheme of equal basic liberties with that of a "fully adequate" one. This amendment helps remind one that Rawls is concerned with a set of fundamental civil and political liberties, roughly those that are traditional in western democracies, and not with some one-dimensional idea of liberty that one might conceive somehow of maximizing. Another controversial aspect of the first principle, aside from its general basis, is its interaction with the principles of distributive justice. Although the first principle has absolute priority over the distributive principles, critics have raised the worry whether the liberties thus protected will nonetheless be subverted by inequalities of wealth and power. In *TJ*, Rawls dealt with this issue by invoking a distinction between liberty and the worth of liberty. Norman Daniels' article (this Vol.) casts doubt on the viability of this distinction. In *PL* (318, 326–8), Rawls admits that this distinction is merely definitional, and by itself does not accomplish the needed work of assuring that the basic liberties are not subverted by material inequalities; to take this step, he develops the idea of the "fair value" of the political liberties (an idea that, he claims, was present in *TJ*).[5] The reprinted article by Thomas Pogge explores many of these same issues independently of (and prior to) Rawls's later reactions to these critics, and pursues a systematic answer to the question, Which liberties are basic?

Rawls's most widely visible contribution to political philosophy is the difference principle, which requires that the basic structure of society (on this notion, see Vol. 1) be structured so that social and economic inequalities are, within the constraints of the first principle, to the greatest advantage of the least well-off representative persons. It has been common for economists to mention just this one Rawlsian principle, isolating it from its context in the broader ideals of justice as fairness. The article by the philosopher and economist Amartya Sen, reprinted in this volume, gives the flavor of this work while putting it in a broader perspective.[6] One should remember that the difference principle is a specification of a more general ideal of reciprocal benefit (where full equality represents the morally privileged baseline of comparison). Reference only to the prospects of the least-well-off representative persons is a convenience of exposition that Rawls achieves only on the basis of some important assumptions about how changes in the expectations of different groups of people are knit together (*TJ*, 81–3). The idea that inequalities could ever redound to the benefit of the least advantaged relies on the possibility that inequalities could provide incentives that stimulate economic growth. Responding to earlier work by Kenneth Arrow and Partha Dasgupta, the article by Wolfgang Leininger purports to be able to fend off inconsistencies that stem from explicitly formulating the difference principle for direct application to a growing economy. Another rather technical question that arises as to the "least well of persons" is how they are to be identified. If we think in terms of particular persons, it will become obvious to us that those who are worst off in one scenario are not the same persons as those who are worst off in another. Clearly, however, Rawls means his principle to have us compare those who are worst off under one set of institutions with others who are worst off in another. Paul Voice's article helps clarify this fundamental point, which leads us to the recognition that when one is comparing alternative basic structures of society, it is indeed necessary to think in terms of abstractly characterized representative groups of citizens, rather than in terms of concrete individuals, actual or otherwise.[7] A more substantive, and still on-going debate concerns whether the difference principle can really be applied only to the basic structure of society, such that it does allow inequalities that, via incentive effects and the like, redound to the benefit of the least well-off representative persons. For, of course, individuals who benefit from these inequalities could make donations or take other actions that would make the less well-off better off still. This issue about whether the difference principle will factor through to individual actions so as to squeeze out any inequality whatsoever, was raised in an article by G.A. Cohen. Here we reprint a responding article by Philippe Van Parijs, which argues that incentive-generating inequalities might be justified under certain conditions, and a later article by Cohen in which he argues that the attempt to limit the difference principle to the basic structure of society will not insulate it from this radically egalitarian implication.

The priority of liberty — of the first principle over the second — is as important to the content of justice as fairness as is either principle taken separately. We have already seen that H.L.A. Hart's article led Rawls to reconsider his argument for the first principle and for its priority. Brian Barry's piece in this Volume, which is focussed more squarely on the priority of liberty, attacks Rawls's argument in the form it was presented in *TJ*, namely, as relying upon generalizations about individuals' preferences. Henry Shue's article is more sympathetic, reconstructing Rawls's argument from the primary good of (the social basis of) self-respect (on which see Vol. 4) to the priority of liberty. Since, as noted, Rawls later recast his argument for the priority of liberty, it is important to examine critically how the newer argument works. David Estlund's essay does that, finding that the priority of liberty established by the later argument is as strong as that proclaimed in *TJ*.

The second set of topics covered in this Volume involve Rawls's most general ideas about justification: the Kantian interpretation of his view, including his so-called "Kantian constructivism," and his ideal of reflective equilibrium.

"The Kantian Interpretation" is the title of sec. 40 of *TJ*. This section gives an alternative accounting of why it is that appeal to the OP should be seen as helping justify the principles that end up there getting endorsed by its hypothetical participants. Rawls explains that the aspect of Kant's ethics that he takes to be most distinctive and central, and that in any case he means to build upon, is the idea of autonomy. He there writes that for Kant, "a person is acting autonomously when the principles of his action are chosen by him as the most adequate possible expression of his nature as a free and equal rational being" (252). But Kant, according to Rawls, did not find a felicitous way to structure his view so as to make apparent that the principles he favored did express the moral nature of persons in this way. The OP, he hopes, makes good this defect, providing a perspicuous interpretation of "the point of view of noumenal selves" (255). In response to these claims, the critical literature pursued two different tacks. The first addressed whether justice as fairness, and its social-contract apparatus, is indeed susceptible to the kinds of interpretation in terms of autonomy, so glossed, that Rawls claims for it. The second focussed on whether the themes that Rawls identifies as "Kantian" really deserve that label, in light of what Kant actually wrote.[8] While Rawls has recently published an article interpreting Kant's moral philosophy,[9] this second question is the less interesting of the two for the purposes of understanding Rawls's own view. In this Volume, we reprint two articles addressed to the first. The one by Oliver A. Johnson, focussing on the motivational assumptions about the parties to the OP, raises doubts about the Kantian features claimed by Rawls. Stephen L. Darwall's article defends Rawls's claims in the section on the Kantian interpretation and attempts to answer Johnson's objections.

Rawls's Dewey Lectures, "Kantian Constructivism in Moral Theory," which appeared in the *Journal of Philosophy* in 1980,[10] struck many readers of Rawls — especially those who had not focussed on the Kantian interpretation — as marking a radical shift in his conception of justification. Although (as we noted in the Introduction to Vol. 1), Rawls explicitly states in *TJ* that the OP, his preferred interpretation of the social-contract apparatus, builds in many important moral assumptions (e.g., 12, 120, 130, 529, 584–6), and although the Kantian interpretation reinforces this point, Rawls had also made statements that suggested quite a different reading. Most notorious of these is his comment that "on the social contract view morality is part of the theory of rational choice" (*TJ*, 47). The debates about whether the maximin rule really reflects a rational approach to choice under uncertainty (Vol. 1) were fueled by this comment. Certainly in light of the terminology that he introduced in the Dewey Lectures and has stuck with since, this comment must be qualified. The idea of rational choice in the furtherance of a given conception of the good — e.g., in the case of the parties, the conception of the good given by their stipulated mutually disinterested pursuit of primary goods (see Vol. 1) — he associates with Kant's hypothetical imperative and classifies as but one branch of practical reason. The other branch, which has to do with what ends ought to be pursued or with how conceptions of the good ought to be framed or constrained to be morally acceptable, he associates with Kant's categorical imperative and labels the "reasonable." In retrospect, at least, it seems clear that the OP embodies constraints of reasonableness that importantly constrain the choice of principles, even if the abstract parties to the constrained choice are defined as proceeding rationally in the narrower sense. In any case, those who had been convinced that Rawls meant to present morality as a branch of the theory of rational choice, in the narrower sense, were quite surprised to see the strongly Kantian turn he took in the Dewey Lectures, in which he centrally invoked the two "highest-order moral powers" of formulating and pursuing a conception of the good and of having and acting upon a sense of justice. The reprinted article by William A. Galston well captures the sense of Rawls's apparent shifts, as they appeared at the time.

It is difficult to glean a general definition of "constructivism" directly from Rawls's writings. What he carefully characterizes are notions that are somewhat more delimited: "Kantian constructivism" in the Dewey Lectures and "political constructivism" in PL (Lect. III). The general idea of constructivism, however, has something to do with regarding principles as the outcome of a procedure of construction. In defining this procedure, we appeal to practical reason in working out the implications, or the best interpretation, of ideals of society and personhood. These ideals, accordingly, must be sufficiently rich to be able to provide such structure. Much of the Dewey Lectures is devoted to developing these ideals of persons' moral capacities, of autonomy, and of public justification. Rawls contrasts constructivism with a realist form of rational intuitionism, which holds that moral (and political) truths are available to be known by theoretical reason, independently of our practical reflections about how ideals of personhood and society are best to be pursued. Accordingly, Rawls's constructivism, at least initially, seemed to stake out a metaphysical position that was neither strongly realist in this way nor yet subjectivist. Taking this stance seriously, David O. Brink subjects it to critical examination in his piece in this Volume.[11]

As it turned out, Rawls himself drew back, to the extent he could, from any such metaphysical commitments. In 1985 he published "Justice as Fairness: Political Not Metaphysical."[12] There he picked up on a theme he first articulated in his Presidential Address to the American Philosophical Association in 1974, "The Independence of Moral Theory."[13] Since matters of moral epistemology, the metaphysics of the person, and the like, seem the subject of perennial dispute, one ought to see if one can make progress in political theory by means that avoid, to the extent possible, taking controversial or controvertible stances on any such issue. This "method" or "precept of avoidance" Rawls increasingly sought to follow (see, e.g., PL 113, 126). For more on the political, as opposed to metaphysical, character of Rawls's approach, see Vol. 4.

The ideas of rational choice, of a choice of free and equal rational persons as representing the point of view of autonomy, and of a procedure of construction informed by the ideal of persons having two highest-order moral powers all bear on the justification of Rawls's view because they provide different lenses through which to view the force of the social-contract argument. More general than any of these ideas about social-contract justification, more influential than any of them, and importantly delimiting their significance, is Rawls's ideal of reflective equilibrium. While hints of this idea were present in his earliest writings (see the Introduction to Vol. 1), it is first explicitly articulated in TJ. Reflective equilibrium is sometimes explained as simply denying both that moral theory is top-down or deductive, deriving concrete conclusions from first principles, and that moral theory is bottom-up or inductive, deriving principles from fixed case intuitions. This is, indeed, part of the idea. As Rawls famously said, "we work from both ends" (20). It is crucial also to note, however, that this use of the first-person pronoun is not incidental: as he writes, "reflective equilibrium . . . is a notion characteristic of the study of principles which govern actions shaped by self-examination" (*TJ*, 48–9). When *we* work from both ends, pruning and adjusting our "considered judgments," we are not simply deciding which data points to pay attention to: we are changing our minds, revising what we think on due reflection. Then, indeed, if we reach an equilibrium, there need be no particular directionality to the mode of argumentation or support in which the justification of our particular stance consists. Instead, "justification is a matter of mutual support of many considerations, of everything fitting together into one coherent view" (*TJ*, 21 and 579). But, again, this will be a mutual supportingness, made clear by arguments and theoretical connections, among the various judgments to which we adhere on due reflection.

Two further aspects of Rawls's account of reflective equilibrium deserve notice here. The first is the notion of "considered judgments" alluded to in the last paragraph. Rawls suggests that, in reflecting about (political) morality, we pay attention only to those judgments of ours that are made in conditions that are relatively unlikely to yield mistakes. His particular characterization of these conditions has drawn some criticism.[14] There is presumably no fundamentally neutral way of characterizing considered judgments: that characterization, too, is something we might well revise on due reflection. The second further aspect is the distinction between "wide" and "narrow" reflective equilibrium.[15] The former, unlike the latter, utilizes all of the resources of abstract thinking — in social theory, political theory, and any relevant subject — to generate arguments that might test and challenge our initial considered judgments. It is wide reflective equilibrium, Rawls notes, "that one is concerned with in moral philosophy" (*TJ*, 49).[16]

The ideal of reflective equilibrium, which enables us to envision how to justify moral claims without depending upon a priori, necessary, or self-evident truths (although, pursuant to the precept of avoidance, without denying their existence, either), now informs the way many working in normative political and ethical theory conceive of what they're doing. Some philosophers, however, reacted quite strongly against the idea that we might simply work within our considered judgments. R.M. Hare's article, reprinted below, well exemplifies this reaction.

As we have seen, the ideal of reflective equilibrium gives priority to no one category of judgments, whether abstract or concrete. Does this mean that reflective equilibrium excludes all forms of "foundationalism," and is best analogized to coherentist epistemologies, in which justification rests simply on the coherence of the elements? One difficulty with this sort of question is that, as noted above and in the Introduction to Vol. 1, Rawls invokes other ideas about the nature of justification besides the ideal of reflective equilibrium. Even so, it is possible to abstract the ideal from Rawls's use of it so as to pursue the question. In doing so, one will naturally want to begin by nailing down the Protean terms "foundationalist" and "coherentist." Carefully doing so, Michael R. DePaul's article in this volume concludes that reflective equilibrium is a coherentist idea. Equally nice in its distinctions among the possible kinds of view, Roger P. Ebertz's article argues, to the contrary, that the appeal to considered judgments introduces an element of foundationalism into the ideal.

Henry S. Richardson

Notes

[1] John Rawls, *A Theory of Justice* (Cambridge: Harvard University Press, Belknap, 1971), 302.

[2] John Rawls, *Political Liberalism* (New York: Columbia University Press, 1996), 9, 15, 20.

[3] See also Jane English, "Justice Between Generations," *Philosophical Studies* 31 (1977): 91–104.

[4] Lecture VIII of *PL*, where this acknowledgment of Hart's influence occurs, is itself a revision of John Rawls, "The Basic Liberties and Their Priority," in *The Tanner Lectures on Human Values III* (Salt Lake City; London: University of Utah Press; Cambridge University Press, 1982), 3–87.

[5] For a rigorous discussion of the fair value of the basic liberties, albeit one preceding *PL*, see Thomas W. Pogge, *Realizing Rawls* (Ithaca: Cornell University Press, 1989), chap. 3.

[6] Sen also summarizes the contributions of Hammond and Strasnick, cited in the introduction to Vol. 1.

[7] For further discussion of the characterization of the least-well-off representative persons, see chap. 4 of Pogge, *Realizing Rawls*.

[8] See, e.g., Otfried Höffe, "Is Rawls' Theory of Justice Really Kantian?" *Ratio* 26, no. 2 (December 1984): 103–24; Arnold I. Davidson, "Is Rawls a Kantian?" *Pacific Philosophical Quarterly* 66 (1985): 48–77.

[9] John Rawls, "Themes in Kant's Moral Philosophy," in *Kant's Transcendental Deductions: The Three* Critiques *and the* Opus Postumum, edited by Eckart Förster (Stanford: Stanford University Press, 1989), 81–113. Rawls's lectures on Kant's moral philosophy are currently being prepared for publication by Harvard University Press.

[10] John Rawls, "Kantian Constructivism in Moral Theory: The Dewey Lectures 1980," *Journal of Philosophy* 77, no. 9 (1980): 515–72. *PL*, first published thirteen years later, fulfilled Rawls's commitment to Columbia University Press to publish the Dewey Lectures; its first three lectures thoroughly recast them. The most important shift is that *PL* presents simply a normative political theory, and refrains from making claims about moral theory more generally.

[11] Onora O'Neill has proceeded to develop this sort of Kantian constructivism independently from Rawls's justice as fairness: see her *Constructions of Reason* (Cambridge: Cambridge University Press, 1989).

[12] John Rawls, "Justice as Fairness: Political not Metaphysical," *Philosophy and Public Affairs* 14 (1985): 223–51.

[13] John Rawls, "The Independence of Moral Theory," *Proceedings of the American Philosophical Association*, November 1975, 5–22.

[14] See, e.g., Martha C. Nussbaum, "Perceptive Equilibrium: Literary Theory and Ethical Theory," *LOGOS: Philosophic Issues in Christian Perspective* 8 (1987): 55–83, reprinted in Martha C. Nussbaum, *Love's Knowledge: Essays on Philosophy and Literature* (New York: Oxford University Press, 1990).

[15] While Rawls first used this terminology in Rawls, "The Independence of Moral Theory," he notes that the distinction was present in *TJ* at 49.

[16] In an influential series of articles, Norman Daniels laid out how Rawls's social contract apparatus allows him to bring these wider theoretical resources to bear on the process of pursuing reflective equilibrium. See Norman Daniels, "Wide Reflective Equilibrium and Theory Acceptance in Ethics," *The Journal of Philosophy* 76 (1979): 256–82; "Moral Theory and the Plasticity of Persons," *Monist* 62 (1979): 265–85; "On Some Methods for Ethics and Linguistics," *Philosophical Studies* 37 (1980): 21–36; "Reflective Equilibrium and Archimedean Points," *Canadian Journal of Philosophy* 10 (1980): 83–103.

The Two Principles
and Their Justification

Rawls on Liberty and Its Priority

H.L.A. Hart†

I. Introductory

No book of political philosophy since I read the great classics of the subject has stirred my thoughts as deeply as John Rawls's *A Theory of Justice*. But I shall not in this article offer a general assessment of this important and most interesting work. I shall be concerned with only one of its themes, namely, Rawls's account of the relationship between justice and liberty, and in particular with his conception that justice requires that liberty may only be limited for the sake of liberty and not for the sake of other social and economic advantages. I have chosen this theme partly because of its obvious importance to lawyers who are, as it were, professionally concerned with limitations of liberty and with the justice or injustice of such limitations. I choose this theme also because this part of Rawls's book has not, I think, so far received, in any of the vast number of articles on and reviews of the book which have been published, the detailed attention which it deserves. Yet, as Sidgwick found when he considered a somewhat similar doctrine ascribing priority to liberty over other values, such a conception of liberty, though undoubtedly striking a responsive chord in the heart of any liberal, has its baffling as well as its attractive aspect,[1] which becomes apparent when we consider, as Rawls intends that we should, what the application of this doctrine would require in practice.

Part of what follows is concerned with a major question of interpretation of Rawls's doctrine and the rest is critical. But I am very conscious that I may have failed to keep constantly in view or in proper perspective all the arguments which Rawls, at different places in this long and complex work, concentrates on the points which I find unconvincing. I would not therefore be surprised if my interpretation could be corrected and my criticisms answered by some further explanation which the author could supply. Indeed I do not write to confute, but mainly in the hope that in some of the innumerable future

---

† Research Fellow of University College, Oxford.

[1] H. Sidgwick, The Methods of Ethics (7th ed. 1907) Book III, Ch. V, § 4. "I admit that it commends itself much to my mind. . . . But when I endeavour to bring it into closer relation to the actual circumstances of human society it soon comes to wear a different aspect."

editions of this book Rawls may be induced to add some explanation of these points.

I hope that I can assume that by now the main features of Rawls's *A Theory of Justice* are familiar to most readers, but for those to whom it is not, the following is a minimum account required to make this article intelligible.

First, there is what Rawls terms the "Main Idea." This is the striking claim that principles of justice do not rest on mere intuition yet are not to be derived from utilitarian principles or any other teleological theory holding that there is some form of good to be sought and maximised. Instead, the principles of justice are to be conceived as those that free and rational persons concerned to further their own interests would agree should govern their forms of social life and institutions if they had to choose such principles from behind "a veil of ignorance" —that is, in ignorance of their own abilities, of their psychological propensities and conception of the good, and of their status and position in society and the level of development of the society of which they are to be members. The position of these choosing parties is called "the original position." Many discussions of the validity of this Main Idea have already appeared and it will continue to be much debated by philosophers, but for the purposes of this article I shall assume that if it could be shown that the parties in the original position would choose the principles which Rawls identifies as principles of justice, that would be a strong argument in their favour. From the Main Idea Rawls makes a transition to a general form or "general conception" of the principles that the parties in the original position would choose. This general conception of justice is as follows:

> All social values—liberty and opportunity, income and wealth, and the bases of self-respect—are to be distributed equally unless an unequal distribution of any, or all, of these values is to everyone's advantage.[2]

This general conception of justice, it should be observed, refers to the equal distribution of liberty but not to its maximisation or extent. However, most of the book is concerned with a special interpretation of this general conception which refers both to the maximisation and the equality of liberty. The principal features of this special conception of justice are as follows:

First Principle ["the principle of greatest equal liberty"][3]
    Each person is to have an equal right to the most extensive total

---

2 P. 62.
3 P. 124.

system of equal basic liberties compatible with a similar system of liberty for all.

Second Principle

Social and economic inequalities are to be arranged so that they are . . . to the greatest benefit of the least advantaged . . . .[4]

To these two principles there are attached certain priority rules of which the most important is that liberty is given a priority over all other advantages, so that it may be restricted or unequally distributed only for the sake of liberty and not for any other form of social or economic advantage.

To this account there must be added two points specially relevant to this article. First, Rawls regards his two principles as established or justified not simply by the fact that they would be chosen, as he claims they would, by the parties in the original position, but also by the general harmony of these principles with ordinary "considered judgments duly pruned and adjusted."[5] The test of his theory, therefore, is in part whether the principles he identifies illuminate our ordinary judgments and help to reveal a basic structure and coherence underlying them.

Secondly, it is an important and interesting feature of Rawls's theory that once the principles of justice have been chosen we come to understand what their implementation would require by imagining a four-stage process. Thus, we are to suppose that after the first stage, when the parties in the original position have chosen the principles of justice, they move to a constitutional convention. There, in accordance with the chosen principles, they choose a constitution and establish the basic rights or liberties of citizens. The third stage is that of legislation, where the justice of laws and policies is considered; enacted statutes, if they are to be just, must satisfy both the limits laid down in the constitution and the originally chosen principles of justice. The fourth and last stage is that of the application of rules by judges and other officials to particular cases.

II. Liberty and Basic Liberties

Throughout his book Rawls emphasises the distinction between liberty and other social goods, and his principle of greatest equal liberty is,

---

[4] P. 302. I have here omitted the provisions for a just savings principle and for equality of opportunity, which Rawls includes in this formulation of his second principle, since they are not relevant to the present discussion.

[5] P. 20. Rawls, in fact, speaks of a "reflective equilibrium" between principles and ordinary judgments, since he envisages that where there are initial discrepancies between these we have a choice of modifying the conditions of the initial position in which principles are chosen or modifying in detail the judgments. Pp. 20 ff.

as I have said, accompanied—in his special conception of justice as distinct from his general conception—by a priority rule which assigns to liberty, or at least to certain forms of liberty institutionally defined and protected, a priority which forbids the restriction of liberty for the sake of other benefits: liberty is only to be restricted for the sake of liberty itself. In the general conception of justice there is no such priority rule and no requirement that liberty must be as extensive as possible, though it is to be equally distributed unless an unequal distribution of it is justified as being to everyone's advantage.[6] The special conception is to govern societies which have developed to the point when, as Rawls says, "the basic wants of individuals can be fulfilled"[7] and social conditions allow "the effective establishment of fundamental rights."[8] If these favourable conditions do not obtain, equal liberty may be denied, if this is required to "raise the level of civilization so that in due course these freedoms can be enjoyed."[9]

I find it no easy matter, on some quite crucial points, to interpret Rawls's complex doctrine, and there is one initial question of interpretation which I discuss here at some length. But it is perhaps worth saying that to do justice to Rawls's principle of greatest equal liberty it is necessary to take into account not only what he says when expressly formulating, expounding, and illustrating this principle, but also what he says about some other apparently separate issues—in particular, natural duties,[10] obligations arising from the principle of fairness,[11] permissions,[12] paternalism,[13] and the common good or common interest,[14] for these may apparently supplement the rather exiguous provision for restrictions on liberty which are all that, at first sight, his principle of greatest equal liberty seems to allow.

The initial question of interpretation arises from the following circumstances. Rawls in his book often refers in broad terms to his first principle of justice as "the principle of greatest equal liberty,"[15] and in similarly broad terms to its associated priority rule as the rule that "liberty can be restricted only for the sake of liberty."[16] These references

---

6 P. 62.
7 P. 543.
8 Pp. 152, 542.
9 P. 152.
10 Pp. 114 ff, 333 ff.
11 Pp. 108 ff.
12 Pp. 116 ff.
13 P. 248.
14 Pp. 97, 213, 246.
15 *E.g.*, p. 124.
16 Pp. 250, 302.

to liberty in quite general terms, and also Rawls's previous formulation in his articles of this first principle as the principle that everyone has "an equal right to the most extensive liberty compatible with a like liberty for all,"[17] suggest that his doctrine is similar to that criticized by Sidgwick.[18] It is probable that Sidgwick had chiefly in mind a formulation of a principle of greatest equal liberty urged by Herbert Spencer in his long forgotten *Social Statics*.[19] This was effectively criticised by Sidgwick as failing to account for some of the most obvious restrictions on liberty required to protect individuals from harms other than constraint or deprivation of liberty, and indeed as forbidding the institution of private property, since to own anything privately is to have liberty to use it in ways denied to others. Spencer attempted to get out of this difficulty (or rather outside it) by simply swallowing it, and reached the conclusion that, at least in the case of land, only property held in common by a community would be consistent with "equal liberty"[20] and hence legitimate. Rawls in his book simply lists without argument the right to hold personal property, but not property in the means of production, as one of the basic liberties,[21] though, as I shall argue later, he does this at some cost to the coherence of his theory.

Rawls's previous formulation of his general principle of greatest equal liberty—"everyone has an equal right to the most extensive liberty compatible with a like liberty for all"—was then very similar to the doctrine criticised by Sidgwick. But Rawls's explicit formulation of it in his book is no longer in these general terms. It refers not to "liberty" but to basic or fundamental *liberties*, which are understood to be legally recognised and protected from interference. This, with its priority rule, as finally formulated, now runs as follows:

> Each person is to have an equal right to the most extensive total system of equal basic liberties compatible with a similar system of liberty for all. . . .

---

[17] Rawls, *Justice as Fairness*, 67 PHILOSOPHICAL REVIEW 164, 165 (1958); *see* Rawls, *The Sense of Justice*, 72 PHILOSOPHICAL REVIEW 283 (1963); J. RAWLS, *Distributive Justice*, in POLITICS, PHILOSOPHY AND SOCIETY 61 (3d Series, Oxford 1967). This formulation in these articles should not be confused with the formulation of the "general conception" of justice in the book. *See* pp. 3 ff.

[18] H. SIDGWICK, *supra* note 1, Book III, Ch. V., §§ 4–5 and Ch. XI, § 5.

[19] *See* H. SPENCER, SOCIAL STATICS (1850). Criticisms of Spencer's theory in terms very similar to Sidgwick's criticisms were made by F. W. Maitland in 1 COLLECTED PAPERS 247 (H. Fisher ed. 1911). Maitland treated Spencer's doctrine of equal liberty as virtually identical with Kant's notion of mutual freedom under universal law expounded in the latter's *Rechtslehre*. I am grateful to Professor B.J. Diggs for pointing out to me important differences between Rawls's doctrine of liberty and Kant's conception of mutual freedom under universal law.

[20] H. SPENCER, *supra* note 19.

[21] P. 61.

> [L]iberty can be restricted only for the sake of liberty. There are
> two cases: (a) a less extensive liberty must strengthen the total sys-
> tem of liberty shared by all; (b) a less than equal liberty must be
> acceptable to those with the lesser liberty.[22]

Even to this, however, for complete accuracy a gloss on the last sentence
is needed because Rawls also insists that "acceptable to those with the
lesser liberty" means not acceptable just on any grounds, but only acceptable because affording a greater protection of their other liberties.[23]

The basic liberties to which Rawls's principle thus refers are identified by the parties in the original position[24] from behind the veil of
ignorance as essential for the pursuit of their ends, whatever those ends
turn out to be, and so as determining the form of their society. Not surprisingly, therefore, the basic liberties are rather few in number and
Rawls gives a short list of them which he describes in the index as an
"enumeration,"[25] though he warns us that these are what they are only
"roughly speaking."[26] They comprise political liberty, that is, the right
to vote and be eligible for public office, freedom of speech and of assembly; liberty of conscience and freedom of thought; freedom of the person, along with the right to hold personal property; and freedom from
arbitrary arrest and seizure.

Now the question of interpretation is whether Rawls's change of language from a principle of greatest equal liberty couched in quite general terms ("everyone has an equal right to the most extensive *liberty*"),
to one referring only to specific basic *liberties,* indicates a change in his
theory. Is the principle of liberty in the book still this quite general
principle, so that under the priority rule now attached to it no form of
liberty may be restricted except for the sake of liberty? It is difficult to
be sure, but my own view on this important point is that Rawls no
longer holds the quite general theory which appeared in his articles,
perhaps because he had met the difficulties pointed out by Sidgwick
and others. There are, I think, several indications, besides the striking
change in language, that Rawls's principle is now limited to the list of
basic liberties, allowing of course for his statement that the actual list
he gives is only rough. The first indication is the fact that Rawls does
not find it necessary to reconcile the admission of private property as a
liberty with any general principle of *maximum* equal liberty, or of "an
equal right to the most extensive liberty," and he avoids the difficulties

---

22 P. 302.

23 P. 233.

24 *E.g.,* "equal liberty of conscience is the only principle that parties in the original
position can acknowledge." P. 207.

25 P. 540.

26 P. 61.

found in Herbert Spencer's doctrine by giving a new sense to the requirement that the right to hold property must be equal. This sense of equality turns on Rawls's distinction between liberty and the value or worth of liberty.[27] Rawls does not require, except in the case of the *political liberties* (the right to participate in government and freedom of speech), that basic liberties be equal in value, or substantially equal, so he does not require, in admitting the right to property as a basic equal liberty, either that property should be held in common so that everyone can enjoy the same property or that separately owned property should be equal in amount. That would be to insist that the value of the right to property should be equal. What is required is the merely formal condition that the *rules*[28] governing the acquisition, disposition, and scope of property rights should be the same for all. Rawls's reply to the familiar Marxist criticism that in this case we shall have to say that the beggar and the millionaire have equal property rights would be to admit the charge, but to point out that, in his system, the unequal value of these equal property rights would be cut down to the point where inequality would be justified by the working of the difference principle, according to which economic inequalities are justified only if they are for the benefit of the least advantaged.[29]

The second indication that Rawls's principle of greatest equal liberty and its priority rule ("liberty can be restricted only for the sake of liberty")[30] is now limited to the basic liberties is his careful and repeated explanation that, though the right to hold property is for him a "liberty," the choice between private capitalism and state ownership of the means of production is left quite open by the principles of justice.[31] Whether or not the means of production are to be privately owned is something which a society must decide in the light of the knowledge of its actual circumstances and the demands of social and economic efficiency. But, of course, a decision to limit private ownership to consumer goods made on such grounds would result in a less extensive form of liberty than would obtain if private ownership could be exercised over all forms of property. Rawls's admission of this restriction as allowable so far as justice is concerned would be a glaring inconsistency if he was still advancing the general principle that there must be "an equal right to the most extensive liberty," for that, under the priority rule, would entail that *no form* of liberty may be narrowed

27 Pp. 204, 225 ff.
28 Pp. 63–64.
29 P. 204.
30 P. 302.
31 Pp. 66, 273–74.

or limited for the sake of economic benefits, but only for the sake of liberty itself.

These considerations support very strongly the interpretation that Rawls's principle of greatest equal liberty, as it is developed in this book, is concerned only with the enumerated basic liberties, though of course these are specified by him only in broad terms. But I confess that there are also difficulties in this interpretation which suggest that Rawls has not eliminated altogether the earlier general doctrine of liberty, even though that earlier doctrine is not, as I have explained above, really consistent with Rawls's treatment of the admissible limitations of the right of property. For it seems obvious that there are important forms of liberty—sexual freedom and the liberty to use alcohol or drugs among them—which apparently do not fall within any of the roughly described basic liberties;[32] yet it would be very surprising if principles of justice were silent about their restriction. Since John Stuart Mills's essay *On Liberty,* such liberties have been the storm centre of discussions of the proper scope of the criminal law and other forms of social coercion, and there is, in fact, just one passage in this book from which it is clear that Rawls thinks that his principles of justice are not silent as to the justice of restricting such liberties.[33] For in arguing against the view that certain forms of sexual relationship should be prohibited simply as degrading or shameful, and so as falling short of some "perfectionist" ideal, Rawls says that we should rely not on such perfectionist criteria but on the principles of justice and that according to these no reasonable case for restriction can be made out.

There is much that I do not understand in this short passage. Rawls says here that justice requires us to show, before restricting such modes of conduct, either that they interfere with the basic liberties of others or that "they violate some natural duty or some obligation." This seems an unexplained departure from the strict line so often emphasised in the case of basic liberties, that liberty may be restricted only for the sake of liberty. Is there then a secondary set of principles for nonbasic

---

32 It has been suggested to me that Rawls would regard these freedoms as basic liberties falling under his broad category of liberty of conscience, which is concerned not only with religious but with moral freedom. But Rawls's discussion of this, pp. 205 ff, seems to envisage only a man's freedom to fulfill moral *obligations* as he interprets them, and sexual freedom would therefore only fall under this category for those to whom the promptings of passion presented themselves as calls of moral duty. Others have suggested that these freedoms would fall under Rawls's category of freedom of the person; but this seems most unlikely to me in view of his collocation of it with property ("freedom of the person along with the right to hold personal property"). It is to be noted also that sexual freedom is spoken of as a "mode of conduct," p. 331, and the possibility of its interference with "basic liberties" (not *"other"* basic liberties) is mentioned.

33 P. 331.

liberties? This solution would have its own difficulties. The natural duties to which Rawls refers here, and the principle from which obligations, such as the obligation to keep a promise, derive, are, according to Rawls, standards of conduct for *individuals* which the parties in the original position have gone on to choose after they have chosen the principles of justice as standards for *institutions*, which I take it include the law. If liberty may be restricted to prevent violation of any such natural duties or obligations, this may rather severly narrow the area of liberty, for the natural duties include the duty to assist others when this can be done at small cost and the duty to show respect and courtesy, as well as duties to support just institutions, not to harm the innocent, and not to cause unnecessary suffering. Further, since the parties in the original position are said to choose the principles of justice as standards for institutions *before* they choose the natural duties for individuals, it is not clear how the former can incorporate the latter, as Rawls suggests they do when he says that principles of justice require us to show, before we restrict conduct, that it violates either basic liberties or natural duties or obligations.

I hope that I have not made too much of what is a mere passing reference by Rawls to liberties which do not appear to fall within his categories of basic liberties, but have been at the centre of some famous discussions of freedom. I cannot, however, from this book see quite how Rawls would resolve the difficulties I have mentioned, and I raise below the related question whether liberties which are plainly "basic" may also be restricted if their exercise involves violation of natural duties or obligations.

III.   Limiting Liberty for the Sake of Liberty

I turn now to consider the principle that basic liberties may be limited only for the sake of liberty. Rawls expresses this principle in several different ways. He says that basic liberties may be restricted or unequally distributed only for the sake of a greater "system of liberty as a whole";[34] that the restriction must yield "a greater equal liberty,"[35] or "the best total system of equal liberty"[36] or "strengthen" that system,[37] or be "a gain for . . . freedom on balance."[38]

What, then, is it to limit liberty for the sake of liberty? Rawls gives a number of examples which his principle would permit. The simplest

---

34 P. 203.
35 P. 229.
36 P. 203.
37 P. 250.
38 P. 244.

case is the introduction of rules of order in debate,[39] which restrict the liberty to speak when we please. Without this restriction the liberty to say and advocate what we please would be grossly hampered and made less valuable to us. As Rawls says, such rules are necessary for "profitable"[40] discussion, and plainly when such rules are introduced a balance is struck and the liberty judged less important or less valuable is subordinated to the other. In this very simple case there seems to be a quite obvious answer to the question as to which of the two liberties here conflicting is more valuable since, whatever ends we are pursuing in debate, the liberty to communicate our thought in speech must contribute more to their advancement than the liberty to interrupt communication. It seems to me, however, misleading to describe even the resolution of the conflicting liberties in this very simple case as yielding a "greater" or "stronger" total system of liberty, for these phrases suggest that no values other than liberty and dimensions of it, like extent, size, or strength, are involved. Plainly what such rules of debate help to secure is not a *greater* or more extensive liberty, but a liberty to do something which is more valuable for any rational person than the activities forbidden by the rules, or, as Rawls himself says, something more "profitable." So some criterion of the value of different liberties must be involved in the resolution of conflicts between them; yet Rawls speaks as if the system "of basic liberties" were self-contained, and conflicts within it were adjusted without appeal to any other value besides liberty and its extent.

In some cases, it is true, Rawls's conception of a greater or more extensive liberty resulting from a more satisfactory resolution of conflicts between liberties may have application. One fairly clear example is provided by Rawls when he says that the principle of limiting liberty only for the sake of liberty would allow conscription for military service in a war genuinely undertaken to defend free institutions either at home or abroad.[41] In that case it might plausibly be said that only the quantum or extent of liberty was at stake; the temporary restriction of liberty involved in military conscription might be allowed to prevent or remove much greater inroads on liberty. Similarly, the restriction imposed in the name of public order and security, to which Rawls often refers,[42] may be justified simply as hindering greater or more extensive hindrances to liberty of action. But there certainly are important cases of conflict between basic liberties where, as in the simple rules of

---

[39] P. 203.
[40] *Id.*
[41] P. 380.
[42] Pp. 97, 212–13.

debate case, the resolution of conflict must involve consideration of the relative value of different modes of conduct, and not merely the extent or amount of freedom. One such conflict, which, according to Rawls's four-stage sequence, will have to be settled at a stage analogous to a constitutional convention, is the conflict between freedom of speech and of the person, and freedom to participate in government through a democratically elected legislature.[43] Rawls discusses this conflict on the footing that the freedom to participate in government is to be considered as restricted if there is a Bill of Rights protecting the individual's freedom of speech or of the person from regulation by an ordinary majority vote of the legislature. He says that the kind of argument to support such a restriction, which his principles of justice require, is "a justification which appeals only to a greater equal liberty."[44] He admits that different opinions about the value of the conflicting liberties will affect the way in which different persons view this conflict. Nonetheless, he insists that to arrive at a just resolution of the conflict we must try to find the point at which "the danger to liberty from the marginal loss in control over those holding political power just balances the security of liberty gained by the greater use of constitutional devices."[45] I cannot myself understand, however, how such weighing or striking of a balance is conceivable if the only appeal is, as Rawls says, to "a greater liberty."

These difficulties in the notion of a greater total liberty, or system of liberty, resulting from the just resolution of conflict between liberties, are made more acute for me by Rawls's description of the point of view from which he says all such conflicts between liberties are to be settled —whether they occur at the constitution making stage of the four-stage sequence, as in the case last considered, or at the stage of legislation in relation to other matters.

Rawls says that when liberties conflict the adjustment which is to secure "the best total system" is to be settled from the standpoint of "the representative equal citizen," and we are to ask which adjustment "it would be rational for him to prefer."[46] This, he says, involves the application of the principle of the common interest or common good which selects those conditions which are necessary for "all to equally further their aims" or which will "advance shared ends."[47] It is, of course, easy to see that very simple conflicts between liberties, such as the de-

---

43 Pp. 228–30.
44 P. 229.
45 P. 230.
46 P. 204.
47 P. 97.

bating rules case, may intelligibly be said to be settled by reference to this point of view. For in such simple cases it is certainly arguable that, whatever ends a man may have, he will see as a rational being that the restrictions are required if he is to pursue his ends successfully, and this can be expressed in terms of "the common good" on the footing that such restrictions are necessary for all alike. But it would be quite wrong to generalize from this simple case; other conflicts between basic liberties will be such that different resolutions of the conflict will correspond to the interests of different people who will diverge over the relative value they set on the conflicting liberties. In such cases, there will be no resolution which will be uniquely selected by reference to the common good. So, in the constitutional case discussed above, it seems difficult to understand how the conflict can be resolved by reference to the representative equal citizen, and without appeal to utilitarian considerations or to some conception of what all individuals are morally entitled to have as a matter of human dignity or moral right. In particular, the general strategy which Rawls ascribes to the parties in the original position of choosing the alternative that yields the best worst position is no help except in obvious cases like the debating rules case. There, of course, it can be argued that it is better to be restricted by reasonable rules than to be exposed to unregulated interruption, so that it is rational to trade off the liberty to speak when you please for the more valuable benefit of being able to communicate more or less effectively what you please. Or, to put the same exceedingly simple point in the "maximin" terms which Rawls often illuminatingly uses, the worst position under the rule (being restrained from interruption but given time to speak free from interruption) is better than the worst position without the rule (being constantly exposed to interruption though free to interrupt).

Such simple cases, indeed, exist where it can be said that all "equal citizens," however divergent their individual tastes or desires, would, if rational, prefer one alternative where liberties conflict. But I do not understand how the notion of the rational preference of the representative equal citizen can assist in the resolution of conflicts where reasonable men may differ as to the value of conflicting liberties, and there is no obviously best worst position which a rational man would prefer. It is true that at the stages in the four-stage sequence where such conflicts have to be resolved there is no veil of ignorance to prevent those who have to take decisions knowing what proportions of the population favour which alternatives. But I do not think Rawls would regard such knowledge as relevant in arguments about what it would be rational for the representative equal citizen to prefer; for it would only be rele-

13

vant if we conceive that this representative figure in some way reflects (perhaps in the relative strength or intensity of his conflicting desires) the distribution of different preferences in the population. This, however, would be virtually equivalent to a utilitarian criterion and one that I am sure is far from Rawls's thoughts. I would stress here that I am not complaining that Rawls's invocation of "the rational preference of the representative equal citizen" fails to provide a decision procedure yielding a determinate answer in all cases. Rather, I do not understand, except in the very simple cases, what sort of argument is to be used to show what the representative's rational preference would be and in what sense it results in "a greater liberty."

Of course, it is open to Rawls to say, as he does, that arguments concerning the representative's rational preference will often be equally balanced, and in such cases justice will be indeterminate. But I do not think that he can mean that justice is to be indeterminate whenever different people value alternatives differently. Indeed, he is quite clear that, in spite of such difference in valuation, justice does require that there be some constitutional protections for individual freedom, though these will limit the freedom to participate in government;[48] the only indeterminacy he contemplates here is as to the particular form of constitutional protection to be selected from a range of alternatives all of which may be permitted by principles of justice. Yet, if opinion is divided on the main issue (that is, whether there should be any or no restrictions on legislative power to protect individual freedom), I do not understand what sort of argument it is that is supposed to show that the representative equal citizen would prefer an affirmative answer on this main issue as securing "the greater liberty."

This difficulty still plagues me even in relatively minor cases where one might well accept a conclusion that principles of justice are indeterminate. Thus, suppose the legislator has to determine the scope of the rights of exclusion comprised in the private ownership of land, which is for Rawls a basic liberty,[49] when this basic liberty conflicts with others. Some people may prefer freedom of movement not to be limited

---

[48] "The liberties of equal citizenship must be incorporated into and protected by the constitution." P. 197. "If a bill of rights guaranteeing liberty of conscience and freedom of thought and assembly would be effective then it should be adopted." P. 231.

[49] It has been suggested to me by Mr. Michael Lesnoff that Rawls might not consider the private ownership of land to be a basic liberty since, as noted above, justice according to Rawls leaves open the question whether there is to be private ownership of the means of production. I am not, however, clear what is included in the scope of the basic liberty which Rawls described as "the right to hold [personal] property." P. 61. Would it comprise ownership or (in a socialized economy) a tenancy from the state in land to be used as a garden? If not, the example in the text might be changed to that of a conflict between pedestrians' freedom of movement and the rights of automobiles.

by the rights of landowners supported by laws about trespass; others, whether they are landowners or not, may prefer that there be some limitations. If justice is indeterminate in this minor case of conflicting liberties, then no doubt we would fall back on what Rawls terms procedural justice, and accept the majority vote of a legislature operating under a just constitution and a fair procedure, even if we cannot say of the outcome that it is in itself a just one. But, presumably, in considering what measures to promote and how to vote, the legislators must, since this is a case, though a minor one, of conflicting basic liberties, begin by asking which of the alternatives a representative equal citizen would, if rational, prefer, even if they are doomed to discover that this question has no determinate answer. But indeterminacy and unintelligibility are different things, and it is the intelligibility of the question with which I am concerned. What do the legislators mean in such cases when they ask which alternative it would be rational for the representative equal citizen to prefer as securing the greater liberty, when they know that some men may value privacy of property more than freedom of movement, and others not? If the question is rephrased, as Rawls says it can be, as a question involving the principle of the common good, then it will presumably appear as the question which alternative will in the long run most advance the good of all, or ends that all share. This might be an answerable question in principle if it could be taken simply as the question which alternative is likely most to advance everyone's general welfare, where this is taken to include economic and other advantages besides liberty. If, for example, it could be shown that unrestricted freedom of movement over land would tend to reduce everyone's food supply, whereas no bad consequences likely to affect everyone would result from the other alternative, then the conflict should be resolved in favour of restriction of movement. But this interpretation of the question in terms of welfare seems ruled out by the principle that liberty may only be limited for the sake of liberty, and not for social or economic advantages. So, I think, that the conception of the rational choice of the representative equal citizen needs further clarification.

IV. LIMITING LIBERTY TO PREVENT HARM OR SUFFERING

I now turn to the question whether the principle of limiting liberty only for the sake of liberty provides adequately for restrictions on conduct which causes pain or unhappiness to others otherwise than by constraining liberty of action. Such harmful conduct in some cases would be an exercise of the basic liberties, such as freedom of speech, for example, or the use of property, though in other cases it may be the exercise of a liberty not classed by Rawls as basic. It would be extraordinary if principles of justice which Rawls claims are in general in harmony with ordinary considered judgments were actually to exclude (because they limited liberty otherwise than for the sake of liberty) laws restraining libel or slander, or publications grossly infringing privacy, or restrictions on the use of private property (e.g., automobiles) designed to protect the environment and general social amenities. These restrictions on the basic liberties of speech and private property are commonly accepted as trade-offs not of liberty for liberty, but of liberty for protection from harm or loss of amenities or other elements of real utility.

There are two ways in which perhaps Rawls's principles can at least partly fill this gap.[50] In some cases more plausibly than others, he might argue that an unrestricted liberty to inflict what we call harm or suffering on others would in fact restrict the victim's liberty of action in either or both of two ways. The physical injury inflicted might actually impair the capacity for action, or the knowledge that such harmful actions were not prohibited might create conditions of apprehension and uncertainty among potential victims which would grossly inhibit their actions. But such arguments seem quite unplausible except in cases of conduct inflicting serious physical harm on individuals, and even there, when such restrictions are accepted as a reasonable sacrifice of liberty, it seems clear that if pain and suffering and distress were not given a weight independent of the tendency of harmful conduct to inhibit the victim's actions or incapacitate him from action, the balance would often, in fact, not be struck as it is.

It is, however, necessary at this point again to take into account those natural duties which are standards of individual conduct, as distinct from principles of justice, which are standards for institutions. These duties include the duty not to harm others or cause "unnecessary suffering" and also the duty to come to the assistance of others. In discussing the acceptance of such duties by the parties in the original position, Rawls represents them as calculating that the burdens of such duties will be outweighed by the benefits;[51] so natural duties represent cases

---

[50] Professor Dworkin and Mr. Michael Lesnoff have suggested to me that what I describe here as a "gap" may not in fact exist, since Rawls's basic liberties may be conceived by him as limited *ab initio* so that they do not include the liberty to act in a way damaging to the interests or liberties of others. But though it is certainly consistent with much of Rawls's discussion of basic liberties to treat his admittedly rough description of them as simply indicating areas of conduct within which the parties in the original position identify specific rights *after* resolving conflicts between the several liberties and the interests or liberties of others, this does not fit with Rawls's account of the basic liberties as liable to conflict, nor with his account of the conflicts as resolved not by the parties in the original position but by constitutional convention or body of legislators adopting the point of view of the representative equal citizen.

[51] P. 338.

where, like the simple rules of debate case, the best worst position for all rational men can be identified, and in these cases even from behind the veil of ignorance. Even there it will appear to the parties as rational self-interested persons that it is, for example, better to be restrained from practising cruelty to others while protected from them than to be exposed to others' cruelty while free to practise it, and better to have to provide modest assistance to others in need than never to be able to rely on such assistance being forthcoming. So it is plain that these natural duties might fill part of the gap left open by the principle that liberty may only be limited for the sake of liberty, if Rawls means (though he does not explicitly say it) that even the basic liberties may be restricted if their exercise would infringe any natural duty. But again, these natural duties chosen from behind the veil of ignorance would only account for very obvious cases where the benefits of the restrictions would, for all rational men, plainly outweigh the burdens. This will not help where divergent choices could reasonably be made by different individuals in the light of their different interests, and it seems to me that this will very often be the case. Some persons, given their general temperament, might reasonably prefer to be free to libel others or to invade their privacy, or to make use of their own property in whatever style they like, and might gladly take the risk of being exposed to these practices on the part of others and to the consequences of such practices for themselves and the general social and physical environment. Other persons would not pay this price for unrestricted liberty in these matters, since, given their temperament, they would value the protections afforded by the restrictions higher than the unrestricted liberty. In such cases restrictions on the basic liberties of speech or private property cannot be represented as a matter of natural duty on the footing that rational men, whatever their particular temperament, would opt for the restrictions just as they might opt for general restrictions on killing or the use of violence.

Of course, it is certainly to be remembered that justice for Rawls does not exhaust morality; there are, as he tells us, requirements, indeed duties, in relation to animals and even in relation to the rest of nature which are outside the scope of a theory of justice as a theory of what is owed to rational individuals.[52] But even if there are such moral duties, regarding even rational beings, I do not think that Rawls would consider them as supplementing principles of justice which apply to institutions. I take it, therefore, that restrictions on the basic liberties excluded by the principles of justice because they are not restrictions of liberty for the sake of liberty could not be independently supported

---

52 P. 512.

as just by appeal to other principles of morality. The point here is not that Rawlsian justice will be shown to be indeterminate at certain points as to the propriety of certain restrictions on liberty; it is, on the contrary, all too determinate since they seem to exclude such restrictions as actually unjust because they do not limit liberty only for the sake of liberty. I take it Rawls would not wish to meet this point by simply adding to his principles of justice a further supplement permitting liberty to be restricted if its exercise violated not only the natural duties but any requirements of morality, for this would, it seems to me, run counter to the general liberal tenor of his theory.

V. THE CHOICE OF BASIC LIBERTIES

I think the most important general point which emerges from these separate criticisms is as follows. Any scheme providing for the general distribution in society of liberty of action necessarily does two things: first, it confers on individuals the advantage of that liberty, but secondly, it exposes them to whatever disadvantages the practices of that liberty by others may entail for them. These disadvantages include not only the case on which Rawls concentrates, namely interference with another individual's basic liberties, but also the various forms of harm, pain, and suffering against which legal systems usually provide by restrictive rules. Such harm may also include the destruction of forms of social life or amenities which otherwise would have been available to the individual. So whether or not it is in any man's interest to choose that any specific liberty should be generally distributed depends on whether the advantages for him of the exercise of that liberty outweigh the various disadvantages for him of its general practice by others. I do not think Rawls recognises this adequately in his discussion of conflicting liberties and his theory of natural duties. His recognition is inadequate, I think, because his doctrine insists that liberty can only be limited for the sake of liberty, and that when we resolve conflicts we must be concerned only with the extent or amount of liberty. This conceals the character of the advantages and disadvantages of different sorts which must be involved in the resolution of such conflicts; and his doctrine also leads him to misrepresent the character of all except those most simple conflicts between liberty and other benefits which are resolved by the parties in the original position when they choose the natural duties. Throughout, I think, Rawls fails to recognise sufficiently that a weighing of advantage and disadvantage must always be required to determine whether the general distribution of any specific liberty is in a man's interest, since the exercise of that liberty by others may outweigh the advantages to him of his own exercise of it. A rather startling sign that this is ignored appears in Rawls's remark that "from the standpoint of the original position, it is rational" for men to want as large a share as possible of liberty, since "they are not compelled to accept more if they do not wish to, nor does a person suffer from a greater liberty."[53] This I find misleading because it seems to miss the vital point that, whatever advantage for any individual there may be in the exercise of some liberty taken in itself, this may be outweighed by the disadvantages for him involved in the general distribution of that liberty in the society of which he is a member.

The detailed criticisms which I have made so far concern the *application* of Rawls's principle of greatest equal liberty. But the general point made in the last paragraph, if it is valid, affects not merely the application of the principles of justice once they have been chosen but also the argument which is designed to show that the parties would in the conditions of the original position, as rational self-interested persons, choose the basic liberties which Rawls enumerates. Even if we assume with Rawls that every rational person would prefer as much liberty as he can get if no price is to be paid for it, so that in that sense it is true that no one "suffers from a greater liberty," it does not follow that a liberty which can only be obtained by an individual at the price of its general distribution through society is one that a rational person would still want. Of course, Rawls's natural duties represent some obvious cases where it can fairly be said that any rational person would prefer certain restrictions to a generalised liberty. In other, less simple cases, whether it would be rational to prefer liberty at the cost of others having it too must depend on one's temperament and desires. But these are hidden from the parties in the original position and, this being so, I do not understand how they can make a rational decision, in terms of self-interest, to have the various liberties at the cost of their general distribution. Opting for the most extensive liberty for all cannot, I think, be presented as always being the best insurance against the worst in conditions of uncertainty about one's own temperament and desires.

VI. THE ARGUMENT FOR THE PRIORITY OF LIBERTY

I will end by explaining a difficulty which I find in the main argument which Rawls uses to show that the priority of liberty prohibiting exchanges of liberty for economic or other social advantages must be included among the requirements of justice. According to Rawls's theory, the rational, self-interested parties in the original position choose

---

53 P. 143.

this priority rule from behind the veil of ignorance as part of the special conception of justice, but they choose it on the footing that the rule is not to come into play unless or until certain favourable social and economic conditions have actually been reached in the society of which they will be members. These favourable conditions are identified as those which allow the effective establishment and exercise of the basic liberties,[54] and when basic wants can be fulfilled.[55] Until this point is reached the general conception of justice is to govern the society, and men may give up liberties for social and economic gains if they wish.

I do not think that Rawls conceives of the conditions which bring the priority rule into play as a stage of great prosperity.[56] At any rate, it is quite clear that when this stage is reached there may still be in any society people who want more material goods and would be willing to surrender some of their basic liberties to get them. If material prosperity at this stage were so great that there could then be no such people, the priority rule then brought into operation could not function as a prohibitory rule, for there would be nothing for it to rule out. As Rawls says, we need not think of the surrender of liberties which men might still be willing to make for greater economic welfare in very extreme terms, such as the adoption of slavery.[57] It might be merely that some men, perhaps a majority, perhaps even all, in a society might wish to surrender certain political rights the exercise of which does not appear to them to bring great benefits, and would be willing to let government be carried on in some authoritarian form if there were good reasons for believing that this would bring a great advance in material prosperity. It is this kind of exchange which men might wish to make that the priority rule forbids once a society has reached the quite modest stage where the basic liberties can be effectively established and the basic wants satisfied.

---

54 P. 152.

55 Pp. 542–43.

56 It is plain that under this identification the conditions for the application of the special conception of justice may be reached at very different levels of material prosperity in different societies. Thus, in a small agrarian society or in a society long used to hard conditions, men might be capable of establishing and exercising political liberties at a much lower standard of living than would be possible for inhabitants of a large, modern industrial society. But in view of the fact that Rawls describes the relevant stage as one where conditions merely "allow" or "admit" the effective establishment and realisation of basic liberties, it is not clear to me whether he would consider the special conception of justice applicable to a very wealthy society where, owing to the unequal distribution of wealth, poverty prevented considerable numbers from actually exercising the basic liberties. Would it be unjust for the poor in such a society to support an authoritarian form of government to advance their material conditions?

57 P. 61.

Why then should this restrictive priority rule be accepted as among the requirements of justice? Rawls's main answer seems to be that, as the conditions of civilisation improve, a point will be reached when *from the standpoint of the original position,* "it becomes and then remains . . . irrational to acknowledge a lesser liberty for the sake of greater material means . . . ." because, "as the general level of well-being rises, only the less urgent material wants remain"[58] to be satisfied and men come increasingly to prize liberty. "The fundamental interest in determining our plan of life *eventually* assumes a prior place" and "the desire for liberty is the chief regulative interest that the parties [in the original position] must suppose they all will have in common *in due course.*"[59] These considerations are taken to show the rationality, from the standpoint of the parties in the original position, of ranking liberty over material goods, represented by the priority rule.

The core of this argument seems to be that it is rational for the parties in the original position, ignorant as they are of their own temperaments and desires and the conditions of the society of which they are to be members, to impose this restriction on themselves prohibiting exchanges of liberty for other goods because "eventually" or "in due course" in the development of that society the desire for liberty will actually come to have a greater attraction for them. But it is not obvious to me why it is rational for men to impose on themselves a restriction against doing something they may want to do at some stage in the development of their society because at a later stage ("eventually" or "in due course") they would not want to do it. There seems no reason why a surrender of political liberties which men might want to make purely for a large increase in material welfare, which would be forbidden by the priority rule, should be permanent so as to prevent men, when great affluence is reached, restoring the liberties if they wished to do so; it is not as if men would run the risk, if there were no priority rule, of permanently losing liberties which later they might wish to have. I think, however, that probably Rawls's argument is really of the following form, which makes use again of the idea that under certain conditions of uncertainty rational beings would opt for the alternative whose worst consequences would be least damaging to one's interests than the worst consequences of other alternatives. Since the parties in the original position do not know the stage of development of their society, they must, in considering whether to institute a priority rule prohibiting exchanges of liberty for economic goods, ask themselves which of the following alternatives, A or B is least bad:

---

58 P. 542.
59 P. 543 (emphasis added).

A. If there is no priority rule and political liberties have been sur-rendered in order to gain an increase in wealth, the worst position is that of a man anxious to exercise the lost liberties and who cares nothing for the extra wealth brought him by surrender.

B. If there is a priority rule, the worst position will be that of a person living at the bottom economic level of society, just pros-perous enough to bring the priority rule into operation, and who would gladly surrender the political liberties for a greater advance in material prosperity.

It must, I think, be part of Rawls's argument that for any rational self-interested person B is the best worse position and for that reason the parties in the original position would choose it. I am not sure that this is Rawls's argument, but if it is, I do not find it convincing. For it seems to me that here again the parties in the original position, ignorant as they are of the character and strength of their desires, just cannot give any determinate answer if they ask which of the positions, A or B, it is then, in their condition of ignorance, most in their interests to choose. When the veil of ignorance is lifted some will prefer A to B and others B to A.

It may be that a better case along the line of argument just considered could be made out for some of the basic liberties, for example, religious freedom, than for others. It might be said that any rational person who understood what it is to have a religious faith and to wish to practise it would agree that for any such person to be prevented by law from practising his religion must be worse than for a relatively poor man to be prevented from gaining a great advance in material goods through the surrender of a religious liberty which meant little or nothing to him. But even if this is so, it seems to me that no *general* priority rule forbidding the exchange, even for a limited period, of any basic liberty which men might wish to make in order to gain an advance in material prosperity, can be supported by this argument which I have ascribed, possibly mistakenly, to Rawls.

I think the apparently dogmatic course of Rawls's argument for the priority of liberty may be explained by the fact that, though he is not offering it merely as an ideal, he does harbour a latent ideal of his own, on which he tacitly draws when he represents the priority of liberty as a choice which the parties in the original position must, in their own interest, make as rational agents choosing from behind the veil of ig-norance. The ideal is that of a public-spirited citizen who prizes polit-ical activity and service to others as among the chief goods of life and could not contemplate as tolerable an exchange of the opportunities for such activity for mere material goods or contentment. This ideal powerfully impregnates Rawls's book at many points which I have been unable to discuss here. It is, of course, among the chief ideals of Liberalism, but Rawls's argument for the priority of liberty purports to rest on interests, not on ideals, and to demonstrate that the general priority of liberty reflects a preference for liberty over other goods which every self-interested person who is rational would have. Though his argument throws much incidental light on the relationship between liberty and other values, I do not think that it succeeds in demonstrating its priority.

Equal Liberty and Unequal Worth of Liberty

NORMAN DANIELS[*]

I

Liberal political theory has traditionally attempted to provide a two-fold justification. On the one hand, liberal theorists have argued for the equality of various political liberties. Of course, different theorists were concerned with different sets of equal basic liberties. Hobbes justified only a narrow set of equal liberties of the person, for example, the liberty to refuse to testify against oneself.[1] Locke argued for a broader set of equal liberties of political participation, and Mill tried to defend broad, equal liberties of thought and expression. On the other hand, while justifying some degree of equality in the political sphere, these liberal theorists at the same time accepted and justified significant inequalities in income, wealth, powers, and authority between both individuals and classes.[2] Usually, they viewed these inequalities as the necessary or fair outcomes of differences in skill, intelligence, or industriousness operating within the framework of a competitive market. Despite the highly divergent theoretical frameworks used to justify these political equalities and socio-economic inequalities, including appeals to natural rights, to social contracts, and to different forms of utilitarianism, there was always a shared assumption. Liberal theorists uniformly assumed that political equality is compatible with significant social and economic inequalities, that they can exist together.

A similar assumption is implicit in John Rawls' 'special conception'[3] of justice as fairness and in his powerful and sophisticated

---

[*] Assistant Professor, Tufts University.

[1] Thomas Hobbes, *Leviathan: or the Matter, Form, and Power of a Commonwealth Ecclesiastical and Civil* (New York: E. P. Dutton & Co., 1950), Everyman Edition, Chapter XXI.

[2] Rawls tends to define classes as in contemporary stratification theory, in terms of weighted parameters of income, prestige, etc. Though I prefer the Marxist treatment, in which classes are defined in terms of relations to production, I shall here follow Rawls' usage unless otherwise indicated.

[3] The *Special* conception of justice as fairness, which gives priority to

arguments for it. Rawls' First Principle requires broad
equality in the political sphere, stipulating a maximally extensive system of equal basic liberties (p. 302). Moreover, this
liberty is given 'priority' and 'can be restricted only for the sake
of liberty' (p. 302). That is, neither the extent nor the equality of
liberty can be traded away for other social goods. Rawls' Second
Principle, however, permits inequalities in the social and economic
sphere. Specifically, inequalities in income, wealth, powers and
authority between individuals or classes are permitted if such
inequalities maximize a suitable index of the 'primary social
goods' enjoyed by the worst-off representative members of society.

The assumption that First Principle equalities and Second
Principle inequalities are compatible is likely to be weak and un-
problematic if the inequalities allowed by the Second Principle
are very small. Rawls certainly hopes they will not be large and
that most of the inequalities we judge unjust or unfair today
would be ruled out by the Second Principle. But he offers no
argument from the social sciences capable of demonstrating, or
even designed to demonstrate, the impossibility or improbability
that large or significant inequalities will always fail to satisfy the
Second Principle. Such an argument would have to show that inequalities greater than a certain magnitude always fail to benefit
the worst-off maximally.[4] Moreover, Rawls sets no moral restriction on the absolute size of 'fair' inequalities, perhaps because he
thinks that envy, which is ruled out of the original position,
would be the only basis for opposing large inequalities. But
lacking assurance from either social theory or special moral
principles, we are forced to assess the compatibility of First and
Second Principle equalities and inequalities in the least favorable
case, where social and economic inequalities may prove to be
large.

The incompatibility that may obtain between First Principle
and significant Second Principle inequalities is not, of course,
logical incompatibility. There is no logical contradiction involved.
But it is not enough that there be no logical contradiction here.
When Rawls proposes his principles as a model for 'ideal theory'

equality of liberty, applies only when a certain level of material well-being
has been achieved in a society. Otherwise, the *general* conception applies
and the difference principle governs all social goods, liberty included. Cf.
Sect. 11, 26, 82.

[4] There may be the basis for just such an argument in Marxist theory, but
there seems to be no theoretical basis for it in non-Marxist social sciences.

(see Sect. 39), he is not concerned with mere logical possibility. Rather, he requires that his ideal must be socially possible (p. 138). It must comprise a workable conception of justice in light of what we know from general social theory, including psychology, sociology, history, economics, and political science (though, of course, we are not told how to achieve the workable ideal). Thus Rawls argues at length that the special conception of justice as fairness is consonant with 'the principles of moral psychology'. Indeed, one of Rawls' arguments for justice as fairness is that it is more stable than other theories because it is more in accord with the principles of moral psychology (cf. Sect. 76). 'Stability' in this sense is one determinant of social possibility and is an important empirical constraint on the content of an adequate moral theory.

There are other determinants of social possibility, however. If the degree to which a moral theory accords with principles of moral psychology provides one measure of stability, then the degree to which a moral theory is in line with principles from other areas of the social sciences presumably would provide other measures of stability and, thus, other determinants of social possibility. For example, if we have good reason to believe that the arrangements authorized by a conception of justice are not in line with the principles of political science or with what we know from history, then that conception of justice is to a certain degree unstable and perhaps not socially possible. Specifically, if social theory gives us good reason to believe that significant individual and class inequalities in wealth and powers cause or produce inequalities of liberty, then this fact becomes relevant to assessing Rawls' ideal.[5] It would indicate a serious form of instability, though not one Rawls discusses when he talks about the stability of conceptions of justice. More generally, this fact, if established, would raise a serious question whether Rawls' ideal is realizable, that is, whether or not Rawls' two principles of justice describe a socially possible or consistent system of justice

My concern in this paper is to explore the consistency of the two principles of justice. In Section II, I argue that it is a serious question in social theory, one not to be ignored, whether or not

[5] The argument for class inequalities causing inequalities of liberty is both clearer and stronger if we restrict attention to the dominant economic class in any given period, defined by its control over the means of production, and consider the various ways in which it has controlled the major institutions, notably the state.

the kinds of inequalities allowable by Rawls' Second Principle are compatible with the demands of his First Principle. Further, I will show that Rawls' steps to accommodate this possibility are inadequate. In Section III, I discuss Rawls' distinction between liberty and worth of liberty, arguing that it is arbitrary. In Section IV, using considerations internal to Rawls' theory, I show that the appeal to worth of liberty cannot reconcile the First and Second Principles. If I am right, then these points raise a serious problem, not just for Rawls, but for this central assumption about compatibility which he shares with earlier theories. As I argue in Section V, Rawls' principles may drive him and other liberal theorists toward far greater egalitarianism than was expected.

II

Our historical experience, as Rawls acknowledges (p. 226), is that inequalities of wealth and accompanying inequalities in powers tend to produce inequalities of liberty. For example, universal suffrage grants the wealthy and the poor identical voting rights. But the wealthy have more ability than the poor to select candidates, to influence public opinion, and to influence elected officials.[6] Consequently, a clear inequality in the liberty to participate in the political process emerges. Similarly, though wealthy and poor are equally entitled to a fair trial, are 'equal before the law', the wealthy have access to better legal counsel, have more opportunity to influence the administration of justice both in specific cases and in determining what crimes will be prosecuted, and have greater ability to secure laws that favor their interests. Again, the wealthy and the poor are equally free to express (non-libelous) opinions in the appropriate circumstances. Yet, the wealthy have more access to and control over the media and so are freer to have their opinions advanced. This inequality in 'free-

[6] To the extent that elected (and appointed) officials are drawn in disproportionate numbers from the better-off and best-off classes, 'influence' and 'control' by the wealthy over public officials becomes less the issue than the awareness of common class interests. To the extent that elected officials initially drawn from the worse-off classes begin to identify their interests with the interests of better-off classes, perhaps even as a result of the kinds of 'incentives' provided for by the Second Principle, then the perception of common interests again supersedes direct 'influence' and 'control'. These processes are accelerated by various ideological factors, like professionalism, elitism, and racism.

dom of speech' is one of the greatest importance since it means views which represent particular interests, that is, those of the best-off classes, are most likely to get advanced. Indeed, whole ideologies reflecting those interests may be promoted in this manner. What is worse, even greater inequalities in liberty emerge when we note that there are combined effects. For example, if the wealthy have greater liberty to affect the political process, then they may also acquire greater influence over the schools and what is taught in them. But the combined effects of control over the schools and the media give the wealthy vastly greater 'freedom of expression' than those less well-off. In turn, their resulting influence over public information and training produces further increases in their political effectiveness. The inequalities in liberty compound each other.

In these generalized examples, the inequality of liberty does not result primarily from abuses, like bribery. Instead, the inequality derives from the (usually) legal exercise of abilities, authority, and powers that come with wealth. Moreover, the examples do not seem to depend primarily, if at all, on violations of what Rawls calls 'fair equality of opportunity' to achieve offices to which advantages are attached (cf. Sect. 14). To the extent that some inequality of opportunity is operative in these examples, it, too, may be an effect of inequalities in wealth and concomitant powers. Indeed, the resulting inequality of opportunity may be as hard to avoid as the inequalities of liberty which here concern us.[7]

Examples such as these do not, of course, prove that inequalities in wealth and power cause inequalities in basic liberties in all workable political systems. If one thought that the mechanisms through which unequal wealth operates to destroy equal liberty were simple and insolatable, then perhaps constitutional provisions could be devised to solve the problem. Rawls, for example, suggests constitutional provisions for the public funding of political parties and for the subsidy of public debate (pp. 225-6). But there is little reason to believe that the mechanisms are so simple and that such safeguards would work. The current United States tax deduction for subsidizing election campaigns, for example, is unlikely to wrest control of the major parties from the hands of the wealthy. From what we do know about cases

[7] Rawls admits practical limitations, such as the continued existence of the family as a social unit, to securing fair equality of opportunity in a context of social and economic inequalities.

of class divided societies, the process of political control by the dominant economic class is highly complicated, and, much more than the direct 'buying' of influence, it involves the combined effect of vast economic powers and control over ideological institutions. At any rate, in the absence of a comprehensive 'political sociology', as Rawls calls it (p. 227), it is safe to say that we fail to know what all, or even the main, causal mechanisms are. Therefore, we fail to know if constitutional safeguards could satisfactorily interfere with them.

Actually, the situation is a bit worse than is indicated by our claiming lack of comprehensive knowledge. Rawls himself admits that it is an open question, even in theory, whether or not we could eliminate the relevant mechanisms. As he suggests, 'The democratic political process is at best regulated rivalry, it does not *even in theory* have the desirable properties that price theory ascribes to truly competitive markets' (p. 226, my emphasis). Part of the problem, of course, is that the 'regulating' becomes the task of those needing regulating and there is no equivalent of market forces to redistribute imbalances.[8]

From the point of view of the original position, then, reliance on reassurances about the possibility of constitutional safeguards seems highly risky. Persons in the original position are aware how little is really known about the relevant mechanisms. They also know that there even are theoretical reasons for skepticism that an adequate set of constitutional safeguards could be devised. Assuming these rational agents value equal liberty as strongly as Rawls says they do, they would not want to risk losing that equal liberty. But if such agents do not know if it is socially possible to prevent unequal wealth and powers from destroying equal liberty, then they would not want to take a chance on an untested constitutional blueprint. Accordingly, they might not be able to accept the conjunction of the First and Second Principles.

[8] The point is put more strongly in Marxist theory of the state. The state cannot exist to 'reconcile' and regulate class conflicts. Rather, both in theory and in practice, it always functions as an instrument of class conflict, controlled by the dominant class. My own view is that formal, procedural guarantees are never sufficient to make sure small groups or classes cannot gain significant advantages in political liberty and power. For example, if a broad class, like the working class, controlled the political apparatus, then only its own developed class consciousness and political understanding, not constitutional guarantees, could protect it against attempts by smaller classes to reinstate a condition of less political equality. Equalizing liberty between antagonistic classes by devising the proper form of government is an impossible dream.

III

Fortunately, Rawls does not rely on the unsupported hope that we can find a constitutional blueprint for eliminating the effects of unequal wealth and powers on liberty. Instead, he tries to circumvent the problem by introducing a distinction between *liberty* and *the worth of liberty*. *Liberty*, 'represented by the complete system of the liberties of equal citizenship' (p. 204), continues to be distributed in accordance with the First Principle. But the new social good, *the worth of liberty* to persons or groups, 'is proportioned to their capacity to advance their ends within the framework the system defines' (p. 204). Apparently, then, it is distributed in accordance with the Second Principle. As a consequence, the incompatibility between equal liberty and unequal wealth and power, between the First and Second Principles, seems to disappear. Unequal wealth and unequal powers no longer cause inequality of liberty itself, only inequality in the worth of liberty:

> Freedom as equal liberty is the same for all; the question of compensation for a lesser than equal liberty does not arise. But the worth of liberty is not the same for everyone. Some have greater authority and wealth and therefore greater means to achieve their aims [p. 204].

We shall consider in turn two questions. In this section we shall ask if Rawls' distinction between 'liberty' and 'worth of liberty' is an arbitrary one, that is, if there is good reason for Rawls to make it. The point here is whether it is useful to talk about something as a 'liberty' when we can not effectively exercise it. Is it useful to be able to say, 'my liberty is equal to Rockefeller's, but I can not exercise "it" equally'? In the next section we will grant Rawls his use of the distinction, and inquire if it really helps him to reconcile the First and Second Principles.

To see if the distinction between liberty and worth of liberty is arbitrary, we must first see how Rawls analyzes liberty. Basically, he follows Felix Oppenheim and Gerald MacCallum in treating liberty as a triadic relation holding between agents, constraints, and acts, and having the general form: 'This or that person (or persons) is free (or not free) from this or that constraint (or set of constraints) to do (or not to do) so and so' (p. 202).

Agents include persons and associations, such as states and classes.
Constraints 'range from duties and prohibitions defined by law to
coercive influences arising from public opinion and social pressure' (p. 202), though Rawls is mainly concerned with legal
restrictions. The crucial point for our discussion is that economic
factors, and perhaps other factors (like ideology) are explicitly
excluded from among the constraints *definitive* of liberty.

> The inability to take advantage of one's rights and oppor-
> tunities as a result of poverty and ignorance, and a lack of means
> generally, is sometimes counted among the constraints defini-
> tive of liberty. I shall not, however, say this, but rather I shall
> think of these things as affecting the worth of liberty, the value
> to individuals of the rights that the First Principle defines
> [p. 204].

Rawls also remarks that 'greater authority and wealth' implies
having 'greater means to achieve . . . aims' and thus greater worth
of liberty (p. 204). Thus the full range of economic factors, and
not just abject poverty, are excluded from the category of constraints defining liberty.

The question whether Rawls' distinction between liberty and
worth of liberty is arbitrary reduces, then, to the question whether
it is arbitrary to exclude economic factors from the category of
constraints defining liberty. It is often assumed that constraints
defining liberty must be legal restrictions, but, as we have seen,
Rawls agrees with Mill and does not view being a legal restriction
as a necessary condition for being a defining constraint. Non-legal,
but legally permissible coercions, like public opinion and social
pressure, are counted among the defining constraints. But, assuming for the moment that economic factors are not reflected in
legal restrictions, why distinguish them from other non-legal
coercions? Presumably, social pressure and public opinion act
as defining constraints because they create obstacles for agents
who might desire to perform certain acts. In exactly the same
way, however, economic factors also act as systematic, socially
produced obstacles (or aids) for hindering agents desiring to perform certain acts.

It might be thought that we should treat economic factors
differently from other non-legal coercions if we can find a relevant difference in the way the obstacles work. Legal constraints
and pressures of public opinion appear as socially produced

obstacles acting outside the agent whose liberty is in question. They appear to be the results of other agents' activities. In contrast, lack of money might appear to function more like the lack of a capacity or an ability than like the effect of another agents' activities. That is, it might appear more like something internal to the agent whose liberty is in question. Since there is some reason to exclude certain 'internal' abilities from among liberty-defining constraints, there might seem to be reason to treat economic factors in the same ways.

This defense of a difference is not quite adequate. However much one might want to exclude obviously psychological abilities or capacities from among the liberty-defining constraints,[9] it ought to be clear that the institutions which define and determine income and wealth, including the rights of transfer, exchange and protection of property, cannot be assimilated to them. There is a much more direct parallel here between public pressure and economic factors than there is between economic factors and capacities. If social pressure prohibits me from sending my children to private school, then I am not at liberty to do so. But, if I cannot afford to send my children, I am not at liberty to do so either. If I send them, they'll be sent home by forces as external as those involved in social pressure. Similarly, if it makes sense to claim that economic factors define only worth of liberty but not liberty itself, then it makes equally good sense to say that other non-legal coercions also define only worth of liberty. The special exclusion of economic factors seems arbitrary.

One way around the charge of arbitrariness might be to exclude all non-legal coercions from the category of defining constraints. That is, since economic factors are to be excluded, then let us exclude social pressures and public opinion as well. Unfortunately, this maneuver will not solve the problem, either. Requiring that constraints definitive of liberty must be legal restrictions will not entail excluding economic factors since economic factors are always reflected in the laws and constitution. In fact, economic factors are constituted by laws which recognize and enforce property rights, including rights for the transferral, exchange and protection of property. If I do not have the money

---

[9] More difficult questions arise when we try to assess the degree to which certain 'internal' capacities, like motivation, are social products, perhaps even developed in accordance with a particular plan for their distribution. Attitudes and beliefs that result from training and indoctrination may similarly function as obstacles to the performance of certain acts and also raise questions about what can count as constraints defining liberty.

to afford adequate legal counsel, then it is because there are laws which establish the rights of lawyers to refuse to counsel me and of police to arrest me if I create a commotion demanding the legal counsel I want. So, if economic factors are to be excluded from constraints defining liberty, Rawls owes us another, hopefully sufficient, criterion for distinguishing economic factors from other legal restrictions.[10] No other criterion is provided us, however.

We might sympathize with the desire to mark *some* distinction between having liberties and having the ability to exercise those liberties, otherwise defined. If I am unable to speak in public because I am shy, it would be a mistake to conclude that I have no liberty to speak.[11] Some kinds of obstacles are not the ones we want to include among liberty-defining constraints. But simply believing it important to make some distinction here does not by itself tell us to draw it where Rawls proposes, since economic factors share important features with both social pressures and legal retrictions.

There is, though, a history to, and perhaps therein an explanation, for the exclusion of economic factors from constraints defining liberty. For example, although MacCullum and Oppenheim say things that seem to allow economic factors to serve as defining constraints,[12] Oppenheim in particular insists that liberty-defining constraints always be identifiable as individuals or groups of individuals. According to this methodological individualism, legal restrictions are to be translatable into the actions and powers of various officers and agents of the state. In contrast, however, economic inequalities have traditionally, for example, in Hobbes and Locke, been construed not as the work of identifiable individuals, but, rather, as the effect of impersonal market forces

[10] Incidentally, as Hugo Adam Bedau has pointed out to me, being a legal restriction is not by itself sufficient condition for being a constraint on liberty since all legal systems, including Rawls' ideal one, leave room for discretion in the prosecution of laws; not all laws in fact, then, constrain anyone.

[11] Although even this obvious case is not entirely clear. Suppose, for example, that people with blue eyes and black skin are the object of an inferiority theory which claims they are always poor public speakers. Suppose this theory is widely believed and acted on, so that people with blue eyes and black skin are rarely listened to and may even be ridiculed. As a result, many such people become extremely shy. Suppose further that it is the shyness, and not the response of others, that acts as the obstacle to speaking. This situation might make it plausible to think that blue-eyed, black-skinned people actually had less liberty to speak.

[12] Felix Oppenheim, *Dimensions of Freedom* (New York: St. Martins, 1961), p. 123.

which operate vis-a-vis individuals or classes much like the laws of nature, i.e., anonymously. Since we do not, in political theory, treat anonymous natural laws as constraints definitive of liberty, then by analogy, market effects would seem equally excludable.[18] This historical explanation, however, cannot serve as justification for Rawls' distinction. If we view, as Rawls does, the market as an institution whose outcomes and processes we can deliberately manipulate, then market operations and outcomes are no longer anonymous, natural-law-like forces and effects to be distinguished from legal restrictions.

Perhaps we are barking up an unnecessary tree. Rawls' exclusion of economic factors from among the constraints defining liberty seems arbitrary because we have sought without success a special rationale for it. But, it might be argued, no rationale is really needed. If the special treatment of economic factors has systematic, beneficial ramifications in Rawls' overall theory, then that may be justification enough. And we did see that Rawls expects just such a systematic, beneficial effect, namely the reconciliation of the First Principle demand for equal liberty and the possible Second Principle effect of destroying equal liberty. Unfortunately, this final defense seems only to beg the question. Reconciling the two principles by appeal to the special definition of liberty is exactly what needs justification in the first place. Besides, there are far more interesting reasons, internal to Rawls' theory, which prevent Rawls from using the distinction between liberty and worth of liberty to reconcile the top two principles of justice. I shall turn to these now.

IV

Considerations internal to Rawls' own theory open him to the charge that equal liberty without equal worth of liberty is a worthless abstraction. No doubt, this charge could be explored directly by trying to discover what value there is to equality of liberty if the liberty cannot effectively be equally exercised. But it will be more illuminating of Rawls' theory to ask the question from the point of view of agents in the original position. Specifically, we shall want to know if it is rational to choose equal liberty without also choosing equal worth of liberty. If the

[18] I am obliged to my colleagues Hugo Bedau and David Israel for helpful discussion of this and other points.

answer is 'no', then Rawls cannot use worth of liberty to reconcile his First and Second Principles.

In answering this question, we will arrive at what might be called a 'relative rationality proof', analogous to relative consistency proofs in mathematics. Our argument will have the overall form: If it is rational to choose x for reasons R in the original position, then, if R constitutes equally good reasons for choosing y, then it is also rational to choose y in the original position. Specifically, if it is rational to choose equal liberty in the original position for the reasons Rawls gives, and the same reasons are equally good reasons for choosing equal worth of liberty, then it is equally rational to choose equal worth of liberty. In short, choosing equal worth of liberty is rational if choosing equal basic liberties is. Being concerned with the relative consistency and not the validity of Rawls' argument, I will not question whether or not Rawls is right in concluding that choosing equal basic liberties is rational in the original position. Accordingly, I shall use, rather than assess, Rawls' reasons for choosing equal liberty, and I shall use, rather than criticize, his contractarian method. Of course, I do have to paraphrase Rawls' argument in order to isolate his reasons for choosing equal liberty.

Rawls gives only two arguments in which he is explicitly concerned with showing that basic liberties must be distributed equally. The first such argument is for equal liberties of conscience. The second, potentially more general, is for equal liberties of political participation. Both arguments draw, as we shall see, on Rawls' general claim that liberty is to be given priority over other primary social goods. The general argument for the priority of liberty, however, leaves open the question how liberty is to be distributed. But the equal distribution of liberty is both what mainly concerns us here and what is special about these two arguments. Accordingly, I will not discuss the general priority argument, especially since it has been widely discussed elsewhere.[14]

The argument for equal liberty of conscience seems to rest on the special importance of moral and religious obligations. It is by appeal to this special importance that Rawls establishes, first, the priority of liberty of conscience and, then, its equal distri-

[14] Discussions of the priority of liberty can be found in several selections in this volume, in particular in the articles by Nagel, Hart, and Scanlon. Brian Barry also discusses the question in *The Liberal Theory of Justice: A Critical Examination of the Principal Doctrines in 'A Theory of Justice' by John Rawls* (Oxford: Clarendon Press, 1973), Chap. 7.

bution. These two phases of the argument are obvious in the following paraphrase (cf. pp. 205–8): (1) Persons in the original position 'have interests which they must protect as best they can'; (2) among these interests there *may be* self-imposed moral or religious obligations which are very important to chosen life-plans; (3) Persons in the original position know that at some level of material well-being, even the worst-off members of any society would prefer (increments in) the liberty to meet moral and religious obligations over any further increments in the index of other primary social goods; (4) accordingly, persons in the original position would choose to give liberty of conscience priority over other primary social goods; (5) liberty of conscience, even if given priority over other goods, could be distributed in accordance with (a) majority will, (b) the utilitarian principle, or (c) the principle of equality; (6) moral and religious obligations are so important, however, that agents in the original position cannot gamble on their being able to meet such obligations; but (7) because of the veil of ignorance, persons in the original position cannot know if they'll be in the majority; and (8) because the freedom to meet such obligations is so important to them, they cannot afford to gamble on being in the majority; so, (9) majority will would not be an acceptable principle for distributing liberty of conscience; similarly, (10) because such obligations are so important, agents in the original position would not gamble that the utilitarian principle will allow for meeting them; consequently, (11) only the principle of equality remains as a rational basis for distribution; and so, (12) rational agents in the original position would choose equal liberty of conscience and give it priority over other primary social goods. Rawls supplements this central argument by claiming that the equality principle, more than other principles, respects the interests of the next generation, which agents in the original position are obliged to consider. We shall ignore this supplementary argument.

Before showing that an analogous argument to (1)–(12) can be made for equal worth of liberty, a few points are worth noting about Rawls' argument itself. First, Rawls views the conclusion of the argument as 'settled', as 'one of the fixed points of our considered judgments of justice' (p. 206). He never considers any of the very serious questions that can be raised about self-imposed demands of conscience. It might be argued, for example, that some religious views tend to impose and emphasize divisions and barriers among people with a generally harmful effect. If people

in the original position know of these effects, why would they
want to risk being exposed to them? Or, it might be objected that
it is hard to grant liberty of conscience to a parent without also
granting the ability to indoctrinate children. From the point of
view of the original position, would a rational agent want to
risk being the child of a parent free to pursue fanatical religious
views?

A more general problem also emerges. Does treating equal
liberty of conscience as a 'fixed point' tend to imply, and therefore to impose, an unnecessary and possibly dangerous relativism
on the assessment of the truth and effects of various religious,
moral and philosophical views? Are not some such views false,
dangerous, and immoral? Why should persons in the original position back away from recognizing this fact by granting the equal
'right' to hold and practice such views? These are questions
worth pursuing, though Rawls does not take them up. Nor, I am
afraid, can we.[15]

A second point worth noting about the liberty of conscience
argument is that Rawls believes 'the reasoning in this case can
be generalized to apply to other freedoms, although not always
with the same force' (p. 206). His 'intuitive idea is to generalize
the principle of religious toleration to a social form, thereby
arriving at equal liberty in public institutions' (pp. 205–6, n. 6).
But there is a serious question whether this generalization can
be made. We have seen that the argument for liberty of conscience
depends at steps (3) and (6)–(10) on appeals to the importance of
obligations of conscience. If such obligations are granted a
special importance, however, then there is serious question
whether other types of wants, beliefs and preferences, which
form the basis for desiring freedom of expression and certain
personal freedoms, can claim a similar importance. But if there
is no claim that a special importance accrues to demands of
conscience, and all chosen features of life plans can give rise to
interests which agents in the original position may feel they have
to protect, then the First Principle rapidly mushrooms to include
far more than what we might pick out as 'basic' liberties. Freedoms spring up whenever the seeds of desire are planted.

Another complaint about the generalizability of arguments for
religious toleration might also be made, in this case challenging

---

[15] Cf. Gerald Dworkin's paper, 'Non-Neutral Principles', reprinted in this
volume, which pursues this issue in some depth. See also Milton Fisk's
and T. M. Scanlon's discussions of freedom of thought, also in this volume.

the attempt to treat religious and moral obligations on the same plane. One might say that the relativism implicit in religious toleration is acceptable because it is fairly harmless, at least when we are concerned with religious practices narrowly construed. But the acceptance of relativism with regard to other kinds of obligations, say moral obligations, may prove to be a more risky business since these obligations affect a wide variety of social interactions. This asymmetry, however, bodes ill for using religious toleration as the intuitive model for justifying other freedoms, even other freedoms of conscience.

Thirdly, it is also worth noting that, although Rawls views equality of liberty of conscience as a 'settled question', the structure of his argument can at best establish only a provisional agreement on equal distribution. If his argument succeeds, it shows only that equality is a preferred distribution principle when compared to majority will or to the utilitarian principle. Nothing in Rawls' argument precludes abandoning equality for another principle. Perhaps a principle weaker than equality but stronger than the utilitarian principle would be chosen if such a principle better meets all of Rawls' empirical constraints on choices in the original position. I shall briefly touch on one plausible alternative to equality shortly.

Before showing that choosing equal worth of liberty of conscience is rational if choosing equal liberty is, it is worth being clear just what worth of liberty is in this case. After all, examples of unequal worth of liberty for other basic liberties, like liberty of expression or political participation, are familiar and the subject of real concern. On the other hand, unequal worth of liberty of conscience seems less familiar and more abstract. Nevertheless, examples of unequal worth of liberty of conscience are readily found. For example, some religions view time-consuming, expensive acts, like pilgrimages, as obligations of the truly faithful. Inequalities in wealth clearly affect the ability to meet such demands and so would create inequalities in the worth of liberty of conscience. If this example is not compelling to us, it is probably because few of us feel compelled to make pilgrimages.

Other examples may be more relevant to our experience. Some religions consider it a matter of religious obligation to avoid killing or violence of any kind, including military service. It is a matter of historical experience in the United States, however, that conscientious objection to military service on religious grounds places a greater burden on lower- than upper-class objectors. The costs of legally establishing or defending objector status, and of facing up to hostile attitudes and discriminatory job practices toward pacifists are substantial and affect different classes differentially. This example is even clearer in the case of 'moral' or 'political' conscientious objectors to the Vietnam war, since these grounds for objector status were not legally recognized and often entailed defying induction, an outcome with far higher cost to working- or lower-class objectors than to upper middle-class objectors. Similarly, differences in wealth make it far easier for upper-class than lower-class opponents of South African apartheid to emigrate when refusal to live under such laws is felt to be a demand of conscience. No doubt, unequal worth of liberty of conscience may not seem as important to many as unequal worth of other liberties, but that may be because liberty of conscience is not as important as other liberties. In any case, we are forced to consider the worth of liberty of conscience because Rawls makes liberty of conscience the focus of his argument for other liberties. We come, then, to our first relative rationality argument.

Showing that equal worth of liberty of conscience would be chosen in the original position requires an argument analogous to (1)–(12), Rawls' argument for equal liberty of conscience. The crux of Rawls' argument is that equality is the only distribution principle which recognizes the importance individuals place on demands of conscience. Because these demands are so important, it is rational for persons in the original position to avoid risking any interference with meeting them. Thus, it is rational to reject majority will [steps (7)–(9)] and the principle of utility [step (10)] in favor of equality of liberty because these principles may yield obstacles, like adverse majority opinion or unfavorable utility calculations, which would interfere with meeting obligations. But whatever the principles of rationality guiding choice here, they do not distinguish among the source of obstacles; they simply require we avoid them. So, the desired analogue follows easily. If it is rational to reject principles producing obstacles like adverse opinion and unfavorable calculations because these obligations of conscience are so important, then it seems equally rational to reject inequalities in wealth and powers if they create similar obstacles.

By Rawls' definition, however, inequalities in the ability to meet demands of conscience, when caused by unequal wealth or powers, just *are* inequalities in worth of liberty of conscience. So the rational choice for those behind the veil of ignorance would be to rule out principles, like the Second Principle, which may reduce the worth of liberty for some. In short, if it is rational to choose equal liberty of conscience for the reasons Rawls gives, then it is equally rational to choose equal worth of liberty of conscience.

The priority of equal worth of liberty of conscience over other primary social goods can also be established. In step (3), Rawls argued that once a given index of the primary social goods was reached, even the worst-off members of society would prefer increments in their liberty to meet demands of conscience to further increments in the index. Thus rational agents would assign priority to liberty of conscience. But it seems equally rational to reject a higher index in favor of increments in the ability to meet demands of conscience. The alternative to this conclusion is the paradox of preferring liberty to other primary goods while at the same time preferring those goods to the ability to exercise the liberty, or at least to exercise it equally.[16]

Rawls' discussion of compensation for inequalities in the worth of liberty seems to verge on this same paradox since, on one interpretation, it fails to respect the *priority* of worth of liberty over other social goods. Inequalities are to be allowed only if they help the worst-off.

> The lesser worth of liberty is, however, compensated for since the capacity of the less fortunate members of society to achieve their aims would be even less were they not to accept the existing inequalities whenever the difference principle is satisfied [p. 204].

If we assume that the 'difference principle' referred to is the Second Principle, then there is an immediate problem. The Second Principle employs an index which includes all primary social goods *other than* basic liberties. It allows inequalities in individuals' indices only if the inequalities act to maximize the

---

[16] Rawls does assume that the level of the index at which preference for liberty emerges is a level at which the means for exercising liberty effectively exists. But the point of our discussion of equal worth of liberty in the cases of liberties of expression and political participation is that the 'effective' exercising of a liberty may require near equality in the ability to exercise the liberty. 'Effectiveness' may well be relative in the sense that the greater effectiveness of some persons' exercise of liberty renders ineffective lesser degrees of effective exercise of the liberty.

index of the worst-off. If worth of liberty is not included among
the goods indexed, then Rawls appears to be authorizing a trade-
off between it and the primary social goods which are indexed,
since he claims that the lesser worth of liberty of the worst-off is
compensated for by maximization of their index. But as we have
just seen by the analogue to Rawls' step (3), once a certain index
is achieved, increments in it are not as valuable to persons as are
increments in the ability to meet demands of conscience. Therefore, such increments would not be accepted as compensation
for lesser worth of liberty of conscience. Nor can this problem be
avoided simply by counting worth of liberty itself as one of the
primary goods included in the index. Since it would still be one
among several goods indexed, worth of liberty will not necessarily
be maximal whenever the index is maximal. Thus, maximization of
even this expanded index would not be acceptable in the original
position as compensation for lesser worth of liberty.

One way to try to compensate lesser worth of liberty while
respecting its priority over other primary social goods would be
to introduce a special Liberty-Restricted Difference Principle
(LRDP), distinct from the Second Principle. This principle would
permit inequalities of worth of liberty only if they act to maximize
the worth of liberty of those with the least worth of liberty. As
stated, the principle seems to capture Rawls' intention when he
says the 'difference principle' will act to maximize 'the capacity
of the less fortunate members of society to achieve their aims . . .'
(p. 204). Its advantage over the Second Principle is that it prohibits direct trade-off of worth of liberty for a higher index of
other primary goods. At the same time, it benefits from the
general rationale Rawls offers for choosing the Second Principle
in the original position.

Unfortunately, appeal to the Liberty-Restricted Difference
Principle does not help to reconcile the First Principle demand
for liberty with the Second Principle effect of generating unequal
worth of liberty. To solve that problem by appeal to the LRDP
requires an assurance that the inequalities in worth of liberty
justified by the LRDP are exactly the same inequalities which are
caused by the Second Principle. Unfortunately, there is no reason
to believe they will be the same. For one thing, the worst-off
groups may not be identical from the point of view of the two
principles. The worst-off representatives, for the purposes of the
Second Principle, are those with the lowest index of primary
social goods. The worst-off representatives, for purposes of the

LRDP, are those with the least worth of liberty. Unless we assume that every variation in the index of primary social goods has a corollary variation in the worth of liberty, which there is no reason to assume, then the worst-off representatives will not be the same individuals (or classes).

But even if the worst-off individuals or classes happen to coincide, the inequalities justified by the two principles will most likely not coincide anyway. Second Principle inequalities of wealth and power which maximize the index of primary social goods may well not maximize worth of liberty for those with the lowest index. Indeed, what is most likely is that worth of liberty is especially sensitive to *relative* differences in the index of primary social goods and is not a simple monotonic function of it.

An example might help illustrate the point. Assume, for the moment, what we are often told, that granting corporation owners particularly high indices of primary social goods maximizes the indices of workers. The assumption is that profit incentive acts to increase investments and, thereby, allows for more jobs, higher wages, and greater tax monies for welfare. Also, grant what I have argued earlier, that significant inequalities of wealth and powers cause, in cases like this, significant inequalities in the worth of liberty. Then, the higher index of primary social goods enjoyed by the worker or welfare recipient does not necessarily produce more worth of liberty, as Rawls apparently assumes (cf. p. 204). Rather, the very inequality of wealth and powers which, we are assuming, acts to *increase* the index of the worst-off individuals can at the same time act to *decrease* his worth of liberty. The increased index of the corporation owner may give him substantial competitive advantage over those with lower indices. This effect is decisive where worth of liberty is affected by comparative access to those resources and institutions such as qualified legal counsel or the mass media, which are needed for the effective exercise of liberty. The result is that the worst-off, despite their increased indices, may be in a relatively worse position to effectively exercise their liberty. Their increased index is worth relatively less when it comes to exercising liberty because extra, even decisive, advantage has been ceded to the best-off.

The fact that the LRDP and Second Principle yield different sets of inequalities of worth of liberty is not the only problem with appeal to this new difference principle. First, let us leave aside the whole issue of conflict with the Second Principle. Next, let us assume that persons in the original position would choose to regulate worth of liberty in accordance with the LRDP. Their reasoning would be analogous to the reasoning for the Second Principle. That is, there is no reason to accept less worth of liberty for the purposes of maintaining equality if accepting certain inequalities in worth of liberty might lead to greater worth of liberty. It now becomes obvious that we can turn our relative rationality argument in the reverse direction. Just as it is rational to distribute worth of liberty according to the LRDP, why should it not be rational to distribute liberty itself according to a liberty-restricted difference principle instead of insisting on equal liberty.[17] In Rawls' original argument for equal liberty of conscience, equality of liberty was chosen because it was less risky than the principle of utility or than majority will. But the LRDP seems no riskier than equality. So if it is rational to choose LRDP for worth of liberty, then it seems equally rational to choose it for liberty itself, since it suffers none of the disadvantages that led to rejecting other distribution principles.

This reversal is not completely acceptable to Rawls. Equal liberty of conscience, we have seen, is viewed by Rawls as a 'settled question', a 'fixed point' in our moral judgments. Therefore Rawls is not likely to abandon the equal distribution in favor of a special difference principle. But if this is so, consistency demands, according to our relative rationality argument, that he also abandon the equal distribution of worth of liberty. Consequently, he must reject the LRDP here as well. In short, the LRDP provides no way around the relative rationality argument in the case of liberty of conscience.

Earlier I noted that Rawls' argument for equal liberty of conscience does not consider distribution principles weaker than equality but stronger than the utilitarian principle or majority will. The LRDP is just such a principle and because of that, creates the tension we have just seen in Rawls' position. On the one hand, Rawls wants equal distribution to be a fixed point. On the other, his argument can at best establish that equality of distribution is preferred to riskier principles. Against an equally non-risky principle, like the LRDP, Rawls has yet to show that equality is the rationally preferred choice.

Our first relative rationality argument establishes that choosing

17 Thomas Nagel objects to this possibility. See his remark in 'Rawls on Justice' (p. 14), this volume.

equal worth of liberty of conscience is rational if choosing equal liberty of conscience is. This argument shows that considerations internal to Rawls' theory prevent him from reconciling possible conflicts between the First and Second Principles by appeal to his distinction between liberty and worth of liberty. A second relative rationality argument can be applied to the liberties of political participation, the only other liberties for which Rawls presents an extended argument for equality of distribution (although, in this case, Rawls uses his argument as much to show the general priority of liberty as to show why it should be equal). The argument for equal participation liberties or 'the participation principle', as Rawls calls it (p. 221), is based on the importance of self-respect, which is classified as a primary good. Although, as we have seen, Rawls intends the equal liberty of conscience to be a model for other liberties, there are problems with generalizing that argument. Because the central primary good of self-respect is at the heart of this second argument for equal liberty, it may provide more promise of being extended to cover other liberties.

Once again, since our purpose is not to analyze it, we shall content ourselves with a rough paraphrase of Rawls' argument.[18] Our paraphrase is composed of points found in Sections 36, 63, 67, and especially 82:
(1) Since without self-respect 'nothing may seem worth doing' (p. 440), self-respect is an important primary social good, basic to all life plans. (2) When the index of primary goods is at a certain level, most urgent needs of the worst-off will be met (p. 542) and 'the fundamental interest in determining our plan of life ... assumes a prior place' (p. 543). (3) At this point, self-respect becomes crucially important and parties in the original position would want 'to avoid at almost any cost the social conditions that undermine self-respect (p. 440) or increase risks to self-respect. (4) Similarly, at this point, parties in the original position would reject further increases in the index in favor of increases in self-respect or at least in favor of eliminating conditions that undermine self-respect. (5) Self-respect (a) could be based on socio-economic status, or 'income share' (p. 544), as it is in current

[18] A detailed discussion of this argument can be found in Henry Shue's paper, 'Liberty and Self-Respect', *Ethics*, 85 (forthcoming), which came to my attention too late to be included in this volume. Shue's analysis of the self-respect argument is similar in outline to my own, though it differs in details. Shue is not concerned with the effects on liberty of unequal wealth.

societies, or (b) it could be based on 'the public recognition of just institutions' and 'the publically affirmed distribution of fundamental rights and liberties' (p. 544), especially the liberties of political participation. But, (6) basing self-respect on socio-economic status is risky; since the Second Principle allows inequalities in the index of primary goods, some persons would have less self-respect than others. What is worse, (7) those with less self-respect have no acceptable compensation. All they have in return for their lower index is the assurance that it is maximal. But the fact that their index is maximal does not mean that their self-respect is; self-respect is based on the *relative* level of the index, not on its absolute level. Moreover, the higher index itself is not acceptable compensation by step (4). So, (8) basing self-respect on the 'publically affirmed distribution of fundamental rights and liberties' would be less risky than basing it on income share, provided that the distribution were equal; unequal distribution would be subject to similar objections to those mentioned in step (7). (9) The liberties most relevant to enhancing self-respect, since they imply one's value to others, are those which recognize as equal the contribution each party can make to determining public policy and action. Therefore, (10) parties in the original position would choose to secure self-respect by the public affirmation of the status of equal citizenship for all.

Some points about this paraphrase of Rawls' argument are worth noting. First, the claim that self-respect is such an important primary goal, appealed to in step (1), depends on a general psychological theory which Rawls argues for elsewhere (cf. Sect. 63 and 67). Discussing this theory would take us too far afield, but discussion is certainly warranted. The general role of self-respect described in premise (1) is what may make this argument more generalizable than Rawls' argument for liberty of conscience. Second, the explicit claim that self-respect emerges as the central primary good only when the index has reached a certain level [steps (2) and (3)] is not made explicit in Rawls' own exposition. I believe, however, it is compatible with his intentions. If Rawls believed that self-respect was always to be viewed as the most important primary social good, he would have given it a more central role in discussions of how the index is constructed and how the Second Principle is to be applied. Third, Rawls may oversimplify the possible bases of self-respect when he suggests the contrast which I characterize in step (5). Though socio-economic status no doubt plays a significant role in determining self-respect, it hardly is the whole story, as Rawls would readily agree. But then the other important bases of self-respect would have to be discussed before we could simply reject disjunct (a) of step (5) and opt for disjunct (b). Finally, step (4) of my reconstruction is not explicit in Rawls' discussion. Yet it is extremely important. Without it, it becomes impossible to show that socio-economic status is not an acceptable basis for self-respect. That is, it is impossible unless we adopt an even stronger premise, one claiming that self-respect must be distributed equally. But Rawls does not make the stronger premise explicit either. Indeed, one wonders how one could guarantee such a distribution, so it is unlikely Rawls would feel committed to equality of self-respect. Therefore, I use the weaker premise (4) since it catches the intention behind steps (2) and (3).

We can now sketch our relative rationality argument for equal worth of citizenship liberties. To carry through the argument, we must assume what was claimed earlier, that Second Principle inequalities in wealth and powers may cause significant inequalities in the worth of these liberties. As we have seen, Rawls cannot rule out this possibility. Indeed, the distinction between liberty and worth of liberty was introduced to cope with it. Also, we must be clear what the core of Rawls' own argument is. Rawls' argument for equal citizenship liberties depends on three claims, that public affirmation of the equal liberties could act as a social basis for self-respect, that enhancement of self-respect would be equal because the liberties are equal, and that this arrangement, viewed from behind the veil of ignorance, minimizes the risk of having relatively low self-respect, making it rational to choose equal citizenship liberties. Are there analogous claims that could be made for worth of liberty? If we can find these analogues, the rest of the relative rationality argument is elementary and we need not take space to spell it out.

One similarity is obvious. Inequalities in worth of citizenship liberties, that is, inequalities in the ability of parties to influence and participate in the political process, would be no less 'publically known' than the equal liberties themselves. But if these inequalities in worth of citizenship liberties are publically known, do they have an effect on self-respect? Could public knowledge of inequalities in worth of citizenship liberties act to undermine the self-respect of those with less worth of liberty?

It seems plausible to say they would, that public recognition of unequal liberty to exercise the 'affirmed' basic liberty is just as likely to undermine self-respect as public recognition of unequal liberties themselves. For example, consider those who are worst-off, as determined by their index of primary goods. They know that those far better off than they not only enjoy a higher index, but also have greater worth of citizenship liberties. They know, for example, that those better-off are more able to have their views and interests put forward in the mass media, are better able to select candidates, and are more effective in influencing office holders. It is likely, then, that their self-respect would be diminished. The mechanism here seems identical to the one Rawls cites in arguing for equal basic liberties: 'This subordinate ranking in the public forum experienced in the attempt to take part in political and economic life and felt in dealing with those who have a greater liberty, would indeed be humiliating and destructive of self-esteem' (pp. 544–5).

Thus, it seems that public knowledge of worth of liberty can act as a basis for self-respect. Moreover, unequal worth of liberties can enhance or diminish self-respect depending on how much worth of liberty one has. What is worse, it is hard to see how the well-ordered society could succeed in guaranteeing that the affirmation of equal liberties would successfully serve as the basis of self-respect but prevent knowledge of unequal worth of liberty from playing any role. The problem is that many people keep their eyes on the doughnut and not on the hole. They would reject the idea that their self-respect would be enhanced and secured by the public affirmation of equal liberties which they know they cannot exercise equally with others. Parties in the original position presumably would also keep their eyes on the doughnut. From the original position, they would believe it as rational to guarantee equal worth of citizenship liberties as they would to guarantee equal basic liberties themselves. Thus all three of Rawls' core claims about the relation between self-respect and equal citizenship liberties have their analogues for the equal worth of those liberties.

It should also be clear, from step (4) in our reconstruction, why we cannot simply compensate those with less worth of citizenship liberties, and therefore, with possibly less self-respect, by reassuring them that their index of primary goods is maximal. Once a certain level of the index is reached, it is not rational to prefer further increments in it to increments in self-respect. Since unequal worth of liberty diminishes self-respect for some, from behind the veil of ignorance it is rational to secure maximal self-respect through maximally equal worth of liberty. Equal worth of citizenship liberties gains its priority over other goods through its causal relation to self-respect, and self-respect enjoys priority by step (4).

As in the previous relative rationality argument, the compensation problem cannot be averted by appeal to a special, Liberty-Restricted Difference Principle (LRDP) applied to worth of citizenship liberties. Such an LRDP would justify inequalities in worth of citizenship liberties only if they acted to maximize the worth of liberty of those with the least worth of liberty. In other words, it would be justified to grant some people greater worth of citizenship liberties, if their having made it possible for those with less worth of liberty to have more than they otherwise would have had. The problem here is that the inequalities justified by the LRDP are not likely to coincide with the inequalities in worth of liberty caused by Second Principle inequalities in wealth and powers. As in the first appeal to an LRDP, the worst-off classes are not likely to coincide unless we make the strong assumption, which is probably not true, that every variation in the index has a corollary variation in the worth of liberty. More important, for the same reasons as before, it is unlikely that the worth of citizenship liberties is a monotonic function of the index. It is more likely that it is affected more by relative differences in the index than by absolute levels of the index.

If, as in the first relative rationality argument, we set aside the problem of reconciling the effects of the LRDP and the Second Principle, and assume it is rational to adopt the LRDP for worth of citizenship liberties, then we run into the same problem we did earlier. The relative rationality argument can be run in reverse. Instead of arguing from the rationality of equal liberty to the rationality of equal worth of liberty, we could argue from the rationality of unequal worth of citizenship liberties to the rationality of unequal citizenship liberties themselves. Rawls does not say that equal citizenship liberties have the status of a 'fixed point', but he surely seems committed to them:[19] 'When it is the

---

[19] One qualification is in order here. Rawls does seem to suggest at points that certain inequalities in citizenship liberties might be justifiable.

The priority of liberty does not exclude marginal exchanges within the system of freedom. Moreover, it allows although it does not require that some liberties, say those covered by the principle of participation, are less essential in that their main role is to protect the remaining freedom [p. 230].

This remark seems to ignore the special relation between self-respect and

278 _The Principles of Justice_

position of equal citizenship that answers to the need for status, the precedence of the equal liberties becomes all the more necessary' (p. 545). So, in general, Rawls would want to resist applying an LRDP to basic citizenship liberties. To be consistent, he would be then forced to reject appeal to the LRDP for worth of citizenship liberties as well.

V

Our two relative rationality arguments, using considerations internal to Rawls' theory, show that choosing equal worth of liberty is just as rational in the original position as choosing equal basic liberty. They show this for liberty of conscience and liberties of participation (citizenship liberties), the only two cases in which Rawls argues explicitly that the liberties are to be distributed equally. But this result means that Rawls' distinction between liberty and worth of liberty cannot be used to reconcile the First and Second Principles, as might have been hoped.

Initially, the distinction between liberty and worth of liberty looked like it might work. It made it seem that the First Principle demand for equality would not be undermined by Second Principle inequalities of wealth and powers, since, by definition, these inequalities did not affect liberty but only worth of liberty. If we could justify these inequalities in worth of liberty by application of a difference principle, perhaps the Second Principle itself, then the conflict would disappear.

Unfortunately, as the relative rationality arguments show, there is no way to accept unequal worth of liberty in the original position. Unequal worth of liberty cannot be compensated for by increases in other primary goods, since the reasons for granting priority to equal basic liberties apply to equal worth of liberty

equal participation liberties appealed to in Sect. 82. So does the following passage:

> The passengers of a ship are willing to let the captain steer the course, since they believe he is more knowledgeable and wishes to arrive safely as much as they do . . . the ship of state is in some ways analogous to a ship at sea; and to the extent that this is so, the political liberties are indeed subordinate to the other freedoms that, so to say, define the intrinsic good of the passengers. Admitting these assumptions plural voting may be perfectly just [p. 233].

Cf. Brian Barry's remarks on this point in _The Liberal Theory of Justice_, p. 145.

with equivalent strength. No other difference principle, even one restricted to maximizing (the minimum worth) of liberty, will work either. The 'fair' inequalities that might result from a Liberty-Restricted Difference Principle, for example, will not in general coincide with the effects of the Second Principle. Since it is these Second Principle effects which need reconciling with the First Principle, the LRDP gives no relief from the force of the relative rationality argument.

The distinction between liberty and worth of liberty thus fails Rawls in two ways. First, it has no satisfactory rationale. The special exclusion of economic factor from constraints definitive of liberty seems arbitrary, as we showed in Section III. Second, it fails to accomplish the task that motivated its introduction. That is, it fails to reconcile the First and Second Principles. What is worse, as was shown in Section IV, it fails for reasons internal to and important to Rawls' theory. These internal reasons, however, also have an import not restricted to Rawls' theory. Showing that equal liberty and equal worth of liberty are equally rational choices in the original position goes part of the way toward showing why equality of basic liberty seems to be something merely formal, a hollow abstraction lacking real application, if it is not accompanied by equality in the ability to exercise liberty. Further, since equality in the ability to exercise liberty is directly affected by the distribution of wealth and powers, our discussion of relative rationality has another consequence not restricted to Rawls' theory. It shows that a strong egalitarian sentiment in the political sphere may not be so isolatable as Rawls and earlier theorists had hoped from strong egalitarian demands in the social and economic sphere.

Perhaps this last point will be better understood if we look a bit more carefully at where Rawls stands as a result of our argument. Rawls seems to have two main alternatives. One is to attempt reconciling the First and Second Principles by refusing to allow any Second Principle inequalities which undermine the First Principle by making worth of liberty unequal. This strategy could be justified by resting very heavily on the priority of the First Principle. Since liberty has priority over other social goods, no trade-off can be allowed between worth of liberty and the index of primary goods. Rawls can accept our contention that significant Second Principle inequalities in wealth and powers can cause inequalities in worth of liberty, yet respond by ruling out all such significant inequalities.

51

Throughout *Theory of Justice*, Rawls uses examples which make it seem that fairly significant inequalities are compatible with justice as fairness. Perhaps the most striking example is the attempt to leave it an open question whether or not inequalities resulting from private ownership of the means of production are compatible with the Second Principle. Operating on the supposition that they are, Rawls describes in some detail a constitutional democracy which has as its basis a private ownership economy. If Rawls follows this first alternative, however, many inequalities which might have been justified by the Second Principle taken in isolation will probably fail the test of compatibility with the First Principle.

In a sense, a more far-reaching egalitarianism may be forced on us as a result of the two principles of justice than we at first expected, and certainly one more far-reaching than Rawls' examples indicate.[20] Rawls, being primarily interested in the argument for the principles themselves, might be willing to roll with the punch. All this means is that his system is not compatible, as a matter of empirical fact, with as diverse a set of social systems as he might have hoped.

But even if Rawls is willing to accept this result, there remains something of a surprise in it. What I have shown is that it is the First Principle, rather than the Second, which carries the egalitarian punch. It is the First Principle, even more than the Second, which is likely to force strong egalitarianism with regard to primary social goods other than liberty. As we have seen, however, Rawls' conjunction of the First and Second Principles is only a contemporary version of earlier attempts to conjoin equality in the political sphere with various social and economic inequalities. The thrust of our argument is that this historical attempt has also consistently underestimated the egalitarian force of the demand for equality in the political sphere.

There is, of course, another alternative. Rawls could reject the claim that significant economic and social inequalities cause inequalities in liberty or worth of liberty. But the attempt to reject this claim would involve Rawls in the 'policy sociology' he had clearly hoped to ignore while developing his 'ideal'

[20] The result is reminiscent of Engels' remark that one form of the proletarian demand for equality arises 'as the reaction against the bourgeois demand for equality, drawing more or less correct and more far-reaching demands from this bourgeois demand . . . in this case, it stands and falls with bourgeois equality itself.' Cf. *Anti-Duhring* (New York: International Publishers, 1966), pp. 117–18.

theory (cf. pp. 226–7). Nevertheless, the alternative does remain as a challenge. The serious point of social theory which Rawls, as well as the earlier liberal theories, would have to answer can be put succinctly: can a maximally extensive and equal system of liberties be successfully achieved without ruling out all significant inequalities of wealth and power?[21] I believe not.[22]

[21] The Marxist would rephrase the question as follows: does the demand for equal liberties make sense except when couched as the demand for the abolition of classes? As such, the question becomes a central focus of debate between liberal and marxist political theory.

[22] I would like to express my thanks to Hugo Adam Bedau and John Rawls for many helpful criticisms they have made of an earlier draft of this paper. A version of this paper was read at the American Philosophical Association Western Division Meetings, Chicago, April 1975.

THE INTERPRETATION OF
RAWLS' FIRST PRINCIPLE OF JUSTICE

Thomas POGGE
Harvard University

The cardinal constraint which Rawls aims to impose on any system of social institutions ("basic structure") is formulated as his First Principle, securing for all citizens certain rights and liberties. This demand may not seem at all new or original. To appreciate its distinctive meaning, one must proceed to interpret and specify this proposal within the context of the Rawlsian conception as a whole. In particular, the question is: How would the parties to the original position — construed in accordance with Rawls' conception of the person, and reasoning from the maximin rule — draw up such a package of rights and liberties? In response. I first hope to clarify the wording of, and rationale for, Rawls' principle — which secondly will lead to a better understanding of the appropriate notion of a basic liberty. The next three sections are then devoted to the substantive question of what liberties should count as basic: Section III will use Rawls' conception of the person — as appealed to in his argument for the priority of liberty — to argue for a triad of fundamental values. This triad may serve as a heuristic for drawing up a preliminary list (section IV), and finally for fitting together into a coherent package (section V), those rights and liberties which Rawlsian considerations might entitle to special protection. Section VI, finally, by way of an appendix. will briefly discuss the political force of these conclusions by comparing them to the presently most influential human rights documents.

I: THE RATIONALE FOR THE FIRST PRINCIPLE

Under the maximin rule. alternatives are ranked according to their worst possible outcomes (TJ 152ff)[1]. The parties will therefore assess

1. The following abbreviations are used in citations:

BR   Henry Shue: *Basic Rights*; Princeton University Press. Princeton 1980.

each (model for the) basic structure from the point of view of its least
advantaged citizens. A scheme permitting unequal life-prospects is
then justified by Rawlsian standards if and only if those least

BSS   John Rawls: 'The Basic Structure as Subject', in A.I. Goldman and J. Kim (eds.): *Values and Morals*: Reidel. Dordrecht 1978.

CPR   International Covenant on Civil and Political Rights: quoted by article as reprinted in HR.

ECHR   European Convention on Human Rights: quoted by article as reprinted in HR.

EMPL   David Hume: *Essays Moral, Political. Literary* in two volumes: Longmans. Green. and Co., London 1875.

ESCR   International Covenant on Economic. Social and Cultural Rights: qouted by article as reprinted in HR.

FEL   Isaiah Berlin: *Four Essays on Liberty*: Oxford University Press. Oxford 1969.

GTP   Immanuel Kant: *On the Old Say: "That May Be Right in Theory But It Won't Work in Practice"*: quoted by volume VIII of the Prussian Academy edition as translated by E.B. Acton; University of Pennsylvania Press. Philadelphia 1974.

HR   Frank E. Dowrick (ed.): *Human Rights*: Saxon House, Westmead 1979.

ILHR   H. Lauterpacht: *International Law and Human Rights;* Preager. 1950.

KCE   John Rawls: 'A Kantian Conception of Equality': in *Cambridge Review* February 1975. pp. 94-99.

KCMT   John Rawls: 'Kantian Constructivism in Moral Theory', in *Journal of Philosophy* 77:9 (September 1980). pp. 515-572.

LN   James L. Brierly: *The Law of Nations*: Clarendon Press, Oxford 1955.

MEW   Karl Marx and Friedrich Engels: *Werke*, volumes 1-39: Dietz, Berlin 1969-1973.

MSR   Immanuel Kant: Metaphysics of Morals Part I: *The Metaphysical Elements of Justice*: quoted by volume VI of the Prussian Academy edition as translated by J. Ladd; Bobbs-Merrill, Indianapolis 1965.

NPF   Gerald MacCallum: 'Negative and Positive Freedom', in *Philosophical Review* 76:3 (July 1967), pp. 312-334.

TJ   Rawls: *A Theory of Justice*: Harvard University Press, Cambridge 1971.

UDHR   Universal Declaration of Human Rights; quoted by article as reprinted in HR.

ULR   John Stuart Mill: *Utilitarianism, Liberty, Representative Government*; H.B. Acton (ed.); Dent, London 1976.

advantaged under it are no worse off than the least advantaged under any alternative arrangement would be[2]. Now by arguing for the priority of the First Principle, Rawls claims that the parties would use the liberties as their primary criterion for identifying the least advantaged under each scheme and for comparing the life-prospects of these least advantaged groups across models. This "lexical" (TJ 42n23) priority of the liberties has two interesting consequences. First, the parties can adopt this ranking only for liberties which are of so fundamental importance to human life-prospects that their loss could not be outweighed by any compensatory allotment of other social primary goods (opportunities, income and wealth, powers and authority, and leisure time). Hence the First Principle only protects certain *basic* liberties. The second consequence derives from a unique formal feature of these liberties: Any liberty that can be guaranteed to more than one person can, without being weakened, also be guaranteed to all.[3] It follows that the parties, reasoning from the maximin rule, would allow no representative group to enjoy either more, or less, than the most extensive package of basic liberties compatible with a like package for all: The former would abridge the liberties of all others, and the latter would make the group in question worse off than any group need be. Hence the First Principle postulates *equal* basic liberties:

2. There are, even in Rawls' own work, many imprecise formulations to the effect that the least advantaged must be as well off as they possibly could be. This demand makes no sense, as it is presumably always possible to make the least advantaged better off. In a perfectly just society this could however only be done in ways which would lead to a new least advantaged group that is worse off than the old one was. So the general requirement is that social institutions be arranged so as to offer the best possible minimal life-prospects.

3. The political liberties constitute an exception here which will be discussed in section V. — I call this feature "formal", because the premise need not in fact be true in non-ideal contexts, and the conclusion is hence asserted only in ideal theory. For example: The right of others to physical security does not abridge my right to the same. Yet the more others are guaranteed physical security, the less protection I am likely to receive, so that, in non-ideal contexts, a violation of my right will become more likely. — Rawls' remark that "the question of compensating for a lesser than equal liberty does not arise" (TJ 204) must then be construed as restricted to ideal theory (cf. case (b) below).

> Each person is to have an equal right to the most extensive total system of equal basic liberties compatible with a similar system of liberty for all (TJ 250,302).

In clarifying the force of this demand, we must keep distinct the two functions of the First Principle: It plays a role in describing a social ideal, and it sets priorities regarding the social changes to be initiated in non-ideal contexts (cp. TJ 245f). Let me briefly address these two functions in turn.

In ideal theory, the adjective "extensive" must be understood as operating *within* the already identified package of *basic* liberties. Otherwise one could argue that the package could be made more extensive by adding further freedoms which would undermine the Second Principle (regulating social and economic inequalities) and hence the plausibility of Rawls' priority ranking:

> It is essential to observe that these liberties are given by a list of liberties: [...] the hypothesis is that the general form of such a list could be devised with sufficient exactness to sustain this conception of justice. Of course, liberties not on this list, for example the right to own certain kinds of property (e.g. means of production), and freedom of contract as understood by the doctrine of laissez-faire are not basic: and so they are not protected by the priority of the first principle (KCE 96).

Moreover, at least the political liberties must be understood as having certain intrinsic limits, so as to forestall the demand that they should be made more extensive by allowing the political process to overrule the Second Principle. The basic liberties are then from the outset so construed that their exercise cannot conflict with the Second Principle. And so the lexical priority of the basic liberties is irrelevant to ideal theory where both principles are fully satisfied. Yet it is of crucial importance in non-ideal contexts on which I shall comment next.

Here Rawls distinguishes two cases: "(a) a less extensive liberty must strengthen the total system of liberty shared by all" (TJ 302), i.e. under difficult circumstances — when the exercise and enjoyment of the full basic liberties, though formally guaranteed to all, is in jeopardy — some guarantees may temporarily be suspended. Such a measure is permissible, if it makes the remaining basic liberties more secure, thereby enhancing citizens' overall enjoyment of their basic liberties (TJ 212f, 229f, 246ff), or if it holds out the credible prospect of attaining, in due course, the secure enjoyment of the complete package (TJ 152,220,542). — "(b) a less than equal liberty must be acceptable to those with the lesser liberty" (TJ 302). Given the point made in the second footnote, this cannot mean that there must be no way of making the basic liberties of "those with the lesser liberty" more extensive or secure[4]. Rather it must mean that any way of doing so would result in some group (the same *or another one*) ending up in an even more unfortunate position with respect to basic liberties. And systematically, of course, Rawls argues exactly in this vein: The freedom of the intolerant may be restricted not only when *their* basic liberties are thus better secured, but also

> when the tolerant sincerely and with good reason believe that their own security and that of the institutions of liberty are in danger. [...] The leading principle is to establish a just constitution with the liberties of equal citizenship (TJ 220).

II: THE APPROPRIATE NOTION OF A BASIC LIBERTY

Once this general structure of Rawls' proposal is understood, our original problem reduces to the question of what liberties the parties would single out for special protection. In what follows, I shall try not only to answer this question, but also to indicate what political consequences this answer would have under present general circumstances. For this latter purpose of illustration, I shall assume that the First Principle must, in *our* world, ultimately be interpreted as global in scope. I cannot argue for this point here, but the main reasons are, briefly, Rawls' insistence on the primacy of background justice (see BSS) in conjunction with the fact of extensive global interdependence; and Rawls' conception of the person which militates against permitting life-prospects at birth to diverge dramatically from country to country so that today a large majority of humankind is abandoned to hunger, disease, and oppression — congenitally excluded from decisions concerning the use of our natural environment or otherwise profoundly affecting our collective future. All things considered, Rawls' conception will support, I believe, not a world republic, but a model akin to Kant's confederation of nations under common laws.

Candidates for inclusion among the basic liberties can be arranged and categorized in a variety of relevant or irrelevant ways, some of

---

4. Although Rawls once says just that: "the freedom of those with the lesser liberty must be better secured" (TJ 244).

which I shall discuss at the outset. A first relevant factor is the dimension of abstractness: Since the Rawlsian conception of justice operates at or above the constitutional level (cf. TJ 31), the basic liberties must be formulated in a suitably abstract way so as to avoid presupposing particular institutional arrangements. Looking at the problem of background justice from the vantage point of individual citizens, we are not yet concerned with endorsing particular institutions, but rather with specifying general features of them which citizens would find indispensable. To the extent that various possible schemes are functionally equivalent in offering a roughly equal prospect of exhibiting these features, the choice between them should be a *political* one, i.e. be left to the legislative stage. This is important, because, as far as possible, we want to avoid forcing other cultures or future societies into the Procrustean bed of our present prejudices and lack of imagination. Or, in terms of the original position: the parties want to insure themselves against abuses without, as far as possible, undermining the political autonomy of the communities to which they belong. The package of basic liberties developed within the framework of Justice as Fairness will then be formulated in more abstract language than present day constitutions and international declarations. Here one must carefully distinguish between the content of a particular liberty and examples of what it demands within given institutional settings. Thus, the "right to a nationality" or the equal protection of children "whether born in or out of wedlock" (UDHR 15.1, 25.2) may be meaningless or irrelevant in a setting in which the institutions of nations and mariage play a different role or none at all.

A second relevant factor is the formal/material dimension. The parties will not be content to demand formal guarantees to be incorporated into the constitution or legislation (in that respect, most states today have a very good record). Their decisive yardstick in evaluating a (model for the) basic structure will rather be the extent to which such guarantees are actually enjoyed: Clearly, the parties want the basic structure to discourage violations, and foster the free exercise, of basic liberties as much as possible[5]. However, this emphasis on the actual enjoyment of liberties does not go all the way. The effective exercise of some liberties may presuppose a certain

5. The criticisms which Hume (EMPL I:443ff) and Marx (e.g. MEW 23:189f) have, in this particular, directed against Locke and the liberalist tradition can thus be avoided by the Rawlsian conception.

educational background, financial resources, or leisure time which it would be unreasonable to subsume under the First Principle. Thus, society need not underwrite the cost of travel (under freedom of movement), of gatherings (under freedom of association) or of publications (under freedom of the media). The means required for effectively exercising these liberties are rather covered by what Rawls calls the *worth* of liberties, which is estimated by the social primary goods falling under, and hence is regulated by, the Second Principle (cf. TJ 204f). As we shall see, Rawls excepts the political liberties here, the fair value of which must also be protected by the First Principle: likewise, I believe, the rule of law must call for an institutional embodiment which ensures that even the poorest and least educated citizens have fair access to the judiciary (cf. p. 139 below).

A third relevant factor concerns the question of what are to count as violations of liberties. Here the parties will e.g. not single out infringments by the official authorities, but rather be concerned to minimize *all* abuse which may seriously endanger their life-prospects. In accordance with their maximin strategy, their reluctance to risk execution or torture pertains to death-squads as much as to governmental security forces, they are as averse to forced labor imposed by a dictator as to slavery and serfdom. Thus starvation, malnutrition, and many eradicable diseases common in the Third World today may constitute violations of basic liberties, as do deaths, injuries, and health-problems which are due to the lack of effective handgun legislation, or caused by products, equipment, or jobs which are unsafe as a consequence of intention or negligence.

The most common traditional categorization of liberties will turn out to be irrelevant to the attempt to (show how the parties would) identify liberties as basic and shape them into a coherent package: The distinction between positive (social, economic, and cultural) and negative (civil and political) liberties[6] is a purely conceptual one. The parties, however, will not adopt any antecedent definition or conceptual analysis of the term 'liberty': The First Principle must safeguard the most fundamental components of a person's life-prospects, regardless of whether these components can be expressed so

---

6. The political liberties, though intrinsically "positive", often — by sleight of hand — end up in the "good" pile of the Western theorist's classification.

as to fit any particular analysis or account of this concept. The parties want to develop a criterion for minimally adequate life-prospects — guarantees which everybody must securely possess if talk about the dignity of every human being is not to remain a mockery — and in this endeavor they pay attention not to the type, but to the severity of various threats, in relation to the cost of preventing or mitigating them. The Rawlsian concern for the least advantaged undercuts then the classical liberalist emphasis on civil and political liberties, because the parties can be presumed to be equally reluctant to risk death from starvation or lack of hygiene as they are to risk being killed through assassination or torture[7]. — Now it could be argued, of course, that a conflict between the parties' demands for the basic civil and political liberties and for elementary subsistence rights would never arise in practice. The parties run no risk, the argument continues, if they accord lexical priority only to civil and political liberties, because their implementation will not cause any significant social costs which could lead to, or perpetuate, unacceptable socio-economic conditions. Yet, however plausible the parties may find this assumption, they have no reason to take chances by relying on it: they might as well guarantee their most elementary necessities straightway by including them under the First Principle[8].

7. For an example of the classival view, see Berlin (FEL). I agree with much of the recent criticism of this position which, I think, has convincingly shown that the distinction between positive and negative liberties is not as clear-cut (NPF) or morally significant (BR chs. 1 and 2) as had been supposed. Still, I believe that the most convincing and systematic alternative conception of basic liberties (or "human rights") can be developed within the framework of Justice as Fairness. Thus, although I agree with Shue's conclusion that subsistence is as basic a right as physical security, I am not convinced by the structure of his argument, nor do I think that it establishes the same status for the political liberties and freedom of movement as he thinks it does (BR ch. 3).

8. This argument is analogous to one Rawls gives for his claim that the parties would not subordinate their demand for the basic liberties to the principle of utility: the parties, he says, "cannot take chances with their liberty by [...] consent[ing] to the principle of utility. In this case their freedom would be subject to the calculus of social interest and they would be authorizing its restriction if this would lead to a greater net balance of satisfaction. Of course, as we have seen, a utilitarian might try to argue from the general facts of social life that when properly carried out the computation of advantages never justifies such limitations, at least under reasonably favorable

Constructing the package of basic liberties with a view to establishing protections against the most severe threats, irrespective of their kind, would also allow the parties to rescind Rawls' proviso restricting the priority of the First Principle to reasonably favorable conditions (TJ 62f, 151f, 247f, 303, and esp. §82): We could then say that civil and political liberties may be curtailed for the sake of social and economic gains only if the latter are themselves required by the First Principle.

III: THE FUNDAMENTAL VALUES: FREEDOM, EQUALITY, PARTICIPATION

In order to get a first idea of how the parties would spell out the First Principle, we must go back to the two reasons Rawls imputes to them for giving priority to the liberties in the first place: On the one hand — by guaranteeing scope for the widest possible variety of diverse life-plans, "conceptions of the good", or ways of life — the basic liberties minimize the chance that as citizen one will find oneself in a social environment in which one's deepest aspirations meet with hostility and repression (cp. TJ 206ff). This provides reason one for the priority of the First over the Second Principle as mentioned in this quote:

> One reason for this I have discussed in connection with liberty of conscience and freedom of thought. And a second reason is the central place of the primary good of self-respect and the desire of human beings to express their nature in a free social union with others (TJ 543).

The second reason, appealing to the crucial need for self-respect, furnishes two arguments: The equal basic liberties uphold a notion of equal citizenship which can support everyone's self-respect (TJ §82), and they engender a pluralistic society in which most citizens can find or form groups in which to share their interest, goals, or aspirations (TJ 441f, §79). — Let me refer to these two elements, determining the quality of human life-prospects, as Freedom and Respect, choosing the latter term to denote Rawls' *deeper* notion of self-respect (not

---

conditions of culture. But even if the parties were persuaded of this, they might as well guarantee their freedom straightway by adopting the principle of equal liberty" (TJ 207).

The guarantee of civil and political liberties is, of course, also not cost-free: It requires the establishment of institutions and subsystems like parliaments, police, and a judiciary (see again BR ch. 2).

the more superficial one signifying a social primary good the distribution of which, together with that of several others, is to be regulated by the Second Principle — cp. KCMT 526). I shall then base my proposal for a package of basic liberties on those two core-values on which Rawls relies in arguing for the priority of the basic liberties. It is assumed that the parties will, on the one hand, want to secure for themselves the freedom to live as they please, requiring the basic structure to be as unrestrictive as possible for individuals: their desire for Freedom supports the social ideal of Pluralism. — On the other hand, they will want to live in a congenial social environment in which cooperation, friendship, and love are possible, in which people acknowledge, respect, and are sensitive to one another: their desire for Respect supports the social ideal of Community.

We can now take a further step towards clarifying the commitment on which the package of basic liberties is to be based by relating it to the notion of equality. Here we must, with respect to Rawls' conception, distinguish three layers. *Every* contractarian conception accommodates the value of equality in the first, weak sense: The contracting parties are represented as equal, no anterior privileges are recognized. Thus, all historically influential social contract doctrines are incompatible with claims to privilege which are based e.g. on having a religiously important forefather or on belonging to a particular ethnic group[9]. Yet, as Hobbes' and Locke's doctrines illustrate, this underlying equality is still compatible with extreme actual inequalities among the parties to the contract in question (cf. also Rawls' example of a contractarian justification for slavery — TJ 167).

The other two layers are peculiar to Rawls' conception and define equality in the strong sense. The second layer is associated with the maximin rule leading, as we have seen (*pp.* 119 ff.), to a presumption in favor of actual equality which is decisive in the special case of the basic liberties. The third layer of equality is enshrined in Rawls' conception of the person. By introducing Respect, beside Freedom, as the second fundamental component through which to understand

---

9. No doctrine describes a contract in which the blacks, for instance, recognizing the inherent moral and intellectual superiority of the whites, concede them certain permanent privileges. To the extent that groups were viewed as naturally inferior (blacks, women, laborers, etc.), they were simply not pictured as being party to the contract.

human aspirations, Rawls originates a further tendency towards equality. This tendency, on the one hand, reinforces the case for *equal* basic liberties, because unequal citizenship (or even slavery and serfdom) is a sure way of undermining mutual and self-respect within a community. Thus, even if inequalities in the distribution of basic liberties could be instituted so as to enhance everyone's liberty, even if, that is, such privileges could be justified by recourse to the core-value of Freedom, they would most likely still be unjust because of their effects on the life-prospects of the underprivileged in terms of Respect[10]. On the other hand — beyond supporting the demand for equal basic liberties, whatever rights these may secure — the core-value of Respect will also play a major role in determining what rights should be secured in the first place, or how the notion of equality is to be conceived. To illustrate: If Freedom were the only core-value, a strong case could be made for including, among the basic liberties, a right to conduct business with whomsoever one chooses, as an equal right for all. This case will now, however, be undermined by the consideration that arbitrary discrimination will tend to be destructive of the core-value of Respect: It will now seem that e.g. black citizens should have a *right* to be served by shopkeepers, businesspersons, etc., who publicly offer their goods and services[11]. — In what follows. I shall then assume that the social ideal of Community has, besides the rather obvious aspect of Participation, also that of Equality in this sense. I shall interpret the core-value of Respect as implying that the self-realization of human persons requires their ability to *participate* in social interaction on *equal* terms.

The moral kernel of Justice as Fairness can then, at least for the purpose of bringing it to bear on the issue of basic liberties, be expanded to the triad of Freedom. Equality, and Participation. There is of course a wealth of historical examples for such a list of

10. In order to forestall an analogous argument against material ine-
qualities, Rawls writes: "The basis for self-esteem in a just society is not then one's income share but the publicly affirmed distribution of fundamental rights and liberties" (TJ 544).

11. One might turn this illustration around: If Respect were the only core-value, one might make a case for including among the basic liberties the right to attend every private party or religious ceremony. This case is undercut by the core-value of Freedom.

fundamental values, and it does perhaps enhance the clarity of my starting point to contrast it with some of those earlier proclamations in which freedom was always, equality sometimes, and participation never at issue. The American declarations of 1776 postulate freedom as the only one of these three, flanked by life, the acquisition and ownership of property, and the pursuit of happiness and security (collapsing the *Viginia Bill of Rights* and the *Declaration of Independence* into one). These demands belong, according to the systematic hierarchy advocated here, to four different levels: While freedom is part of, and thus on the same level with, the triad here proposed, the pursuit of happiness seems to intend something more general, being roughly equivalent to the parties' striving for optimal life-prospects. The pursuit of happiness requires Freedom — and, I would add, Respect, as the equal chance to participate. The claims to life and security, on the other hand, are more concrete, and thus rather obvious candidates for inclusion in the package of basic liberties which is to be constructed through the triad. Property is again one level more concrete, because it refers to an institution which may be chosen as part of a model which instantiates the basic liberties. We have yet to see whether and how my proposal of three fundamental values would accommodate these more concrete demands.

The French Revolution, both in the *Déclaration des Droits de l'Homme et du Citoyen* and in the constitution of 1793, reiterates the concerns for property and security which are juxtaposed with those for freedom and equality, thus replacing the original popular demand for *fraternité* which — to the extent that it can give orientation for the task of developing a public and enforcable system of basic liberties — I take to be absorbed by the core-value of Respect. The purported "right to resist oppression" involves, I think, a category mistake (like a law to uphold laws), as oppression *already* violates fundamental values[12].

Kant proposes a triad of freedom, equality and independence (GTP 290ff, MSR 314f) in which, as in the American and French cases, equality has the weak sense discussed above:

> equality of persons as subjects of a state is quite consistent with the greatest inequality in the quantity and degree of their possessions,

12. This thought seems to be operative in the Declaration of Rights of 1793 which lays down (Article 33) that the right to "resistance to oppression is the consequence of all other rights of man".

whether these be [...] external gifts of fortune or simply rights (of which there can be many) with respect to others. [...] And yet, as subjects all of them are equal before the law (GTP 292)

In order to be independent, one is required "to be *his own master* (sui iuris): that he own some sort of property — among which may be counted any skill, craft, fine art or science that supports him" (GTP 295). This demand for independence of citizens is a very reasonable one, except for the fact that Kant, in blatant disanalogy to his discussion of freedom and equality, does not address it so social institutions but to the individuals themselves: If they are not independent, they cannot be citizens, says Kant, and thereby he excludes all women, and all workers from the hairdresser on down. As a demand on institutions, a certain independence is, as we shall see, supported by, and hence reducible to, the core-values of Freedom and Respect.

IV: THE PRELIMINARY LIST OF LIBERTIES

Even if the contrast with these historical examples may serve to make the proposed triad somewhat more persuasive, it will ultimately stand or fall with its capacity to generate a plausible unified package of basic liberties. This task of using the triad in a heuristic way may best be approached through a procedure which first identifies the paradigmatic threat to each of the fundamental values (F, P, E): The basic liberties must protect persons against these threats as far as possible. To these *fundamental* basic liberties we can then add those which, although not absolutely required by any of the fundamental values, are strongly supported by the core-value of Freedom and by at least one aspect of Respect. This will add another three categories of basic liberties (FPE, FP, and FE).

In developing these six categories one must keep in mind that liberties can guarantee protection only against threats which can be averted or mitigated by social institutions. Let me also emphasize that liberties, to count as basic, must protect against *vital* threats or receive *strong* support, because the parties will want to be reasonably certain that the liberties they selct would maximally benefit the least advantaged under virtually any circumstances: They will try to avoid the inclusion of liberties which might undermine or erode other, more vital ones. (To illustrate: the inclusion of *any* liberty will have costs by restricting political decision-making and thus reducing the extent of the political liberties.) Finally, the constraints of unity and consistency must also be accommodated: A basic liberty must be compatible with the fundamental value(s) which it is not directly based upon: and it must be generalizable and consistent with all other basic liberties so as to minimize the possibilities of conflict in which somebody's basic liberties *must* be sacrificed. — The six categories of basic liberties will then look roughly as follows.[12b]

(F) In the case of Freedom, the threat is mainly one to a person's bodily and mental *integrity*. Persons lose their Freedom when they are subjected to torture or forced labor, are afflicted with starvation or serious disease, suffer confinement or major violations of their home and privacy, or undergo any other forms of severe physical or psychological violence or duress. Now, evidently, social institutions cannot guarantee a right to life and health. What they can underwrite is the right not to be murdered, maimed, tortured, assaulted, enslaved, coerced; not to be abandoned to relievable hunger and malnutrition, hazardous natural or climatic conditions, or eradicable or curable disease; not to be needlessly deprived of one's personal effects, or compromized in one's privacy; not to be severely humiliated, degraded, abused; and not to be threatened with any of these evils.

(P) The standard threat to Participation is isolation or, more generally, *exclusion* from social interaction, culture, education, health-care. To isolate the really basic component of the right to Participation, it helps to focus on those aspects which can never reasonably be abridged, even in cases of convicted criminals and those with dangerous mantal defects or contagious diseases. Even these persons must be allowed to engage in correspondence, receive visitors (subject to appropriate precautions), communicate with wardens and fellow-inmates, read books, and follow events on the outside; they must also be given some access to health-care and education.

(E) The paradigmatic threat to equality is arbitrary *discrimination*, resulting in unequal access to offices and positions, social benefits, goods and services, and natural resources. Constitutional protections against arbitrary discrimination must however be restricted to the public realm where the loss of Freedom of those who would otherwise disciminate is clearly less vital than the alternative loss of

12b. The content of each category is here treated very briefly, and mostly for illustrative purposes, as each of them will ultimately require a much more elaborate discussion.

Respect due to discrimination. In the private realm, where this is not clearly the case, people must be left free (certainly by the First Principle) to seek or decline friendship and other relations as they see fit. The distinction between the public and the private realms should not cause any major difficulties: Apart from executive, legislature and judiciary, the former comprises economic transaction, the educational and healthcare systems, and recognized associations. This would rule out arbritrary discrimination within e.g. political parites, schools and universities (public and private), hospitals, and news-media, with respect to both their internal organization (officers, staff, etc.) and their dealings with outsiders (availability, admission, etc.). — The issue of when discrimination is arbitrary should likewise be clear enough. Even if there are no features of persons which *always* constitute arbitrary grounds (think of mannequins, actors, or team-athletes to disqualify race and sex), it is generally not difficult to determine what features would constitute arbitrary grounds for discrimination in a particular case.

(FPE) The political liberties are an important expression of Freedom by securing people's right to live under rules of their own making (autonomy), to shape the political conditions which shape their lives. They are regulated by the fundamental principle of *democratic self-determination* which has two components. The first is a demand for political equality, as paradigmatically reflected in the equal right to vote — on political issues and/or for candidates for political office. This demand is supported by both *Rawlsian* layers of Equality discussed above (*pp. 128f*): The maximin rule favors strict equality, because the chance to shape political decisions is a zero-sum good in that the greater political weight of some must entail a lesser share for others. The conception of the person also favors equality, especially if we view people as arguing and voting for what they believe is right, rather than for what they prefer (cp. TJ 357, 230f): Unequal political liberties symbolize unequal moral competence and thus create a psychological climate of disrespect which, in conjunction with the real lack of political influence, constitutes a particularly vicious and intolerable disadvantage. Laws enacted by the political process are then protected by the political liberties only if they are adopted in a democratic fashion. — In addition, such laws must meet two provisos: They must not impose unacceptable hardships (by abridging any basic liberties); and they must not discriminate against the least advantaged (i.e. must satisfy the Second Principle). These two provisos are required by the maximin rule: The parties will not authorize institutions which permit human sacrifices or torture, say, even if supported by a majority, because the victims of such practices would clearly be (among) the least advantaged whose collective position would then be much worse than necessary. And they will permit socio-cultural conditions to be imposed or maintained only if any burdens arising from them are distributed so that the least advantaged could rationally agree to them. In this way the political process is subordinate to the constitution in which the parties specify, and require institutional protections for, the two principles.

The domain of the political process has however also *internal* boundaries correlative to the demand that people's right to exert political influence be confined to those political decisions by which they are affected. This demand constitutes the second component of the principle of democratic self-determination, which is more closely associated with the value of Participation: As far as possible, political decision-making should be decentralized so as to allow persons a meaningful, responsible role within a surveyable process involving others familiar with the social context which their dicisions will be affecting. The second component both entails and constrains the liberties regulating the formation of communities smaller than humankind. and thus, in particular, places upper and lower bounds on the extent of sovereignty which national communities may claim, as well as on the autonomy of different kinds of associations. A global legislature would therefore only be authorized to make decisions of global significance (in general including those of transnational significance where appropriate regional institutions are lacking). Other issues must be left to national and local communities which will therefore — insofar as these matters qualify as political at all — have a rather free hand in organizing education, health-care, and their domestic economy; in stipulating traffic regulations, opening hours, holidays, etc.; and in detailing the responsibilities arising from marriage, child-birth, contracts, and so forth. Here it is obviously not always evident on which level a particular issue ought to be decided; the general principle should however be clear enough so that particular conflicts can be settled by the judiciary. — Now the private sphere, at the bottom of this hierarchy of (de-) centralization, can be pictured as separated by either an external or an internal boundary. On the former picture, a group would be capable of *political* decisions only if it has a certain, quite arbitrary, minimum size. On the latter, the term "political" would, against common usage, be stretched to the limit of individual decisions. Both terminologies are thus somewhat imperfect; yet the latter is the systematically appropriate one, since it emphasizes that the principle of self-determination reaches all the way down: A law prohibiting homosexual relations between consenting adults is unjust not because a non-political matter has been usurped by a political body, but because a decision has been made on too high a level. i.e. by people not legitimately concerned. (This is also, I think, the most elegant way of accommodating Mill's classic argument in *On Liberty* — ULR 131-149.)

(FP) Freedom of thought and liberty of conscience (cp. TJ §§33-35), as well as the freedoms of association, speech, and the media, are supported by the fundamental value of Participation in that they guarantee the opportunity to take part — implicitly (through example) or explicitly — in the exchange of ideas and information and in the collective life of a variety of communities at all levels. They are likewise grounded in Freedom, because they guarantee the rights to hold, practice. and advocate religious, moral, and political beliefs and convictions. as well as to assemble in peace and to create. join, shape, change. leave, or dissolve political, religious. regional. or cultural associations. These rights need not be protected. however, if and to the extent that their exercise would violate or endanger the basic liberties of others, either directly or through a general disruption of public order and security.

(FE) What is commonly referred to as the rule of law (cp. TJ §38) enhances people's Freedom by protecting them from (the fear of) arbitrary treatment. This is achieved if a body of rules (standardly a constitution and legislation), and its application (ultimately by the judiciary), generate a legal framework comprehensive. precise. and intelligible enough so as to allow the formation of stable and secure expectations. This demand implies that persons be equal before the law: the same general rules must be applied to them in an identical manner (establishing commitments to due process and the force of precedent)[13]. The rule of law embodies Equality also through the

13. This is perfectly compatible with the laws' themselves being grossly inequitable. by unjustly according differential treatment to e.g. the high-and the low-born, the faithful and the pagans, men and women. Such inequities do not violate the rule of law, but are rather excluded by the protection against arbitrary discrimination.

demand that all people must actually (not only formally) have access to the judiciary. — On a global interpretation, the main responsibility of the international judiciary — although it would also be charged with safeguarding the (specified) Second Principle and any global legislation — would lie in the area of the First Principle, issuing in an International Bill of Human Rights which would form the center-piece of international law. If this Bill is to be effentive in protecting the basic liberties, the following six features are essential:

(1) The Bill is to be *legally* (rather than only morally) binding on all national governments.

(2) Alleged infractions are, once domestic legal remedies have been exhausted, tried and judged before *international* courts, i.e. the legal obligation is one "in foro externo".

(3) The rights enumerated in the Bill are *absolute*, and thus protect not only foreign nationals, but equally shield persons against their own national institutions.

(4) Individuals are *subjects*, rather than objects, of (rights under) international law, i.e. they enjoy full procedural capacities (a legal personality or locus standi) before international courts.

(5) Not only states, but also *state officials* can be held accountable under international law.

(6) Judgments passed by international courts are *enforcable* against national governments — by coercive sanctions, if necessary[14].

14. This sketch is indebted to Lauterpacht (ILHR). The six features do not imply that international courts function as a last recourse for all domestic litigation. They need not be authorized to enforce national or regional legislation by reviewing the verdicts of com-petent courts — except insofar as such legislation (as construed and enforced by the judiciary) might be found to violate international law, in which case it would be declared void ab initio by an international court. (This model resembles that in the U.S. where the state judiciaries are supreme in the interpretation of state legislation — the federal judiciary can annul, but does not supervise the application of, state law.) The annulment of a national law by reference to the International Bill of Human Rights might come about in two ways: An international court might be confronted with a legal case in which a person's basic liberties were violated by enforcement of the law in question. Or it may hear a general complaint charging that the law was not properly enacted (thus violating the political liberties of the citizenry) or that it e.g. unduly discriminates against segments of the population.

V: THE PACKAGE OF BASIC RIGHTS AND LIBERTIES

The preliminary list of liberties developed in the last section must now be combined into a consistent package. The parties' perspective, here as always, is defined by their concern for the least advantaged of whom we have an intuitive notion via the conception of the person which is given, in turn, by the two core-values. The parties will therefore attempt to shape the package of basic liberties so as to maximally benefit the least advantaged, both under (A:) ideal and (B:) non-ideal circumstances:

(A)   Under conditions which allow the basic liberties to be fully and equally enjoyed by all, the package should raise the minimum life-prospects as high as possible. In particular, the parties will include an additional liberty only if they are at least reasonably sure that the least advantaged under the wider scheme would in fact be better off than those under the narrower one: Thus. for example, granting any liberty to the more advantaged must not depress the life-prospects of the least advantaged more than granting the same liberty to the least advantaged will improve them.

(B)   When the basic liberties are unequally abridged[15], the package should facilitate a maximally plausible identification of the least advantaged. The parties must redeem the lexical priority of the First over the Second Principle which stipulates that those with a lesser liberty are automatically to count as less advantaged.

The following table illustrates these two desiderata for the simplified case of only two representative groups, each either enjoying or not enjoying a particular liberty. Any other basic liberties are assumed to be equal for both groups in all four cases; the other social primary goods are however variable — being lexically subordinate to the liberty in question. they should not affect the outcome.

Liberty enjoyed by		Life-prospects of	
Group 1	Group 2	Group 1	Group 2
Yes	Yes	A_1	A_2
Yes	No	B_1	B_2
No	Yes	C_1	C_2
No	No	D_1	D_2

15. I neglect here the non-ideal case where the basic liberties are uniformly abridged. because it does not pose any additional problem for shaping the package.

The first desideratum specifies that Amin should be better than Bmin, Cmin, and Dmin. The second one stipulates that B_1 should be preferable to B_2, and C_2 to C_1. Any liberty satisfying the latter desideratum can be expected to satisfy the former one as well.

Both these considerations will support the inclusion of liberties which, by being preconditions for the secure enjoyment of any social primary goods whatever, are of so crucial importance to human life-prospects that the parties can plausibly assume that persons deprived of them should *ipso facto* count as less advantaged than all others. Among these will be those in categories (F), (P), and (E). — Some of the remaining candidates are such that their inclusion is supported by the first, but made problematic by the second desideratum: Granting such liberties to the better off as well does not significantly endanger the life-prospects of the least advantaged; yet, these liberties may not be so crucial that their abridgment would be incommensurably worse than, say, severe poverty. Among this second group will be the liberties of categories (FE) and (FP), excepting freedom of the media. — Neither of our two considerations will, however, support the inclusion of the political liberties and of freedom of the media: Even though the parties may hope that the Second Principle will ideally work to keep economic inequalities fairly small, they cannot just assume that this will be the case. And in a rather inegalitarian society, it is not obvious that freedom of the media (effective use of which may require substantial financial resources) or equal political liberties (without special provisions for the poor) will work in the best interest of the least advantaged. Similarly, the parties would not want to commit themselves to identifying, in non-ideal contexts, the procurement of these liberties, e.g. for the otherwise most advantaged, as the first priority of justice (assuming the other basic liberties to be secure): If, in the U.S. today, millionaires were not allowed to run for public office, this would hardly constitute an infinitely graver injustice than the educational, health, and housing conditions among the very poor (which violate only the Second Principle).

Surely the parties cannot leave all these problems to be solved by the political process, because one doesn't know how the latter should work before they have solved the problem. Moreover, in leaving such questions open, the parties would, on behalf of the least advantaged, be gambling with very high stakes, a practice discouraged by the maximin rule. — There are essentially two solutions. The parties can relegate the political liberties and freedom of the media to the Second

Principle making them commensurable either with the opportunities or with income and wealth, powers and prerogatives, and leisure time. Apart from being rather tedious, this proposal has the major disadvantage of undermining the notion of equal citizenship which the parties hope to support for the sake of the core-value of Respect/Community and for which at least the political liberties are particularly central. Also it does not take care of the rule of law, freedom of thought and speech, and the liberties of association yet to be decided about. — On the other hand, the parties might follow Rawls and, within the First Principle, underwrite an even *more* extensive package which would provide adequate safeguards against political preponderance and impotency arising from social and economic inequalities. Rawls writes that

> there is a maximum gain permitted to the most favored on the assumption that, even if the difference principle would allow it, there would be unjust effects on the political system and the like excluded by the priority of liberty (TJ 81). And:
>
> Historically one of the main defects of constitutional government has been the failure to ensure the fair value of poltical liberty. [...] Disparities in the distribution of property and wealth that far exceed what is compatible with political equality have generally been tolerated oy the legal system (TJ 226).

Thus the parties could affirm the political liberties as basic, if they also include in the First Principle the demand that their *value* be not too unequal due to social and economic inequalities. This demand could be met by restricting such inequalities[16], and to some extent also by fostering the autonomy of the political as against the economic process, which former could e.g. be publicly financed. An analogous solution, demanding that the judiciary be independent from the economic system and accessible to all regardless of their social or economic position, would also allay doubts about including the rule of law. The hope is that the limitation on social and economic inequalities can be defined stringent enough to reassure the parties with respect to all the liberties still pending, yet not so stringent as to undermine the Second Principle by ruling out those

16. For this purpose, the parties could make use of the index (TJ 92ff) taking account of income and wealth, position, and leisure time, as all of these have an important bearing on a person's ability to exert political influence. Within the confines of this paper, I cannot offer my ideas about how the parties might construct that index and define the limitation in terms of it.

moderate inequalities due to incentives which might raise productivity sufficiently to make those least favored by those inequalities
still significantly better off than they would be under perfect equality.

Provisionally accepting the Rawlsian priority rules, the parties
would then be led to adopt a scheme of basic liberties which again
involves a lexical ordering:

(I) freedoms which are fundamental regardless of whether or not
     the limitation on social and economic inequalities is main-
     tained: integrity of the person (F), freedom of participation (P),
     and freedom from arbitrary discrimination (E); and

(II) liberties which, in importance for the least advantaged, are
     commensurable with, and therefore have to be balanced against,
     that limitation: the political liberties (FPE), the liberties of
     association plus liberty of conscience with freedom of thought,
     speech and the media (FP), the rule of law (FE), and the
     limitation on index-inequalities (to be defined along with the
     index itself)[17].

17. The formulation of several of these basic liberties — particularly
those belonging to the first three categories in group (b) — will of course
contain clauses restricting their guarantee to persons of a certain minimum
age, those not mentally disturbed (cp. Rawls on paternalism — TJ 248ff),
and/or those who are not, on the basis of past actions and in accordance
with fair juridical procedures, judged likely unjustly to infringe upon the
life-prospects of others. In general, these restrictions will present no
problem, because the least advantaged under such a scheme will, over a
complete life-time, be better off than the least advantaged under one of
unrestricted liberties. The stronger claim that *everybody* will be better off
fails however in the case of those with permanent mental illnesses or
retardations who constitute a *natural* group of persons *permanently* falling
outside the scope of some basic liberties. There are essentially two ways of
accommodating our treatment of the mentally ill: Either *we* decide not to
represent them in the original position on the grounds that, like animals (cp.
TJ 512), they lack the capacity for a sense of justice (we then assume the
parties to know themselves mentally healthy). Or we argue that *the parties*
would decide that adopting the relevant restrictions is the most rational way
of benefitting the least advantaged, because the mentally ill will constitute
only a small fraction of that representative group for whom the basic
liberties in question would moreover be of rather marginal value. It is
obvious, I trust, that the second solution is much to be preferred from a

VI: COMPARISON WITH INTERNATIONAL DECLARATIONS AND COVENANTS

Now that the main outlines of my proposed specification of Rawls' First Principle have become visible, it makes sense, by way of an appendix, to sketch the political consequences of this suggestion. I shall do so by comparing it to the *Universal Declaration of Human Rights*, which will also, I hope, make it more difficult to contend that the hope for a global realization of the First Principle is unrealistic and utopian, and that we are far from a cross-cultural consensus on basic rights. In response, one can point out that even the present governments of most major states — whatever their actual conduct — do not openly advocate this view, but rather have committed themselves to no less ambitious a catalogue of basic rights and liberties. In substantiating this claim, I shall concentrate on the UDHR, adopted by the U.N. in 1948, as this document (though not legally binding) still has a far more fundamental status than the two covenants of 1966 (in effect since 1976) which have not been ratified by the majority of states. I shall however cite the latter two pacts where they might clarify, or diverge from, the text of the Declaration.

Before discussing specifics, let me emphasize the crucial fact that the UDHR has been intended to be fully global in scope: Neither the ascription of these rights, nor the responsibility for their implementation and maintenance, is in any way limited by national borders. The former point is already epitomized in the very title of the Declaration which insists on its universality and also stresses the intention that certain rights be secured for persons as human beings, not as members of this or that, or any, society. The preamble reiterates that what is at stake are "the equal and inalienable rights of all members of the human family". The United Nations do not, then, view the question of what more fundamental rights persons have as falling within the jurisdiction of individual countries. — Yet, it might still be thought that the responsibility for protecting these rights is located on the national level. The U.N., however, decided otherwise:

> Everyone is entitled to a social *and international* order in which the rights and freedoms set forth in this Declaration can be fully realized (UDHR 28 — my emphasis).

moral point of view, since it enjoins upon us obligations towards the mentally ill which far transcend those which govern our treatment of animals.

Some part of the effort on behalf of human rights must then be undertaken on the global plane so as to create a global basic structure which provides a favorable environment within which individual nations *can* succeed in realizing the postulated rights and liberties. Another part of the effort is assigned to the national level, as is implied by the choice of "can be" instead of "are". Yet, even with respect to problems due to a particular national (rather than the global) basic structure, the responsibility is not a purely domestic one, but rather extends at least throughout the U.N. membership:

> every individual and every organ of society [...] shall strive [...] to promote respect for these rights and freedoms and by progressive measures, national and international, to secure their universal and effective recognition and observance, both among the peoples of Member States themselves and among the peoples of territories under their jurisdiction (UDHR preamble).

Thus, any attack on the idea of globalizing the concern for basic rights and liberties as such, *ipso facto* stands in opposition to the UDHR which has, at least verbally, been taken for granted during the past thirty-odd years.

Now it could still be claimed that the basic liberties proposed here are, by comparison, so extravagant as to allow a complaint against them (as "utopian" or "totalitarian") which would not equally constitute an attack on the UDHR. Instead of supporting the claim of relative extravagance, the examination of the rights and liberties postulated by the U.N. will show extensive overlap between the two proposals, interspersed with a number of interesting differences which may serve to elucidate further the distinctive viewpoint embodied by Justice as Fairness.

The UDHR deals with the liberties of category (F) in articles 3-5, 12, 13, and 25. There are three minor areas of divergence: First, although article 3 guarantees "the right to life, liberty, and the security of the person", CPR 6, while reaffirming the right to life and clearly expressing the hope for its eventual global abolition (esp. CPR 6.6), permits the death penalty "for the most serious crimes". Within Justice as Fairness, by contrast, capital punishment could be justified only in circumstances where fundamental basic liberties could not otherwise be protected, i.e. where confinement would not be a feasible option. — Secondly, though the Declaration forbids "slavery and the slave trade" (UDHR 4), a general prohibition against forced labor is provided only in CPR 8.3a. Forced labor is, however, permitted as a form of punishment imposed by courts (CPR 8.3b) — a provision which the parties would licence only for the truly exceptional case in which its economic benefits would be necessary to avoid or mitigate the abridgment of other fundamental basic liberties (e.g. hunger or malnutrition). CPR 8.3c specifically allows forcible induction into the armed forces (or into an equivalent service mandated for conscientious objectors) — a topic which I cannot deal with here. — Thirdly, the right to privacy is specified to safeguard family, home, and correspondence, and extended to protect also against attacks on a person's honor and reputation (UDHR 12, cp. CPR 17). The parties would not protect the latter under the First Principle, because such attacks do not clearly constitute a graver threat to people's life-prospects than, say, severe poverty, and might thus lead to an implausible identification of the least advantaged. The parties could subsume honor and reputation under the social primary good of self-respect, leaving the details to be worked out by the political process on the assumption that the least advantaged need no special protection in this regard, as their interests are likely to coincide with those of the majority[18]. — Elementary subsistence rights are fully protected by the Declaration:

> Everyone has the right to a standard of living adequate for the health and well-being of himself and his family, including food, clothing, housing and medical care and necessary social services, and the right to security in the event of [...] lack of livelihood in circumstances beyond his control (UDHR 25.1)[19].

The global scope of this right is underscored by ESCR 11.2:

> The States Parties of the present Covenant, recognising the fundamental right of everyone to be free from hunger, shall take, individually and through international co-operation, the measures, including specific

---

18. The same considerations apply, *mutatis mutandis*, to "the right to the protection of the moral and material interest resulting from any scientific, literary or artistic production" (UDHR 27.2).

19. The exclusive use of the male pronoun, in conjunction with the mysterious addition "and of his family", might create the unfortunate impression that women and children are not meant to fall within the scope of the universal quantifier. One should treat this as a simple infelicity, however, given that the Declaration elsewhere emphatically demands equal rights for men and women (UDHR preamble, 2, and 7) and special concern for children (UDHR 25.2).

programmes, which are needed: [...] Taking into account the problems of both food-importing and food-exporting countries, to ensure an equitable distribution of world food supplies in relation to need.

The liberties of category (P) are protected by UDHR 5, 16.1, 20.1, 27.1, 25.1, and 26.1 which, respectively, prohibit cruel and inhuman treatment and guarantee to all the rights to marry and found a family, and to enjoy freedom of association, free participation in the cultural life of their community, as well as minimal health-care and education. In addition, a "right to work" is postulated which, I believe, the parties would also recognize, but rank below the basic liberties.

Although the U.N. instruments emphasize that the rights they stipulate must be extended to all persons without discrimination (UDHR 2; CPR 2.1, 3; ESCR 2.2, 3) and that all must within their country be equally eligible for public office (UDHR 21.2; CPR 25c) and be equal before its laws, they do not fully deal with discrimination in other respects, e.g. in the economy. There are two exceptions: "Everyone, without any discrimination, has the right to equal pay for equal work" (UDHR 23.2). The second, possible exception is CPR 26 which states:

> All persons are equal before the law and are entitled without any discrimination to the equal protection of the law. In this respect, the law shall prohibit any discrimination and guarantee to all persons equal and effective protection against discrimination on any ground.

It is unclear whether, in addition to equality before the law, this article requires that the law should protect persons equally or that it also prohibit discrimination even outside the legal sphere. Unless the latter were the intended meaning, the liberties of category (E) would not be fully protected by the U.N. instruments.

The political liberties are addressed in UDHR 21 (cp. CPR 25). In contrast to the provisions of category (FPE) above, this article allows individuals only to exert political influence over domestic institutions, i.e. does not deal with political decisions of transnational significance. CPR 1.1 and ESCR 1.1 both guarantee to all peoples a right to self-determination without, however, answering the crucial question of how a people is to be identified.

UDHR 18-20, 23.4, and 27 protect, and go beyond, the liberties of category (FP), specifically including the right to communicate information and ideas across borders (UDHR 19).

The rule of the law is safeguarded through UDHR 6-11. So far, little progress has been made, however, towards a supranational juridical system, as members of the U.N. have been very reluctant to cede elements of their sovereignty to this end. Let me comment in turn on the six features postulated above (p. 136)

(1) Although the UDHR imposes a merely moral obligation, it is believed that the "fundamental human rights" repeatedly referred to in the U.N. Charter are legal rights (e.g. ILHR 34). Likewise the ESCR, the CPR, and the ECHR - although acceded to by only a minority of states - involve specific legal obligations.

(2) The ECHR sets a precedent for supranational jurisdiction which will be significantly strengthened once ten states will have consented to submit to the jurisdiction of the U.N. Human Rights Committee under CPR 41.

(3) That rights are due persons as individuals rather than as members of particular states is by now a standard feature of international human rights documents.

(4) The right of individual petition to the U.N. Human Rights Committee is recognized by the signatories of the Optional Protocoll of the CPR. It is likewise guaranteed by ECHR 25.

(5) The Nuremberg trials furnish a precedent for holding also state officials accountable under international law.

(6) Thus far, supranational courts have no means of enforcement at their disposal.

In sum, the United Nations have not only given a mandate for (in UDHR 28), but have also inspired at least a tendency towards, the establishment of a international juridical system protecting at least basic rights and liberties. This tendency has become manifest also on the regional level, most impressively perhaps in the successful functioning of the European Court and Commission of Human Rights (cf. Fawcett in HR 78ff).

No international instrument imposes any limitation on social and economic inequalities for the sake of protecting the fair value of the political liberties. Yet all citizens are to have at least some share in the wealth and economic growth of their society.

> Everyone, as a member of society, [...] is entitled to realization, through national effort and international co-operation and in accordance with the organization and resources of each State, of the economic, social and

cultural rights indispensable for his dignity and the free development of his personality (UDHR 22).

Still, it seems that once these indispensable rights are secure, social and economic inequalities can increase indefinitely without violating the article. It seems, moreover, that inequalities across national borders — and, incidentally, persons without citizenship — are left out of account, as the right in question is, in a unique deviation from the Declaration's title, postulated only for people as "members of society": Other nations are not required to make an effort, but need only cooperate, presumably by allowing free trade on whatever terms the market will bear. — Whether or not UDHR 22 was meant to be read in this narrow way, both restrictions are clearly absent in ESCR 11 and 12:

> The States Parties to the present Convention recognise the right of everyone [...]
> to the continuous improvement of living conditions [...]
> to the enjoyment of the highest possible standard of physical and mental health.

Although these articles are not motivated by the concerns which would lead the parties to limit social and economic inequalities, they have a similar effect and are certainly no less ambitious.

The main provisions have now been categorized and, at least briefly, discussed, leaving out only those few which presuppose the existence of certain social institutions: nations (UDHR 14,15), the family (UDHR 16.2 16.3), and property (UDHR 17)[20]. The result, on the whole, is quite encouraging, as the differences we found were rather insignificant when viewed against a proposal on which the global basic structure would be constrained merely by the familiar principles of the law of nations (cp. LN): However small the real progress achieved (if any), our aspirations for global justice have become very much more ambitious in the period after the Second World War. — With respect to the basic liberties absolute in character (categories (F), (P), (FP)), the differences are minor: Under modern conditions, Justice as Fairness would mandate the abolition of capital punishment, forced prison labor, and, probably, conscription. With respect to the remaining basic liberties, the differences are somewhat more

---

20. The latter two provisions are also objected to, on similar grounds, by Lauterpacht (ILHR 342n39).

substantial. Here, on my global interpretation, Justice as Fairness would raise two major additional demands:

— Global social and economic inequalities must be limited so that children, wherever they may be born, have a reasonable prospect of becoming respected members of the world-community with a stake and a say in its future.

— International juridical and political institutions (both global and regional) must be strengthened and democratized to the point where they will effectively protect the rights, and represent the will, of all people within their scope.

Acknowledging these two additional goals is particularly important, because they seem crucial for the attempt finally to bridge the enormous gap between political reality and the aspirations enshrined in the U.N. documents: If, over time, we could bring states under the rule of law, and better enable the world's marginal persons and peoples to fend for themselves, the high hopes of the post-war years may yet be realized.

AMARTYA SEN

WELFARE INEQUALITIES AND RAWLSIAN AXIOMATICS *

ABSTRACT. This paper is concerned with ordinal comparisons of welfare inequality and its use in social welfare judgements, especially in the context of Rawls' 'difference principle'. In Section 1 the concept of ordinal inequality comparisons is developed and a theorem on ordinal comparisons of welfare inequality for distributional problems is noted. Section 2 is devoted to Harsanyi's (1955) argument that a concern for reducing welfare inequalities among persons must not enter social welfare judgements. In Section 3 an axiomatic derivation of Rawls' lexicographic maximim rule is presented; this relates closely to results established by Hammond (1975), d'Aspremont and Gevers (1975) and Strasnick (1975). In the last section the axioms used are examined and some alternative axioms are analysed with the aim of a discriminating evaluation of the Rawlsian approach to judgements on social welfare.

1. ORDINAL EQUALITY PREFERENCE

Usual measures of economic inequality concentrate on income, but frequently one's interest may lie in the inequality of welfare rather than of income as such.[1] The correspondence between income inequality and welfare inequality is weakened by two distinct problems: (i) welfare — even in so far as it relates to economic matters — depends not merely on income but also on other variables, and (ii) even if welfare depends on income alone, since it is not likely to be a linear function of it, the usual measures of inequality of income will differ from that of welfare. The first problem incorporates not merely the basic difficulties of interpersonal comparison of welfare, but also those arising from differences in non-income circumstances, e.g., age, the state of one's health, the pattern of love, friendship, concern and hatred surrounding a person. The second reflects the fact that the usual measures, such as the coefficient of variation, or the standard deviation of logarithm, or the Gini coefficient, or the inter-decile ratio, will not be preserved under a strictly concave transformation of income as the welfare function is typically assumed to be, when it is taken to be cardinally measurable. And when welfare is measurable only ordinally, then the usual measures of inequality are not even defined.

There is an obvious need for investigating inequality contrasts when welfare comparisons are purely ordinal. There is likely to be much greater agreement on the *ordering* of welfare levels of different persons than on a particular

Theory and Decision 7 (1976) 243–262. *All Rights Reserved*
Copyright © 1976 by D. Reidel Publishing Company, Dordrecht-Holland

85

numerical interpersonal welfare function unique up to a positive linear transformation. However, the meaning of more or less inequality is not altogether clear when comparisons of welfare levels are purely ordinal.

There are, nevertheless, some unambiguous cases. Let (x, i) stand for the position of being person i in social state x. Taking two persons 1 and 2 and two states x and y, consider the following strict descending orders:

1	2	3	4
$(y, 2)$	$(y, 1)$	$(y, 2)$	$(y, 1)$
$(x, 2)$	$(x, 1)$	$(x, 1)$	$(x, 2)$
$(x, 1)$	$(x, 2)$	$(x, 2)$	$(x, 1)$
$(y, 1)$	$(y, 2)$	$(y, 1)$	$(y, 2)$

Note that irrespective of the relative values of the 'differences', in each case y displays more inequality than x in an obvious sense. This type of comparison will be referred to as 'ordinal inequality comparison'.[2]

To formalize this criterion, let $\widetilde{R}$ stand for an agreed 'extended ordering'[3] over the Cartesian product of X (the set of social states) and H (the set of individuals), i.e., over pairs of the form (x, i). The meaning of $(x, i) \widetilde{R} (y, j)$ is that i is at least as well off in x as is j in y. $\widetilde{P}$ and $\widetilde{I}$ stand for the corresponding concepts of 'strictly better' and 'indifference'. Let ρ stand for any one-to-one correspondence between the pair of persons to itself.

Two-person ordinal inequality criterion (TOIC): For any pair of social states x, y, for a two-person community, if there is a one-to-one correspondence ρ from the pair of persons (i, j) to the same pair such that:

$$(y, i) \widetilde{P} (x, \rho(i)), \quad (x, \rho(i)) \widetilde{R} (x, \rho(j)), \quad (x, \rho(j)) \widetilde{P} (y, j),$$

then x has less ordinal inequality than y, denoted $x \, \theta \, y$.[4]

The criterion can be extended to n-person communities also, by requiring the additional antecedent that all persons other than these two are equally well off under x and y. This implies an assumption of 'separability', which is however more debatable, and will be debated (see Section 4).

Strengthened two-person ordinal inequality criterion (STOIC): If for any n-person community with $n \geqslant 2$, for any two persons i and j, and any two social states x and y for some ρ: $(y, i) \widetilde{P} (x, \rho(i))$, $(x, \rho(i)) \widetilde{R} (x, \rho(j))$, $(x, \rho(j)) \widetilde{P} (y, j)$, and for all $k \neq i, j$: $(x, k) \widetilde{I} (y, k)$, then x has less ordinal inequality than y, denoted $x \, \theta^* \, y$. The transitive closure of θ^* is θ^{**}.

Of course, for a two person community $\theta = \theta^*$, and STOIC implies TOIC in this sense.

Note that no condition of constancy of total welfare has been used in the definitions, and indeed no such concept is definable given utility comparisons that are purely ordinal. It is, however, possible to use these definitions in the particular context of ranking alternative distributions of a fixed total income. Indeed, for that particular problem of 'pure distribution', ordinal inequality comparisons can be linked with some well-known results in the normative approach to inequality measurement based on Lorenz curve comparisons (see Kolm, 1966; Atkinson, 1970; Dasgupta *et al.*, 1973; Rothschild and Stiglitz, 1973). Our motivation here differs, however, from those exercises in the sense that our current concern is to look at welfare inequalities as such without necessarily saying anything about social welfare by invoking some group welfare function, and this contrasts with comparing values of social welfare given by a group welfare function, or a class of such functions.

Let the ranking relation λ stand for strict 'Lorenz domination', i.e., $x \lambda y$ if and only if the Lorenz curve of x is nowhere below that of y and somewhere strictly above it.

(T.1)   In the 'pure distribution' problem with welfare rankings preserving the order of income rankings, if $x \lambda y$, then $x \theta^{**} y$.

The proof follows immediately from a well-known result of Hardy, Littlewood and Polya (1934), which in this context implies that $x \lambda y$ holds if and only if x can be obtained from some inter-personal permutation y^0 of y through a finite sequence of transfer operations with income being transferred from a richer person to a poorer one without reversing their income ranking.[5] Since in each of these operations taking us from x^s to x^{s+1}, the incomes of others except the two involved (say, $1(s)$ and $2(s)$ respectively) in that operation remain the same, and since more income implies higher welfare, clearly:

$$(x^s, 1(s)) \, \widetilde{P} \, (x^{s+1}, 1(s)), (x^{s+1}, 1(s)) \, \widetilde{R} \, (x^{s+1}, 2(s)), (x^{s+1}, 2(s)) \, \widetilde{P} \, (x^s, 2(s)).$$

Thus $x^{s+1} \, \theta^* \, x^s$. Since x and y^0 are the two extreme members of this sequence, and by virtue of STOIC it makes no difference whether we start from y^0 or from y, clearly $x \, \theta^{**} \, y$.

Notice that (T.1) provides a welfare basis for comparisons of inequality which is not dependent on taking 'more social welfare' to be 'less unequal', and in this sense departs from the normative approach of Kolm (1966), Atkinson (1970) and others. Indeed, nothing is said about social welfare as such, and this welfare interpretation of inequality simply looks at the inequality of the welfare distribution (in ordinal terms).

Note also that no assumption of concavity (or quasi-concavity, or S-concavity) of welfare functions is required in establishing (T. 1) in contrast with the earlier results on Lorenz comparisons referred to above, e.g., Kolm (1966), Atkinson (1970), Dasgupta *et al.* (1973), Rothschild and Stiglitz (1973).

It is, however, possible to introduce the additional assumption that less welfare-inequality is socially preferred, or at least regarded to be as good. Let R stand for the weak relation of social preference, with P and I its asymmetric and symetric parts: 'strict preference' and 'indifference' respectively.

Two-person equality preference (TEP): In a 2-person community for any x, y, if $x \, \theta \, y$, then $x \, R \, y$.

Strengthened two-person equality preference (STEP): In any community, for any x, y, if $x \, \theta^* \, y$, then $x \, R \, y$.[6]

Again, STEP obviously implies TEP. Note, however, that STEP has been defined in terms of θ^* and not θ^{**}. Of course, if R is transitive, then the two are equivalent.

How appealing a condition is STEP? That would seem to depend on three types of considerations. The first applies to STEP only, while the last two apply to both STEP and TEP.

(1) STEP involves a 'separability' assumption being based on θ^* (rather than θ in a 2-person community). A reduction of ordinal inequality between two persons is rather more definitive for a community of those two persons than for a community where there are others also, even though they are equally well off under x and y.[7] In Section 4 we shall examine the far-reaching consequences of this extension from a 2-person to a n-person comparison in the presence of other conditions, e.g., 'independence of irrelevant alternatives'.

(2) TEP and STEP both give overriding importance to the reduction of welfare inequality without bringing in any consideration of relative gains and losses of different persons.[8] How disturbing this criticism is will depend partly on the 'informational basis' of welfare comparisons, i.e., on the mea-

surability and interpersonal comparability assumptions.[9] If individual welfare is not cardinal, or if interpersonal comparisons must be ordinal only (whether or not individual welfares are cardinal), then clearly the concept of 'gains' and 'losses' in welfare lose meaning. If, however, cardinal interpersonal comparisons can be made, then one can consider a choice in which x involves less ordinal inequality than y, but the loss of person 2 is so much and the gain of person 1 is so little, that a reasonable case can be made for the choice of y. With 'full comparability' this conflict of ethics (e.g., *vis-à-vis* utilitarianism) must be faced, but with 'level comparability' only, this objection to STEP or TEP cannot be sustained.[10]

(3) The approach of STEP or TEP shares with utilitarianism and other needs-based ethics, a disregard of the concept of desert (see Sen, 1973, Chapter 4 on the contrast between need-based and desert-based approaches). Arguments such as 'person i is better off than j both in x and in y and gains less than j loses, but the additional gain is his just desert', are not entertainable in this approach.[11]

2. HARSANYI'S CRITICISM OF CONCERN FOR WELFARE INEQUALITY

In the context of social evaluation taking note of welfare inequalities, we should consider an objection of John Harsanyi (1975) to attempts at using social welfare functions that are non-linear on individual welfares. We know, of course, that with some assumptions of interpersonal comparability (e.g., 'unit comparability'), individual welfare levels cannot be interpersonally compared even though gains and losses can be compared (see Sen, 1970, Chapter 7). Harsanyi's attack is, however, not based on any subtlety of the comparability assumption.[12] It takes mainly the form of quoting his justly celebrated result that if individual preferences and social preference can both be given von Neumann-Morgenstern cardinal representation, and if Pareto indifference must imply social indifference, then social welfare must be a *linear combination* of individual welfares (Harsanyi, 1955), and then of defending the acceptability of the von Neumann-Morgenstern axioms. Harsanyi thus sees social welfare simply as an average welfare (unweighted if a further assumption of symmetry is made), and there is no question of reflecting a concern for welfare equality in the value of social welfare by choosing a non-linear form.

The first question to ask is whether the von Neumann-Morgenstern axioms are acceptable, especially for social choice. Diamond (1967) raised this question effectively, especially questioning the use of the strong independence axiom. Harsanyi (1975) has analysed the issue (pp. 315–8), but seems to me to take little account of Diamond's main concern, viz, that our assessment of alternative policies from an *ethical* point of view, which is what Harsanyi means by 'social preference', may not depend only on the *outcomes* but also on the fairness in the *process* of interpersonal allocation. Harsanyi may well be right in claiming that "when we act on behalf of other people, let alone when we act on behalf of society as a whole, we are under an obligation to follow, if anything *higher* standards of rationality than when we are dealing with our own private affairs" (Harsanyi, 1975, p. 316), but the bone of contention surely is *whether* the strong independence axiom represents a 'higher' standard of rationality in the social context than a rule that takes note of the allocational *process*.

The strong independence axiom is, of course, not the only axiom of the von Neumann-Morgenstern system that has been questioned. The continuity postulate raises difficulties that are well-known, and even the assumption of there being a complete social ordering over all lotteries is a fairly demanding requirement.

But suppose the von Neumann-Morgenstern axiom system is obeyed in social choice as well as in individual choices. In what sense does this rule out non-linear social welfare functions? Obviously, the von Neumann-Morgenstern values − let us call them the V-values − of social welfare will be a linear combination of the V-values of individual welfares. But when someone talks about social welfare being a non-linear function of individual welfares, the reference need not necessarily be to the V-values at all. The V-values are of obvious importance for predicting individual or social choice under uncertainty, but there is no obligation to talk about V-values only whenever one is talking about individual or social welfare.

What gives Harsanyi's (1955) concern with V-values a central role in his own model of social choice, is his concept of 'ethical' preference (the 'social preference of a person') being derived from the *as if* exercise (done by that person) of placing oneself in the position of everyone in the society with equal probability. (Note that Rawls' (1958) concern with 'ignorance' as opposed to 'equi-probability' is different and makes it impossible to define the von Neumann-Morgenstern 'lotteries' for social choice except with some additional axiom, e.g., 'insufficient reason'.) These are lotteries that apply to a person's 'social' (or 'ethical') preference only, and need not figure in his actual preferences — what Harsanyi calls their 'subjective' preferences. It will, of course, still remain true that if the social preference follows the von Neumann-Morgenstern axioms, then welfare numbers W_i will be attributed to individuals in the V-value system for social preference such that social choice will be representable in terms of maximizing $W = \frac{1}{n} \Sigma W_i$. But this linear form asserts very little, since $W(x)$ is simply the value of the lottery of being each person i with $1/n$ probability in state x, and the set of W_i need not necessarily have any other significance.

Consider the following conversation:

1: "Let (x, i) be the position of being person i in state x. Tell me how you would rank $(x, 1), (x, 2), (y, 1), (y, 2)$, please."

2: "The best is $(y, 2)$. Then $(x, 2)$. Then $(x, 1)$. Worst $(y, 1)$."

1: "And the welfare gaps between each pair of adjacent positions? Scale them with $(y, 2)$ being 10 and $(x, 1)$ marked zero."

2: "I can't on weekdays, when I feel ordinal."

1: "So on weekdays you are lost and don't know whether to recommend x or y as your ethical judgement for society?"

2: "No, I would recommend x. I even accept TEP on weekdays."

1: "On weekends you are not so ordinal?"

2: "On weekends, on your normalization, I would put 10 for $(y, 2)$, 5 for $(x, 2)$, 2 for $(x, 1)$ and 0 for $(y, 1)$, though I don't like making the 'origin' quite so arbitrary."

1: "Never mind the origin! Since the welfare sum is 10 with y and 7 with x, you clearly will recommend y on weekends?"

2: "No, no, I would recommend x."

1: "So you don't follow von Neumann-Morgenstern axioms in these choices?"

2: "On Saturdays not. But on Sundays yes."

1: "But on Saturdays what do these cardinal welfare numbers stand for? What meaning can we attach to them since they are not von Neumann-Morgenstern numbers?"

2: "They reflect my views of the welfare levels and gaps. I can axiomatize them in many different ways.[13] The welfare numbers have quite nice properties."

1: "But I can't relate them to your observed behaviour."

2: "I should think not. Nor can I relate your von Neumann-Morgenstern numbers over *interpersonal* choices to your observed behaviour; there is not much to go by. No, these numbers reflect my introspection on the subject as do yours, I presume."

1: "Okay, forget the Saturdays. But on Sundays you say your hypothetical interpersonal choices satisfy the von Neumann-Morgenstern axioms. Then you must choose y since social welfare must be the *sum* of these individual welfare numbers."

2: "No, not of these; social welfare is non-linear over these values. It is linear over the V-values, of course. The V-values, which take my distributional attitude into account (to the extent it is possible to do this within the von Neumann-Morgenstern system), are, with the normalization suggested by you: 10 for $(y, 2)$, 7 for $(x, 2)$, 4 for $(x, 1)$ and 0 for $(y, 1)$."

1: "I am relieved. I thought you were about to take social welfare to be a non-linear function of the V-values in von Neumann-Morgenstern representation."

2: "You must be joking."

1: "Anyway, I am so glad that on Sundays you are a utilitarian as far as V-values are concerned."

2: "I am also glad that your pleasures are inexpensive."

I end this section with two final comments. First, 'Sen's utility-dispersion argument', to which Harsanyi (1975) makes extensive references (pp. 318–324), and which according to him "shows a close formal similarity ... to the view that the utility of a lottery ticket should depend, not only on its *expected (mean) utility*, but also on some measure of *risk*" (p. 320), and which "is an illegitimate transfer of a mathematical relationship for money amount, for which it does hold, to utility levels, for which it does not hold" (p. 321), is — in that form — a figment of Harsanyi's imagination. There is, alas, no 2-parameter "Sen's theory which would make social welfare depend, not only on the mean, but also on some measure of *inequality*, i.e., of *dispersion*" (Harsanyi, 1975, pp. 319–320). More importantly, there is no proposal, which would have been grotesque, to define a non-linear social welfare function on *von Neumann-Morgenstern utilities*.[14] Even the axioms for additive separability of the social welfare function over individuals was explicitly criticised (Sen, 1973, pp. 39–41).

Second, whether we use utilitarianism or not is an important moral issue,[15] and is not disposable by carefully defining individual utilities in such a way that the only operation they are good for is addition. An axiomatic justification of utilitarianism would have more content to it if it started off at a place somewhat more distant from the ultimate destination.[16]

3. AXIOMATIZATION OF THE LEXICOGRAPHIC MAXIMIN RULE

The Rawlsian (1958, 1971) 'maximin' rule ranks social states in terms of the welfare of the worst-off individual in that state. This rule can violate even the Pareto principle. The lexicographic version of the maximin rule (Rawls, 1971; Sen, 1970) does not. This rule, which for brevity, and not out of disrespect, I shall call 'leximin', can be formalized in the following way. Let the worst-off person in state x be called $1(x)$, the second worst-off $2(x)$, and in general the jth worst-off $j(x)$. When there are ties, rank the tied persons in *any* strict order. For an n-person community, for any x, y in X:

(i) $x \, P \, y$ if and only if there exists some $r: 1 \leqslant r \leqslant n$ such that
        $(x, i(x)) \, \widetilde{I} \, (y, i(y))$ for all $i: 1 \leqslant i < r$,
        and
        $(x, r(x)) \, \widetilde{P} \, (y, r(y))$;

(ii) $x \, I \, y$ if and only if $(x, i(x)) \, \widetilde{I} \, (y, i(y))$ for all $i: 1 \leqslant i \leqslant n$.

Leximin has been recently illuminatingly analysed in axiomatic terms by Hammond (1975), d'Aspremont and Gevers (1975) and Strasnick (1975). The axiomatization presented here is on similar lines but it differs in some important respects. In particular, the strategy adopted here is first to propose axioms such that the lexicographic maximin rule emerges for 2-person communities, and then to ensure by additional axioms that the lexicographic maximin rule holding for 2-person communities should guarantee the same for n-person communities.

There are, it seems to me, two advantages in this procedure. First, in the 2-person case the axioms are easier to assess and the proof of the theorem is extremely brief. It is my belief that the rationale of the leximin comes out best in this case, and it is worth noting that. Second, this procedure permits the isolation of what appears to me to be the least acceptable feature of leximin, which emerges in the move from 2-person leximin to n-person leximin. The issues raised are discussed in Section 4.

Consider first a 2-person community with persons 1 and 2. The following axioms are defined for a GSWF (generalized social welfare function): $R = f(\widetilde{R})$, where R is the social ordering over X and $\widetilde{R}$ the extended ordering over the product of X and H.

U(Unrestricted domain): Any logically possible $\widetilde{R}$ is in the domain of f.

I(Independence of irrelevant alternatives): If the restrictions of $\widetilde{R}$ and $\widetilde{R}'$ on any pair in X are the same, then the restrictions of $f(\widetilde{R})$ and $f(\widetilde{R}')$ on that pair are also the same.

J(Grading principle of justice): For any x, y in X, if for some one-to-one correspondence μ from $(1,2)$ to $(1,2)$: $(x, 1)\,\widetilde{R}\,(y,\mu(1))$ and $(x, 2)\,\widetilde{R}\,(y, \mu(2))$, then $x\,R\,y$. If, furthermore, one of the two $\widetilde{R}$'s is a $\widetilde{P}$, then $x\,P\,y$.

T(Two-person ordinal equity): For any x, y in X, if one person, say 1, prefers x to y, and the other prefers y to x, and if person 1 is worse off than 2 both in x and in y, then $x\,R\,y$.

U and I are standard parts of the Arrow framework applied to extended orderings for a 2-person community. J is proposed by Suppes (1966). T corresponds to Hammond's Equity Axiom E in the two-person case, without the separability requirement built into it in the n-person case (for $n > 2$). It corresponds to E in the same way as TEP corresponds to STEP.

(T.2)   For a 2-person community, given at least three social states in X, leximin is the only generalized social welfare function satisfying U, I, J and T.

Proof. Since it is easily checked that leximin satisfies U, I, J and T, we need concentrate only on the converse. Suppose U, I, J and T are satisfied, but not leximin. Leximin can be violated in one of three alternative ways. For some x, y in X:

(I) $(x, 1(x))\,\widetilde{P}\,(y, 1(y))$, but not $x\,P\,y$.
(II) $(x, 1(x))\,\widetilde{I}\,(y, 1(y))$ and $(x, 2(x))\,\widetilde{P}\,(y, 2(y))$, but not $x\,P\,y$.
(III) $(x, i(x))\,\widetilde{I}\,(y, i(y))$ for $i = 1, 2$, but not $x\,I\,y$.

Since (II) and (III) contradict J directly, we need be concerned only with (I). Suppose (I) holds.

If $(x, 2(x))\,\widetilde{R}\,(y, 2(y))$, then $x\,P\,y$ by J. Hence it must be the case that $(y, 2(y))\,\widetilde{P}\,(x, 2(x))$. *A fortiori*, $(y, 2(y))\,P(x, 1(x))$. Consider now $\widetilde{R}'$ reflecting the following strict descending order involving x, y and a third social state z:

$$(y, 2(y)), (x, 2(x)), (x, 1(x)), (z, 2(z)), (z, 1(z)), (y, 1(y)).$$

By T and J, $z R' y$, where $R' = f(\widetilde{R}')$, and by $J, x P' z$. Hence $x P' y$. But then by $I, x P y$. So (I) is impossible. This establishes (T.2).

Consider now a family of GSWFs, one for each subset of the community H. In what follows only those for pairs and for H will be used.

In addition to the axioms for 2-person communities, two axioms with a wider scope are now introduced. Let the social states x and y be called 'rank-equivalent' for $\widetilde{R}$ if everyone's relative welfare rank is the same in x as in y, i.e., $i(x) = i(y)$ for all i.

B(*Binary build-up*): For any $\widetilde{R}$, for any two rank-equivalent social states, for a set π of pairs of individuals in the community H such that $\cup \pi = H$, if $x R y$ (respectively, $x P y$) for each pair in π, then $x R y$ (respectively, $x P y$) for H.

J^* *(Extended grading principle)*: If $\widetilde{R}'$ is obtained from $\widetilde{R}$ by replacing i by $\mu(i)$ in all positions (x, i) for some x and all i, where $\mu(\cdot)$ is a one-to-one correspondence from H to H, then $f(\widetilde{R}) = f(\widetilde{R}')$ for H.

J^* is an extension of J and is in the same spirit. Notice that it is not satisfied by many conditions, e.g., the method of majority decision; the majority method does not satisfy J either. J^* stipulates essential use of interpersonal comparison information in an anonymous way, e.g., taking note of $(x, i) \widetilde{R}$ (y, i) but in the same way as $(x, i) \widetilde{R} (y, k)$.

(T.3)   Given at least three social states, if for each pair of persons in H, there is a 2-person GSWF satisfying U, I, J and T, then the only GSWF for H satisfying U, J^* and B is leximin.

Proof. It is clear from (T.2) that the GSWF for each pair of individuals is leximin. If the community H has only two members, then (T.3) is trivial. In general for any community H, leximin clearly satisfies U and J^*. It remains to be established that it must satisfy B also, and then to establish the converse proposition.

Suppose the GSWF is leximin, but B is violated. This is possible only if x and y are rank-equivalent, and

(I) $x R y$ for all pairs in π, but not $x R y$ for H.

(II) $x P y$ for all pairs in π, but not $x P y$ for H.

Consider (I) first. Since each R is an ordering, $y P x$ must hold for H. Given the leximin nature of the GSWF for H, this is possible only if there is some rank r such that: $(y, r(y)) \widetilde{P}(x, r(x))$, and $(y, i(y)) \widetilde{I}(x, i(x))$, for all $i < r$. Given rank-equivalence, $i(x) = i(y) = i$, say, for all i. Thus: $(y, r) \widetilde{P}(x, r)$, and $(y, i) \widetilde{I}(x, i)$, for all $i < r$. Since r must belong to at least one pair included in π, for that pair, by leximin, $y P x$. So the supposition (I) leads to contradiction.

Next consider (II). If not $x P y$ for H, then either $y P x$, which leads to the same problem as (I), or $x I y$, which is now considered. For leximin this implies, given rank equivalence, $(x, i) \widetilde{I}(y, i)$ for all i. Clearly then $x P y$ is impossible for any pair contained in π, thus contradicting (II).

Now the converse. Let the stated axioms hold. To establish that the GSWF for the community H must be leximin, we have to show that:

(III)   If $(x, i(x)) \widetilde{I}(y, i(y))$ for all i, then $x I y$ for H.

(IV)   If there is some r such that $(x, r(x)) \widetilde{P}(y, r(y))$, and for all $i < r$: $(x, i(x)) \widetilde{I}(y, i(y))$, then $x P y$ for H.

Let the antecedent in (III) hold. Take the one-to-one correspondence μ such that $i(x) = \mu(i(y))$ for all i, and let this transformation applied to the y-invariant elements convert $\widetilde{R}$ to $\widetilde{R}'$. Note that x and y are rank-equivalent for $\widetilde{R}'$. Note also that $f(\widetilde{R}) = f(\widetilde{R}')$ for all subset of H by J^*. Consider now any set π of pairs of persons in H such that $\cup \pi = H$. Leximin guarantees $x I' y$ for all such pairs with $R' = f(\widetilde{R}')$. By Binary build-up B: $x I' y$ for H. By J^*: $x I y$.

Finally, let the antecedent of (IV) hold. Consider μ and $\widetilde{R}'$ as defined in the last paragraph with x and y rank-equivalent for $\widetilde{R}'$. Consider now the set π of pairs $(r(x), i)$ for all $i \neq r(x)$. Since the GSWF for each pair is leximin, clearly $x P' y$ for all pairs in π. Furthermore $\cup \pi = H$. Hence $x P' y$ for H by Binary build-up. By J^*: $x P y$, which completes the proof.

4. RAWLSIAN AXIOMS: A DISCRIMINATING ASSESSMENT

The axiom structure used in the last section to derive the Rawlsian leximin rule was not chosen to provide an axiomatic 'justification' of the rule. Rawls himself did not seek such a justification (see especially his 'Concluding Remarks on Justification', Rawls (1971, pp. 577–587)), and was much more concerned with being able 'to see more clearly the chief structural features' of the approach chosen by him (p. viii). In (T.2) and (T.3) axioms have been chosen with a view to distinguishing between different aspects of Rawlsian ethics, which would permit a discriminating evaluation.

Before examining the axioms one by one, it is important to clarify the type of aggregation that is involved in the exercise as a whole. Social choice problems can be broadly divided into the aggregation of personal 'interests' and that of 'judgements' as to what is good for society, and as I have tried to argue elsewhere (Sen, 1975), the 'theory of social choice' seems to have suffered persistently from a failure to make clear which particular problem is being tackled. It seems reasonable to take leximin as a proposed solution to the interest aggregation exercise. The contrast between giving priority to the welfare ranking of the worst off person as opposed to the welfare ranking of the person who 'gains more' (as under utilitarianism) is a contrast between two alternative approaches to dealing with interest conflicts. The problem of aggregating people's different judgements on what should be done (e.g., aggregating different 'views' on the 'right' public policy), while central to Arrow's (1951) analysis of social choice, is not a problem to which leximin can be sensibly addressed.

It is perhaps easiest to think of a generalized social welfare function GSWF as an exercise by a person of deriving ethical judgements from his assessment of everyone's interests implicit in the particular $\widetilde{R}$ in terms of which he does the exercise. (This is the sense in which Harsanyi (1955) also uses 'social preference': "When I speak of preferences 'from a social standpoint', often abbreviated to social preferences and the like, I always mean preferences based on a given individual's value judgements concerning social welfare" (p. 310).) The exercise can be institutional also, e.g., taking a person with a lower money income to be invariably worse off as a 'stylized' assumption in a poverty programme (see Atkinson, 1969). These exercises are done with one given $\widetilde{R}$ in each case. The problem of basing a 'social judgement' on the n-tuple of 'extended orderings' $\{\widetilde{R}_i\}$ – one for each person – is a different issue, raising problems of its own (see Sen, 1970, Theorems 9*2, 9*2.1, and 9*3, pp. 154–156, and Kelly, 1975, 1975a).

The fact that a GSWF is defined as a function of $\widetilde{R}$, an extended *ordering*, without any information on preference intensities, is of some importance, since this rules out the possibility of varying the ethical judgements with cardinalization. Formally the axiom in question is 'unrestricted domain' U, since if cardinalization made any difference in any particular case, R will not be a *function* of $\widetilde{R}$ in that case, and such an $\widetilde{R}$ will not be an element in the domain of $f(\cdot)$. However, even if R were not defined as a function of $\widetilde{R}$, and the possibility of using intensities of welfare differences were kept open, no essential difference will be made in the axiom structure used in the derivation of leximin. In the 2-person case in (T.2), axioms J(Grading principle of justice) and T(Two-person ordinal equity) along with I (independence of irrelevant alternatives) do 'lock' the social preferences leaving no room for cardinal intensities to exert themselves. In (T.3) there is formally a bit of room which is, however, easily absorbed by a slight variation of the axioms. For the responsibility of elimination of intensity considerations we must critically examine axioms other than U.

Axiom J (Grading principle of justice) is, however, quite harmless in this respect since it operates on utilitizing dominance. Indeed, the preference relation generated by J is not merely a subrelation of the Rawlsian leximin relation, it is a subrelation also of the utilitarian preference relation (see Sen, 1970, pp. 159–160).[17] J incorporates the Pareto relation but also all similar dominance relations obtained through interpersonal permutations.[18]

The eschewal of intensities of welfare differences as relevant considerations is, however, an important aspect of T(Two-person ordinal equity). There is no dominance here, and person i's preference for x over y is made to override j's for y over x if i is worse off in each of the two states without any reference to the relative magnitudes of i's gain and j's loss. This was one reason for our hesitation with TEP also (Section 1) and the same applies to T. Both give priority to reducing welfare inequality in the ordinal sense without any concern for 'totals' and for comparing welfare 'differences'. If cardinal welfare comparisons were ruled out *either* because of ordinality of individual welfare, *or* because of level comparability, T like TEP would be a lot more persuasive. In so far as T is a crucial aspect of the Rawlsian approach, this point about 'informational contrast' is of great importance.[19] The hazier our notion of welfare differences, the less the bite of this criticism of the Rawlsian rules.

The usual criticisms of Arrow's use of the independence of irrelevant alternatives (see Sen, 1970, pp. 39, 89–92, and Hansson, 1973), also apply to the use of I for a GSWF. It rules out postulating cardinal measures of intensity based on rank positions (as in 'positional rules' discussed by Gärden-fors (1973), Fine and Fine (1974) and others). This, as it were, puts the last nail in the coffin of using welfare difference intensities.[20]

Turning now to (T.3), axioms J^* and B have to be considered. J^* uses the interpersonal permutation approach pioneered by Suppes (1966). While J uses it for 'dominance' only, J^* uses this more generally, to the extent of not discriminating between two extended orderings where positions of indi-viduals for some social state are switched around. The objections that apply to the usual 'anonymity' postulates apply here too, and it is particularly serious when considerations of personal liberty are involved (see Sen, 1970, Chapter 6, 1975b; Kelly, 1975).[21]

Binary build-up B is in some ways the least persuasive of the axioms used. It permits a lexicographic pattern of dictatorship of *positions* (being least well off) as opposed to persons (as in Arrow's (1951) theorem). The worst off person rules the roost not merely in a 2-person community, but in a community of any size no matter how many persons' interests go against his.[22]

Leximin can be derived without using B (see Hammond, 1975; d'Aspre-mont and Gevers, 1975 and Strasnick, 1975), and using instead conditions that look less narrow in their focus (e.g., d'Aspremont and and Gevers' 'Elimination of Indifferent Individuals'). However, leximin must satisfy B, as we establish in (T.3). And no matter how we 'derive' leximin, B is an integral part of the Rawlsian set-up. This seems to bring out a rather disagreeable feature of leximin. In a 2-person community in the absence of information on welfare difference intensities, it might seem reasonable to argue that the worse off person's preference should have priority over the other's, but does this really make sense in a billion-person community even if everyone else's interests go against that of this one person? The transition from 2-person leximin to n-person leximin (making use of Binary build-up) is a long one.

It may be interesting to observe how Binary build-up creeps into axioms that look rather mild. Consider Hammond's Equity axiom E. It differs from the 2-person equity axiom T used here in being extendable to n-member communities also if all others are *indifferent* between x and y. This may look innocuous enough, but in the presence of U and I, this 'separability' assumption is quite overpowering. The 'elimination of indifferent individ-uals', as d'Aspremont and Gevers (1975) call it, is not merely (as it happens) spine-chilling in the choice of words, but also quite disturbing in its real

implications. The condition is defined below in a somewhat different form
(to permit ready comparability with Hammond's E).

EL (Elimination of the influence of indifferent individuals): For any $\widetilde{R}$, for
any x, y, if $(x, i) \widetilde{I} (y, i)$ for all i in some subset G of H, and if f^H and f^{H-G}
are the GSWF's for the communities H and $(H - G)$ respectively, then $x f^H (\widetilde{R})$
y if and only if $x f^{H-G} (\widetilde{R}) y$.

Notice that our T (Two-person ordinal equity) and EL together imply Hammond's Equity axiom E. What may, however, not be obvious is that for the
class of GSWF satisfying unrestricted domain (U) and independence (I), T
and EL together eliminate the influence not merely of indifferent individuals
but also of non-indifferent ones, leading to a single-minded concern with one
person. The same effect is achieved by Hammond's E itself in the presence
of the other axioms.

$SFE(n)$ *(Single-focus equity for n-member communities)*: If for an n-member
community, for any x and y, $\widetilde{R}$ involves the strict extended order: (y, n),
$(x, n), (y, n-1), (x, n-1), ..., (y, 2), (x, 2), (x, 1), (y, 1)$, then $x R y$.

$SFE(2)$ is equivalent to two-person equity T (and trivially to Hammond's E
also), and may not be thought to be exceptionally objectionable (especially
in the absence of preference intensity information). But $SFE(n)$ for relatively
large n is very extreme indeed, since everyone other than 1 is better off under
y than under x, and still $x R y$.

(T.4)   Given at least three social states, if U, I and EL hold for the
         GSWF for each subset of the community H, then T implies
         $SFE(k)$ for GSWF for each subset of the community including
         the one for the entire community H (i.e., $k \leqslant n$).

Proof. Suppose $SFE(m)$ holds for some $m < n$. We first show that SFE
$(m+1)$ holds. Consider the following extended order (with indifference
written as $=$) for the triple x, y and some z: $(y, m+1), (x, m+1) = (z, m+1)$,
$(y, m) = (z, m), (x, m), (y, m-1), (z, m-1), (x, m-1), ..., (y, 2), (z, 2), (x, 2)$,
$(x, 1), (z, 1), (y, 1)$. By U, this is admissible. By $SFE(m)$, for the m-member
community $(1, ..., m)$, $x R z$. By EL, for the $(m+1)$-member community
$(1, ..., m+1)$, $x R z$ also. Again, by $SFE(m)$, for the m-member community

$(1, ..., m-1, m+1)$, $z R y$. By EL, for the $(m+1)$-member community $(1, ..., m+1)$, $z R y$ also. By the transitivity of R, $x R y$. By independence I, this must be due solely to the restriction of $\widetilde{R}$ over the pair (x, y), and this establishes SFE$(m+1)$.

The proof is completed by noting that SFE(2) holds since it is equivalent to Two-person equity T, and then obtaining SFE(k) for all $k \leqslant n$ by induction.

While the Rawlsian leximin can be established from axioms that look more appealing, it must end up having the extreme narrowness of focus that is represented by SFE(n) for large n. This in itself is obvious enough, since leximin clearly does satisfy SFE(n). What (T.4) does is to show precisely how it comes about that such apparently broad-focussed conditions together produce such a narrow-focussed property.

It should be observed that the force of the Rawlsian approach as a critique of utilitarian ethics stands despite the limitation of SFE(n). SFE(2) is equivalent to T — an appealing requirement — and while Rawlsian leximin satisfies it, utilitarianism may not. As large values of n are considered, SFE(n) becomes less appealing and so does — naturally — Rawlsian leximin, but the criticism of utilitarianism is not thereby wiped out. In this paper a 'warts-and-all' view of Rawlsian leximin has been taken, choosing a set of axioms with the focus on transparency rather than on immediate appeal. This 'warts and all' axiomatization does not, however, give any reason for disagreeing with Rawls' (1971) own conclusions about his theory: (i) "it is not a fully satisfactory theory", and (ii) "it offers ... an alternative to the utilitarian view which has for so long held the pre-eminent place in our moral philosophy" (p. 586). Rawls was, of course, referring to his theory in its broad form including his contractual notion of fairness and justice, but the observations seem to apply specifically to leximin as well.

London School of Economics

NOTES

* Based on the text of a lecture delivered at the International Congress of Logic, Methodology and Philosophy of Science in London, Ontario, Canada, on August 29th, 1975. Thanks are due to Peter Hammond and Kevin Roberts for helpful comments and criticisms.
[1] See Hansson (1975).

[2] Cf. the concept of 'ordinal intensity' in comparisons of preference intensity used by Blau (1975) and Sen (1975b).

[3] See Sen (1970), Chapters 9 and 9*, for a discussion of the concept of extended ordering.

[4] Note that this criterion permits $(x, \rho(i)) \ \bar{I}(x, \rho(j))$, in contrast with the examples noted above. But obviously if $\bar{I}$ holds, then there is no inequality in x at all, and this must be less than whatever inequality there is in y.

[5] See Dasgupta et al. (1973), or Sen (1973), pp. 53–56.

[6] Note that STEP subsumes Hammond's (1975) axiom of 'Equity' (E), which extends and generalizes Sen's (1973) 'weak equity axiom' (WEA). Preferring inequality reduction irrespective of any consideration of the 'total' (as in STEP) has the effect of giving priority to the person who is going to be worse off anyway (as in these equity axioms).

[7] Note, however, that the characteristic of 'separability' is shared by STEP with many other criteria, e.g., utilitarianism, or the lexicographic maximin. Cf. the condition of 'elimination of indifferent individuals' (E1) of d'Aspremont and Gevers (1975).

[8] In the special case of 'pure distribution' problem however, there will be no conflict between the welfare sum and the equality of the welfare distribution if everyone shares the same concave welfare function on individual income. This is, however, a very special case, and the condition can be somewhat relaxed without introducing a conflict; on this see Hammond (1975a).

[9] See Sen (1970, 1973), d'Aspremont and Gevers (1975), and Hammond (1975).

[10] However, even with *partial* unit comparability there will be a quasi-ordering of the total (see Sen, 1970; Fine, 1975; Blackorby, 1975). With level comparability only, this quasi-ordering will shrink only to the weak n-person version of Suppes' 'grading principle of justice', which will never contradict θ or θ^*.

[11] Contrast Nozick (1973). See also Williams (1973, pp. 77–93).

[12] Indeed the interpretation of Harsanyi's (1955) own theorems on social choice is seriously hampered by his silence on the precise comparability assumption (on which and related issues, see Pattanaik (1968)).

[13] See, for example, Krantz et al. (1971).

[14] The only page reference Harsanyi gives on this point, which he discusses so extensively, is to p. 18 of Sen (1973). I see nothing there that justifies Harsanyi's presumption that I had non-linear designs on utilities in the *von Neumann-Morgenstern representation*, let alone a 2-parameter non-linear design on them.

[15] For an illuminating debate on this see Smart and Williams (1973).

[16] For some extremely interesting recent contributions in this direction, see d'Aspremont and Gevers (1975), Hammond (1975a), and Maskin (1975), even though more work may still need to be done in terms of starting off from individual welfare functions which are not necessarily confined precisely to the class of positive affine transformations.

[17] Blackorby and Donaldson (1975) demonstrate that with cardinal interpersonal comparability the convex hull of the 'at least as good as' set according to the grading principle is a subset of the intersection of the utilitarian and leximin 'at least as good as' sets, and in the 2-person case exactly equals the intersection.

[18] Hammond's axioms for leximin include the symmetric part of the grading relation (his S) as well as the asymmetric part in the case coinciding with the Pareto strict preference (his P^*), but the remainder of J follows from his remaining axioms U, I, P^* and S (as he notes in Theorem 5.1).

[19] See Sen (1973, 1974), and d'Aspremont and Gevers (1975).

[20] Furthermore, combined with the 'separability' assumption implicit in Binary build-up B (or in Hammond's E, or in d'Aspremont and Gevers' EL, to be defined below), independence of irrelevant alternatives can be very demanding from the point of view of inter-pair consistency (see (T.4) below). In this its role here is not dissimilar to that in

the class of possibility theorems on social welfare functions without interpersonal comparisons.
[21] In this sense it seems a bit misleading to call Rawls' theory a 'liberal theory of justice' (see, for example, Barry (1973), which is very helpful contribution otherwise).
[22] It should be remarked that utilitarianism does not satisfy Binary build-up B. For example it is possible that in a 3-person community with 1 preferring x to y and the others y to x that $W_1(x) - W_1(y) > W_i(y) - W_i(x)$, for $i = 2, 3$, but $W_1(x) - W_1(y) < \sum_{i=2,3} [W_i(y) - W_i(x)]$. So $x P y$ for the 2-person communities $(1, 2)$ and $(1, 3)$, but not for their union $(1, 2, 3)$. However, utilitarianism satisfies another − and in some ways weaker − binary build-up condition B^*, viz, if $x R y$ for a set of pairs which *partition* the community (with no person belonging to more than one pair), then $x R y$ for the community (and similarly with P). Strasnick's (1975) condition of 'unanimity' incorporates B^* for any partition of the community (not necessarily into pairs), and is more reasonable and much less demanding than B, in this sense.

BIBLIOGRAPHY

Arrow, K. J., 1951, *Social Choice and Individual Values*, Wiley, New York, 2nd edition, 1963.
Arrow, K. J., (1973, 'Some Ordinalist-Utilitarian Notes on Rawls' Theory of Justice', *Journal of Philosophy* 70.
Atkinson, A. B., 1969, *Poverty in Britain and the Reform of Social Security*, Cambridge University Press.
Atkinson, A. B., 'On the Measurement of Inequality', *Journal of Economic Theory* 2.
Barry, B., 1973, *The Liberal Theory of Justice*, Clarendon Press, Oxford.
Blackorby, C., 1975, 'Degrees of Cardinality and Aggregate Partial Orderings', *Econometrica* 43.
Blackorby, C. and Donaldson, D., 1975, 'Utility vs. Equity: Some Plausible Quasi-orderings', mimeographed.
Blau, J. H., (1975), 'Liberal Values and Independence', *Review of Economic Studies* 42.
Daniels, N. (ed.), 1975, *Reading Rawls*, Basil Blackwell, Oxford.
Dasgupta, P., Sen, A., and Starret, D., 1973, 'Notes on the Measurement of Inequality of Incomes', *Journal of Economic Theory* 6.
d'Aspremont, C. and Gevers, L., 1975, 'Equity and the Informational Basis of Collective Choice', presented at the Third World Econometric Congress, mimeographed.
Diamond, P., 1967, 'Cardinal Welfare, Individualistic Ethics and Interpersonal Comparisons of Utility: A Comment', *Journal of Political Economy* 61.
Fine, B., 1975, 'A Note on "Interpersonal Comparison and Partial Comparability" ', *Econometrica* 43.
Fine, B. and Fine, K., 1974, 'Social Choice and Individual Ranking', *Review of Economic Studies* 42.
Gärdenfors, P., 1973, 'Positionalist Voting Functions', *Theory and Decision* 4.
Hammond, P. J., 1975, 'Equity, Arrow's Conditions and Rawl's Difference Principle', mimeographed; forthcoming *Econometrica*.
Hammond, P. J., 1975a, 'Dual Interpersonal Comparisons of Utility and the Welfare Economics of Income Distribution', mimeographed, Essex University.
Hansson, B., 1973, 'The Independence Condition in the Theory of Social Choice', *Theory and Decision* 4, 25.
Hansson, B., 1975, 'The Measurement of Social Inequality', text of lecture at the Congress of Logic, Philosophy and the Methodology of Science, London, Ontario.

Hardy, G., Littlewood, J. and Polya, G., 1934, *Inequalities*, Cambridge University Press.

Harsanyi, J.C., 1955, 'Cardinal Welfare, Individualistic Ethics and Interpersonal Comparisons of Utility', *Journal of Political Economy* 63.

Harsanyi, J.C., 1976, 'Nonlinear Social Welfare Functions', *Theory and Decision* 6.

Kelly, J.S., 1975, 'The Impossibility of a Just Liberal', mimeographed; forthcoming *Economica*.

Kelly, J.S., 1975a, 'Arrow's Theorem, Grading Principle of Justice and the Axiom of Identity', mimeographed, University of Minnesota.

Kolm, S.Ch., 1966, 'The Optimum Production of Social Justice', paper presented in the Biarritz Conference on Public Economics; published in J. Margolis (ed.), *Public Economics*, Macmillan, London.

Krantz, D.H., Luce, R.D., Suppes, P. and Tversky, A., 1971, *Foundations of Measurement*, Academic Press, New York.

Maskin, E., 1975, 'A Theorem on Utilitarianism', mimeographed, Cambridge University.

Nozick, R., 1973, *Anarchy, State and Utopia*, Basil Blackwell, Oxford.

Pattanaik, P.K., 1968, 'Risk, Impersonality and the Social Welfare Function', *Journal of Political Economy* 76.

Pattanaik, P.K., 1971, *Voting and Collective Choice*, Cambridge University Press.

Phelps, E.S. (ed.), 1973, *Economic Justice*, Penguin, Harmondsworth.

Rawls, J., 1958, 'Justice as Fairness', *Philosophical Review* 67.

Rawls, J., 1971, *A Theory of Justice*, Harvard University Press, Cambridge, Mass., and Clarendon Press, Oxford.

Rothschild, M. and Stiglitz, J.E., 'Some Further Results on the Measurement of Inequality', *Journal of Economic Theory* 6.

Sen, A.K., 1970, *Collective Choice and Social Welfare*, Holden-Day, San Francisco, and Oliver & Boyd, Edinburgh.

Sen, A.K., 1973, *On Economic Inequality*, Clarendon Press, Oxford, and Norton, New York.

Sen, A.K., 1975, 'Social Choice Theory: A Re-examination', text of lecture at the Third World Econometric Congress; forthcoming *Econometrica*.

Sen, A.K., 1975a, 'Interpersonal Comparisons of Welfare', mimeographed; forthcoming in a festschrift for Tibor Scitovsky.

Sen, A.K., 1975b, 'Liberty, Unanimity and Rights', mimeographed, London School of Economics; forthcoming *Econometrica*.

Smart, J.J.C. and Williams, B., 1973, *Utilitarianism: For and Against*, Cambridge University Press.

Strasnick, S., 1975, 'Arrow's Paradox and Beyond', mimeographed, Harvard University.

Suppes, P., 1966, 'Some Formal Models of Grading Principles', *Synthese* 6; reprinted in P. Suppes, *Studies in the Methodology and Foundations of Science*, Dordrecht, 1969.

Williams, B., 1973, 'A Critique of Utilitarianism', in Smart and Williams (1973).

Review of Economic Studies (1985) LII, 505–513
© 1985 The Society for Economic Analysis Ltd.

0034-6527/85/00340505$02.00

Rawls' Maximin Criterion and Time-Consistency: Further Results

WOLFGANG LEININGER
University of Bonn

The paper is concerned with the implications of a maximin welfare function for an intertemporal society which has a nonlinear technology at its disposal, but holds conflicting preferences over time. The complete solution given shows that time-consistency and optimality of plans may or may not be compatible. The time-consistent case is generalized to a very wide class of models. This leads to the partial invalidation of a result stated in the earlier literature on the subject.

1. INTRODUCTION

The principle of justice laid down in the work of Professor Rawls (1971) is of great interest to economists since it provides an alternative to the widely applied utilitarian point of view.

The principle requires a society to maximize the well-being of its poorest member. It is applicable in an atemporal as well as an intertemporal context. Applications of the principle to intertemporal models which describe "society" as the union of present and future generations have unfortunately resulted in time-inconsistent solutions (Arrow (1973), Dasgupta (1974)). The plan chosen as best according to the maximin criterion by one generation may not be identical to the plan chosen by the next generation. In recognition of the possibility of such an incompatibility of optimality and time-consistency Peleg and Yaari (1973) have argued that the conceptual description of a resonable course of action in intertemporal models cannot dispense with the requirement of time-consistency. This would preclude the use of Rawls' principle. On the other hand it was shown in two recent contributions to this journal (Calvo (1978), Rodriguez (1981)) that the presence of this incompatibility depends on the specific model under consideration.

The present paper reinvestigates this issue with reference to a model which neither postulates a linear technology nor a perfectly altruistic intertemporal preference structure. The complete characterization of the maximin solution in this model (Theorem 1) gives rise to a very general compatibility result for time-consistency and optimality of plans (Theorem 2). Comparison of this result with previous work points out an error in the analysis of Rodriguez (1981) which for certain parameter constellations invalidates the given solution in his model.

2. THE PROBLEM AND THE MODEL

We introduce a simple model of production with an infinite time horizon. There is only one good in the economy which can either be consumed or used as an input into a production process which yields output at the beginning of the next time period. Each generation consists of a fixed number of identical individuals and lives for one period. Hence we can for simplicity assume that there is just one individual per generation.

105

Let y_t denote the capital stock at the beginning of period t and $\{y_t\} = \{y_0, y_1, \ldots, y_t, \ldots\}$ denote a sequence of capital stocks.

Such a sequence is called feasible if

$$y_t \geq 0 \quad \text{for all } t \geq 0 \tag{1}$$

and

$$y_{t+1} \leq y_t + f(y_t) \quad \text{for all } t \geq 0, \tag{2}$$

where the (incremental) production function f satisfies the following conditions (see Rodriguez (1981)):

    (i) $f(y)$ is twice continuously differentiable,
    (ii) $f'(0) > 0$ and $f(0) = 0$,
(P)   (iii) $f(y) + y$ is strictly increasing over the interval $[0, \bar{y}]$, $\bar{y} > 0$,
    (iv) $f(\bar{y}) = 0$,
    (v) f is strictly concave.

The feasibility conditions (1), (2) and (P) can be rewritten in the form of

$$y_t = y_{t-1} + f(y_{t-1}) - c_{t-1} = y_{t-2} + f(y_{t-2}) - c_{t-2} + f(y_{t-1}) - c_{t-1}$$

$$= y_0 + \sum_{i=0}^{t-1} [f(y_i) - c_i] \geq 0, \tag{3}$$

i.e. a feasible consumption sequence $\{c_t\}$ derived from the capital sequence $\{y_t\}$ must satisfy

(F) $\sum_{t=0}^{T} [c_t - f(y_t)] \leq y_0 \quad \text{for all } T = 0, 1, 2, \ldots$.

(F) says that along a feasible consumption sequence the sum of "excess" consumption (i.e. consumption per period in excess over the capital increment $f(y_t)$ realized in that period) over all periods cannot exceed y_0, the initial capital level. In particular, initial capital y_0 is kept constant by $\{c_t\} = \{f(y_0), \ldots, f(y_0), \ldots\}$.

With respect to preferences we will follow Arrow (1973) and Dasgupta (1974) in assuming that utility of each generation t is represented by a utility function u_t of the form

(U) $u_t = u(c_t, c_{t+1}) = v(c_t) + bv(c_{t+1}), \quad b \in (0, 1),$

where v is a twice differentiable, strictly increasing and strictly concave function.

Note that (U) makes a generation care about its direct descendant but—at the same time—ignore the altruism of the next generation towards its descendant. This source of intergenerational conflict is not present in the model of Rodriguez (1981) (which includes Calvo's as a special case).

The celebrated Rawls maximin criterion of maximizing the utility of the worst-off generation now takes the form

(M) $\max \inf_{t \geq 0} \{u(c_t, c_{t+1})\}$ over all feasible consumption sequences $\{c_t\}$.

An optimal consumption sequence $\{c_t^*\}$ is called time-consistent, if (given y_0)

$$\inf \{u(c_t^*, c_{t+1}^*)\} = \max_{\{c_t\}} \inf_{t \geq 0} \{u(c_t, c_{t+1})\}$$

implies that (given $y_{t_0}^*$)

$$\inf_{t \geq t_0} \{u(c_t^*, c_{t+1}^*)\} = \max_{\{c_t\}} \inf_{t \geq t_0} \{u(c_t, c_{t+1})\} \quad \text{for } t_0 = 1, 2, \ldots.$$

($y_{t_0}^*$ is taken from the capital sequence $\{y_t^*\}$ which generates $\{c_t^*\}$ from y_0.)

Time-consistency requires an optimal plan calculated at $t = 0$ to stay optimal if followed; i.e. renewed application of the maximin criterion at $t = t_0$, relative to the then realized capital stock $y_{t_0}^*$, should produce $\{c_t^*\}_{t=t_0}^\infty$ as a solution. The definition indicates that both technology and preference structure matter.

Previous studies have either used "static" preference structures which reflect no intergenerational conflict (Calvo (1978), Rodriguez (1981)) or a linear technology which allows for no trade-off with respect to productivity (Arrow (1973), Dasgupta (1974)). Both restrictions are absent in the present paper.

3. EXISTENCE OF TIME-CONSISTENT MAXIMIN SOLUTIONS

To prove our main result a generalization of the notion of "utility productiveness" (Arrow (1973)) proves very helpful. With a linear technology this property of an economy is *independent* of the amount of capital used in production. With a non-linear technology, however, the question arises whether an economy can change its "mode" from "utility productive" to "utility non-productive" (or vice versa) under the maximin criterion. Two particular capital levels turn out to be of interest:

Definition. Let y^G be the (unique) solution of the equation $f'(y) = 0$, and y^1 be the (unique) solution of the equation $b \cdot (1 + f'(y)) = 1$ ($y^1 = 0$ if there is no solution).

y^G is the "golden-rule"-capital level maximizing steady-state consumption. At y^1 the marginal productivity of capital equals the inverse of the discount factor, it is the point where a utility productive economy ($y_0 < y^1$) turns into a utility non-productive one ($y_0 > y^1$). Of course, $y^1 < y^G$ by (P).

With these preparations we can state the full solution to Problem (M).

Theorem 1. *Assume* (P) *and* (U).
   (i) *If* $0 < y_0 < y^1$ *then the unique maximin optimal consumption sequence is given by* $\{c_t^*\} = \{c_0^*, c_1^*, c_0^*, c_1^*, \ldots, c_0^*, c_1^*, \ldots\}$ *where* (c_0^*, c_1^*) *solves the problem*

$$\max v(c_0) + bv(c_1) \quad \text{subject to } y_2 = y_0 + f(y_0) - c_0 + f(y_1) - c_1 = y_0.$$

$\{c_t^*\}$ *is time-inconsistent.*
   (ii) *If* $y^1 \leq y_0 \leq y^G$ *then the unique optimal consumption sequence is given by*

$$\{c_t^*\} = \{f(y_0), f(y_0), \ldots, f(y^0), \ldots\}.$$

$\{c_t^*\}$ *is time-consistent.*
   (iii) *If* $y^G < y_0 \leq \bar{y}$ *then there exists an infinite number of optimal consumption sequences. They are all non-stationary and time-consistent.*

Theorem 1 is proved in the appendix. It shows that solution paths can be classified with respect to initial capital levels. The initial "mode" of the system always is preserved. However, the much criticized "conservative" tendency inherent in the maximin criterion only applies for the cyclical nature of the solution in part (i) and the stationary case of part (ii), which are both familiar patterns from the Arrow–Dasgupta analysis. A new qualitative feature of the maximin-solution appears in part (iii) of Theorem 1: at y^G the maximal sustainable ("golden rule") consumption level, $f(y^G)$, is reached; thereafter steady-state consumption is declining. Under these circumstances the maximin-criterion *does* allow the run down of capital from a position above y^G if it is done in such a way that every generation "on the way to y^G" consumes at least the amount $f(y^G)$. The crucial feature—well-known from optimal growth theory—is that with too much capital a society can consume more *in the present and the future*. It does not pay (from a maximin point of view) to maintain a capital level in excess of y^G since the consumption level can be raised in the steady state (at y^G) *and* the adjustment process to y^G. If the adjustment path is chosen in such a way that the "worst-off" generation lives "at infinity" (realizing utility $u(f(y^G), f(y^G))$) the consumption sequence is time-consistent (the time-inconsistency problem precisely arises when the "worst-off" generation lives at a finite date, because after time has elapsed beyond that date a new generation gets the worst spot and this might alter the optimal plan). There exist infinitely many ways to approach y^G in this way.

In fact, given (P), the nature of the maximin solution for $y_0 > y^G$ is in no way confined to or dependent on (U). It generalizes to a very broad class of preferences. Specifically, let u_t, the utility function of generation t, be defined as follows:

$$(U') \qquad\qquad u_t = u(_t c) \quad \text{where } _t c = \{c_t, c_{t+1}, \ldots\}$$

where u is Paretian in the sense that it is strictly increasing in all its arguments. We also assume it to be strictly concave.[1]

Then the following Theorem, which is proved in the Appendix, holds:

Theorem 2. *Assume (P) and (U') and let $y_0 > y^G$. Then there exists an infinite number of time-consistent solutions to the maximin problem. They are all non-stationary.*

Theorem 2 is important. As an ethical norm the maximin criterion was criticized on the grounds that a society adopting it seems to be "imprisoned in perpetual poverty if it begins in poverty" (Dasgupta (1974)). However, it is much more accepted and appealing for a better off society in which the need for further accumulation of capital is less desirable. It is for this case that Theorem 2 demonstrates that time-consistency and optimality of plans are always comptabile.

Since (U') contains the utility structure used in Rodriguez (1981) as a special case, Theorem 2 contradicts a result stated there, namely that the maximin optimal policy for all $y_0 \geq y^1$ (i.e. for all utility non-productive states) is to keep initial capital constant.[2] Intuitively, it is quite clear that it can never be optimal to keep the capital stock $y_0 = \bar{y} > y^1$ constant. At $\bar{y}$ *all* capital is needed to maintain the capital stock; i.e. nothing is left for consumption. But strictly positive consumption for all generations is feasible.

CONCLUSION

Economists' assessment of the maximin criterion as a way to determine intergenerational distributive justice was based on models which either postulate a very "static" production sector (i.e. a linear technology) or a very "static" intertemporal preference structure (i.e. one which "hooks together" preferences of succeeding generations in a non-conflicting way). This paper dissociates itself from both of these assumptions. As a result a qualitatively new solution pattern for certain parameter constellations emerges in which there are a multiplicity of time-consistent maximin consumption paths. This pattern which demonstrates the *compatibility* of time-consistency and optimality of plans, is shown to generalize to an extensive class of economies with a non-linear technology. One consequence of this is that a result stated in the earlier literature on the subject turns out to be incorrect since it failed to identify this possibility.

APPENDIX

Proof of Theorem 1.   (P) implies that

Lemma 1.   (i) *If* $y_0 \leq y^G$ *then the maximal feasible constant level of consumption is*
$\bar{c} = f(y_0)$.
(ii) *If* $y_0 > y^G$ *then the maximal feasible constant level of consumption is* $\bar{c} = f(y^G)$.

Proof.   (i) $y_0 \leq y^G$: Suppose the claim is not true. Then there exists a feasible
consumption sequence $\{\bar{c}\}$ such that $\bar{c} = f(y_0) + \delta$ with $\delta > 0$. Look at the associated
sequence $\{\bar{y}_t\}$:

$$\bar{y}_1 = y_0 + f(y_0) - \bar{c} = y_0 - \delta \quad \text{by (3)}$$
$$\bar{y}_2 = \bar{y}_1 + f(\bar{y}_1) - f(y_0) - \delta \leq \bar{y}_1 - \delta - y_0 - 2\delta$$
$$\vdots$$
$$\bar{y}_t = \bar{y}_{t-1} + f(\bar{y}_{t-1}) - f(y_0) - \delta \leq \bar{y}_{t-1} - \delta$$
$$\leq (y_0 - (t-1)\delta) - \delta$$
$$= y_0 - t \cdot \delta$$

For t big enough $\bar{y}_t \leq y_0 - t\delta$ must violate the condition $\bar{y}_t \geq 0$; thus $\{\bar{c}\}$ is not feasible
and we created a contradiction.
(ii) $y_0 > y^G$: The argument of (i) analogously applies with $\bar{c} = f(y^G) + \delta$ since $f(y^G) \geq$
$f(y)$ for all y (by definition of y^G). ‖

Proposition 1.   *For any feasible consumption sequence* $\{c_t\}$

$$\inf_{t \geq t_0} \{u(c_t, c_{t+1})\} \leq u(f(y^G), f(y^G)) = \bar{u} \qquad (*)$$

holds $(t_0 = 0, 1, 2, \ldots)$.

Proof.   Assume there exists $\{c_t\}$ such that $\inf_t u(c_t, c_{t+1}) = \bar{u} + \varepsilon$. Then by (U) and
concavity of v we have for all $t \geq 0$

$$[v(c_t) - v(f(y^G))] + b[v(c_{t+1}) - v(f(y^G))] \geq \varepsilon > 0,$$
$$\Rightarrow (c_t - f(y^G))v'(f(y^G)) + b(c_{t+1} - f(y^G))v'(f(y^G)) \geq \varepsilon$$

or

$$(c_t - f(y^G)) + b(c_{t+1} - f(y^G)) \geq \varepsilon' > 0$$

with

$$\varepsilon' = \frac{\varepsilon}{v'(f(y^G))}.$$

The last inequality holds for all t. Let $\{y_t\}$ denote the capital sequence associated with
$\{c_t\}$ and use the fact that $f(y^G) \geq f(y_t)$ for all t (by definition of y^G) to get

$$(c_t - f(y_t)) + b(c_{t+1} - f(y_{t+1})) \geq \varepsilon' \quad \text{for all } t.$$

Summation over t then yields

$$A = \sum_{t=0}^{\infty} [(c_t - f(y_t)) + b(c_{t+1} - f(y_{t+1}))] = \infty.$$

But

$$A = (c_0 - f(y_0)) + (1 + b) \sum_{t=1}^{\infty} [c_t - f(y_t)]$$

which implies that $\sum_{t=1}^{\infty} [c_t - f(y_t)]$ cannot be bounded. This violates the feasibility condition (F). Such a $\{c_t\}$ therefore cannot exist. ‖

Because of Lemma 1 the value on the right-hand side of (∗), $\bar{u}$, is always attainable if $y_0 > y^G$. Any of the infinitely many feasible consumption sequences doing so is therefore optimal. Time-consistency is guaranteed since (by Proposition 1) $\bar{u}$ cannot be improved upon from any $t = t_0$. This proves part (iii) of Theorem 1.

In order to prove parts (i) and (ii) of Theorem 1 it is helpful to study the following problem of generation 0:

(I)   max $\{v(c_0) + bv(c_1)\}$ subject to $y_2 \geqq y_0$,

where y_0 is the given initial capital stock and (c_0, c_1) has to be feasible.

(I) always has a unique solution lying on the boundary of the constraint set:

The contour lines of u (c_0, c_1) are strictly convex and by use of (3) we see that $y_2 \geqq y_0$ is equivalent to

$$c_0 + c_1 - f(y_0) - f(y_0 + f(y_0) - c_0) \leqq 0,$$

which defines a convex set in (c_0, c_1)-space for any $y_0 \geqq 0$ since f is strictly concave.

The first-order conditions for (I) (with $y_2 \geqq y_0$ replaced by $y_2 = y_0$) then yield that

$$\frac{v'(c_0^*)}{v'(c_1^*)} = b \cdot (1 + f'(y_1^*))$$

and therefore (by concavity and monotonicity of v)

$$c_0^* \gtreqqless c_1^* \Leftrightarrow b(1 + f'(y_1^*)) \lesseqqgtr 1 \tag{4}$$

must hold.

On the other hand it is not difficult to see that along the constraint (written as $c_1 = f(y_0) - c_0 + f(y_0 + g(y_0) - c_0)$) we have:

$$c_1 \gtreqqless c_0 \quad \text{as} \quad c_0 \lesseqqgtr f(y_0) \quad \text{as} \quad y_1 \gtreqqless y_0. \tag{5}$$

(5) combined with (4) yields

$$c_0^* > c_1^* \Leftrightarrow b(1 + f'(y_1^*)) < 1 \Rightarrow b(1 + f'(y_0^*)) < 1 \quad (\text{since } y_1 < y_0)$$

and

$$c_0^* < c_1^* \Leftrightarrow b(1 + f'(y_1^*)) > 1 \Rightarrow b(1 + f'(y_0^*)) > 1 \quad (\text{since } y_1 > y_0)$$

and this is sufficient to establish

Lemma 2. *Let* (c_0^*, c_1^*) *be the unique solution to Problem* (I). *Then*

$$c_0^* \gtreqqless c_1^* \Leftrightarrow b[1 + f'(y_0)] \lesseqqgtr 1$$

$$\Leftrightarrow b[1 + f'(y_1)] \lesseqqgtr 1 \Leftrightarrow y_0 \gtreqqless y^1$$

where y^1 *is defined on page 6.*

This Lemma shows that the solution to (I) always implies a next period capital level y_1 that lies on the same side of y^1 as y_0. This allows us to prove

Proposition 2. *Let (c_0^*, c_1^*) be the solution to* (I) *and assume* $y_0 \leqq y^1$. *Then* $\{c_t^*\} = \{c_0^*, c_1^*, c_0^*, c_1^*, \ldots, c_0^*, c_1^*, \ldots\}$ *is the unique maximin optimal consumption sequence.*

· *Proof.* Let $W(y_t, z_t)$ denote the following function:

$$W(y_t, z_t) = \max_{\{c_t, c_{t+1}\}} u(c_t, c_{t+1}) \quad \text{subject to } z_t = f(y_t) - c_t + f(y_t + f(y_t) - c_t) - c_{t+1}$$

(Note that $W(y_t, 0)$ is identical with the optimal value function of Problem (I)). W is increasing in y_t (at least for $y_t < y^G$) and decreasing in z_t. These properties of W allow us to conclude that any consumption sequence $\{c_t\}$ such that

$$\inf_t \{u(c_t, c_{t+1})\} = u(c_0^*, c_1^*) + \varepsilon, \qquad \varepsilon > 0,$$

cannot be feasible.

For $u(c_0, c_1) \geqq u(c_0^*, c_1^*) + \varepsilon$ implies that (by definition of W)

$$W(y_0, y_2 - y_0) \geqq u(c_0, c_1) \geqq W(y_0, 0) + \varepsilon$$

and therefore $y_2 < y_0$ must hold. By the same argument $u(c_2, c_3) \geqq u(c_0^*, c_1^*) + \varepsilon$ implies $y_4 < y_2$, etc.

We claim:

$$y_{2(t+1)} - y_{2(t+2)} > y_{2t} - y_{2(t+1)} \quad \text{for all } t.$$

But clearly, such a program eventually would violate the feasibility condition $y_{2t} \geqq 0$. Indeed define the function $\delta(y)$ implicitly by

$$W(y, -\delta(y)) = W(y_0, 0) + \varepsilon \tag{6}$$

(then $y_2 \leqq y_0 - \delta(y_0)$, $y_4 \leqq y_2 - \delta(y_2)$ etc.) It is readily shown that δ is strictly decreasing; for, total differentiation of (6) yields:

$$W_1(y, -\delta(y)) + W_2(y, -\delta(y)) \cdot (-\delta'(y)) = 0$$

i.e.

$$\delta'(y) = \frac{W_1(y, -\delta(y))}{W_2(y, -\delta(y))} < 0 \quad (\text{since } W_1 > 0, W_2 < 0).$$

Thus, $u(c_0^*, c_1^*) = \max_{\{c_t\}} \inf_t \{u(c_t, c_{t+1})\}$ if $u(c_0^*, c_1^*) \leqq u(c_1^*, c_0^*)$. This, in fact, holds with strict inequality if $y_0 < y^1$. For by Lemma 2 $c_0^* < c_1^*$, which implies that $(1-b)v(c_0^*) < (1-b)v(c_1^*)$ and this gives us $u(c_0^*, c_1^*) = v(c_0^*) + bv(c_1^*) < v(c_1^* + bv(c_0^*)) = u(c_1^*, c_0^*)$. This proves that $\{c_t^*\} = \{c_0^*, c_1^*, \ldots\}$ is the maximin solution if $y_0 \leqq y^1$. The solution is time-inconsistent since (c_1^*, c_0^*) cannot be the solution to (I) relative to $y_1^* = y_0 + f(y_0) - c_0^*$. That solution must have the property that $\bar{c}_0^* < \bar{c}_1^*$ (Lemma 2). ‖

The reasoning of Proposition 2 cannot be applied to the case where $y_0 > y_1$, since then the solution to (I) (c_0^*, c_1^*), is such that $c_0^* > c_1^*$; then $u(c_0^*, c_1^*)$ is *not* the maximin optimal utility level. But neither is $u(c_1^*, c_0^*)$: we show that the plan $\{c_t\} = \{f(y_0), f(y_0), \ldots\}$, which keeps initial capital constant, is better.

Claim. *If $y_0 > y^1$ then $u(f(y_0), f(y_0)) > u(c_1^*, c_0^*)$.*

Proof. Assume that $u(c_0^*, c_1^*) > u(c_1^*, c_0^*) \geqq u(f(y_0), f(y_0))$. (The first inequality follows from Lemma 2.) Then $u(\frac{1}{2}c_0^* + \frac{1}{2}c_1^*, \frac{1}{2}c_1^* + \frac{1}{2}c_0^*) > u(f(y_0), f(y_0))$ which implies $\frac{1}{2}c_0^* + \frac{1}{2}c_1^* > f(y_0)$. But the consumption plan $\{c_t\} = \{\frac{1}{2}c_0^* + \frac{1}{2}c_1^*, \frac{1}{2}c_0^* + \frac{1}{2}c_1^*, \ldots\}$ is feasible since f is concave and $\frac{1}{2}c_0^* + \frac{1}{2}c_1^* < c_0^*$. This contradicts Lemma 1 which states that $\{\bar{c}\} = \{f(y_0), \ldots\}$

is the maximal feasible constant consumption level for $y_0 < y^G$. Thus, $u(c_1^*, c_0^*) \geqq u(f(y_0), (y_0))$ is not possible. ‖

We now prove that $\{c_t\} = \{f(y_0), f(y_0), \ldots\}$ also dominates any other feasible plan.

Proposition 3. *If* $y^1 \leqq y_0 \leqq y^G$ *then* $\{\bar{c}\} = \{f(y_0), f(y_0), \ldots\}$ *is the maximin optimal consumption sequence.*

Proof. $u(f(y_0), f(y_0))$ is strictly increasing in y_0 over $[y^1, y^G]$ and strictly concave in y_0. Since one cannot improve upon $u(f(y_0), f(y_0))$ from a maximin point of view *under the restriction* $y_{t+1} \geqq y_t$, any plan giving higher utility than $u(f(y_0), f(y_0))$ for the first generation must leave less capital than y_0 to the third generation; i.e. $W(y_0, z_0) = u(f(y_0), f(y_0)) + \varepsilon$ implies $z_0 < 0$. But then the argument in the proof of Proposition 2 precisely shows that to maintain this utility level from lower and lower initial capital levels requires higher and higher 'excess' consumption and such a sequence eventually must violate the feasibility condition $y_{2t} \geqq 0$. This completes the proof of Theorem 1. ‖

Proof of Theorem 2. We prove that $\bar{u} = u(f(y^G), f(y^G), \ldots)$ is the maximal utility level attainable by means of a feasible consumption sequence: Assume this is not so; i.e. there exists a feasible consumption sequence $\{c_t\}$, such that

$$\inf_t \{u(_t c)\} = \bar{u} + \varepsilon, \qquad \varepsilon > 0,$$

where $\bar{u} + \varepsilon$ is the optimal utility level (this number exists and is finite since consumption is bounded by $\bar{y}$).

Then $\{c_t\}$ cannot be a constant consumption sequence, since that could maximally yield a utility level $\bar{u}$ according to Lemma 1. Neither can any of the subsequences $_t c = \{c_t, c_{t+1}, \ldots\}$ be constant. Hence we have that for any t, $_t c$ contains two adjacent elements, c_{t_0} and $c_{t_0} + 1$, such that $c_{t_0} \neq c_{t_0} + 1$. Without any loss of generality we can assume $c_{t_0} > c_{t_0+1}$ because otherwise $\{c_t\}$ would be infeasible. Now examine $u(_t c)$ for every t. Keep $_t c = \{c_t, \ldots, c_{t_0}, c_{t_0+1}, \ldots\}$ constant except for c_{t_0} and c_{t_0+1}. Use the strict concavity of u to conclude that $u(_t c)$ can be improved upon for all t:
The function

$$v(c_{t_0}, c_{t_0+1}) = u(\bar{c}_t, \bar{c}_{t+1}, \ldots, \bar{c}_{t_0-1}, c_{t_0}, c_{t_0+1}, \bar{c}_{t_0+2}, \ldots)$$

is strictly concave and therefore $v(\frac{1}{2}c_{t_0} + \frac{1}{2}c_{t_0+1}, \frac{1}{2}c_{t_0} + \frac{1}{2}c_{t_0+1}) > v(c_{t_0}, c_{t_0+1})$ holds. Furthermore, $(\frac{1}{2}c_{t_0} + \frac{1}{2}c_{t_0+1}, \frac{1}{2}c_{t_0} + \frac{1}{2}c_{t_0+1})$ is feasible in the sense that, given $\bar{y}_{t_0}$ it leads to $y'_{t_0+2} > \bar{y}_{t_0+2}$. This follows from the fact that $\frac{1}{2}c_{t_0} + \frac{1}{2}c_{t_0+1} < c_{t_0}$.

Thus, for every t, $u(_t c)$ can be improved upon. If there exists a $\delta > 0$ such that any improvement is greater or equal to δ, we have a contradiction to the fact that inf$_t (u(_t c)) = \bar{u} + \varepsilon$ is the optimal utility level; $\{c_t\}$ could not be feasible. If such a δ does not exist the sequence $\{c_t\}$ must eventually become stationary (by construction of the improvements). But stationarity implies inf$_t \{u(_t c)\} \leqq \bar{u}$ by Lemma 2. This contradicts the hypothesis $\varepsilon > 0$; i.e. inf$_t \{u(_t c)\} \leqq \bar{u}$ for all feasible $\{c_t\}$. The observation that $\bar{u}$ is always attainable if $y_0 > y^G$ completes the proof. ‖

First version received December 1983; final version accepted January 1985 (Eds).

The author is grateful to John Lane, Martin Hellwig and Walter Trockel for helpful discussions and suggestions. He is also indebted to an anonymous referee and gratefully acknowledges support by the Deutsche Forschungsgemeinshacft and the VW Foundation.

NOTES

1. Note that (U') includes the cases in which u_t only depends on a finite number of consumption levels after c_t; e.g. (c_t, c_{t+1}). u_t describes altruistic preferences if it depends on a c_i with $i > t$.

2. Rodriguez (1981) confuses production function and *net* production function and attributes properties to the latter which only the former possesses. Specifically, in the proofs of Proposition 1 and 2 it is assumed that the net production function is increasing, which is *not* true. It is the production function which is increasing. This error invalidates the conclusions.

REFERENCES

ARROW, K. J. (1973), "Rawls' Principle of Just Saving", *Swedish Journal of Economics*, 75, 323-335.

CALVO, G. (1978), "Some Notes on Time Inconsistency and Rawls' Maximin Criterion", *Review of Economic Studies*, 45, 97-102.

DASGUPTA, P. (1974), "On Some Alternative Criteria for Justice Between Generations", *Journal of Public Economics*, 3.

PELEG, B. and YAARI, M. (1973), "On the Existence of a Consistent Course of Action when Tastes are Changing", *Review of Economic Studies*, 40, 391-401.

RAWLS, J. (1971), *A Theory of Justice* (Cambridge: Harvard University Press).

RODRIGUEZ, A. (1981), "Rawls' Maximin Criterion and Time-Consistency: A Generalization", *Review of Economic Studies*, 48, 599-605.

Rawls's difference principle and a problem of sacrifice

Paul Voice

Department of Philosophy, University of South Africa, P.O. Box 392, Pretoria 0001,
Republic of South Africa

Received May 1990; revised July 1990

G.A. Cohen makes a distinction between the 'strict' interpretation of Rawls's difference principle and a 'mis-construed' interpretation. In this article it is argued that when understood 'strictly' the difference principle may demand sacrifices of life prospects comparable to the sacrifices Rawls finds unacceptable on a utilitarian account of justice. This problem arises once one introduces alternative economic systems which one must if the difference principle is to be properly understood. The author argues in favour of this point before attempting to meet a range of possible objections to his thesis. The results of the author's argument conflict with Rawls's main reasons for believing that the parties to the original position would opt for the difference principle before a utilitarian principle of justice.

G.A. Cohen maak 'n onderskeid tussen 'n 'streng' interpretasie van Rawls se verskilsprinsipe (difference principle) en 'n 'verdraaide' interpretasie daarvan. In hierde artikel is die argument dat wanneer mens Rawls se verskilsprinsipe streng interpreteer, dit opofferings mag verg wat Rawls self onaanvaarbaar sou vind t.o.v. 'n utilistiese geregtig-heidbegrip. Hierdie probleem kom voor sodra die alternatiewe ekonomiese sisteme wat die verskilsprinsipe eis ter sprake kom. Dit is die argument wat die outeur aanvoer voordat hy probeer om 'n reeks objeksies teen sy tesis te weerlê. Die gevolgtrekking is dat die outeur se argument strydig is met Rawls se siening dat die oorspronklike partye die verskilsprinsipe sal verkies bo 'n utilistiese prinsipe van geregtigheid.

In a recent article on Robert Nozick, G.A. Cohen (1985) makes some important clarificatory remarks on John Rawls's difference principle. They are important not only because they clear up a vagueness in Rawls's exposition of the principle, but also, I will argue, they point to substantial difficulties with the coherence of the principle itself, and the work it is assigned to do in Rawls's theory of justice.

First, let me give an interpretation of Cohen's claims. He says that 'In its strict meaning the difference principle is satisfied by a given economic system only if those who are worst off under it are not more badly off than the worst off would be under any alternative to it' (Cohen 1985:102). In other words, the position of the worst-off representative person will determine which economic system is to be preferred where there is a range of possible economic systems with differing distributions of primary goods. The following matrix gives a clearer picture:

Matrix I

	i	ii	iii
A	11	12	13
B	10	11	12
C	9	10	11

The least advantaged group is represented by C and satisfaction of the difference principle demands that economic system iii be adopted over either i or ii because under iii C is in the best worst position with respect to its holdings of primary goods. Note that in this matrix and the ones that follow it is assumed that the least advantaged benefit by the inequality in holdings and that they would not be better off under an equal distribution.

This interpretation is to be contrasted with what Cohen calls the 'misconstrual' of the difference principle. Under this inter-pretation the difference principle would be satisfied only if the worst-off representative person in a given economic system would not *herself* be better off under some alternative system. The contrast with the strict interpretation is not immediately

obvious because the 'misconstrued' under-stand-ing would have the same satisfaction conditions in matrix I as the 'strict' understanding of the difference principle. The worst-off repre-sentative person in C would herself be better off under system iii than under either i or ii. But, it is easy to see why Rawls cannot intend the difference principle to be understood in the 'misconstrued' way. The distribution of primary goods in matrix 2 shows why.

Matrix 2

	i	ii	iii
A	10	5	1
B	5	1	10
C	1	10	5

The worst-off representative person under i is C who would be better off under either ii or iii. If the principle states that the position of the worst off is be maximized *simpliciter*, as the 'misconstrued' version appears to demand, then there is an obligation when in i to move to system iii. However, once in iii it is now A who represents the worst off and whose posi-tion would be maximized by a return to i. So, for as long as there are at least two economic systems in which the least advantaged are not identical in both systems, and where the worst off would be better off in the other system, the 'mis-construed' difference principle would require a continuous swapping from one system to the other. This is, of course, a fatal source of instability and in the context of Rawls's theory wholly unacceptable.

The 'misconstrued' version goes wrong because of a failure to recognize that the worst-off group is not necessarily the same group under alternative economic systems. The problem is disguised in matrix 1 precisely because it is assumed that C is the worst off in each of the alternatives. The mistake is to compare the position of the members of a designated worst-off group with some position they might hold in another system. This is because any designated worst-off group will be better off under some other imaginable economic system.

Thus, the 'misconstrued' interpretation of the difference principle is not only a misconstrual as Cohen claims, but also an interpretation which prevents any stable choice of a just economic system. Since the purpose of the difference principle is to enable us to choose, or at least understand, a just economic arrangement, the principle must be understood differently or be charged with incoherence.

Let us look at the favoured interpretation, as extrapolated from Cohen. In matrix 3 it is quite clear which economic system will satisfy the difference principle.

Matrix 3

	i	ii	iii	iv
A	8	11	12	10
B	8	10	11	7
C	8	9	10	13

There can be no charge of incoherence because iii is a stable choice since it realizes the best worst position. Nevertheless, a new, and more substantive, problem looms for the difference principle. I will argue that the difference principle as 'strictly' understood is open to exactly the same arguments which Rawls offers as reasons for rejecting a utilitarian principle of justice.[1]

Rawls's argument against a utilitarian principle of justice is summed up in the following passage:

> 'The principles of justice apply to the basic structure of the system and to the determination of life prospects. What the principle of utility asks is precisely a sacrifice of these prospects. We are to accept the greater advantage of others as a sufficient reason for lower expectations over the whole course of our life. This is surely an extreme demand. In fact, when society is conceived as a system of cooperation designed to advance the good of its members, it seems quite incredible that some citizens should be expected, on the basis of political principles, to accept lower prospects of life for the sake of others' (Rawls 1972:178).

The core of the argument states that no principles of justice are acceptable which demand a sacrifice of life prospects for the benefit of others. There are two reasons for this. Firstly, the parties to the original position, given their mutual disinterest in each others' welfare and their desire to maximize their own life prospects, would not under the veil of ignorance accept principles of justice which may demand sacrifice for the good of others. The veil of ignorance prevents them from knowing in advance what their own position in society would be and whether they would be the ones required to make a sacrifice. This together with reasoning according to the maximin principle and their lack of willingness to take chances, would lead them to reject any principle which may demand substantial sacrifice of the kind required by the principle of utility. Secondly, the parties to the original position want to be able to 'rely on each other to understand and to act in accordance with whatever principles are finally agreed to' (Rawls 1972:145).

They therefore take note of the 'strains of commitment' involved in the principles they adopt. A too great strain of commitment would make compliance difficult and undermine the stability of the system. A demand for sacrifice of one's life prospects which may be required under a utilitarian regime is a clear example of a case in which the strain of commitment is too high.

However, a second look at matrix 3 reveals that sacrifices of just the kind required by a utilitarian may be demanded by a Rawlsian. Economic system iii is to be preferred even though C would be better off under iv because B would be worse off under iv than C is under iii. C is therefore expected to accept lower life prospects in order that B not suffer still lower prospects. C is in effect expected to make what could be substantial sacrifices so that others may enjoy a better life. Considerations of the strains of commitment apply equally to the difference principle and, given the above, count equally against the difference principle.

Rawls is therefore wrong to think that considerable sacrifice for the sake of the good of others could not occur through the application of the difference principle. Some indeed may benefit at the expense of others. Thus the chief reason for opting for Rawls's principles over utilitarian principles has been removed if the difference principle is understood according to the 'strict' interpretation, as I have argued above it must.

A Rawlsian has some obvious replies to this line of argument. Although Rawls does state that everyone benefits from the application of the difference principle, the above argument takes this claim too literally. Of course some sacrifice of life prospects is required in order to realize a just society, and the parties to the original position would be aware of this. The most obvious case is the sacrifices made by the best off. They sacrifice prospects they would have otherwise enjoyed had they been beneficiaries of an unjust system, a system in which the distribution of primary goods is both unequal and not to the benefit of all. Nevertheless these sacrifices are not arbitrarily imposed. Firstly, the best off would recognize and accept the claim that they would have agreed to such sacrifices in the original position. Secondly, they would enjoy a general recognition that they are entitled to the benefits and advantages they possess which they would not under an unjust regime.

The difficulty arises with respect to the sacrifices the worst off are called upon to make. This is especially so because one of the founding premises upon which Rawls's theory of justice is based is the idea that the perspective of the least well off is to be privileged. The matrices above do show that this group is required to sacrifice life prospects. This is so because the least advantaged in a particular economic arrangement may be called upon to sacrifice life prospects they would have otherwise enjoyed under an alternative system in order that others are not placed in an even worse position. The question to be asked is whether or not this sacrifice can be justified within the parameters of Rawls's theory.

Much of Rawls's argument in favour of the difference principle is conducted in conscious opposition to a utilitarian alternative. Rawls's main argument against the idea that the parties to the original position would opt for utilitarian principles of justice is based on the argument from the strains of commitment. I have tried to argue that the strains of commitment argument does not favour the difference principle since this principle may require substantial sacrifice. Nevertheless, a Rawlsian may maintain that I have missed what looks like a decisive difference between utilitarian and Rawlsian positions with respect to sacrifice.

It may be claimed that the difference principle stipulates a limit on the extent of sacrifice that anybody can be expected to endure. That limit is defined by the ruling that an inequality in the distribution of primary goods is justified only if such an inequality is to the benefit of all, otherwise an equal distribution is to be preferred. Now, no such limit applies to utilitarian principles, since any amount of sacrifice can be justified by appeal to the common good. So it may be argued that even if I am correct in saying that the worst off are expected to make sacrifices, such sacrifices are limited. This, then, is the decisive difference between the difference principle and a utilitarian principle of justice.

The first point in reply is to say that Rawls does not argue like this. His claim is not that the difference principle limits sacrifice, whereas a utilitarian principle offers the prospect of unlimited sacrifice. As the earlier quotation shows, Rawls's argument turns simply on the extent of possible sacrifice, that is, whether or not a substantial sacrifice may be required.

The second point is to question whether a real difference has been identified here or not. Rawls's concern in speaking of substantial sacrifice is the idea that persons under a utilitarian regime may be expected to live a miserable and hopeless life just so that others may live a better one. In practice this can be so under a Rawlsian regime. Those who are required to sacrifice their prospects for the good of others under the difference principle may face a choice between leading a miserable and hopeless life by foregoing benefits they would have enjoyed under a different economic system or leading an even more miserable and hopeless existence under an equal distribution. The difference principle does not guarantee a particular quality of life any more than a utilitarian principle of justice does.

It would be useful here to distinguish two kinds of sacrifice. The first kind is a sacrifice in one's material welfare, and the second kind is a sacrifice of goods such as liberties, rights, etc. The difference principle may require, if my argument is correct, sacrifices of the first kind, namely, in material welfare, but the principle of greatest equal liberty, which is lexically prior to the difference principle, would prevent sacrifices of the second kind. The level of material welfare enjoyed by a community under an equal distribution may be so low and the benefits of an unequal distribution so marginal for the worst-off group, that the difference between the life prospects of the worst off under either Rawlsian or utilitarian regimes is in fact negligible. So, to claim that the difference principle limits sacrifice whereas a utilitarian principle does not is not a particularly strong claim with respect to sacrifices of material goods.

Where limitation does play a role is in sacrifices of goods such as liberty. Conditions such as slavery are ruled out on Rawls's scheme by the principle of greatest equal liberty. It is this principle which does the work in limiting the sacrifice of non-material goods and not the difference principle. So, if we are charitable to Rawls and argue that under a Rawlsian regime sacrifices are limited, whereas they may be unlimited under a utilitarian regime, we must note that this argument cannot be used in support of the difference principle, since the limits are defined not by the difference principle but by the principle of greatest equal liberty. Therefore, the question of the limits on sacrifice is largely irrelevant when we assess the reasoning leading to the parties in the original position to opt

Another objection may be stated as follows: a utilitarian principle may demand sacrifices in order to *increase* the overall prospects of an entire community, whereas the sacrifices which may be demanded by the difference principle would be required in order to prevent the prospects of a particular group from *falling below* the prospects of the actual worst-off group. So, it might be argued, the sacrifices are not strictly comparable.

But, of course, a Rawlsian has no recourse to such an argument. The difference between the types of sacrifice only makes sense if we attribute to the Rawlsian agent a *moral* concern which includes not only regard for others, but also a regard which is capable of overriding considerations of self-interest. However, given Rawls's insistence on a mutual disinterestedness between the parties to the original position, the other-regarding criteria which would justify a distinction between the types of sacrifice is absent. Therefore, from the point of view of the parties to the original position, the sacrifices possible under a utilitarian regime and a Rawlsian regime are comparable and the considerations of the strains of commitment apply to both.

The issue of sacrifice would not arise at all if we assume, either that only one economic system can in fact satisfy the difference principle, or that a particular group would always be worst off in *any* economic system. Clearly Rawls does think that a property owning market society would best satisfy the difference principle, given considerations of efficiency, but wisely does not exclude possible alternatives. The difference principle has to go beyond a single instantiation on pain of appearing as an apologia for capitalism. But, once alternatives are entertained, the problem of sacrifice arises.

The idea that the worst-off group would be identical in any future economic system is not only improbable but points to a conservatism which takes present economic arrangements as historically rigid and closes off radical future change.

Lastly, it may be objected that my argument depends on an unrealistic multiplication of economic systems and an unrealistic swapping around of groups. In reply, Rawls himself acknowledges a variety of possible economic arrangements: free market capitalism, command economy socialism, and market socialism. Rawls argues in favour of market over command economies and in favour of private over public ownership of property, but states that 'The theory of justice does not by itself favour either form of regime. As we have seen, the decision as to which system is best for a given people depends upon the circumstances, institutions, and historical conditions' (Rawls 1972:280).

Further, it could be argued that my use of 'economic system' is misleading (I merely followed Cohen in this). In the matrices above it appears that an economic system is defined by its distribution of primary goods. This is misleading because the same economic system can distribute primary goods in different ways at different times and in different historical and political circumstances. In addition, different economic systems may distribute primary goods in precisely the same way, although this is unlikely. An economic system may favour certain patterns of distribution, but it is a contingent matter what the distribution profile in fact turns out to be for any given economic system.

So, it is misleading to simply define economic systems in

materially affect the argument since the alternative economic systems represented in the matrices may be read as true alternative systems, or differently placed and managed single systems, or as combinations of both. This reading of 'economic system' yields an even greater multiplicity of possible systems and so reinforces the point made in the article.

In summary, the 'misconstrued' interpretation of the difference principle compared the position of the representative worst-off person with some position she might hold in another economic system. This leads to instability of choice between systems and to incoherence. The 'strict' interpretation allowed for stability of choice, but also allowed that some members of society may be required to sacrifice better life prospects for the good of others. This latter consequence conflicts with Rawls's main reasons for our accepting his difference principle over a principle of utility. Therefore, under both interpretations the difference principle fails to do the work Rawls assigns to it.

Acknowledgements

I would like to thank George Carlson for his comments on a early draft of the this article and Geoffrey Warnock for his suggestions, as well as two anonymous referees.

Notes

1. The problem of stability naturally arises in the context of a discussion of sacrifice, and although what I have to say concerning sacrifice has consequences for Rawls's remarks on stability, I do not pursue these here beyond the following comments.

    Stability, in one sense, is achieved by the 'strict' interpretation of the difference principle. We know, given a range of options, which economic system the principle picks out as fulfilling its conditions. This is not the case with the 'misconstrued' interpretation, as I showed. Stability in another sense though is weakened.

    Rawls calls on a principle of reciprocity (e.g. Rawls 1972:102) in an attempt to demonstrate that the principles of justice as fairness afford greater stability in social arrangements than a principle of utility. The principle of reciprocity rests on the idea of mutual advantage. Clearly, the sacrifices which I will argue are demanded by the 'strict' interpretation undermine the idea of mutual advantage and thus rebound on Rawls's arguments concerning stability. If, as I will argue, the sacrifices demanded by the difference principle and a principle of utility are comparable, then the difficulties Rawls finds with a utilitarian conception of justice with respect to stability (see Rawls 1972:496ff) apply as much to his own principles as they do to utilitarian principles.

References

Cohen, G.A. 1985. Nozick on appropriation. *New Left Review*, 150:89–105.

Rawls, J. 1972. *A theory of justice*. Oxford. Oxford Univ. Pr.

Ratio Juris. Vol. 8 No. 1 March 1995 (40–63)

Social Justice and Individual Ethics*

PHILIPPE VAN PARIJS

Abstract. If one is committed to a "Rawlsian" conception of justice, is one not also necessarily committed to a "Christian" personal ethics? More explicitly, if one believes that social justice requires the maximinning of material conditions, should one not use one's time and resources as well as one can in order to assist the poorest? The paper offers a very partial answer to these questions by arguing for the following two claims:

(1) Contrary to what is implied by some egalitarian critics of Rawls, the idea of a well-ordered society does not require maximin-guided choices at the individual level, and hence leaves room for legitimate incentive payments.

(2) Despite Rawls's own neglect of this fact, a limited form of patriotism does constitute an individual "natural duty" following from a commitment to maximin social justice.

It happened to me when bargaining over the price of a hammock on a Mexican beach, when checking my purse in my back pocket on a packed

* This article is a significantly abridged version of a paper that grew, in directions I did not anticipate, out of a sequence of talks given in various places in the course of the academic year 1992–93: at a meeting of the Institut International de Philosophie on "Public and Private Morality" (Liège, 2 September 1992), at the Philosophy Department of Bristol University (Bristol, 12 February 1993), at the conference on "Consensus and Democracy: A Debate around John Rawls" (Oxford, 13 February 1993), at the Philosophy Department of the Université du Québec (Montréal, 7 April 1993), at the Legal Theory Workshop of Yale Law School (New Haven, 8 April 1993), at the Séminaire de philosophie contemporaine of the Université Catholique de Louvain (Louvain-la-Neuve, 22 April 1993), at the Faculty of Economic and Social Sciences of the Université Catholique de Fribourg (Fribourg, 11 May 1993), at the Theology Faculty of the Université de Genève (Geneva, 12 May 1993), at the Philosophy Department of Fu Jen University (Taipei, 29 May 1993), and at the Faculty of Sociology and Politics of the Universitat Autonoma de Barcelona (Barcelona, 19 June 1993). I am particularly grateful to Bruce Ackerman, Karl-Otto Apel, Christian Arnsperger, Ruth Barcan-Marcus, Brian Barry, Chris Bertram, John Broome, Jerry Cohen, Jocelyne Couture, Geneviève de Pesloüan, Toni Domènech, Paul Dumouchel, Ronald Dworkin, Owen Fiss, Marc Fleurbaey, Andreas Follesdal, Keith Graham, Steven Lukes, Adam Morton, Robert Nadeau, Kai Nielsen, Onora O'Neill, John Passmore, Michael Rosen, Dan Weinstock, and above all John Baker and Joe Carens, for stimulating oral and/or written comments. All of them forced me and helped me to think harder about the issues touched upon in the article, but only some of this further thinking found its way into this abridged version. See Van Parijs (1993) for the full version.

Italian bus, and when running into a legless beggar on a Russian souvenir market. It happens to me every year when wondering whether I should report on my tax form the fees or royalties I earned abroad. It happens to me every week when chucking out unread yet another leaflet from yet another charity that caught my name on its mailing list. And it happens to me nearly every day when hearing one of my children ask for something more, or nicer, or bigger than what (s)he has already been spoiled with. On all these occasions—and on countless others—I hit upon the nagging, discomforting question of what, if anything, my professed beliefs about social justice entail for my personal conduct, of what constraints, if any, a person's conception of justice imposes on her personal ethics,[1] or of what it means to be ethically consistent across the political/individual boundary.

In particular—I cannot help asking—if one is committed—as I am—to some broadly "Rawlsian" conception of justice, is one not also necessarily committed to a broadly "Christian" personal ethics?[2] More explicitly, if one believes that justice requires the maximinning of material conditions—however the latter are precisely defined, and possibly subject to respect for self-ownership, fundamental liberties, or the like—should one not use one's time and resources as well as one can in order to assist the poorest, the most vulnerable—subject, presumably, to not making oneself worse off than them in the process and also possibly, again, to respect for other people's fundamental liberties, self-ownership and the like? Or more succinctly, does it make ethical sense to advocate maximin institutions while recoiling from maximin conduct? Can one consistently be a "Rawlsian" without also being a "Christian"?

1. Managerial Dilemmas, Utilitarian Distinctions

Those anxious to find reasons to support what I shall call the dichotomic view, i.e., a positive answer to this last question, may first appeal to the following sort of example, which suggests that if you are a Rawlsian, consistency does not only allow you not to be a Christian, but prevents you from being one. Consider the choice of a manager committed to a maximin conception of justice who has to sack one of her workers. Does her commitment to (a lexical version of) maximin demand that she should sack, not her worst worker, for whom it is likely to be most difficult to find another job, but her best worker, for whom this is likely to be easiest? Or suppose she has to hire someone. Should she seek out the person who most needs the job and is likely to be the least employable, the least productive among the applicants? Surely, this inference from maximin at the macro-level to maximin at

[1] Here, and throughout the remainder of this paper, "her" stands for "his or her" or "him or her", and "she" for "he or she".
[2] As a professor in a Catholic University, I may perhaps be forgiven for using this convenient but admittedly parochial formulation.

the micro-level is spurious, as the latter, when consistently practiced, is bound to undermine the former, by gravely impairing the economy's performance, and hence making the best material condition that can sustainably be granted to the worst off considerably worse than is necessary. Far from implying a maximin personal ethics, commitment to a maximin conception of social justice seems to rule it out.

But one should not make too much of this sort of example. For all it does, in the present context, is warn against a naive interpretation of the policy implications of maximin at both the political and the personal level. If one can sufficiently trust the efficiency of the institutional framework, and especially of its redistributive component, it will generally be best, for the sake of the worst off in our society, if managers do not try, when hiring or firing, when buying or selling, and in any other professional circumstances, to benefit the worst off, but maximize instead their firms' expected profits. However, this does not exemplify a discrepancy between social justice and individual ethics. It simply reflects the fact that the behavioural rule which maximin-designed institutions should impose or which maximin-minded agents should follow in some specific role, need not be maximin itself.[3] In the same spirit, rule utilitarians are likely to recommend that judges take decisions in line with their convictions about who is guilty, rather than on the basis of their conjectures about which decision would be best for aggregate welfare. What is shown by examples of this sort is not that maximin social justice rules out maximin personal conduct, but that neither must be understood and implemented in too simplistic a fashion.

Does the utilitarian tradition not provide a second, and more relevant, type of support to those who would like to cut the link from maximin justice to maximin conduct? True, if you believe that some version of utilitarianism provides the correct answer to the question of how each individual ought to behave, then it is hard to see how you could deny that the same version of utilitarianism provides the criterion in terms of which alternative institutional setups are to be evaluated. If your individual ethics is utilitarian, how could your conception of justice be anything else? But it does not follow that it is impossible to be utilitarian on the social level—a just social framework is one that maximizes expected aggregate welfare—while having, for example, a hedonistic life ideal. Indeed, this possibility seems emphatically asserted when utilitarians stress that the content of each person's welfare is "liberally" left entirely open or, even more perhaps, when they want to cleanse people's preferences of any "other-regarding" element the latter may

---

[3] See James Meade's (1973, 52) statement that "the ideal society would be one in which each citizen developed a real split personality, acting selfishly in the market place and altruistically at the ballot box" (quoted by Barry 1989, 394–95). Split personalities are not the outcome of a conflict between two moralities, but the instrument of a single morality.

contain, in order to avoid the inappropriate discounting or multiple counting of some people's preferences.[4]

On reflection, however, all this can be reconciled with the claim that if we must try to maximize aggregate welfare in the choice of institutions, then we must also do so in our personal conduct. For suppose all members of society are committed utilitarians at both the individual and the social level. If utilitarianism, at both levels, is to avoid unwelcome biases and double counting, it will have to care equally for the satisfaction of every person's *self-regarding* preferences only: The filtering out of other-regarding preferences at both levels has nothing to do with the separation of the two levels. Moreover, the fact that people's self-regarding preferences, as aggregated by any unbiased utilitarian calculus, can be allowed to vary without limits shows that utilitarianism, at both the personal and the social level, is in some sense "liberal" or "non-perfectionistic." It does not show that the ethical principle that defines appropriate personal conduct can consistently diverge from the ethical principle that defines appropriate institutional design, let alone that it must do so.

Thus, despite some appearances, utilitarian distinctions have proved no more able than our managerial dilemmas to support the strong claim that the principles of individual moral behaviour cannot coincide with the principles of social justice. The dichotomic view, however, only makes the weaker claim that the former need not coincide with the latter. This view is forcefully expressed in John Rawls's recent writings.

2. Rawls's Conception of a Well-ordered Society

According to Rawls's (1971, 453–54) original characterization, a well-ordered society is "a society in which everyone accepts and knows that the others accept the same principles of justice, and the basic institutions satisfy and are known to satisfy these principles." Hence, "its members have a strong and normally effective desire to act as the principles of justice require." In so far as the difference principle is concerned, the concrete meaning of this "normally effective desire" is vividly suggested in the connection Rawls (1971, 105) establishes earlier between this principle and "a natural meaning of fraternity": "Members of a family commonly do not wish to gain unless they can do so in ways that further the interests of the rest. Now wanting to act on the difference principle has precisely this consequence." Such formulations strongly support the view that in Rawls's ideal of a just society, maximin does not only shape the institutions, but also guides people's personal conduct.

[4] On the former, see the discussion between Scanlon (1991) and Rawls (1993a, 179–80) on whether utilitarianism is a form of liberalism. On the latter, see the discussion between Dworkin (1977, 232–38) and, for example, Ten (1980, 30–33) and Ezorsky (1981) on the notion of "personal" preferences.

This is, however, the most fundamental point on which Rawls (1993a, xvi) has changed his position since the publication of his first book. In his more recent writings, he still defines a well-ordered society, the subject of "strict compliance theory," as a society in which "(nearly) everyone strictly complies with, and so abides by, the principles of justice" (Rawls 1990, §5.1). But he stresses that the account of the well-ordered society he offered in *A Theory of Justice* (*TJ*) was inconsistent.

The fact of plurality of reasonable but incompatible comprehensive doctrines—the fact of reasonable pluralism—shows that, as used in *TJ*, the idea of a well-ordered society of justice as unfairness is unrealistic. This is because it is inconsistent with realizing its own principles under the best of foreseeable conditions. (Rawls 1993a, xvii)

To understand this, one needs to see that, according to *TJ*'s account, "the members of any well-ordered society [...] accept not only the same conception of justice but also the same comprehensive doctrine of which that conception is a part, or from which it can be derived" (Rawls 1990, §55.4). But this "fails to take into account the condition of pluralism to which [*TJ*'s] own principles lead" (ibid. §55.5).

Given the free institutions that conception itself enjoins, we can no longer assume that citizens generally, even if they accept justice as fairness [i.e., Rawls's two principles of justice] as a political conception, also accept the particular comprehensive view to which it might seem in *TJ* to belong. We now assume citizens hold two distinct views; or perhaps better, their overall view has two parts: one part can be seen to be, or to coincide with, a political conception of justice; the other part is a (fully or partially) comprehensive doctrine to which the political conception is in some manner related. (Ibid. §55.5)

Whereas a comprehensive moral doctrine is "one that applies to all subjects and covers all values," a political conception "focuses on the political (in the form of the basic structure), which is but a part of the domain of the moral" (ibid. §5.3). And it is precisely because commitment to the political doctrine does not entail commitment to the corresponding comprehensive doctrine that realizing the former can be "*realistically* utopian" (ibid. §5.1, my emphasis).

By contrast, a free democratic society well-ordered by any comprehensive doctrine, religious or secular, is surely utopian in the pejorative sense. Achieving it would in any case require the oppressive use of state power. This is as true of the liberalism of rightness as fairness [the comprehensive moral doctrine corresponding to justice as fairness], as it is of the Christianity of Aquinas and Luther. (Ibid. §55.5)

Does this new formulation of the ideal of a well-ordered society provide the dichotomists with the support they are looking for? Does it provide the resources required to resist the entailment from maximin justice to maximin conduct? Certainly not, according to a lineage of critics who have accused Rawls of explicitly allowing a far wider range of inequalities than consistency with his own conception should permit.[5] For this criticism—which has been articulated most recently and systematically by Gerry A. Cohen (1992a, 1992b) but goes back to Thomas Grey (1973, 316-25) in a leftish variant and to Jan Narveson (1976, 7–19) in a rightish variant—presupposes, as we shall see that such a division between the two parts of a citizens' overall morality cannot be made, and in particular that strict compliance with a maximin conception of justice must entail maximin conduct. Let us briefly examine the general structure of this line of criticism by focusing on the version offered by Cohen, before scrutinizing the threat it poses for the dichotomists' stance.

3. Cohen's Egalitarian Challenge

Suppose that everyone is committed to a maximin conception of justice such as the one encapsulated in Rawls's (1971) difference principle. It is commonly believed and said, including by Rawls himself, that even in this sort of context maximin will diverge from equality, because the incentives created by income inequalities make it possible to give more to the worst off than the latter would get under strict equality. But why should that be the case? If I am committed to maximin and could get more than others on the market because of the talents I possess, surely I shall not exploit this possibility and shall instead accept the same job for no more pay than the others, thus making it possible (say, through lower prices or higher transfers) to maximize the real income of the worst off without any departure from equality. If everyone's behaviour conforms to the difference principle, the latter will justify no such inequalities. Or, put differently, if you take seriously Rawls's idea that, in a just or well-ordered society, people are committed to the principles of justice that underlie the institutions, then maximin justice demands that incomes be equalized. This is the claim, in its simplest formulation.

But there are two compelling reasons, both acknowledged by Cohen, why this proposition cannot possibly be sustained in this form. Firstly, income on its own does not provide an appropriate metric for a plausible interpretation of the difference principle. This is the case not only because restricting attention to income would lead one to neglect the other dimensions of socio-economic advantages explicitly mentioned in canonical formulations of the difference principle (wealth, powers and prerogatives, the social bases of self-respect), but also, more relevantly, because it would lead one to neglect the unequal distribution of the length and irksomeness of labour. It is in no

---

[5] I shall return below (section 6) to the question of what does follow for individual conduct, according to Rawls himself, from a commitment to justice as fairness as a purely political conception.

© Blackwell Publishers Ltd. 1995.

way inconsistent with a commitment to the difference principle, plausibly interpreted, to say: "I claim more income than others, but no more than what is required to match the burden of doing more hours of work or a more strenuous job" or "I accept less income than others, but on condition that my work load is correspondingly decreased, using some meaningful metric for measuring burdens." Asking whether the difference principle justifies incentive-providing inequalities amounts to asking whether it justifies rewards that go beyond sheer compensation for arduous work, which can be construed as equalizing unequal situations. Cohen's (1992a, 296–97; 1992b, section 4) claim is that there is no justification for payments to talented people that go *beyond* this compensation and thereby constitute genuine inequalities. The many philosophers who have pondered at length about the fortunes of basketball player Wilt Chamberlain and his younger brother, hockey player Wayne Gretzky, will need little convincing to believe that such inequalities can still be very considerable.

Secondly, some inequalities may be needed to make it possible (as opposed to attractive) for the talented to perform the job at which they would be socially most useful. I think I can remember, for example, that during the week preceding the Oxford-Cambridge rowing contest, the Oxford University rowing team was hosted by its captain's college and given lavish meals, in order to *enable* them (not motivate them) to win a victory that would bring great pride to all Oxonians. Similarly, a stressed manager's expensive holidays are arguably needed to *enable* her and her family to live the sort of life they have to live without going crazy. In such cases, genuine inequality (beyond sheer compensation for doing the job: Both the rowers and the manager may actually enjoy it) may be justified, though not justified *qua* subjective incentives. To use Cohen's (1992a, 311; 1992b, section 8) formulations, such inequalities are "strictly necessary," "necessary apart from human choice," "necessary apart from people's chosen intentions," they reflect "purely objective feasibility sets." Their point is to enable, not to stimulate. Such genuine inequalities, Cohen (1992b, section 4) concedes, are consistent with everyone being committed to the difference principle, but he ascribes them to "special circumstances" and distinguishes them from the "normal case," in which inequalities work as incentives.

4. Subjective Compensation; or the Convergence of Maximin, Equality and Self-interest

What matters to us here, however, is not the empirical question of how much inequality would still find room in Rawls's well-ordered society in the event that Cohen's claim (appropriately qualified) proves valid, but whether the latter is indeed valid. In a society whose institutions are shaped by the difference principle and whose members are committed to it, are the only legitimate inequalities those that are required to compensate for special burdens or to generate worthwhile capacities? In other words, do incentive payments have no place in a just society?

To get a better grip on this question, let us try to imagine the functioning of a society that is not only equipped with institutions governed by the difference principle, but also consists in people committed to that principle. Should one, for example, require these people to find out how hard they would work spontaneously in the absence of institutions designed to maximally favour the worst off and then to work just as hard despite the redistributive mechanisms (a rather problematic and underspecified counterfactual exercise)? Or should one require them to be constantly on the lookout for the worst off in order to display their generosity? There seems to be a far simpler approach which asks the members of such a well-ordered society no more than a willing and honest participation in the working of appropriately designed institutions. Leaving out, for the sake of simplicity, the possibility of enabling inequalities, one particularly convenient construal of these institutions goes like this.[6]

First, select at random some no-work-some-income option common to all the members of the society concerned, and call it the *zero option*. Next, ask each person what her reservation wage would be for each occupation (defined by type and length of labour) she could do, and accordingly draw her *fair compensation curves*, which specify, for each type of labour, the (possibly negative) level of pay required to make that person indifferent between various lengths of labour time and the zero option. Next, determine each person's productivity for each such occupation. Finally, require people to choose occupations in such a way that the social surplus is maximized. The *social surplus* is here understood as the difference between the aggregate social product (net of capital used up) and the aggregate compensation of those who have contributed to it, as determined by the reservation wages just mentioned. This social surplus is to be distributed equally to all members of the society concerned, thus providing the common zero option. There is of course no reason why the fair compensation curves associated with any particular zero option picked at random should lead to socially optimal assignments that will generate a social surplus per head that matches exactly the chosen zero option. The associated social surplus may fall short of or exceed what is needed to fund this option. The level of income that defines the latter is appropriately chosen when the funds required to finance it exactly match the social surplus generated as a result of people taking up their socially optimal assignment among those they regard as equivalent to the zero option. Within this institutional framework, people's commitment to the difference principle simply requires them (1) to reveal the true pattern of their reservation wages and productivity patterns, so that their fair

[6] The present section and the following two are heavily indebted, more than is acknowledged in the footnotes of this abridged version, to discussions of equality and compensation by Joseph Carens (1981, 1985, 1986), John Baker (1987, 1992) and Brian Barry (1992).

compensation curves can be worked out and their socially optimal assignment determined, and (2) to willingly accept the latter, as characterized by a particular type and length of labour.

Before turning to the problems the scheme poses, let us note that it painlessly combines maximin, equality and free choice of occupation within each person's legitimate choice set made up of all subjectively equivalent occupations (with appropriate compensatory payments). It even seems able to generate, with choice sets thus shaped, a smooth convergence between commitment to justice and self-interest, the latter negatively defined as whatever, among the things a person cares about, does not reduce to or derive from a commitment to justice. For it suffices to increase very slightly (say, by ε) the payment as associated with the socially optimal option, for each person to choose out of self-interest the occupation which will most contribute to the situation of the worst off, i.e., of everyone, since everyone enjoys a situation equivalent (in her own eyes, and forgetting about the ε's) to the zero option. Consequently, this picture of the implied institutional framework seems to fully substantiate Cohen's defensive insistence that he "do[es] not aim to impugn the integrity of a conception of justice which allows the agent a certain self-regarding prerogative" (Cohen 1992a, 314), and that "it is not true that, in the society [he has] in mind, a person would have to worry about unfortunate people every time he made an economic decision" (ibid., 316).

Moreover, the basic setup just sketched can easily be extended from the choice of occupation to the choice of levels of effort within an occupation. Material incentives, and hence inequalities, are not only said to be required to induce the talented to choose occupations which put their talents to productive use. Under the standard version of the so-called efficiency-wage approach to unemployment, for example, the effort is assumed to be a positive function of the wage rate because the higher the latter, the greater the fear of being dismissed. If the employer gave the worker no more than the latter's reservation wage, the worker would be indifferent between working and being sacked, and hence would not put as much effort into her work. But here again, if workers are committed to the difference principle, they would reveal truthfully what levels of pay would exactly compensate them for various levels of effort. They could then be told not only what job to do, but also what level of effort to muster (which would not be the maximum feasible level, given the need for compensation), and they would comply, without thereby sacrificing themselves, since they would not be worse off (and could even be made better of by ε) than at lower levels of effort.

Furthermore, the same framework can conceivably be extended from working to saving, i.e., to an area which Cohen does not consider but in which claims about the need for incentives are no less relevant. Given some common no-work, no saving, some-income option, we could then (1) construct for each person the set of combinations of (financially compensated) work and (financially compensated) saving that are equivalent, using her own preferences, to this option, and (2) ask each person (possibly with an ε signal) to select from this legitimate choice set the combination of work and saving behaviour that maximizes the sustainable social surplus.

Whether in its simpler or in its more complex variant, one striking feature of this egalitarian institutional framework is that it does not require any sacrifice of people's self-interest in addition to the truthful provision of the information the working of the institutions requires. The situation of the worst off will be maximized without any incentive payment (apart from the negligible ε's), just as a result of people pursuing their self-interest within the choice set designed for each of them by the institutional framework. The proposal, however, also raises a number of difficulties, at least one of which I believe to be decisive. One essential feature of the proposed institutional setup is that the same type and amount of work (or the same type and amount of saving) will have to be rewarded differently depending on who performs it: The more distaste a person has for contributing to social production in a certain way, the higher the rate at which she will have to be compensated, at least if her contribution is worth having at that rate.

Clearly, this feature makes the institutional scheme practically unworkable: Each worker or saver would need to face a personalized, preference-specific set of wage and interest rates. But at the level of abstraction on which the present exercise is being conducted, this can hardly count as a decisive defect. More seriously, in order to determine the appropriate differentiation of payments, one needs information that is entirely private: Since the self-interest reflected in the fair compensation curves is not definitionally equivalent to the preference schedule that guides a person's choices, there is no way of checking the truth of a person's statements about her reservation wage or interest payments. And this arguably violates the publicity requirement which Rawls and others want any just institutional set-up to meet. But above all, the key feature singled out above makes the scheme most questionable as an adequate expression of the egalitarian ideal. For although every person's situation will be, in her own eyes, equivalent to (or, taking the ε's into account, no worse than) some common baseline situation (the zero option), some people may end up in an objective situation that is far worse, in everyone's eyes, than some others, simply owing to their having more accommodating preferences. Suppose, for example, that you and I can do only the same single job and that, whatever the number of working hours, I resent doing the job more than you do. Consequently, for any given number of hours, the criterion of fair compensation will require paying me more than you. (Surplus maximization may, but need not require that you perform more hours than me.) And my assignment (with the associated compensation) is then most likely to be universally preferred to yours. A set-up that ends up giving me a universally preferred job because of my being fussier than you—or, to put it differently, because of my having, relative to you, an expensive taste for leisure—is not very credible as an adequate expression of the egalitarian ideal.

5. Objective Compensation; or Maximin, Equality and Self-Interest at Odds

Cohen (1992a, 296; 1992b, section 4) is not very explicit about the notion of "special burden" which allows higher remuneration to work as a "counter-balancing equalizer" "where work is specially arduous, or stressful." But the most plausible ways of spelling out the institutional framework called forth by his egalitarian ideal do not rest—if the arguments just stated are cogent, fortunately so—on a subjective notion of fair compensation, as does the proposal examined above. Along with Baker (1992, 109–10), he might rather be taken to assume that some objective, individually undifferentiated notion of burden can be used to play the role ascribed above to the subjective, person-specific disutility of working or saving.

The formal structure sketched above then remains relevant: (1) For each level of the zero option, each type of activity and each individual, one draws a fair compensation curve—a set of work-income combinations equivalent to the zero option—which indicates the remuneration needed to cover the special burden incorporated in a certain number of hours of that activity; (2) among these equivalent combinations, people are asked to select the one that maximizes the social surplus (to be distributed equally to all and thereby provide the income entering the zero option); and (3) the zero option is pitched at the highest sustainable level consistent with this process. But because of the objective interpretation of the notion of burden, the implementation of this framework no longer raises the same problems of untractability and lack of publicity—there are no longer different rates of pay depending on some features of a person which only that person can know—nor the same objection of unfairness—the work-shy no longer get a premium.

But while solving these difficulties, the shift to an objective notion of burden creates another problem, of central importance, as we shall see, for the question of the relationship between maximin justice and individual ethics.[7] For one can now no longer bank on a guaranteed harmony between the maximal improvement of the situation of the worst off and self-interested choice within the choice sets shaped by egalitarian institutions. Obviously, the various occupations (*cum* compensation) deemed equivalent

---

[7] I should say that I am exploring this interpretation of the egalitarian ideal because it is present in Cohen's critique of Rawls, not because I believe it provides the most appealing approach. Some metric of opportunities (rather than of income-burden bundles) makes for a better fit with (at least) my moral intuitions, generalizes easily beyond the sphere of production, and dispenses with the problematic notion of objective burden (see Van Parijs 1990, 1991). However, some version of the central issues raised in this article arises also under the opportunity-egalitarian interpretation.

by virtue of the objective notion of burden are no longer automatically equivalent according to the agents' preferences. Consequently, it can no longer be taken for granted that picking the surplus-maximizing element in the choice set drawn by the egalitarian institutions will involve no substantial cost, relative to other options in that set, in terms of the person's self-interest. The level of fair compensation associated with various occupations by this objective assessment will in general exceed for some people what is needed to match the disutility incurred, while falling short of it for some other people. Given the choice, the latter's self-interest may therefore strongly favour the zero option over the zero-option-objectively-equivalent occupation (for short, ZOE) which surplus maximization would recommend, and this time, therefore, an insignificant ε would be incapable of reconciling maximin and self-interest by steering people's self-interested choices in the socially optimal direction. Note, moreover, that this tradeoff would not only arise for those who would be undercompensated, relative to the disutility incurred, if they were assigned to their surplus-maximizing ZOE, but also for those who would then get exactly the right compensation or be overcompensated, as overcompensation may be even greater for some other, non-surplus-maximizing ZOE.

This may seem to point to an unbridgeable conflict between equality, maximin and free occupational choice. If you let people free to choose their occupation, there is no reason to expect that people's choices in their egalitarian choice sets will select the surplus-maximizing option, and maximin will therefore generally diverge from equality. For example, choice-respecting egalitarian institutions seem bound to make you lose the services of an exceptionally gifted manager whose tastes are such that she would be subjectively undercompensated at the rate of pay that matches the objectively assessed burden of a managerial job. Given the choice, she may choose to do no work at all or opt for another, more relaxed occupation (say, being a sculptor) whose objective burden, and hence pay, have been assessed at a lower level but for which she has a far greater liking, so that the lower pay is more than offset by the reduced stress, or by the greater instrinsic pleasure she derives from the job, or by the importance she attaches to her children and spouse no longer having to suffer her being away at unsuitable times. As a result of occupational choice being guided by this preference, exceptional managerial skills are left unused, and both the social surplus and the situation of the worst off remain at a lower level than would have been the case if the absence of free occupational choice had made it possible to effectively assign the sculptor to the managerial job instead.

However, formulating the conflict as one between maximin equality and *freedom of occupation* begs the central question of this article. For if commitment to the difference principle (whether constrained by freedom of choice or unconstrained) implies accepting the surplus-maximizing assignment, then there is no conflict, in a well-ordered society, between maximin equality and free occupational choice, nor any reason to expect freely choosing but appropriately committed individuals to prevent equality from achieving the maximin. What the example of our managerially gifted sculptor illustrates is rather the possibility of a sharp conflict between maximin equality *and self-interest*, even when the choice is restricted to objectively equivalent options.

Realizing this possibility forces us to ask the following question: Does the ideal of a just society require that people should always sacrifice their self-interest to their commitment to the difference principle, by accepting the surplus-maximizing assignment, however much they would (self-interestedly) prefer another, objectively equivalent occupation? Under the subjective compensation interpretation of equality, the question did not arise. But under the objective compensation interpretation, unless there is a close fit, not just an (uncontroversial) positive correlation, between what people like and what they are good at, it can take a very acute and worrying form. For what people need, if they are to sacrifice their self-interested preferences, is not just a strong commitment to the difference principle, but also a full trust in the way in which the objective burden of the various occupations is being assessed. This puts a lot of weight on the possibility of working out a meaningful objective notion of burden. While it is clear that the latter should not be person-specific, it is also clear that it cannot be completely disconnected from the disutility incurred by the people per-forming the activity concerned. If everyone prefers doing A to doing B, one cannot sensibly associate a heavier objective burden, and hence a higher level of fair compensation, with the doing of A. But how is this burden to be defined? Perhaps as average disutility, the latter being measured by the reservation wage with the zero option as the only alternative option? But what is the relevant sample? The whole of the active population of the society concerned? Only those among them who have the skills required to do the job? Only those among them who know what they are talking about, because they have had an opportunity to try the job? And what if some would not do the job whatever the wage, thus making the job's average disutility infinite? If simple (or more sophisticated) averaging is no good, perhaps we could appeal to some democratic procedure. But even leaving aside the fact that any workable democratic procedure would involve delegating the assessment to an appropriate group of experts, which would take us back to square one, what would be the credentials of majority rule on the presumably factual issue of how burdensome a particular activity is?

I am not claiming that these few remarks make total nonsense of the notion of objective burden. But they suffice to show, I believe, that any such notion is bound to remain conceptually problematic. Consequently, one could never feel on firm ground when turning down the complaint of some-one who believes that she is being unfairly treated, i.e., considers herself unjustifiably made worse off than others in terms of income-burden bundles, as a result of being asked to accept, out of commitment to the difference principle, her surplus-maximizing ZOE. This does not force us to abandon the whole approach. But it seems hard to escape the need to protect oneself against serious injustices by providing every worker with the following sort of safeguard: Apart from her surplus-maximizing option, she can also choose, if she prefers, the common zero option to which the latter is supposed to be objectively equivalent.

This seems to be, given the specific interpretation of the egalitarian institutional framework adopted here, a natural way of interpreting Cohen's concession to Scheffler that "every person has a right to pursue self-interest to some reasonable extent" (1992a, 302) or his emphatic refusal "to impugn the integrity of a conception of justice which allows an agent a certain self-regarding prerogative" (ibid., 314). One could of course think of more restrictive or complicated ways of making some room for the pursuit of self-interest. For example, one could exempt a worker from her socially optimal assignment only if the cost to her of accepting it would be great, and the benefit to society rather small. Or one could imagine that each person would be allowed to choose from a subset of ZOE's involving some contribution on her part rather than to go for the zero option. But apart from its simplicity, the safeguard has the great advantage of meeting what would seem to be a minimum condition of any fair scheme of work compensation, namely that it should make sure that no worker ends up worse off than if she had been left to do nothing. Even those who feel inclined towards more subtle or guarded ways of making room for self-interest should therefore find it worthwhile exploring what follows from introducing the safeguard.

6. Why Incentive Payments Can be Just After All

But here comes the crux. For once such a safeguard is introduced (arguably as a minimalist way of spelling out Cohen's concession), there is no longer any reason to believe that, in a well-ordered society of suitably committed people (and abstracting, as usual, from enabling inequalities), maximin will necessarily coincide with equality, nor therefore that incentive payments should be ruled out. Once people are left the choice between their socially optimal occupation and the zero option, the (largest sustainable) social surplus and hence the zero option will obviously be smaller than if their choice had been restricted to the former. One way of weakening this negative effect consists in assigning to each worker who would otherwise choose the zero option the socially most beneficial among the ZOE's not blocked by the safeguard. This is no doubt better as far as maximin is concerned, while still being perfectly egalitarian according to the objective metric. But there is better still. It may be possible, consistently with the safeguard, to generate a higher social surplus if people are not only given access to some suboptimal ZOE's, but also to some supra-ZOE's, to some options that are superior to the zero option according to the objective metric. Paying more than the objectively fair compensation may make a productive worker relinquish the zero option in favour of an occupation that will contribute more to the surplus than any of her safeguard-proof ZOE's, despite the additional compensation required.

In the case of the exceptionally gifted but not very keen manager referred to above, for example, it may be better, as far as maximin is concerned, to ask her to be a sculptor rather than remain idle. But it may be even better to provide her with a wage sufficiently high to make her prefer being a manager to doing nothing. For if this higher wage still allows the manager's net contribution to the social surplus to be greater than it would have been with the best ZOE occupation she would have accepted, then, assuming the other workers' compensation is unaffected, social surplus maximization, and hence maximin, will deviate from (burden-sensitive) equality. Ignoring this potential by sticking to payments that do not exceed the assessed objective burden, in other words, amounts to keeping the social surplus, and hence the situation of the worst off, lower than it could be. Maximin no longer necessarily coincides with equality once a person's commitment to the difference principle is no longer interpreted as entailing the lexical priority of accepting her surplus-maximizing ZOE over all the other moral and non-moral considerations that make up her self-interest.

Once this is admitted, incentives of the standard type are not much further down the road. For what has been said so far supposes that one can identify the gifted but reluctant workers and award them the premium required to make them self-interestedly prefer their optimal assignment to the zero option. This supposes in turn that different people may receive different incomes for the same job, depending on the nature of their preferences. This does not take us completely back to the subjective compensation scheme and to the expensive-taste difficulty which proved fatal to it. For paying the fussy more than the keen is now no longer an embarrassing component of the egalitarian ideal, but a by-product of the pursuit of maximin in a context in which self-regarding considerations are allowed to play some role. Nonetheless, this person-specific compensation scheme raises the other difficulties mentioned in connection with the subjective compensation scheme, notably those grounded in its reliance on essentially private information, and this can reasonably be deemed sufficient to discard it.

The alternative consists in conceding the supra-ZOE pay, not only to the reluctant managers, but to any one else doing the same job. While increasing the net contribution of the reluctant manager, the introduction of the premium now also reduces the net contribution of her no less productive but keener fellow managers. This will no doubt make the labour allocator very cautious about awarding any significant premium. It will also further complicate her job, for what was socially optimal for a person to do if she were paid no more than the objectively fair compensation may no longer be socially optimal once she is paid an extra premium. So, instead of adding this further headache to a job that was already unmanageable anyway, the labour allocator may wisely decide to give over to a sufficiently competitive and self-interest-guided labour market the task of allocating people to jobs and determining their gross incomes, while converting herself into a tax collector. The social surplus is then being maximized, not through the filling of jobs and the fixing of wages, but through the sustainable-yield-maximizing taxation of every type of job, taking both supply and demand reactions into account, and the equal distribution of this yield.

The two approaches are not quite equivalent. For example, whereas the central allocation method described allows only upward deviations from the ZOE baseline, nothing in principle prevents taxation from turning some jobs which a sufficient number of appropriately skilled workers are keen to do into infra-ZOE's, i.e., occupations paid less than is justified by the objective assessment of the associated burden. Indeed, in the taxation approach, the very notion of objective burden has become superfluous. But I very much doubt this makes any significant difference. Let us bear in mind, in particular, that the equal and unconditional distribution of the surplus guarantees that no worker will be worse off while working than under the zero option. Let us also bear in mind that scarce talents may command large gross incomes as potential employers compete to hire them, but that yield-maximizing taxation should manage to extract the bulk of this factor rent. How much the resulting income distribution would diverge from objective-burden-sensitive equality is of course a question that can only be settled on an empirical basis. But on the plausible assumption that there cannot be that many people who particularly hate doing what they are particularly good at, one can safely conjecture that the income inequalities that would survive yield-maximizing taxation will not be far greater nor far different from those implied by any sensible notion of fair compensation.

In this light, it remains quite possible—indeed, if the facts are not wildly different from what I think they are, extremely plausible—that "a modest right of self-interest [of the sort acknowledged above] seems insufficient to justify the range of inequality, the extremes of wealth and poverty, that actually obtain in [contemporary Britain]" (Cohen 1992a, 302–03). But is the range of inequality thus justified any narrower than the range of inequality allowed by the conventional interpretation of the difference principle? Cohen's concession, as elaborated above step to step, seems to lead to legit-imizing all incentive payments that boost the social surplus, and hence the situation of the worst off. Does this mean that people's commitment to the difference principle, once softened by the safeguard, has no impact whatever on legitimate inequalities? Not quite.

To start with, in the institutional context sketched above, each person committed to the difference principle can be expected to report truthfully her gainful activities and pay honestly whatever tax rates the surplus-maximizing institutions attach to the pay and perks these activities give access to. Being able to bank on this sort of behaviour will enable a well-ordered society to collect and distribute a higher social surplus than would be the case in a society whose members are not so committed. Even in such a society, higher tax rates will induce, owing to the safeguard, lower levels of performance. But they will not widen the gap between actual and reported activities. Thus, safeguard-checked commitment demands that people should not *cheat*. It also demands that they should not use their bargaining power, especially their collective bargaining power as exercised in strikes and similar actions, in order to resist tax pressure more than they would do by adjusting parametrically to the tax structure, i.e., by simply reducing individually their supply of labour or capital as the tax rate increases. In a well-ordered society, the availability of the highest zero option that can be made available to all provides the legitimate safeguard. Free collective bargaining, or an unrestricted right to strike, cannot be part of the picture. In other words, it is not enough not to cheat the institutions, it is equally important not to *bend* them.[8]

These are two important features of economic behaviour, whether individual or collective, that follow from a commitment to maximin justice, understood as willing compliance with institutions that aim to maximize the situation of the worst off. But among the choices left open by such institutions and the two constraints on individual behaviour just mentioned, people can and should be left free to pursue their self-interest broadly understood, remember, as anything that does not reduce to or derive from a concern with achieving justice as characterized, including for example visiting an old aunt or supporting Greenpeace's action in the Antarctic. And if this is conceded, it follows, along the path followed above, that incentive payments—the rewarding of talents over and above what is needed to compensate the objective burden associated with their productive use (and to make the latter possible)—are legitimate in some quite plausible circumstances, namely in those circumstances in which the sustainable social surplus would be smaller without them, owing to the room granted to self-interest-guided choice.

There will of course be people who will book a substantial "producer's surplus," i.e., enjoy the benefit of a large difference between their actual pay and their reservation pay, as a result of such incentive payments being allowed. But this also happens if the pay exactly matches the assessed burden, as soon as the latter is not defined in terms of person-specific disutility. More seriously, even with perfectly enforced maximin institutions,

---

[8] This twofold restriction on individual behaviour bears at least some resemblance to Rawls's (1990, §37.1) stipulation that, in a well-ordered society, "citizens accept existing institutions as just and usually have no desire to *violate*, or to *renegotiate*, the terms of social cooperation, given their present and prospective social position. Here we suppose that political and social cooperation would quickly break down if everyone, or even many people, always acted self- or group-interestedly in a purely strategic, or game-theoretic fashion" (my emphasis).

skills inequalities and/or various obstacles to the clearing of the labour market may well generate situations of dominance, i.e., of unanimous strict preference for one job situation over another or over the zero option. There is no question that these would be genuine inequalities. But once the concern to maximize the objectively worst income-burden bundle is constrained, as a way of making room for legitimate self-regarding considerations, by the possibility of choosing the zero option (or other, socially superior alternatives), then such inequalities are justified. Under perfectly operating maximin institutions, some job situations may be superior to others in everyone's eyes. But any attempt to tax away such universally recognized advantages necessarily leads to a smaller redistributable surplus, as a result of some of the people taxed more heavily legitimately shifting to occupations that yield smaller net contributions to this surplus.

7. Why Most Incentive Payments Are Nonetheless Unjust, or the Unexpected Alliance of Justice and Patriotism

Even on Cohen's premises, it thus turns out, some genuine incentive payments are justified. But my guess is that the inequalities so justified are of such a modest scope that not only Rawls but also Cohen would feel quite comfortable about condoning them. If this is the case, the apparent clash between left liberalism and radical egalitarianism has melted away. And since there is no point in insisting stubbornly on differences that vanish under scrutiny, radical egalitarians would simply have to shelve their interesting but misguided challenge and rally behind the left liberal flag. Or at least so they would have to do if one could reason, as we have done so far, within the boundaries of a closed economy. But once this assumption is lifted, the picture becomes very different indeed. We are then led to considerations that rescue the importance of Cohen's challenge, but also have some other, rather puzzling implications. Let me briefly sketch these considerations and return, by the same token, to our initial question about the implications of a maximin theory of justice for individual ethics.

Suppose first that people can legitimately leave the country with their skills and other assets, if this is what their self-interest tells them to do. The agents' legitimate choice sets are then no longer basically shaped by the fact that the zero option should be available to all and that institutions should maximin people's situations, bearing this safeguard in mind. If agents have the option of supplying their labour and capital abroad and if the country concerned can attract valuable factors from the outside world, then, whether or not the other countries each have their own maximin institutions, the situation is deeply altered. For the condition that needs to be met if a person is to choose her socially preferred occupation is no longer that she should regard it as preferable to the zero option (and other ZOE's), but that she should regard it as preferable to the most attractive option abroad. How attractive this possibility is to the person concerned obviously depends on the subjective cost of supplying abroad the factors one owns, and on the prices these factors command in other countries, which will in turn depend both on the overall level of development of these countries and on their distributive institutions. Clearly, under such circumstances, just as in the actual world, the owners of potentially mobile and widely valued factors of production will be able to earn, even without any cheating or bending, far higher returns than in the world assumed so far. For the tax elasticity of the supply of these factors (essentially capital and highly skilled labour) tends to be very high, i.e., the amounts of these factors which a country can hope to retain or attract tends to be highly responsive to increases or decreases in their post-tax returns, and the maximin criterion will therefore lead to selecting very low, though yield-maximizing, tax rates.

But is this picture consistent with the assumption that all members of the society concerned are committed to the difference principle? In other words, must disloyalty to one's country be assimilated to cheating or bending, and hence ruled out, or rather to choosing the zero option, and hence legitimized by some variant of our safeguard? There is a strong *prima facie* case in favour of the first answer. If commitment to the difference principle implies that people will not want to cheat by concealing some of their gains in their home country, while still conceivably making a very sizeable contribution to the situation of the worst off in their country through the taxes they pay or the employment they create, then surely commitment to the difference principle must also rule out that people may care so little about their countrymen that they may want to send their capital abroad or to move out altogether with their productive talents in a way that avoids maximin taxation in their home country. In other words, if one is committed to contributing as much as possible to improving the situation of the worst off in one's society, one must *a fortiori* be committed to sticking with this society—not whatever happens perhaps, but as long as the society's institutions remain just.

This argument, however, cannot be right. For if it were, then it would be even less legitimate to opt for the zero option. At least those who choose to leave the country altogether are not sucking the social surplus. So, if commitment to the difference principle makes it bad to quit, it must make it even worse to take a free ride or, more generally, to take a share in the surplus that exceeds the productive contribution one chooses to make. Or conversely, if a safeguard legitimately protects the desire I may have to surf rather than work, should it not also allow me to move abroad, at a lesser cost to my society, because I fell in love with a foreign culture, a foreign land-scape or a foreign woman?

The argument, however, can be rephrased in a way that is not vulnerable to this objection. Let us look at the issue from the standpoint of the original position: We do not know what conception of the good life we shall have nor what talents we shall be endowed with, but we do know which society we belong to. In order to keep our life options open both at home and abroad, we shall certainly not commit ourselves to contributing to the surplus as much as we can. But in order to give ourselves the firmest possible real basis for making any choice we may want to make in case we turn out to have the poorest endowment, we shall not only choose to introduce maximin institutions but also commit ourselves to not cheating nor bending them. These institutions will have to involve the yield-maximizing taxation of incomes earned abroad as well as at home, and the matching individual duties will have to require the truthful reporting of foreign no less than of domestic earnings.

Nothing said so far requires that the members of a well-ordered society be subjected to a special duty of patriotism. For the duty not to cheat, and in particular to honestly report any foreign income, seems sufficient to check the downward pressure on the social surplus that would otherwise result from actual or potential international factor mobility. This ignores, however, the crucial question of what defines, for redistribution purposes, membership in the society concerned. Whether it is permanent residence or formal citizenship, it is clear that the duty not to cheat offers only very poor protection against the pressure of international mobility if membership can easily be changed. If the institutions were to prohibit emigration (whether interpreted as a change of permanent residence or of citizenship status), the duty not to cheat would encompass the duty not to emigrate and the problem would disappear. But such an institutional prohibition would clearly violate what Rawls and many others would count among people's fundamental liberties. And so would, presumably, the imposition of prohibitive costs on prospective emigrants, such as the reimbursement of educational expenses, or of the present value of one's skills, to the society they are leaving.

This is why a special duty of patriotism needs to enter the picture. Such a duty does not need to require that one should never use the institutionally guaranteed right to emigrate. What it must require is rather that one should not emigrate for the wrong reason, i.e., modify one's residence or citizenship status in order to enjoy a more favourable tax treatment. What generates strong constraints on the effective operation of an open economy's maximin institutions in a large world is not that its members may want to relinquish their membership because they fell in love with foreign people or foreign landscapes, but only that they may want to do so because of their interest in maximizing their post-tax incomes. If they endorse maximin institutions, it would be inconsistent for the best endowed members of a society not only to consider cheating but also to consider escaping in response to high taxation. For the consequence would be that the objective of the maximin institutions would be defeated: Precious little could be collected for redistribution to the worst off, both because of actual cheating or escaping and even more because of credible threats to cheat or escape. Knowing which society they belong to, people in the original position will protect themselves against this risk by committing themselves to behaving not only honestly but also patriotically, in the restricted sense of refusing to consider relinquishing membership in their society for the wrong sort of reason.

If the society's members can be relied on not only to refrain from cheating (and bending), but also to refrain from moving out in search of higher returns, then the constraints on the society's attempt to make its worst off members as well off as possible are greatly loosened, and the size of the incentive payments that will sustainably maximize the situation of the worst off will be far smaller than if tax rates had to keep subjecting themselves to the ruthless discipline of a highly responsive world financial market or of an increasingly integrated international market for skilled labour. Of course, how great a loss can be avoided in this way will greatly vary as a function of the size of the territory controlled by the relevant tax authority, the society's relative prosperity, the distinctness of its language and culture, the charm of its climate and countryside, and many other factors. But the very modest extent to which people actually alter their place of residence or their citizenship in order to avoid taxes should not make us underestimate the impact of potential emigration on the current and, even more, the future shape and size of redistributive policies. The growing asymmetry between the taxation of capital and labour income and the erosion of the progressiveness of income taxation in several countries can plausibly be interpreted as two clear signs of growing pressures in an ever more open—and unpatriotic—world.

One implication of this argument, if it is correct, is that—after all—Cohen is right and Rawls is wrong on the issue of whether (the bulk of) surplus-enhancing incentive payments are justified, or at least that Rawls would be wrong if what he had in mind was an open economy in a large world of the sort we live in. In a hypothetical closed economy, whatever incentive payments would be paid to self-interest-guided economic agents under maximin institutions can be justified, because maximin requires them, despite a universal commitment to the difference principle, as soon as self-regarding considerations are allowed to guide people's choice with the zero option as a common baseline. In an open economy, this would not be the case. Some part, and probably by far the greatest part, of the incentive payments paid to self-interest-guided economic agents under maximin institutions would then remain unjustified, because they would only be needed as a consequence of the widespread adoption of an attitude that is inconsistent with a commitment to the difference principle.

8. Rawlsians: not Christians but Patriots?

What constraints, if any, does a commitment to maximin justice impose on one's individual ethics? The (very partial) answer we are arriving at can be summed up as follows. Once maximin institutions are in place, commitment to maximin does entail a duty not to cheat or bend these institutions, and strict compliance with this duty will enable the maximin to be far more egalitarian than it would otherwise be. But it does not entail a moral duty to help those poorer than oneself. It is not inconsistent with such a duty, but performance of the latter would be an expression of love, charity or caring, not an implication of a commitment to maximin justice, as we have come to interpret it. In a well-ordered society, being committed to the difference principle does not force us to find it despicable or objectionable to spend much of one's time and money collecting Indian totems or supporting the local soccer team, at the expense of doing everything within one's power to improve the situation of the worst off, providing of course the time and money thus used do not exceed what we are allotted by maximin institutions.

To be honest, this negative conclusion is not particularly relevant to the moral choices we face in our daily lives, such as those mentioned in the first few sentences of this article. For we undoubtedly live in a badly ill-ordered society, and this leads to a different set of questions. In such circumstances, could we, for example, allow ourselves to be less honest, less cooperative, less patriotic than we would need to be in a well-ordered society, whether because the institutions are not to be trusted to generate, collect and distribute the social surplus in an efficient way, or because others do not do what the institutions expect them to do? Or should we rather be more demanding on ourselves, for example because it is up to us, in our private conduct, to do part of what the institutions of a well-ordered society would do, and because it is also up to us, in our political conduct, to fight energetically for a juster institutional setup? I am not sure what overarching criterion could be applied in this balancing exercise, and there is little in the arguments of this article that may be helpful on this issue. My hunch, however, is that the second set of considerations is bound to weigh far more heavily, at any rate for all those (probably you and certainly me among them) who are better off than they would be in a just society. One cannot consistently claim to be committed to a maximin conception of justice and complacently enjoy privileges one can only be granted because the institutional set-up violates this conception. Even if Rawlsians need not be Christians in a well-ordered society, they may well, after all, have to be (something like) Christians in the real world.

Even in a hypothetical well-ordered society, however, it is not enough for Rawlsians to refrain from cheating their maximin institutions and from using their bargaining power in order to force redistribution down. They may not have to be Christians, but they will have to be patriots, in the limited sense of refusing to pull out of their society for the sake of collecting higher post-tax incomes elsewhere. Unless the members of our society—and also those of other societies—are patriotic in this sense, concern with maximin will force our institutions to pay large unjustified incentive payments to the holders of valuable factors. There is, it must be conceded, one alternative to such a patriotic commitment. It consists in hoisting the maximin institutions from the local to the global level, from the nation state to the world community. This is not, however, the way Rawls (1993b) himself conceives of global justice. The just law of peoples, in his view, is not the one on which the representatives of individuals would settle in a global original position in which they ignore which society they belong to. It is one on which the representatives of well-ordered societies would settle behind a suitably redesigned veil of ignorance, and it will include no stronger redistributive institution than mutual aid in the event of famines and other disasters. But if this is the way Rawlsians need to conceive of global justice, then, as the world market strengthens its grip on a growing number of countries, it becomes every day more crucial that Rawlsians should also be patriots. In so far as Rawlsianism rejects the global maximin of a world society while at the same time shying away from patriotism, it can only turn into the ideological justification of a world-wide breakdown of redistributive institutions in the name of maximin constrained by free exit.[9] And even if the global maximin is recognized, as I believe it should be, as the only coherent long-term ideal, patriotic commitments would provide a welcome help to relieve pressure on each country's (or each region's or each confederation's) redistributive setup in the long interim period that is bound to elapse before sufficiently powerful interpersonal transfer systems can be introduced at the global level.

Hence, whether or not consistent Rawlsians can stop short of advocating a global maximin, patriotism is a central ingredient in the individual ethics called forth by the conception of justice they assert.

Université Catholique de Louvain
Chaire Hoover d'éthique économique et sociale
3, Place Montesquieu
B-1348 Louvain-la-Neuve
Belgium

References

Baker, John. 1987. *Arguing for Equality*. London: Verso.
———. 1992. An Egalitarian Case for Basic Income. In *Arguing for Basic Income. Ethical Foundations for a Radical Reform*. Ed. P. Van Parijs, 101–27. London: Verso.
Barry, Brian. 1989. *Theories of Justice*. London: Harvester Wheatsheaf.
———. 1992. Equality Yes, Basic Income No. In *Arguing for Basic Income. Ethical Foundations for a Radical Reform*. Ed. P. Van Parijs, 128–40. London: Verso.

[9] Rawls (1990, §26.5; 1993b) speaks of a "suitably qualified right of emigration." But the qualifications he has in mind have nothing to do with the patriotic duty advocated here: "I shan't discuss these qualifications. I have in mind, for example, that those properly convicted of certain sufficiently serious crimes may not be allowed to emigrate, pending serving their sentence" (Rawls 1990, §26.5, n. 15).

Carens, Joseph H. 1981. *Equality, Moral Incentives and the Market*. Chicago: University of Chicago Press.

————. 1985. Compensatory Justice and Social Institutions. *Economics and Philosophy* 1: 39–67.

————. 1986. Rights and Duties in an Egalitarian Society. *Political Theory* 1: 31–49.

Cohen, Gerald A. 1992a. Incentives, Inequality and Community. In *The Tanner Lectures on Human Values*. Vol. XIII, 261–329. Salt Lake City: University of Utah Press.

————. 1992b. *The Pareto Argument for Inequality*. Oxford: All Souls College.

Dworkin, Ronald. 1977. *Taking Rights Seriously*. Cambridge, Mass.: Harvard University Press.

Ezorsky, Gertrud. 1981. On Refined Utilitarianism. *Journal of Philosophy* 78: 156–59.

Grey, Thomas C. 1973. The First Virtue. *Stanford Law Review* 25: 286–327.

Meade, James E. 1973. *Theory of Economic Externalities*. Leiden: Sijthoff.

Narveson, Jan F. 1976. A Puzzle about Economic Justice in Rawls's Theory. *Social Theory and Practice* 4: 1–27.

Rawls, John. 1971. *A Theory of Justice*. Cambridge, Mass.: Harvard University Press.

————. 1990. *Justice as Fairness. A Restatement*. Harvard University, unpublished lecture notes.

————. 1993a. *Political Liberalism*. New York: Columbia University Press.

————. 1993b. The Law of Peoples. In *On Human Rights. The Oxford Amnesty Lectures 1993*. Eds. S. Shute and S. Hurley. New York, N.Y.: Basic Books.

Scanlon, Tim M. 1991. The Moral Basis of Interpersonal Comparisons. In *Interpersonal Comparisons of Well-being*. Eds. J. Elster and J.E. Roeme, 17–44. Cambridge: Cambridge University Press.

Ten, C.L. 1980. *Mill on Liberty*. Oxford: Clarendon.

Van Parijs, Philippe. 1993, Rawlsians, Christians and Patriots. Maximin Justice and Individual Ethics. *European Journal of Philosophy* 1: 309–42.

————. 1995. *Real Freedom for All. What (If Anything) Can Justify Capitalism?* Oxford: University Press.

G. A. COHEN

Where the Action Is: On the Site of Distributive Justice

I

In this paper I defend a claim which can be expressed in the words of a now familiar slogan: the personal is political. That slogan, as it stands, is vague, but I shall mean something reasonably precise by it here, to wit, that principles of distributive justice, principles, that is, about the just distribution of benefits and burdens in society, apply, wherever else they do, to people's legally unconstrained choices. Those principles, so I claim, apply to the choices that people make *within* the legally coercive structures to which, so everyone would agree, principles of justice (also) apply. In speaking of the choices that people make *within* coercive structures, I do not include the choice whether or not to comply with the rules of such structures (to which choice, once again, so everyone would agree, principles of justice [also] apply), but the choices left open by those rules because neither enjoined nor forbidden by them.

The slogan that I have appropriated here is widely used by feminists.[1] More importantly, however, the idea itself, which I have here used the slogan to formulate, and which I have tried to explicate above, is a feminist idea. Notice, however, that, in briefly explaining the idea that I shall defend, I have not mentioned relations between men and women in particular, or the issue of sexism. We can distinguish between the substance and the form of the feminist critique of standard ideas about

For comments that influenced the final version of this paper, I thank Gerald Barnes, Diemut Bubeck, Joshua Cohen, Margaret Gilbert, Susan Hurley, John McMurtry, Derek Parfit, Thomas Pogge, John Roemer, Amelie Rorty, Hillel Steiner, Andrew Williams, Erik Wright, and Arnold Zuboff.

1. But it was, apparently, used by Christian liberation theologians before it was used by feminists: see Denys Turner, "Religion: Illusions and Liberation," in Terrel Carver, ed., *The Cambridge Companion to Marx* (Cambridge: Cambridge University Press, 1991), p. 334.

justice, and it is the form of it which is of prime concern to me here,[2] even though I also endorse its substance.

The substance of the feminist critique is that standard liberal theory of justice, and the theory of Rawls in particular, unjustifiably ignore an unjust division of labor, and unjust power relations, within families (whose legal structure *may* show no sexism at all). That is the key point of the feminist critique, from a political point of view. But the (often merely implicit) form of the feminist critique, which we get when we abstract from its gender-centered content, is that choices not regulated by the law fall within the primary purview of justice, and that is the key lesson of the critique, from a theoretical point of view.

In defending the claim that the personal is political, the view that I oppose is the Rawlsian one that principles of justice apply only to what Rawls calls the "basic structure" of society. Feminists have noticed that Rawls wobbles, across the course of his writings, on the matter of whether or not the family belongs to the basic structure and is therefore, in his view, a site at which principles of justice apply. I shall argue that Rawls's wobble on this matter is not a case of mere indecision, which could readily be resolved in favor of inclusion of the family within the basic structure: that is the view of Susan Okin,[3] and, in my opinion, she is wrong about that. I shall show (in Section V below) that Rawls cannot admit the family into the basic structure of society without abandoning his insistence that it is to the basic structure only that principles of distributive justice apply. In supposing that he could include family relations, Okin shows failure to grasp the *form* of the feminist critique of Rawls.

II

I reach the conclusion announced above at the end of a trail of argument that runs as follows. Here, in Section II, I restate a criticism that

2. Or, more precisely, that which *distinguishes* its form. (Insofar as the feminist critique targets government legislation and policy, there is nothing distinctive about its form.)

3. Okin is singularly alive to Rawls's ambivalence about admitting or excluding the family from the basic structure: see, e.g. her "*Political Liberalism*, Justice and Gender," *Ethics* 105, no. 1 (Oct. 1994): 23–24, and, more generally, her *Justice, Gender and the Family* (New York: Basic Books, 1989), Chapter 5. But, so far as I can tell, she is unaware of the wider consequences, for Rawls's view of justice in general, of the set of ambiguities of which this one is an instance.

Where the Action Is: On the
Site of Distributive Justice

I have made elsewhere of John Rawls's application of his difference principle,[4] to wit, that he does not apply it in censure of the self-seeking choices of high-flying marketeers, which induce an inequality that, so I claim, is harmful to the badly off. In Section III, I present an objection to my criticism of Rawls. The objection says that the difference principle is, by stipulation and design, a principle that applies only to social institutions (to those, in particular, which compose the basic structure of society), and, therefore, not one that applies to the choices, such as those of self-seeking high fliers, that people make *within* such institutions. Sections IV and V offer independent replies to that *basic structure objection*. I show, in Section IV, that the objection is inconsistent with many statements by Rawls about the role of principles of justice in a just society. I then allow that the discordant statements may be dropped from the Rawlsian canon, and, in Section V, I reply afresh to the basic structure objection, by showing that no defensible account of what the basic structure *is* allows Rawls to insist that the principles which apply to it do not apply to choices within it. I conclude that my original criticism of Rawls rests vindicated, against the particular objection in issue here. (Section VI comments on the implications of my position for the moral blamability of individuals whose choices violate principles of justice. The Endnote explores the distinction between coercive and noncoercive institutions, which plays a key role in the argument of Section V).

My criticism of Rawls is of his application of the difference principle. That principle says, in one of its formulations,[5] that inequalities are just if and only if they are necessary to make the worst off people in society better off than they would otherwise be. I have no quarrel here with the difference principle itself,[6] but I disagree sharply with Rawls on the matter of *which* inequalities pass the test for justifying inequality that it sets

4. See "Incentives, Inequality, and Community," in Grethe Peterson, ed., *The Tanner Lectures on Human Values*, Vol. 13 (Salt Lake City: University of Utah Press, 1992), and "The Pareto Argument for Inequality," *Social Philosophy and Policy*, 12 (Winter 1995). These articles are henceforth referred to as "Incentives" and "Pareto," respectively.

5. See "Incentives," p. 266, n. 6, for four possible formulations of the difference principle, all of which, arguably, find support in *A Theory of Justice* (Cambridge, Mass.: Harvard University Press, 1971). The argument of the present paper is, I believe, robust across those variant formulations of the principle.

6. I do have some reservations about the principle, but they are irrelevant to this paper. I agree, for example, with Ronald Dworkin's criticism of the "ambition-insensitivity" of the difference principle: see his "What Is Equality? Part 2: Equality of Resources," *Philosophy & Public Affairs*, 10, no. 4 (Fall 1981): 343.

and, therefore, about how *much* inequality passes that test. In my view, there is hardly any serious inequality that satisfies the requirement set by the difference principle, when it is conceived, as Rawls himself proposes to conceive it,[7] as regulating the affairs of a society whose members themselves accept that principle. If I am right, affirmation of the difference principle implies that justice requires (virtually) unqualified equality itself, as opposed to the "deep inequalities" in initial life chances with which Rawls thinks justice to be consistent.[8]

It is commonly thought, for example by Rawls, that the difference principle licenses an argument for inequality which centers on the device of material incentives. The idea is that talented people will produce more than they otherwise would if, and only if, they are paid more than an ordinary wage, and some of the extra which they will then produce can be recruited on behalf of the worst off.[9] The inequality consequent on differential material incentives is said to be justified within the terms of the difference principle, for, so it is said, that inequality benefits the worst off people: the inequality is necessary for them to be positioned as well as they are, however paltry their position may nevertheless be.

Now, before I mount my criticism of this argument, a *caveat* is necessary with respect to the terms in which it is expressed. The argument focuses on a *choice* enjoyed by well-placed people who command a high salary in a market economy: they can choose to work more or less hard, and also to work at this occupation rather than that one, and for this employer rather than that one, in accordance with how well they are remunerated. These well-placed people, in the foregoing standard presentation of the argument, are designated as "the talented," and, for reasons to be given presently, I shall so designate them throughout my criticism of the argument. Even so, these fortunate people need not be thought to be talented, in any sense of that word which implies something more than a capacity for high market earnings, for the argument to possess whatever force it has. All that need be true of them is that *they are so positioned that, happily, for them, they do command a high salary*

7. "Proposes to conceive it": I use that somewhat precious phrase because part of the present criticism of Rawls is that he does not succeed in so conceiving it—he does not, that is, recognize the implications of so conceiving it.

8. *A Theory of Justice,* p. 7.

9. This is just the crudest causal story connecting superior payment to the better off with benefit to the worst off. I adopt it here for simplicity of exposition.

and they can vary their productivity according to exactly how high it is.
But, as far as the incentives argument is concerned, their happy position
could be due to circumstances that are entirely accidental, relative to
whatever kind of natural or even socially induced endowment they pos-
ses. One need not think that the average dishwasher's endowment of
strength, flair, ingenuity, and so forth falls below that of the average
chief executive to accept the argument's message. One no doubt does
need to think some such thing to agree with the different argument
which justifies rewards to well-placed people in whole or in part as a fair
return to exercise of unusual ability, but Rawls's theory is built around
his rejection of such desert considerations. Nor are the enhanced rewards justified because extra contribution warrants extra reward on
grounds of proper reciprocity. They are justified purely because they
elicit more productive performance.

I nevertheless persist in designating the relevant individuals as "the
talented," because to object that they are not actually especially talented
anyway is to enter an empirical claim which is both contentious and, in
context, misleading, since it would give the impression that it should
matter to our assessment of the incentives argument whether or not
well-placed people merit the contestable designation. The particular
criticism of the incentives argument that I shall develop is best understood in its specificity when the apparently concessive word "talented"
is used: it does not indicate a concession on the factual question of how
top people in a market society get to be where they are. My use of the
argument's own terms shows the strength of my critique of it: that critique stands even if we make generous assumptions about how well-
placed people secured their powerful market positions. It is, moreover,
especially appropriate to make such assumptions here, since the
Rawlsian difference principle is lexically secondary to his principle that
fair equality of opportunity has been enforced with respect to the attainment of desired positions: if anything ensures that those who occupy
them possess superior creative endowment, that does. (Which is not to
say that it indeed ensures that: it is consistent with fair equality of opportunity that what principally distinguishes top people is superior cun-
ning and/or prodigious aggressivity, and nothing more admirable.)

Now, for the following reasons, I believe that the incentives argument
for inequality represents a distorted application of the difference principle, even though it is its most familiar and perhaps even its most persua-

sive application. Either the relevant talented people themselves affirm the difference principle or they do not. That is: either they themselves believe that inequalities are unjust if they are not necessary to make the badly off better off, or they do not believe that to be a dictate of justice. If they do not believe it, then their society is not just in the appropriate Rawlsian sense, for a society is just, according to Rawls, only if its members themselves affirm and uphold the correct principles of justice. The difference principle might be appealed to in justification of a government's toleration, or promotion, of inequality in a society in which the talented do not themselves accept it, but it then justifies a public policy of inequality in a society some members of which—the talented—do not share community with the rest:[10] their behavior is then taken as fixed or parametric, a datum vis-à-vis a principle applied to it from without, rather than as itself answerable to that principle. That is not how principles of justice operate in a just society, as Rawls specifies that concept: within his terms, one may distinguish between a just society and a just government, one, that is, which applies just principles to a society whose members may not themselves accept those principles.

So we turn to the second and only remaining possibility, which is that the talented people do affirm the difference principle, that, as Rawls says, they apply the principles of justice *in their daily life* and achieve a sense of their own justice in doing so.[11] But they can then be asked why, in the light of their own belief in the principle, they require more pay than the untalented get, for work that may indeed demand special talent, but which is not specially unpleasant (for no such consideration enters the Rawlsian justification of incentives-derived inequality). The talented can be asked whether the extra they get is *necessary* to enhance the position of the worst off, which is the only thing, according to the difference principle, that could justify it. Is it necessary *tout court*, that is, independently of human will, so that, with all the will in the world, removal of inequality would make everyone worse off? Or is it necessary only insofar as the talented would *decide* to produce less than they now

10. They do not, more precisely, share *justificatory community* with the rest, in the sense of the italicized phrase that I specified at p. 282 of "Incentives."

11. "Citizens in everyday life affirm and act from the first principles of justice." They act "from these principles as their sense of justice dictates" and thereby "their nature as moral persons is most fully realized." (Quotations drawn from, respectively, "Kantian Constructivism in Moral Theory," *The Journal of Philosophy*, 77, no. 9 (Sept. 1980): 521, 528, and *A Theory of Justice*, p. 528.)

do, or not to take up posts where they are in special demand, if inequality were removed (by, for example, income taxation which redistributes to fully egalitarian effect[12])?

Talented people who affirm the difference principle would find those questions hard to handle. For they could not claim, *in self-justification*, at the bar of the difference principle, that their high rewards are necessary to enhance the position of the worst off, since, in the standard case,[13] it is they themselves who *make* those rewards necessary, through their own unwillingness to work for ordinary rewards as productively as they do for exceptionally high ones, an unwillingness which ensures that the untalented get less than they otherwise would. Those rewards are, therefore, necessary only because the choices of talented people are not appropriately informed by the difference principle.

Apart, then, from the very special cases in which the talented literally *could* not, as opposed to the normal case where they (merely) would not, perform as productively as they do without superior remuneration, the difference principle can justify inequality only in a society where not everyone accepts that very principle. It therefore cannot justify inequality in the appropriate Rawlsian way.

Now, this conclusion about what it means to accept and implement the difference principle implies that the justice of a society is not exclusively a function of its legislative structure, of its legally imperative rules, but also of the choices people make within those rules. The standard (and, in my view, misguided) Rawlsian application of the difference principle can be modeled as follows. There is a market economy all agents in which seek to maximize their own gains, and there is a Rawlsian state that selects a tax function on income that maximizes the income return to the worst off people, within the constraint that, because of the self-seeking motivation of the talented, a fully equalizing taxation system would make everyone worse off than one which is less than fully equalizing. But this double-minded modeling of the implementation of the difference principle, with citizens inspired by justice endorsing a state policy which plays a tax game against (some of) them in their manifestation as self-seeking economic agents, is wholly out of

12. That way of achieving equality preserves the information function of the market while extinguishing its motivational function: see Joseph Carens, *Equality, Moral Incentives, and the Market* (Chicago: University of Chicago Press, 1981).

13. See "Incentives," p. 298 *et circa*, for precisely what I mean by "the standard case."

accord with the (sound) Rawlsian requirement on a just society that its citizens themselves willingly submit to the standard of justice embodied in the difference principle. A society that is just within the terms of the difference principle, so we may conclude, requires not simply just coercive *rules*, but also an *ethos* of justice that informs individual choices. In the absence of such an ethos, inequalities will obtain that are not necessary to enhance the condition of the worst off: the required ethos promotes a distribution more just than what the rules of the economic game by themselves can secure.

To be sure, one might imagine, in the abstract, a set of coercive rules so finely tuned that universally self-interested choices within them would raise the worst off to as high a position as any other pattern of choices would produce. Where coercive rules had and were known to have such a character, agents could choose self-interestedly in confidence that the results of their choices would satisfy an appropriately uncompromising interpretation of the difference principle. In that (imaginary) case, the only ethos necessary for difference principle justice would be willing obedience to the relevant rules, an ethos which Rawls expressly requires. But the vast economics literature on incentive-compatibility teaches that rules of the contemplated perfect kind cannot be designed. Accordingly, as things actually are, the required ethos must, as I have argued, guide choice within the rules, and not merely direct agents to obey them. (I should emphasize that this is not so because it is *in general* true that the point of the rules governing an activity must be aimed at when agents pursue that activity in good faith: every competitive sport represents a counterexample to that generalization. But my argument for the conclusion stated above did not rest on that false generalization.)

III

There is an objection which friends of Rawls's *Theory of Justice* would press against my argument in criticism of his application of the difference principle. The objection is that my focus on the posture of talented producers in daily economic life is inappropriate, since their behavior occurs within, and does not determine, *the basic structure* of society, and it is only to the latter that the difference principle applies.[14] What-

14. For a typical statement of this restriction, see, John Rawls, *Political Liberalism* (New York: Columbia University Press, 1993), pp. 282–83.

ever people's choices within it may be, the basic structure is just provided that it satisfies the two principles of justice. To be sure, so Rawls
acknowledges, people's choices can themselves be assessed as just or
unjust, from a number of points of view. Thus, for example, appoint-
ment to a given job of candidate A rather than candidate B might be
judged unjust, even though it occurs within the rules of a just basic
structure.[15] But injustice in such a choice is not the sort of injustice that
the Rawlsian principles are designed to condemn. For, *ex hypothesi*, that
choice occurs within an established basic structure: it therefore cannot
affect the justice of the basic structure itself, which is what, according
to Rawls, the two principles govern. Nor, similarly, should the choices
with respect to work and remuneration that talented people make be
submitted for judgment at the bar of the difference principle. So to
judge those choices is to apply that principle at the wrong point. The
difference principle is a "principle of justice for institutions."[16] It governs the choice of institutions, not the choices made within them. The
development of the second horn of the dilemma argument at pp. 8–9
above misconstrues the Rawlsian requirement that citizens in a just society uphold the principles that make it just: by virtue of the stipulated
scope of the difference principle, talented people do count as faithfully
upholding it, as long as they conform to the prevailing economic rules
because that principle requires those rules.

Call that "the basic structure objection." Now, before I develop it further, and then reply to it, I want to point out that there is an important
ambiguity in the concept of the basic structure, as that is wielded by
Rawlsians. The ambiguity turns on whether the Rawlsian basic structure
includes only coercive aspects of the social order or, also, conventions
and usages that are deeply entrenched but not legally or literally coercive. I shall return to that ambiguity in Section V below, and I shall show
that it shipwrecks not only the basic structure objection but also the
whole approach to justice that Rawls has taught so many to pursue. But,
for the time being, I shall ignore the fatal ambiguity, and I shall take the
phrase "basic structure," as it appears in the basic structure objection,

15. See the first sentence of Sec. 2 of *A Theory of Justice* ("The Subject of Justice"): "Many
different kinds of things are said to be just and unjust: not only laws, institutions, and
social systems, but also particular actions of many kinds, including decisions, judgments,
and imputations" (*ibid.*, p. 7). But Rawls excludes examples such as the one given in the
text above from his purview, because "our topic ... is that of social justice. For us the
primary subject of justice is the basic structure of society" (*ibid.*).

16. *A Theory of Justice*, p. 303.

as denoting *some* sort of structure, be it legally coercive or not, but whose key feature, for the purposes of the objection, is that it is indeed a structure, that is, a framework of rules within which choices are made, as opposed to a set of choices and/or actions.[17] Accordingly, my Rawlsian critic would say, whatever structure, precisely, the basic structure is, the objection stands that my criticism of the incentives argument misapplies principles devised for a structure to individual choices and actions.

In further clarification of the polemical position, let me make a background point about the difference between Rawls and me with respect to the site or sites at which principles of justice apply. My own fundamental concern is neither the basic structure of society, in any sense, nor people's individual choices, but the pattern of benefits and burdens in society: that is neither a structure in which choice occurs nor a set of choices, but the upshot of structure and choices alike. My concern is *distributive justice*, by which I uneccentrically mean justice (and its lack) in the distribution of benefits and burdens to individuals. My root belief is that there is injustice in distribution when inequality of goods reflects not such things as differences in the arduousness of different people's labors, or people's different preferences and choices with respect to income and leisure, but myriad forms of lucky and unlucky circumstance. Such differences of advantage are a function of the structure *and* of people's choices within it, so I am concerned, secondarily, with *both* of those.

Now Rawls could say that his concern, too, is distributive justice, in the specified sense, but that, for him, distributive justice obtains just in case the allocation of benefits and burdens in society results from actions which display full conformity with the rules of a just basic structure.[18] When full compliance with the rules of a just basic structure obtains, it follows, on Rawls's view, that there is no scope for (further) personal justice and injustice which affects *distributive* justice, whether it be by enhancing it or by reducing it. There is, Rawls would, of course,

---

17. The contrast between structure and action is further explained, though also, as it were, put in its place, in the Endnote to this article.

18. *A Theory of Justice*, pp. 274–75: "The principles of justice apply to the basic structure. . . . The social system is to be designed so that the resulting distribution is just however things turn out." Cf. *ibid.*, p. 545: ". . . the distribution of material means is left to take care of itself in accordance with the idea of pure procedural justice."

Where the Action Is: On the
Site of Distributive Justice

readily agree, scope, within a just structure, for distribution-affecting meanness and generosity,[19] but generosity, though it would alter the distribution, and might make it more equal than it would otherwise be, could not make it more *just* than it would otherwise be, for it would then be doing the impossible, to wit, enhancing the justice of what is already established as a (perfectly) just distribution by virtue merely of the just structure in conformity with which it is produced. But, as I have indicated, I believe that there is scope for relevant (relevant, that is, because it affects justice in distribution) personal justice and injustice *within* a just structure, and, indeed, that it is not possible to achieve distributive justice by purely structural means.

In discussion of my claim (see p. 10 above) that social justice requires a social *ethos* that inspires uncoerced equality-supporting choice, Ronald Dworkin suggested[20] that a Rawlsian government might be thought to be charged with a duty, under the difference principle, of promoting such an ethos. Dworkin's suggestion was intended to support Rawls, against me, by diminishing the difference between Rawls's position and my own, and thereby reducing the reach of my criticism of him. I do not know what Rawls's response to Dworkin's proposal would be, but one thing is clear: Rawls could not say that, to the extent that the indicated policy failed, society would, as a result, be less just than if the policy had been more successful. Accordingly, if Dworkin is right that Rawlsian justice requires government to promote an ethos friendly to equality, it could not be for the sake of making society more distributively just that it was doing so, *even* though it would be for the sake of making its distribution more *equal*. The following threefold conjunction, which is an inescapable consequence of Rawls's position, on Dworkin's not unnatural interpretation of it, is strikingly incongruous: (1) the difference principle is an egalitarian principle of distributive justice; (2) it imposes on government a duty to promote an egalitarian ethos; (3) it is not for the sake of enhancing distributive justice in society that it is required to promote that ethos. Dworkin's attempt to reduce the distance between Rawls's position and my own threatens to render the former incoherent.

19. This is a different point from the one made at p. 11 above, to wit, that there is scope within a just structure for justice and injustice in choice in a "nonprimary" sense of "justice."
20. At a seminar in Oxford, in Hilary Term of 1994.

Now, before I mount my two replies to the basic structure objection, a brief conceptual digression is required, in clarification of the relationship between a just *society*, in Rawls's (and my own) understanding of that idea (see p. 8 above) and a just *distribution*, in my (non-Rawlsian) understanding of that different idea (see pp. 12–13). A just society, here, is one whose citizens affirm and act upon the correct principles of justice, but justice in distribution, as here defined, consists in a certain egalitarian profile of rewards. It follows that, as a matter of logical possibility, a just distribution might obtain in a society that is not itself just.

To illustrate this possibility, imagine a society whose ethos, though not inspired by a belief in equality, nevertheless induces an equal distribution. An example of such an ethos would be an intense Protestant ethic, which is indifferent to equality (on earth) as such, but whose stress on self-denial, hard work, and investment of assets surplus to needs somehow (despite the asceticism in it) makes the worst off as well off as is possible. Such an ethos achieves difference principle justice in distribution, but agents informed by it would not be motivated by the difference principle, and they could not, therefore, themselves be accounted just, within the terms of that principle. Under the specifications that were introduced here, this Protestant society would not be just, despite the fact that it displays a just distribution. We might say of the society that it is accidentally, but not constitutively, just. But, whatever phrasings we may prefer, the important thing is to distinguish "society" and "distribution" as candidate subjects of the predicate "just." (And it bears mentioning that, in contemporary practice, an ethos that achieves difference principle equality would almost certainly have to be equality-inspired: the accident of a non-equality-inspired ethos producing the right result is, at least in modern times, highly unlikely. The Protestantism described here is utterly fantastic, at least for our day.)

Less arresting is the opposite case, in which people strive to govern their behavior by (what are in fact) just principles, but ignorance, or the obduracy of wholly external circumstance, or collective action problems, or self-defeatingness of the kinds studied by Derek Parfit,[21] or something else which I have not thought of, frustrates their intention, so that the distribution remains unjust. It would perhaps be peculiar to

21. See his *Reasons and Persons* (Oxford: Oxford University Press, 1984), Chapter 4.

call such a society *just*, and neither Rawls nor I need do so: justice in citizens was put, above, as a *necessary* condition of a just society.

However we resolve the secondary, and largely verbal, complications raised in this digression, the point will stand[22] that an ethos informing choice within just rules is necessary in a society that is committed to the difference principle. My argument for that conclusion did not rely on aspects of my conception of justice which distinguish it from Rawls's, but on our shared conception of what a just society is. The fact that distributive justice, as I conceive it, causally requires an ethos (be it merely equality-promoting, such as our imaginary Protestantism, or also equality-inspired) that goes beyond conformity to just rules, was not a premise in my argument against Rawls. The argument of Section II turned essentially on my understanding of Rawls's well-considered requirement that the citizens of a just society are themselves just. The basic structure objection challenges that understanding.

IV

I now present a preliminary reply to the basic structure objection. It is preliminary in that it precedes my interrogation, in Section V, of what the phrase "basic structure" denotes, and also in that, by contrast with the fundamental reply that will follow that interrogation, there is a certain way out for Rawls, in face of the preliminary reply. That way out is not costless for him, but it does exist.

Although Rawls says often enough that the two principles of justice govern only justice in basic structure, he also says three things that tell against that restriction. This means that, in each case, he must either uphold the restriction and repudiate the comment in question, or maintain the comment and drop the restriction.[23]

---

22. If, that is, my argument survives the basic structure objection, to which I reply in Secs. IV and V.

23. Because of these tensions in Rawls, people have resisted my incentives critique of him in two opposite ways. Those convinced that his primary concern is the basic structure object in the fashion set out in Sec. III. But others do not realize how important that commitment is to him: they accept my (as I see it, anti-Rawlsian) view that the difference principle should condemn incentives, but they believe that Rawls would also accept it, since they think his commitment to that principle is relevantly uncompromising. They therefore do not regard what I say about incentives as a *criticism* of Rawls.

Those who respond in that second fashion seem not to realize that Rawls's liberalism is jeopardized if he takes the route that they think open to him. He then becomes a radical

First, Rawls says that, when the difference principle is satisfied, society displays *fraternity*, in a particularly strong sense: its citizens do not want

> to have greater advantages unless this is to the benefit of others who are less well off. . . . Members of a family commonly do not wish to gain unless they can do so in ways that further the interests of the rest. Now wanting to act on the difference principle has precisely this consequence.[24]

But fraternity of that strong kind is not realized when all the justice delivered by that principle comes from the basic structure, and, therefore, whatever people's motivations may be. Wanting not "to gain unless they can do so in ways that further the interests of the rest" is incompatible with the self-interested motivation of market maximizers, which the difference principle, in its purely structural interpretation, does not condemn.[25]

Second, Rawls says that the worst off in a society governed by the difference principle can bear their inferior position with dignity, since they know that no improvement of it is possible, that they would lose under any less unequal dispensation. Yet that is false, if justice relates to structure alone, since it might then be necessary for the worst off to occupy their relatively low place only because the choices of the better off tend strongly against equality. Why should the fact that no purely structurally induced improvement in their position is possible suffice to guarantee the dignity of the worst off, when their position might be very inferior indeed, because of unlimited self-seekingness in the economic choices of well-placed people?[26] Suppose, for example, that, as many politicians claim, raising rates of income taxation with a view to enhancing benefits for the badly off would be counterproductive, since the higher rates would induce severe disincentive effects on the productivity of the better off. Would awareness of that truth contribute to a sense of dignity on the part of the badly off?

Third, Rawls says that people in a just society act with a sense of justice *from* the principles of justice in their daily lives: they strive to apply

---

egalitarian socialist, whose outlook is very different from that of a liberal who holds that "deep inequalities" are "inevitable in the basic structure of any society" (*A Theory of Justice*, p. 7).

24. *A Theory of Justice*, p. 105.
25. See, further, "Incentives," pp. 321–22, "Pareto," pp. 178–79.
26. See, further, "Incentives," pp. 320–21.

those principles in their own choices. And they do so because they

> have a desire to express their nature as free and equal moral persons, and this they do most adequately by acting *from* the principles that they would acknowledge in the original position. When all strive to comply with these principles and each succeeds, then individually and collectively their nature as moral persons is most fully realized, and with it their individual and collective good.[27]

But why do they have to act *from* the principles of justice, and "apply" them "as their circumstances require"[28] if just behavior consists in choosing as one pleases within, and without disturbing, a structure designed to effect an implementation of those principles? And how can they, without a redolence of hypocrisy, celebrate the full realization of their natures as moral persons, when they know that they are out for the most that they can get in the market?

Now, as I said, these inconsistencies are not decisive against Rawls. For, in each case, he could stand pat on his restriction of justice to basic structure, and give up, or weaken, the remark that produces the inconsistency. And that is indeed what he is disposed to do at least with respect to the third inconsistency that I have noted. He said[29] that *A Theory of Justice* erred by in some respects treating the two principles as defining a *comprehensive* conception of justice:[30] he would, accordingly, now drop the high-pitched homily which constitutes the text to footnote 27. But this accommodation carries a cost: it means that the ideals of dignity, fraternity, and full realization of people's moral natures can no longer be said to be delivered by Rawlsian justice.[31]

V

I now provide a more fundamental reply to the basic structure objection. It is more fundamental in that it shows, decisively, that justice re-

27. *A Theory of Justice*, p. 528, my emphasis. See, further, footnote 11 above, and "Incentives," pp. 316–20.

28. John Rawls, "Justice as Fairness: A Briefer Restatement," Harvard University, 1989, typescript, p. 154.

29. In reply to a lecture that I gave at Harvard in March of 1993.

30. That is, as (part of) a complete moral theory, as opposed to a purely political one: see, for explication of that distinction, *Political Liberalism*, *passim*, and, in particular, pp. xv–xvii.

31. See "Incentives," p. 322.

quires an ethos governing daily choice that goes beyond one of obedience to just rules,[32] on grounds which do not, as the preliminary reply did, exploit things that Rawls says in apparent contradiction of his stipulation that justice applies to the basic structure of society alone. The fundamental reply interrogates, and refutes, that stipulation itself.

A major fault line in the Rawlsian architectonic not only wrecks the basic structure objection but also produces a dilemma for Rawls's view of the subject[33] of justice from which I can imagine no way out. The fault line exposes itself when we ask the apparently simple question: what (exactly) *is* the basic structure? For there is a fatal ambiguity in Rawls's specification of the basic structure, and an associated discrepancy between his criterion for what justice judges and his desire to exclude the effects of structure-consistent personal choice from the purview of its judgment.

The basic structure, the primary subject of justice, is always said by Rawls to be a set of institutions, and, so he infers, the principles of justice do not judge the actions of people within (just) institutions whose rules they observe. But it is seriously unclear *which* institutions are supposed to qualify as part of the basic structure. Sometimes it appears that coercive (in the legal sense) institutions exhaust it, or, better, that institutions belong to it only insofar as they are (legally) coercive.[34] In this widespread interpretation of what Rawls intends by the "basic structure" of a society, that structure is legible in the provisions of its constitution, in such specific legislation as may be required to implement those provisions, and in further legislation and policy which are of central importance but which resist formulation in the constitution itself.[35]

32. Though not necessarily an ethos embodying the very principles that the rules formulate: see the last four paragraphs of Sec. III above. Justice will be shown to require an ethos, and the basic structure objection will thereby be refuted, but it will be a contingent question whether the ethos required by justice can be read off the content of the just rules themselves. Still, as I suggested at p. 14, the answer to that question is almost certainly "Yes."

33. That is, the subject matter that principles of justice judge. I follow Rawls's usage here (e.g. in the title of Lecture VII of *Political Liberalism*: "The Basic Structure as Subject"; and cf. n. 15 above).

34. Henceforth, unless I indicate otherwise, I shall use "coercive," "coercion," etc. to mean "legally coercive," etc.

35. Thus, the difference principle, though pursued through (coercively sustained) state policy, cannot, so Rawls thinks, be aptly inscribed in a society's constitution: see *Political Liberalism*, pp. 227–30.

Where the Action Is: On the Site of Distributive Justice

The basic structure, in this first understanding of it, is, so one might say, the *broad coercive outline* of society, which determines in a relatively fixed and general way what people may and must do, in advance of legislation that is optional, relative to the principles of justice, and irrespective of the constraints and opportunities created and destroyed by the choices that people make within the given basic structure, so understood.

Yet it is quite unclear that the basic structure is *always* thus defined, in exclusively coercive terms, within the Rawlsian texts. For Rawls often says that the basic structure consists of the *major* social institutions, and he does not put a particular accent on coercion when he announces *that* specification of the basic structure.[36] In this second reading of what it is, institutions belong to the basic structure whose structuring can depend far less on law than on convention, usage, and expectation: a signal example is the family, which Rawls sometimes includes in the

36. Consider, for example, the passage at pp. 7–8 of *A Theory of Justice* in which the concept of the basic structure is introduced:

> Our topic . . . is that of social justice. For us the primary subject of justice is the basic structure of society, or more exactly, the way in which the major social institutions distribute fundamental rights and duties and determine the division of advantages from social cooperation. By major institutions I understand the political constitution and the principal economic and social arrangements. Thus the legal protection of freedom of thought and liberty of conscience, competitive markets, private property in the means of production, and the monogamous family are examples of major social institutions. . . . I shall not consider the justice of institutions and social practices generally. . . . [The two principles of justice] may not work for the rules and practices of private associations or for those of less comprehensive social groups. They may be irrelevant for the various informal conventions and customs of everyday life; they may not elucidate the justice, or perhaps better, the fairness of voluntary cooperative arrangements or procedures for making contractual agreements.

I cannot tell, from those statements, what is to be included in, and what excluded from, the basic structure, nor, more particularly, whether coercion is the touchstone of inclusion. Take, for example, the case of the monogamous family. Is it simply its "legal protection" that is a major social institution, in line with a coercive definition of the basic structure (if not, perhaps, with the syntax of the relevant sentence)? Or is the monogamous family itself part of that structure? And, in that case, are its typical usages part of it? They certainly constitute a "principal social arrangement," yet they may also count as "practices of private associations or . . . of less comprehensive social groups," and they are heavily informed by the "conventions and customs of everyday life."

Puzzlement with respect to the bounds of the basic structure is not relieved by examination of the relevant pages of *Political Liberalism*, to wit, 11, 68, 201–202, 229, 258, 268, 271–72, 282–83, and 301. Some formulations on those pages lean toward a coercive specification of the basic structure. Others do not.

basic structure and sometimes does not.[37] But once the line is crossed, from coercive ordering to the non-coercive ordering of society by rules and conventions of accepted practice, then the ambit of justice can no longer exclude chosen behavior, since the usages which constitute informal structure (think, again, of the family) are bound up with the customary actions of people.

"Bound up with" is vague, so let me explain how I mean it, here. One can certainly speak of the structure of the family, and it is not identical with the choices that people customarily make within it; but it is nevertheless impossible to claim that the principles of justice which apply to family structure do not apply to day-to-day choices within it. For consider the following contrast. The *coercive* structure arises independently of people's quotidian choices: it is formed by those specialized choices which legislate the law of the land. By contrast, the non-coercive structure of the family has the character it does only because of the choices that its members routinely make. The constraints and pressures that sustain the non-coercive structure reside in the dispositions of agents which are actualized as and when those agents choose to act in a constraining or pressuring way. With respect to coercive structure, one may fairly readily distinguish the choices which institute and sustain a structure from the choices that occur within it.[38] But with respect to informal structure, that distinction, though conceptually intelligible, collapses extensionally: when A chooses to conform to the prevailing usages, the pressure on B to do so is reinforced, and no such pressure exists, the very usages themselves do not exist, in the absence of conformity to them.

Now, since that is so, since behavior is *constitutive* of *non*-coercive structure, it follows that the only way of protecting the basic structure objection against my claim that the difference principle condemns maximizing economic behavior (and, more generally, of protecting the restriction of justice to the basic structure against the insistence that the personal, too, is political) is by holding fast to a purely coercive specification of the basic structure. But that way out is not open to Rawls,

---

37. See the final paragraph of Sec. I of this paper.

38. For more on structure and choice, see the Endnote to this article. Among other things, I there entertain a doubt about the strength of the distinction drawn in the above sentence, but, as I indicate, if that doubt is sound, then my case against Rawls is not weakened.

because of a further characterization that he offers of the basic structure: this is where the discrepancy adverted to in the second paragraph
of this section appears. For Rawls says that "the basic structure is the
primary subject of justice because its effects are so profound and present from the start."[39] Nor is that further characterization of the basic
structure optional: it is needed to explain why it *is* primary, as far as
justice is concerned. Yet it is false that only the *coercive* structure causes
profound effects, as the example of the family once again reminds us.[40]
Accordingly, if Rawls retreats to coercive structure, he contradicts his
own criterion for what justice judges, and he lands himself with an arbitrarily narrow definition of his subject matter. So he must let other
structure in, and that means, as we have seen, letting chosen behavior
in. What is more, even if behavior were not, as I claim it is, constitutive
of non-coercive structure, it will come in by direct appeal to the profun-
dity-of-effect criterion for what justice governs. So, for example, we
need not decide whether or not a regular practice of favoring sons over
daughters in the matter of providing higher education forms part of the
structure of the family to condemn it as unjust, under that criterion.[41]

Given, then, his stated rationale[42] for exclusive focus on the basic
structure—and what *other* rationale could there be for calling it the *primary* subject of justice?—Rawls is in a dilemma. For he must either

39. *A Theory of Justice*, p. 7.

40. Or consider access to that primary good which Rawls calls "the social basis of self-
respect." While the law may play a large role in securing that good to people vulnerable
to racism, legally unregulable racist attitudes also have an enormous negative impact on
how much of that primary good they get.

But are the profound effects of the family, or of racism, "present from the start" (see the
text to n. 39)? I am not sure how to answer that question, because I am unclear about the
intended import, here, of the quoted phrase. Rawls probably means "present from the
start of each person's life": the surrounding text at *Theory*, p. 7 supports this interpretation. If so, the family, and racial attitudes, certainly qualify. If not, then I do not know how
to construe the phrase. But what matters, surely, is the asserted profundity of effect, not
whether it is "present from the start," whatever may be the sense which attaches, here, to
that phrase.

41. Note that one can condemn the said practice without condemning those who engage in it. For there might be a collective action problem here, which weighs heavily on
poor families in particular. If, in addition to discrimination in education, there is discrimination in employment, then a poor family might sacrifice a great deal through choosing
evenhandedly across the sexes with whatever resources it can devote to its children's
education. This illustrates the important distinction between condemning injustice and
condemning the people whose actions perpetuate it: see, further, Sec. VI below.

42. See the text to n. 39 above.

admit application of the principles of justice to (legally optional) social practices, and, indeed, to patterns of personal choice that are not legally prescribed, *both* because they are the substance of those practices, *and* because they are similarly profound in effect, in which case the restriction of justice to structure, in any sense, collapses; or, if he restricts his concern to the coercive structure only, then he saddles himself with a purely arbitrary delineation of his subject matter. I now illustrate this dilemma by reference to the two contexts that have figured most in this paper: the family, and the market economy.

Family structure is fateful for the benefits and burdens that redound to different people, and, in particular, to people of different sexes, where "family structure" includes the socially constructed expectations which lie on husband and wife. And such expectations are sexist and unjust if, for example, they direct the woman in a family where both spouses work outside the home to carry a greater burden of domestic tasks. Yet such expectations need not be supported by the law for them to possess informal coercive force: sexist family structure is consistent with sex-neutral family law. Here, then, is a circumstance, outwith the basic structure, as that would be coercively defined, which profoundly affects people's life-chances, *through the choices people make in response to the stated expectations, which are, in turn, sustained by those choices.*[43] Yet Rawls must say, on pain of giving up the basic structure objection, that (legally uncoerced) family structure and behavior have no implications for justice in the sense of "justice" in which the basic structure has implications for justice, since they are not a consequence of the formal coercive order. But that implication of the stated position is perfectly incredible: no such differentiating sense is available.

John Stuart Mill taught us to recognize that informal social pressure can restrict liberty as much as formal coercive law does. And the family example shows that informal pressure is as relevant to distributive justice as it is to liberty. One reason why the rules of the basic structure, when it is coercively defined, do not by themselves determine the justice of the distributive upshot is that, by virtue of circumstances that are

43. Hugo Adam Bedau noticed that the family falls outside the basic structure, under the coercive specification of it often favored by Rawls, though he did not notice the connection between non-coercive structure and choice that I emphasize in the above sentence: see his "Social Justice and Social Institutions," *Midwest Studies in Philosophy*, 3 (1978): 171.

relevantly independent of coercive rules, some people have much more
power than others to determine what happens *within* those rules.

The second illustration of discrepancy between what coercive structure commands and what profoundly affects the distribution of benefits
and burdens is my own point about incentives. Maximinizing legislation,[44] and, hence, a coercive basic structure that is just as far as the
difference principle is concerned, are consistent with a maximizing ethos
across society which, under many conditions, will produce severe inequalities and a meager level of provision for the worst off, yet both have
to be declared just by Rawls, if he stays with a coercive conception of
what justice judges. And that implication is, surely, perfectly incredible.

Rawls cannot deny the difference between the coercively defined
basic structure and that which produces major distributive consequences: the coercively defined basic structure is only an instance of the
latter. Yet he must, to retain his position on justice and personal choice,
restrict the ambit of justice to what a coercive basic structure produces.
But, so I have (by implication) asked: why should we *care* so dispropor-
tionately about the coercive basic structure, when the major reason for
caring about it, its impact on people's lives, is *also* a reason for caring
about informal structure and patterns of personal choice? To the extent
that we care about coercive structure because it is fateful with regard to
benefits and burdens, we must care equally about the ethi that sustain
gender inequality, and inegalitarian incentives. And the similarity of our
reasons for caring about these matters will make it lame to say: ah, but
only the caring about coercive structure is a caring about *justice*, in a
certain distinguishable sense. That thought is, I submit, incapable of
coherent elaboration.

My response to the basic structure objection is now fully laid out, but
before proceeding, in the sections that remain, to matters arising, it will
be useful to rehearse, in compressed form, the arguments that were presented in Sections II through V.

My original criticism of the incentives argument ran, in brief, as follows:

(1) Citizens in a just society adhere to its principles of justice.

---

44. That is, legislation which maximizes the size of the primary goods bundle held by
the worst off people, given whatever is correctly expected to be the pattern in the choices
made by economic agents.

But

(2) They do not adhere to the difference principle if they are acquisitive maximizers in daily life.

∴ (3) In a society that is governed by the difference principle, citizens lack the acquisitiveness that the incentives argument attributes to them.

The basic structure objection to that criticism is of this form:

(4) The principles of justice govern only the basic structure of a just society.

∴ (5) Citizens in a just society may adhere to the difference principle whatever their choices may be within the structure it determines, and, in particular, even if their economic choices are entirely acquisitive.

∴ (6) Proposition (2) lacks justification.

My preliminary reply to the basic structure objection says:

(7) Proposition (5) is inconsistent with many Rawlsian statements about the relationship between citizens and principles of justice in a just society.

And my fundamental reply to the basic structure objection says:

(8) Proposition (4) is unsustainable.

VI

So the personal is indeed political: personal choices to which the writ of the law is indifferent are fateful for social justice.

But that raises a huge question, with respect to *blame*. The injustice in distribution that reflects personal choices within a just coercive structure can plainly not be blamed on that structure itself, nor, therefore, on whoever legislated that structure. Must it, then, be blamed, in our two examples, on men[45] and on acquisitive people, respectively?

I shall presently address, and answer, that question about blame, but, before I do so, I wish to explain why I could remain silent in the face of it, why, that is, my argument in criticism of Rawls's restricted applica-

---

45. We can here set aside the fact that women often subscribe to, and inculcate, male-dominative practices.

tion of the principles of justice requires no judgment about blaming individual choosers. The conclusion of my argument is that the principles of justice apply not only to coercive rules but also to the pattern in people's (legally) uncoerced choices. Now, if we judge a certain set of rules to be just or unjust, we need not add, as pendant to that judgment, that those who legislated the rules in question should be praised or blamed for what they did.[46] And something analogous applies when we come to see that the ambit of justice covers the pattern of choices in a society. We can believe whatever we are inclined to do about how responsible and/or culpable people are for their choices, and that includes believing that they are not responsible and/or culpable for them at all, while holding that on which I insist: that the pattern in such choices is relevant to how just or unjust a society is.

That said, I return to the question of how blamable individuals are. It would be inappropriate to answer it, here, by first declaring my position, if, indeed, I have one, on the philosophical problem of the freedom of the will. Instead,I shall answer the question about blame on the prephilosophical assumptions which inform our ordinary judgments about when, and how much, blame is appropriate. On such assumptions, we should avoid two opposite mistakes about how culpable chauvinistic men and self-seeking high fliers are. One is the mistake of saying: there is no ground for blaming these people *as individuals*, for they simply participate in an accepted social practice, however tawdry or awful that practice may be. That is a mistake, since people do have choices: it is, indeed, *only* their choices that reproduce social practices; and some, moreover, choose *against* the grain of nurture, habit, and self-interest. But one also must not say: look how each of these people shamefully decides to behave so badly. That, too, is unbalanced, since, although

46. We can distinguish between how unjust past practices (e.g. slavery) were and how unjust those who protected and benefited from those unjust practices were. Most of us (rightly) do not condemn Lincoln for his (conditional) willingness to tolerate slavery as strongly as we would a statesman who did the same in 1997, but the institution of slavery itself was as unjust in Lincoln's time as it would be today.

What made slavery unjust in, say, Greece, is exactly what would make slavery (with, of course, the very same rules of subordination) unjust today, to wit, the content of its rules. But sound judgments about the justice and injustice of people are much more contextual: they must take into account the institutions under which they live, the prevailing level of intellectual and moral development, collective action problems such as the one delineated in n. 41 above, and so forth. The morally best slaveholder might deserve admiration. The morally best form of slavery would not.

there exists personal choice, there is heavy social conditioning behind it and there can be heavy costs in deviating from the prescribed and/or permitted ways. If we care about social justice, we have to look at four things: the coercive structure, other structures, the social ethos, and the choices of individuals, and judgment on the last of those must be informed by awareness of the power of the others. So, for example, a properly sensitive appreciation of these matters allows one to hold that an acquisitive ethos is profoundly unjust in its effects, without holding that those who are gripped by it are commensurately unjust. It is essential to apply principles of justice to dominant patterns in social behavior—that, as it were, is where the action is—but it doesn't follow that we should have a persecuting attitude to the people who emit that behavior. We might have good reason to exonerate the perpetrators of injustice, but we should not deny, or apologize for, the injustice itself.[47]

On an extreme view, which I do not accept but need not reject, a typical husband in a thoroughly sexist society, one, that is, in which families in their overwhelming majority display an unjust division of domestic labor, is literally incapable of revising his behavior, or capable of revising it only at the cost of cracking up, to nobody's benefit. But even if that is true of typical husbands, we know it to be false of husbands in general. It is a plain empirical fact that some husbands are capable of revising their behavior, since some husbands have done so, in response to feminist criticism. These husbands, we could say, were moral pioneers. They made a path which becomes easier and easier to follow as more and more people follow it, until social pressures are so altered that it becomes harder to stick to sexist ways than to abandon them. That is a central way in which a social ethos changes. Or, for another example, consider the recent rise in ecological consciousness. At first, only people that appear to be freaky because they do so bother to save and recycle their paper, plastic, and so forth. Then, more do that, and, finally, it becomes not only difficult not to do it but easy to do it. It is pretty easy to discharge burdens that have become part of the normal round of everybody's life. Expectations determine behavior, behavior determines expectations, which determine behavior, and so on.

Are there circumstances in which a similar incremental process could

---

47. See the preceding note.

occur with respect to economic behavior? I do not know. But I do know
that universal maximizing is by no means a necessary feature of a market economy. For all that much of its industry was state-owned, the
United Kingdom from 1945 to 1951 had a market economy. But salary
differentials were nothing like as great as they were to become, or as
they were then in the United States. Yet, so I hazard, when British executives making five times what their workers did met American counter-
parts making fifteen times what their (anyhow better paid) workers did,
many of the British executives would *not* have felt: *we* should press for
more. For there was a social ethos of reconstruction after war, an ethos
of common project, that restrained desire for personal gain. It is not for
a philosopher to delimit the conditions under which such, and even
more egalitarian ethi, can prevail. But a philosopher can say that a maximizing ethos is not a necessary feature of society, even of market society, and that, to the extent that such an ethos prevails, satisfaction of the
difference principle is prejudiced.

In 1988, the ratio of top executive salaries to production worker wages
was 6.5 to 1 in West Germany and 17.5 to 1 in the United States.[48] Since
it is not plausible to think that Germany's lesser inequality was a disincentive to productivity, since it is plausible to think that an ethos that
was relatively friendly to equality[49] protected German productivity in
the face of relatively modest material incentives, we can conclude that
the said ethos caused the worst paid to be better paid than they would
have been under a different culture of reward. It follows, on my view of
things, that the difference principle was better realized in Germany in
1988 than it would have been if its culture of reward had been more
similar to that of the United States. But Rawls cannot say that, since the
smaller inequality that benefited the less well off in Germany was not a
matter of law but of ethos. I think that Rawls's inability to regard Germany as having done comparatively well with respect to the difference
principle is a grave defect in his conception of the site of distributive
justice.

48. See Lawrence Mishel and David M. Frankel, *The State of Working America*, 1990-1991
(Armonk, N.Y.: M. E. Sharpe, 1991), p. 122.

49. That ethos need not have been an egalitarian one. For present purposes, it could
have been an ethos which disendorses acquisitiveness as such (see n. 32, and the digression at the end of Sec. III), other than on *behalf of* the worst off.

ENDNOTE ON COERCIVE AND OTHER STRUCTURE

The legally coercive structure of society functions in two ways. It *prevents* people from doing things by erecting insurmountable barriers (fences, police lines, prison walls, etc.), and it *deters* people from doing things by ensuring that certain forms of unprevented behavior carry an (appreciable risk of) penalty.[50] The second (deterrent) aspect of coercive structure may be described counterfactually, in terms of what would or might happen to someone who elects the forbidden behavior: knowledge of the relevant counterfactual truths motivates the complying citizen's choices.

Not much pure prevention goes on within the informal structure of society: not none, but not much. (Locking an errant teenager in her room would represent an instance of pure prevention, which, if predictable for determinate behavior, would count as part of a society's informal structure: it would be a rule in accordance with which that society operates.) That being set aside, informal structure manifests itself in predictable sanctions such as criticism, disapproval, anger, refusal of future cooperation, ostracism, beating (of, for example, wives who refuse sexual service) and so on.

Finally, to complete this conceptual review, the ethos of a society is the set of sentiments and attitudes in virtue of which its normal practices, and informal pressures, are what they are.

Now, the pressures that sustain the informal structure lack force save insofar as there is a normal practice of compliance with the rules they enforce. That is especially true of that great majority of those pressures (beating does not belong to that majority) which carry a moral coloring: criticism and disapproval are ineffective when they come from the mouths of those who ask others not to do what they do themselves. To be sure, that is not a conceptual truth, but a social-psychological one. Even so, it enables us to say that what people ordinarily do supports and partly constitutes (again, not conceptually, but in effect) the informal structure of society, in such a way that it makes no sense to pass judgments of justice on that structure while withholding such judgment from the behavior that supports and constitutes it: that point is crucial

50. The distinction given above corresponds to that between the difficulty and the cost of actions: see my *Karl Marx's Theory of History* (Oxford: Oxford University Press, and Princeton: Princeton University Press, 1978), pp. 238–39.

to the anti-Rawlsian inference at p. 20 above.[51] Informal structure is not a behavioral pattern, but a set of rules, yet the two are so closely related that, so one might say, they are *merely* categorially different. Accordingly, so I argued, to include (as one must) informal structure within the basic structure is to countenance behavior, too, as a primary subject of judgments of justice.

Now, two truths about legally coercive structure might be thought to cast doubt on the contrast I drew between it and informal structure in Section V above. First, although the legally coercive structure of society is indeed discernible in the ordinances of its constitution and law, those ordinances count as delineating it only on condition that they enjoy a broad measure of compliance.[52] And, second, legally coercive structure achieves its intended social effect only in and through the actions which constitute compliance with its rules. To be more accurate, those propositions are true provided that we exclude from consideration "1984" states in which centralized brute force prevails against nonconformity even, if necessary, at the cost of half the population being in jail. But it is appropriate to ignore 1984 scenarios here.[53]

In light of those truths, it might be objected that the dilemma that I posed for Rawls (see pp. 21–22 above), and by means of which I sought to defeat his claim that justice judges structure *as opposed to* the actions of agents, was critically misframed. For I said, against that claim, that the required opposition between structure and actions works for coercive structure only, with respect to which a relevantly strong distinction can be drawn between structure-sustaining and structure-conforming action, but that coercive structure could not reasonably be thought to

51. See the sentence beginning "But once" on the top of that page.

52. It does not follow that they are not *laws* unless they enjoy such compliance: perhaps they are nevertheless laws, if they "satisfy a test set out in a Hartian rule of recognition, even if they are themselves neither complied with nor accepted" (Joshua Cohen, in comment on an earlier draft of this paper). But such laws (or "laws") are not plausibly represented as part of the basic structure of society, so the statement in the text can stand as it is.

53. That is because of Rawls's reasonable stipulation that, in a just society, the threat of coercion is necessary for assurance game reasons only: each is disposed to comply provided that others do, and coercion is needed not because, in the absence of its threat *to me*, I might not comply, but because in the absence of its threat to others I cannot be sure that *they* will comply (see *A Theory of Justice*, p. 315). This stipulation makes formal law less *essentially* coercive than one might otherwise suppose and therefore less contrastable with custom than I have supposed.

exhaust the structure falling within the purview of justice: accordingly, so I concluded, justice must also judge everyday actions.

The truths rehearsed two paragraphs back challenge my articulation of the distinction between coercive structure and action within it. They thereby also challenge the contrast that I drew between two relationships, that between coercive structure and action, and that between informal structure and action.

This problem needs more thought than I have to date spent on it. For the moment I shall say this: even if coercive structure counts as such only if appropriate compliance obtains, that structure may nevertheless be *identified* with a set of laws which are not themselves patterns of behavior. And one can distinguish sharply between behavior forbidden and directed by those laws, and behavior that is optional under them, however systematic and widespread it may be. By contrast, the identity of informal structure is less separable from practice: no distinction is sustainable between widespread practices which manifest or represent informal structure and widespread practices which do not.

If the would-be saving contrast which I there essay is an unrealistic idealization, then the distinction, vis-à-vis action, between coercive and informal structure, may be more blurred than I have been disposed to allow. Yet that would not be because informal structure is more separable from action than I claimed, but because coercive structure is less separable from it. Therefore, even if the dilemma constructed on pp. 21–22 was for the stated reasons misframed, the upshot would hardly be congenial to Rawls's position, that justice judges structure rather than actions, but, if anything, congenial to my own rejection of it, if not, indeed, to the terms in which some of the argument for that rejection was cast.

BRIAN BARRY　　　　　　　　John Rawls and
　　　　　　　　　　　　　　　the Priority of Liberty

"Grub first, then ethics."
Brecht.[1]

A short review of the whole of John Rawls's *A Theory of Justice*[2] could hardly do more than state the outlines of the argument and offer a few comments. Since this has already been done in other places by a number of other people I should prefer in this review to concentrate on one topic. The one I have chosen has the advantage of being one of Rawls's central preoccupations while at the same time it can be discussed without too much reference to the complexities of the whole theory. It is also of great significance as a problem in political theory in its own right.

"The priority of liberty" is a proposition concerning the relation between the first of Rawls's two principles of justice, that of equal liberty, and the second of his two principles, which says that inequalities of wealth and power should work to the benefit of the least advantaged representative man. For the purposes of this discussion I shall not bother with another part of the second principle, which requires equal opportunity to secure favorable positions, nor shall I place any weight on the particular (maximin) form given to the second principle or to the question how representative men are to be defined. Nothing in this discussion will turn on the most characteristic feature of Rawls's theory of justice, the one everybody knows about, which insists on making evaluations where wealth and power

1. Quoted in W. H. Auden and Louis Kronenberger, *The Faber Book of Aphorisms* (London, 1964), p. 368.
2. John Rawls, *A Theory of Justice* (Cambridge, Mass., 1971). Page references throughout the text are to this book.

are concerned in terms of minima rather than averages. I shall similarly not get involved in the problems of equal liberty, as against
average or maximin liberty. The interest here is focused at another
point with quite general ramifications: the question whether it is
possible, and if so in what sense, to assert a priority relationship between liberty and wealth.

Rawls maintains that there is a simple priority relationship between
the two: "*First Priority Rule* (The Priority of Liberty). The principles
of justice are to be ranked in lexical order and therefore liberty can
be restricted only for the sake of liberty" (p. 302). In the section
"The Priority of Liberty Defined" (§39) Rawls spells this out a little
more fully: "By the priority of liberty I mean the precedence of the
principle of equal liberty over the second principle of justice. The
two principles are in lexical order, and therefore the claims of liberty
are to be satisfied first. Until this is achieved no other principle comes
into play" (p. 244).

"Lexical" is Rawls's private version of the word "lexicographic,"
which is a term of art meaning a way of ordering criteria such that
the smallest discernible difference on the first-ranking criterion off-
sets any amount of difference on the second-ranking criterion, and
so on. As the word suggests, the paradigm is the arrangment of words
in a dictionary, where alphabetic position on the first letter of a word
is decisive in ordering two words unless they begin with the same
letter, in which the same decision process is applied to the words'
second letters. Another way of putting it is that the second-rank
criterion comes into operation only to break ties between things which
cannot be distinguished on the basis of the first-rank criterion.

In the present case the implications of lexicographic ordering are
that as between two situations the smallest superiority on the first
principle outweighs any amount of superiority on the second principle, and that the smallest amount of improvement on the first principle is worth sacrificing any amount of loss on the second principle.
The contrast is with a "pluralistic" relation, in which each of the
principles would be ascribed a weight and choices made between
alternative situations by "trading off" gains and losses on the two
principles at the prescribed rate of exchange. Rawls makes it clear
that it is precisely such "trading off" that he wishes to reject. "Now it

is possible, at least theoretically, that by giving up some of their fundamental liberties men are sufficiently compensated by the resulting social and economic gains. . . . Imagine . . . that men forego certain political rights when the economic returns are significant and their capacity to influence policy by the exercise of these rights would be marginal in any case. It is this kind of case which the principles as stated rule out; being in serial order they do not permit exchanges between basic liberties and economic gains" (pp. 62-63).

This might be called Rawls's official doctrine, and it is the one he refers to most frequently in the book. It is, as stated, so outlandishly extreme that it is scarcely worth devoting any space to a discussion of it. It can be accepted only if wealth is assigned a value that is literally infinitesimally small in relation to liberty, so that it would be judged worth dropping from general affluence to general poverty in order to score a minute gain on the "equal liberty" criterion, if such a choice were presented to a society. In the end, however, Rawls does not defend this official view. Indeed, even when introducing the notion of lexicographic ordering (in § 8, "The Priority Problem") he writes: "While it seems clear that, in general, a lexical order cannot be strictly correct, it may be an illuminating approximation under certain special though significant conditions (§ 82)" (p. 45). Almost five hundred pages later, near the end of the book, we finally arrive at section 82, which is entitled "The Grounds for the Priority of Liberty." Here at last we get a chance to see what is covered by the qualification "certain special though significant conditions," and it is to Rawls's discussion in this section of the book that I shall address myself in the remainder of this essay.

Actually, it is not clear what exactly Rawls does want to say here, though there is no doubt that he wishes to arrive at a particular conclusion; namely, that it is rational for a society to pursue increased wealth up to some point even at the expense of the equal basic liberties guaranteed by the first principle. The most easily comprehensible statement of his position makes it appear that he intends to relax the lexicographic priority of the first principle so that at low levels of economic development a degree of "pluralistic" trading off between liberty and wealth can be allowed. This interpretation is especially suggested by the talk of "marginal significance" in the following passage: "Now the basis for the priority of liberty is roughly as follows: as the conditions of civilization improve, the marginal significance for our good of further economic and social advantages diminishes relative to the interests of liberty, which become stronger as the conditions for the exercise of the equal freedoms are more fully exercised. Beyond some point it becomes and then remains irrational from the standpoint of the original position to acknowledge a lesser liberty for the sake of greater material means and amenities of office" (p. 542).

Now, the most convenient way to discuss trading-off relationships between two goods is to represent them graphically by means of indifference curves. (Rawls does this himself to illustrate his discussion of "pluralism" on page 37.) Figure 1 is an attempt to draw the indifference map implied by the passage just quoted. Several points about the construction may be noted. First, the axes. Along the vertical axis are amounts of "equal liberty," increasing with distance from the origin in the bottom left-hand corner. This dimension is shown as having an upper bound, indicating that it makes sense to think of the maximum possible equal liberty being achieved within a society. Position along the horizontal axis indicates the level of the society's wealth. It is not conceived as having any definite upper limit. In this connection it is worth remembering that wealth is treated within Rawls's theory as a "primary good" in itself; it is thus the kind of thing measured by indices of Gross National Product rather than something that might be captured by a more sophisticated conception of economic welfare explicitly relating production to the satisfaction of human needs.

Let us now consider the indifference curves. An indifference curve connects points representing different combinations of the two goods which are equally desirable. Following what would appear to be the implications of Rawls's reference to the diminishing marginal significance of wealth as the society has more of it, we show a family of indifference curves with a downward slope at low levels of wealth to indicate that at these levels it is worth trading some equal liberty for any increase in wealth. These curves are shown as gradually flattening out as they move to the right until at the point P they all become horizontal. This means that beyond P no gain in wealth compensates for a reduction in the degree to which the "equal liberty" criterion is

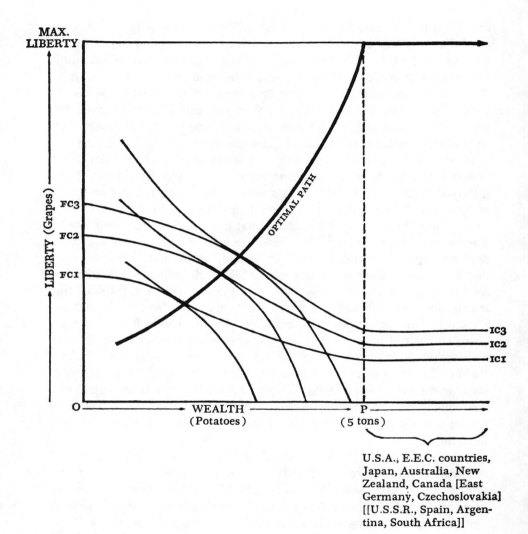

Figure I

satisfied. P is thus the "point [at which] it becomes and then remains irrational from the standpoint of the original position to acknowledge a lesser liberty for the sake of greater material means and amenities of office."

We cannot attach a quantitative figure, in terms of GNP per capita, to the point P on the basis of Rawls's discussion. But we can in a rough and ready way use the names of contemporary societies as surrogates. It is clear from the whole drift of Rawls's discussion, here and at other places in the book, that he thinks some contemporary societies are past the point P, so that he is talking about an actual rather than a hypothetical situation.[3] Since he is an American and often uses terms such as "we" in connection with social choices, it is safe to put the United States to the right; and if the United States, then presumably also the other countries listed without brackets. The countries in a single pair of brackets would seem plausible candidates while those in double brackets raise questions of diverse kinds which it would have been nice to have Rawls's ruling on. We cannot, on the basis of anything Rawls says, assign actual positions to countries in relation to the point P or attach any definite date to the time when those that are to the right of P passed it.

There are three technical points which are worth making here. First, it is surely clear that it is misleading to describe the relation between the two principles as one of lexicographic priority. Suppose, for example, that we replace equal freedom with grapes and economic development with potatoes, and provide that the goods cannot be sold if they are not used. Point P might then be (as shown in Figure 1) five tons of potatoes. Rawls would have us say that, given we have five tons of potatoes, grapes have a lexicographic priority. There are surely better ways of describing the position.

Second, we should note that Rawls makes statements that are inconsistent with his assertion that beyond a certain point it is not worth sacrificing equal liberty for increased wealth. As Figure 1 shows, the implication of being able to say that when we have five tons of potatoes no offer of further potatoes will induce us to part with a single grape, is that once we have five tons of potatoes, any more potatoes

3. "For the most part I shall assume that the requisite circumstances for the serial [lexicographic] order obtain" (p. 152).

are totally without value. But Rawls remarks, in the paragraph following that just quoted: "To be sure, it is not the case that when the priority of liberty holds, all material wants are satisfied. Rather these desires are not so compelling as to make it rational for the persons in the original position to agree to satisfy them by accepting a less than equal freedom" (p. 543). But if wants for material goods, even if not "compelling," still have some value in fulfillment, this is inconsistent with the indifference curves being parallel to the axis; it suggests a shallow slope. Rawls might reply to this that the apparent inconsistency arises because we can only represent the priority relation graphically by a line parallel to the axis, and that such a mode of representation leaves out the fact that the second principle acts as a tiebreaker. This, however, is a point of trivial significance in the present context. It means that, in Figure 1, point x is less good than point y, instead of being just as good, but it still means that point x is better than a point y', which we may define as a point an infinitesimal distance below y. In other terms, it means that if we get ten thousand grapes anyway, we would sooner have ten tons of potatoes than five tons; but we would prefer five tons of potatoes and ten thousand grapes to ten tons of potatoes and nine thousand nine hundred and ninety-nine grapes. This is surely not giving economic goods the kind of value which Rawls implies that they still have at the point where the priority of liberty becomes absolute. There is thus, it would appear, an unresolved contradiction between Rawls's claim that beyond a certain point an additional increment of wealth is not worth the sacrifice of the smallest amount of "equal liberty" and his statement that at this point there are still unsatisfied material wants which are merely less "compelling" than at lower levels of wealth. The second thesis seems to me a good deal more sensible than the first, and if it is accepted then the lexicographic priority of the first principle has to be dropped altogether. Nothing in Rawls's derivation of the value of "primary goods" from the pattern of choices in the "initial position" prepares us to admit that while there are still unsatisfied wants for material "primary goods" the satisfaction of these should ever be regarded as having in effect no value.

A third, and more intriguing, point is that this artificial and dubious notion of a threshold beyond which "equal liberty" has absolute priority does not have the logical consequences that Rawls seems to suppose that it has. He writes as though, once the priority of liberty (in this sense) has been established, it follows immediately that as a society developed economically it would at some stage reach the threshold (the point P) at which equal liberty has priority; at that point, and not before, the society would pursue equal liberty only. But the optimal path cannot be deduced in this way from a bare knowledge of the indifference curves. The path which a society ought to follow in order to act in accordance with its principles depends not only on the principles but on what possibilities the world allows. In the present context this means that it depends partly on the feasible set of combinations of liberty and wealth open to the society at each stage. In Figure 1, lines showing three feasible sets ("feasibility curves" marked FC) have been drawn in. The shape of these curves is that usually assumed for production functions; e.g., in the famous example for the choice in a given economy between guns and butter. For each feasible set of combinations of liberty and wealth, the point the society should choose is that which puts it on the highest attainable indifference curve. If we connect up these points, we can show what is the optimal path for the society as it "develops" or increases its level of "civilization" so as to proceed from one feasible set to the next. A plausible one (given Rawlsian indifference curves and standard-shaped feasibility curves) is shown in Figure 1. There are two interesting points about it.

The first point to notice is that although we have followed Rawls's prescription for the indifference curves, the optimal path at no point becomes vertical, so the society would never be pursuing equal liberty as its only goal. This is not an arbitrary matter of drawing the optimal path in one place rather than another. Rather, it is inevitable with feasible sets of the kind assumed here unless there is a very sharp discontinuity in the indifference curves at the point P. For what we are saying is that at point P further increments of wealth are virtually devoid of value. Surely if this is so, we are entitled to assume, in the absence of any definite argument to the contrary, that increments of wealth are not worth very much at a point just to the left of the point P. And any indifference curves which approach the horizontal smoothly will generate a sloping optimal path of the kind shown in Figure 1.

The second point to notice is that in the end the horizontal indifference curves which Rawls has worked so hard to establish are not crucial to the optimal path. We could make the indifference curves slope down gently beyond the point P instead of being flat without making the optimal path change its course one iota, so long as we left the points of tangency to the left of the point P in the same place.

If Rawls is concerned to show that at some level of economic development equal freedom should be pursued single-mindedly, his indifference curves do not give him this result. I have also suggested that the kind of result he wants can be arrived at without these indifference curve assumptions, and this I shall now explain. Instead of taking funny indifference curves and standard feasibility curves, I propose that we do the reverse: let us take indifference curves of ordinary shape but try to make an argument for unusually shaped feasibility curves. This I think can be done quite plausibly, since there are good reasons for suggesting that freedom and GNP are not related in the same way as guns and butter. The relation I wish to argue for is one of the general kind shown in Figure 2, where eight lines represent increasing ranges of choice, that is to say, increasing levels of "civilization" or "development." The significance of their shapes is that countries at a low level of development (those with feasible sets shown by lines near the origin) can obtain a fairly large increase in wealth by sacrificing a given amount of liberty, but that as countries become more developed the amount of extra wealth that can be gained by moving along the feasibility curve so as to sacrifice that same amount of equal liberty becomes less. As the economy becomes more sophisticated, the need for managerial initiative and for predictability in the operation of the law becomes more pressing, while at the same time the working population becomes more accustomed to the routines of industrialism, and the traumatic social changes of the initial stages are not paralleled in scale or severity by those which accompany increasing economic development.

As I have drawn the curves, several have at least a section which is vertical or outward sloping. This implies that a certain minimum of liberty is either neutral with respect to the production of material goods or actually conducive to it. The further from the origin the line showing feasible combinations of the two, the more marked this com-

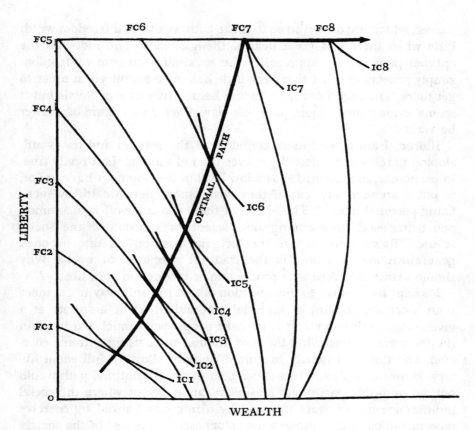

Figure 2

patibility between them becomes. This seems to me to correspond with common sense, and in fact I think the societies in the unbracketed list in Figure 1 are in a position where a reduction in personal liberty would have little or no effect on productivity. If this is so, then it means there is no need for choice (and indeed no possibility of a choice) between wealth and liberty. This is reflected in the shape of the optimal path, which quickly rises to near the maximum amount of liberty, though the bulging shape of the feasibility curves prevents it from hitting the maximum until the line is outward-sloping all the way. Recall that this analysis is carried out with standard indifference

181

curves, which are drawn so as to make both wealth *and* freedom worth little when there is a great deal of them already. The fact that the optimal path rapidly approaches the maximum amount of freedom simply reflects the fact that very little has to be sacrificed in order to get there. The argument may be less heroic than that of Rawls but it seems to me a much more plausible way of getting the kind of answer he wants.

Indeed, I am myself more confident of the vertical and backward-sloping parts of the feasibility curves than of the rest. Is it really true, in particular, that countries at a low level of development have to (or, to put it another way, can if they wish) have more wealth by sacrificing personal liberty? The idea that there is a trade-off is a common one, better established among social scientists than some of the "social science" Rawls imports into the "original position" as unquestioned generalizations. But how is the trade-off supposed to work? Why should liberty interfere with production or production with liberty?

Perhaps the answer to this question is that the only way to get more than a certain amount of material production out of a society at a given stage of development is to make people work much harder than they want to, by enslaving them or in other ways using extreme coercion, and this is obviously incompatible with allowing full equal liberty. However, it should be noticed that a society's optimal path would not get onto this part of its feasibility curve except where the social indifference curves were imposed by a minority backed by coercive powers sufficient to overcome the reluctance of the rest of the society to follow this path. A society would never get into this position if its collective indifference curve were in some way based on the aggregated indifference curves of the members of the society.

The worry motivating Rawls's theory of the (conditionally) absolute priority of liberty is that people might prefer more wealth to more liberty even when they were not desperately poor. But what I am suggesting is that to the extent that they want wealth they probably cannot get more by giving up liberty; there is only the possibility of getting increased material production at the expense of liberty to the extent that they do not want the extra material production (at the price that has to be paid in extra work). It is not therefore necessary for Rawls to make such strenuous efforts to rule out the rationality of selling one's birthright for a mess of pottage. For if I am right, the only way of getting more pottage by selling one's birthright would be by choosing to be coerced into working harder than one thought worthwhile; and this it would clearly be irrational to do. If I am not right, and it would be possible to get a great increase of production with little more work by making, say, a small sacrifice of equal liberty, then I do not see why it would be irrational to accept this trade. If the feasibility curve were almost horizontal in its upper part, Rawls's stipulation of horizontal indifference curves beyond the point P would affect the optimal path. (This is the only exception to my earlier statement that it would not make any difference if they sloped down at a shallow angle to the right of the point P.) At the point P, the society would be obliged to pursue only increased liberty even though (*ex hypothesi*) each increment of liberty involved foregoing a great deal of additional wealth. But it does not appear to me that Rawls ever argues persuasively that the men in the "original position" would be rational to bind themselves in advance to making this decision if the world happens to pose them with this particular choice.

So far I have done three things in this essay. First, I proposed an interpretation of Rawls in terms of indifference curves such that at a certain point each curve becomes parallel with the "wealth" axis. Second, I drew attention to some difficulties in this analysis, in particular that it is not consistent with ascribing value to the satisfaction of material wants beyond the point at which the indifference curves become horizontal and that it does not produce the implication which Rawls seems to be after, namely, that at a certain stage of economic development it is rational for a society to pursue solely "equal freedom" until the maximum degree of "equal freedom" has been achieved. And third, I suggested that the desired conclusion could be derived more plausibly by making special assumptions about the shapes of the feasibility curves than by having indifference curves of a different shape from those usually assumed.

To conclude, I should like to offer an alternative interpretation of what Rawls may have in mind when he speaks of the conditional priority of liberty. The advantages of this interpretation are, first, that it produces (if the units are chosen suitably) exactly the right shape of optimal path; and, second, that it makes sense of certain ideas to which Rawls seems to attach importance since he repeats them in two different places in the book. Its disadvantage is that it involves the creation of a new key variable, "effective liberty" or "exercised liberty," on the basis of only the most sketchy guidance from the text about its significance and behavior. But the idea is one that has certainly been put forward by other liberals, so it may be of interest to work it out briefly here; and in any case, it seems very difficult to understand the passages I shall quote unless something of the kind is attributed to Rawls.

On pages 151-152, Rawls says that "roughly, the idea underlying this [lexicographic] ordering is that if the parties assume that their basic liberties can be effectively exercised, they will not exchange a lesser liberty for an improvement in economic well-being. It is only when social conditions do not allow the effective establishment of these rights that one can concede their limitation; and these restrictions can be granted only to the extent that they are necessary to prepare the way for a free society. The denial of equal liberty can be defended only if it is necessary to raise the level of civilization so that in due course these freedoms can be enjoyed. Thus, in adopting a serial order, we are in effect making a special assumption in the original position; namely, that the parties know that the conditions of their society, whatever they are, admit the effective realization of the equal liberties." And on page 542, in the paragraph immediately preceding the one quoted from earlier, which is said to provide "the basis for the priority of liberty," there is an almost word for word repetition of this passage, now referred to as containing "the intuitive idea behind the precedence of liberty." There is however one new clause which, if taken seriously, would introduce a major modification. Rawls now says that "if the persons in the original position assume that their basic liberties can be effectively exercised, they will not exchange a lesser liberty for an improvement in their economic well-being, *at least not once a certain level of wealth has been attained.*" The italicized clause suggests that until some (unspecified) level of wealth has been reached, it would be rational to give up liberty for economic improvement even if the level reached was already such as to allow the basic liberties to be effectively exercised.

Let us leave this clause aside and stick to the elements common to the two widely separated passages. These are: (1) that the basic liberties covered by the first principle of justice acquire value only to the extent that they can be "effectively exercised," "effectively established" or "effectively realized" (all three expressions are used); (2) that the conditions of "effectiveness" are material ones; and (3) that of any two situations the one with more "effective liberty" is always better, even if the other has a much higher level of wealth, though of two situations with equal amounts of "effective liberty" that with more wealth is better. Unfortunately, Rawls nowhere spells out the political philosophy implied by items (1) and (2) above. But presumably the idea is that the "basic liberties" cannot be "enjoyed" (another expression Rawls uses in the same context) unless people reach some necessary level of economic prosperity. Why this should be so is not at all clear to me. Is there anything in the *material* situation of, say, a group of nomadic Bedouins eking a bare subsistence from the desert, or a population of poor peasant cultivators, which would prevent them from being able to use personal liberty? Perhaps, however, Rawls has in mind that the material conditions should make it possible for children to be given some form of education (including at least literacy), and that adults should have enough leisure to read and talk, and so on. This would relate him to those nineteenth century liberals who wished to emphasize the social preconditions for the enjoyment of freedom.[4]

I shall not pursue further the question: what is the nature of the connection between "basic liberty," "effective exercise" and wealth? I shall now ask what the *form* of the connection is, and hope that the answer to this does not depend too critically on the answer to the other question. Taking two extreme cases, it would seem reasonable to say that a zero level of basic liberty accompanied by any amount of wealth gives a zero level of "effective exercise" of liberty; and similarly that any amount of "basic liberty" accompanied by no wealth at all would give a zero level of "effective exercise," since the people involved would soon die of starvation. A relatively simple kind of relationship satisfying these conditions is a multiplicative relationship; we would

---

4. For a sympathetic reconstruction of such a view, see W. L. Weinstein, "The Concept of Liberty in Nineteenth Century English Political Thought," *Political Studies* 13 (1965): 145-162.

say that the amount of "effective exercise" was the product of the amount of "basic liberty" and the amount of wealth. However, we must add that the multiplicative relationship is limited in its scope. At some point, as Rawls emphasizes, no increments of "effective exercise" are produced by a further increase in wealth.

These ideas are illustrated in Figure 3. Budget lines of a standard shape are drawn to connect "basic liberty" with wealth. But it is also assumed that to each combination of these two there corresponds a single value on the new variable of "effective exercise of liberty." In Figure 3, we take it that at no units of wealth, "effective liberty" is always zero; at one unit of wealth, the number of units of "effective liberty" is the same as the number of units of "basic liberty"; at two units of wealth, the number of units of "effective liberty" is twice the number of units of "basic liberty"; and at three units it is three times. But further increases of wealth beyond three units do not produce any greater increase in the value of "effective exercise" for any given level of "basic liberty." The number of units of "effective exercise" stays at three times the number of units of "basic liberty."

By performing the appropriate multiplication we can construct from the given curves relating "basic liberty" and wealth a new set of curves relating wealth and "effective liberty." These curves are shown as dashed lines in Figure 3. The scale for units of "effective exercise" on the vertical axis is the same as that used for units of "basic liberty." It will be seen that, as before, we are assuming that there is an upper bound to the possible amount of basic liberty. Since this is set here at five units and the most by which units of "basic liberty" can be multiplied to give units of "effective exercise" is a factor of three, it follows that there is a maximum of "effective exercise" at fifteen units.

Now, of course, the optimal path for a society is not given until we also have the shape of the indifference curves specified. But this is governed by point (3) in our statement of assumptions above, which provided that, except as a tie-breaker, wealth should have value only insofar as it offered the material conditions for the "effective exercise" (etc.) of "basic liberty." Following this we can immediately deduce that the indifference curves relating "effective exercise" to wealth will run parallel to the "wealth" axis. We can add a lexicographic relation between the two by saying that of two positions on the same indiffer-

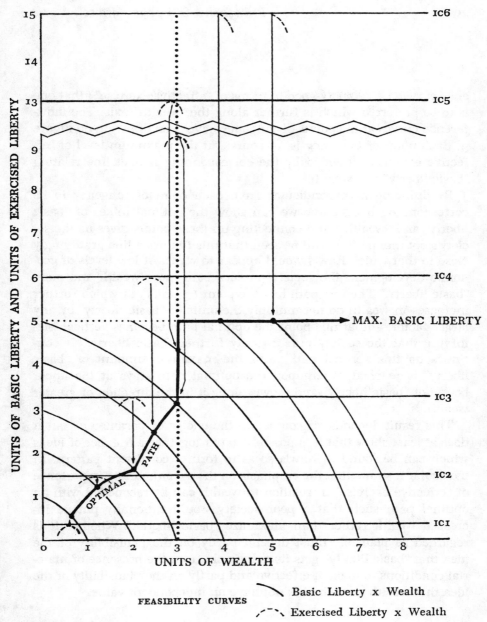

FEASIBILITY CURVES

—— Basic Liberty x Wealth

--- Exercised Liberty x Wealth

Figure 3

ence curve (i.e., equally good in terms of "effective exercise") that one is to be preferred which is further along the "wealth" axis. The indifference curves at the points of tangency have been drawn in on Figure 3. Each point of tangency is, of course, at the maximum level of "effective exercise" provided by the corresponding budget line relating "basic liberty" and wealth.

By dropping a perpendicular from each point of tangency to its corresponding budget line we can show the optimal mixes of "basic liberty" and "wealth," and connecting up these points gives us the society's optimal path. It will be seen that this follows a line gratifyingly close to that which Rawls would appear to want. At low levels of economic development the society pursues both more wealth and more "basic liberty." Then its path hits the point (3 units) at which further increases in wealth do not multiply the units of "basic liberty" by any larger factor, and at this point the optimal path becomes vertical, signifying that the society pursues only further "basic liberty." It continues on this vertical path until the maximum amount of "basic liberty" is reached, whereupon the optimal path stays at the upper bound of "basic liberty" and moves along it in the direction of greater wealth.

This result depends, of course, on the choice of parameters, but it does at least show that it is possible to put together a number of ideas which can be found in Rawls so as to form a consistent pattern. In particular it shows that the emphasis on the overwhelming importance of "effective exercise" in relation to wealth can be reconciled with an optimal path such that a poor society would rationally pursue increased wealth rather than maximize "basic liberty." Whether it is regarded as plausible must depend partly on the plausibility of the idea that "basic liberty" gets its value only from the presence of material conditions to make it effective and partly on the plausibility of the idea that wealth as such does not have an independent value.

Liberty and Self-Respect

Henry Shue
Wellesley College

An original philosophical position is often most difficult to understand just where it is most important that it be understood. This is certainly the case with "The Grounds for the Priority of Liberty" in John Rawls's *A Theory of Justice*. [1] Nothing is more important in Rawlsian theory than the priority of liberty, although the difference principle is equally important: "The force of justice as fairness would appear to arise from two things: the requirement that all inequalities be justified to the least advantaged, and the priority of liberty" (250). Rawls's inference to the priority of liberty is the final, carefully designed logical bridge for the long train of reasoning to the ordered pair of principles of justice. And this highly compressed argument contains in microcosm all the most important themes of justice as fairness. But the logical structure of this argument is difficult to separate from the strands of other arguments on other fronts, all of which Rawls conducts simultaneously in the densely written pages of this critical section 82 of his book. So it may be of some use to try to lay out, as plainly as possible, the five premises from which Rawls hopes finally to deduce the priority of liberty. [2] Before we examine the argument for the thesis, we might recall the basic meaning of the thesis itself. [3]

1. John Rawls, *A Theory of Justice* (Cambridge, Mass.: Harvard University Press, Belknap Press 1971). Since this is the only work quoted in the text, references are given by page number only.
2. I take Rawls to be quite serious in his commitment to the construction of deductive arguments: "The argument aims eventually to be strictly deductive. To be sure, the persons in the original position have a certain psychology, since various assumptions are made about their beliefs and interests. These assumptions appear along with other premises in the description of this initial situation. But clearly arguments from such premises can be fully deductive, as theories in politics and economics attest. We should strive for a kind of moral geometry with all the rigor which this name connotes" (121).
3. The thesis has received a rich and stimulating critique in H. L. A. Hart, "Rawls on Liberty and Its Priority," *University of Chicago Law Review* 40 (1973): 534–55, reprinted in Norman Daniels, ed., *Reading Rawls: Critical Studies of John Rawls' "A Theory of Justice"* (New York: Basic Books, 1975). There is also an interpretation of the thesis, although no exploration of its derivation, in Brian Barry, *The Liberal Theory of Justice* (Oxford: Clarendon Press, 1973), chap. 7 ("The Derivation of the Priority of Liberty").

Those who have wrestled with *A Theory of Justice* know that Rawls's theory of justice as fairness provides for historical change by means of a distinction between, on the one hand, a general conception of justice (constituted by a single principle), which might be described as a principle for the just transition to a just society, and, on the other hand, a special conception of justice (constituted by two principles of justice), which are meant to be the final principles for the governance of a just society (60–63, 150–52, 244–48, 541–43). All his versions of the principles of justice describe distributions of what Rawls calls the social primary goods, the most important three general types of which he maintains to be self-respect, the basic liberties, and material wealth (62). The general conception of justice permits inequalities in any primary good (83, 150). The special conception, by the means of apportionment into two principles, requires equality in one kind of primary good through the first principle of justice but permits continued inequality in some other kinds of goods through the second principle of justice (151–52). The thesis that the liberties are to take priority over other primary goods means, first, that the basic liberties are to be the primary good which is selected to be kept equal and to be governed by the first principle of justice in the special conception (244–48). Second, the priority of liberty means that a lesser liberty is not to be accepted in exchange for greater wealth, even if everyone's liberty were thus to be reduced equally (302, 542). While it is rational, according to Rawls, to pursue more wealth even after one's wealth is adequate for one's urgent needs, what is not rational after a level of adequate wealth has been attained is to pursue greater wealth at the cost of one's liberties (543). However, the meaning of this thesis is made most clear by exploration of Rawls's rationale for advancing it.[4] In reconstructing the Rawlsian argument here I present the premises in what I believe is the most perspicuous order, which is not entirely the order of Rawls's exposition.

THE PREMISES OF THE ARGUMENT

I.   *The Priority of Self-Respect*

The first premise of the argument for the priority of liberty is itself the conclusion of a long chain of argumentation running through most of chapter 7 of *A Theory of Justice*. The logical order, although not the expository order, of this earlier argument (1) begins by assuming the correctness of the psychological law which Rawls names "the Aristotelian Principle," (2) infers

---

4. Actually there are two separate arguments for the priority of liberty, as Rawls notes in these important but buried summary statements: "One reason for this I have discussed in connection with liberty of conscience and freedom of thought. And a second reason is the central place of the primary good of self-respect and the desire of human beings to express their nature in a free social union with others" (543). The bulk of Rawls's section 82, entitled "The Grounds for the Priority of Liberty," is devoted to the argument from self-respect (543–46), the formulation of an objection to the argument (547), and a reply to the objection (547–48); while the argument from freedom of conscience has, as Rawls indicates here and elsewhere (248), already been formulated (205–9). Since there is insufficient space to consider adequately both of Rawls's arguments for the priority of liberty, I will set aside the argument from freedom of conscience in favor of his final and far-reaching argument from self-respect.

from the Aristotelian Principle to a principle of rational choice called "the principle of inclusiveness" (414), and (3) concludes, chiefly on the basis of the Aristotelian Principle and the principle of inclusiveness (433–34), "that perhaps the most important primary good is that of self-respect" (440).[5]

The argument for the priority of liberty, then, takes it as already established that self-respect is the supreme primary good: "The account of self-respect as perhaps the main primary good has stressed the great significance of how we think others value us. . . . The basis for self-esteem in a just society is not then one's income share but the publicly affirmed distribution of fundamental rights and liberties" (544).[6] What I have just quoted is not part of Rawls's argument for the priority of liberty but only his advance notice that the argument will rest on the connection between the basic liberties and the main primary good, self-respect (or, self-esteem). The argument for the priority of liberty over the other primary goods (except, of course, self-respect itself, which liberty serves) will take the form of maintaining that a guarantee of the priority of liberty is the most effective means available for guaranteeing self-respect, while assuming that self-respect is of the very first importance. Hence, the general form of the argument for the priority of liberty is the following hypothetical: if self-respect has first priority among the primary goods, . . . then liberty is to take priority over the remaining primary goods.

From a different perspective we can also characterize the general kind of argument Rawls gives in the following terms. An assumption of the supreme importance of self-respect can serve, logically, as a premise for the conclusion that liberty is to take priority over other goods, because an establishment of the priority of liberty would serve, causally, as the most effective social basis available for self-respect. The following example has the same logical structure: the first priority is to assassinate the emperor; the best source of assassins available is discontented intellectuals; therefore, we must keep the intellectuals discontented. The supreme importance of achieving the end serves logically as support for the importance of taking a causally effective means to that end.

In the example, once it has been shown that the first priority is to assassinate the emperor, the next task would be to explain why it is that the best source of assassins is discontented intellectuals. Similarly, assuming that he has already shown that the most important primary good is self-respect, Rawls takes as his task in section 82 an explanation—if possible, a deductive one—of why the best source of self-respect is a guarantee of the priority of liberty.

---

5. Acceptance of the account in this article of Rawls's argument from his thesis about self-respect to this thesis about the priority of liberty depends, of course, in no way upon acceptance of the above outline of some of Rawls's yet more basic premises for his thesis about self-respect. Documentation of the outline and examination of its first inference will be found in Henry Shue, "Justice, Rationality, and Desire: On the Logical Structure of Justice as Fairness," *Southern Journal of Philosophy*, vol. 13 (April 1975).

6. I shall quote this same passage twice again in an effort successively to highlight various facets of it.

II.   *Equal Distribution of Self-Respect*

Having isolated the assumption about the importance of self-respect, we should make explicit another assumption. This one is so fundamental for Rawls that it evidently does not seem to him to need to be stressed, although the argument for the priority of liberty will not work without it: self-respect is to be distributed equally. I am not aware of any point at which Rawls actually argues for equality of self-respect; and I suspect that once Rawls concluded that self-respect is the supreme primary good he simply found it inconceivable that an inequality of self-respect would ever be justifiable in the proper manner, that is, as being to the advantage of those with least self-respect.[7] In short, the requirement of an equality of self-respect may be thought to follow from the supreme importance of self-respect. Certainly no argument springs to mind in support of the conclusion that some citizens would themselves be better off if they had less self-respect than other citizens.

On the other hand, the equality of self-respect may be a fresh, additional assumption. Whether the argument this far is to be construed, strictly speaking, as one premise about self-respect or as two premises, one about the importance of self-respect and one about equality, is probably of no great moment. But, for the sake of clarity, I will treat them as two. In any case, Rawls's focus throughout most (544–48) of "The Grounds for the Priority of Liberty" is on how to guarantee self-respect which is equal; and the insistence on the equality of self-respect, however arrived at, is indispensable to the structure of the argument for the priority of liberty.

III.   *Equal Distribution of the Social Basis*

We might glance back at the meaning of the priority of liberty. What we find is that Rawls is proposing the priority of liberties which are distributed equally. The more obvious aspect of the assignment of priority to liberty is the prohibition against trading liberty for wealth: we are not allowed to accept a lesser liberty in order to gain greater wealth. But the more important aspect of the assignment of priority to liberty is that everyone's liberties are to be kept equal to everyone else's: "The basis for self-esteem in a just society is . . . the publicly affirmed distribution of fundamental rights and liberties. And this distribution being equal, everyone has a similar and secure status when they meet to conduct the common affairs of the wider society" (544). Thus, if liberty is to serve as the social basis for equal self-respect, liberty too must be distributed equally. Rawls's assumption evidently is that since self-

---

7. That an inequality in any primary good is justifiable only if it is to the advantage of the inferior party to the inequality (here, the person with less self-respect) is, of course, Rawls's difference principle. It would be extremely valuable to be able to establish precisely the logical relation of the difference principle and the priority of liberty. At this point Rawls's argument for the priority of liberty seems to presuppose the difference principle. Elsewhere (152, 156, 158) there are suggestions that the argument for the difference principle presupposes the priority of liberty. A contradiction on this question of logical order would, presumably, be nearly fatal to Rawls's theory.

respect is to be equal whatever serves as the social basis for self-respect must also be equal.[8] This is a third important premise.

By combining these three premises about self-respect, its equality, and the equality of its social basis, we can begin to state the question about the priority of liberty in the form it has for Rawls. Given (1) that self-respect is the most important primary good, and given (2) that the most important primary good is to be distributed equally, and given (3) that whatever provides the social basis for equal self-respect must itself be distributed equally, why is liberty to be that basis? Or, more simply, why should we think that the equal distribution of self-respect must rest on an equal distribution of liberty rather than an equal distribution of something else?

IV.   *Incentive Value of Economic Inequality*

What else, Rawls next asks, might equal self-respect rest on? And the one serious alternative, as Rawls and his critics seem to agree, is equal wealth: "The basis for self-esteem in a just society is not then one's income share but the publicly affirmed distribution of fundamental rights and liberties" (544). The priority of liberty is especially the priority of liberty over wealth, its leading rival. The inference to the priority of equal liberty is also an inference to the subordination of wealth and its equality. Rawls will enthrone his candidate for priority, equal basic liberties, by undercutting the claims of its rival, equal wealth. And it will be wealth over which equal liberty will then take priority.

Rawls's attack against priority for wealth has two stages. I will quote Rawls's own statement of the first stage in full: "Suppose . . . that how one is valued by others depends upon one's relative place in the distribution of income and wealth. In this case having a higher status implies having more material means than a larger fraction of society. Thus not everyone can have the highest status, and to improve one person's position is to lower that of someone else. Social cooperation to increase the conditions of self-respect is impossible. The means of status, so to speak, are fixed, and each man's gain is another's loss. Clearly this situation is a great misfortune. Persons are set at odds with one another in the pursuit of their self-esteem" (545).

The zero-sum game for self-respect which Rawls conjures up is indeed horrible (and thoroughly familiar). But why must it come to a cutthroat competition for more self-respect? Rawls is searching for a society which provides equal self-respect. Even if people's relative degree of self-respect is based on their relative economic position, there could be, one might suggest, equal self-respect provided only that there was equal wealth, as the third premise requires. Everyone could cooperate in seeing to it that wealth was kept equally distributed—and perhaps also that the general level of wealth was increased for all.

But the consideration of increasing the wealth brings us to the second stage of Rawls's attack, which seems intended to counter proposals advocat-

8. While this premise may have an air of self-evidence, it is not indisputable.

ing equal wealth as the source of equal self-respect. Consider Rawls's second move: "Moreover, as I mentioned in the discussion of envy, if the means of providing a good are indeed fixed and cannot be enlarged by cooperation, then justice seems to require equal shares, other things the same. But an equal division of all primary goods is irrational in view of the possibility of bettering everyone's circumstances by accepting certain inequalities. Thus the best solution is to support the primary good of self-respect as far as possible by the assignment of the basic liberties that can indeed be made equal, defining the same status for all. At the same time, distributive justice as frequently understood, justice in the relative shares of material means, is relegated to a subordinate place" (546).

What is the thrust of this not entirely lucid passage? Since equal self-respect needs to have, as its basis in society, a good which is itself equally distributed throughout society, either the basic liberties or wealth might be made equal. But, quite independent of questions of self-respect there is a compelling ground for allowing an unequal distribution of wealth. This other, independent ground favoring an inequality of wealth is the very reason why it would not be rational to enforce equal wealth as the basis for equal self-respect. And this other ground, Rawls is recalling, is the incentive force which is provided by some inequality: "But an equal division of all primary goods is irrational in view of the possibility of bettering everyone's circumstances by accepting certain inequalities" (546). We can all have more primary goods than we have at any given time if some of us are allowed even more wealth than the rest of us, as an incentive for performing activities which will carry us all forward. Rawls is harking back to one of the most basic psychological assumptions of the theory of justice as fairness: the value of material inequality as an incentive to move some citizens to act in ways which will improve the positions of all citizens. "If there are inequalities in the basic structure that work to make everyone better off in comparison with the benchmark of initial equality, why not permit them? The immediate gain which a greater equality might allow can be regarded as intelligently invested in view of its future return" (151).[9]

---

9. Rawls's argument would be greatly strengthened by a fuller explanation of why an inequality in liberties would not function equally well, in the role of incentive for greater effort, as an inequality in wealth is said to function. For example, why not promise a certain special liberty (say, exemption from conscription) as a reward for anyone who uncovered major government repression of the society's poorest members? Evidently Rawls assumes that liberty, unlike wealth, is the sort of good of which it is the case that "the means of providing a good are indeed fixed and cannot be enlarged by cooperation" (546). The contrasting pictures of wealth and liberty seem to be roughly as follows. Our increasing our wealth can be a cooperative enterprise which is mutually (even if unequally) beneficial, because we can all work together to wrest greater production from recalcitrant Nature. But increasing liberty, according to Rawls, cannot be a matter of all of us working together against some sort of common enemy. The question is: why not? I suspect that part of the reason is that Rawls sees one person's liberty largely as liberty from other people. Hence, to offer someone else more liberty as incentive would be to reduce one's own liberty and to defeat in advance the purpose of offering the incentive—the system of liberties is a zero-sum game. This raises serious problems, which require a careful analysis of the Rawlsian concept of liberty before they may be treated systematically.

A person's degree of self-respect could be based on his relative wealth —this is psychologically feasible. Indeed, this is the actual situation in many existing societies, which is perhaps the main reason Rawls explores this alternative. But since, in existing societies, wealth is unequal, self-respect based on relative wealth is also unequal. Obviously the possibilities include: (*a*) trying to equalize the wealth and (*b*) trying to break the psychological connection between wealth and self-respect. Rawls advocates the latter, because he believes the incentive value of (limited) inequalities of wealth is beneficial to all, especially the least wealthy. This assumption is at the heart of the argument for the difference principle, and it is also vital here. Whether it is true is, of course, another, very important subject. But here the judgment is that, in order that all citizens may gain still greater amounts of other primary goods, some citizens must sometimes have the prospect of gaining greater wealth than others gain.

V.   Economic Adequacy for the Worst-off Man

If an equality of wealth and an equality of basic liberties are the only psychologically feasible social bases for equal self-respect, then the argument against wealth would, by elimination, establish the claim of the basic liberties. And certainly an equality of wealth is the only rival arrangement which Rawls views with sufficient seriousness to construct an argument against it.

But Rawls does also offer in section 82 an additional consideration in favor of the equality of basic liberties. Strictly speaking, this consideration takes the form of contending that what is, during one period, a good reason against assigning priority to liberty, will after a certain date no longer hold. Under the general conception of justice, which holds sway until the special conception assigning priority to liberty is justified, no priority is assigned to any one primary good, and it is permissible to accept less of any good, including liberty, than other citizens have in order to increase one's quantity of any other good. The chief reason for this arrangement is that the enjoyment of any primary good is dependent on the possession of an adequate amount of other primary goods (204–5). Most notably, to assign priority to equal basic liberties when some citizens are too poor to be able to enjoy their liberties is a cruel charade. Until all have attained an adequate minimum of wealth it is not unreasonable of them to accept less liberty in exchange for more wealth, if they must and can.

The movement away from this general conception of justice to the special conception (which is simply an alternative description for the assignment of priority to liberty) occurs at a certain point in the economic development of a given society which we may call the date of economic adequacy. Economic adequacy is attained when the search for food, shelter, and work has become routine rather than urgent, and when citizens now freed from constant preoccupation with mere survival are enabled to devote some of their energy to what we used to call the pursuit of happiness. The economic condition for the the priority of the basic liberties is not, therefore, abundance but adequacy, that is, sufficient wealth for basic liberties to be "effectively exercised" (542).

And adequacy must extend to the citizens who are economically the worst off in a society in order for that society to meet this condition. Much of the distinctiveness of justice as fairness rests in the requirement that all judgments about structural inequalities are to be made from the perspective of the worst-off man (231, 250). If conditions of unequal wealth are not adequate for the economically worst-off man, conditions are not adequate. Since basic liberties are to be given priority for every citizen and distributed equally, every citizen must at the least have his basic wants already fulfilled. Otherwise those liberties can have little value for him. " . . . The basic structure is to be arranged to maximize the worth to the least advantaged of the complete scheme of equal liberty shared by all" (205). Accordingly, the date of economic adequacy must be determined from the perspective of the economically worst-off representative man. Economic adequacy has been reached only when "the equal freedoms can be enjoyed by all" (542). Equal liberties are not to be guaranteed formally until there is no one for whom the guarantee will be merely formal.

But once the guarantee will be effective for everyone, because everyone will be able to enjoy his equal liberty, the only good reason against giving priority to equal liberty is removed. Therefore, given that the best reason against a priority for equal liberty will cease to apply once economic adequacy for all is reached, and given the positive consideration that a priority for equal liberty will provide an effective social basis for an equality of self-respect, we have sufficient grounds for the assignment of priority to an equality of basic liberties.

THE ARGUMENT FOR THE PRIORITY OF LIBERTY

For the sake of one type of clarity I have so far concentrated on the five major notions underlying Rawls's argument. For the sake of a different type of clarity now, I would like to conclude by reconstructing in full detail the most compelling deduction which Rawls's text supports. The major premises I–V above are restated as follows: I yields 1, II yields 2, III yields 4 and 9, IV yields 5 and 6, and V yields 10 and 11. The other steps follow logically.

1. Self-respect is the most important primary good.

2. The most important primary good must be guaranteed an equal distribution.

3. Therefore (from 1 and 2), self-respect must be guaranteed an equal distribution (i.e., if there is an acceptable means for guaranteeing an equal distribution of self-respect, this means must be undertaken).

[Argument against wealth]

4. A distribution of wealth is an acceptable means for guaranteeing an equal distribution of self-respect if and only if an equal distribution of wealth could always reasonably be maintained after a given date in a given society.

5. If an unequal distribution of wealth (as an incentive to some) might

ever be beneficial to all, an equal distribution of wealth could not always reasonably be maintained after any date.

6. An unequal distribution might often be beneficial to all.

7. Therefore (from 5 and 6), an equal distribution of wealth could not always reasonably be maintained after any date.

8. Therefore (from 4 and 7), the distribution of wealth is not an acceptable means for guaranteeing an equal distribution of self-respect.

[Argument for liberty]

9. A distribution of liberty is an acceptable means for guaranteeing an equal distribution of self-respect if and only if an equal distribution of liberty could always reasonably be maintained after a given date in a given society.

10. If wealth is adequate (for the effective exercise of liberty by everyone) after a given date in a given society, an equal distribution of liberty could always reasonably be maintained after that date in that society.

11. Wealth is adequate after time, t, in society, S.

12. Therefore (from 10 and 11), an equal distribution of liberty could always reasonably be maintained after t in S.

13. Therefore (from 9 and 12), an equal distribution of liberty after t in S is an acceptable means for guaranteeing an equal distribution of self-respect.

14. Therefore (from 3 and 13), an equal distribution of liberty after t in S must be undertaken.

This is why, according to Rawls, equal liberty would take priority in a just society. If granted all the premises which we have teased from the text, Rawls can mount a valid argument. Whether each of those premises is true is another matter.

The Journal of Political Philosophy: Volume 4, Number 1, 1996, pp. 68–78

Debate

The Survival of Egalitarian Justice in John Rawls's *Political Liberalism*[1]

DAVID ESTLUND

Philosophy, Brown University

In John Rawls's second Book, *Political Liberalism*,[2] the doctrines of his historic book, *A Theory of Justice*,[3] are placed in a new light. It is not, however, the new book's primary purpose to reflect upon and 'rethink' the theory of the first book.[4] It is no exaggeration to say that the two books are not about the same subject. The first is primarily about justice; the second is primarily about political legitimacy, a topic essentially ignored in *TJ*. The requirements of legitimacy (roughly, the permissibility of using coercive public powers) are different from the requirements of justice, and if this change in topic is ignored many of the distinctive contributions of the second volume will be mistaken for revisions in the original theory of justice. In this short comment I hope to illustrate this danger by arguing, contrary to the suggestions of some commentators,[5] that there is no retreat from the egalitarianism of the original theory of justice. Rather than defending or criticizing Rawls in any significant respect, I confine myself to the interpretive question. Nevertheless, this will count as a defense of his own claim[6] that the doctrines of *TJ*, including the egalitarian 'difference principle,' and the

---

[1] I am grateful to Liam Murphy, Thomas Pogge and Lewis Yelin for helpful comments.

[2] Columbia University Press 1993, hereafter *PL*.

[3] Harvard University Press, 1971, hereafter *TJ*.

[4] Columbia University Press advertises *PL* with the slogan 'Rawls Rethinks Rawls.' This is true in many respects, as Bernard Williams also says in his review (*London Review of Books*, May 13, 1993). However, the 'rethinking' is secondary to Rawls's pursuit of a new project, which the slogan encourages us to neglect. The fact that Rawls recognizes many political liberalisms, a fact exploited by some who think the requirements of justice have been weakened, suggests that many of the most important ideas in *PL* could have been conceived independently of *TJ*, such as the liberal principle of legitimacy itself, the idea of public reason, overlapping consensus, and even political constructivism.

[5] Bernard Williams, in his review of *PL*, writes that 'Now that it has taken on its new aspect of a political theory of the tolerant liberal state, the Difference Principle has come to play a distinctly secondary role compared to the elements that help to define a constitutional structure within which the debates of politics can go on' (op. cit., p. 8). In her review of *PL*, Susan Moller Okin echoes Williams: 'Rawls's focus on the liberties that constitute the conditions for toleration . . . virtually drowns out the redistributive part of his original theory . . . The priority of liberty that Rawls has always argued for has become a virtual monopoly' ('Book Review,' *American Political Science Review*, December 1993, p. 1010). Brian Barry claims that, unlike the first principle, 'the second principle is abandoned at the second [overlapping consensus] stage . . . The implication is surely that the second principle has to be sacrificed.' 'John Rawls and the Search for Stability,' *ETHICS*, July 1995, p. 913.

[6] My thesis is not merely that Rawls *makes* this claim. That is settled beyond dispute by the quotation at the end of this essay. I attempt to *defend* his claim about the implications of his view.

arguments for them ought to be seen as presupposed rather than as revised in the new book.[7] This is also a defense inasmuch as those who have purported to see such a change have lamented it. The important question is not whether Rawls can be convicted of changing his mind. Rather, if his view has not changed on this matter, it will be impossible to understand and appreciate the theory in *PL* as if it were a further and corrective reflection on the question of what social justice requires. And if *PL* is not about justice, what is it about? It is about a liberal conception of political legitimacy.

In *TJ*, social justice is said to require a basic social structure that conforms to two principles, with the first having absolute priority over the second. The first requires a system of equal basic political and civil liberties. Once this is met, a second principle comes into play requiring that primary social goods be equally distributed except where inequality would benefit even the very worst off ('The Difference Principle'), and that offices and positions attached to these goods be open to all in certain ways ('Fair Equality of Opportunity').[8] The priority of the first over the second means that no compromise of the required system of basic political liberties could be justified as a way of better meeting the imperative of the second principle. However, once the first principle is met, the second principle presses in a strongly egalitarian direction, permitting deviations from equality only on the narrowest of grounds: the unequal system's capacity to provide more primary goods for the least well off than they would have under perfect equality, or under other feasible unequal schemes.[9]

The question is whether this specific egalitarian doctrine of the second principle is revised into a weaker view, or given a less demanding status in *PL* than in *TJ*. It may clarify things to present the strongest case I can devise for interpreting *PL* in this way, before advancing the contrary interpretation—that there is no such change. It might be argued that:

> It is a basic shift from *TJ* to *PL* to now regard it as a necessary condition for the appropriateness of a conception of justice that it be acceptable to an overlapping consensus of reasonable comprehensive conceptions of life and value. Rawls admits that this new requirement of consensus is, at the very least, more difficult for the second, egalitarian principle of *TJ* to meet than it is for the first principle guaranteeing only equal and extensive civil and political liberties. While Rawls still holds to both principles as his preferred conception of justice, only the first principle is required by his new political conception of justice. He now admits that there are many political liberalisms, his 'justice as fairness' being only one, and says that others may prefer some criterion other than his second principle, although any political liberalism must come very close to the first principle. Furthermore, he explicitly denies that the second principle is a 'constitutional essential,' primarily because

---

[7]See *PL*, p. 7 including note 6 (quoted below, p. 20).
[8]*TJ*, p. 302.
[9]For statements of the two principles see *TJ*, p. 302, and *PL*, pp. 5–6, where Rawls adds, 'much exposition would be needed to clarify the meaning and application of these principles. Since in these lectures *such matters are not our concern, I* make only a few comments' (emphasis added).

principles serving that sort of distributive role are less amenable to political consensus. Apparently, then, any 'political liberalism' is as just as any other, including those that include the difference principle and those that reject it. This marks a fundamental move away from the egalitarian claim in *TJ* that social justice requires compliance with the difference principle.

It is impossible to deny that Rawls holds in *PL* that there are many political liberalisms, justice as fairness being but one;[10] or that the difference principle is not a constitutional essential;[11] or that this fact is connected with the inherently greater controversy surrounding such principles;[12] or that the central theme in *PL* *is* a certain requirement that a political conception of justice be acceptable to all reasonable comprehensive views.[13]

There are at least three ways of accommodating all of these points in which Rawls can still be read as endorsing the difference principle as a requirement of justice. The first is included in the indented view, and weakens this endorsement enormously: Rawls endorses the difference principle from within a comprehensive conception, but not as a requirement of justice within a political liberalism. This has little to be said for it. It is entirely clear that the two principles of justice are held to comprise one admissible political liberalism, and that all political liberalisms are conceptions of justice.

The second has Rawls endorsing the two principles together as one among many acceptable political liberalisms, all equally just.

The third has Rawls staying closer to *TJ*, endorsing both principles as comprising a political liberalism *and* as requirements of justice, but allegedly departing from *TJ* in removing the difference principle from the status of a constitutional essential.

The fourth interpretation, which I shall defend, is like the third except that it claims that it is no departure from *TJ* at all to treat the first principle as a constitutional essential but not the second principle.

The second interpretation accepts this, but supposes that many or all political liberalisms and their conceptions of justice present equally reasonable conceptions of justice. This would imply that whether a conception includes the difference principle or not does not bear on the reasonableness of the conception or on the justice of the society it envisages. On this reading, Rawls must believe that justice, as conceived within a political liberalism, does not demand conformity to the difference principle.

This reading takes Rawls's claim that 'there are many political liberalisms' to imply that, from a political point of view, all such conceptions are on a normative par. On this interpretation, Rawls must be seen to advance justice as fairness as only one reasonable conception of justice, not necessarily any more reasonable than a conception that substituted some other principle for the difference principle. This is difficult to square with the fact that Rawls gives reasons in *TJ*[14] and reaffirms them in *PL*,[15] in favor of the difference principle over the major alternatives. The question is how to reconcile the doctrine of many political liberalisms with the thesis that justice as fairness is superior to other conceptions of justice.

Rawls says:

> Keep in mind that political liberalism is a kind of view. It has many forms [all of which] have in common substantive principles of justice that are liberal and an idea of public reason . . . Accepting the idea of public reason and its principle of legitimacy emphatically does not mean, then, accepting a particular liberal conception of justice down to the last details . . . We agree that citizens share in political power as free and equal, and that as reasonable and rational they have a duty of civility to appeal to public reason, yet we differ as to which principles are the most reasonable basis of public justification. The view I have called 'justice as fairness' is but one example of a liberal political conception; its specific content is not definitive of such a view' (*PL*, 226).

What do the partisans of different political liberalisms agree about, and what do they disagree about? They agree that citizens share in political power as free and equal, and that they have a duty to appeal to public reason in deliberations about constitutional matters and matters of basic justice. They differ 'as to which principles are the most reasonable basis of public justification.' A partisan of justice as fairness, for example, believes that Rawls's two principles of justice are 'the most reasonable basis of public justification,' more reasonable than the principles preferred by other political liberalisms. In short, partisans of different political liberalisms disagree about what counts as just within a liberal framework.

If different political liberalisms disagree about justice, what is it that they agree about? What is their shared political liberalism about? It is primarily about legitimacy.

> [P]olitical liberalism says: our exercise of political power is fully proper only when it is exercised in accordance with a constitution the essentials of which all citizens as free and equal may reasonably be expected to endorse in the light of principles and ideals acceptable to their common human reason. This is the liberal principle of legitimacy. To this it adds that all questions arising in the legislature that concern or border on constitutional essentials, or basic questions of justice, should also be

[14]See esp. *TJ*, sections 26–30, pp. 150–93.
[15]*PL*, p. 7, including note 6, and pp. 281–2.

settled, so far as possible, by principles and ideals that can be similarly endorsed. Only a political conception of justice that all citizens might be reasonably expected to endorse can serve as a basis of public reason and justification (*PL* 137).

The liberal principle of legitimacy is the core of political liberalism, and is accompanied by the closely related idea of public reason. ('The liberal principle of legitimacy makes this the most appropriate, if not the only, way to specify the guidelines of public inquiry' (*PL* 224).)[16] What defines a conception of justice as a version of political liberalism is that it meets this standard of legitimacy and the additional idea of public reason that it 'makes . . . appropriate.'

Political legitimacy, on this reckoning, does not require conformity to one single complete conception of justice, since it does not specify the terms of equality beyond what is essential to a political constitution. The use of collective political power is justified so long as the constitution guarantees a list of equal civil and political liberties to each citizen; these are the 'constitutional essentials,' and they 'can be specified in but one way, *modulo* relatively small variations. Liberty of conscience and freedom of association, and the political rights of freedom of speech, voting and running for office are characterized in more or less the same manner in all free regimes' (*PL* 228). Beyond this, the government can be constitutionally structured in various ways (*PL* 228), and the 'principles covering social and economic inequalities' can vary to some extent without violating the liberal criterion of legitimacy.[17] These further matters do bear on justice: justice as fairness is put forward as the most reasonable of the liberal conceptions of justice, as a better conception of justice within a liberal framework. Nevertheless, what the other views lack as conceptions of justice does not detract from the legitimacy of the regimes they endorse, so long as they include the constitutionally essential civil and political liberties. Justice as fairness disagrees with these other

---

[16]They are also treated as related but distinct at *PL*, p. 225.

[17]There is an important detail about Rawls's guarantee of the 'fair value of the political liberties.' It stems from a passage in Lecture VIII, 'The Basic Liberties And Their Priority':

> . . . those with relatively greater means can combine together and exclude [from the political process] those who have less in the absence of the guarantee of fair value of the political liberties. We cannot be sure that the inequalities permitted by the difference principle will be sufficiently small to prevent this. Certainly, in the absence of the second principle of justice, the outcome is a foregone conclusion (*PL*, p. 328).

The demands of the difference principle are apparently necessary but not sufficient to satisfy the guarantee of the 'fair value of the political liberties' which is explicitly included in the first principle (*PL* 327). In that case, the demands of the second principle are no more egalitarian than those of the first. (As Thomas Pogge has pointed out to me, where they conflict, the difference principle would apparently sacrifice the absolute position of the least well off for the sake of greater equality and political fairness.) This suggests that while the first principle in justice as fairness includes the fair value guarantee, this guarantee is not part of the required content of a liberally legitimate conception. For if it were, there would be no possibility of the other legitimate yet less egalitarian liberalisms that Rawls seems to allow. What liberal legitimacy requires, then, is only the guarantees of the first principle *minus* the fair value guarantee—merely formal equal political liberties. This reading seems to accord with all the text. It is technically wrong then to say that legitimacy requires meeting the demands of Rawls's first principle, since that principle includes the fair value guarantee. This interpretation has the consequence that the first principle of Justice as Fairness already entails at least as much social and economic equality as the Difference Principle (although I see no obvious problem in this).

conceptions, and the disagreement is about what justice requires, but political liberalism regards justice as fairness and many of its competitors alike as each sufficient to justify the use of public coercive political power. In short, legitimacy does not require justice.[18]

SAME AS IT EVER WAS

Even if not all political liberalisms are regarded as equally just, all must include the formal rights and liberties of the first principle of justice. In this way, the first principle (minus the fair value guarantee)[19] is given a special role, even beyond its lexical priority within the theory of justice. The formal rights of the first of Rawls's two principles are not only a requirement of justice but also a requirement of the more basic property: legitimacy. The difference principle is not. Is this asymmetry with regard to legitimacy a change from TJ, reducing the clout of the egalitarian difference principle?[20] If so, PL could fairly be regarded as less egalitarian than TJ, even if there is no change as to what justice requires.

The answer, however, is that there is no such change. The topic of legitimacy is not taken up directly in TJ, and so it could be argued, with some sterility, that there is no view there with which to conflict. Fortunately, however, there is some attention in TJ to the question of which among the requirements of justice as fairness are constitutional matters and which are not. If TJ treated both alike as constitutional requirements then there would be a change from TJ to PL, since matters of social and economic inequality are not regarded as necessarily constitutional in PL. In PL, we are told that:

> The distinction between the principles covering the basic freedoms and those covering social and economic inequalities is . . . that the basic structure of society has two coordinate roles, the [former] specifying the first role, the [latter] covering the second (PL 229).

In TJ, we find the same asymmetry, and the same general reasons:

> I imagine then a division of labor between stages in which each deals with different questions of social justice. This division roughly corresponds to the two parts of the basic structure. The first pinciple . . . is the primary standard for the constitutional convention . . . The second principle comes into play at the stage of the legislature . . . Thus the priority of the first principle of justice to the second is reflected in the priority of the constitutional convention to the legislative stage (TJ 199).

[18]Rawls has recently stated this relationship between legitimacy and justice explicitly, acknowledging an earlier version of the present essay. (See 'Reply to Habermas,' The Journal of Philosophy, 92, 1995, pp. 175–6.) It should be noted, however, that his discussion there is not limited, as mine is here, to liberal legitimacy, but understands the concept in a broader way.

[19]See note 16.

[20]Okin asserts such a change explicitly: '[B]oth the difference principle and fair equality of opportunity—arrived at in TJ through the "original position"—are no longer "constitutional essentials" and are relegated to the legislative stage of the theory' (op. cit., p. 1010).

Furthermore, in both volumes, the greater weight given to the basic liberties is explained by the greater tendency to reasonable disagreement about matters of social and economic inequality. In *TJ*, 'The application of the difference principle in a precise way normally requires more information than we can expect to have and, in any case, more than the application of the first principle. It is often perfectly plain and evident when the equal liberties are violated' (*TJ* 199). In *PL*, the account is the same:

> There are four grounds for distinguishing the constitutional essentials specified by the basic freedoms from the principles governing social and economic inequalities.
> a. The two kinds of principles specify different roles for the basic structure.
> b. It is more urgent to settle the essentials dealing with the basic freedoms.
> c. It is far easier to tell whether those essentials are realized.
> d. It [is] much easier to gain agreement about what the basic rights and liberties should be, not in every detail of course, but about the main outlines (*PL* 230).

In both books, (c) is presented as a reason for the asymmetry: it is easier to tell when principles governing the basic liberties are met. This is used to explain why matters of the second principle are not constitutional essentials. The issue of legitimacy only arises explicitly in the second book. Thus, Rawls adds a consideration explaining why the division between the constitutional essentials and matters of justice not constitutionally essential is also appropriate as the division between requirements of legitimacy and other requirements of basic justice *not* required for legitimacy. This further reason, (d), is that in the case of the constitutional essentials it is easier to agree about what the principle should be—easier than agreeing on a principle for matters of distributive justice. This further difference bears on legitimacy, while the case of determining when certain *given* principles are *met* determines only what ought to be fixed in a constitution. Matters of social and economic inequality are more subject to controversy in both respects. The criterion of legitimacy in *PL* is in harmony, then, with *TJ*'s division between constitutional essentials and other matters of basic justice.

Are principles of distributive justice excluded from the requirements of legitimacy because no principle is beyond reasonable objection? Is the overlapping consensus test conceded to be too hard for the difference principle to meet? Is that what is meant by saying that it is harder to get agreement on distributive principles than on basic rights and liberties? If so, this would make hash of the theory, since it would concede that no principle of distributive justice could properly guide political actors (including voters). Political liberalism requires that matters of basic justice be settled by principles and ideals that all reasonable citizens could endorse. If no principle of distributive justice could meet this standard, then none can 'serve as a basis of public reason and justification' (*PL* 8).

However, saying that agreement about distributive matters is more *difficult* is compatible with holding that there is a principle that can be accepted from all reasonable points of view. Together these two positions merely entail that where citizens who are otherwise reasonable claim that the difference principle violates important aspects of their world view, they are *mistaken*. This, of course, needs to be shown, and the argumentative edifice built around the original position attempts to show it.[21] Showing that the hold-out is in error is possible even if the hold-out fails to recognize the error.

Rawls's claim is that the questions about the best distributive principle are difficult. You don't have to be *as unreasonable* to reject the difference principle as you have to be to reject the list of basic rights and liberties. That is why it is inappropriate to suppose that a regime has to get this *right* in order to be legitimate. Nevertheless, the claim continues, these difficult matters have answers, and the difference principle can be shown to be acceptable from all reasonable points of view. It is thus an appropriate basis for public reason and justification and may properly be pursued in legislation and voting. The 'no reasonable objection' requirement and the closely related standard of 'overlapping consensus' are not the obstacles that keep distributive matters off the list of requirements of legitimacy. According to Rawls, the difference principle clears these hurdles, even if less easily than the basic liberties clear them.

Rawls writes at one point that owing to the Supreme Court's duty to stay within 'the political values covered by the public political conception of justice . . . an appeal cannot be made to the difference principle unless it appears as a guideline in a statute.'[22] This may seem to imply the view that the difference principle is not within the public political conception of justice, contrary to the interpretation I have been advancing. However, this passage is easily brought into line when it is noticed that justices may appeal to the difference principle when it is 'a guideline in a statute.' Rawls is unequivocal in requiring legislation to conform to public reason at least where it bears on 'constitutional essentials' and 'matters of basic justice.' The present passage refers the reader to an earlier passage in which he says explicitly that the issues addressed by the difference principle, 'although they are not constitutional essentials, fall under questions of basic justice and so are to be decided by the political values of public reason.' The court may not appeal to the difference principle because it is not a constitutional essential, that being the limit of their purview. But it is a matter of basic justice subject to the requirement of public reason even in the case of legislation, a standard he plainly implies that it can meet.

The idea of overlapping consensus is often misunderstood as a standard of *de facto* stability or social concord. The fact that the difference principle is controversial is then taken to show that it does not lie within an overlapping consensus. In fact, all it shows is that it is controversial. Rawls uses the term 'stability' in connection with the idea of overlapping consensus, and this has misled many. The question about overlapping consensus is, however, always

---

[21]See the edifying footnote on the relation between reasonable pluralism, overlapping consensus, and the veil of ignorance: *PL*, p. 24, note 27.

[22]*PL*, pp. 236–7, note 23.

only whether a conception of justice would be acceptable to the *reasonable* comprehensive views that would be likely to arise in a society governed by it.[23] Widespread controversy certainly raises the question whether any of the objections is fully reasonable and defensible. But the answer may be no, and so controversy itself does not violate political liberalism's standard of legitimacy. Therefore, even intractable disagreement about such matters as the permissible limits of social and economic inequality is compatible with the difference principle lying within an overlapping consensus of reasonable comprehensive doctrines.

This is not the place to evaluate Rawls's argument for this claim. My aim throughout is to clarify *PL*'s ambitions as I understand them. They are higher than has been widely thought.

LEGITIMACY AND THE LAW OF PEOPLES

Rawls's recent treatment of 'The Law of Peoples' might tempt similar misunderstandings. Rawls argues that his political liberalism can be extended to account for the tolerance owed to some other societies that are unjust and illiberal.[24] I have argued that it is a mistake to assume that, for Rawls, any society justified in its use of political power must, as the basis for this judgment, be counted as just; it may, on Rawls's account, be legitimate without being just. Similarly, it would be a mistake to assume that any society deserving of recognition in a reasonable society of societies could only deserve this as a result of being counted as legitimate. Rawls's view is apparently that a state's legitimacy—its being warranted in the use of coercive political power—is not necessary to its being appropriately recognized within a reasonable law of peoples. Constructivism tailors its principles to the subject at hand, and, 'whenever the scope of toleration is extended . . . the criteria of reasonableness are relaxed.'[25] It takes less to count as a reasonable party to the society of peoples than it takes to count as a reasonable member of a single political society. Nevertheless, Rawls argues that one criterion of a reasonable society in the international context is that the society be 'legitimate in the eyes of its own people.' This may not require that it be legitimate in the eyes of Rawls or of any outsiders.[26]

It is unclear whether Rawls believes a form of society that would be illegitimate for an advanced pluralistic society can nevertheless be legitimate for other societies. It is clear that no society needs to meet the demands of justice as fairness in order to be legitimate. If I am right, however, the first principle of that

---

[23]*PL*, p. 15.

[24]'The Law of Peoples,' *Amnesty Lectures 1993*, Oxford University Press, 1993.

[25]op. cit., p. 78.

[26]There are, in any case, other substantial requirements. The view is far from amoral. See, e.g., 'The Law of Peoples,' op. cit., pp. 60–5.

conception[27] is a requirement of legitimacy for an advanced pluralistic society. Now, is it also a requirement of legitimacy for *any* society? That is, even apart from whether a society meets the more relaxed standards for admission into a reasonable community of nations, can any society deviating severely and formally from the first principle be justified in enforcing internal compliance to its laws and commands? In other words, is the 'liberal principle of legitimacy' itself of universal application? Is it *the* principle of legitimacy, or only the *liberal* principle, one among other principles of legitimacy each applying in its own appropriate setting?[28] Rawls's text seems to be silent on this question. Widespread concerns that Rawls's theory is 'relativistic' will not be allayed by an account of the law of peoples. The question is whether Rawls's theory of justice and legitimacy have critical force against illiberal regimes in very different societies. The theory of the law of peoples has not yet addressed this question.

The point for present purposes is that Rawls's willingness to include certain illiberal societies within a reasonable moral community of nations is no evidence that he regards them as just or even legitimate. It is not a revision of the central doctrines of either *TJ* or *PL*.

CONCLUSION

There is no dilution of the role and weight of the egalitarian difference principle from *TJ* to *PL*. It was, and is, held to be one of two principles of justice which together comprise the most reasonable public conception of justice for an advanced pluralistic society. It was, and is, held to be subordinate to the first principle guaranteeing equal basic liberties. It was, and is, held to be subject to more reasonable controversy than the basic liberties of the first principle. This was, and is, held to give the basic liberties the special role of being placed in the political constitution. *PL* takes a further step: owing to greater controversy about what would be an appropriate principle of social and economic inequality, these matters are allowed to vary more within the bounds of legitimacy. The 'constitutional essentials,' on the other hand, are relatively rigid requirements of legitimacy.

PL is a second book, not merely an extended reflection on a first book. As such, it has its own subject matter: the liberal principle of legitimacy. The claim that legitimacy can exist without the justice of the difference principle simply does not imply or suggest that the requirements of social justice have been adjusted downward, made less demanding. Rawls's enormous influence on philosophical debates about the requirements of social justice may lead many to hear his recent

---

[27]*Minus* the guarantee of the fair value of the political liberties. See note 17.

[28]In 'Reply to Habermas' (op. cit., p. 175) Rawls is plainly willing to speak of legitimacy of non-liberal regimes. He says that legitimacy always requires some measure of justice, though not complete. Still, it is not clear whether he thinks that even illiberal kinds of legitimacy morally warrant coercive enforcement and duties of compliance to law.

views as contributions to that continuing discussion. Perhaps it was in anticipation of this reaction that Rawls sought to dispel this misunderstanding right at the beginning:

> All [the elements of justice as fairness] are still in place, as they were in *Theory*; and so is the basis of the argument for them. Hence I presuppose throughout these lectures the same egalitarian conception of justice as before; and though I mention revisions from time to time, none of them affect this feature of it. [footnote:] I make this comment since some have thought that my working out the ideas of political liberalism meant giving up the egalitarian conception of *Theory*. I am not aware of any revisions that imply such a change and think the surmise has no basis (*PL* 7).

It is well understood that Rawls's recent views propose a certain relationship between comprehensive moral and philosophical world-views and the idea of a public liberal conception of justice. What has been less well appreciated is that with his second book Rawls also begins another new conversation, about how best to conceive the relation between the requirements of (a public conception of) social justice and the requirements of political legitimacy. His thesis that justice is not necessary for legitimacy goes unnoticed from within a conversation about the demands of justice alone.

Oliver A. Johnson

University of California, Riverside

Paragraph 40 of John Rawls's book *A Theory of Justice* bears the title "The Kantian Interpretation of Justice as Fairness."[1] In this section the author makes the claim that the argument supporting the notion of justice he develops in his book can be interpreted in Kantian terms—thus, that his theory is consonant, in its foundations, with the ethics of Kant. In this paper I shall take issue with Rawls, arguing that he is mistaken in believing that his theory can be given a Kantian interpretation. Rather, to fit his views into the ethics of Kant, he must radically misinterpret Kant. For the conception that he has of man's nature as a moral being is basically opposed to, rather than consonant with, that held by Kant.

To make my case I shall concentrate on three concepts that play a central role in the ethics of Kant and that Rawls in paragraph 40 holds to be interpretable in terms of his own theory—autonomy, the categorical imperative, and rationality. In analyzing these I shall be led to consider other notions, like will and desire, "the original position," hypothetical imperatives, heteronomy, "the veil of ignorance," respect for the moral law, happiness, etc. I shall begin by explaining briefly the meanings Rawls gives to the concepts in question and the roles he assigns them in his theory. I shall then go on to describe and, at some length, to criticize his attempt to establish that his views can be given a Kantian interpretation. I shall end with a few general remarks regarding the incompatibility between the Rawlsian and Kantian conceptions of man as a moral being.

As a background for our discussion, it is necessary to give a brief sketch of the main features of Rawls's theory of justice as fairness. This, in turn, must be set in its place within the context of his general theory of society, which is a reformulation of the classical social contract view.[2] The principles of justice that he believes should govern human relations in an ideal society can be discovered by postulating an "original position"[3] in which individuals get together and reach a unanimous agreement to

1. John Rawls, *A Theory of Justice* (Cambridge, Mass.: Harvard University Press, 1971), pp. 251–57.

2. Cf. ibid., p. 11. The main exposition of this general theory appears in chaps. 1–3.

3. Cf. ibid., par. 4. Rawls sometimes uses the term "initial situation" as roughly equivalent to "original position." Both represent his formulation of the condition classical theorists referred to as the "state of nature" (cf. p. 12).

accept a set of rules to regulate their social activities. In his words: "The guiding idea is that the principles of justice for the basic structure of society are the object of the original agreement. They are the principles that free and rational persons concerned to further their own interests would accept in an initial position of equality as defining the fundamental terms of their association. . . . The choice which rational men would make in this hypothetical situation of equal liberty . . . determines the principles of justice."[4] The logic of Rawls's argument is this: given the characteristics of the individuals reaching agreement, as well as the conditions under which they must make their decision, any set of principles acceptable to all will likewise be fair to all. For if it were not fair to some, it would be unacceptable to them as well, and hence would never be unanimously chosen. What is chosen by all, thus, is fair to all, therefore just, and Rawls draws the conclusion that justice is fairness.

But this entire argument rests on an assumption: that the individuals in question will arrive at an agreement. But if, as Rawls points out, everyone involved is concerned only to advance his own interests, each will attempt to warp the principles that are to govern society to his own advantage; hence, it is obvious that no unanimous agreement can ever be reached. Rawls solves this thorny problem by a novel device, which he labels "the veil of ignorance." Briefly put, he postulates among the assumptions governing the original position that the individuals who must reach agreement do so in ignorance of most kinds of particular facts about themselves, such as their place in society, class position, and social status; their natural abilities, such as strength and intelligence; the special features of their personal psychology; and their conception of the good. Without this kind of knowledge they are unable to warp the principles selected in their own favor because any attempt they might make to do so could equally lead to their own undoing. Thus, they can make a disinterested decision; indeed, given the veil of ignorance, such a move would be, from the point of view of individual self-interest, the most rational decision anyone could make. Since the individuals are assumed to be rational, Rawls concludes that they will so decide; hence, unanimous agreement can be reached. As he puts it: "The veil of ignorance makes possible a unanimous choice of a particular conception of justice."[5]

With the problem of agreement resolved, Rawls then goes on to work out the

4. Ibid., pp. 11–12. As Rawls makes clear, the original position is a hypothetical, and not a historical, situation. Nevertheless, it is of crucial importance in his theory, not only for the role it plays in the social contract mechanism, but also because it is the paradigm example of individuals reaching a practical decision on the basis of a consideration of what is just. As he says (p. 19), any of us can enter the original position at any time to determine what is just. By extension, when he offers the Kantian interpretation of his theory, the agreement reached in the original position becomes the paradigm example of a decision reached on moral grounds (see p. 252). For this reason, in the discussion that follows I shall refer to the original position and the characteristics of the individuals who reach agreement in it when I compare Rawls's theory with that of Kant.

5. Ibid., p. 140. Rawls's main discussion of the veil of ignorance is in sec. 24. In further elaboration of his argument, Rawls appeals to what he calls the "maximin rule" as a guide to control the decision-making process. This rule states that it is rational for a person who must make a choice in a situation in which he does not know what the personal results of choosing any alternative would be to rank each alternative by its worst possible outcome and then adopt the alternative whose worst outcome is better for him than the worst outcome of the others. For his discussion, see pp. 152–61.

principles of social relationship that would be acceptable to individuals constituted as he conceives them to be and placed in the (hypothetical) situation he describes. These principles thus make up his concrete theory of justice. Since our concern here is not with this aspect of his theory, I shall not pursue it in any detail, but simply note that he lays down two basic principles of justice, one having to do with liberty, and the other with equality.[6]

With these preliminary matters concerning Rawls's social contract theory clarified, we are ready to turn directly to the question of whether his views can be given a Kantian interpretation. In support of his thesis, Rawls begins by making the point that the central notion in Kant's ethics is the concept of autonomy.[7] So I shall start with this notion in my comparison of his theory with that of Kant. However, before turning to that task, it will be helpful to have before us a general statement of Rawls's understanding of the main features of the Kantian ethics, as a point of departure in our assessment of their consonance with the views of human nature and moral action that he offers. Rawls writes:

> [Kant] begins with the idea that moral principles are the object of rational choice. They define the moral law that men can rationally will to govern their conduct in an ethical commonwealth. . . . Kant supposes that this moral legislation is to be agreed to under conditions that characterize men as free and equal rational beings. The description of the original position is an attempt to interpret this conception. . . .
>
> Kant held, I believe, that a person is acting autonomously when the principles of his action are chosen by him as the most adequate possible expression of his nature as a free and equal rational being. The principles he acts upon are not adopted because of his social position or natural endowments, or in view of the particular kind of society in which he lives or the specific things that he happens to want. To act on such principles is to act heteronomously.
>
> . . . by categorical imperative Kant understands a principle of conduct that applies to a person in virtue of his nature as a free and equal rational being. The validity of the principle does not presuppose that one has a particular desire or aim. Whereas a hypothetical imperative by contrast does assume this: it directs us to take certain steps as effective means to achieve a specific end.[8]

I shall now analyze and evaluate the Kantian interpretation of Rawls's theory, as he understands it. My inquiry will be under three closely related heads, corresponding to the central concepts that Rawls believes himself to share with Kant; namely, (1) autonomy, (2) the categorical imperative, and (3) rationality. My aim will be to show that the two theories are basically disparate, rather than consonant, because the writers do not share a common, but espouse a widely divergent, conception of man's nature as a moral being.

1. *Autonomy.* —Although there is room for disagreement regarding the best full interpretation of Kant's notion of autonomy, the main idea he is attempting to elucidate by this term is fairly clear. It is with the will that he is concerned when he speaks of autonomy—or its counterpart, heteronomy—and his argument turns on the diverse nature of two kinds of motives that can lead men to act. He describes the situation in which we are motivated to act by desire or inclination as heteronomy of the will; we perform the act in question because we want to gain the object to which

6. Cf., for example, ibid., par. 11.
7. Cf. ibid., p. 251.
8. Ibid., pp. 251–53. Whether, and to what extent, this is an accurate interpretation of Kant, I shall discuss later. Rawls himself expresses some doubt on this score, but does not pursue it.

the action leads. Autonomy of the will, on the other hand, describes action in which our motive (maxim) is respect for the moral law. In such action our wants and inclinations play no role; in acting autonomously we do what we believe to be our duty because we believe it to be our duty and for no other reason whatsoever. That our wants would lead us in another direction is a point we refuse to take into consideration when we act autonomously. As Kant sums up the difference between autonomy and heteronomy: "Autonomy of the will is that property of it by which it is a law to itself independently of any property of objects of volition. . . . [However], if the will seeks the law which is to determine it anywhere else than in the fitness of its maxims to its own universal legislation, and if it thus goes outside itself and seeks this law in the property of any of its objects, heteronomy always results."[9]

Let us now turn to Rawls's construal of the meaning of autonomy, to evaluate his claim that it is consonant with the concept as understood by Kant. As Rawls puts it: "Kant held, I believe, that a person is acting autonomously when the principles of his action are chosen by him as the most adequate possible expression of his nature as a free and equal rational being. The principles he acts upon are not adopted because of his social position or natural endowments, or in view of the particular kind of society in which he lives or the specific things he happens to want. To act on such principles is to act heteronomously. Now the veil of ignorance deprives the persons in the original position of the knowledge that would enable them to choose heteronomous principles."[10] The crucial point Rawls makes here is that the individuals in the original position reach their decision[11] regarding the principles of justice autonomously, rather than heteronomously, because they are led to adopt these principles, not because of specific considerations or contingencies and, in particular, not because of the things they happen to want. The reason they choose autonomously is that, because of the veil of ignorance, they are precluded from taking such heteronomous factors into consideration.

The inference Rawls invites us to make is that, since decisions motivated by specific, contingent wants constitute heteronomy, decisions in which these can play no part must be autonomous. It is this inference that we must examine. To do so we need to recollect the role played by the veil of ignorance in Rawls's contract theory. Its purpose, as we saw earlier, is to guarantee unanimous agreement to a set of principles. Because the individuals concerned are all motivated by a desire to advance their own interests, they will never reach agreement if they are given sufficient information to make predictions regarding the future, since each one will opt for principles designed to enhance his personal welfare. The veil of ignorance breaks this impasse because, since all now decide in the dark, no one is able to determine whether a set of principles, apparently favorable to him, would in fact turn out to his advantage.

Although the veil of ignorance solves Rawls's decision problem, it is important to

9. Immanuel Kant, "Foundations of the Metaphysics of Morals," in *Critique of Practical Reason and Other Writings in Moral Philosophy*, trans. L. W. Beck (Chicago: University of Chicago Press, 1949), p. 97.

10. Rawls, p. 252.

11. It is understood that, for Rawls, this decision offers the paradigm example of moral choice (see n. 4 above).

note the terms of that solution. In particular, we must examine the motivations of the individuals in question. And here the point to be made is that their motivations are not changed by the veil of ignorance. Only the conditions under which they reach their decision have been changed. They still choose the principles they do motivated by the desire to promote their own interests in the best way they can. Each man's decision, in other words, still has its basis in want or desire.

For Kant the distinction between autonomous and heteronomous acts lies not in the circumstances in which the acts are performed, but in the motive from which they are performed. An action originally heteronomous is not rendered autonomous, even though performed under a veil of ignorance, if the nature of its motivation is unchanged. Such an act remains heteronomous because the individual chooses as he does because of his desire to gain an object by his action, in this case the set of controlling principles for human relations in his society most favorable to his personal interests. To act autonomously, in Kant's sense, everyone would have to eliminate all such motivations and reach his decision on different grounds altogether, namely, respect for the moral law. For this conception of autonomy, Rawls's theory of the original position, with a decision reached under the veil of ignorance, provides no place. Thus, his understanding of autonomy is not consonant with that of Kant; rather, action he calls autonomous Kant would without hesitation label as heteronomous.

2. *The categorical imperative.* —In Kant the distinction between autonomy and heteronomy is parallel to that between the categorical imperative and hypothetical imperatives. The fact that Rawls misconstrues the former distinction, therefore, offers presumptive evidence that he will misconstrue the latter as well. Let us see if this presumption is borne out by the text.

By a categorical imperative Kant understands a principle of conduct that applies to a person in virtue of his nature as a free and equal rational being. The validity of the principle does not presuppose that one has a particular desire or aim. Whereas a hypothetical imperative by contrast does assume this: it directs us to take certain steps as effective means to achieve a specific end. The argument for the two principles of justice does not assume that the parties have particular ends, but only that they desire certain primary goods. . . . The preference for primary goods is derived, then, from only the most general assumptions about rationality and the conditions of human life. To act from the principles of justice is to act from categorical imperatives.[12]

It is hardly necessary to comment on this passage as an interpretation of Kant, for all too obviously it is a misinterpretation. Nevertheless, it is worth examining to see exactly where Rawls has gone wrong, as well as why he has done so. As for the nature of his error, this lies in his belief that the distinction between a hypothetical and the categorical imperative can be explained in terms of the nature and, in particular, the breadth of the ends that we desire and seek. If we are motivated to act by the desire for a specific end, the imperative is hypothetical; if we are motivated to act by the desire for a "primary good" (which Rawls believes that all humans seek),[13] however, the imperative is categorical. Now it is true that the distinction Rawls makes between types of imperatives resembles a Kantian distinction, but it is not that between

12. Rawls, p. 253.
13. Cf. ibid., par. 15.

hypothetical imperatives and the categorical imperative, but rather that between "rules of skill" and "counsels of prudence."[14] However, for Kant, both of these are types of hypothetical imperative. The reason why Kant calls them hypothetical—as opposed to categorical—is that they presuppose the desire for some end, whether specific or general. But the categorical imperative commands absolutely, without reference to any end: "The hypothetical imperative, therefore, says only that the action is good to some purpose, possible or actual. . . . The categorical imperative, which declares the action to be of itself objectively necessary without making any reference to a purpose, i.e., without having any other end, holds as an apodictical (practical) principle."[15]

For Rawls to give the imperatives he has described the label "categorical" is, thus, to apply a misnomer. That his theory is non-Kantian is once again affirmed. But more than this, it is a theory radically opposed to Kant's—one in which the categorical imperative can have no more place than the Kantian notion of the autonomy of the will. This conclusion leads us to our second question: why does Rawls describe a form of hypothetical imperative and call it categorical (and why does he describe heteronomous action and call it autonomous)? These misinterpretations of Kant, I believe, rest on Rawls's conception of rationality, which he contends also to be consonant with that of Kant. It is to this (most important) contention that we now turn.

3. *Rationality.*—As we have already seen, Rawls believes that his description of rationality as it functions in his contract theory is an interpretation of the Kantian conception of moral reason. To repeat his views on this subject:

> [Kant] begins with the idea that moral principles are the object of rational choice. They define the moral law that men can rationally will to govern their conduct in an ethical commonwealth. Moral philosophy becomes the study of the conception and outcome of a suitably defined rational decision. This idea has immediate consequences. For once we think of moral principles as legislation for a kingdom of ends, it is clear that these principles must not only be acceptable to all but public as well. Finally Kant supposes that this moral legislation is to be agreed to under conditions that characterize men as free and equal rational beings. The description of the original position is an attempt to interpret this conception.[16]

To decide whether Rawls is correct in claiming his conception of the role of reason in the moral life to be an interpretation of that of Kant, we must return to the original position and the individuals who there agree on a set of principles to govern their conduct. As we saw when we described Rawls's argument earlier, he assumes that the individuals in the original position act rationally. This assumption is essential to his argument that they will reach agreement on the principles of justice that he formulates. They accept these principles, he contends, because they recognize that, even though they must reach their decision from behind the veil of ignorance, they will have chosen principles of such a nature that, whatever is revealed regarding their own situation, abilities, and social status once the veil is lifted, they will have made the best bargain possible for themselves. It is because the principles he then formulates constitute such a bargain for each individual that Rawls maintains that these principles would be accepted by choosers assumed to be rational.

14. Cf. Kant, pp. 72–76.
15. Ibid., p. 74.
16. Rawls, pp. 251–52.

I shall consider three questions raised by Rawls's claim that his notion of rationality is an acceptable interpretation of Kant's conception of practical reason.[17] The first is Rawls's idea that, to make a rational choice, one must choose whatever will best further his own ends, with the ends of anyone else irrelevant to the decision. The second is that, in choosing the principles of justice, reason functions as the instrument of desire; it chooses rules of social action which the individual believes will best satisfy his long-range wants. The third is that Rawls makes no provision for reason to function in moral decision beyond those just mentioned. I shall examine each in turn.

Although Rawls is unwilling to describe his theory of rational choice as egoistic, preferring instead to say that the decisions of the individuals in the original position are "mutually disinterested," the line he draws between these types of motivation is an unusual one. As he puts it: "One feature of justice as fairness is to think of the parties in the initial situation as rational and mutually disinterested. This does not mean that the parties are egoists, that is, individuals with only certain kinds of interests, say in wealth, prestige, and domination. But they are conceived as not taking an interest in one another's interests."[18] As this quotation makes clear, Rawls avoids the charge of egoism not by affirming that an individual making a rational, moral decision takes into account the interests of others, but only by affirming that he does not limit the personal interests he considers to a certain range of ends, which apparently encompass for him the limits of egoistic motivation. Whether Kant would allow such "mutually disinterested" action to qualify as moral need hardly be argued. For the question is immediately put beyond dispute by his conception of what it means to act morally, as he formulates it in the statement of the categorical imperative: act so that you treat humanity, whether in your own person or in that of another, always as an end and never as a means only.

Nevertheless, the crucial point in the comparison between Rawls's conception of the role of reason in moral decision and that of Kant is not the question of Rawls's egoism, but rather of his view regarding the relationship between reason and desire. According to Rawls, the decision the individual makes in choosing the principles of justice is rational insofar as it serves his long-range best interests. For him, thus, reason is instrumental; its function is to select means that will lead to ends determined by desire. He begins the discussion of his theory of justice by offering the following description of the function of reason in moral decision: "The concept of rationality must be interpreted as far as possible in the narrow sense, standard in economic theory, of taking the most effective means to given ends."[19] Developing his theory, he stipulates further what he means by rationality as the "taking the most effective means to given ends." His account is clear and pointed and requires no further explanation: "I have assumed throughout that the persons in the original position are rational. In choosing between principles each tries as best he can to advance his interests. . . . A rational person is thought to have a coherent set of preferences between the options open to him. He ranks these options according to how well they further his purposes; he follows the plan which will satisfy more of his desires rather than less. . . . The

17. My concern, of course, will be with what Kant calls pure practical reason.
18. Rawls, p. 13.
19. Ibid., p. 14.

assumption of mutually disinterested rationality, then, comes to this: the persons in the original position try to acknowledge principles which advance their system of ends as far as possible."[20]

How does this account, held by Rawls to be the paradigm example of the function of reason in moral action, compare with Kant's conception of moral action? The answer is not far to seek. Early in the first section of the *Foundations*, Kant distinguishes two roles of reason in the realm of practical affairs. On the one hand, it can be used as an instrument for the attainment of happiness, for planning our life activities and guiding our decisions to yield us a maximum of enjoyment and satisfaction. Rawls is clearly describing the same function of reason in the quotation I have just reproduced, as well as in his remark: "A rational plan of life establishes the basic point of view from which all judgments of value relating to a particular person are to be made and finally rendered consistent. Indeed . . . we can think of a person as being happy when he is in the way of a successful execution (more or less) of a rational plan of life drawn up under (more or less) favorable conditions, and he is reasonably confident that his plan can be carried through."[21] But Kant, after delineating a Rawlsian conception of reason, immediately adds the somewhat startling judgment that reason cannot successfully perform the role described: "The more a cultivated reason deliberately devotes itself to the enjoyment of life and happiness, the more the man falls short of true contentment."[22] Assuming that nature has given us our faculties to serve some purpose, Kant then argues, the conclusion we must draw is that reason's proper role is not to promote happiness. "Now if its preservation, welfare —in a word, its happiness—were the real end of nature in a being having reason and will, then nature would have hit upon a very poor arrangement in appointing the reason of the creature to be the executor of this purpose."[23] Or, to put Kant's point in Rawlsian terminology, to gain the end of happiness it is futile to adopt a "rational plan of life" because reason cannot achieve the desired goal. Better, as Kant adds, to leave the whole undertaking to instinct.

This negative conclusion prepares the way for Kant to make his main point—that nature has given us reason to perform a second, quite different, and higher role in human affairs: "But reason is given to us as a practical faculty, i.e., one which is meant to have an influence on the will. As nature has elsewhere distributed capacities suitable to the functions they are to perform, reason's proper function must be to produce a will good in itself and not one good merely as a means, for to the former reason is absolutely essential."[24] It is clear that Kant, in assigning a second (and proper) role to reason, is describing the function that reason performs in moral decision and action. Reason, for him, is not functioning as a moral faculty (that is, is not in his terms pure practical reason) if it is being used as an instrument for the satisfaction of our various desires or even for the attainment of a goal we all seek —happiness. On the contrary, the moral and proper function of reason is to produce a

20. Ibid., pp. 142–44. For the further elaboration of this conception of rationality, see esp. pars. 63 and 64.
21. Ibid., p. 409.
22. Kant, p. 57.
23. Ibid., p. 56.
24. Ibid., p. 58.

will good in itself. That Kant's conception of moral or practical reason is not only different from, but opposed to, the account offered by Rawls is apparent. For Rawls's paradigm example of the moral use of reason Kant would deny to have anything to do with morality at all. And Kant's description of the proper moral function of reason is nowhere echoed in Rawls's theory. Rather than being consonant with each other, these two conceptions of the role of reason in the moral life stand, in relation to each other, very near the limits of incompatibility. No "Kantian interpretation" is remotely possible.

I turn now to my third question: why did Rawls (mistakenly) identify his notion of reason as the instrument of desire with Kant's pure practical reason, failing to include in his theory any conception of the role of reason in the moral life comparable to the latter? This question can be answered only in part. It is clear from what Rawls writes that he disagrees with Kant on the nature of reason and the range of its activities. Specifically, he limits the competence of reason in such a way as to preclude it from functioning in the manner that Kant describes in his moral theory. As he writes: "By definition rationality is taking effective means to achieve one's ends.[25] It is on the basis of such a definition that he describes the moral choice in the original position as being rational: "I have assumed throughout that the persons in the original position are rational. In choosing between principles each tries as best he can to advance his own interests."[26]

It is obvious that, if reason is defined in such a way that it can only be an instrument to be used in the satisfaction of personal interests, it cannot also be employed in the production of a will good in itself; for these are different—indeed, incompatible—activities. Thus, Rawls rules out the Kantian moral conception of reason by definition. The further question, however, still remains: why does he define reason in such a way? To this question I have not been able to find any answer in his book. So I shall simply conclude by pointing out that the divergence between Rawls and Kant, which generates Rawls's abortive attempts to identify heteronomy with autonomy and hypothetical imperatives with the categorical imperative, rests on the incompatibility between his conception of the nature of reason and that of Kant. Unless reason is given the powers that Kant attributes to it, no "Kantian interpretation" of a moral theory is possible. Further, Kant would claim, unless reason does have such powers, man cannot rise to the level of moral action at all. Whether this last claim is true or whether, on the contrary, a theory like that of Rawls, with its anti-Kantian conception of human rationality, can ever provide a viable foundation for morality is an issue far beyond the scope of the present paper.

25. Rawls, p. 401.
26. Ibid., p. 142.

A DEFENSE OF THE KANTIAN INTERPRETATION*

Stephen L. Darwall

University of North Carolina

I

Oliver Johnson argues that Rawls's claim to a Kantian interpretation of his theory of justice is unsupportable.[1] Indeed, Johnson holds that the main lines of Rawls's theory are such that it is in profound conflict with Kant's at three basic points. He argues that the Rawlsian theory of justice has no place for, and conflicts with, the Kantian notions of autonomy, the categorical imperative, and pure practical reason.

I find the idea that there is a Kantian interpretation of Rawls's theory a very attractive one. And though I shall not give a sustained argument for this position, I will try to give a defense of this view against Johnson's criticisms of it.

II

Just what does Rawls mean by the thesis that his theory has a Kantian interpretation? I take the main force of this claim to be that "the original position may be viewed, then, as a procedural interpretation of Kant's conception of autonomy and the categorical imperative."[2]

The interest in this thesis is not merely to locate Rawls's views within the history of moral philosophy. If the thesis is correct, it provides the hope of a deeper justification for Rawls's principles of justice. Rawls's two main arguments for his theory are well known: first, that the principles best systematize the considered judgments about justice that one would be prepared to accept in "reflective equilibrium," and second, that the principles would be chosen from a position (the original position) which embodies constraints that would seem compelling from reflective equilibrium. Both of these "coherence" justifications for the principles of justice may seem ultimately unsatisfying for a number of reasons. To begin with, the method seems to presuppose a rather substantial agreement in our considered judgments about justice in reflective equilibrium. Second, this justifica-

*I am indebted to the editor of *Ethics* for helpful comments on an earlier version of this paper.

1. Oliver A. Johnson, "The Kantian Interpretation," *Ethics* 85 (1974): 58–66.

2. John Rawls, *A Theory of Justice* (Cambridge, Mass.: Harvard University Press, 1971), pp. 147–48.

tion of the principles leaves unanswered the deeper question of why one should be interested in justice, even if it is true that our considered judgments about it can be organized by the principles. That is, it does not imbed a theory of justice in a theory of practical reason.

The Kantian interpretation suggests that there may be a deeper justification for the principles—namely, that they would be chosen from a perspective which, since it is the "procedural interpretation of Kant's conception of autonomy and the categorical imperative," it is compellingly rational to adopt.[3] To be sure, the attractiveness of this line of argument would depend on being able ultimately to make out the Kantian connections between autonomy, the categorical imperative, and pure practical reason. But, at the very least, this claim suggests the direction that a deeper justification of his theory might take and is of interest for that reason.

Thus, to my mind, the substance of Rawls's invocation of Kant in support of his theory is that there is a Kantian justification for the constraints on choice of principles imposed in the original position. I will not, therefore, be concerned with other proposed dissimilarities between Rawls and Kant. For example, it may be, as Joe Hicks has argued, that the notion of a social contract plays a rather different role in Kant's theory of justice than in Rawls's theory.[4] Whether or not that is the case does not directly affect the question of whether there is a justification in terms of the Kantian concept of autonomy (and related notions) for adopting the perspective embodied in the original position and accepting principles which one would choose from it.

III

Johnson's criticisms proceed "under three closely related heads, corresponding to the central concepts that Rawls believes himself to share with Kant; namely, (1) autonomy, (2) the categorical imperative, and (3) rationality."[5] His strategy is to argue, in each instance, that Rawls's claim that the respective Kantian concepts can be used to interpret his theory of justice is a mistake. Since on Kant's view there are fundamental connections between the three concepts in question, and since, therefore, Johnson's arguments against Rawls under each of these heads are

---

3. Notice that it is the coherence method of argument to Rawls's principles which Joe Hicks centers on as distinctly unKantian in "Philosophers' Contracts and the Law," *Ethics* 85 (1974): 20–21: "Rawls's manner of explication appears more economic: a quasi-bargaining process which weighs the available resources, as to regulative principles, against the objectives, as to ordinary judgments to be explained, and seeks the maximizing balance of the least expensive principles to secure the greatest richness of judgments." I think that Hicks is right to contrast Kant and Rawls on this point. Still, this is not directly relevant to the question of whether or not the thesis of the Kantian interpretation is valid. For, as I understand that thesis, it provides a different argument for, or explication of, the principles—namely, that they would be chosen from a position which is the "procedural interpretation of Kant's conception of autonomy and the categorical imperative." Thus, the question of whether or not the thesis advanced as the Kantian interpretation is true is independent of the sort of difference between Kant and Rawls that Hicks points out.

4. Hicks, "Philosophers' Contracts and the Law."

5. Johnson, p. 60.

at root the same argument, I propose to treat in depth only his argument with respect to autonomy and then to indicate how my points would apply to the other two concepts.

IV

Johnson's argument with respect to the Kantian notion of autonomy is that it is a mistake to think of principles arrived at from the original position as autonomous rather than heteronomous principles. This is a mistake because the principles are chosen by the parties in the original position in order to promote the interest of each. As long as decisions in the original position are so motivated, such decisions are necessarily heteronomous, since they spring from interest rather than respect for the practical law as such.

It is easy to be misled here. One may think that in order for principles arrived at from the original position to be autonomous principles (or laws of freedom as Kant calls them), the choice from the original position must itself be an autonomous choice. And it seems that as Rawls conceives the choice in the original position it is not an autonomous choice. In particular, the parties are conceived as choosing principles on grounds of interest, given the constraints of the veil of ignorance. Thus one is led to Johnson's conclusion.

But to be so led one must accept the initial premise, and I wish to argue that there is no good reason for doing so. It may well be the case that the choice of principles in the original position is a heteronomous choice because it is an interested choice and still be true that the decision of actual rational beings, not in the original position, to act under such principles is an autonomous decision, and hence that action on such principles is autonomous. Even if it is true that if one were under the constraints of the original position (most importantly, the veil of ignorance) one would want a particular principle adopted in one's own interest, it by no means follows that all, or even any, rational beings as they are actually placed in the world would want that same principle adopted in their interest. Thus, if a rational being chooses to act on principles which would be acceptable to him if he were under the veil (on the grounds that they would be acceptable to him under the veil), such a choice is by no means a choice on the basis of his interests and thus is not, on those grounds, a heteronomous choice.

Interestingly enough, Rawls seems to have anticipated the confusion which underlies Johnson's argument, and he explicitly warns against it:

Since the persons in the original position are assumed to take no interest in one another's interests, . . . it may be thought that justice as fairness is itself an egoistic theory. It is not, of course, one of the three forms of egoism mentioned earlier, but some may think, as Schopenhauer thought of Kant's doctrine, that it is egoistic nevertheless. Now this is a misconception. For the fact that in the original position the parties are characterized as not interested in one another's concerns does not entail that persons in ordinary life who hold the principles that would be agreed to are similarly disinterested in one another. Clearly the two principles of justice and the principles of obligation and natural duty require us to consider the rights and claims of others. And the sense of justice is a normally effective desire to comply with these restrictions. The motivation of the persons in the original position must not be confused with the motivation of persons in everyday life who accept the principles that would be chosen and who have the corresponding sense of justice. . . . [Such an individual] voluntarily takes on the limitations expressed by this interpretation of the moral point of view.[6]

Rawls's claim is that if one is willing to act only on the basis of principles acceptable from the original position, then, and only then, is one acting autonomously. To secure this claim one would have to be able to make a connection between being willing to act only on principles which one would will qua rational being (that is, to act on practical laws—principles which would be followed if "reason had full power over the faculty of desire")[7] and principles which one would find acceptable from the original position. This is the crucial connection to be made, since Kant understands autonomy in terms of the capacity of the will (as pure practical reason) to be a law to itself.[8] It is this connection which Rawls expresses by saying that the original position may be seen as "a procedural interpretation of Kant's conception of autonomy . . ." and on which, therefore, a Kantian justification for adopting the constraints of the original position would depend.

v

That such a connection can be made is at least suggested by the following commentary by Kant on the so-called realm of ends formulation of the categorical imperative:

The concept of each rational being as a being that must regard itself as giving universal law through all the maxims of its will, so that it may judge itself and its actions from this standpoint, leads to a very fruitful concept, namely, that of a *realm of ends*.

By "realm" I understand the systematic union of different rational beings through common laws. Because laws determine ends with regard to their universal validity, *if we abstract from the personal difference of rational beings and thus from all content of their private ends*, we can think of a whole of all ends in systematic connection, a whole of rational beings as ends in themselves as well as the particular ends which each may set for himself.[9]

The point here is that to will something as a practical law is to will it as a principle governing the behavior of all rational beings and hence to will it as a common law for all rational beings. Thus, one constraint on what one can will as a practical law is that one be capable of regarding it as a principle which could be willed by all other rational beings also.

Kant suggests that we can arrive at such a conception of rational beings under common laws only if we abstract from their own private ends and focus on what all would will as rational beings. Rawls's point is that the device of the original position, utilizing the veil-of-ignorance constraint, provides a methodological tool for performing such an abstraction. It allows one to derive what rational beings would will as common universal principles by forcing them to abstract from idiosyncratic differences between them.

6. Rawls, pp. 147–48.
7. Immanuel Kant, *Foundations of the Metaphysics of Morals*, trans. Lewis W. Beck (Indianapolis: Bobbs-Merrill Co., 1959), p. 17n. .
8. Ibid., p. 65.
9. Ibid., p. 51 (emphasis added, except for the phrase "realm of ends").

VI

Johnson's rejoinder at this point would be that even though the parties in the original position operate under constraints which force such an abstraction, still the choice in the original position is one which is motivated by interest, and thus egoistic. Two things can be said in reply to this.

First, as I have argued, even if the choice in the original position is egoistic, it by no means follows that the willingness of actual rational beings to act only on principles acceptable from the original position is in any sense egoistic and thus heteronomous. Second, it is arguable that what is in one's interest under the constraints of the original position (in particular, under the constraint of the veil of ignorance) is in one's interest as a rational agent and not merely in one's interest in virtue of some desire one happens to have ("as belonging to the world of sense under laws of nature").[10]

The root idea here is that rational agency itself (or, in any case, rational human agency) requires the having of certain goods. A modicum of health, education, liberties, and wealth are necessary for one to exercise agency at all. Indeed, it is arguable that Rawls's primary goods are best thought of as goods from the point of view of rational agency, goods vital to one's existence as a rational agent. So much is entailed by Rawls's claim that "These [primary goods] are things that it is rational to want whatever else one wants. Thus given human nature, wanting them is part of being rational."[11] These goods are goods not just from the point of view of this or that particular end but from the point of view of one's having any ends at all—that is, from the point of view of one's being a rational agent.[12]

If this is correct, then the charge that the choice in the original position is an interested choice loses much of its bite. For it can now be conceived of as a choice from the point of view of one's interests as a rational agent. And thus it is arguably connected to what one would will as a rational agent, abstracting from one's own idiosyncratic desires, conception of the good, social position, etc.

VII

A rather important caveat is in order here. Although the veil of ignorance forces an abstraction from specific information about oneself (including one's

---

10. Ibid., p. 71. That a decision is motivated by an interest does not entail that it is heteronomous for Kant. After all, Kant entitles this section "Of the Interest Attaching to the Ideas of Morality." A choice can be autonomous and still be motivated by an interest (for example by an interest in morality) though not by an interest in some "external condition."

11. Rawls, p. 253.

12. It is important to note that the idea of primary goods is implicit in some of Kant's remarks also. One instance occurs in his discussion of the third example following the initial formulation of the categorical imperative in the *Foundations of the Metaphysics of Morals*. There he offers the following as support for the claim that a person could not will that everyone (or even that he himself) not develop his talents: "For, as a rational being, he necessarily wills that all his faculties should be developed, inasmuch as they are given him *for all sorts of possible purposes*" (p. 41, emphasis added). John Rawls reminded me of this passage. I am also indebted to Arthur Kuflik and Allen Buchanan for discussions of the view that primary goods are good from the point of view of rational agency. The idea is worked out in greater detail in a dissertation by Buchanan, "Autonomy, Distribution and the State" (Ph.D. diss., University of North Carolina, 1975), pp. 45–94.

desires and interests), there is a great deal of more general information that one has about oneself over and above the fact that one is a rational agent. Thus, one will know that one is a human being in the circumstances of justice. Since one has general knowledge of a psychological and sociological sort available to one, one will know in more or less detail interests, desires, and needs that one will have as a human being in such circumstances. Such information would be relevant to a choice of principles in one's own interest in the original position. Furthermore, one is to decide on principles for the basic structure of a society where this presumably means a group of human beings occupying some particular geographical area (though one knows nothing about that area in particular). All of this significantly restricts the generality of the choice from the original position. For even though one is forced to abstract from desires, interests, and features which would be idiosyncratic within the class of human beings in the circumstances of justice, one will have, as information relevant to a choice of principles, a great deal of information which may be idiosyncratic to human beings (in the circumstances of justice) within the potentially larger class of all rational beings. How does this effect any line of argument to the principles of justice on Kantian grounds?

It may well be the case that the principles of justice (even if arguable to from the original position) are not practical laws in the sense of laws which are valid for all rational beings. Still, if we conceive of principles of justice as principles which the basic structure of a human society ought to realize in the circumstances of justice, then the Kantian argument may still go through. For clearly the general information about the circumstances of justice and about human beings will be directly relevant here. The principles of justice may not possess universal validity in the sense of being valid for all rational beings, even though it is the case that they are valid for rational beings who are human beings placed in the circumstances of justice. Thus, were it true that the original position forces an abstraction from everything but information about oneself as a rational human being in the circumstances of justice, then it would be arguable that if there were principles which would be chosen by anyone so situated (that is, any rational being under those conditions), then such principles would be practical laws for rational beings under those conditions. The Kantian argument to the principles of justice would then be that they would be willed by any rational human being in the circumstances of justice if he were to attend to only those general features which characterize him as such a being, and hence would be willed by all such beings as common principles. Since the validity of such principles arises out of features of oneself qua rational agent (subject to the constraints of being human and in the circumstances of justice), they could be characterized as autonomous principles in that sense.

VIII

To recapitulate the argument: (*a*) Even if the choice from the original position is a heteronomous choice, it by no means follows that the decision to act only on principles acceptable from the original position (and hence action on such principles) is not fully autonomous. (*b*) It is arguable that the methodological device of the original position gives an interpretation to the Kantian idea of willing something as a practical law, a common law in a realm of ends subject to the constraints of being human and in the circumstances of justice. Indeed, so much is hinted at in parts of the Kantian text itself.

IX

Johnson's arguments against Rawls's use of the Kantian notions of the categorical imperative and pure practical reason are similar to his objection to the Rawlsian use of the notion of autonomy. In each case, Johnson makes the mistake of supposing that since something characterizes the parties' choice of principles within the original position (and hence their grounds for accepting the principles), it must therefore characterize the principles themselves or the grounds of any actual person (outside the original position) for holding the principles. In the first instance, Johnson argues that the choice of the principles in the original position is conditional on the desire of the parties for primary goods, and as such the principles are mere hypothetical imperatives, conditional on one's having such a desire. Two things can be said about this. First, if someone accepts the principles of justice on the ground that he would choose them if he were in the original position (behind the veil, etc.), he does not accept them on the ground that the basic social structure's satisfying the principles is most likely to provide him with the highest index of primary goods as he is actually placed outside the veil. Thus, the principles are not hypothetical in that sense. Furthermore, the desire for primary goods is not merely one desire among others. It is arguable that it is a desire which is preeminently rational for one to have, given that one is a rational human being in the circumstances of justice.

With respect to the Kantian notion of pure practical reason, Johnson argues that since the parties within the original position are characterized as (*a*) mutually disinterested and (*b*) rational in the economic sense of choosing whatever will be most in their own interest, Rawls's notion of rationality is at odds with Kant's. Clearly Johnson has again misidentified the sense of 'rational' in which the parties within the original position are assumed to be rational with Rawls's notion of reason per se. Though Rawls is not terribly explicit about his conception of reason, in the final section of the book he alludes to a conception of rationality rather different than the narrow economic notion: "Within the framework of justice as fairness we can reformulate and establish Kantian themes by using a *suitably general conception of* rational choice."[13]

To be sure, one would want to emphasize the same caveat here as before. Principles which one would will from the original position are not categorical imperatives or practical laws in the sense that they are valid for the will of any rational being—though it is arguably the case that they are valid for any rational human being who happens to be in the circumstances of justice.

As I said at the outset, this paper is not intended to be a sustained argument for the Kantian interpretation. Much greater clarity is yet required about Rawls's views, Kant's views, and the connection between the two. Nevertheless, I hope that I have shown that such a program has not been rendered otiose by Johnson's criticisms.

13. Rawls, p. 584 (emphasis added).

MORAL PERSONALITY AND
LIBERAL THEORY
John Rawls's "Dewey Lectures"

WILLIAM A. GALSTON
University of Texas at Austin

I

The past generation has witnessed a much-discussed revival of normative political theory. It has been less frequently remarked that this revival has rested to an extraordinary degree on Kantian foundations. From Robert Nozick on the libertarian right to Jürgen Habermas on the participatory left have come appeals to Kantian concepts and premises, variously interpreted. John Rawls is of course the chief representative of this tendency within contemporary Anglo-American liberal thought. Largely as a consequence of his efforts, present-day liberals are far more likely to invoke Kant, as opposed to (say) John Stuart Mill, than they were only two decades ago.

Why has Kant so unexpectedly become the preeminent practical philosopher of our day? To begin with, discontent with utilitarianism has been growing steadily, for both technical and moral reasons, within Anglo-American philosophy, reducing the plausibility of utilitarian justifications of political institutions. At the same time, many European thinkers on the left have felt compelled to discard the orthodox Marxist illusion that justifications of policies and institutions are somehow immanent in the historical process. As Bernard Crick has said, "Theories of socialism without a critical moral philosophy are as undesirable as they are impossible."[1] But to most theorists it no longer seems acceptable to base moral theory on divine authority, on cultural tradition, on the *consensus gentium*, on the direct intuitive perception of moral truth, or on any form of naturalism. The remaining possibility is a law of reason in the Kantian sense: a standard immanently derived from the fact and form of moral rationality itself. Not only is Kantian

POLITICAL THEORY, Vol. 10 No. 4, November 1982 492-519
© 1982 Sage Publications, Inc.
0090-5917/82/040492-28$3.05

practical philosophy the right *type* of moral theory; it is also thought to provide the right *content*. Kant's account of moral personality allows us to speak of the dignity and inviolability of every individual and to understand individuals as bearers of rights, simply by virtue of their humanity. Kantian moral theory provides a philosophical foundation for the derivation of legitimate authority and rational principles of social organization from freedom, equality, and autonomous consent— the predominant values of our democratic age.

Rawls's *A Theory of Justice* invokes Kant's authority at many junctures. But on one crucial point—Rawls's understanding of individual personality—the Kantian legacy is at best ambiguously expressed. There are in fact three discernibly different—and not wholly compatible—accounts of individual motivation in *A Theory of Justice*. Rawls offers what he calls the "Kantian interpretation," in which adherence to the dictates of justice is advantageous (and fully voluntary) because such action expresses our nature as free and equal rational beings. A second interpretation superimposes the constraints of the "moral point of view" on individuals understood as the narrowly self-interested rational calculators of modern economic and social choice theory. Yet a third interpretation (the Aristotelean) understands individuals as moved to develop and to exercise their innate abilities. These conflicting motivational assumptions generate serious, perhaps unresolvable, tensions within the overall account of justice as fairness presented in Rawl's magnum opus.

Recently, in three John Dewey lectures collectively titled "Kantian Constructivism in Moral Theory,"[2] Rawls has offered a comprehensive restatement of his argument. As he says, these lectures consider previously neglected aspects of justice as fairness, they lay out more clearly the Kantian roots of that conception, and they seek to display the general features of Kantian moral argument as a distinctive and attractive "method" (in Sidgwick's sense) of ethics.

Rawls unequivocally rests his revised case on a fuller Kantian interpretation of personality. In so doing, he significantly increases the clarity and coherence of his theory. He does not, however, increase its appeal commensurately. Quite the reverse. The Kantian reconstruction enables us to specify more precisely the questionable assumptions underlying justice as fairness and to identify the points at which Rawls misunderstands both Kant's argument and his own. It also highlights the extent to which Rawls abandons a truly Kantian understanding of the epistemological status of moral principles, an understanding propounded, not without equivocation, in *A Theory of Justice*. In all these respects, I shall argue, Rawls inadvertently illuminates some basic defects of contemporary liberal theory and points us toward a more adequate understanding of the liberal tradition.

II

The general strategy of the Dewey lectures is straightforward. Rawls sets forth three *model-conceptions*: the moral person, the well-ordered society, and the original position. The conception of the moral person contains all (but *only*) those features of human personality relevant to the choice of principles of justice. The conception of the well-ordered society contains quasi-formal features that both constrain possible principles of justice and delimit the domain of those principles. That is, the conception of the well-ordered society is intended to depict those aspects of human social life that principles of justice must encompass and support. Finally, the conception of the original position models the manner in which individuals, viewed solely as moral persons, should select first principles of justice for a well-ordered society.

At first glance, then, each of these model-conceptions is independent of the others. A determinate theory of justice emerges because, taken together, three independent sets of constraints—on choosers, on the object of choice, and on the circumstances of choice—radically narrow the range of principles that individuals, so constrained, may rationally select.

But this surface impression is misleading. The three model-conceptions are not independent of one another. Consider the well-ordered society. It has, Rawls emphasizes, three basic features. First, members of a well-ordered society are, and view themselves and one another as, free and equal moral persons (521). Second, it satisfies the *publicity* condition: That is, it is "effectively regulated by a public conception of justice" (521). Third, a well-ordered society exists under what Rawls calls the "subjective circumstances of justice": deep and pervasive differences of religious, philosophical, and ethical doctrine on which public agreement cannot be reached (539).

Clearly, the first feature merely builds the model-conception of the moral person into the well-ordered society. Moreover, it turns out that the publicity condition is derived from—or at least justified through—the conception of the free and equal moral person. Full publicity, Rawls asserts, is a "precondition of freedom" (539). Thus, a different conception of personality might not entail publicity as an element of the well-ordered society. It follows, I believe, that the publicity condition adds nothing to Rawls's specification of moral personality. It does not, and cannot, serve as a second filter screening out principles judged consistent with Rawlsian moral personality, because the personality condition, by itself, rules out everything inconsistent with publicity, and more.

The diversity assumption raises more complex problems, to which we shall return later. For now, suffice it to say that Rawls's professed reasons for adopting this assumption call into question its independence from the conception of moral personality. The diversity assumption, Rawls insists, "does not imply either skepticism or indifference about religious, philosophical, or moral doctrines." Nor does it imply that unanimity on these questions is entirely impossible. It rests, rather, on the belief that "uncoerced agreement is not to be expected," that diversity is bound to prevail "in the absence of a sustained and coercive use of state power that aims to enforce the requisite unanimity" (542). This is to say that the diversity assumption rests on the opposition to coercion, even in the name of truth—that is, on the privileged position of individual freedom. But for Rawls, the social freedom individuals enjoy is grounded in the freedom characteristic of moral personality.

This interpretation of Rawls's intention is strengthened by the reasons he gives for rejecting any prior and independent conception of desert, capable of overriding or restricting individual consent, as a possible element of a theory of justice. "To suppose that there is such a notion," Rawls asserts, "would violate the autonomy of free and equal moral persons" (551-552). The point is, it seems, of general application. Any appeal to external moral norms—whatever their ground or justification—would violate autonomy, so conceived. And, Rawls suggests, the fact of autonomy by itself constitutes a sufficient reason to reject anything that would breach it. Thus, all coercion designed to impose moral, philosophical, or religious principles must be rejected *as a violation of free and equal moral personality.* (That this is a sufficient reason does not mean that there are not other reasons, perhaps also sufficient, for rejecting such coercion. I shall return to this point.)

When we turn to Rawls's new formulation of the original position, matters are much the same: Every significant feature can be shown to rest on moral personality. Let me cite just two examples. The famous "veil of ignorance" excludes information about individuals in the name of moral personality. For if it did not do so, Rawls argues, it would

231

represent parties to the agreement "not solely as free and equal moral persons, but instead as persons also affected by social fortune and natural accident" (523). Second, the original position incorporates pure procedural justice—the thesis that there is no independent criterion of justice external or anterior to the parties' agreement. The reason for this, Rawls says, is that it "enables us to explain how the parties, as rational agents of construction, are also autonomous" (523). But the core of Rawlsian autonomy turns out to be a special account of motivation—the desire to exercise the powers that characterize the parties as moral persons (527).

If I am correct, then, Rawls's reconstructed theory in the Dewey lectures radiates from a single core—his conception of moral personality. To bring out the force of this fact, let us briefly glance back at *A Theory of Justice*. In that work, Rawls sought to preserve a sharp distinction between individual agents and the circumstances within which they are required to act. He explicitly denied that his conception of justice rested on an ideal conception of the person, and he "avoided attributing to the parties [in the original position] any ethical motivation." Instead, he depicted them as the rational prudential agents of neoclassical economics or social choice theory. The original position, on the other hand, incorporated morally nonneutral constraints on rational agents in the form of conditions that express the "moral point of view" or are "widely recognized as fitting to impose on the adoption of moral principles" (*A Theory of Justice* [TJ], 584-585). In *A Theory of Justice*, then, an ideal of the person enjoys at most derivative status. Choices in the original position generate principles of justice, which may in turn be employed to define a "partial ideal of the person." The ideal of the person is not the foundation, but rather the outcome, of the theory of justice.

In the Dewey lectures, the ideal of the person plays a direct rather than derivative role. First, as we shall see, Rawls now depicts individuals in the original position as moral agents, in the sense that their choices are seen as pursuing, or expressing, basic features of moral personality. Second, the elements of the original position lose their previous character as reasonable but ad hoc moral constraints on individual choice, and become instead representations of the moral personality of the individuals themselves.

Of course, in *A Theory of Justice* Rawls had already opened the door to this revised view, through what he called the Kantian interpretation of justice as fairness. Here, both the principles we choose and our desire to honor them in our conduct are viewed as expressions of our nature as free and equal rational beings. But I think it is fair to say that this "interpretation" is in important respects an *alternative* account. Certainly its depiction of the motivation of rational agents diverges widely from the motivational assumptions of neoclassical economics. For if we take the Kantian interpretation seriously, the "sense of justice" ceases to be a *constraint* on the pursuit of self-interest and becomes instead a defining *element* of our interest (rightly understood) as human agents.

I suggest, then, that the Dewey lectures can be seen as resolving the tension, which runs through *A Theory of Justice*, between the Kantian and the rational-prudential account of human agency, by offering a thoroughgoing reconstruction of justice as fairness along frankly Kantian lines. The philosophical advantages of this strategy are obvious. I shall argue, however, that it has its costs as well.

III

It is now time to inspect more closely Rawls's concept of moral personality. Moral persons are, he tells us,

> characterized by two moral powers and by two corresponding highest-order interests in realizing and exercising these powers. The first power is the capacity for an effective sense of justice, that is, the capacity to understand, to apply and to act from (and not merely in accordance with) the principles of justice. The second moral power is the capacity to form, to revise, and rationally to pursue a conception of the good [525].

Moral persons, so characterized, are said to be *free*, in two senses. They are thought of as "self-originating sources of valid claims [that] carry weight on their own without being derived from prior duties or obligations owed to society or to other persons" (543). They are regarded as free, second, because they "do not view themselves as inevitably tied to the pursuit of the particular conception of the good and its final ends which they espouse at any given time" (544). And moral persons are said to be *equal* because each is equally capable of "understanding and complying with the public conception of justice . . . and of being full participants in social cooperation throughout their lives" (546).

This new conception of moral personality leads directly to a drastically revised account of primary goods. In *A Theory of Justice*, we recall, these goods were defined relative to the objectives of prudential calculators. They were, Rawls specified, a class of goods "that are normally wanted as parts of rational plans of life which may include the most varied sorts of ends." The account of these goods depends on "psychological premises" (TJ, 260). In the Dewey lectures, on the other hand,

> primary goods are singled out by asking which things are generally necessary as social conditions and all-purpose means to enable human beings to realize and exercise their moral powers . . . the conception of moral persons as having certain specified highest-order interests selects what is to count as primary goods. . . . Thus these goods are not to be understood as general means essential for achieving whatever final ends a comprehensive empirical or historical survey might show people usually or normally have in common under all social conditions [526-527][3]

The account of moral personality in the Dewey lectures alters, not only the understanding of primary goods, but also the character of Rawls's theory, taken as a whole. *A Theory of Justice* rejected "perfectionism" as both improper and superfluous. Perfectionism, Rawls alleged, violates our considered judgments about human liberty and equality. Moreover, "to find an Archimedean point [for appraising institutions] it is not necessary to appeal to . . . perfectionist principles" (TJ, 263).

But the revised theory of the Dewey lectures verges on perfectionism. Clearly the ideal of the person functions as a moral goal, in two respects. Individuals choosing principles of justice will seek, first and foremost, to create circumstances in which they can realize and express their moral powers. Second, we as observers will appraise social institutions in light of their propensity to promote the realization and facilitate the expression of these powers, and this standard will take priority over our other concerns.

In what sense is this theory distinguishable from the perfectionism Rawls continues to reject? There are, it seems, two major distinctions. First, perfectionism as Rawls describes it takes as its goal nonmoral excellence, while his own theory focuses on the development of moral powers. Second, perfectionism focuses on the excellence achievable only by the few, whose claims are given disproportionate (if not absolute) weight relative to ordinary individuals, while the moral powers Rawls emphasizes are, he supposes, within the capacity of every normal person to develop and to exercise, at least in favorable circumstances.

Now (to take the first point) it would appear that Rawls's new theory and perfectionism differ, not generically, but rather as species within a single genus. In each case, philosophical reflection must somehow pick out normatively favored individual ends and interests. Rawls would perhaps argue that while individuals may differ about criteria for nonmoral excellence, they are in substantial agreement about at least the main features of moral excellence. Thus, for both theoretical and practical reasons, it makes sense to set controverted ideals to one side and to build social institutions on a more solid normative foundation.

There are two difficulties with this contention. First, it is by no means obvious that we are in hopeless disagreement about the components of nonmoral excellence. Clearly we have a pluralistic conception. There are many dimensions of excellence, no one of which enjoys clear priority. But to admit this is not to deny that we have a criterion sufficiently determinate for purposes of social judgment and public policy. Second, even if we restrict our attention to moral excellence, matters are more complex than Rawls suggests. Some might wish to argue that the ideal of the moral person should incorporate a wider range of virtues (those sketched in Aristotle's *Ethics*, say). It is by no mean clear why a sense of justice should be emphasized while courage and a variety of social virtues are altogether excluded from Rawls's model-conception. In this respect, at least, it is not self-evident that moral excellence is simpler or less open to reasonable disagreement than is nonmoral excellence.

Rawls believes he has answered this kind of objection in the Dewey lectures by grounding his view of moral personality in the conception "implicitly affirmed in . . . the public culture of a democratic society" (518). As I shall later argue, this defense of a Kantian view of moral personality is doubly questionable: It misrepresents what is in fact our shared cultural understanding of personality, and it entails the abandonment of the fundamental aims of Kantian moral philosophy

Let us now turn to the second point of difference, between perfectionism as a hierarchical doctrine and Rawls's theory as egalitarian. It cannot be denied that some perfectionist thinkers have given something approaching absolute priority to the sorts of excellence achievable only by the few. But this is *not* a defining characteristic of perfectionism. Many perfectionists have believed that unusual development along a particular dimension of excellence differs quantitatively, not qualitatively, from ordinary competence. The rare genius raises to a higher power traits characteristic of normal human beings. Thus, in cases where societies face a stark choice between the normal development of the many and the extraordinary development of the few, perfectionism as an ideal-teleological theory is likely to give more weight to the aggregate good of the many, unless it can be shown that favoring the few here and now will eventually produce a greater social good.

Of course, it is possible to construct a quantitative measure that gives rare excellence many times the weight of normal development. But it is as least as plausible to argue for the diminishing marginal weight of incremental individual development. Suppose that a society must choose between two policies. Under A, all available resources are devoted to the full development of X (a potential genius), while Y (a potentially normal individual) is wholly ignored and allowed to remain illiterate, unskilled, and brutish. Under B, the same resources are used to develop both X and Y up to the point of normality. Naturally, egalitarians and contractarians will select B over A. But so will perfectionists who believe that the gain to Y under B exceeds the loss to X—who believe, that is, that to deprive an individual of the chance to achieve normal development and to lead a normal life is to subject that individual to the greatest conceivable harm.

IV

As a point of departure for social theory, the Rawlsian view of personality is remarkable at least as much for what it *excludes* as for what it *affirms*. In *A Theory of Justice*, Rawls had excluded knowledge of individual conceptions of the good from the original position. Pressed to defend this exclusion, he subsequently argued that

> our final ends . . . depend on our abilities and opportunities, on the numerous contingencies that have shaped our attachments and affections. That we have one conception of the good rather than another is not relevant from a moral standpoint. In acquiring it we are influenced by the same sort of contingencies that lead us to rule out a knowledge of our sex and class.[4]

But in light of the revised account in the Dewey lectures, this thesis is no longer tenable. The power to form a conception of the good, Rawls now argues, is a core aspect of developed moral personality, a manifestation, not of heteronomous contingency, but rather of autonomous reflection and choice. There is no longer any basis to argue that the specific exercise of this power is arbitrary from a moral point of view.

Not surprisingly, the Dewey lectures offer a different argument for excluding conceptions of the good. By assumption, Rawls contends,

> in a well-ordered democratic society under modern conditions, there is no settled and enduring agreement on [conceptions of the good. This disagreement seems] bound to obtain in the absence of a sustained and coercive use of state power that aims to enforce the requisite unanimity.... Because [the principles of justice] are to serve as a shared point of view among citizens with opposing ... conceptions of the good, [the veil of ignorance] needs to be appropriately impartial among these differences [542-543].

Strikingly, Rawls does not argue that rational judgment about the worth of different conceptions of the good is impossible. Rather, he emphasizes the practical difficulties of institutionalizing a specific conception. The implicit argument is that even if a conception is valid, the evil of the coercion that would be required to give it public effect would outweigh the benefits of inculcating general belief in its validity.

This is, of course, a classical premise of liberalism. It originated in the seventeenth-century wars of religion and in the desperate efforts of Locke and others to shape a doctrine of toleration that could serve as a basis of peace and mutual accommodation. But to arrive at his doctrine, Locke went a long way toward denying the truth-claims of the sectarian combatants. If he had accepted the view of any party that its beliefs and practices were required for eternal salvation, the relative evils of coercion and toleration would have appeared in a very different light. Similarly, Rawls's admission that some contending conceptions of the good may be superior to others makes it difficult to maintain without further ado that coercion is *always* inferior to impartiality among these conceptions.

The continued exclusion of conceptions of the good seems arbitrary from another standpoint as well. Rawls insists that the original position must be impartial among opposed conceptions. But there is no reason to believe that impartiality requires ignorance. Presumably, impartiality would prevail if every conception of the good may be freely expressed and each is given equal weight. That is, impartiality requires only that no conception of the good be accorded a privileged position from which other conceptions can be coercively repressed.

Rawls's remaining objections to what we may call full-information impartiality reduce to two: that no agreement will be possible in such circumstances, or that any agreement reflecting knowledge of the good will somehow be biased. Neither objection seems tenable. Suppose, to begin with, that individuals are asked to agree on principles governing

237

the relation between church and state. Rawls grants to them the knowledge that they differ profoundly in religious belief. But how would the situation differ if, instead of this general knowledge, each individual knew what his or her beliefs were? For as long as unanimity is required, each individual can block an outcome adverse to his or her convictions. Quickly the group will realize that its alternatives reduce to no agreement and some form of toleration for all religions. Indeed, history presented precisely this choice to the religious combatants of the early modern period. Some decades of no agreement, replete with civil conflict, international convulsions, and unspeakable brutalities on all sides, sufficed to bring home the lesson that a moderation of claims all around was preferable to the consequences of futilely pressing one's maximal demands.

Nor is it clear why agreements made in full awareness of differing conceptions of the good will necessarily be "biased." Of course, individual A's conception may require considerable resources while B's can be realized much more simply. If total resources are insufficient for the full realization of both, the individuals are likely to agree on a division that provides each with the same proportionate share of what he or she requires, or on some other end-regarding scheme. To be sure, the more expensive one's conception of the good, the more dependent one is likely to be on the advantages of social cooperation. Those with cheaper conceptions lose less from no agreement, and they may therefore be able to exploit their stronger bargaining position to achieve a greater-than-proportionate share of the advantages of cooperation. But this possibility does not tell decisively against full-information bargaining, for two reasons. First, as we have seen, conceptions of the good are *not* just like race and sex. They are (or so Rawls now insists) within our power to choose and to alter. If so, it is not unreasonable to expect individuals selecting expensive conceptions to take into account the risk that the resources they require will not be (wholly) available. Second, Rawls's index of primary goods takes no notice whatever of differences in cost among conceptions of the good. It is thus far *more* biased against expensive conceptions than any full-information agreement is likely to be.[5]

V

Bernard Williams has argued that if, as Rawls contends, utilitarianism fails to take seriously the *separateness* of persons, Kantianism gives insufficient weight to their *distinctiveness*. Kantian theories ask us to arrive at principles valid for all human beings (or, in Kant's own view, all rational beings) without taking into consideration the specific features that distinguish us one from another. Our obligations are independent of our identity or character. This abstraction from character is, Williams contends, a fundamental mistake. My character—my predilections, projects, and conceptions of the good—are conditions of my taking any interest in the world at all, either on my own account or on anyone else's. By detaching us, not just from our social circumstances, but also from our selves, Kantian impartiality makes it impossible for us to take any interest in, or to regard as binding, the conclusions to which it gives rise.[6]

In the Dewey lectures, Rawls attempts without notable success to respond to this charge. He distinguishes between the conceptions of the person appropriate to the public world and to "personal affairs." In the latter, something like Williams's view prevails: Individuals cannot regard themselves as detached from their specific ends and beliefs. In the former, they must adopt the Kantian perspective. This dualism, Rawls adds, is in no way vicious: "Within different contexts we can assume diverse points of view toward our person without contradiction so long as these points of view cohere together when circumstances require" (545).

But Williams's point is that they do *not* cohere. Kantian impartiality requires us to nullify core aspects of our character, not just in original-position reflection, but also in concrete moral conduct. As Rawls himself says, our ends *must* be revised whenever they conflict with principles of justice—principles constructed without concrete reference to these ends (544).

To clarify this issue, we may distinguish four different interpretations of the relation between justice and character:

(1) *The neutral interpretation:* principles of justice are defined without reference to conceptions of the good actually held by individuals, and these principles override conceptions of the good in cases of conflict.

(2) *The full-information interpretation:* principles of justice are defined in a manner sensitive to actually held conceptions of the good but, as in the neutral interpretation, justice overrides these conceptions.

(3) *The personal-identity interpretation:* principles of justice are defined in a manner sensitive to actually held conceptions of the good, but in cases of conflict, justice has no clear (lexical) priority over individual projects and attachments.

(4) *The perfectionist interpretation:* principles of justice are defined relative to ideal standards of the good; in cases of conflict, justice has no clear priority over individual excellence conforming to that ideal.[7]

Williams's critique of the neutral interpretation is directed both at the manner in which it defines principles of justice and at the lexical priority it accords them. But the latter point seems contingent on the former. If—as in the full-information interpretation—principles of justice are sensitive to actually held conceptions of the good, the case for according priority to those principles is considerably strengthened. After all, individual identity has *already* been given fair weight. For a particular individual to demand exemption from the requirements of justice, so defined, is a form of selfishness. Thus, persons who refuse to fight for their country during wartime on the ground that their characters would be degraded by brutality would hardly be entitled to our respect, for they ignore the harm to others their refusal may engender. In particular, they ask someone else to do their dirty work and to risk undergoing the same fundamental transformations of attitude and character.

Thus, Williams's critique of Rawls rests on the tacit assumption that there is no alternative lying between the personal-identity interpretation and the neutral interpretation. But there *is* an alternative—what I have called the full-information interpretation—and it is hardly implausible on its face. Rawls's insistence on the priority of justice is not (as he supposes) undermined, but rather supported, by the full-information interpretation. And, as we have seen, there are a number of other reasons to prefer it to the neutral interpretations.

It is not clear, however, that Rawls continues to espouse the neutral interpretation. To the extent that my earlier argument is correct, the reconstructed theory of the Dewey lectures is a kind of perfectionism. If so, Williams's critique must be recast. The problem with Rawls's revised Kantian doctrine is not that it abstracts completely from conceptions of character, but rather that it prescribes, as valid for all, a single, substantive, eminently debatable ideal of moral personality that gives pride of place to the capacity for just action.[8]

The manner in which Rawls develops this ideal gives rise to a familiar difficulty. The history of political philosophy virtually begins with the query: Assuming that I know what justice is, is it to my advantage to act justly, and if not, why should I do so? As every reader of the *Republic* knows, Plato resolves the "motivational" problem—the irrationality of self-sacrifice—by interpreting justice as the highest form of self-interest: the harmonious ordering of one's soul that engenders the profoundest and most lasting contentment. In so doing, however, he leaves unresolved the precise relation between these goods of the soul and the "external" goods that constitute the subject matter of justice in the political arena. And he opens a breach between his self-regarding conception of justice and the duties toward others that characterize principles of justice as ordinarily understood.

In the Dewey lectures, Rawls adopts a version of Plato's strategy. The capacity for an effective sense of justice is declared to be one of our fundamental moral powers, corresponding to which is the "highest-order interest" to realize and to exercise this power. And, Rawls adds, this interest is supremely regulative as well as effective. Whenever circumstances are relevant to its fulfillment, this interest governs the deliberation and conduct of moral persons (525). Thus, the conclusion that just actions performed on principle promote the highest good of the agent is built into the very definition of moral personality. Rawls even goes beyond Plato by defining primary goods relative to moral personality, thus ruling out any possibility of conflict between internal and external advantage. The external world is understood as "good" only insofar as it serves the interests of moral personality.

This strategy of argument is a pronounced change—and in some respects a regress—from *A Theory of Justice*. In the earlier work, Rawls had defined primary goods, and hence the "thin" theory of rational self-interest, independently of the sense of justice. Rational agents can therefore ask themselves whether this "regulative sentiment" is "consistent with their good"; that is, they "assess the goodness of the desire to adopt a particular point of view, that of justice itself" (TJ, 568). Rawls then proceeds to offer a series of empirical/psychological arguments to show that the just life is, all things considered, the rationally advantageous life. At the same time, he characterizes as "trivial" the answer that if an individual has an effective sense of justice, he or she will then have a regulative desire to act justly, a desire that determines the content of the rationally advantageous life for him or her—the very argument he offers in the Dewey lectures! We should not, he contends,

> rely on the doctrine of the pure conscientious act . . . the desire to act justly is not a final desire like that to avoid pain, misery, or apathy. . . . The theory of justice supplies other descriptions of what the sense of justice is a desire for [TJ, 569].

But this is p.ecisely what the revised theory of the Dewey lectures *cannot* supply.

To be sure, Rawls does suggest a way out of this impasse. The "'Kantian interpretation" sketched in *A Theory of Justice* foreshadows the doctrine of the Dewey lectures, that persons acting from the principles of justice express their nature as free and equal rational beings. And, he continues, "since doing this belongs to their good, the sense of justice aims at their well-being" (TJ, 476).

But this line of argument exposes Rawls to two serious difficulties. First, it undermines what he regards as the central feature of Kant's ethics and of his own theory—the priority of right, and hence of justice, over the good (TJ, 31). If justice is desirable because it aims at our good as moral persons, then justice as fairness rests on a specific conception of the good, from which the "constraints" of right and justice are ultimately derived. "Once this is understood," Rawls asserts in the Dewey lectures, "the constraints of the original position are no longer external" (532). To which he should have added—they are no longer contraints at all, but rather the objects of rational desire.

Second, to the extent that justice as fairness rests on a theory of the objective good, applicable to every human being, regulative of every desire, Rawls must defend this theory both against its competitors and against the sorts of objections he elsewhere raises against notions of rationally justified final aims. That is, he must enter into precisely that arena of conflicting perfectionist claims that the formal structure of justice as fairness was designed to sidestep. And he must answer more fully the contentions of those who—with Williams—see in Rawls's Kantian universalism a systematic violation of the individualistic particularity that characterizes the human good.

VI

So far we have discussed the implications of excluding individual character and conceptions of the good from free and equal moral personality. We now reach the most controversial exclusion: differences of natural endowment, that is, of skills and talents and of the propensity to develop and exercise them. Rawls's argument, familiar since *A Theory of Justice* and reinforced in the Dewey lectures, is that natural differences are as much the product of accident and chance as are differences of family background and social circumstance. Because natural differences, like those of family and social class, are arbitrary from a moral point of view, they are in principle unsuited to serve as the bases of distributive outcomes.

To this argument Robert Nozick and, more recently, Michael Zuckert have offered a powerful retort. Rawls's rejection of the moral force of natural assets rests on the proposition that desert claims cannot be based on something undeserved. But this proposition is questionable, perhaps incoherent. To begin with, there is nothing self-contradictory about basing a claim on some undeserved feature of yourself, as long as you did not come to possess it by arbitrarily depriving someone else of his or her legitimate possession.[9] Second, the demand that desert bases be deserved amounts to a nullification of the entire procedure of claiming. As Zuckert says, we "either have an infinite regress of bases of desert or arrive at some basis, some beginning point, which the individual cannot claim to have deserved or to be responsible for."[10] Moral personality is no exception, for one's existence as a moral person is every bit as accidental and undeserved as are any special abilities and traits of character.

Now, one can imagine Rawls replying to this by dismissing altogether the relevance of desert for distributive justice. There is no dilemma: Desert *is* an incoherent concept, but a properly constructed theory of justice can get along perfectly well without it. Indeed, justice as fairness is the theory that results from denying the existence of any "prior and independent notion of desert, perfectionist or intuitionist, that could override or restrict the agreement of the parties" (551-552).

But matters are not so simple, for you can only get to be a party to the agreement if you are a moral person. If you are not (if you are, say, a chimpanzee), then your interests are of no weight in determining acceptable principles of justice. Or—to put it the other way around— moral personality is the basis of your claim to be taken into account. As Rawls himself puts it, all moral persons (and, he might have added, only moral persons) think of themselves and of one another as "self-originating sources of claims," which they are not required to justify further (548). And thus, if by desert we mean "the possession of some attribute in light of which an individual's claims are accorded moral weight," then Rawls does not (as he seems to believe) dispense with desert altogether. Rather, he establishes, as the sole relevant desert basis, a feature of our lives (moral personality) that equally character- izes nearly all of us. But—to repeat—he cannot employ the distinction between the arbitrary and the nonarbitrary to do this, because moral personality is every bit as contingent as any other feature of our existence. The exclusion of natural endowments from Rawls's theory of valid claims represents a *choice* of equal over unequal claims.

Rawls is hardly unaware that he has made this choice. He attempts to justify it in the Dewey lectures by appealing to the formal features of a theory of justice. In constructing such a theory, we are not really interested in individual cases. Rather,

> we seek principles to regulate the basic structure into which we are born to live a complete life. The thesis is that the only relevant feature in connection with these principles is the capacity for moral personality [551].

The question then becomes: Why is the principle of "fair equality of opportunity"—expectations of success based on effort and ability, without regard to background or social class—unsuited to govern the basic structure of society? As far as I can tell, Rawls gives only one answer: As long as the institution of the family is allowed to exist, fair equality can be only imperfectly realized (TJ, 74).

This is of course true. But it hardly constitutes a decisive argument against fair equality of opportunity. *If* effort and ability ought to be reflected in distributive outcomes, then the pattern that emerges when natural endowments are filtered through the family may be the best we can attain, even though there will be significant deviations from pure equality of opportunity. From the fact that there will be deviations, it does *not* follow that the second-best solution is a basic structure that ignores effort and ability altogether.

Besides, few proponents of fair equality of opportunity insist that it must be the sole principle governing the basic structure of society. Most recognize that other principles and institutions must be given due weight. Typically, fair equality of opportunity is only part (albeit an important part) of a broader conception of an ideal society in which opportunities for development of individual talents are maximized. Taken as a whole, the evidence suggests, the institution of the family plays a key role in individual development. Thus, proponents of the thesis that natural endowments have moral weight will be willing to balance pure fairness against (say) the average level of individual development. Pure fairness at a lower level (*ex hypothesi*, without the family) may reasonably be regarded as inferior to a measure of unfairness at a higher level. And this is especially likely to be true if social institutions other than the family—property, education, compensatory programs— are arranged so as to mitigate unfairness.

The issue between Rawls and proponents of fair equality of opportunity, then, turns on differing conceptions of what political society is *for*. Rawls looks to the development and exercise of moral personality; his opponents emphasize a fuller range of human powers.

Rawls cannot legitimately criticize proponents of fair equality of opportunity as teleologists, for his own theory is teleological in exactly the same sense: "Free persons," as Rawls conceives of them, "have a regulative and effective desire to be a certain kind of person" (548). Nor can Rawls simply appeal to the greater parsimony of his conception, for, as Bernard Williams has forcefully reminded us, parsimony in moral theory is hardly a neutral or formal criterion. It entails, rather, an abstraction from concrete individual moral life, which ought to enjoy a natural primacy in our moral reflection, at least as a point of departure. It is therefore the movement toward—not away from—a narrower conception of personality that requires special justification.

Rawls's most powerful objection to the "full development" theory underlying fair equality of opportunity is that is presupposes, as a ground of agreement on principles of justice, knowledge of a specific conception of the good. But this is precisely the sort of knowledge that should be excluded "in order to have a lucid representation of the notion of freedom that characterizes a Kantian view" (550). But it is at this point that Rawls *diverges* from the Kantian view. In *The Doctrine of Virtue*, Kant argues that

> it is a command of morally practical reason and a duty of man to himself to cultivate his powers . . . and to be, from a pragmatic point of view, a man equal to the end of his existence.[11]

As Patrick Riley has recently argued, it is hardly possible to make sense of Kant's moral philosophy unless this teleological component is given due weight. To treat "rational nature" as an "end in itself" is to treat the development of human powers, *broadly* conceived, as a duty.[12] Without this premise, Kant's treatment of the South Sea Islands example in the *Foundations of the Metaphysics of Morals* is unintelligible. Because Kant sees this teleology of natural powers as *contained* in the conception of the person, he does not regard it as conflicting in any way with his understanding of moral freedom. Thus, Rawls is quite correct to identify Kantian "autonomy" with whatever is contained in Kant's concept of moral personality and to stress that "in a Kantian doctrine a relatively complex conception of the person plays a central role" (559-560). But, ironically, Rawls departs from Kant's understanding of freedom because his conception of the person is *less* complex than Kant's. And it is only this deviation that permits Rawls to rule out—as a breach of freedom—the view of individual personality and development that underlies the doctrine of fair equality of opportunity.

245

VII

The conceptual arguments supporting Rawls's view of personality as the appropriate point of departure for social theory are, we have seen, far from persuasive. But his view cannot be adequately understood on this plane alone, for it is embedded in a broader vision of the nature and purpose of political philosophy.

The highest task of traditional political philosophy was the comparative evaluation of regimes. To this end, philosophers in the tradition developed ideal accounts of desirable political orders, in the form either of discursive principles or of concrete depictions of utopias. The "death" of political philosophy proclaimed a generation ago was the loss of confidence in the possibility of political evaluation, so conceived. Rawls's *A Theory of Justice* was greeted with excitement in large measure because it moved boldly to restore the legitimacy of political evaluation. His "ideal theory," abstracted from the empirical contingencies that differentiate existing political orders, was designed to judge and (when possible) to improve them. And, Rawls contended, his theory was neither produced by specific historical or social circumstances nor intended to defend any existing order. The theory was rather "impartial," for it was constructed *sub specie aeternitatis*, regarding the human situation "not only from all social but also from all temporal points of view" (TJ, 587).

There was, however, a striking difference between Rawls and the tradition. Previously, ideal theory had been a prelude to the severe critique of existing orders, for reflections on images of good politics had always highlighted the imperfections of actuality. But in Rawls's case, theory was a prelude to the celebration of a political order that bore a remarkable resemblance to the modern liberal-democratic welfare state. Naturally the left wing of the Democratic party was delighted to hear its platform ringingly intoned by the Voice of Eternity. Marxists and conservatives were, predictably, less enthralled. They argued that Rawls's theory was solidly rooted in place and circumstance, ideological in nature and effect if not in intention and appearance.[13]

In the Dewey lectures, Rawls has conceded the substance of conservative and Marxist allegations about the provenance of his theory. Gone are the references to eternity:

We are not trying to find a conception of justice suitable for all societies regardless of their particular social or historical circumstances. We want to settle a fundamental disagreement over the just form of basic institutions within a

democratic society under modern conditions. . . . How far the conclusions we reach
are of interest in a wider context is a separate question [518].

This is a shift of epistemology as well as of intention. Political
philosophy, Rawls now contends, is always addressed to a specific
"public culture." It appeals to the principles latent in the common sense
of that culture or proposes principles "congenial to its most essential
convictions and historical traditions." In particular, Kantian constructivism (Rawls's reconstruction of justice as fairness) addresses the public
culture of a democratic society, and it rests on a "conception of the
person implicitly affirmed in that culture, or else one that would prove
acceptable to citizens once it was properly presented and explained"
(518). Thus, the basic materials from which Rawls's principles of justice
are constructed are embedded in, and determined by, a specific public
culture. But, Rawls adds, "apart from the procedure of constructing the
principles of justice, there are no moral facts" (519). It follows that there
are no general principles or particular judgments *external* to the shared
understanding of a public culture that can be employed to judge the
worth of that culture, taken as a whole.

This conclusion has an important bearing on the central metaethical
thesis of the Dewey lectures. Rawls develops a distinction between two
types of ethical theory. *Rational intuitionism* asserts that the first
principles of morality are

fixed by a moral order that is prior to and independent of our conception of the
person and the social role of morality. This order is given by the nature of things
and is known . . . by rational intuition [557].

Kantian constructivism, by contrast, specifies a "particular conception
of the person" and a "reasonable procedure of construction" (516).
Principles of justice are constructed by persons, so conceived, through
that procedure, without appealing to any prior moral facts. In Rawls's
view, the very possibility of Kantian constructivism blunts the strongest
argument in favor of intuitionism, that some form of intuitionist theory
is necessary if objectivity is to be achieved (570).

If the only issue between intuitionism and constructivism were the
location of key premises (the natural order and the person, respectively),
Rawls's point would be well taken. The difficulty, of course, is that
constructivists must offer some support for the specific conception of
the person they choose to employ. Here they encounter a dilemma. If
they appeal to something external to the person to justify their choice,

they return to intuitionism through the back door. If they do not, they must concede that the formal *concept* of personality is compatible with a wide variety of *conceptions*, each of which would lead to somewhat different moral conclusions through the procedure of construction.

As we have seen, Rawls constrains this choice by looking for a conception appropriate to democratic culture. But unless one has some prior reason for preferring democratic to nondemocratic culture, this either pushes the problem of justification back one step, without resolving it, or it changes the question entirely. Objectivity within a culture is *not* what intuitionists mean by objectivity. The moral order on which they rest their case is (or so they think) accessible to human beings as such, not just to Britons and Americans. Thus, Rawls defends constructivism against the charge of relativism only by altering the very conception of objectivity, in a manner that has the effect of conceding the substance, if not the letter, of the intuitionist critique.

Rawls's reconstructed theory is divided against itself. It is explicitly Kantian, but implicitly Hegelian. It avoids formalism only at the cost of abandoning the Kantian standpoint above history and culture. Instead, the content of its principles is provided by the shared beliefs of the democratic community. The new task of political philosophy is to develop these implicit principles into a coherent structure, that is, to display the community to itself by bringing it to full consciousness of itself.[14]

Rawls deviates even farther from Kant by stressing the "practical" task of political philosophy. We are to look for principles that can achieve a "public and workable agreement on matters of social justice which suffices for effective and fair social cooperation" (560). We must thus set to one side the difficult issues raised by relations between societies and between the human species and other living things (524). We must accept, as fixed constraints, the basic features of modern democratic society. We must discard first principles that cannot be generally understood and easily applied. We must rule out certain moral considerations as irrelevant because eliminating them increases the capacity of the remaining considerations to fulfill their social role. We must lay aside inconvenient facts about unfortunate human beings— congenitally inadequate mental powers, unusual and costly needs—with which social theory and practice must eventually come to grips (546). And we must employ concepts that, as far as possible, are publicly verifiable and "less open to dispute" (563). If the publicity condition is to be satisfied, therefore, we must sacrifice some portion of what we believe to be morally relevant, making do instead with rough-and-ready approximations. It is in this light, Rawls explains, that such features of his theory as the basic structure, priority rules, and primary goods, are to be understood (561-563). Rawls sums up this strategy of argument as follows:

> We are accustomed to the idea that secondary norms and working criteria, by which our views are applied, must be adjusted to the normal requirements of social life as well as to the limited capacities of human reasoning.... But we tend to regard these adjustments as made in the light of various first principles, or a single principle. First principles themselves are not widely regarded as affected by practical limitations and social requirements. [But in Kantian constructivism, the] very content of the first principles of justice ... is determined in part by the practical task of political philosophy [543].

The contrast with Kant's own views could not be starker. For Kant, first principles lose all their moral force if they are shaped by the requirements of social practice. Kant concedes (as any theorist must) that "ought implies can." But Kant defines "possibility" relative, not to the social world as we know it, but rather to conceivable transformations of that world. And he places the burden of proof on the proponents of impossibility. Unless it can be *shown* that an otherwise compelling moral proposition rests on an assumption that cannot ever be realized, the proposition must be accorded full normative weight, even though it cuts radically against the grain of prevailing beliefs and practices, even though it makes the most stringent demands on our powers of moral reflection and action. For Kant, it is *reason*—not the need for agreement, not the circumstances of agreement—that determines the content of our appropriate social undertakings.

Rawls has an answer to this: His deviation from Kant in the name of social practice is necessary and proper because it helps to overcome the "dualisms" that disfigure Kant's doctrine (516). But matters are not so simple. From Aristotle to the present day, the point of ideal theory has been to elucidate the first principles that would be fully actualized in the most favorable circumstances conceivable, as a guide for action in the much less hospitable circumstances of ordinary political life. To build the circumstances of ordinary life into our first principles is of course to reduce the gap between theory and practice. But it is also to forget the point of having first principles—to judge our practices, not merely to codify them.[15]

Moreover, the "practical" conception of first principles opens the door to the arbitrary selection of practical constraints. For example, Rawls refuses to rest the content of first principles on highly developed powers of reflection, because such powers cannot be regarded as widely shared. But he does not hesitate to presuppose (against all evidence) that a sense of justice (or at least a capacity for it) *is* widely shared. I confess that I do not see the ground for distinguishing these two cases. If we are allowed to take our bearings from fully developed moral powers, even though most individuals do not possess them, then why cannot the content of first principles reflect fully developed intellectual powers, rather than the average powers of the individuals we encounter in daily life? Why is Rawls willing to be so noumenal, so counterfactual in the one case, so phenomenal and practical in the other?

I suspect that in this case (as in so many others), the conclusions Rawls wishes to reach dictate the premises he chooses to employ. It is at least possible to conjecture that under the most favorable circumstances, all or nearly all individuals will develop roughly equal capabilities for moral conduct. This conjecture becomes especially plausible if we focus, in good Kantian fashion, on intention rather than performance. But the parallel conjecture in the case of intellectual powers would be wholly incredible. Under the most favorable circumstances, the undeniable inequalities of natural intellectual endowment would necessarily be reflected in inequalities of intellectual performance. To incorporate fully developed moral powers into our first principles of justice is to support the moral legitimacy of equality. To incorporate fully developed intellectual powers would be to open the door to—if not to legitimate—various forms of social hierarchy. For if principles of social organization are complex and difficult to apply, then the cause of justice itself may require a ruling class selected on the basis of superior intellectual competence. Rawls's practical *conception* of political philosophy is, I suspect, governed by his overall practical *intention*—to uphold the principle of equality that stands at the heart of democratic culture.

VIII

The Dewey lectures thus set aside the central concern of traditional political philosophy and put in its place a new set of questions, to which justice as fairness purports to provide the answer. How are "we"— reflective citizens of a liberal democracy—to understand freedom and equality, the ideals to which we are individually and collectively committed? How are we to resolve the recurrent conflict between these ideals? Which principles of justice are most consistent with them, and how are we to transform these principles into workable institutions?

These new questions are well worth asking. But justice as fairness departs so sharply from our shared self-understanding that Rawls cannot plausibly claim to be making our intuitions explicit, or to be providing a foundation for what we already believe.

For there is (at least in broad outline) a contemporary American consensus concerning just principles and institutions. Every citizen is entitled to at least a minimally decent existence. Those who are able to work receive the wherewithal to live decently in the form of wages. Those who cannot work—either because they are incapable of working or because they cannot find work to do—are to be compensated by the community. Those who can work but choose not to have no valid claims against other individuals or against the community. Above the level of minimal decency defined by the minimum wage, the welfare system, unemployment insurance, and social security, individuals are permitted to achieve unequal rewards by developing their natural talents and persuading others to employ and remunerate them. The community supervises this domain of competitive inequality by equalizing opportunities to develop talents and by ensuring that the distribution of rewards is governed by task-related factors rather than such irrelevant characteristics as race, sex, and family background. But it is recognized that this supervision will necessarily remain imperfect, because fair equality of opportunity could be fully achieved only through a system of total regulation that would gravely impede the ability of individuals to lead their lives as they see fit.

Underlying this broad consensus about justice are general conceptions of equality and freedom. Individuals are held to be morally equal, in the sense that membership in the human species suffices to engender certain minimal claims that other members are obliged to honor. At the same time, individuals are naturally unequal, in ways that both generate and legitimate differences of occupation, income, and status. Individuals are held to be morally free in several respects. They enjoy a sphere of privacy within which coercive interference by other individuals or by the state is thought to be illegitimate. They may select and pursue their own plans of life. And they are free, finally, because they are considered—and consider themselves to be—responsible for the choices they make. But individual freedom is far from unlimited. It is circumscribed by duties both to ourselves and to others. We owe it to ourselves to develop our gifts so that we may lead lives of independence and self-respect. We owe it to others to honor the valid claims they have against us, claims that precede (and to some extent govern) our collective choice of social principles and institutions.

Rawls's conception of free and equal moral personality diverges radically from this American understanding of freedom and equality and leads to principles of justice significantly different from those most Americans embrace. Rawlsian moral freedom liberates us from all antecedent principles—all duties and obligations, all intrinsic values other than freedom itself. Rawlsian moral equality reduces to moral nullity the respects in which we are naturally unequal. And Rawlsian justice severs the link between what we *do* and what we *deserve*. The valid claims we address to one another are based on being rather than doing, on bare abstract existence, shorn of any of the features that distinguish us from one another.

Rawls is well aware of the extent of his divergence from prevailing beliefs. In a telling sentence he declares that "the way in which we think about fairness in everyday life all prepares us for the great shift in perspective required for considering the justice of the basic structure itself" (551). But it is *Rawls* who ill prepares us for this shift. The conceptual foundation of the basic structure—free and equal moral personality—is supposedly addressed to the citizens of our society. But Rawls's reconstruction of justice as fairness does *not* invoke—indeed, it flatly rejects—the conception of the person underlying our beliefs and practices. There is little evidence to support—and much to refute— Rawls's hope that his conception of personality will prove acceptable to us once its implications are fully grasped. Yet his "constructivist" metatheory leaves him no other grounds of persuasion or verification.

What has led Rawls to this impasse? I conclude with two hypotheses, one rooted in the itinerary of modern social philosophy, the other in the vagaries of contemporary politics.

Rawls is of course a leading figure in the recent revival of nor- mative social philosophy. In crucial respects, however, this revival remains rooted in the climate of moral skepticism that it has supplanted. Few contemporary theorists (and Rawls is surely no exception) are more willing than were their overtly skeptical predecessors to entertain perfectionist, intuitionist, or naturalist theses. But modern liberal- democratic culture contains many elements of this sort. Thus, any philosophic attempt to reconstruct this culture on quasi-skeptical foundations is bound to do violence to the beliefs of its members. As we have seen, Rawls's proposed reconstruction, carried out in Kant's name, goes so far as to reject perfectionist principles that Kant found it necessary to affirm as elements of both his moral and his political philosophy, principles that we continue to embrace.

It is, in the second place, not accidental that Rawls's thought came to fruition and burst into prominence at the very moment that "advanced" liberal politics, preoccupied with the plight of the worst-off groups in our society, severed its bonds with the moral convictions of the working class. For it is the American working class that clings most fervently to the principle of fair equality of opportunity, to desert as the basis of distribution, to ability, effort, and self-denial as the bases of desert. In their zeal to right the wrongs inflicted on the least advantaged, liberal politicians employed rhetoric and adopted programs that, in effect if not in intention, rejected the beliefs and undercut the interests of the working class.

What these politicians initiated in practice, Rawls brought to completion in theory. It was one thing for moral philosophers to advocate sacrifice in the name of fair equality of opportunity, but quite another for the leading philosopher of the age to discard this principle altogether. For justice as fairness was a systematic effort to reject, as morally irrelevant, precisely those features of human life on which the claims, and the self-respect, of the lower middle class rested. Rawls severed the connection between the willingness to produce and the right to consume; he replaced claims based on achievement with those based on bare existence; he dismissed, as unrelated or even hostile to the conduct of our public life, the claims of natural duty, of particularity, and of religion.

The practical results of this strategy are now all too clear. The high ground yielded by liberal politicians was quickly seized by the forces of reaction. A similar process is likely on the plane of theory, unless contemporary philosophers of liberalism remain open to the historic principles of liberalism. Rawls offers us a dangerously one-sided reconstruction of the liberal tradition. It is the responsibility of his critics to show how those elements of this tradition that he has so unwisely repudiated may be restored to their rightful place.[16]

NOTES

1. Bernard Crick, quoted in Norman Daniels, ed., *Reading Rawls* (New York: Basic Books, 1975), p. xvi.

2. John Rawls, "Kantian Constructivism in Moral Theory," *Journal of Philosophy*, vol. 77, no. 9, pp. 515-572. Unless otherwise noted, all page references in the text will be to this work.

3. Remarkably, this alteration in the *basis* of primary goods effects no changes whatever in the *enumeration* of these goods. Rawls simply sketches a brief explanation of why the interest in moral personality will lead parties in the original position to pursue the primary goods set forth in *A Theory of Justice*. But the fit between the new basis of primary goods and their unchanged content seems less than perfect. For example, Rawls argues that basic liberties "allow for the development and exercise of the sense of . . . justice" (526). This is in a way true. But one might rather argue that basic liberties allow for the development and expression of a *wide range* of moral positions and characteristics, many of which pull—directly or indirectly—against the sense of justice. Basic liberties enable those who doubt the rationality of justice, or scorn it altogether, to constitute a portion of the public culture that educates the young. In modern democracies, anyway, basic liberties seem to promote license at least as much as self-restraint—hardly a promising backdrop for the inculcation of virtues, such as justice, that demand restraint. This problem is especially serious if, as Aristotle argued, an effective sense of justice cuts across the grain of human nature, at least for most people, and can only be fostered through a rigorously directive system of moral education, backed by the full power of political and social institutions. Thus, the question whether the sense of justice is more effectively promoted in an open society or in a suitably designed closed society cannot be regarded as settled.

4. John Rawls, "Fairness to Goodness," *Philosophical Review*, vol. 84 (October 1975), p. 537.

5. For more than a decade, Rawls's critics have charged that his theory is in principle incapable of dealing with the problem of special needs. To the best of my knowledge, Rawls has never attempted a response. The Dewey lectures continue and even deepen this odd silence by ruling the question out of court. Rawls now stipulates that no party in the original position "suffers from unusual needs that are especially difficult to fulfill . . . the fundamental problem of social justice arises between those who are full and active . . . participants in society" (546). He goes on to talk vaguely about extending the theory, so conceived, to hard cases. But he never does so, and it is difficult to see how he could do so in a manner consistent with his basic approach. Unusual and costly needs present difficulties that simply cannot be addressed by an index of primary goods.

6. Bernard Williams, "Persons, Character and Morality," in Amelie Oksenberg Rorty, ed., *The Identities of Persons* (Berkeley: University of California Press, 1976), pp. 210, 215.

7. This is roughly the Platonic/Aristotelean view as I understand it. One can imagine a variant of the perfectionist interpretation that does give priority to justice, so defined.

8. In this respect, at least, Rawls is squarely in the Kantian tradition. Early on in the *Foundations of the Metaphysics of Morals* Kant declares that nothing is good without qualification except a good will. He proceeds to examine the classical virtues—wisdom, courage, moderation—showing that each can be viewed as evil in certain circumstances. But he excludes justice from this critique, apparently because he cannot see how justice could ever be evil. Indeed, Kant comes very close to equating the good will with justice.

9. Robert Nozick, *Anarchy, State, and Utopia* (New York: Basic Books, 1974), pp. 224-227.

10. Michael Zuckert, "Justice Deserted: A Critique of Rawls' *A Theory of Justice*," *Polity*, vol. 13, no. 3, pp. 477.

11. Immanuel Kant, *The Doctrine of Virtue*, Mary J. Gregor, trans., (New York: Harper & Row, 1964), p. 111.

12. Patrick Riley, "Practical Reason and Respect for Persons in the Kantian Republic," (paper delivered at the 1981 Annual Meeting of the American Political Science Association).

13. For an example of the conservative critique, see David Lewis Schaefer, *Justice or Tyranny?: A Critique of John Rawls's "Theory of Justice"* (Port Washington, NY: Kennikat, 1979), ch. 5. For an example of the Marxist version, see Milton Fisk, "History and Reason in Rawls' Moral Theory," in Daniels, 1975, pp. 53-80.

14. Obviously this parallel with Hegel cannot be extended very far. Hegel contended that to bring a community to full self-consciousness is to make manifest its latent contradictions. Rawls appears to believe that this very process is the vehicle for *eliminating* contradictions. Specifically, Rawls believes in the possibility of a recognizably liberal society (and theory) in which all significant internal tensions have been overcome.

15. For a fuller discussion of these points, see William A. Galston, *Justice and the Human Good* (Chicago: University of Chicago Press, 1980), pp. 13-16.

16. For a preliminary attempt to do this, see William A. Galston, "Defending Liberalism," *American Political Science Review*, vol. 76, no. 3, pp. 621-629.

William A. Galston is Associate Professor in the Department of Government, University of Texas at Austin. From September 1980 to January 1982 he was a Visiting Fellow at the Institution for Social and Policy Studies, Yale University. Since June 1982, he has served as Director of Policy Planning for Walter F. Mondale. Among his recent works is Justice and the Human Good *(University of Chicago Press, 1980). He is currently working on a book about liberalism.*

CANADIAN JOURNAL OF PHILOSOPHY   71
Volume 17, Number 1, March 1987, pp. 71-90

Rawlsian Constructivism in Moral Theory

DAVID O. BRINK
Case Western Reserve University
Cleveland, OH 44106
U.S.A.

I Introduction

Since his article, 'Outline for a Decision Procedure in Ethics,' John Rawls has advocated a coherentist moral epistemology according to which moral and political theories are justified on the basis of their coherence with our other beliefs, both moral and nonmoral (1951: 56, 61).[1] A moral theory which is maximally coherent with our other beliefs is in a state which Rawls calls 'reflective equilibrium' (1971: 20). In *A Theory of Justice* Rawls advanced two principles of justice and claimed that they are in reflective equilibrium. He defended this claim by appeal to a hypothetical contract; he argued that parties in a position satisfying certain informational and motivational criteria, which he called 'the original position,' would choose the following two principles of justice to govern the basic structure of their society.

1. Each person is to have an equal right to the most extensive total system of equal basic liberties compatible with a similar system of liberty for all.

---

1 Cf. 1971: 19-21, 46-51, 579-81; 1974: 7; 1980: 534. References to Rawls' writings are by year of publication and page. My discussion will draw on 'Outline for a Decision Procedure in Ethics,' *Philosophical Review* **60** (1951) 177-97 reprinted in J. Thomson and G. Dworkin, eds., *Ethics* (New York: Harper and Row 1968); *A Theory of Justice* (Cambridge, MA: Harvard University Press 1971); 'The Independence of Moral Theory,' *Proceedings and Addresses of the APA* **48** (1974) 5-22; 'Fairness to Goodness,' *Philosophical Review* **84** (1975) 536-54; 'A Well-Ordered Society' in P. Laslett and J. Fishkin, eds., *Philosophy, Politics, and Society*, fifth series (New Haven: Yale University Press 1979); 'Kantian Constructivism in Moral Theory' *The Journal of Philosophy* **77** (1980) 515-72; and 'Social Unity and Primary Goods' in A. Sen and B. Williams, eds., *Utilitarianism and Beyond* (New York: Cambridge University Press 1982).

2. Social and economic inequalities are to be arranged so that they
are both (a) to the greatest benefit of the least advantaged and
(b) attached to offices and positions open to all under fair conditions of equality of opportunity (1971: 302).

Rawls refers to this conception of justice as 'justice as fairness.'

Although Rawls claimed that theories of the person play an important part in the justification of theories of justice (1971: 258-65, 584)
and explored a Kantian interpretation of his theory of justice (1971:
251-7), he did not provide a systematic justification of his use of the
original position or the contract device. Instead, he claimed only that
features of the original position represent various considered judgments
about conditions of fairness in choice.

But Rawls' recent Dewey Lectures, 'Kantian Constructivism in Moral
Theory,' make good this weakness. There Rawls does provide a
systematic justification of the original position; he offers rich and subtle argument to show that a Kantian ideal of the person which conceives of persons as free, equal, rational, and socially cooperative
motivates the use of a contract device, underlies the original position
and explains its various features.

There is a wealth of interesting and persuasive argument in Rawls'
Dewey Lectures which I will not discuss. Instead, I want to focus on
his defense of Kantian constructivism. Someone who had followed the
development of Rawls' views to this point might easily have concluded that Rawls had now completed a realist defense of his theory of
justice. Rawls claims that his two principles of justice would be chosen
by contractors in the original position, and the original position is supposed to represent the constraints of a Kantian ideal of the person.
One would have thought that he was claiming that this ideal of the
person is true independently of anyone's beliefs or evidence, from
which it would follow that Rawls' theory of justice purports to be objectively true. But Rawls resists this interpretation. In fact, I will argue,
he can be understood to claim that this appeal to a Kantian ideal of
the person supports an anti-realist, constructivist thesis about ethics.

I am fully aware that this anti-realist construal of Rawls' constructivism will be controversial. But, then, any consistent interpretation
of Kantian constructivism is likely to be controversial. Rawls' statements
of and justification for his constructivist thesis are neither always clear
nor always consistent. What I claim is that the text of the Dewey Lectures supports an anti-realist construal of Kantian constructivism and
that the Dewey Lectures and Rawls' other writings contain an argument for Kantian constructivism, so construed. Though I think that
this reconstruction provides the best interpretation of the disparate
claims Rawls makes about Kantian constructivism, I do not think that

I need be committed to this strong exegetical claim. This anti-realist reading is a possible, natural, and fairly common interpretation of Rawls' claims, and so it is worth seeing how plausible Kantian constructivism is when construed in this way.

To anticipate the results of my reconstruction: constructivism is or implies an anti-realist metaethical view according to which moral truth is constituted by our moral beliefs, in particular, by our ideals of the person. Kantian constructivism is that set of moral truths constituted by a Kantian ideal of the person. Rawls believes that ideals of the person play a very important role in framing and justifying moral theories. But ideals of the person are themselves underdetermined and so underdetermine theory choice in ethics. The best explanation of this underdetermination is that there are no evidence-independent moral facts; moral facts or truth must be relativized to or defined in terms of ideals of the person. Hence, moral realism is false; constructivist anti-realism is true.

If this reconstruction of Kantian constructivism is correct, we can identify a tension in Rawls' epistemological views. Rawls' argument for constructivism requires him to assign to ideals of the person an evidential role incompatible with a coherentist moral epistemology. But, I shall argue, a coherence theory of justification in ethics of the sort Rawls himself has advocated allows one to recognize the importance of ideals of the person in moral theory and the existence of competing ideals without conceding any anti-realist claims.

As I have indicated, Rawls' argument for constructivism requires reconstruction, largely because his own position and argument at various points are obscure or ambiguous. Therefore, before we can properly examine and assess Rawls' argument, we need to reconstruct his claims.

II Intuitionism and Coherence in Ethics

Rawls' official epistemological position is clear; in explaining the justification of his theory of justice, Rawls writes: 'Here the test is that of general and wide reflective equilibrium, that is, how well the view as a whole meshes with and articulates our more firm considered convictions, at all levels of generality, after due examination, once all adjustments and revisions that seem compelling have been made. A doctrine that meets this criterion is the doctrine that, so far as we can now ascertain, is the most reasonable for us' (1980: 534). Wide reflection equilibrium represents a coherence theory of justification in ethics. A coherence theory of justification in ethics claims that A's moral belief p is justified insofar as (a) p is part of a coherent system of moral and nonmoral beliefs, and (b) p's coherence at least partially explains why A holds p.[2] The degree of A's justification in holding p varies directly with the degree of coherence exhibited by the belief system of which p is a member. The degree of a belief system's coherence is a function of its comprehensiveness and of the logical, probabilistic, and explanatory relations holding among members of the system.

Coherence theories of justification contrast with foundationalist theories. Foundationalist theories claim that A's moral belief p is justified just in case p is either (a) foundational (i.e. non-inferentially justified or self-justifying) or (b) based on the appropriate kind of inferences from foundational beliefs. Versions of foundationalism differ according to how they specify the nature and content of foundational beliefs and what kind of inferences they recognize as justifying non-foundational beliefs. Almost all defenders of moral foundationalism have been intuitionists; Clarke, Price, Reid, Sidgwick, Moore, Prichard, Ross, and Broad were all intuitionists. Intuitionism is that version of moral foundationalism which holds that A's moral belief p is justified just in case p is either (a) foundational or (b) based on the appropriate kind of inference from foundational *moral* beliefs. The intuitionist requires of every justified moral belief that it be foundational or that the termini of its justification include foundational moral beliefs. Moreover, intuitionism is non-skeptical; it claims that there are foundational moral beliefs and that we have knowledge of evidence-independent moral facts.

Intuitionism claims, among other things, that all moral knowledge is or rests upon non-inferentially justified moral beliefs, while coherentism claims that all moral justification is inferential and that moral beliefs are justified insofar as they cohere with other beliefs we do or might hold. This contrast between intuitionism and coherentism will be important to both the identification and assessment of Rawls' constructivist position.

III Kantian Constructivism

What is Kantian constructivism? Rawls sometimes distinguishes between constructivism and Kantian constructivism; Kantian constructivism is apparently one kind of constructivist doctrine. The Dewey

---

2 Cf. Norman Daniels, 'Wide Reflective Equilibrium and Theory Acceptance in Ethics' *Journal of Philosophy* **76** (1979) 256-82 and my *Moral Realism and the Foundations of Ethics* (New York: Cambridge University Press forthcoming), chapters 5 and 6.

Lectures represent, among other things, Rawls' recognition of the importance of theories of the person in moral theory and of the way in which his own conception of justice as fairness depends upon a Kantian theory of the person. This suggests, what will be confirmed below, that constructivism in some way recognizes the importance of theories of the person and incorporates them into moral theory; Kantian constructivism is a constructivist view incorporating a Kantian ideal of the person.

Though this gives us some idea of constructivism, Kantian constructivism, and their relation to each other, it leaves many questions unanswered. How does constructivism incorporate theories of the person? Rawls claims that constructivism yields a conception of objectivity in ethics. What view of objectivity is it supposed to imply? How is this conception of objectivity related to other conceptions? Why does recognition of the importance of theories of the person in moral theory imply any conception of objectivity? Unfortunately, Rawls is not as clear about these issues as one would like. It is necessary for us to reconstruct his claims here.

Since constructivist views are usually metaphysical views which contrast with realist views, it would be natural to interpret Kantian constructivism as a form of anti-realism about ethics. Indeed, I do think that this is a natural and defensible construal of Kantian constructivism. However, it is worth comparing this metaphysical construal of Kantian constructivism with two other construals, since Rawls makes a variety of different claims about Kantian constructivism.

A *methodological* construal of constructivism relies on Rawls' distinction in 'The Independence of Moral Theory' between moral *theory* and moral *philosophy* (1974: 5-7, 21). Moral theory merely articulates given moral conceptions or structures and is not concerned with the truth or plausibility of these conceptions or structures. So moral theory is neutral with respect to the metaphysical, epistemological, and semantic questions about ethics which moral philosophy addresses. Indeed, at the beginning of the Dewey Lectures Rawls claims that the aim of political philosophy as well as that of political theory is '... to articulate and make explicit those shared notions and principles thought to be already latent in common sense; or, as is often the case, if common sense is hesitant and uncertain, and doesn't know what to think, to propose to it certain conceptions and principles congenial to its most essential convictions and historical traditions' (1980: 518). On this construal, constructivism represents no more than an articulation of a particular moral and political structure, in particular, a particular theory of the person. Kantian constructivism would then articulate a moral structure based on a Kantian theory of the person. As a methodological constructivist, Rawls would simply be agnostic about the truth or plausibility of a Kantian theory of the person and of the moral structure which it supports.

Rawls does claim that the contractors are agents of construction and that they view themselves as determining, rather than discovering, principles of justice (1980: 524, 564, 568), and this may seem to threaten the metaphysical neutrality (and, hence, a methodological construal) of constructivism. But these are claims which hold *within* the social contract device and so should have no metaphysical import. The contract is an analytical device to be used in moral theory and is not intended to represent the way the world is. Just as the disinterestedness of the contractors shows nothing about human motivation, the contractors' view of themselves as agents of construction (if, indeed, they do or should so view themselves) has no implications for the metaethical status of the two principles of justice which result from the contract device. A methodological construal of constructivism, therefore, would be metaphysically, epistemologically, and semantically neutral and so would presuppose no anti-realist metaethical view.

An *epistemological* construal of constructivism results from taking it to represent a coherence theory of justification in ethics. Epistemological constructivism represents recognition of the importance of theories of the person within a coherentist moral epistemology. Rawls clearly advocates a coherentist moral epistemology. Though an epistemological construal of constructivism could not, of course, be epistemologically agnostic, it could be agnostic about the sort of metaphysical issues about ethics which moral realism and anti-realism concern. In particular, as long as a coherence theory of justification does not require a coherence theory of truth, an epistemological construal of Kantian constructivism does not require an anti-realist metaethical view.

Finally, a *metaphysical* construal of constructivism results from taking it to represent an anti-realist metaethical view. Realist theories about a subject matter x usually claim that (a) there are facts or truths of kind x, and (b) these facts or truths are metaphysically or conceptually independent of our evidence (beliefs) and our methods of verification. Anti-realist theories about that subject matter typically deny either (a) or (b); nihilists deny (a), and idealists and constructivists deny (b). The moral realist claims that there are moral facts and true moral propositions whose existence and nature are independent of our moral beliefs and theories. Moral anti-realists include both nihilists, noncognitivists, and others who deny that there are moral facts or true moral propositions and others, whom we might call constructivists, who claim that there are moral facts and true moral propositions but who insist that these facts and truths are constituted by our moral beliefs in some way. A constructivist in ethics who accepts a coherence theory of justification, as Rawls does, would be committed to a kind of coherence theory of moral truth according to which a moral belief is true just in case it is part of (a) reflective equilibrium.[3] On this construal, moral facts and truth are constituted by our moral beliefs in reflective equilibrium, in particular, by our ideals of the person; Kantian constructivism refers to those moral facts, including justice as fairness, which are constituted by a Kantian ideal of the person.

Given this metaphysical sense of 'constructivism,' it would be natural to regard Kantian constructivism as this kind of anti-realist metaethical view. For this reason, there is perhaps presumptive evidence against both methodological and epistemological construals of Kantian constructivism and in favor of a metaphysical construal.

But, against this metaphysical construal, someone might cite Rawls' apparent denial that Kantian constructivism is or implies an anti-realist metaethical view. Near the end of the Dewey Lectures, Rawls writes: 'Furthermore, it is important to notice here that no assumptions have been made about a theory of truth. A constructivist view does not require an idealist or verificationist, as opposed to realist, account of truth' (1980: 565). But this denial of a metaphysical construal of Kantian constructivism is only apparent, for the passage continues: 'Whatever the nature of truth in the case of general beliefs about human nature and how society works, a constructivist moral doctrine requires a distinct procedure of construction to identify the first principles of justice' (1980: 565). This part of the passage indicates that Rawls claims only that Kantian constructivism does not imply an anti-realist theory of truth for certain *nonmoral* propositions. For all that this passage claims, Kantian constructivism may imply moral anti-realism.

There are two important sources of evidence against the methodological construal. First, there is Rawls' task in the Dewey Lectures. Presumably, Rawls wants to argue that justice as fairness is the correct conception of justice to govern the basic structure of society, or at least, as he sometimes suggests, the basic structure of a constitutional democracy. That is, justice as fairness is supposed to state terms

---

3 We can distinguish between relativist and nonrelativist forms of constructivism. Relativist constructivism (relativism) is true just in case there are a plurality of sets of moral facts each constituted by different moral beliefs or different bodies of moral beliefs. According to moral relativism, x is a moral fact for S (x is true-for S) just in case S believes x, S would believe x upon reflection, S is part of a social group the majority of whom believe x, or some such thing. Nonrelativist constructivism (constructivism) holds that there is a single set of moral facts which are constituted by some function of our moral beliefs, e.g., by our moral beliefs in reflective equilibrium. Identifying the moral facts with those moral beliefs in reflective equilibrium will be a form of constructivism if there is a unique equilibrium point; it will be a form of relativism if there are only equilibria.

of social cooperation which are in fact just. This task is not fulfilled merely by showing how justice as fairness depends upon a Kantian theory of the person; knowing this does not establish that justice as fairness states terms of social cooperation which are in fact just. If Rawls were to claim that this Kantian theory of the person is true or that we have good reason to believe that it is true, then the fact that justice as fairness depends upon and draws support from a Kantian theory of the person would justify justice as fairness. Since the methodological construal of Kantian constructivism is agnostic about the truth or plausibility of the moral structure built around a Kantian theory of the person, that construal would seem inadequate to Rawls' task. This is so even if the Kantian moral structure is, as Rawls sometimes suggests, implicit or latent in our political culture (1980: 517f.). To show that justice as fairness states terms of social cooperation for our society which are just, he must claim that the Kantian theory of the person is part of a reflective equilibrium (as the epistemological construal could), that it is true (as a moral realist could), or that its truth consists in its being deeply embedded in our political culture (as the metaphysical construal could).[4] The methodological construal can make none of these claims.

Second, there is Rawls' contrast between Kantian constructivism and intuitionism (1980: 557-60, especially 557). Since the methodological construal is metaphysically and epistemologically neutral, it is in no way inconsistent with intuitionism's claims and so would not seem to explain Rawls' contrast between Kantian constructivism and intuitionism. The epistemological construal, on the other hand, does provide an explanation of the contrast; a coherence theory of justification in ethics is incompatible with the foundationalist element of intuitionism. But the epistemological construal does not provide the only explanation of this contrast. As Rawls observes, intuitionism also contains a metaphysical component, namely, a realist view about moral facts and truth. Intuitionism claims that we have foundationally justified knowledge of moral facts whose existence and nature are independent of our evidence for them. So the metaphysical construal of Kantian constructivism also explains the contrast between constructivism and intuitionism; constructivism's anti-realism is inconsistent with intuitionism's moral realism.

---

4 Another alternative would be for Rawls to make the normative claim that it is always right for a society to maintain and pursue those assumptions which can be ascribed to its political tradition, regardless of the moral content of those assumptions. I assume that it is obvious why this sort of moral and political conservativism makes this alternative not very promising.

Finally, and most importantly, the Dewey Lectures contain a number of metaphysical characterizations of Kantian constructivism. Although the methodological construal cannot underwrite the sort of claims which Rawls needs to defend justice as fairness and cannot account for the contrast between Kantian constructivism and intuitionism, the epistemological construal fares well enough on these issues to make the choice between the metaphysical and epistemological construals difficult. However, against the epistemological construal (as well as the methodological construal) and in favor of the metaphysical construal, there is the weight not only of the constructivist contrast with realism but also of several passages in which Rawls implies that Kantian constructivism involves an anti-realist, constructivist view about the nature of moral facts and truth. For instance, early in the Dewey Lectures, Rawls describes Kantian constructivism as follows: 'Kantian constructivism holds that moral objectivity is to be understood in terms of a suitably constructed social point of view that all can accept. Apart from the procedure of constructing principles of justice, there are no moral facts' (1980: 519). Later, he repeats the anti-realist commitments of Kantian constructivism. 'The parties in the original position do not agree on what the moral facts are, as if there already were such facts. It is not that, being situated impartially, they have a clear and undistorted view of a prior and independent moral order. Rather (for constructivism), there is no such order, and therefore no such facts apart from the procedure of construction as a whole; the facts are identified by the principles that result' (1980: 568).[5] These are straightforward statements of the anti-realist commitments of Kantian constructivism. Kantian constructivism implies that there are no moral truths independent of, or antecedent to, a full justification of some set of moral prin-

---

5 Someone might try to offer a methodological reading of the first two sentences of this passage as descriptions of how the contract device looks, as it were, from the inside. We saw that a methodological construal could claim that *the contractors do not view themselves* as discovering moral truth but as creating it. But the availability of this reading cannot save Kantian constructivism from anti-realism. For (a) the previous passage, the last sentence of this passage, and other passages (listed below) are straightforward statements of the anti-realist commitments of Kantian constructivism, and (b) as we have seen, a methodological construal cannot support Rawls' defense of justice as fairness or explain his contrast between Kantian constructivism and intuitionism. Compare: 'The search for reasonable grounds for reaching agreement rooted in our conception of ourselves and in our relation to society replaces the search for moral truth interpreted as fixed by a prior and independent order of objects and relations, whether natural or divine, an order apart from how we conceive of ourselves' (1980: 519). Cf. Rawls 1980: 516, 537-8, 551-2, 564, 569.

ciples; moral truth is constituted by the moral principles which result from the investigation.

Thus, despite the availability of competing construals of Kantian constructivism, we make most sense of Rawls' various claims if we construe Kantian constructivism as an anti-realist metaethical view. Indeed, as I will now explain, Rawls' writings contain an argument for Kantian constructivism, so construed.[6]

IV Rawls' Argument for Constructivism

What is Rawls' argument for constructivist anti-realism? He clearly thinks that the way we justify moral theories supports constructivism. Some critics of *A Theory of Justice* seemed to assume that a coherence theory of justification in ethics requires constructivism, because coherence could be evidence of truth only if coherence were constitutive of truth. If Rawls were to accept this reasoning, his defense of a coherentist moral epistemology would commit him to constructivism in ethics. (See section VI below.) But Rawls' explicit statements about constructivism suggest a different motivation for constructivism. As I have already suggested, he claims that the role of theories of the person in framing and justifying moral theories supports constructivism. 'This [Kantian constructivism's] rendering of objectivity implies that, rather than think of the principles of justice as true, it is better to say that they are principles that are reasonable for us, given our conceptions of persons as free, equal, and fully cooperating members of society' (1980: 554).

---

6 After this paper was accepted for publication, Rawls published 'Justice as Fairness: Political not Metaphysical' *Philosophy & Public Affairs* **14** (1985) 223-51. In this paper, Rawls claims to eschew controversial philosophical and metaphysical claims and to defend his conception of justice as no more than a reasonable basis of agreement among members of a constitutional democracy. This claim (which itself seems to make controversial philosophical assumptions) runs counter to my metaphysical interpretation of Kantian constructivism and accords more closely with what I call the methodological interpretation. However, I don't think this need affect the merits or interest of my interpretation of the Dewey Lectures. First, Rawls concedes that his new paper may not be entirely consistent with his previous writings (1985: 224). Second, the 'political' interpretation which he offers there, like what I call the methodological interpretation of 1980, cannot, I think, adequately support his defense of justice as fairness or explain his contrast between Kantian constructivism and intuitionism. Finally, whether or not Rawls intends the metaphysical interpretation of Kantian constructivism, his writings suggest it and others have so understood them. Indeed, as I will now explain, his writings suggest an argument for constructivist anti-realism. For these reasons, it is worth exploring the metaphysical interpretation.

Why should the importance of theories of the person in moral theory support constructivism? Rawls, reasoning is not transparent, but we can reconstruct it. This reconstruction draws primarily upon 'The Independence of Moral Theory' and the Dewey Lectures and requires us to make explicit a distinction, which Rawls implicitly recognizes, within theories of the person between *conceptions* of the person and *ideals* of the person.[7] Conceptions of the person are the province of philosophy of mind, and ideals of the person are the province of moral philosophy. Conceptions of the person provide accounts of the concept of a person, that is, of the nature of synchronic and diachronic personal identity or survival; ideals of the person provide accounts of what kind of persons we really are and want or ought to be. For example, Locke, on one interpretation, offers us a conception of the person according to which diachronic personal identity consists in the continuity of memory from one stage of a person's life to another.[8] Aristotle offers us an ideal of the person in the *Nicomachean Ethics* when he claims that *eudaimonia* consists in the exercise of a certain set of practical and intellectual virtues.

We need make no claim that conceptions and ideals of persons are unrelated. Nor need we claim that conceptions of persons are morally neutral while ideals of the person are morally loaded (although we can and should claim that ideals of the person are *more* morally loaded than conceptions of persons are). However difficult the distinction may be to draw precisely, the distinction between conceptions and ideals of the person is a distinction of which we have an intuitive grasp.

Relying on this distinction, we can reconstruct Rawls' argument from the role of theories of the person in moral theory to constructivism in ethics. In 'The Independence of Moral Theory' Rawls claims that standard moral theories embody ideals of the person and that conceptions of the person set feasibility constraints upon ideals of the person. A moral theory can be rejected if the ideal of the person which it embodies prizes physical or psychological characteristics whose realization the philosophy of mind can show would violate conditions necessary for personal identity or survival. But, Rawls claims, this feasibility constraint is very weak; all standard moral theories are compatible with the conditions for personal identity or survival laid down by plausible conceptions of the person. So, the concept of the person radically underdetermines choice among competing moral theories in

---

7 Rawls seems to recognize this distinction; see Rawls 1974: 17, 21; 1980: 534, 571. But he typically fails to mark or observe it.

8 See John Locke, *An Essay Concerning Human Understanding*, ed. P.H. Nidditch (New York: Oxford University Press 1975) II, xxvii.

the sense that no plausible conception of the person alone provides conclusive evidence for the truth of one moral theory over all others. Rawls concludes that determinacy in theory choice in ethics is possible only if we appeal to the morally more robust ideal of the person (1974: 15-21).[9] In 'Kantian Constructivism in Moral Theory' Rawls develops the role of ideals of the person in moral theory. He claims that ideals of the person play a uniquely important role in the justification of moral theories. '... [First] principles of justice must issue from a conception [an ideal] of the person through a suitable representation of that conception [ideal] as illustrated by the procedure of construction in justice as fairness' (1980: 560). In an earlier paper, 'A Well-Ordered Society,' Rawls makes this claim still plainer. 'When fully articulated, any conception of justice expresses a conception [an ideal] of the person, of the relations between persons, and of the general structure and ends of social cooperation. To accept the principles that represent a conception of justice is at the same time to accept an ideal of the person; and in acting from these principles we realize such an ideal. Let us begin, then, by trying to describe the kind of person we might want to be and the form of society we might wish to live in and to shape our interests and characters. In this way we might arrive at the notion of a well-ordered society' (1979: 6).[10] There are closer and

---

9 Cf. Norman Daniels, 'Moral Theory and the Plasticity of Persons,' *The Monist* **62** (1979), 274.

10 Cf. Rawls 1974: 17-20; 1980: 516-7, 535-6; 1982: 169, 180-1. Also see Daniels, 'Moral Theory and the Plasticity of Persons' and 'Reflective Equilibrium and Archimedian Points,' *Canadian Journal of Philosophy* **10** (1980) 83-103 and Samuel Scheffler, 'Moral Skepticism and Ideals of the Person' *The Monist* **62** (1979), 297.

Someone might resist the claim that Rawls assigns a uniquely important role in moral theory to ideals of the person by appeal to the public conception of justice in the justification of Rawls' two principles of justice. 'The model-conception of the well-ordered society,' as well as 'the model-conception of the moral person,' helps to determine the selection of the two principles of justice (1980: 517, 537-8, 555). However, even if, contrary to fact, the model-conception of the well-ordered society were independent of the model-conception of the moral person, Rawls' texts make clear the greater importance of the model-conception of the moral person (1971: 584; 1979; 6, 20; 1980: 516-17, 518, 520, 535-6, 547-52, 554, 559-60, 571; 1982: 172f.). Cf. Allen Buchanan, 'Revisability and Rational Choice' *Canadian Journal of Philosophy* **5** (1975) 395-408; T.M. Scanlon, 'Rawls' Theory of Justice' in N. Daniels, ed., *Reading Rawls* (New York: Basic Books 1975), 171, 178-9; Daniels, 'Moral Theory and the Plasticity of Persons' and 'Reflective Equilibrium and Archimedian Points'; and Scheffler, 295. In fact, the model-conception of the well-ordered society is not independent of the model-conception of the moral person; the former is heavily influenced by the latter. The various features of the well-ordered society depend in important ways upon the Kantian ideal of persons as free, equal, rational, and socially cooperative (1979: 6, 20; 1980: 519-22, 543-7; 1982: 172).

more important evidential relations between ideals of the person and moral theories than between conceptions of the person and moral theories. Ideals of the person thus provide greater determinacy in the choice among competing moral theories than do conceptions of the person. But even ideals of the person in a certain sense underdetermine theory choice in ethics. Rawls' claim is not that particular ideals of the person cannot require particular moral theories, for he clearly thinks that a Kantian ideal of the person which conceives of persons as free, equal, rational, and socially cooperative requires or makes uniquely reasonable his two principles of justice.[11] But Rawls does seem to hold that there are competing ideals of the person and that we cannot adjudicate this disagreement (1980: 516-17, 534-5, 537-8, 554).[12] Thus, because ideals of the person are themselves underdetermined, ideals of the person may be said to underdetermine theory choice in ethics in the sense that that part of moral philosophy concerned with ideals of the person does not itself provide conclusive evidence for one moral theory over all others. Because of the importance of ideals of the person in moral theory and the underdetermination of ideals of the person, the truth of moral theories must be defined in terms of, or relativized to, those moral beliefs about persons upon which those theories depend (evidentially). But this implies that moral facts are evidence-dependent rather than evidence-independent. So moral realism is false and constructivism in ethics is true.[13]

V Ideals of the Person and Moral Realism

Does Rawls' argument from the role of ideals of the person in moral theory undermine moral realism and support constructivism in ethics? Rawls claims that ideals of the person play an important role in the justification of moral theories and that ideals of the person underdetermine theory choice in ethics. He concludes that there can be no

---

11 Rawls 1971: 251-65, 584; 1979: 6-7, 19-20; 1980: 516, 519-22, 534-6, 547-52, 554, 559-60, 571; 1982: 169, 172, 180-1. For useful discussion of Rawls' ideal of the person and how it supports his two principles of justice, see Buchanan; Scanlon; Scheffler; and Daniels, 'Moral Theory and the Plasticity of Persons' and 'Reflective Equilibrium and Archimedian Points.'

12 Cf. Scheffler, 295-300.

13 Indeed, since Rawls' argumentative strategy contains an argument for underdetermination, it supports a relativistic version of constructivism. Thus, Rawls' argument for constructivism creates a tension with his official agnosticism in the Dewey Lectures between relativism and nonrelativism. Cf. Rawls 1980: 569-70.

evidence-independent moral facts; moral facts must be constituted by the moral beliefs about persons which serve as evidence in moral theory. I will argue that Rawls' argument neither undermines realism nor supports constructivism, because a coherence theory of justification in ethics allows us to claim that appeal to ideals of the person may determine theory choice and that, even if it does not, it does not follow that theory choice in ethics is underdetermined.

First, I should say something about the role of underdetermination in Rawls' argument. Rawls, as I reconstruct him, seeks to establish the underdetermination of theory choice in ethics and concludes that there are no moral facts save those that can be defined by different ideals of the person. As such, Rawls' argument may assume that underdetermination implies indeterminacy. Many philosophers have assumed that if a choice among competing claims is genuinely underdetermined by all of the available evidence (both deductive and non-deductive) then there can be no (evidence-independent) fact of the matter as to which of those claims is correct.[14] If this were true, then genuine underdetermination in ethics would imply that there are no evidence-independent moral facts and that moral facts must be defined relative to different bodies of evidence, for instance, to different ideals of persons. Of course, since moral realism claims that moral facts are evidence-independent, it denies that underdetermination *implies* indeterminacy. Strictly speaking, all that follows from genuine underdetermination among claims is that there are no grounds for believing that any one of the claims in question (rather than another) is true. So, someone might argue, we ought not to attribute this argument to Rawls, since it presupposes a connection between justification and truth and, hence, between underdetermination and indeterminacy which the realist will deny. But, even if this argument did require the implication from underdetermination to indeterminacy, the popularity of this inference pattern would allow us to include it as part of a reconstruction of Rawls' argument for constructivism. Moreover, Rawls' argument does not require the implication from underdetermination to indeterminacy. While moral realism and genuine underdetermination are *compatible* (we may have no good grounds for distinguishing true and false moral theories), there is little *motivation* for us to believe in the existence of evidence-independent moral facts *if there is good reason* to believe that there is in principle no way to decide among competing moral theories. In this way, the falsity of moral realism and the truth of constructivism in

---

14 See, e.g., W.V.O. Quine, *Word and Object* (Cambridge, MA: MIT Press 1960), chapter 2 and 'Ontological Relativity' in *Ontological Relativity and Other Essays* (New York: Columbia University Press 1969).

ethics may provide the *best explanation* of genuine underdetermination in ethics.

Someone might think that nihilism, rather than constructivism, was the proper conclusion to draw from the sort of genuine underdetermination for which I claim Rawls argues. Nihilism is also an anti-realist thesis. But notice that nihilism is the best explanation of underdetermination only if we have already ruled out the claim of constructivism that moral facts are to be relativized to different sets of coherent beliefs which include different ideals of the person. I suppose that Rawls might think that it is unacceptable to conclude simply that there are *no* moral facts; once we deny the existence of evidence-independent moral facts, we must reconstruct the objectivity of moral claims as best we can. The natural way to do this, given underdetermination, is to make the moral facts evidence-dependent, as constructivism does.

Does Rawls' argument provide good reason for thinking that theory choice in ethics is genuinely underdetermined? We can agree that theories of the person play an important role in the justification of moral theories. We can also agree that conceptions of the person underdetermine theory choice in ethics. Perhaps Derek Parfit is right that the conception of the person which we adopt can make some moral theories more plausible than others;[15] even if this is so, I think we should concede that no plausible conception of the person determines theory choice in ethics in the sense that it alone provides conclusive evidence for the truth of one moral theory over all others. We can, with Rawls, conclude that if theories of the person are to determine theory choice in ethics, then ideals of the person had better do the job. But Rawls goes on to claim that, even if particular ideals of the person require particular moral theories, there are competing ideals of the person among which we cannot adjudicate. A Kantian ideal may require Rawls' two principles of justice, but there are alternative ideals of the person (e.g. utilitarian and libertarian ideals) which require other moral principles. Since we have no way of deciding among these ideals, Rawls claims, appeal to the ideal of the person cannot determine theory choice in ethics. Because of the importance of ideals of the person in moral theory, theory choice in ethics is therefore underdetermined.

We can deny this underdetermination thesis by resisting Rawls' claim that ideals of the person underdetermine theory choice in ethics. Appeal to the ideal of the person would underdetermine theory choice in ethics if, in addition to the existence of competing ideals, these ideals were unrevisable. But ideals of the person, like other moral beliefs,

---

15 Parfit, *Reasons and Persons* (New York: Oxford University Press 1984), chapter 15. Cf. Daniels, 'Moral Theory and the Plasticity of Persons,' 267-9.

are revisable, and so we can at least begin to adjudicate among competitors. According to a coherentist moral epistemology, ideals of the person are revisable upon the basis of their coherence with moral theories which seem plausible and with considered moral beliefs. For instance, we can demand coherence between our beliefs about what sorts of character are admirable or valuable and our beliefs about which actions are praiseworthy and which are reprehensible. Rawls himself seems to think that there are only a small number of competing ideals of the person. If so, there is good reason to suppose (at least Rawls has given us no reason to doubt) that coherentist reasoning about the support for these ideals can, at least in principle, decide among the competitors. If we accept the sort of holistic epistemology which a coherence theory of justification in ethics represents, we can concede the existence of competing ideals of the person without conceding that appeal to the ideal of the person underdetermines moral theory.

Moreover, we can deny Rawls' conclusion about underdetermination by resisting his tacit assumption that ideals of the person provide the only, or the decisive, support for moral theories. Rawls claims that ideals of the person underdetermine theory choice in ethics and concludes that theory choice in ethics is underdetermined. This conclusion would follow only if ideals of the person provided not only important but exclusive, or necessarily decisive, support for moral theories. But there is little reason (and Rawls has provided none) to suppose that ideals of the person are the only, or the decisive, evidence for moral theories. In fact, according to a coherence theory of justification in ethics, moral theories receive support from nonmoral beliefs about such things as sociology, economics, and psychology and from considered moral beliefs about concrete moral issues as well as from ideals of the person. Indeed, a coherentist moral epistemology should lead us to *expect* that moral theory is underdetermined by appeal to the ideal of the person (or any other subset of our total set of beliefs). If moral theories are justified by their coherence with considered moral beliefs about particular cases and social theories as well as ideals of the person, then it should come as no surprise that appeal to the ideal of the person does not itself decide between competing moral theories. But precisely because coherence with considered moral beliefs and various nonmoral beliefs is evidential, we can concede that ideals of the person do underdetermine moral theory without concluding that theory choice in ethics is underdetermined.

These two lines of resistance to Rawls' thesis about underdetermination in ethics illustrate a tension in Rawls' epistemological views in the Dewey Lectures which becomes apparent only after his argument for constructivism is fully articulated. A coherence theory of justification in ethics is compatible with an emphasis on the importance of theories of the person, in particular, ideals of the person, in justifying moral theories. But Rawls' argument for constructivism presupposes a different justificatory role for ideals of the person. The inference from the underdetermination of ideals of the person to the underdetermination of theory choice in ethics presupposes something like an intuitionist epistemology in which ideals of the person play the part of incorrigible foundational moral beliefs. Assigning *this* justificatory role to ideals of the person is incompatible with a coherentist moral epistemology. This intuitionist view about the role of ideals of the person in moral theory represents an implausibly restrictive view of moral justification and conflicts with Rawls' own considered epistemological views. A coherentist epistemology of the sort Rawls himself advocates elsewhere allows one to concede the importance of ideals of the person in moral theory and the existence of competing ideals of the person without conceding that theory choice in ethics is underdetermined. If Rawls' grounds for believing that moral theory is underdetermined are weak, as I have argued they are, then he has provided us with no good reason for denying the existence of evidence-independent moral facts or for believing constructivism.

VI Coherence and Realism in Ethics

Rawls might think that underdetermination is avoided only by giving in to constructivism. Perhaps he believes, not that competing ideals of the person cannot be adjudicated among, but that they can be adjudicated among only by coherentist reasoning from moral beliefs whose truth is evidence-dependent. Moral principles justified on the basis of the most plausible ideal of the person would then have a constructivist status.

Of course, this argument would beg the question. We expect Rawls to provide an argument for constructivism in ethics; he cannot do this by appealing to constructivism about particular moral beliefs.

Constructivism in ethics need not presuppose constructivism about particular moral beliefs. One might argue that a coherentist defense of cognitivism commits one to constructivism in ethics. Some philosophers have thought that coherence theories of justification require coherence theories of truth, because they have thought that coherence could be evidence of truth only if coherence were constitutive of truth. The constructivist might appeal to this reasoning and conclude that a coherence theory of justification in ethics requires constructivism in ethics, in particular, a coherence theory of moral truth.

This epistemological argument is interesting and poses a serious challenge to moral realists who defend a coherentist moral epistemology. Many critics of Rawls' epistemological position in *A Theory of Justice* relied on this epistemological argument in claiming that Rawls' use of the method of reflective equilibrium commits him to a 'subjectivist' position in ethics.[16] Perhaps Rawls' Dewey Lectures reflect his acceptance of the kind of epistemological argument underlying their criticisms.[17]

I can here only sketch replies to this epistemological argument.[18] Realists can and should claim that coherentist reasoning is both *reliable* and *evidential*. Coherentist reasoning is reliable just in case a sufficient number of beliefs one already holds are sufficiently approximately true. Accepting beliefs which cohere with other beliefs one holds is a reliable method just in case a sufficient number of beliefs in one's inference base are approximately true. The same is true of coherentist reasoning about moral beliefs. Accepting, say, a moral theory because it coheres in the appropriate way with, among other things, considered moral beliefs which one holds is a reliable method of theory choice in ethics if a sufficient number of one's considered moral beliefs are sufficiently approximately true. An independent argument is required, which the epistemological argument does not contain, for doubting that the inference base of considered moral beliefs contains a sufficient number of approximately true beliefs.

Moreover, coherentist reasoning can provide evidence of objective truth. The thesis that coherence could provide evidence of truth only if coherence were constitutive of truth seems to assume that justification must guarantee truth. But this overstates the connection between justification and truth. Justification does not entail truth; we can be perfectly justified in holding false beliefs and beliefs which could have been false. In this way, the epistemological argument threatens to collapse the distinction between justification and knowledge. Instead, justification need only provide evidence of truth. Coherence will pro-

---

16 See, e.g., R.M. Hare, 'Rawls' Theory of Justice' reprinted in Daniels, ed. *Reading Rawls* and *Moral Thinking* (New York: Oxford University Press 1981), 12, 40; Ronald Dworkin, 'The Original Position' reprinted in Daniels ed., *Reading Rawls*; Peter Singer, 'Sidgwick and Reflective Equilibrium,' *The Monist* 57 (1974) 490-517; David Lyons, 'The Nature and Soundness of Contract and Coherence Arguments' in Daniels ed., *Reading Rawls*; and Richard Brandt, *A Theory of the Good and the Right* (New York: Oxford University Press 1979), 16-23. Actually, unlike the others, Dworkin embraces, rather than criticizes, the constructivist implications of the epistemological argument.

17 Here one might compare Rawls 1975 and 1980 with Dworkin, 'The Original Position.'

18 See my *Moral Realism and the Foundations of Ethics*, chapters 2, 5, and 6 and appendix 2 for fuller discussion of these issues.

vide evidence of truth if there are second order beliefs — beliefs about our belief formation mechanisms and their reliability — with which our first order beliefs may cohere. A belief's coherence, then, with, among other things, such second order beliefs will be evidence of its objective truth.[19] A moral belief's coherence with, among other things, background moral beliefs will be evidence of its objective truth just in case there are second order beliefs about morality — such as belief in the general reliability of considered moral beliefs or judgments — with which our moral beliefs may cohere. If we take considered moral beliefs to be moral beliefs which are well informed, which result from good inference patterns, which are held with confidence, which are not the result of obvious distorting influences (such as prejudice, social ideology, or excessive self-concern), and which are based on an imaginative consideration of the interests of those involved in the situations which the moral beliefs concern, then we have reason to regard considered moral beliefs as reliable (cf. Rawls 1951). Considered moral beliefs, so construed, are reliable, because they have been formed under conditions of general cognitive reliability and under conditions whose moral importance is recognized by a wide variety of substantive moral theories. Considered moral beliefs are hardly infallible, and, because it is coherence with these beliefs *among others* which a coherence theory of justification in ethics demands, considered moral beliefs are certainly revisable. But considered moral beliefs do play an important role in the justification of moral beliefs. Because there is reason to regard them as generally reliable, coherence with, among other things, considered moral beliefs can be evidence of objective moral truth. An independent argument is required, which the epistemological argument does not contain, for doubting that considered moral beliefs are reliable and that coherentist reasoning in ethics can be evidential.

Moreover, I *need* only sketch replies to the epistemological argument for constructivism. In assessing Rawls' argument for constructivism, we can avoid a comprehensive assessment of the epistemological argument. Not only does Rawls not advance this argument; it is quite independent of the one argument he does advance for constructivism, viz. the argument based on the role of theories of the person in moral theory.

---

19 Cf. Lawrence Bonjour, 'The Coherence Theory of Empirical Knowledge,' *Philosophical Studies* **30** (1976) 281-312 and Michael Williams, 'Coherence, Justification, and Truth,' *Review of Metaphysics* **34** (1980) 243-72.

VII Conclusion

A significant part of my discussion has been reconstructive exegesis. Thoughtful readers of Rawls' discussion of constructivism will appreciate the need for this reconstruction. We make best sense of Rawls' various claims, I argued, by construing constructivism as an anti-realist metaethical view which he defends as follows. Ideals of the person are underdetermined. Hence, appeal to the ideal of the person underdetermines moral theory. Because of the importance of ideals of the person in moral theory, the underdetermination of moral theory by appeal to the ideal of the person implies the underdetermination of moral theory. The best explanation of the underdetermination of moral theory is that there are no evidence-independent moral facts; moral facts and truth must be defined relative to different bodies of evidence, in particular, relative to different moral beliefs about persons (ideals of the person). Hence, moral realism is false and constructivism in ethics is true.

Once Rawls' argument is fully articulated, its assessment is more straightforward. Though ideals of the person play a central role in moral epistemology, Rawls' argument commits him to a moral epistemology which is incompatible with the sort of coherence theory of justification in ethics which he has long advocated. A coherence theory of justification in ethics allows us to recognize the importance of ideals of the person in moral theory and the existence of competing ideals of the person without conceding the underdetermination of theory choice in ethics or any other anti-realist claims. Since ideals of the person are revisable upon the basis of coherentist reasoning, there is no reason to deny that there is a uniquely plausible ideal of the person, which, in turn, determines theory choice in ethics. Moreover, even if ideals of the person do underdetermine theory choice in ethics, a coherence theory of justification in ethics allows us to concede this point without concluding that theory choice in ethics is underdetermined. Despite the importance of ideals of the person in moral theory, moral theories do not depend exclusively or decisively upon ideals of the person. Moral theories are justified on the basis of their coherence with all of our beliefs, both moral and nonmoral. Recognition of the importance of ideals of the person in moral theory, therefore, commits us to neither the truth of constructivism nor the falsity of moral realism.[20]

Received February, 1985

20 I would like to thank John G. Bennett, T.H. Irwin, Alan Sidelle, Nicholas Sturgeon, Jennifer Whiting, audiences at Cornell University and Bates College, and a referee for the *Canadian Journal of Philosophy* for helpful comments on earlier versions of this paper.

CRITICAL STUDY

RAWLS' THEORY OF JUSTICE—I[1]

By R. M. HARE

A Theory of Justice. By JOHN RAWLS. (Cambridge, Mass. : Harvard U.P., 1971. Oxford : Clarendon Press, 1972. Pp. xv + 607. Price £5.00, U.S. paperback, $3.95.)

Any philosopher who writes on justice or on any other subject in moral philosophy is likely to propound, or to give evidence of, views on one or more of the following topics :

(1) *Philosophical methodology*—i.e., what philosophy is supposed to be doing and how it does it. Rawls expresses some views about this, which have determined the whole structure of his argument, and which therefore need careful inspection.

(2) *Ethical analysis*—i.e., the meanings of the moral words or the nature and logical properties of the moral concepts. Rawls says very little about these, and certainly does not treat them as fundamental to his enquiry (51/10)[2].

(3) *Moral methodology*—i.e., how moral thinking ought to proceed, or how moral arguments or reasonings have to be conducted if they are to be cogent.

(4) *Normative moral questions*—i.e., what we ought or ought not to do, what is just or unjust, and so on.

I shall leave discussion of Rawls' views on (4) to the second, forthcoming part of this review, this first part being devoted to (1), (2) and (3). I shall argue that, through misconceptions about (1), Rawls has not paid enough attention to (2), and that therefore he has lacked the equipment necessary to handle (3) effectively ; so that what he says about (4), however popular it may prove, is unsupported by any firm arguments.

(1) Rawls states quite explicitly how he thinks moral philosophy should be done : " There is a definite if limited class of facts against which conjec-

---

[1]Although the Editor has been kind enough to allow me to spread this review over two parts, I do not hope to explore in it all the convolutions of the book. I shall concentrate on what seems most important. I feel excused from discussing Rawls' treatment of liberty by my general agreement with an article which Professor Hart is to devote to this topic in the *Chicago Law Review*, and of which he has kindly shown me a draft. Of the many other people with whom I have discussed the book, and who have kept my courage up during two readings of it, I should like especially to thank Mr. Derek Parfit, who seems to me to see deeper and more clearly into these problems than any of us. [The second part of this Critical Study is to appear in the July number of this volume.]

[2]References are to pages/lines of Rawls' text.

tured principles can be checked, namely our considered judgments in reflective equilibrium " (51/3). It is clear from the succeeding passage that Rawls does not conceive of moral philosophy as depending primarily on the analysis of concepts in order to establish their logical properties and thus the rules of valid moral argument. Rather, he thinks of a theory of justice as analogous to a theory in empirical science. It has to square with what he calls " facts ", just like, for example, physiological theories. But what are these facts ? They are what people will *say* when they have been thinking carefully. This suggestion is reminiscent of Sir David Ross.[3] But sometimes (though not consistently) Rawls goes farther than Ross. Usually he is more cautious, and appeals to the reflections of *bien pensants* generally, as Ross does (e.g., 18/9, 19/26). But at 50/34 he says, " For the purposes of this book, the views of the reader and the author are the only ones that count ". It does not make much practical difference which way he puts it ; for if (as will certainly be the case) he finds a large number of readers who can share with him a cosy unanimity in their considered judgments, he and they will think that they adequately represent " people generally ", and congratulate themselves on having attained the truth.[4] This is how phrases like ' reasonable and generally acceptable ' (45/16) are often used by philosophers in lieu of argument.

Rawls, in short, is here advocating a kind of subjectivism, in the narrowest and most old-fashioned sense. He is making the answer to the question " Am I right in what I say about moral questions ? " depend on the answer to the question " Do you, the reader, and I agree in what we say ? ". This must be his view, if the considered judgments of author and reader are to occupy the place in his theory which is occupied in an empirical science by the facts of observation. Yet at 516/15 he claims objectivity for his principles.

It might be thought that such a criticism can be made only by one who has rejected (as Rawls has apparently accepted) the arguments of Professor Quine and others about the analytic-synthetic distinction and the way in which science confronts the world. But this is not so. Even Quine would hardly say that scientific theories as a whole are to be tested by seeing what people say when they have thought about them (it would have been a good thing for medieval flat-earthers if they could be) ; but that is what Rawls is proposing for moral principles.

In order not to be unfair to Rawls, it must be granted that *any* enquirer, in ethics as in any other subject, and whether he be a descriptivist or a prescriptivist, is looking for an answer to his questions which he can accept. I have myself implied this in my *Freedom and Reason*, page 73 and elsewhere. The element of subjectivism enters only when a philosopher claims that he can " check " his theory against his and other people's views, so

---

[3] Cf. *The Right and the Good*, pp. 40 ff.

[4] See 104/3-14 for a " considered judgment " with which many of us now would agree, but which differs from the views of most writers of other periods than the present, and is not argued for.

that a disagreement between the theory and the views tells against the theory. To speak like this (as Rawls does constantly throughout the book) is to make the *truth* of the theory *depend on* agreement with people's opinions. I have myself been so often falsely accused of this sort of subjectivism that it is depressing to find a self-styled objectivist falling as deeply into it as Rawls does—depressing, because it makes one feel that this essentially simple distinction will never be understood : the distinction between the view that thinking something can make it so (which is in general false) and the view that if we are to say something sincerely, we must be able to accept it (which is a tautology).

Intuitionism is nearly always a form of disguised subjectivism. Rawls does not call himself an intuitionist ; but he certainly is one in the usual sense. He says, " There is no reason to suppose that we can avoid all appeals to intuition, of whatever kind, or that we should try to. The practical aim is to reach a reasonably reliable agreement in judgment in order to provide a common conception of justice " (44/34, cf. 124/38). It is clear that he is here referring mainly to moral intuitions ; perhaps if he appealed only to linguistic intuitions it would be all right. He reserves the name ' intuitionist ' for those (including no doubt Ross) who advocate a *plurality* of moral principles, each established by intuition, and not related to one another in an ordered structure, but only weighed relatively to each other (also by intuition) when they conflict. The right name for this kind of intuitionism would be ' pluralistic intuitionism '. Rawls' theory is more systematic than this, but no more firmly grounded. There can also be another, non-pluralistic kind of intuitionist—one who intuits the validity of a single principle or ordered system of them, or of a single method, and erects his entire structure of moral thought on this. Sidgwick might come into this category—though if he were living today, it is unlikely that he would find it necessary to rely on moral intuition.

' Monistic intuitionism ' would be a good description of this kind of view. It might apply to Rawls, did it not suggest falsely that he relies only on one great big intuition, and only at one point in his argument. Unfortunately he relies on scores of them. From 18/9 to 20/9 I have counted in two pages thirty expressions implying a reliance on intuitions : such expressions as ' I assume that there is a broad measure of agreement that ' ; ' commonly shared presumptions ' ; ' acceptable principles ' ; ' it seems reasonable to suppose ' ; ' is arrived at in a natural way ' ; ' match our considered convictions of justice or extend them in an acceptable way ' ; ' which we can affirm on reflection ' ; ' we are confident ' ; ' we think ' ; and so on. If, as I have done, the reader will underline the places in the book where crucial moves in the argument depend on such appeals, he may find himself recalling Plato's remark : " If a man starts from something he knows not, and the end and middle of his argument are tangled together out of what he knows not, how can such a mere consensus ever turn into knowledge ? " (*Rep.* 533 c). Since the theoretical structure is tailored at every point to fit Rawls' intuitions, it is hardly surprising that its normative consequences fit them too—if they did not, he would alter the theory (19/26 ff., cf. 141/23) ; and the fact that Rawls is a fairly typical man of his times and society, and will therefore have many adherents, does not make this a good way of doing philosophy.

Rawls' answer to this objection (581/9) is that *any* justification of principles must proceed from some consensus. It is true that any justification which consists of a " linear inference "[5] must so proceed ; but Rawls' justification is not of this type. Why should it not *end* in consensus as a result of argument ? There may have to be a prior consensus on matters of fact, including facts about the interests of the parties (though these themselves may conflict) ; and on matters of logic, established by analysis. But not on substantial moral questions, as Rawls seems to require. A review is not the place for an exposition of my own views of how moral argument can succeed in reaching normative conclusions with only facts, *singular* prescriptions and logic to go on ; all that I wish to say here is that the matter will never be clarified unless these ingredients are kept meticulously distinct, and the logic carefully attended to (see further footnote 6).

(2) I shall mention only in passing Rawls' views about the meanings of the moral words or the natures, analyses and logical properties of the moral concepts. It would be wrong to take up space on something which Rawls evidently thinks of little importance for his argument. He wishes to " leave questions of meaning and definition aside and to get on with the task of developing a substantive theory of justice " (579/17). There is in fact a vast hole in his 600-page book which should be occupied by a thorough account of the meanings of these words, which is the only thing that can establish the logical rules that govern moral argument. If we do not have such an account, we shall never be able to distinguish between what we have to avoid saying if we are not to contradict ourselves or commit other *logical* errors, and what we have to avoid saying if we are to agree with Rawls and his coterie.[6] So far as he does say anything about the meanings of the moral words, it is mostly derivative from recent descriptivist views, my arguments against which it would be tedious to rehearse. I found this reliance surprising, in view of the fact that what he says about justice, at any rate, clearly commits him to some form of prescriptivism : the principles of justice determine how we *are to* behave, not how we are to *describe* certain kinds of behaviour (61/7, 145/12, 14, 33, 149/16, 351/15). My quarrels with Rawls' main theory do not depend at all on the fact that I am a prescriptivist.

[5]See my *Freedom and Reason*, pp. 87 f.

[6]See the paper " The Argument from Received Opinion " in my *Essays on Philosophical Method*, which might have been written with Rawls' book in mind, although in fact at that time I had not had the opportunity of reading it. For my latest shot at the project of giving such an account, see the paper " Wrongness and Harm " in my *Essays on the Moral Concepts*.

There are significant passages in which Rawls compares moral philosophy with mathematics (51/23) and linguistics (47/5, 49/8). The analogy with these sciences is vitiated by the fact that they do not yield substantial conclusions, as moral philosophy is supposed, on Rawls' view, to do, and in some sense clearly should. It is quite all right to test a linguistic theory (a grammar) against what people actually say when they are speaking carefully ; people's *linguistic* " intuitions " are indeed, in the end, authoritative for what is correct in their language. The kind of interplay between theory and data that occurs in all sciences can occur here, and it is perfectly proper for the data to be the utterances of native speakers. But the only " moral " theories that can be checked against people's actual moral judgments are anthropological theories about what, in general, people *think* one ought to do, not moral principles about what one ought to do. That these latter can be so checked is not, indeed, what Rawls is suggesting in this passage ; but do not the whole drift of his argument, and the passage quoted above (51/3), suggest it ?

The case of mathematics is more controversial. Rawls seems to imply that if we had a " moral system " analogous to the systems of logic and mathematics, then we could use such a system to elucidate the meanings of moral judgments, instead of the other way about, as I have suggested. There is no objection, so far as I can see, to such a claim in mathematics and logic, provided that we realize that the concepts used in the formal systems may be different from (perhaps more useful for certain purposes than) our natural ones. Such a procedure is all right in logic and mathematics, since the construction of artificial models can often illuminate the logic and the meaning of our ordinary speech ; but whichever way the illumination goes (why not both ways ?) it can work only if the system in question is purely formal. If what Rawls calls " the substantive content of the moral conceptions " (52/7) is part of the system, then what will be revealed by it are not the meanings of moral judgments but the moral opinions of those who adhere to the system. And when he proposes (111/6) to *replace* our concept of right by the concept of being in accordance with the principles that would be acknowledged in the original position, he is in effect seeking to foist on us not a new meaning for a word, but a substantial set of moral views ; for he thinks that he has tailored the original position so as to yield principles which fit his own considered judgments.

(3) Rawls' moral methodology takes the form of a picture or parable— and one which is even more difficult than most to interpret with any confidence. We are to imagine a set of people gathered together (hypothetically, not actually), to agree upon a set of " principles of justice " to govern their conduct.[7] The " principles of justice " are those principles to which these

---

[7]It is tempting to say " their *subsequent* conduct " ; but the tenses in Rawls' account are one of its most baffling features. On the one hand, these " people in the original position " (POPs) are to make a " contract " ; this, and terms like ' original position '

" people in the original position " (POPs) would agree for the conduct of all of them as " people in ordinary life " (POLs), if, when making the agreement, they were subject to certain conditions.

It is obviously these conditions which determine the substance of the theory (indeed they *are* its substance, the rest being mere dramatization, useful for expository purposes, but also potentially misleading). Rawls' theory belongs to a class of theories which we may call " hypothetical choice theories "—i.e., theories which say that the right answer to some question is the answer that a person or set of people *would* choose if subject to certain conditions. The best-known example of such a theory is the " ideal observer " theory of ethics, about which Rawls says something, and which we shall find instructive to compare with his own. The important thing to notice about all such theories is that *what* this hypothetical person would choose, if it is determinate at all (which many such theories fail to make it) has to be determined by the conditions to which he is subject. If the conditions, once made explicit, do not deductively determine the choice, then the choice remains indeterminate, except in so far as it is covertly conditioned by the prejudices or intuitions of the philosopher whose theory it is. Thus intuition can enter at two points (and in Rawls' case enters at both ; cf. 121/7-15). It enters in the choice of the conditions to which the chooser is to be subject ; and it enters to determine what he will choose in cases where the conditions, as made explicit, do not determine this (see Part II, forthcoming).

The more important of the conditions to which Rawls' POPs are subject are the following (§§22-5) :

(1) They know certain facts about the world and the society in which POLs live, but have others concealed from them by a " veil of ignorance ". It is obviously going to be crucial *which* facts they are allowed to know, and which they are not.

(2) They are motivated in certain ways, especially in being selfish or mutually disinterested, and also in lacking envy and in being unwilling to use the principle of insufficient reason. They are also " rational " (i.e., take the most effective means to given ends (14/5)).

(3) They are subject to " the formal constraints of the concept of

---

and ' initial situation ' (20/18), seem to indicate that this conclave is temporally prior to the time at which these same people are to enter the world as we know it, become " people in ordinary life " (POLs) and carry out their contract. But on the other hand Rawls seems to speak commonly in the present tense (e.g., 520/27 ff.), as if they were somehow simultaneously POPs and POLs. Not surprisingly this, and other obscurities, make it often difficult, and sometimes (to me at any rate) impossible, to determine whether some particular remark is intended to refer to POPs or POLs. Who, for example, are " they " in 206/5 ? And in 127/25, is it the POLs who are being said to be mutually disinterested, as the passage seems to imply, and as is suggested by the reference to " circumstances of justice " on 128/5 (which seems usually, though not on 130/1-5, to mean circumstances of POLs, not POPs) ? But if so, how are 129/14-18 or 148/2 ff. consistent ? Again, do POLs lack envy, or only POPs ? (see 151/22-24, 143-4, §§ 80-81.) A review as long as Rawls' book itself could be spent on such questions of interpretation ; I was intending to set a few more of these exercises for the reader, but have not had time to compile them.

right ". Rawls explicitly says that he does not " claim that these conditions follow from the concept of right, much less from the meaning of morality " (130/16). Instead, he as usual says that it " seems reasonable " to impose them (130/14). He does not tell us what he would say to somebody to whom they did not " seem reasonable ".

(4) There are also certain important procedural stipulations, such as that the POPs should all agree unanimously in their choice of principles. Later in the book, the procedure is very much elaborated, and takes the form of a series of stages in which the " veil of ignorance " is progressively lifted ; but I shall ignore this complication here.

In comparing Rawls' theory with other theories, it is most important to notice the roles played by these groups of conditions. If I may be allowed to mention my own theory, I would myself place almost the whole emphasis on (3), and would at the same time aim to establish the " constraints " on the basis of a study of the logical properties of the moral words. This still seems to me the most rigorous and secure procedure, because it enables us to say that *if* this is how we are using the words (*if* this is what we mean by them), then we shall be debarred from saying so-and-so on pain of self-contradiction ; and this gives moral arguments a cutting edge which in Rawls they lack. In a similar way, Achilles should have answered the Tortoise by saying, " If you mean by ' if ' what we all mean, you have to accept *modus ponens* ; for this is the rule that gives its meaning to ' if ' ". It is of course in dispute how much we can do by this method ; but I think, and have tried elsewhere to show, that we can do much more than Rawls allows.

The " ideal observer " theory (in a typical form) differs from Rawls' theory in the following respects. Under (1), it allows the principle-chooser to know everything ; there is no " veil of ignorance ". On the other hand, under (2), he is differently motivated ; instead of being concerned with his own interest only, he is impartially benevolent. Now it is possible to show that on a certain simple and natural " rational contractor " theory of the Rawls type (though not, it is fairly safe to say, on Rawls' own version of this type of theory) these two changes exactly cancel one another, so that the normative consequences of the " ideal observer " and " rational contractor " theories would be identical. To see this, let us remember that the main object of these conditions is to secure impartiality. This is secured in the case of the rational contractor theory by not allowing the POPs to know what are to be their individual roles as POLs in the society in which the contract has to be observed ; they therefore cannot choose the principles to suit their own selfish interests, although they are selfishly motivated. It is secured in the case of the ideal observer theory by express stipulation ;

he is required to be impartially benevolent. It looks, therefore, as if *these* versions of the two theories are, as I have said elsewhere,[8] practically equivalent.

We must next ask *how much* the POPs have to be ignorant of, in order to secure impartiality. It must be noticed that much of the work is already done by the " formal constraint " that the principles have to be " general ".[9] Rawls himself says that the formal constraints rule out egoism (136/13) ; it might therefore be asked what there is left for the " veil of ignorance " to do, since to abandon egoism (and for the same formal reasons the pursuit of the interests of any other particular person or set of them) is *eo ipso* to become impartial. I do not think that this objection sticks ; for a POP, if he had full knowledge of his own role as a POL, might adopt principles which were formally " general " or universal but were rigged to suit his own interest. Rawls, however, thinks (wrongly[10]) that such rigged principles can be ruled out on the formal ground of lack of " generality ", and so is open to the objection *ad hominem*. That is to say, *he* has left nothing for the veil of ignorance to do as regards impartiality.

Be that as it may, however, we need to be clear how thick a veil of ignorance is required to achieve impartiality. To be frugal : all that the POPs need to be ignorant of are their roles as individuals in the world of POLs. That is to say, it would be possible to secure impartiality while allowing the POPs to know the entire history of the world—not only the general conditions governing it, but the actual course of history, and indeed the alternative courses of history which would be the result of different actions by individuals in it, and in particular to know that there would be in the world individuals $a, b, \ldots n$ who would be affected in specific ways by these actions—*provided* that each of the POPs did not know which individual he was (i.e., whether he was a or b, etc.). Impartiality would be secured even by this very economical veil, because if a POP does not know whether he is a or b, he has, however selfish, no motive for choosing his principles so as to suit the interests of a rather than those of b when these interests are in conflict.

A superficial reading of Rawls' rather ambiguous language at 137/4, 12/12 and 198/20 might lead one to suppose that this " economical veil " is what he has in mind. But this cannot be right, in view of 200/17 and other passages. We need to ask, therefore, why Rawls is not content with it, if it suffices to secure impartiality. The answer might just be that he is un-

---

[8] " Rules of War and Moral Reasoning ", *Philosophy and Public Affairs* 1, 1971/2, p. 166.

[9] Rawls' word ; I have commented on his use, and given reasons for preferring the word ' universal ', which *he* uses for something else, in my paper " Principles ", *P.A.S.* 73 (1972/3), p. 2.

[10] I have hinted why in " Principles " (*op. cit.*), p. 4. For my own answer to the " rigging " difficulty, see my *Freedom and Reason*, p. 107.

clear as between two things : (1) the POPs' not knowing which of them is going to be *a* and which *b* ; (2) their knowing this, but not knowing how *a* and *b* are going to fare. Much of his language could bear either interpretation. And 141/25 seems to imply that Rawls thinks that the " economical veil " would allow the POPs to use threats against each other based on the power which as individual POLs they would have ; but this is obviously not so if they do not know *which* individuals they are going to be, however many particular facts about individuals they may know.

Nevertheless, sooner than accuse Rawls of a mere muddle, let us look for other explanations. One is, that he wants, not merely to secure impartiality, but to avoid an interpretation which would have normative consequences which he is committed to abjuring. With the " economical veil ", the rational contractor theory is practically equivalent in its normative consequences to the ideal observer theory and to my own theory (see above and below), and these normative consequences are of a utilitarian sort. Therefore Rawls may have reasoned that, since an " economical veil " would make him into a utilitarian, he had better buy a more expensive one. We can, indeed, easily sympathize with the predicament of one who, having been working for the best part of his career on the construction of " a viable alternative to the utilitarian tradition " (150/12), discovered that the type of theory he had embraced, in its simplest and most natural form, led direct to a kind of utilitarianism. It must in fairness be said, however, that Rawls does not regard this motive as disreputable ; for he is not against tailoring his theory to suit the conclusions he wants to reach (see above, and 141/23, where he says, " We want to define the original position so that we get the desired solution "). I shall be examining in the second part of this review the question of whether Rawls' thicker veil *does* help him to avoid utilitarianism ; it is fairly clear from §28 that he *thinks* it does.

A further motive for the thicker veil is a desire for simplicity both in the reasoning and in the principles resulting from it (140/31 ; 142/8 ; but cf. 141/22). By letting the POPs know only the general facts about the world in which the POLs live, and also by other devices (e.g., 95/14, 96/6, 98/28), Rawls effectively prevents them from going into much detail about the facts. This means that his principles can and must be simple ; but at the same time it raises the question of whether they can be adequate to the complexities of the actual world. Rawls is, in fact, faced with a dilemma. If he sticks to the " economical veil ", then there will be no difficulty of principle in doing justice even in highly specific and unusual cases in the actual world ; but this will involve very complex calculations, in advance, on the part of his POPs. On the other hand, if, in order to avoid these complex calculations, he limits the POPs' knowledge to " general " facts about the world, he is in danger of having his POPs choose principles which may, in particular cases, result in flagrant injustice, because the facts of these cases are peculiar.

This is merely the analogue, in Rawls' system, of the dilemma which afflicts utilitarians, and which I have tried to solve in two articles already referred to.[11] The solution lies in distinguishing between two levels of moral thinking, in one of which (for use " in a cool hour ") we are allowed to go into all the details, and in the other of which (for normal use under conditions of ignorance of the future, stress and temptation, and in moral education and self-education) we stick to firm and simple principles which are most likely in general to lead to right action—they are not, however, to be confused with " rules of thumb ", a term whose undiscriminating use has misled many. The first kind of thinking (let us call it " level-2 ") is used in order to select the principles to be adhered to in the second kind (" level-1 "), choosing those principles which are best for situations likely to be actually encountered. If this kind of solution were applied to Rawls' system, he would allow his POPs to know everything but their individual roles as POLs (the " economical veil ") ; but since their task would be to choose the best *level-1* principles for the thinking of POLs, they could still, since these principles have to be simple and observed only in general, attend only to the general facts about the POL society and the general run of cases. The contract would then not be a contract to act universally in certain ways, but rather a contract to employ certain firm principles in the moral education of POLs themselves and their children, and to uphold such principles as the norm in their society. For unusual cases, and for those in which the principles conflicted, the POLs would be allowed (in Aristotelian fashion)[12] to do a bit of POP-thinking for themselves.

Rawls does not adopt this solution, although he shows some awareness of the distinction between level-1 and level-2 thinking on 28/19. Ross's different but related distinction between " *prima facie* duties " and " duties all things considered " is referred to and indeed used on 340/15. On the whole Rawls' principles are treated as unbreakable ones for universal observance (e.g., 115/36) ; but they are supposed to have the simplicity which in fact only level-1 principles can, or need, have (132/17). Other passages which *might* be relevant to this question are 157/32, 159/16 ff., 161/17, 304/13, 337/11, 340/28, 341/14, 454/6 ; but I have been unable to divine exactly what Rawls' view is.

He has tried to get over the difficulty of conflicts between principles and unusual cases in two ways. The first is by means of a rigid " lexical " ordering of his principles (which could be guaranteed in unusual cases to yield absurd results) ; the second is by his " four-stage sequence " (195 ff.), whereby the " veil of ignorance " is progressively lifted, and at each " lift " the knowledge of extra facts is absorbed and the principles expanded to deal with them. The sequence ends with the complete disappearance of the veil. Since Rawls can say this, he cannot have any objection on grounds

[11]" Principles " (*op. cit.*), pp. 7 ff. ; *Philosophy and Public Affairs* 1 (1971/2), p. 166.
[12]*Eth. Nic.* 1137 b 24 ff. (cf. Rawls 19/9, 138/20).

of practicability to unrestricted knowledge from the start, and his reasons for forbidding it must be theoretical ones.

The four-stage sequence would only work if at each later stage the principles inherited from the stage before *determined*, in the light of the new information, what further principles were to be adopted. At least this is so, if the method is required to be rigorous ; Rawls can perhaps escape this requirement by using intuitions all down the line. But if the principles chosen in the original position do *determine*, in conjunction with each new batch of facts, all the additional principles that are to be adopted at each stage, then the moral law is likely to turn out to be an ass. Some victim of the application of one of these lower-order principles may be found complaining that if the POPs had only *known* about him and his situation, likes and dislikes, then they would have complicated their principles a little to allow them to do justice to him (perhaps he does not give a fig for the " priority of liberty " ; or perhaps his preferences do not coincide with the POPs' ranking of the " primary goods "). If it were rigidly applied, Rawls' system would be like a constitution having a legislature in which reading of the newspapers was forbidden, and law-courts without any judicial discretion. But of course he does *not* apply it rigidly.

I will conclude this part of the review by showing why the ideal observer theory, the rational contractor theory and my own theory must, on certain interpretations of each of them, yield the same results. As pointed out above, the " economical veil " version of the rational contractor theory secures impartiality between the individuals in society. The ideal observer theory includes impartiality as an express stipulation. My own theory secures impartiality by a combination of the requirement that moral judgments be universalizable and the requirement to prescribe for hypothetical reversed-role situations as if they were actual (I am not sure whether the second is an independent condition or not). So, as regards impartiality, the theories are on all fours. Next, some degree of benevolence is required by all three theories ; the ideal observer is expressly required to be impartially benevolent ; my universal prescriber, since he has to treat everybody as one and nobody as more than one, and since one of the persons included in " everybody " is himself, to whom he is benevolent, has to be positively and equally benevolent to everybody ; the rational contractor, although he is selfish, does not know which individual POL it is whose interests he should favour (since he does not know which is himself) and so his selfish or partial benevolence has the same results as impartial benevolence. For the same kind of reason the ideal observer and the universal prescriber, though they have additional knowledge (viz., knowledge of their own individual roles, if any, in the situations for which they are prescribing) are prevented by the previous requirements from using it for selfish ends.

Rawls himself says that the ideal observer theory leads to utilitarianism

(185/24) ; and—at least if it takes a certain form, if it involves what Rawls calls ' sympathetic identification ' with all affected parties—this seems plausible. In stating this form of the theory, he echoes some phrases of my own,[13] and later treats my theory and the ideal observer theory as equivalent.[14] So, then, the rational contractor theory, in the version I have been discussing (which is not Rawls') should also lead to utilitarianism. Rawls is aware of this possibility (121/33). He even seems to imply on 149/3 that *his own* theory is practically equivalent to the ideal observer theory ; but this is not his usual view. I shall leave to the second part of this review the difficult task of deciding whether Rawls, by the departures he makes from this simple version of the rational contractor theory, succeeds in establishing a non-utilitarian conclusion.

Of the three theories that I have just shown to be practically equivalent, it is largely a matter of taste which one adopts. Philosophers will differ in the use they like to make of dramatizations of their theories, and in the particular scenarios chosen. Such dramatizations do not help the argument, though they may help to expound it ; Rawls himself seems to agree (138/31). For myself, I think such devices useful (though they can also mislead), and I had much greater hopes of Rawls' enterprise than have in fact been realized. For, knowing that the simplest and most natural version of the rational contractor theory was practically equivalent to my own position, I was optimistic enough to hope that Rawls' elaborate exploration of the normative consequences of such a theory might illuminate those of my own, and thus enable me (in the most favourable outcome) simply to plug in to his results. Such good luck, however, seldom befalls philosophers ; and in fact Rawls' constant appeal to intuition instead of argument, and his tailoring of his theory to suit his anti-utilitarian preconceptions, have deprived it of the value which it could have had as a tracing of the normative consequences of views about the logic of the moral concepts.

It is interesting that in his peroration (587) Rawls as good as drops into an ideal-observer way of speaking. I myself should be happy to use any of these images (including C. I. Lewis's " all lives *seriatim* " picture[15]). But the work needs to be done on the logic of the argument, which has to be shown to be valid by the procedures of philosophical logic, involving the analysis of concepts, natural, or if need be artificial. Without this, a " theory of justice " is nothing but a suggestive picture.

Corpus Christi College, Oxford

[13]186/30, 34 ; *Freedom and Reason*, p. 123.

[14]See *Freedom and Reason*, p. 94 n.

[15]*Analysis of Knowledge and Valuation*, p. 547 ; Rawls 189/12 ; cf. my *Freedom and Reason*, p. 199, where through ignorance I failed to acknowledge Lewis's use of this picture.

CANADIAN JOURNAL OF PHILOSOPHY
Volume 18, Number 1, March 1988, pp. 67-86

The Problem of the Criterion and Coherence Methods in Ethics

MICHAEL R. DEPAUL
University of Notre Dame
Notre Dame, IN 46556
U.S.A.

I Introduction

The resurgence of interest in systematic moral theory over the past ten to fifteen years has brought to the fore debates concerning issues in moral epistemology, in particular, questions regarding the correct method for moral inquiry. Much of the controversy has focused on John Rawls' method of reflective equilibrium.[1] One merit claimed for this coherence method is that it transcends the traditional two tiered approach to moral inquiry according to which one must choose as one's starting points either particular moral judgments or general moral principles.[2] Several of Rawls' prominent critics[3] have charged that Rawls' loosely assembled rabble of starting points are not epistemically hefty enough to hoist a moral theory upon their shoulders. Perhaps unwittingly, these critics cling to the two level conception of theory construction, for they both defend general principles as the only appropriate

---

1 John Rawls, 'The Independence of Moral Theory,' *Proceedings and Addresses of the American Philosophical Association* **68** (1974-75) 5-22, and *A Theory of Justice* (Cambridge, MA: Harvard University Press 1971)

2 Cf. Norman Daniels, 'Wide Reflective Equilibrium and Theory Acceptance in Ethics,' *Journal of Philosophy* **76** (1979) 256-82.

3 For example, Richard Brandt, *A Theory of the Good and the Right* (Oxford: Clarendon Press 1979), R.M. Hare, 'Rawls' Theory of Justice-I,' *Philosophical Quarterly* **23** (1973) 144-55, and Peter Singer, 'Sidgwick and Reflective Equilibrium,' *The Monist* **58** (1974) 490-517.

starting points for theory construction and insist upon viewing Rawls as one working within the two tiered conception who opts for more particular judgments as starting points.

The two-level conception of theory construction has not been confined to ethics. Indeed, the most detailed exposition of the conception can be found in R.M. Chisholm's various discussions of the problem of the criterion.[4] Chisholm identifies approaches to theory construction with reference to the following two pairs of questions:

(A) *What* do we know? What is the *extent* of our knowledge?

(B) How are we to decide *whether* we know? What are the *criteria* of knowledge?[5]

Assuming that a philosophical theory of knowledge should provide a systematic answer to these questions, we immediately confront a sceptical argument, which constitutes the problem of the criterion.

> You cannot answer question A until you have answered question B. And you cannot answer question B until you have answered question A. Therefore you cannot answer either question.[6]

Two ways of avoiding this argument are apparent: one could assume that one begins the task of constructing a theory of knowledge with the answer to one or the other of the two question pairs. Chisholm labels those who think that we begin with an answer to A and that we can work out an answer to B on this basis *particularists*, and those who think that we begin with an answer to B and that we can work out an answer to A on this basis *methodists*.[7]

---

4 R.M. Chisholm, *The Foundations of Knowing* (Minneapolis: University of Minnesota Press 1982), Ch. 5; *The Theory of Knowledge*, 2nd ed. (Englewood Cliffs: Prentice-Hall 1977), Ch. 7; and *The Problem of the Criterion* (Milwaukee: Marquette University Press 1973)

5 Chisholm, *The Problem of the Criterion*, 12

6 Ibid., 14

7 Perhaps the most significant point Chisholm makes about methodism, particularism and scepticism is that there is no way of proving which of these positions is correct. When a proponent of any attempts to do so he or she will eventually be forced to beg the question against the others. Although I shall try to add to Chisholm's taxonomy and even to argue for one of the positions I describe, I do not claim to avoid this point.

While the problem of the criterion and the possible responses Chisholm describes have played a major role in structuring the way epistemologists think about method, they have not similarly influenced the deliberations of moral theorists. But moral philosophers are not the only ones with myopia, for Rawls' coherentist approach to theory construction as well as a classical moral methodology, viz., the form of intuitionism defended by H.A. Prichard[8] and David Ross,[9] do not appear in Chisholm's taxonomy. One of my aims is to correct the vision of both parties by expanding Chisholm's taxonomy of approaches to normative theory construction in order to make clear how intuitionism and Rawls' coherentist method are related to the methods identified by Chisholm. Although I shall conduct the discussion in terms of constructing a moral theory, I intend the discussion to be of interest to epistemologists as well as ethicists.

My other goal is to argue for coherentism of the sort defended by Rawls against the other non-sceptical methods I consider.[10] I wish to emphasize, however, that I do not take this to be my primary aim, to which the taxonomy I present is subservient. I take the similarities between the two most highly developed inquiries into evaluative properties, i.e., ethics and epistemology, to be very significant. So it is unfortunate that the most influential methodological discussions in the respective areas have not interacted. I conceive of providing a taxonomy relating the methodological positions outlined by Chisholm and Rawls to be as significant as any argument I present.

---

8 H.A. Prichard, 'Does Moral Philosophy Rest on a Mistake?' reprinted in Wilfrid Sellars and John Hospers, eds., *Readings in Ethical Theory* (Englewood Cliffs: Prentice-Hall 1970) 86-96

9 David Ross, *The Right and the Good* (Oxford: Clarendon Press 1930)

10 Some might think that my argument cannot be very strong, since the non-sceptical methods I consider do not exhaust the field. In particular, one might think that the approaches of authors, e.g., R.M. Hare, *Moral Thinking* (Oxford: Clarendon Press 1981), and Richard Brandt, *A Theory of the Good and the Right*, who attempt to deduce moral principles, or establish them in some other way, on the basis of non-moral propositions do not fit into my taxonomy. I maintain that such positins can be fit into my taxonomy, and hence, that my defence of coherentist methods is quite strong. However, because of space limitations, I shall not be able to argue here for this claim, so my 'official' position must be that I offer a partial defence of coherentism.

II Methodism, Particularism, Coherentism and Intuitionism

As I shall conduct the discussion in terms of moral rather than epistemological theories, I shall henceforth understand methodism, particularism and scepticism to be the positions defined in terms of the following analogues of Chisholm's questions.

(A) Which of our actions are morally right?

(B) What are the criteria of right action?

Chisholm tells us that a methodist begins with an answer to B while a particularist begins with an answer to A. Hence, characterizing the answers to A and B provides a good first step towards a more precise understanding of the approaches to theory construction. Presumably these answers will be sets of propositions (henceforth, A*and B* respectively). Three characteristics A* and B* must have in order to answer the respective questions easily come to mind:
(1) The propositions in A* will be particular in some sense and the elements of B* will be, in some sense, general. The distinction between particular and general propositions is more difficult to draw than one might expect. For example, it cannot be purely formal since A* might contain propositions that concern abstractly described hypothetical cases or group actions together in terms of a characteristic that is 'accidental' to their shared moral status.[11] Perhaps the best I can do is to say that the general propositions in B* are conditionals that provide necessary or sufficient non-moral conditions for the presence of moral properties.[12]

---

11 The statement that all killings of Jews at Auschwitz in 1944 were wrong selects a group of actions that are wrong by appeal to a property that is accidental to the wrongness of the action, i.e., the time and place of the killing. For if the world were very different it might have been that only one Jew was killed at that place during that year, and that this person was killed in self defense.

12 This is no benign assumption. For one thing, by understanding the answer to B in this way I side with the second of the two questions that make up B, the question that asks for a criterion of right action. In fact it is not even clear that I side with this member of the pair, since my specification of B* is somewhat weaker than Chisholm's traditional understanding of a criterion would require. Chisholm adopts Cardinal Mercier's requirement that an answer to B be internal, objective and immediate. Chisholm, *The Problem of the Criterion*, 6-8 and 36-7. The first question of the pair seems to ask for a procedure that one might follow in order to determine which actions are right. It is, therefore, more general than the second question in the pair, since a criterion of right action would provide only one sort of procedure for determining which actions are right, i.e., find the actions

(2) A* and B* will have to be consistent.[13]

(3) The propositions in A* and B* will have to cover a sufficiently broad range of actions. One way of capturing this condition is to require that A* and B* be complete with respect to a certain class of actions in the sense that they determine[14] for every action in that class whether or not it is right. I assume that this class will include actions performed in the actual world and in possible worlds inhabited by beings rather like us where the material circumstances of these beings are similar to ours in terms of such things as the scarcity of the resources necessary for a desirable life.[15]

---

that have the criterial property. Other procedures are possible, as illustrated by the many moral methodologies that philosophers have proposed. For example, one might be inclined to think that Rawls' method of reflective equilibrium provides an answer to B. We are to decide whether an action is morally right by bringing our moral beliefs into a state of wide reflective equilibrium, and then seeing whether our moral beliefs in wide reflective equilibrium entail that the action is right. The simplest way I can explain why we cannot understand question B in this very broad and general way is to point out that it collapses the distinction between A and B, and thus, between particularism and methodism. For surely even the particularist proposes a procedure in the broad sense. He tells us to take our particular moral beliefs, and if one of these doesn't concern the case we are interested in, generalize from these cases and apply the principle this generalization yields to the case in question.

13 For simplicity I here ignore problems that might arise if real moral dilemmas are possible. I assume any such problems could be resolved simply by amending the definition of consistency. Although I do not think the definition of consistency she proposes is adequate, on this issue see Ruth Marcus, 'Moral Dilemmas and Ethical Consistency,' *Journal of Philosophy* 77 (1980) 121-36.

14 I intend by 'determine' a logical relation that will be deductive in the case of B* and inductive for A*. For a discussion of a weaker way in which one might wish moral principles to determine the moral status of actions see John Rawls, 'Outline of a Decision Procedure for Ethics,' *Philosophical Review* 60 (1951) 184-6, who requires that moral principles 'explicate' particular moral judgments.

15 Dan Brock has pointed out to me that there is a serious question here about whether completeness with respect to any determinate class of actions should be required of the beliefs which are to base moral inquiry. The point is not that there might be some 'smaller' class of actions that a moral theory must be able to deal with if it is to be adequate. Rather, it is that there might be indefinitely many different and possibly disjoint classes of actions such that, a moral theory should be considered adequate if it could deal with the actions in one of these classes. I can respond to this objection only by pointing out that, even if we might be willing to settle for less in the end, ideally we would want a moral theory to be complete in the sense I've identified. I do not think I will go too far wrong if I begin by considering methods that assume this ideal to be readily attainable. I hope it will be clear below which methods are wedded to this naive assumption, and which are compatible with the more sober estimation that we certainly do not begin with complete moral beliefs, and perhaps never will be able to attain them.

The first characteristic of the starting points for theory construction preferred by methodism and particularism respectively makes it clear that they do not exhaust the field. For why should one suppose that a person must choose between her particular moral beliefs and her general moral beliefs when selecting the starting points for moral inquiry? If a person initially believes both particular and general moral propositions, it would seem to be possible for her to make use of both types of belief in constructing a moral theory. Perhaps neither the person's particular beliefs nor her general beliefs are complete in the sense specified above, but the 'gaps' in each type of belief are filled by beliefs of the other type so that using both would enable the person to answer both questions. *Coherentism* is the position that denies that we begin with an answer to just one of A and B. The coherentist maintains that, in general, we begin believing some particular and some general propositions, i.e., with a partial answer to each of Chisholm's questions, and that by using these partial answers we can construct a systematic answer to both A and B. (We shall let C* be a set of general and particular propositions that is consistent and complete.)

Chisholm's descriptions of the particularist as one who begins with A* and attempts to work out an answer to B on this basis and the methodist as one who has things the other way around, and our similar understanding of coherentism, might suggest that these positions are purely methodological. However, the fact that Chisholm introduces methodism and particularism as alternatives to scepticism indicates that they have a substantive epistemological component as well as a methodological component. The sceptical position to which methodism and particularism are opposed is, so to speak, doubly sceptical, for it denies both that we can know any moral propositions and that there is a method we should adopt for moral inquiry. This position combines substantive scepticism with methodological scepticism. Methodism, particularism and coherentism agree in denying both elements of this sceptical position: they hold that we can have moral knowledge and that there is a method by which we can construct moral theories.

While positions that deny only methodological scepticism have received little serious consideration in epistemology,[16] such positions

---

16 One exception is provided by Ernest Sosa who has commented favorably on a classical intuitionist position regarding epistemic justification ('Foundations of Foundationalism,' *Nous* **14** [1980] 554-6 and 563-4).

have received considerable attention in ethics. Classical intuitionism seems to be an intermediate position, lying between scepticism and either methodism, particularism, or coherentism. H.A. Prichard provides an example of one who held a position between particularism and scepticism. He maintained that we can know immediately in any particular instance what our duty is, but that there is no criterion of right action which can be discovered on this basis (unless it is the trivial criterion of being the act which, upon careful consideration, we *see* to be the one which we ought to perform). Thus, Prichard held that we have, at least potentially, knowledge of all particular propositions about right action, but that no answer to B can be derived from this knowledge.

One might interpret David Ross as holding a form of intuitionism more closely related to methodism. According to Ross we know all the principles regarding right action that there are prior to philosophical reflection, but these principles identify acts that are prima facie right rather than right per se. One can understand this position as follows. There is a finite number of properties that make actions right, and we know what these properties are. However, in various circumstances more than one of a number of mutually exclusive alternative actions might have one of these properties, while only one of these actions would be right. In such a case, 'right making' properties had by actions that it would not be right to perform are said to be 'overridden' or 'defeated.' Thus, according to this view we begin moral inquiry with a set of principles of the form 'if an act is c, and c is not overridden, then it is right,' where 'c' is replaced by a right making property. If there were in addition some principle that determined which right making properties overrode which, this position would be a form of methodism. However, since Ross held that there was no such principle, he was committed to holding that, although we know the answer to B, or more accurately, all there is to know about the answer to B, this answer is incomplete and cannot be used to determine whether or not any particular act is right.

The classical intuitionists took up a sceptical position less radical than the one considered above, allowing that we can have knowledge of some moral propositions, either those in A* or those in B*, while denying that there is a method which tells us how to use this knowledge to construct an ethical theory that provides a systematic answer to both questions. Although these versions of intuitionism are worthy of consideration, and may even be more plausible than the positions I shall evaluate in detail, I will not be giving them further attention. My justification for overlooking them is that their best defense would be provided by the continued frustration of our attempts to work out adequate moral theories. We therefore do well to avoid adopting such pessimistic positions as classical intuitionism before we've given the more positive alternatives a fair shot at completing their projects.[17]

The combination of their commitments regarding the starting points for ethical inquiry with an opposition to methodological and substantive scepticism constrains methodism, particularism and coherentism to some degree, but there is still a wide range of positions compatible with this combination. The various forms of each approach can differ with respect to methodological issues, such as which general or particular propositions are to be used as starting points as well as how these propositions are to be used, and epistemological issues, for example, the epistemic status of the propositions which base theory construction and the account given for the epistemic status of these and the theory constructed.

The most simple minded version of, e.g., particularism might hold the following. (i) The moral beliefs we have before we begin philosophical inquiry satisfy the requirements on A*. (ii) All of these beliefs are known and therefore should not be altered. (iii) We generalize from these beliefs, along with facts about various particular actions, the general propositions necessary to answer B. (iv) These beliefs will be knowledge since they will have been derived via an appropriate form of inference from known propositions.[18]

Among the many faults of this absurdly simple approach one deserves special mention: It understands the idea that we *begin* theory construction with an answer to A quite literally, holding that the moral beliefs we happen to hold prior to any philosophical inquiry constitute an answer to this question. Surely we should not construe the particularist's commitment regarding the starting points for theory construction along these lines. We must rather take the beliefs in A* to be drawn from those that are intuitional or pre-philosophical for us in the rather weak sense that we do not accept them on the basis of any other of our beliefs, but hold them simply because they seem to us as though they must be true.

Even if one corrects the simple version of particularism in the light of the preceding reflection, it is still quite clearly inadequate. Its attribution of a significant positive epistemic status to our pre-philosophical moral beliefs is open to question. In addition, the position faces methodological problems. It holds that our pre-philosophical beliefs

---

17 The same point is made in Sosa, 554-5.

18 A position that is perhaps slightly less implausible might be obtained by weakening the epistemic status claimed for our moral beliefs and claiming that they are justified rather than known.

satisfy the conditions on A*, which means that they must be complete and consistent in the senses specified above. Yet it seems highly unlikely that the pre-philosophical moral beliefs of ordinary persons have the sort of orderly, coherent structure that this entails. The existence of difficult moral problems bears this fact out, for such problems generally do not arise because of great complexity or unseen consequences, but because the moral beliefs brought into conflict by such cases are strongly held intuitions that persons are not inclined to give up even after it has become apparent that they are inconsistent. It is easy to see that similar versions of methodism and coherentism would face the same objections. There are two general strategies for avoiding these problems which a particularist, methodist, or coherentist might employ: (1) One might try restricting our pre-philosophical beliefs in some way, or (2) One might specify circumstances where revisions of these beliefs would be allowed.

III Restricting Our Initial Moral Beliefs

In an early paper John Rawls[19] described what I take to be the paradigm for the restrictive versions of coherentism, methodism and particularism, which hold that at least some of us have initial moral beliefs that can provide a suitable base for constructing moral theories if only we cull some of these beliefs.[20] According to Rawls we should take as our starting points for theory construction the considered moral judgments of competent moral judges. Rawls claims that the defining characteristics of a competent moral judge (e.g., being intelligent, experienced, reasonable and sympathetic) are 'those characteristics which, in the light of experience, show themselves as necessary conditions for a reasonable expectation that a given person may come to know something.'[21] He makes a similar claim for the characteristics that define considered moral judgments, which must be certain, stable, formed disinterestedly on the basis of all the relevant facts, and shared by other competent judges: 'they select those judgments most likely to be

---

19 'Outline of a Decision Procedure for Ethics'

20 Since Rawls limits the class of starting points to particular beliefs, the method he describes is in fact a form of particularism. In order to extend the spirit of his restrictions to coherentism and methodism I shall omit or alter this and a few others of his restrictions.

21 Rawls, 'Outline of a Decision Procedure for Ethics,' 180

decided by those habits of thought and imagination deemed essential for a competent judge.'[22]

If Rawls is right in making these claims, it would seem that the considered judgments of competent judges are likely to have a higher epistemic status than the ordinary moral beliefs of ordinary persons.[23] Thus, one might be tempted by a version of methodism, particularism, or coherentism, that held this class of judgments to provide an appropriate starting point for the construction of a moral theory.[24] Unfortunately, I suspect that the cost for selecting a class of judgments with such favorable epistemic credentials in the way Rawls has proposed is that the class will not allow the construction of a moral theory.

For Rawls' or a similar restrictive method to succeed, it must be the case that the considered moral judgments of competent moral judges meet the conditions of either A*, B* or C*. After eliminating all the pre-philosophical beliefs of competent judges that the judges disagree about, are uncertain of, or have no settled opinion on, there is little question that the remaining propositions will form a consistent set. However, these same requirements on considered moral judgments threaten to limit the beliefs that can be used for theory construction so severely that no moral theory could be constructed *solely* on their basis. Surely if we understand certainty in a standard sense, persons will feel certain of relatively few moral beliefs. Moreover, given the characteristics of competent moral judges we could reasonably expect them to be even less likely to feel certain in their judgments about interesting cases than ordinary people since competent judges would be sensitive to *all* competing interests. We would also expect the moral beliefs of such fair and open minded persons to undergo a sort of evolution so that relatively few of their beliefs would be stable over time. Finally, the restriction to judgments that are agreed to by all competent moral judges is likely to cause problems, if the current degree of agreement among moral philosophers is any indication of the beliefs of such judges.[25] To be sure, there is a class of propositions about which

---

22 Ibid., 183

23 The appearance may be deceptive. Stefan Sencerz has recently argued that the 'filtering' involved in obtaining considered moral judgments does not insure that these judgments will have a significant positive epistemic status (*Philosophical Studies* **50** [1986] 77-95).

24 The method endorsed by Rawls is just such a version of particularism.

25 Others obviously have a different opinion about the chance for intersubjective agreement, e.g., Norman Daniels, 'Wide Reflective Equilibrium and Theory Acceptance in Ethics,' but I do not think it would be helpful to argue the point. For

all competent moral judges are likely to be certain, settled and agree, and this class is perhaps even quite large. In fact it will most likely contain the kinds of judgments that commonly figure in the counterexamples offered against precisely stated moral theories. In my opinion, however, even competent moral judges would agree about too few cases for them to do much more than make a start at constructing a moral theory, as is suggested by the fact that the little agreement there is about moral theories all seems to concern their refutation.

It is quite clear that if the class of initial moral beliefs to be used in constructing a moral theory is restricted in accordance with Rawls' requirements, the beliefs of few, if any, will allow the construction of a moral theory. If a correct approach to moral theory construction should allow the possibility of any competent inquirer completing the task, and also say something about the moral knowledge of ordinary persons, then this result is unsatisfactory. One could attempt to correct Rawls' restrictions, or to produce an entirely new set of restrictions, in order to avoid the problems I have mentioned. However, it seems that all such approaches would either face problems concerning the breadth of propositions in the base class, or if these were avoided, problems concerning the epistemic merits of the propositions. I shall therefore leave behind the restrictive versions of methodism, particularism and coherentism, and attempt to decide whether versions of these positions that allow for the revision of the base class for theory construction open the possibility of constructing a moral theory to a reasonably wide range of inquirers.

IV Revising Our Initial Moral Beliefs

According to the positions I've rejected so far our pre-philosophical moral beliefs are epistemologically privileged, in that we know or are justified in believing them, and methodologically privileged, in the sense that we should use them to base the construction of moral theories. Although one might doubt that there is a class of propositions

---

one thing, it is an empirical question that should not be decided on the basis of philosophical speculation. More importantly, I do not think that proving my claim about the likelihood of intersubjective agreement is essential to my project. My aim in this paper is to categorize certain approaches to the construction of moral theories and to provide some reasons for thinking that one of these is more promising than the others. My interest, then, is in part strategic, and adopting a method which can be successful only if a controversial empirical assumption turns out to be true when one can avoid doing so is a poor strategy indeed.

with these privileges, such a general scepticism did not ground my objections to the simple and restrictive versions of methodism, particularism, and coherentism. Rather, I rejected them because of where they held the privileged class of propositions could be found, i.e., among our pre-philosophical moral beliefs. One can find ample ground for rejecting these positions simply by reflecting on the nature of our moral beliefs. However, such reflections do not call into question the assumption that there is a class of propositions that are epistemologically and methodologically privileged. More plausible versions of methodism, particularism, and coherentism can therefore hold onto the claim that a class of privileged propositions exists, and simply tell us to look for these propositions in a place where we are likely to find them.

Consider the following view. We begin with our initial particular beliefs about right action. We then eliminate those beliefs that fail to satisfy a set of requirements similar to those Rawls places on considered moral judgments. The beliefs would be intuitive, but formed after due consideration and an inquiry into the relevant facts about cases in which one has no significant personal interest. The beliefs will not have to meet any stability condition, nor must they be certain. The latter condition will be replaced with a requirement that the beliefs seem more likely to be true than their negations, or perhaps that the person who holds them feels sure enough of them that she does not think that it would be best to withhold judgment. Consistency is not required, since inconsistencies will be eliminated later.

The really significant difference between this method and the views considered above is that instead of stopping with the restricted class of beliefs, we attempt to correct the beliefs that are excluded by those views: we attempt to eliminate the effects of bias, acquire more information, and think things through more carefully. All of this will serve to lessen our doubts and make us more confident of our beliefs. In addition, we could strive to increase the breadth of cases about which we have opinions by considering new and different situations in which moral questions arise. We could obviously do all of this without relying on any general moral principles, so, although the particular judgments we formed might not be intuitional or pre-philosophical in the strictest sense, they would be in a relevant sense. We would be attempting to answer B on the basis of a set of propositions that constitutes the result of our best effort to answer A.

This method is obviously a form of particularism. Indeed, it is almost certainly the position most particularists hold, interpreting the claim that we begin with an answer to A to mean that we 'implicitly' know the answer to this question, and hence, should base our beliefs in general principles on our judgments about particular cases. Their view is that we can work out an answer to A without relying on any general moral principles, rather than that we can find the answer to A among our pre-philosophical moral beliefs.

It is also obvious that there are analogous forms of methodism and coherentism. The common idea behind these positions is not to restrict our initial moral beliefs in some way and hope that the remaining beliefs will be suitable for constructing a moral theory. Instead, these positions direct us to revise and to expand our moral beliefs until they are suitable for constructing a moral theory. Since there is in principle nothing to stop one who adopted one of these methods from working at his moral beliefs until they determine a moral theory, it would seem that these positions are much better off with respect to the difficulties that faced their simpler predecessors. Although in fact we may not be able to complete the task, it is not obvious at the outset that we cannot, and given that we could keep at it, there is hope that we might meet with success. Not only does allowing revisions of our initial moral beliefs increase the chances that we will be able to construct a moral theory, it also makes better epistemological sense. For we are all more confident of those things that we believe after due consideration than we are of our initial opinions about a topic, and rightly so.

My criticisms of the simple and restrictive versions of methodism, particularism and coherentism rest on considerations about the nature of our pre-philosophical moral beliefs and the idea that moral theory construction is an activity open to most ordinary persons. Considerations of this sort will not count against any of the positions I am now considering. In order to critically evaluate these revisionary positions I must appeal to epistemological considerations. In particular, consideration of how it is rational to resolve conflicts between beliefs will show that revisionary methodism and particularism are likely to lead to irrational beliefs in a way that revisionary coherentism is not.

Let us suppose that a particularist finds that one of her initial particular beliefs about right action is inconsistent with one of the general moral principles she accepts without reflection. This circumstance should not be uncommon, since most people have both general and particular initial beliefs and our unreflective moral beliefs are often in conflict. We can suppose, in addition, that following the particularist method for revising particular beliefs does not lead this person to alter her particular belief. This could easily happen, since the particularist does not use her general moral beliefs in making revisions, but revises initial particular beliefs depending upon how these beliefs were formed or are presently held and their relations with other particular beliefs.

It is, of course, no mystery how the particularist would resolve the conflict: the particularist must favor particular moral beliefs over beliefs in general principles. For this reason particularism can lead one to form irrational beliefs. Suppose, for example, that after comparing the conflicting beliefs and considering matters as thoroughly as she can, our particularist feels quite certain that the general belief is true and the particular belief false. I maintain that in such a circumstance it would simply be irrational to follow the dictates of particularism.

It should be clear that a methodist can get into a precisely similar circumstance and be lead to form a belief that is irrational in just the same way. The problem with revisionary methodism and particularism is that, in general, the way in which it is rational for a person to resolve a conflict between beliefs will not be determined by which of those beliefs is general and which is particular, but by which belief seems most likely to be true to the person after thoroughly considering the matter.

I wish to consider two defenses a particularist or methodist might offer. First, they might claim that, as a matter of fact, we always favor either our general or our particular beliefs in cases of conflict. Certainly one problem with this response is that it rests on a dubious empirical claim. A deeper problem is that the response is inconsistent with methodism and particularism. This is because it allows the class of privileged propositions to be defined without reference to the form of the propositions that go into that class, i.e., to be defined as those favored on reflection. Thus, the methodist or particularist who adopts this solution ends up accepting a form of coherentism. We must note that a person following a coherentist approach might look like a methodist or particularist, if the propositions he accepts after revising his initial moral beliefs are either exclusively general or exclusively particular, or, if after reflecting on cases of conflict, he always favors beliefs of one sort over those of the other.

A more thoughtful defender of methodism or particularism might claim that it would not be irrational to favor a less strongly held particular or general belief if one had a reason for doing so. We have touched upon no reason for supposing that a person's choice of methodism or particularism must be groundless. One will presumably be led to adopt one of these methods because one holds a belief about what it would be rational or irrational for a person to do about her moral beliefs, e.g., the belief that general or particular beliefs respectively should be favored in cases of conflict.

This point is well taken, but I'm not sure it can make much difference.[26] The number of us for whom it will not be irrational to favor

---

26 I should also note that bringing philosophical beliefs that are not 'moral' to bear upon moral theory construction in the way here suggested is characteristic of wide reflective equilibrium, the version of coherentism I shall end up endorsing. I shall therefore have occasion to return to this point when we consider that version of coherentism below.

a belief on the basis of its being particular or general, that is, the number of us for whom it will be rational to accept either particularism or methodism, will be very small. For nearly all of us are much more confident of at least some particular and general beliefs about what we ought to do than we are of relatively theoretical epistemological principles concerning how it is rational to resolve conflicts between moral beliefs. Such a general epistemological principle need not be held without reason. It may, indeed probably will, be held on the basis of less general, more common place epistemological beliefs that are more plausibly placed on a par with our moral beliefs. However, I do not think that we can say a priori that all persons hold such epistemological beliefs more firmly than moral beliefs, so while it may be rational for some to adopt methodism or particularism, it will not be rational for all or even most. I wish to make my charge clear: It is not that revisionary methodism and particularism will necessarily lead one to form irrational beliefs, but only that they are likely to lead many of us to form irrational beliefs. Surely a method that would do this is justly criticized for it.

V Revisionary Coherentism and Full Moral Coherentism

Revisionary coherentism does not direct anyone to form irrational beliefs in the way that revisionary methodism and revisionary particularism might. Nonetheless, I do not think that it is an acceptable position. All of the positions I have examined thus far hold that some class of propositions grounds moral theory construction. It is time to take a closer look at what proponents of these positions would say about the nature of moral theories and their construction.

Particularism seems to take an orthodox approach. A moral theory is a set of general moral principles that satisfies the conditions on B*. Moral theorizing consists in generalizing from our knowledge of particular cases to such a set of principles. In contrast, methodism seems to have things backward. We begin with the theory, and the theorizing consists in our deriving consequences for particular cases from this theory. This stretches our idea of constructing a theory, but the methodist can easily bring his view into line with common sense by pointing out that just any set of propositions which satisfies the conditions on B* will not count as a moral theory, but rather, only the simplest, most elegant set of principles. As it is unlikely that our considered general moral beliefs will be the simplest set of propositions that has a given set of entailments for particular cases, there is plenty of theorizing left for the methodist to do. The coherentist can assume the same notion of theory as the methodist, and claim that it is unlike-

305

ly both that the general beliefs among our considered moral judgments cover enough cases to satisfy the conditions on B* and that these beliefs are as simple and elegant as they might be. Thus, the coherentist can also allow for what we would all regard as theory construction on the basis of our considered moral beliefs.

No matter which of these approaches one takes, one must allow that there is a certain amount of tension between the moral principles strictly determined by one's considered moral beliefs, and considerations of simplicity and elegance. It will most probably be the case that a set of moral propositions somewhat different from one's considered moral beliefs will determine a simpler, more elegant moral theory than the one determined by one's considered moral beliefs. Because the positions I've considered thus far hold that our considered moral beliefs are methodologically and epistemologically privileged, and that the epistemological status of the moral theory eventually accepted is dependent upon these beliefs, none of these positions can take this tension very seriously. This fact opens all of the revisionary positions to objections similar to the objection against revisionary methodism and particularism I just considered, an objection to which coherentism in particular should be sensitive.

Suppose while constructing a theory of right action a person realizes that by altering a few of his considered moral beliefs he could accept a far simpler and more elegant moral theory. Suppose further that the considered moral beliefs involved in the changes are not among those the person is most strongly committed to, and that, upon thinking the matter through, it seems to the person that the revised set of moral beliefs and simpler theory of right action are much more likely to be true than the original set and theory. The new set of moral beliefs and moral theory the person is considering would not simply be another set of considered moral beliefs, since they would have been formed on the basis of theoretical considerations, so the revisionary versions of methodism, particularism and even coherentism would dictate that the person stick stubbornly with his considered beliefs about right action. I do not think that this would be a rational thing for the person to do in the circumstances described.

The obvious way of avoiding this sort of irrationality is to allow a revision of considered moral beliefs on theoretical grounds, with such revisions guided by what seems most likely to be true to one after thinking things through as completely as one can. Both the methodist and the coherentist can avail themselves of this option, but the particularist cannot. The revision may require the methodist and coherentist to alter the epistemological side of their position, since they can no longer hold that the epistemic status of the theory one constructs is determined simply by its having been derived from a set of considered moral beliefs which have a privileged epistemic status, but they can retain the methodological heart of their view. They can hold that theory construction should be guided by either the general moral principles that seem to us to be most likely to be true after due consideration or simply by the moral beliefs that seem to us to be most likely to be true after due consideration. Due consideration here includes considering how plausible the theory determined by one's considered judgments seems to one on its own, i.e., apart from any plausibility it might have in virtue of being determined by judgments that initially seemed to one to be very likely to be true. However, in order to revise particularism in this way one would have to give up the methodological heart of the position, for one would have to allow that it is possible for particular propositions that seem to one to be more likely to be true than any other particular propositions to be rejected in favor of general propositions that seem to the person to constitute a more plausible theory than the one determined by her particular beliefs.

Since only coherentism can avoid leading one to form irrational beliefs in both of the situations I've considered, I conclude that it is superior to both methodism and particularism. The form of coherentism I have been led to, which I shall call full moral coherentism, allows our initial particular and our initial general beliefs about right action to be used in theory construction. According to full moral coherentism we revise these initial beliefs to obtain a set of considered moral beliefs which we then use to construct a theory of right action. On the way to this theory full moral coherentism allows us to revise even our considered beliefs about right action, if by doing so we can attain a more simple and elegant theory that also seems to us to be more likely to be true than the theory based only on our considered judgments, and the altered set of considered beliefs seems more likely to us to be true than the initial set of considered judgments now seem.

Because of this, the proponent of full moral coherentism must give up, or weaken, the claim that our considered moral beliefs have a privileged epistemological status. For example, these beliefs can certainly not all count as knowledge if it is correct to alter them in order to arrive at a better theory, nor can they be justified in any strong sense. Moreover, the epistemic status of the theory accepted can hardly be maintained by the full coherentist to depend solely upon its being constructed on the basis of our considered moral beliefs about right action. Thus, full moral coherentism falls in line with traditional forms of coherentism, since it denies our considered moral beliefs any serious epistemic priority, and therefore, any foundational status. These beliefs serve a purely methodological function for the full coherentist: they are a starting point for theory construction, but it is quite possible for them to be overridden, and theory construction is guided primarily not by these beliefs, but by what seems to be true to the theory constructor upon careful consideration.

VI Wide Reflective Equilibrium

Full moral coherentism is essentially the same as the method of narrow reflective equilibrium described by John Rawls and Norman Daniels. The method they defend, wide reflective equilibrium, differs from full moral coherentism in that it requires persons to bring their non-moral beliefs into coherence with their moral beliefs. Thus, considered moral judgments or moral theory might be altered on the basis of beliefs other than particular or general beliefs about right action. I have already considered one example where this might happen when I described how a person might resolve conflicts between general and particular moral beliefs on the basis of an epistemological belief either that general beliefs should be favored in such situations or that particular beliefs should be favored. The important point for the proponent of wide reflective equilibrium is that all such conflicts are to be resolved on the basis of what seems most acceptable to the theory constructor after considering matters as fully as she can.

It is easy to see that both of the arguments I used to support full moral coherentism can be used to show that wide reflective equilibrium is better still. For first, it would seem irrational for a person to go on believing the moral theory that is fully coherent with his moral beliefs if he were to realize that it does not cohere with non-moral beliefs, e.g., about personal identity or the possibility of human freedom, which the person finds more compelling that any of his moral beliefs. And second, it would be unreasonable for a person to refuse to alter certain of his peripheral considered moral judgments, even if they are fully coherent with his other moral judgments and moral theory, when by doing so he could, e.g., avoid accepting a baroque epistemology that makes the justification of moral beliefs bizarre and utterly unlike the justification of any other beliefs.

It will doubtless seem to the critics of coherence methods that in these last remarks I am perversely looking at matters from the wrong vantage point. The question, they will maintain, is not whether it is rational for a person to allow non-moral beliefs to influence her moral beliefs, but whether we should place any confidence *at all* in moral beliefs apart from their connection with non-moral beliefs, let alone allow the possibility that it might be rational to alter non-moral beliefs in the face of moral beliefs.

My defense of coherentism on this point rests upon the consideration I have used to defend coherentism throughout this paper: If a person has two beliefs, and comes to see that these beliefs are inconsistent, and after careful reflection on these beliefs in connection with the other propositions she accepts or rejects finds herself more strongly committed to one of these beliefs than the other, then it would be irrational to alter the belief to which she is more strongly committed in order to retain the belief to which she is less strongly committed. As I see it this idea forms the core of coherentism. It grounds the view that decisions between competing beliefs must be made on the basis of the person's degree of commitment to these and related beliefs after due reflection, and not on the basis of the type of beliefs involved. It does not matter whether we are considering a conflict between general and particular moral beliefs or between some moral belief and a metaphysical, epistemological, or even a logical belief.

We are now in a position to see why a coherentist will hold there to be no rational alternative to the method of wide reflective equilibrium. Indeed, that even those who take themselves to be opposed to this method are following it. For suppose that there is some person who is unwilling to grant any of his moral beliefs any credibility at all. That is to say, this person is dubious of these beliefs, and will at least hope that he can resist placing any confidence in them until he can show that they are related to other beliefs he finds more credible, say beliefs about practical reason or the meanings and logic of moral terms. Needless to say, this person will alter any moral belief in the face of any non-moral belief with which it conflicts.

How can such a person be thought to be abiding by the method of wide reflective equilibrium, even if unwittingly? Presumably this person does not hold his moral beliefs in such low epistemic esteem, ignoring his degree of commitment to some of these beliefs, for no reason at all. He must have other beliefs, presumably epistemic beliefs or perhaps beliefs regarding the logic of moral terms or metaphysics of moral properties, which ground his rejection of the moral beliefs he naturally holds. Now, all things considered, this person must either be more strongly committed to these non-moral beliefs than he is to his moral beliefs or he must be less strongly committed to them.[27] If the former, then he would seem to be behaving rationally in rejecting his moral beliefs, but doing nothing other than the method of wide reflective equilibrium recommends. He would be attempting to mold his considered moral judgments, moral theory and non-moral beliefs into a

---

27 Ignoring, of course, the off chance that he is equally committed to both.

coherent whole, being guided by his degree of commitment to the various propositions involved after due consideration. It is just that in this person's case his moral beliefs systematically lose out to certain of his non-moral beliefs, which gives the appearance that he is following something other than a coherence method. If the situation is otherwise, and the person is in fact more strongly committed to his moral beliefs than to any of the non-moral beliefs that he rejects them in favor of, I cannot but hold that his behavior is epistemically perverse.[28]

Received November, 1985
Revised November, 1986

---

28 I am indebted to a number of persons for discussions of these issues and comments on earlier versions of this paper, most especially Philip Quinn, Richard Foley, Dan Brock, David Solomon and the referees for the *Canadian Journal of Philosophy*.

CANADIAN JOURNAL OF PHILOSOPHY 193
Volume 23, Number 2, June 1993, pp. 193 - 214

Is Reflective Equilibrium a Coherentist Model?

ROGER P. EBERTZ
University of Dubuque
Dubuque, IA 52001
USA

Over the last twenty years, John Rawls has developed an approach to political philosophy which appeals to the notion of reflective equilibrium.[1] This notion has proven suggestive to those attracted to coherence approaches to justification, in ethics and in other domains as well.[2] In this paper, I explore the question whether Rawls's approach provides a model for a coherentist account of justification, concluding that although the discussion of reflective equilibrium has provided helpful insights it has not produced a coherentist model of justification.

I What Is Reflective Equilibrium?

It will be helpful to briefly outline Rawls's use of the notion of reflective equilibrium.[3] Rawls wants to justify a particular conception of justice

---

1 See, for example, John Rawls, *A Theory of Justice* (Cambridge, MA: Harvard University Press 1971); and 'Kantian Constructivism in Moral Theory,' *Journal of Philosophy* **78** (1980) 515-72.

2 See, for example, Michael Resnik, 'Logic: Normative or Descriptive? The Ethics of Belief or A Branch of Psychology?' *Philosophy of Science* **52** (1985) 221-38; and Ernest Sosa, 'Equilibrium in Coherence?' in J.W. Bender, ed., *The Current State of the Coherence Theory* (Kluwer: Academic Press 1989) 242-50.

3 Norman Daniels has written much to help clarify Rawls's notion of reflective equilibrium. See his 'Reflective Equilibrium and Archimedean Points,' *Canadian Journal of Philosophy* **10** (1980) 83-103, and 'Reflective Equilibrium and Theory

which can be spelled out in terms of two basic principles. The justification of these principles includes arguments at two levels. On one level he needs to show that these principles are those which would be agreed upon by a representative group of free and rational persons, each having their own individual self-interest in mind, in a carefully defined 'initial situation' or 'the original position.' But along with justification on this level, Rawls must also justify the approach to ethics (contractarian constructivist) and a particular definition of the initial situation. To carry out these two justificatory tasks, Rawls introduces the notion of reflective equilibrium. Reflective equilibrium is the state of one's beliefs (about justice, in this case) when 'principles and judgments coincide.' When a person's beliefs are in reflective equilibrium, the structure of those beliefs, from the particular to the most general, cohere. They are 'in order.'[4] I find it helpful to speak also of 'the reflective process' to refer to the activities which lead one to reflective equilibrium. These include carefully considering individual beliefs, comparing them with one another, considering the beliefs of others, drawing out consequences of beliefs, and so forth. A description of the original position and a set of principles are justified, according to Rawls, when one has engaged in the reflective process and come to believe the principles in a state of reflective equilibrium. It is too simple to conceive of reflective equilibrium as a coherence of two elements: considered judgments and principles. In *A Theory of Justice*, and even more explicitly in more recent writings, Rawls has made it clear that it is not simply considered moral judgments and moral principles which play into the balance, but 'common presumptions,' mediating conceptions and background theories as well. Figure 1 illustrates the various elements which must 'fit together' in reflective equilibrium:

Acceptance in Ethics,' *Journal of Philosophy* 76 (1979) 264-73. As an early expositor of Rawls on reflective equilibrium, Daniels has greatly influenced the discussion of this concept. In the following exposition, I stick primarily to Rawls's text itself, yet my interpretation is no doubt influenced by that of Daniels.

4   *A Theory of Justice*, 20

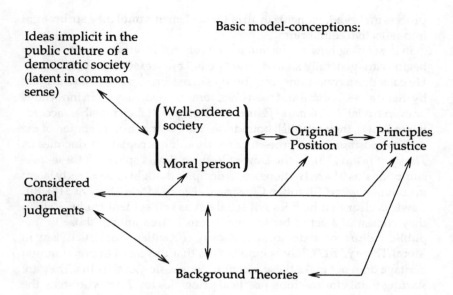

Figure 1: Reflective Equilibrium in Political Theory

One line of reflection passes from commonly shared presumptions (which Rawls refers to as 'ideas implicit in the public culture of a democratic society'), through 'model-conceptions' which focus and systematize the ideas in the presumptions, to principles. Reflection moves in both directions along this line. As a person reflects, she may make changes in any of the elements along this line to reach equilibrium.[5] A second, branching pattern of reflection involves our 'considered judgments' more directly. These considered judgments provide an outside check on all of the elements in the balance. Finally, Rawls also suggests that 'wide reflective equilibrium' will bring psychological and social (background) theories into our reflection on the plausibility and acceptability of the various other elements in the balance.[6] The reflective

---

5 In 'Kantian Contructivism in Moral Theory,' Rawls suggests that the justification of ethical principles is not so much to show that they are true, as with justification in epistemology, but to show that they are reasonable for persons living in a free and democratic society. Given this purpose it is not entirely clear that one could move radically away from the common presumptions we share and still justify principles for all who share those presumptions. I will return to this issue below.

6 Norman Daniels, in 'Reflective Equilibrium and Archimedean Points,' is particu-

process makes adjustments in all of these elements until they are brought into reflective equilibrium.

In describing how we formulate the original position, Rawls says we begin with 'generally shared' and 'weak,' but 'reasonable' conditions.[7] He calls these conditions 'commonly shared presumptions,' which are by themselves 'natural and plausible, some of them may seem innocuous or even trivial' (*A Theory of Justice*, 18). But when taken together, according to Rawls, they establish boundaries for a proper interpretation of the original position and a procedure for choosing acceptable principles (*A Theory of Justice*, 18). In the Dewey lectures Rawls speaks of these 'presumptions' as 'shared notions and principles thought to be already latent in common sense' ('Kantian Constructivism in Moral Theory,' 518). But Rawls is clear that he does not see them as self-evident truths. Rather, they consist of a set of broad convictions shared among those in 'the public culture of a democratic society' ('Kantian Constructiyism in Moral Theory,' 517). Rawls emphasizes that this basis in our common heritage does not make these presumptions basic moral truths. They are starting points for reaching practical principles for those who share the presumptions. One example of such a presumption that becomes central to Rawls justification of his principles is 'a conception of the person implicitly affirmed in' our democratic culture ('Kantian Constructivism in Moral Theory,' 518). This conception, Rawls says 'regards persons as both free and equal, as capable of acting both reasonably and rationally, and therefore as capable of taking part in social cooperation among persons so conceived' ('Kantian Constructivism in Moral Theory,' 518).

Rawls focuses these shared presumptions into three 'model-conceptions.' 'Justice as fairness,' Rawls says, 'tries to uncover the fundamental ideas (latent in common sense) of freedom and equality, of ideal social cooperation, and of the person, by formulating what I shall call "model-conceptions"' ('Kantian Constructivism in Moral Theory,' 520). Most closely related to our presumptions are the model conceptions of a

---

larly helpful in clarifying the relevance of these broader theoretical issues to reflective equilibrium. Daniels clarifies Rawls's distinction between 'narrow reflective equilibrium' and 'wide reflective equilibrium.' See, however, Margaret Holmgren's 'The Wide and Narrow of Reflective Equilibrium,' *Canadian Journal of Philosophy* 19 (1989) 43-60, for an argument that Daniels overdraws this distinction.

7   'We begin by describing [the original position] so that it represents generally shared and preferably weak conditions. We then see if these conditions are strong enough to yield a significant set of principles. If not, we look for further premises equally reasonable. But if so, and these principles match our considered convictions of justice, then so far well and good' (*A Theory of Justice*, 20).

well-ordered society and that of the moral person. Out of these Rawls develops a third, that of the original position, which he calls a 'mediating model-conception,' the purpose of which is to provide a framework from which to choose (or construct) principles of justice. In general these 'model-conceptions' are ways of formulating and organizing common presumptions such that we can use them to further develop and test a theory.

Turning to considered moral judgments, these are those judgments which we would affirm under the conditions favorable to rational deliberation, when we are not swayed by strong emotion, fatigue and the like. They are those we affirm with confidence and without hesitation (*A Theory of Justice*, 47-8). Some considered judgments are very specific, affirming or denying the justice of particular actions or circumstances. Others are not so specific. Rawls provides these examples: '... we are confident that religious intolerance and racial discrimination are unjust' (*A Theory of Justice*, 19). And elsewhere Rawls suggests that these considered judgments can be 'at all levels of generality' ('Kantian Constructivism in Moral Theory,' 534). No matter how general, considered judgments seem to be pretheoretical convictions that arise more directly from our experience of circumstances and our upbringing than from the application of principles. They stand somewhat isolated from one another until they are brought together into a systematic unity in reflective equilibrium. Rawls repeatedly emphasizes that they are to be seen neither as self-evident nor necessary truths, stressing that considered judgments are open to revision, and may even be rejected in the process of reflection on alternative sets of principles.[8]

Thus Rawls describes a reflective process which considers a number of different kinds of beliefs and unites them into a coherent system, which is then said to be in reflective equilibrium. This is a picture which is attractive in domains beyond moral theory. Reasoning in these other domains, it might be suggested, aims at reflective equilibrium between various kinds of beliefs. Figure 2 illustrates a generic conception of reflective equilibrium.

---

8 See *A Theory of Justice*, 21, 578.

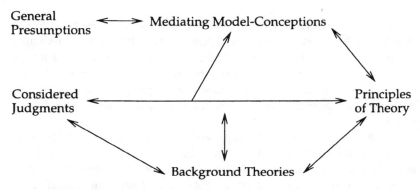

Figure 2: General Model of Reflective Equilibrium

II Does Reflective Equilibrium Require Coherentism?

It has been repeatedly suggested in the literature on reflective equilibrium that Rawls's method provides a nonfoundationalist approach to justification in ethics.[9] But using the notion of reflective equilibrium as such a model will yield a coherentist view of justification in general only if it really does reflect a fully nonfoundationalist approach to ethics. And in spite of the fact that many have suggested that it is a nonfoundationalist approach, it is not clear that it is. I will argue below that it is not.

First, however, we must note the reasons why many find it quite natural to take reflective equilibrium to be a purely coherentist approach to justification. Most obviously, Rawls's emphasizes the role of coherence in the justification of a conception of justice. Rawls writes,

---

9 Rawls himself suggests this through his use of the term 'coherent' to describe beliefs in reflective equilibrium. Norman Daniels seems to suggest that (wide) reflective equilibrium is a coherentist method, although he most explicitly contrasts it with a strong version of foundationalism represented by moral intuitionism ('Reflective Equilibrium and Archimedean Points,' 100-3; and 'Wide Reflective Equilibrium and Theory Acceptance in Ethics,' 264-73). More recently, Kai Nielsen presents his own modification of the concept of wide reflective equilibrium as 'a coherentist model of justification' ('Reflective Equilibrium and the Transformation of Philosophy,' *Metaphilosophy* **20** [1989], 240). Similarly, Mark Timmons has called reflective equilibrium 'the most popular version of moral coherentism' ('On the Epistemic Status of Considered Moral Judgments,' *Southern Journal of Philosophy* **29** [1990] Supplement).

I have not proceeded then as if first principles, or conditions thereon, or definitions either, have special features that permit them a peculiar place in justifying a moral doctrine. They are central elements and devices of theory, but justification rests upon the entire conception and how it fits in with and organizes our considered judgments in reflective equilibrium. As we noted before, justification is a matter of the mutual support of many considerations, of everything fitting together into one coherent whole. (*A Theory of Justice*, 579)

Similarly, in the Dewey lectures Rawls writes that the proper assessment of any doctrine is 'how well the view as a whole meshes with and articulates our more firm considered convictions, at all levels of generality, after due examination, once all adjustments and revisions that seem compelling have been made' ('Kantian Constructivism in Moral Theory,' 534). Two more specific themes in Rawls's thought also point away from foundationalism. First, he denies that there are any elements in the system which are either self-evident or necessary truths, clearly rejecting 'intuitionism.' Second, Rawls emphasizes that all of the elements can be revised in light of the others. This suggests that the individual elements are not dependent on foundations, but on all the other elements.

To gain the full force of this point we must emphasize the radical extent of the revision that the reflective process might bring about. Here Michael DePaul provides a helpful distinction between 'conservative' and 'radical' conceptions of the method of reflective equilibrium.[10] On the conservative conception, a person's *initial* considered moral judgments are crucial. Although they might be refined, they are relatively fixed and authoritative. Here the reflective process is seen as that which aims at the set of principles most coherent with the set of one's initial considered moral judgments, with some minor adjustments being made in these initial judgments.[11] In contrast, the radical conception allows the reflective process to involve major changes in belief which are not called for by inconsistencies in the initial beliefs. All that is crucial is that the

---

10 Michael DePaul, 'Two Conceptions of Coherence Methods in Ethics,' *Mind* 96 (1987) 463-81

11 This seems similar to the way Daniels has exposited the notion of 'narrow reflective equilibrium' in contrast to 'wide reflective equilibrium,' although there the focus is not merely on the relative stability of the initial considered moral judgments but on the kind of judgments which are relevant. The two issues are related. Narrow reflective equilibrium tends to be conservative since all that is brought into balance are the considered moral judgments and moral principles. Wide reflective equilibrium introduces background theories and other beliefs and thus provides many more factors which could force revision of the initial considered moral judgments. Thus it tends to be more radical.

end result is a system which is in equilibrium. The considered moral judgments in this resulting system *may in theory be entirely different from* the considered moral judgments with which one began. Background theories, model-conceptions derived from common assumptions, and the attractiveness of a set of principles may all combine to move a person to alter one's judgments significantly away from their initial form.[12]

Rawls's rejection of self-evident moral truths and his emphasis on the revisability of considered moral judgments provide prima facie reasons for taking his method to be a coherentist approach to ethics.[13] Yet in spite of this, my thesis is that the reflective equilibrium method Rawls describes is in fact best construed as involving modest foundationalism.[14] To set the stage for the argument I will apply some standard definitions to ethics. I will define *classical ethical foundationalism* as the view that one's ethical views are justified when (i) some of these beliefs are directly justified and unrevisable because they are self-evidently true, and (ii) all of the rest of one's ethical beliefs are justified in virtue of being based upon the directly justified, self-evident beliefs.

Classical ethical foundationalism is parallel to classical foundationalism in general epistemology, of which Descartes is usually seen as a primary paradigm. It is committed to very strong foundations. In contrast to classical foundationalism, modest foundationalists in general epistemology argue that justified beliefs need not be based on self-evident or unrevisable beliefs, but merely that they must have a special epistemic status apart from their coherence with other beliefs. Beliefs are

---

12 Although I am not entirely convinced that Rawls has room for the radical extreme suggested by this conception of reflective equilibrium, some proponents are quite open to it.

13 Normal Daniels places significant weight on these two themes in taking wide reflective equilibrium to be a coherentist approach.

14 In 'Reflective Equilibrium and Foundationalism,' *American Philosophical Quarterly* 23 (1986) 59-69, Michael DePaul concludes that reflective equilibrium is consistent with some forms of foundationalism. DePaul argues that Rawls's method of reflective equilibrium is compatible with foundationalism because the two are really positions on different, but related topics. Reflective equilibrium is 'a method of theory construction,' while foundationalism is 'a type of account of the epistemic status of our beliefs' (68). I find his argument well-reasoned and persuasive. His conclusion alone would undermine the thesis that reflective equilibrium provides a coherentist model of justification. The conclusion I am defending, however, is even stronger than DePaul's. I will argue below that the method of reflective equilibrium, at least when taken as a method of seeking justification, is best construed as involving a form of modest foundationalism.

qualified to be foundations only if their justification is not merely a result of their relationships to other beliefs.

We can define *modest ethical foundationalism* as the view that ethical beliefs are justified when (i) some of these beliefs have a prima facie direct justification and (ii) all of the other beliefs are justified in a way that depends on their relationship to these directly justified beliefs. To say that a moral belief is prima facie directly justified, is to say that either (a) its justification is not derived solely from inferences from other beliefs, or (b) it is justified by inference from some *non-moral* belief(s). Thus, modest ethical foundationalism contends that some beliefs must be justified in virtue of some source or sources of direct prima facie justification. Provision (a) suggests that some of these beliefs or judgments may be justified non-inferentially. Provision (b) allows that one such source may be inference from non-moral beliefs. In either case, the beliefs serve as foundations within the structure of moral beliefs. Finally, to say that belief *p* is prima facie justified is to say that it is reasonable to hold *p* only if there are no other factors which undermine or defeat it. Thus modest ethical foundationalism contends that if any of a person's moral beliefs are justified, then at least some of that person's moral beliefs must serve as modest foundations. But even these foundational beliefs are not immune from alteration or defeat in light of other relevant considerations.

Finally let us define *ethical coherentism* as the view that (i) one's ethical beliefs are justified by their systematic relationship to other beliefs, and (ii) none of these beliefs receive any direct justificatory support apart from these systematic relationships. Coherentism, as defined here, holds that a belief can *only* be justified by coherence considerations, and that it is coherence *alone* which justifies. It is important to note a feature of these definitions that is often blurred in discussions about coherentism and foundationalism, in both general and moral epistemology. The modest foundationalist is best construed as claiming that justification requires some source of justificatory input into a system of beliefs. Mere coherence between beliefs is not enough. Some kind of 'foundations,' on this view, are *necessary*. This necessity claim is inconsistent with the coherentist claim that coherence alone justifies. Pure coherentism denies that justification is a matter of any kind of special input into a system of beliefs, claiming that it is solely a matter of coherence between the beliefs in the system. In other words the coherentist claims that coherence between beliefs is *sufficient* for justification. This claim is usually linked with a claim that coherence is *necessary* for justification. Some might be inclined to defend a weaker coherence view, claiming only that coherence is *necessary* for justification. In my argument below, I assume that this weaker view is *not* what is meant by 'coherentism' since if taken alone the coherence necessity claim is consistent with modest foundationalism. Thus the crucial question is whether or not justification requires special justificatory input beyond relationships between beliefs.

Let us apply these definitions to reflective equilibrium. It is clear that Rawls rejects classical ethical foundationalism. But is his doctrine of reflective equilibrium a form of coherentism or of modest foundationalism? I will argue that within reflective equilibrium both considered judgments and common presumptions function as foundational beliefs. We can approach considered moral judgments from at least two angles. First, we can view the system of beliefs *historically*, or in other words, in terms of the process by which beliefs and judgments come to be in reflective equilibrium. As a person begins the reflective process his considered moral judgments have a privileged status in the evaluation of other beliefs. Without committing ourselves to the existence of any special moral sensory faculty, but merely to a person's ability to respond evaluatively to situations around her, we could say that these considered convictions arise from her 'sense of justice.' Out of this 'sense' a person forms judgments about the justice or injustice, rightness or wrongness, and so forth, of actions and situations which she encounters in life. Arising from moral experience, these convictions are sorted and screened out. Those that stand up under rational considerations become 'considered judgments' and are taken as preliminary standards by which to judge the acceptability of principles. Thus they have a prima facie privileged justificatory status in the structure, a status which is not derived merely from their relationship to other beliefs, but in virtue of expressing the way things seem to the individual person morally. As she sees a particular action, she judges it to be unjust. If she thinks about it carefully and still judges the action to be unjust, the judgment becomes a considered moral judgment. Thus these judgments play the initial role they do because they receive support from something other than their relationships to other beliefs. And this is to say that they have prima facie direct justification. It is not to say that they will be justified in the end. For these considered moral judgments enter into the give and take of the search for equilibrium. In the reflective process they may be defeated or thrown out. Nevertheless, if they do survive the process, we have no reason to believe they somehow lose their direct justification.

But approaching considered moral judgments from this 'historical' angle leaves out an important feature of the wider, radical conception of reflective equilibrium. On the radical conception all the original considered moral judgments may end up being rejected, the initial set being replaced by an entirely new set of judgments. If this is possible and the resulting system of beliefs is justified, then surely it is mistaken to say that the justification of the system depends on the prima facie justification of one's initial considered moral judgments. Since the resulting set of moral judgments, principles and other beliefs emerges from the use of a coherence method, and since all the initial 'foundations' have been rejected, it is natural to conclude that it is coherence alone which justifies the final system of moral beliefs. Further still, the proponent of reflective equilibrium may argue that if the justification of a set of beliefs resulting from a radical shift is solely a result of their coherence and not dependent on the foundations, then the same must be true even in the less radical cases. For the fact that the initial beliefs remain is a result, not of any privileged status, but of their coherence with the rest of the elements in the system. Thus when reflective equilibrium is understood widely, it begins to appear that coherence, and not the presence of foundational judgments, produces justification.

The preceding argument fails to demonstrate that considered moral judgments do not have a special justificatory status in reflective equilibrium. To see this we must shift to a second angle. We have been assuming that the relevant foundations would be some subset of the initial considered moral judgments. But the fact that an individual's initial considered moral judgments are all rejected as she seeks reflective equilibrium does not entail that in the end there are no considered moral judgments in the system. In fact, it is crucial to Rawls's understanding of reflective equilibrium, and to all other discussions of it of which I am aware, that *when reflective equilibrium is reached* the resulting system of beliefs involves a balanced set of considered moral judgments and other moral and theoretical beliefs. After a radical shift away from one's initial considered moral judgments, a new set of considered moral judgments is an important part of the resulting equilibrium.

Are these new considered moral judgments foundations? Do these considered moral judgments play a special justificatory role in the system in reflective equilibrium in virtue of support they receive from some feature other than coherence with other beliefs? The answer is 'Yes.' First, in the resulting state of reflective equilibrium, considered judgments play a special justificatory role. At one point Rawls says, 'There is a definite if limited class of facts against which conjectured principles can be checked, namely, our considered judgments in reflective equilibrium' (*A Theory of Justice*, 51). Many, and perhaps Rawls himself, have wished that Rawls had never written these words. And they can be easily misunderstood. Clearly, they should not be understood as committing Rawls to the existence of self-evident or unchangeable moral truths. But these words do point to an important element at the heart of the idea of justification through reflective equilibrium. On this understanding a set of principles could never be justified if they did not match the judgments we reach when we hold the beliefs in question and carefully and reflectively judge the justice or injustice, goodness or badness, rightness or wrongness of particular actions or kinds of actions. To be justified principles must always cohere with judgments of this kind. Part of the reflective process is the continual asking of the question, 'Do these principles really fit what seems to me to be just? right? etc.?' As the quotation above suggests, there is a kind of test by which principles can always be tested — the test of whether they fit the considered moral judgments we are committed to *at that point in the reflective process*. If they do not they are not justified. Thus considered moral judgments do play a special justificatory role in reflective equilibrium, even after a radical shift.

These new judgments could not play this special justificatory role merely in virtue of cohering with other beliefs. For if coherence were the only factor which qualified considered moral judgments for this role there would be an easy way to reach reflective equilibrium. One could simply begin with a set of principles (with the requirement that it be coherent with relevant background theories) and apply them to real and possible situations, producing a judgment for each situation. Unfortunately the coherence between these considered moral judgments on the one hand and the principles and background theories on the other hand would be rather trivial, since they are merely generated as implications of the principles. Any set of principles has a large number of implications waiting to become considered moral judgments which are perfectly coherent with the principles. On this reading, the coherence criterion is too easily met.

It would seem, then, that considered moral judgments must derive their clout at least in part from some feature other than their coherence with the other elements in the system. What could this feature be? A reasonable answer is suggested by our previous discussion of the initial considered moral judgments. A considered judgment is a way of judging a situation, an action, or perhaps a kind of situation or action. Regardless of how one acquired the ability to make these judgments, there is a kind of directness that cannot be captured by the notion of applying general principles to particular situations. Once one enters into the reflective process one does not lose this ability to make direct judgments, even if the process leads to radical shifts. In fact, these judgments continue to serve as criteria for acceptability of principles. The agent may simply come to judge differently. But the judgments continue to have direct justificatory force. This understanding of considered judgments is much more consistent with the spirit behind the introduction of the notion 'considered judgments' in the first place. They serve as a genuinely significant element which must be brought into the balance if a set of principles is to be justified. As Rawls says, '... justification rests upon the entire conception and *how it fits in with and organizes our considered judgments*' (*A Theory of Justice*, 579, emphasis added). Thus considered moral judgments both play a crucial justificatory role and acquire their ability to play this role from a feature other than mere coherence with other beliefs. In short, they serve as modest foundations.

We must turn more briefly to 'common presumptions.' First, it is not entirely clear that these are not merely highly generalized considered convictions. Inasmuch as they are we could say the same thing we have said about considered judgments above. Second, we might want to say that these beliefs are nonmoral, or that they are justified at least in part by reference to nonmoral beliefs. If some moral beliefs can be justified on the basis of nonmoral beliefs, then within the structure of moral beliefs these beliefs constitute foundational beliefs. Finally, there is an argument that these presumptions have a special status which is more closely tied to the use to which Rawls wants to put reflective equilibrium. In the Dewey lectures he suggests that the justification of principles of justice is not an epistemological matter but a 'practical social' one. The goal is to find principles upon which we can agree as persons living in a democratic society. As he writes, 'The task is to articulate a public conception of justice that all can live with who regard their person and their relation to society in a certain way' ('Kantian Constructivism and Moral Theory,' 519). The goal is not to find principles that are true, but to find principles which are reasonable for us to live by, given our own common situation and assumptions about persons and society.[15] Although this conception of the justificatory task does take Rawls further from classical 'intuitionist' foundationalism, it is not at all clear that it takes him away from foundationalism per se. In fact there is a sense in which this move toward practical reasonableness actually ties him more closely to a foundationalist structure. If the goal is to articulate principles which persons in our society can reasonably accept and live with, then the presumptions we hold and the beliefs we share become very important. It is difficult to see how a system of beliefs which does not cohere with our fundamental assumptions and beliefs will be a reasonable one for us to accept. Thus these presumptions play the role of criteria in virtue of being deeply ingrained in our society and our consciousness. Because of this they have a kind of guiding force in the construction of

---

15 We have already seen that Rawls rejects the traditional 'intuitionist' interpretation of moral judgments. In seeing justification in the practical way he does, Rawls makes another move that takes him away from classical 'intuitionist' foundationalism, which would picture the task of justification as the epistemological one of having reasons for believing that certain principles are objectively true. A careful look at Rawls's constructivist alternative would take us away from our theme in this paper. For a critical look at several constructivist proposals, including Rawls's, see Margaret Holmgren, 'Wide Reflective Equilibrium and Objective Moral Truth,' *Metaphilosophy* **18** (1987) 108-24.

livable principles which does not arise from their coherence with other beliefs.[16] So even when Rawls's alternative view of justification is taken into consideration, the structure of beliefs in reflective equilibrium seems best construed as foundational.

Both considered moral judgments and the common presumptions turn out to serve as modest foundations in a system of ethical beliefs in reflective equilibrium. The reflective equilibrium model does take at least one step in the coherentist direction, however, by suggesting that coherence between beliefs is *necessary* for justification. But as we have seen this claim is consistent with modest foundationalism. Thus reflective equilibrium is a model not of coherentism but of modest foundationalism combined with the claim that coherence between beliefs is an additional necessary condition for justification.

III Some Modest Foundationalist Approaches

Why is it important that considered moral judgments serve as foundations in the structure of beliefs in reflective equilibrium? Before we answer, we must note one thing that has *not* been established. The fact that reflective equilibrium incorporates elements playing a modestly foundational role does not entail that Rawls is committed to any form of moral 'intuitionism,' even in a weak form. If my argument has been correct, spelling out moral justification in terms of reflective equilibrium implicitly grants that certain elements in the structure have special justificatory status. But this alone does not commit the proponent of reflective equilibrium to the view that these elements represent 'intuitions' of moral truth. This is one way in which the special status of considered judgments could be accounted for, but it is not the only possible way.

---

16 Although I will not develop it here, it would be possible to argue that presumptions must play the role of foundations even if we grant that the 'common presumptions' could radically change through a kind of communal reflective process. The argument would take a form parallel to that taken in considering the possibility of radical change in considered moral judgments. But the possibility of radical change is much less plausible here than in the case of moral judgments, since the whole point seems to be the articulation of principles for persons who see things as we now do in our free and democratic society. If we were to change our common presumptions radically, we would no longer see things in this way. Thus the principles would not be those which are reasonable for persons with the presumptions we share in our free and democratic society.

But the conclusion of section II does have an important implication. Although my argument does not demonstrate that reflective equilibrium entails any particular account of considered moral judgments (and common presumptions), it does place a burden of responsibility on the shoulders of those who spell out justification in terms of reflective equilibrium. My primary purpose has been to consider the notion of reflective equilibrium in general and whether this idea provides a model for a coherentist approach to justification, not just in moral theory, but in other domains as well. If my argument has been correct, then in whatever domain this model is applied it will have a similar structure, with something like considered judgments playing the role of modest foundations. In each domain, a full account of justification must explain why these considered judgments can play this role.

Let us focus on moral theory. Why should principles which are coherent with considered moral judgments and our common presumptions be justified? This question could be raised by a skeptic about reflective equilibrium. For if reflective equilibrium depends on certain kinds of beliefs playing a special justificatory role and no account can be given of why they can do so, perhaps the idea of reflective equilibrium is really not that helpful after all. But the question may also be raised by a nonskeptic. We may be convinced that considered moral judgments and deeply held common presumptions do legitimately guide moral reflection and the search for principles. I'd like to explore three directions one might go in search of a positive account of the justificatory role of considered moral judgments.[17]

The first suggestion is that considered moral judgments serve as foundations simply because we strongly believe them. Let us call this approach *modest conservatist foundationalism*. Conservatist foundationalism seems the least plausible alternative. It is difficult to see why strongly believing considered moral judgments should enable these judgments to play any role in justifying moral principles. The mere fact that we accept a moral judgment doesn't seem to justify us in accepting it.[18] Surely we can accept judgments unjustifiedly. If we go on to base other

---

17 It is not my intention to suggest that these three directions are exhaustive or even mutually exclusive. The following explorations are meant to merely suggest some possible ways of accounting for the status of considered moral judgments, not to map all the possible approaches.

18 There are, of course, some who defend 'epistemic conservatism' according to which the fact that we believe a proposition does increase our justification for beliefs based on that proposition. For a critical discussion of this view, see Richard Foley, 'Epistemic Conservatism,' *Philosophical Studies* **43** (1983) 165-82.

judgments on these unjustified judgments, it is difficult to see why these further judgments would be justified. Furthermore, it is difficult to see why the fact that I am *strongly* committed to a moral judgment should in any way add to its justificatory force. So it is difficult to see why holding moral beliefs strongly would qualify them to play the justificatory role they do in reflective equilibrium. Although this seeming implausibility does not demonstrate conclusively that a conservatist account cannot be defended, it does motivate a search for more plausible approaches.

A second view is suggested by a modest foundationalist application of some of the points made by Rawls himself. Rawls seeks to divorce moral justification from the epistemological question of moral truth, emphasizing that the task of moral theory is the practical one of constructing moral principles which can guide our actions.[19] Combining this approach with modest foundationalism results in *modest foundationalist constructivism*. Here the goal is to construct moral principles we can live with and employ in our interactions with one another. Considered moral judgments and basic shared ideas have a special role in reaching this goal because our deeply held beliefs determine how we are willing to relate to others and have others relate to us. Thus this second general approach has a nice answer to the question of why certain elements play the special justificatory role they do in reflective equilibrium. The key to moral justification is what we would be willing to accept. Since our deep convictions determine what we would be willing to accept, any moral principles which do not cohere with our considered moral judgments and other shared convictions would fail to be justified.

Modest constructivist foundationalism is worthy of further exploration. It is one plausible way in which reflective equilibrium could be applied to moral theory. It builds upon the argument of section II by recognizing that reflective equilibrium requires modest foundations. But these foundations are not claimed to be such that the principles built upon and around them are 'more apt to be true.' Instead they serve as a test for determining the practical usefulness of the principles. This suggests an interesting approach to the construction of moral principles. The appropriate starting point is empirical enquiry. To construct moral principles for any group of people, we should begin by seeking to discover the way in which these people judge morally and the deeply held presumptions they share. If the group is the group we are a part of, we would seek to uncover our own judgments and presumptions. Once

---

19 See, for example, 'Kantian Constructivism in Moral Theory,' 519.

we have discovered these 'foundations' we could move on to seek principles which cohere with these foundations. It is easy to see how other elements would be brought into the balance as well. Surely the best way to predict what principles we or others would be willing to live with would include an understanding of our best empirical theories about what people are in fact willing to live with in various situations. Taking these empirical theories and our common presumptions and considered judgments into consideration we could make adjustments until we find a set of principles which coheres with the other elements, thus arriving at a 'justified' set of moral principles for that group. One feature of this view which may be attractive to some is its strongly empirical basis both in the place it gives to relevant background theories and in the discovery of common beliefs.

But the modest constructivist foundationalist picture just sketched is not without its difficulties. First, it is not clear in what sense this picture reveals to us how *moral* principles are justified. Although it may be a way to determine what principles we (or others in a specific group) would be willing to live with, it does not give an account of why we (or anyone) *should* live in this way. 'The way we would be willing to live' and 'the way we should live' are not connected in any obviously necessary way.

A second difficulty with the constructivist foundationalist view concerns a tension between the method of reflective equilibrium and the goal of arriving at practical principles. If the considered moral judgments of a group of people are taken as the guide to constructing principles for these people, it is not clear that the reflective process leading to these principles can be as radical as proponents of reflective equilibrium suggest. If the moral theorist ends up rejecting the initial considered moral judgments, she may have a set of principles which are coherent with *her* final considered moral judgments, but she will not have a set which are consistent with the considered moral judgments of those for whom the principles are intended. The 'practical' goal of the reflective process seems to place important limits on changes that reflection can make in its search for equilibrium. This would suggest that constructivism should defend narrow, rather than wide, reflective equilibrium. Yet many constructivists seem attracted to the possibility of radical change more closely related to wide reflective equilibrium. Thus there is a tension between the constructivist goal and the method proposed to reach this goal.

A third difficulty with the constructivist foundationalist view involves a fuzziness concerning the nature of justification. As we have seen the constructivist defends a practical sense of 'justification' — claiming no connection between justification and truth. It would seem, however, that other elements in the balance must be justified in a more traditionally epistemological sense. The most obvious examples are the background theories which must cohere with the judgments and principles. Surely these background theories must be *epistemically*, and not just practically justified. We must have reason to think they are *true*, and not merely useful. And yet the proponents of reflective equilibrium suggest that the reflective process involves the adjustment of each element in the system in light of the others until equilibrium is reached. In endorsing the reflective process, the implication seems to be that empirical theories can and should be modified on the basis of practical considerations. Although such modifications in theory on the basis of practical considerations *may* be appropriate in some cases, it seems troublesome to advocate such a procedure apart from carefully constructed restraints. Practical justification by means of reflective equilibrium, it would seem, cannot be entirely divorced from questions of epistemological justification.

Finally, in light of the constructivist goal, it is unclear why coherence is important at all. On this view it is the practical value, not the truth value, of a set of propositions which produces justification. But it is not obvious that the most coherent set of principles and judgments will be the most practical. So it is not clear why aiming at coherence in the form of reflective equilibrium will produce the set of principles with the highest *practical* justification. Thus in spite of the attractiveness of setting aside thorny epistemological and metaphysical questions surrounding the concept of moral truth, modest constructivist foundationalism faces a number of *prima facie* objections.[20]

A third approach resists the attempt by constructivists to sever moral justification from epistemological justification. On this view, the justificatory task is not to show how principles can be constructed out of our convictions, but to show that we have reason to believe that they are in some sense objectively true. Adding this approach to the foundationalist interpretation of reflective equilibrium defended in section II, results in *modest objectivist foundationalism*. Within this framework considered moral judgments and common presumptions are taken to be, in some sense, indicators of moral truth. It is this which enables them to play the special justificatory role that they do. Yet the modest objectivist would seek to avoid the pitfalls of classical ethical foundationalism, emphasizing the fallibility of these 'foundations.' Because of this, the reflective equilibrium model becomes quite important. Since the 'foundations' provided by our considered judgments and common presumptions are weak and fallible, they must be tested against one another, and against

---

20   I will leave a discussion of whether these objections can be overcome to a future occasion. For a further criticism of constructivist approaches to ethics see Margaret Holmgren, 'Wide Reflective Equilibrium and Objective Moral Truth.'

principles and background theories. The reflective process is aimed at finding principles and considered judgments which reinforce one another, building a solid structure on foundations which are independently very weak. Although coherence alone is not a reason for taking principles and judgments to be true, seeking reflective equilibrium can be an aid for sorting out accurate from inaccurate input.

The modest objectivist foundationalist view offers a second plausible framework for incorporating the notion of reflective equilibrium into an account of moral justification. Yet it too has its problems. By far the most central of these is the difficulty of providing a plausible account of why considered moral judgments should be taken as indicators of moral truth, even if they are only fallible indicators. Standard objections can be raised against attempts to account for considered moral judgments in terms of 'intuition' or 'moral sense.' Such notions have often been employed to defend the moral beliefs of the cultural and historical period of which the proponent is a part. Furthermore, it is difficult to unpack the mechanism by which such 'intuitions' or 'sensations' would arise. Unlike sense perception, there does not seem to be an obvious causal connection between objective moral truth and our moral beliefs and judgments. Thus many have argued that if considered moral judgments play a special role, it cannot be in a way parallel to sensation or intuition.

Nevertheless there is work being done which may provide the keys to plausible forms of modest objectivist foundationalism. Not all of this work points toward the same type of view, nor would all who contribute the relevant insights feel comfortable with the 'foundationalist' label. Nevertheless, if foundationalism is understood in the modest way I am suggesting in this paper, there are some possibilities worthy of further investigation. First, one important development in the recent literature has been a growing appreciation for the concept of supervenience and the suggestion that moral properties supervene on non-moral properties. If moral properties do supervene on non-moral properties, then it may be possible to explain our knowledge of moral properties on the basis of our knowledge of natural, empirically observable properties which serve as the supervenience base for the moral properties.[21] Second, not all have been convinced that the wholesale rejection of the rationalist tradition in ethics is warranted. Although it is currently a minority view, some have argued that moral principles may

---

21 For one naturalist moral realist view of the supervenience of moral on non-moral properties see Peter Railton, 'Moral Realism,' *The Philosophical Review* **95** (1986) 163-207.

be knowable a priori.[22] This rationalist approach, if successful, would provide an a priori link between observable properties and moral properties, or an a priori source of at least some considered moral judgments. Third, new insights are being suggested on the nature of 'moral truth' and justification. In response to the objection that the affirmation of moral truths implies a commitment to 'queer' entities, moral realists are seeking to develop more plausible accounts of how moral judgments could be 'true' which do not involve the positing of new entities. The truth of a moral judgment may, for example, be a matter of its relation to what rational beings would be willing to accept. On such an account moral truths could be understood as both objective and practical. Thus there may be important ways in which a proper understanding of the practical nature of moral justification can be incorporated within an epistemological understanding of the justification of moral principles.[23] What must be emphasized is that all of these contemporary suggestions differ from many earlier versions of foundationalism in that they recognize the fallibility of the foundations. Yet they suggest that the view that moral justification involves moral truth, which is in some sense objective, is still a plausible option. If so, reflective equilibrium might well provide a model of the kind of moral reasoning which helps us attain moral justification.

My purpose in this section has not been to defend a particular metaethical theory, but to spell out ways in which the conclusion of

---

22 For arguments in the defense of rationalist approaches to ethics see Robert Audi, 'Moral Epistemology and the Supervenience of Ethical Concepts,' *Southern Journal of Philosophy* 29 Supplement (1990) 1-24; and Caroline Simon, 'On Defending a Moral Synthetic A Priori,' *Southern Journal of Philosophy* 26 (1988) 217-34. In general, a number of philosophers have published recent articles exploring possibilities in the modest objectivist foundationalist direction. Mark Timmons, in 'Foundationalism and the Structure of Ethical Justification,' argues that there are 'a plethora of foundationalist views of justification that are at least worthy of consideration' (*Ethics* 97 [1987] 595-609, at 595). Margaret Holmgren has also published several articles which present helpful arguments in this direction. See, especially, 'Wide Reflective Equilibrium and Objective Moral Truth'; and 'The Poverty of Naturalistic Moral Realism: Comments on Timmons,' *Southern Journal of Philosophy* 29 Supplement (1990) 131-35. See also Caroline J. Simon, 'The Intuitionist Argument,' *Southern Journal of Philosophy* 28 (1990) 91-114. Both Holmgren and Simon argue that elements of the 'intuitionist' view should be taken more seriously than they have been in the contemporary discussion.

23 Along these lines, David Copp, in 'Normativity and the Very Idea of Moral Epistemology' (*Southern Journal of Philosophy* 29 Supplement [1990] 189-210) suggests that normative propositions are justified epistemologically in virtue of their relationship to moral standards, but that these moral standards are justified practically.

section II, that reflective equilibrium is implicitly a version of modest foundationalism, can be accepted and built upon in an attempt to spell out the nature of moral justification. This illustrates a more general point about applications of the notion of reflective equilibrium. In whatever area of philosophy it is applied, the proponent of reflective equilibrium must also spell out why it is that the 'considered judgments' in that domain can play the role they do in reflective equilibrium. Without such an explanation, appeal to reflective equilibrium supplies an incomplete view of justification. But when added to an account of fallible foundations, it becomes a useful concept for understanding both the process and the structure of justification.

IV Important Insights and Issues

To conclude, I will mention three important insights the reflective equilibrium discussion has produced. First, although it is sometimes taken as an attack on foundationalism in general, the argument for reflective equilibrium is more accurately seen as an alternative to *strong* foundationalism. In any domain in which reflective equilibrium is used, it must be the case that the foundations are subject to criticism and revision. This is inconsistent with classical foundationalism which asserts that justification and knowledge are based on self-evident, indubitable or incorrigible beliefs. But it is unlikely that there are enough of this kind of beliefs, if there are any, in most domains to provide an adequate basis for knowledge. Thus the defenders of reflective equilibrium as a method of justification are correct in rejecting the classical model which seeks to build on unchanging and unchangeable foundational beliefs.

This leads us to the second insight. The discussion of reflective equilibrium is not valuable because it points us to a different understanding of the structure of justified beliefs, but because it gives us insight into the process that is used, or perhaps should be used, in arriving at a system of justified beliefs. Indeed the reflective process spelled out by Rawls can be taken as a model for responsible belief formation, at least at the level of reflective activity. In coming to reflective equilibrium, the person sorts through her beliefs for those which are most strongly justified. She then seeks to gain systematic understanding by ordering these beliefs and forming higher order beliefs and principles to explain and unify the lower ones. Part of this process is the consideration of alternatives suggested by others or suggested by the reflective thinker's own imagination. In the process she may change some of her beliefs at any level in order to arrive at a set of beliefs and principles which stand firmly on strongly held conviction. This is the process suggested by the discussion of reflective equilibrium. And it seems to be a paradigm of epistemic responsibility.

Third, the reflective process leading to reflective equilibrium plays epistemically valuable roles. It plays the negative role of enabling the believer to discover inconsistencies and defeaters for beliefs in her doxastic system and make changes to eliminate them. It plays the positive role of enabling the believer to establish her beliefs more firmly on reasons she has for those beliefs. Reasons she has, but may not be aware of as reasons, for believing propositions can, through reflection, become reasons *for which* she believes them. Sometimes she may come to form new beliefs on the basis of others which then support still other beliefs. Thus various elements of her system are evidentially reinforced by reflection in various ways. Both the negative and positive roles are particularly appropriate within the modest foundationalist framework. Since it is always possible that a person's basic beliefs are mistaken, they could be defeated by other beliefs. Thus it is appropriate for the epistemic agent to be aware of any other propositions he believes that could count against his foundational beliefs. By discovering defeaters and making appropriate changes he can minimize the likelihood, at least from his own perspective, that his basic beliefs are false. And by establishing positive connections between beliefs, the reflective process strengthens the reasons for which he believes the propositions he does.[24]

Received: August, 1991
Revised: May, 1992

---

24   I am grateful to Robert Audi, Albert Casullo, and Joseph Mendola for helpful comments on an earlier version of this paper, and to Peter Vallentyne for his comments at the 1990 APA Eastern Division Meeting. I have also benefited greatly from suggestions made by the referees of this journal.

Acknowledgments

Hart, H.L.A. "Rawls on Liberty and Its Priority," *University of Chicago Law Review* 40 (1973): 534–55. Reprinted with the permission of the University of Chicago Law School.

Daniels, Norman. "Equal Liberty and Unequal Worth of Liberty." In *Reading Rawls: Critical Studies on Rawls'* A Theory of Justice (New York: Basic Books, 1975): 253–81. Reprinted with the permission of HarperCollins Publishers.

Pogge, Thomas. "The Interpretation of Rawls's First Principle of Justice," *Grazer Philosophische Studien* 15 (1982): 119–47. Reprinted with the permission of Editions Rodopi B.V.

Sen, Amartya. "Welfare Inequalities and Rawlsian Axiomatics," *Theory and Decision* 7 (1976): 243–62. Reprinted with the permission of Kluwer Academic Publishers.

Leininger, Wolfgang. "Rawls's Maximin Criterion and Time-Consistency: Further Results," *Review of Economic Studies* 52 (1985): 505–13. Reprinted with the permission of Blackwell Publishers, Ltd.

Voice, Paul. "Rawls's Difference Principle and a Problem of Sacrifice," *South African Journal of Philosophy* 10 (1991): 28–31. Reprinted with the permission of the Foundation for Education, Science and Technology.

Van Parijs, Philippe. "Social Justice and Individual Ethics," *Ratio Juris* 8 (1995): 40–63. Reprinted with the permission of Basil Blackwell Ltd.

Cohen, G.A. "Where the Action Is: On the Site of Distributive Justice," *Philosophy and Public Affairs* 26 (1997): 3–30. Copyright 1997 by Princeton University Press. Reprinted by permission of Princeton University Press.

Barry, Brian. "John Rawls and the Priority of Liberty," *Philosophy and Public Affairs* 2 (1973): 274–90. Copyright 1973 by Princeton University Press. Reprinted by permission of Princeton University Press.

Shue, Henry. "Liberty and Self-Respect," *Ethics* 85 (1975): 195–203. Reprinted with the permission of the University of Chicago Press.

Estlund, David. "The Survival of Egalitarian Justice in John Rawls's *Political Liberalism*," Journal of Political Philosophy 4 (1996): 68–78. Reprinted with the permission of Blackwell Publishers Ltd.

Johnson, Oliver A. "The Kantian Interpretation," *Ethics* 85 (1974): 58–66. Reprinted with the permission of the University of Chicago Press.

Darwall, Stephen L. "A Defense of the Kantian Interpretation," *Ethics* 86 (1976): 164–70. Reprinted with the permission of the University of Chicago Press.

Galston, William A. "Moral Personality and Liberal Theory: John Rawls's `Dewey Lectures,'" *Political Theory* 10 (1982): 492–519. Reprinted with the permission of Sage Publications, Inc.

Brink, David O. "Rawlsian Constructivism in Moral Theory," *Canadian Journal of Philosophy* 17 (1987): 71–90. Reprinted with the permission of the University of Calgary Press.

Hare, R.M. "Rawls' *Theory of Justice* – I," *Philosophical Quarterly* 23 (1973): 144–55. Reprinted with the permission of Basil Blackwell Ltd.

DePaul, Michael R. "The Problem of the Criterion and Coherence Methods in Ethics," *Canadian Journal of Philosophy* 18 (1988): 67–86. Reprinted with the permission of the University of Calgary Press.

Ebertz, Roger P. "Is Reflective Equilibrium a Coherentist Model?" *Canadian Journal of Philosophy* 23 (1993): 193–214. Reprinted with the permission of the University of Calgary Press.